**Doña Ursulina's bejeweled hand took a gentle hold
of Reina's braid, running her thumb along the
coarse texture of the hair, turning it over.**

Reina felt the sting of a challenge, of her invasion of space, but she remained frozen, as was her place.

"If you want to cement your position in this house, you must make yourself necessary to its masters. That includes Doña Laurel, Celeste, *and* Javier and Don Enrique."

Reina nodded obediently.

"But most importantly, Reina, I summoned you because the day I finalize my legacy will arrive soon. It will come as a reward from a god." Doña Ursulina's nod was sure, firm. "You're here to be an instrument for that legacy, which you will benefit from if you do exactly as I say."

"Sí, señora."

"Remember that you are a Duvianos before anything else. I was the one who saved your life, and it was Juan Vicente who gave you his name."

Reina curled a fist over her chest, the back of her hand feeling the raggedness beneath her clothes. With the iridio heart, she was a monster. She was everything the humans feared. And perhaps her grandmother wouldn't have accepted her any other way.

THE
SUN
AND THE
VOID

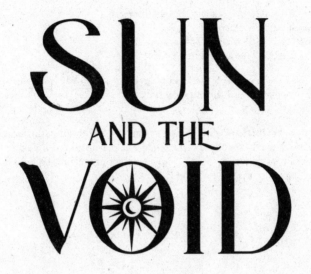

The Warring Gods: Book One

GABRIELA
ROMERO LACRUZ

orbit

orbitbooks.net

Copyright © 2023 by Gabriela Romero Lacruz
Excerpt from *The Jasad Heir* copyright © 2023 by Sara Hashem
Excerpt from *The Phoenix King* copyright © 2021 by Aparna Verma

Cover design by Lisa Marie Pompilio
Cover illustrations by Shutterstock
Cover copyright © 2023 by Hachette Book Group, Inc.
Map by Gabriela Romero Lacruz
Illustrations by Gabriela Romero Lacruz
Author photograph by Hassan Sefidrou

Orbit
Hachette Book Group
1290 Avenue of the Americas
New York, NY 10104
orbitbooks.net

First Edition: July 2023

Orbit is an imprint of Hachette Book Group.
The Orbit name and logo are trademarks of Little, Brown Book Group Limited.

The publisher is not responsible for websites (or their content) that are not owned by the publisher.

The Hachette Speakers Bureau provides a wide range of authors for speaking events. To find out more, go to hachettespeakersbureau.com or email HachetteSpeakers@hbgusa.com.

Orbit books may be purchased in bulk for business, educational, or promotional use. For information, please contact your local bookseller or the Hachette Book Group Special Markets Department at special.markets@hbgusa.com.

Library of Congress Cataloging-in-Publication Data
Names: Romero Lacruz, Gabriela, author.
Title: The sun and the void / Gabriela Romero Lacruz.
Description: First edition. | New York, NY : Orbit, 2023. | Series: The warring gods
Identifiers: LCCN 2022057433 | ISBN 9780316336543 (trade paperback) |
    ISBN 9780316336642 (ebook)
Subjects: LCGFT: Fantasy fiction. | Novels.
Classification: LCC PS3618.O64 S86 2023 | DDC 813/.6—dc23/eng/20230323
LC record available at https://lccn.loc.gov/2022057433

ISBNs: 9780316336543 (trade paperback), 9780316336642 (ebook)

Printed in the United States of America

LSC-C

Printing 1, 2023

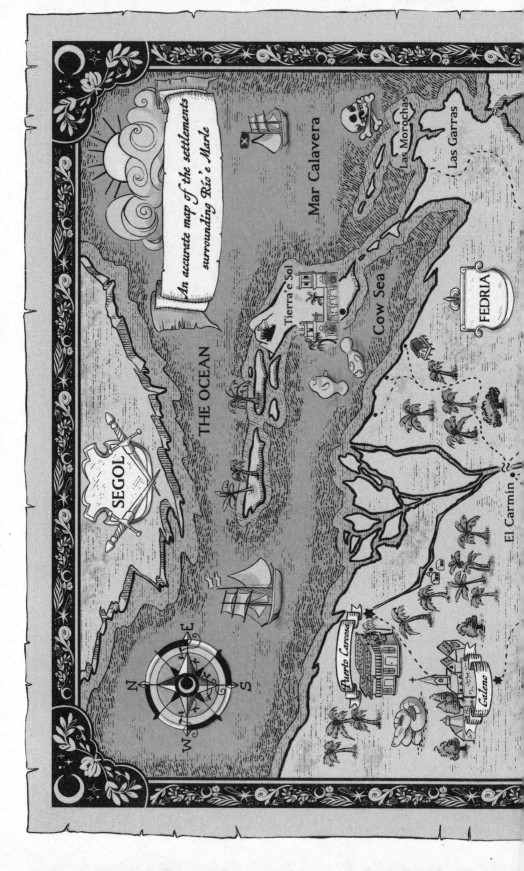

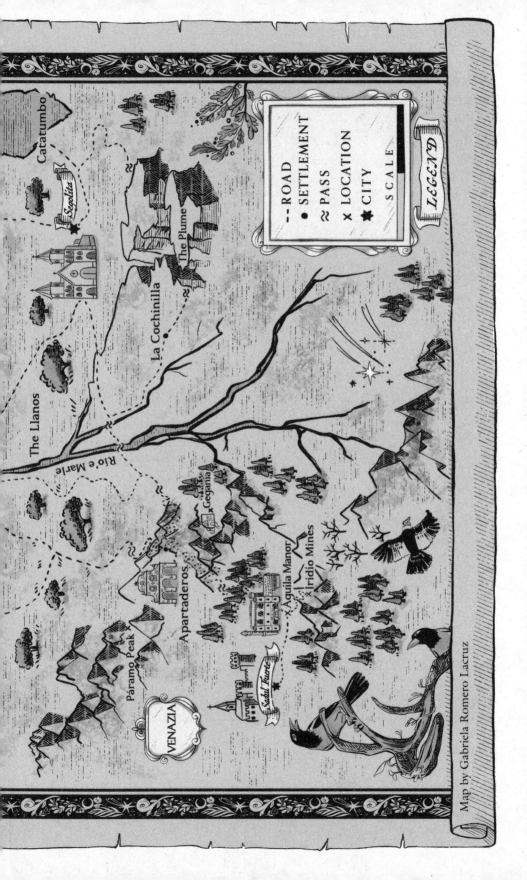

Map by Gabriela Romero Lacruz

Timeline

THE KING'S DISCOVERY (KD)

1 KD: Segol's voyagers first arrive in the lands that later
become the Viceroyalty of Venazia, colony of Segol

326 KD: Rahmagut's Claw becomes visible to the naked eye

344 KD: Samón's and Feleva's declaration of independence

344 KD: Establishment of the sovereign countries of
Venazia and Fedria

348 KD: Fall of the Viceroyalty of Venazia and Segol's
defeat

368 KD: Rahmagut's Claw becomes visible to the naked eye

Major Families

Silva

Seat: Puerto Carcosa, the coast of the Cow Sea
Banner: an onyx crocodile on scarlet fabric, for the red
blood of felled armadas over a crocodile coast
Notable Members:
- Don Rodrigo Agustín Silva Zamorano, king of Venazia,
  appointed by La Junta de Puerto Carcosa
- Doña Orsalide Belén Zamorano de Silva, queen mother
- Marcelino Carlos Silva Pérez

Águila

Seat: outskirts of Sadul Fuerte, the Páramo
Banner: a soaring golden eagle on ivory fabric, for the
riches amassed beneath the Páramo peaks
Notable Members:
- Doña Feleva Lucero Águila Cárdenas, full-blooded valco,
  deceased caudilla of Sadul Fuerte
- Don Enrique Gavriel Águila de Herrón, half human,
  half valco, born in the year 328 KD, caudillo of Sadul
  Fuerte
- Doña Laurel Divina Herrón de Águila, born in the year
  328 KD

- Celeste Valentina Águila Herrón, three-quarters human, one-quarter valco, born in the year 346 KD
- Javier Armando Águila, half human, half valco, born in the year 344 KD

Serrano

Seat: Galeno, the Llanos

Banner: three stripes—brown, blue, and yellow—for the rich soil of Galeno, the plentiful rivers, and the nourishing sun

Notable Members:

- Don Mateo Luis Serrano de Monteverde, governor of Galeno
- Doña Antonia Josefa Monteverde de Serrano
- Doña Dulce Concepción Serrano de Jáuregui, born in the year 326 KD
- Doña Pura Maria Jáuregui de Valderrama
- Décima Lucía Serrano Montilla
- Eva Kesaré de Galeno, three-quarters human, one-quarter valco, born in the year 348 KD

Duvianos

Seat: Sadul Fuerte, the Páramo

Banner: an orange flower with a red sun rising over mauve fabric, for the fields of flowers under Páramo dawns

Notable Members:

- Doña Ursulina Salma Duvianos Palacios, born in the year 305 KD
- Don Juan Vicente Duvianos, born in the year 328 KD
- Reina Alejandra Duvianos Torondoy, half human, half nozariel, born in the year 347 KD

Contador

Seat: Galeno, the Llanos
Banner: a diagonal partition of black and white, crossed
by a golden key, for the establishment of order in the
colonies
Notable Members:
- Don Jerónimo Rangel Contador Miarmal
- Doña Rosa de El Carmín

Villarreal

Seat: Galeno, the Llanos
Notable Members:
- Don Alberto Ferrán Villarreal Pescador

Castañeda

Seat: Los Morichales, the Llanos

Bravo

Seat: Tierra'e Sol, the coast of the Cow Sea
Banner: two mirrored laurels on a diagonal partition of
navy and yellow, for the abundance of Fedria and
its sea
Notable Members:
- Don Samón Antonio Bravo Días, half human, half valco,
born in the year 326 KD, former chancellor of Fedria, the
Liberator
- Ludivina Gracia Bravo Céspedes, three-quarters human,
one-quarter valco

A note on names—

Persons are given a first name, a middle name, and a single family name by each parent. Upon marriage, persons can attach their partner's family name to their own and drop one of their last names. A single parent only bestows a single family name to their offspring. When neither parent is able to bestow a family name upon birth, persons are given the name of the city or settlement where they were born. Full names are seldom mentioned in everyday speech. *Don* and *Doña* are honorifics to express respect. Married persons, heirs, landowners, and elders are addressed by their honorific. When neglected, it is a sign of disrespect.

Part 1

*Year 366 of
the King's Discovery*

Reina Alejandra Duvianos Torondoy

EVA KESARÉ DE GALENO

1

Food for Tinieblas

There were many warnings about the Páramo Mountains, tales of ghosts and shadows now bound to the land after their tragic demise. Yet no one had warned Reina about the cold. How the air filtered through the inadequate layers of her vest and jacket. How every breath she took was a sliver of sustenance, so thin that each gulp left her starving. They'd never told her crossing the Páramo would feel like a journey without end.

The mountains rose ahead of her with their sugar-powdered peaks showered in the violet hues of the arriving dusk. And they opened up behind her like boundless rolling hills blanketed by cold-burned shrubberies and the jutting frailejón trees, which stood alone on a territory perhaps too cold or elevated to be hospitable to anything else.

An icy wind buffeted her forward. Reina fell to her knees like a scared child, her scabs splitting and streaking red on the jagged rock beneath her, but her prehensile tail looped around the rock, reassuring her with balance. When she gathered the courage to continue her climb, she glimpsed the gray fogginess of smoke far ahead, and it filled her with hope. A fire meant a hearth, which meant civilization wasn't too far off.

The way forward was treacherous, but so was the way back. One more day on foot, and Reina was sure she would reach the lower valleys. Images of an inn's warm bed kept her company. She entertained herself with dreams of reaching the farmsteads bordering Sadul Fuerte, when she finally arrived in the city and could share the reason for her journey with the first stranger who asked. She imagined pulling out the invitation marked by the mauve wax seal of the Duvianos family, the elegant loops of Doña Ursulina Duvianos's cursive beckoning Reina to come meet a grandmother estranged by Reina's father's broken heart. From her breast pocket she would produce a golden badge proving the missive's legitimacy, which had been delivered along with the letter.

The engraved medallion was a metal translation of the Duvianos banner: an orange flower crowned by a red sun rising over a mauve sky. Reina recognized the crest, for she had seen it on jackets and correspondence her father owned from his time as a revolutionary, before he had renounced his old life. Juan Vicente Duvianos had never spoken much of his mother, and when he had, it had been with the rancor and disappointment of a schism. Even after he'd died, Reina had discarded the possibility of a relationship with her grandmother. But after reading the words inviting her to the faraway Águila Manor, where Doña Ursulina was employed, Reina couldn't be sure who had disowned whom.

When the cold ached her bones and the mountain rebelled against her, Reina clutched her objective and reminded herself why she was fleeing to Sadul Fuerte to begin with. Behind her, in Segolita, she was nothing more than a jobless nozariel living on the charity of humans. The laws enslaving nozariels to humans had changed, but not the attitudes. The streets of Segolita had been her home—all crooked townhomes of peeling baroque façades and roads muddied from shit and the latest rainfall—and her hell. Reina was of age, too old for the family for whom she had worked as a criada and accidentally caught the eye of the oldest son, and too undesirable to be welcomed by any other human family or employer. The invitation gave her an opportunity, and hope.

Her path opened up to a crossroads, where a naked, knobby tree sustained two planks with carved directions: Apartaderos, where she had come from, to the north, and Sadul Fuerte to the west. A chill ran through Reina as the air grew cooler and the shadows elongated. No longer was the sky streaked in the stark mauve she imagined had been the inspiration for the Duvianos banner. Dusk spread through the mountains, and with it came a howling wind and faraway yaps that turned her jumpy. "There's nothing but frailejones and demons in the Páramo," the inn owner at the foot of the mountain had warned her, shaking his head in disapproval. She would gladly trade the devils of Segolita for the ghosts of the Páramo.

Camping for the night was the last thing she wanted to do, but the path ahead was long and even more treacherous in the dark. Reina broke off course from the well-trodden road and followed a small creek downstream, looking for a burrow or shelter. The creek entered a patch of frailejones, each tree reaching for the sky with its cluster of hairy succulent leaves. Reina followed the stream, plucking the marcescent leaves hanging from the frailejón trunks to build a fire. The night was still. Her huffs of condensing breaths and footsteps crackling the underbrush were all that disturbed an otherwise deathly quiet, which was odd. Just moments ago she had noted the rising cacophony of night: crickets and the croak of amphibians and the occasional hooting bird. The moon was rising, its light creating odd bipedal shapes in the shadows of the trees she passed.

A branch snapped. Reina paused, thinking it must have been the wind. Then a second rustle set the hairs of her back on end. She whirled around. There was nothing but the moonlight and the shadows it created. Fear fell over her. The shadows breathed. Like they were hunting her.

When the silence was shattered by a second snapping twig, she ran.

Guttural snarls erupted behind her, and stomps. With her blood pumping hot in her ears and her heart panicked, Reina breathlessly pelted through the underbrush. Could there be bears in the Páramo, or lions? The sounds were wet, and the hunting creature sounded heavy. She glanced behind her, cursing when it slowed her down, and saw a shadow crowned with horns. She cried and tripped on a protruding root.

Pain lanced through her ankle, but she had no time to nurse it. She pushed herself back to her feet as several pairs of stomps joined the pursuit. The bared trees closed in around her, their marcescent leaves stretching like claws to pull at her clothes. Thorny bushes sliced her calves and ankles. Fog blanketed the mountain. Unable to see, she stumbled into a gully. She shot another glance at her pursuers as she scrambled up. They carried the shape of people, bipedal, with long, naked limbs coated in the grime of the wild. They had the ears of a bovine and the curved horns of a goat. Moonlight gleamed off small eyes reflecting a single line of intention: the desire to devour. But the worst part of it all—what made Reina realize this would be the brutal, bloody end of her journey—were the grinning teeth. They were blunt, like a human's, but with twice too many shoved into the hanging mandible of a monster.

The first one yanked her by the tail. Its clammy touch leeched all the heat from her. The thing tossed her against a bush, thorns impaling her side and scratching her cheeks open.

Reina brandished her knife, which was a rusty, untrustworthy thing she'd brought for skinning game—not for fighting. She screamed as she slashed at her attackers' limbs to no effect. They regarded her with snarling laughter, the sounds warped as if they originated from her own imagination. As if they had one foot in this world and another in the Void. Tears flooded her eyes and blurred an already black night. They slapped the knife away, their claws ripping her clothes and skin.

Desperate, Reina kicked at one with all her strength, sending it toppling back. She scrambled to all fours and sprang up for another getaway. One jerked her braid, then clutched her tail; another grabbed her by the wrist; and the third reached for her collar and ripped her jacket open.

"Stop!" she cried uselessly, for deep down she knew there would be no stopping them until they had all of her.

She shrieked as one of the creatures dug its teeth into her flesh. One moment its face was close, blank eyes reflecting nothing but instinct, and the next it was pulling out her skin and muscle and sinew as it ripped her forearm open.

White-hot pain surged through her. Reina's screams reverberated across the mountain. The other monster tore her cotton shirt open. Her grandmother's badge flew out, and she caught it, by instinct or by a miracle. The thing was heavy in her hand. She smacked the creature gnawing on her forearm with all her strength, imprinting her family's sigil on its sickly forehead.

A glow spread from the badge upon impact. A bubble of yellow light swallowed Reina and the creatures devouring her, revealing their hairless bodies covered in black welts and boils. The light burst out of the badge like a spring of water. Anywhere it touched, their hideous skin sizzled and smoked, earning their wet, agonized hisses.

The creatures were relentless. Their claws went for her chest as if digging for a treasure within, scraping her ribs, her final barrier. Reina swung their mucus-covered arms away with the lighted badge. She swiped left, then right, forcing the light to repel them. Bloodied and battered, she twisted around to her feet and scrambled away. The monsters remained at the perimeter of the badge's light, their growls following her. They wanted her flesh, but something about the light deterred them.

The frailejones opened to a clearing showered in moonlight. Reina limped to it, her wounded arm gripping the remains of her ripped shirt and jacket over the bloody opening on her chest. Her other arm waved the badge like a beacon. She wasn't sure if the monsters still followed.

Swaying deliriously, she stepped on loose mountain terrain, and the stones beneath her gave. She slipped. Her limbs and head crashed against stone and bramble as she rolled down a scree. When the fall finally ended, Reina took a desperate gasp of air, then curled into a ball. Her spine and skull were miraculously unbroken. Somehow, she was alive. But every inch of her ached and burned, and maybe, just maybe, she would have been better off dead.

"Is that another one?"

"No—that's a person."

Voices echoed in the vast void of Reina's darkness, stirring her. Grime coated the inside of her throat when she took in a big gulp of crisp Páramo air. The brightness of a cloudy sky blinded her as she turned her head. She was rewarded with a headache. Reina found herself cushioned by a mossy blanket. A beetle scuttled dangerously close to her eyelashes. She sat up, and a sharp pain lanced her arm. There was a bloody, gaping bite on her forearm.

She had nearly been eaten.

Tears flooded the edges of her vision. Reina felt a renewed vigor to live. She moaned a reply to the voices, which approached with several pairs of squelching footsteps. With the effort came a thunderous ache in her chest, which was crusted with blood, her skin reduced to flaps barely hanging on. Trembling, her hand hovered over the injury. Her broken skin burned, but the ache came from within. A blazing pain. Even the simple act of curling into a ball, to shield her soul from squeezing out of her wound, was torturous. She cried again. She would never make it to Sadul Fuerte.

The footsteps reached her. Someone grabbed her by the shoulder and twisted her around for a better look.

A "No!" blurted out of her from the pain, but she hadn't the strength to fight them off.

"This one's basically dead," a man said.

"But she lives," the second voice said. This one belonged to a woman who crouched close. Her leather gloves gently wiped the grime from Reina's cheeks, and she shushed Reina's sobs.

A pair of blue eyes peered down at her, brilliant, like the sunny skies in Segolita when not a single cloud marred the sky. The woman had clear pale skin and a sharp nose. Blunt black bangs covered her forehead, and the rest of her silky hair was pulled up into a high ponytail. From the crown of her head curled a short pair of antlers, smooth, the color of alabaster.

The young woman was valco.

Reina couldn't believe it...to be able to see one in the flesh, even if right before her death.

The woman's hand hovered over Reina's torn chest without touching the wound. "You were attacked by tinieblas. But you lived—how?"

"I would hardly call that *living*," the man behind her said, covering his nose with his jacketed forearm. He was crowned with a pair of antlers, too, but his were taller and better developed, with sharp edges surely capable of being made a weapon to impale. His hair was as silvery as the clouded sky. Boiled leather armor peeked out from underneath his ruana—a black shawl-like covering, triangular in shape, which covered him from neck to waist.

"The wretch is nozariel," he added, noting her tail with a grimace. A typical reaction from humans when they realized her parents hadn't cut it off after birth to conform. Perhaps valcos were also in agreement.

The pair had other companions lingering behind, awaiting orders or standing as sentinels.

"The rot is going to get to her one way or another. Leave the creature be," he said.

Reina reached for the woman's hand. She gripped it without permission and begged, "Help, please."

"Unhand her!"

"Oh, hush, Javier," the young woman said. She couldn't be older than Reina, but she was beautiful, in the regal sort of way Reina imagined the princesses of the Segolean Empire were raised to be. She was wearing a woolen ruana like Javier, woven in blue and white with fringes decorating the bottom. She took it off and draped Reina in her warmth, and her scent. "Don't you care to know how she survived the tinieblas? They went for her heart."

"Not particularly. We banished them. Our work here is done."

Panic bubbled in Reina's belly. She knew what the man's look meant. She'd been a recipient of it time and time again in Segolita— had seen it directed at the starved and wounded nozariels on the streets. They were going to leave her to die because of the part of her that wasn't human.

Her heart palpitated uselessly. The spasms shot up her chest again, leaving her without the words to beg for mercy. Tears streaked her cheeks as she lifted the engraved badge with her bitten hand. The trinket was half-coated in the red crust of her blood, but the faint light emitting from it was unmissable. Warm magic pulsed from within the metal.

The woman was even more beautiful when her eyes and mouth rounded inquisitively. She took the badge from Reina, despite the dried blood. "It's the crest of Duvianos," she said, rising to her feet and taking the badge with her to show it to her companions.

"No—please," Reina begged, desperate not to be abandoned. Her chest flared again, punishing her. She moaned and twisted in agony like an earthworm under the sun.

"Javier, you must heal her!" The woman's words were faint and far away. "Use healing galio."

Reina couldn't keep her eyes open any longer. She knew she was slipping away.

"Do I look like a nurse to you?"

In some ways, Reina was grateful for it.

"Please, act like you have a droplet of human blood in you for once in your life. I command it."

She had failed in her journey, right as she was reaching Sadul Fuerte. If anything, she was a fool for thinking she could escape her fate at all.

"Please, Celeste, pay no heed to her baubles. The wretch is a thieving nozariel. How else would she get her hands on something like this?"

Reina's trembling fingers reached into the torn jacket and produced the letter. She had the strength for a few last words. And if this was going to be the end, then she might as well say them. "I am no thief. I'm here to meet my grandmother, Ursulina Duvianos."

The impact of her head against a hard surface yanked Reina back to reality. It flared every nerve of pain like jabbing knives. She had been thrown into a shadowed room, where the scent of dust and manure pervaded the stagnant air. At least it was warmer than it had been, and the bedding was softer than the mountain ground. Voices approached and someone entered.

Reina bit down the ache to sit up and take stock of her surroundings. The dormitory was small, with plain walls and a wooden rosary nailed to the wall opposite her. The young valco woman named Celeste stood by the doorway. She fidgeted with Reina's badge, which was the only source of light as dusk settled over the world outside.

As if she'd been waiting for Reina to wake, Celeste said, "Stay here, and don't go anywhere else."

"I couldn't move even if I wanted to." Her heart pounded in a mad race to outrun the pain. A contest it couldn't win. "Please return my badge."

"If you are who you say you are, then I must take it with me." Celeste didn't give Reina a chance for rebuttal, and Reina would have howled at her for leaving the room with her badge were she not so weak.

She wished sleep would claim her a second time. Was she going to die? The memory of the shadowed devils with the grinning, blunt teeth returned the moment her eyes closed. So she forced herself to stare at the ceiling instead.

Soon, the hum of a hushed argument filled the hall outside the room. The argument ended the moment the newcomers reached the doorway. Celeste brought reinforcements: a middle-aged woman who commanded Reina's complete attention as she entered the room. The woman wore a billowing long-sleeved blue dress with fine golden embroidery. She had bobbed black hair, pale skin, and a strong resemblance to Celeste. Her mother, a human lacking the valco antlers.

She approached Reina's bedside, cautiously, and sat on the stool positioned next to it. Another woman also entered, heralded by the clicking footsteps of heeled black boots on the stone floor. "Doña Laurel?" she said. "What is the meaning of this?"

The second woman was the tallest in the room. Her umber skin was lustrous and free of marks, and her black hair was braided in a circle behind her head. She wore black pants, and her high-necked jacket was partitioned into red silk sleeves and a black silk bodice embroidered with golden laurels down the middle.

"Doña Ursulina," Doña Laurel said by way of welcoming her to the room. "That is precisely what I'm trying to figure out."

Stunned, Reina looked to the taller woman, her heart racing again. Suddenly everything about her features became familiar. The high cheekbones; the fullness of her lips. Yet there were other things Reina never saw in herself: The confidence and commanding presence. The opulence of her clothes.

"She was a victim of tinieblas. We found her on our way down from the Páramo," Celeste said.

"There are tinieblas on my lands?" Doña Laurel raised her voice, accusation dripping off her words. "*You* found her?"

"Yes, mami."

"I've told you time and time again that I do not want to see you hunting tinieblas," Doña Laurel said, disappointment and concern simmering beneath the surface. The words took Reina back to that moment with those creatures, reminding her of the determined hunger in their eyes, how their blunt teeth tore chunks off her skin. Every mother *should* be concerned.

"It was Javier's idea," Celeste added, quick like a white lie.

Doña Laurel pursed her lips, her attention drawn to Reina, who was finding it hard to restrain herself from squirming in pain in front of these women. Cautiously, the woman lifted the covers shielding Reina's chest for a peek at the wound. A metallic stink filled the room.

"The tinieblas' rot," Doña Ursulina said.

Doña Laurel clicked her tongue, but her façade was unbothered. She reached out and wiped the sticky bangs away from Reina's temple, her pity clear in her eyes. "You survived the tinieblas? With your heart intact?" Then she turned to Doña Ursulina and asked, "How is that possible?"

"My badge," Reina croaked.

Celeste presented Doña Ursulina with the trinket, then the letter. The taller woman's eyes doubled in size, then her face contorted into a scowl as she recognized the medallion. She hesitated before accepting the letter with fingers bedazzled in fat gem-encrusted rings.

"What is your name?" she asked without lifting her gaze.

Reina choked on her own spit but answered.

Doña Ursulina unfolded the stained letter, her jaw rippling as she read her own words inviting Reina to these cold lands across the mountains.

Reina met her black gaze as a chill shook her from neck to toes. This was the moment she had dreamed of during those lonely days as she crossed the Llanos and the Páramo. This reunion with her grandmother. How flat and painfully disappointing it had turned out to be.

Doña Laurel watched them. "Do you know this woman?"

"This badge belongs to me, just like it used to belong to my father, and his father before him," Doña Ursulina said, slowly turning it over in her hands. "I enchanted it with a powerful ward of litio protection and bismuto—enough to allow you to see the tinieblas and ward them away. I knew the journey here would have its dangers—I just didn't expect to be...so right." She crossed the distance to Reina and lifted her chin for a better look. "A nozariel like your mother, aren't you?" she said, eyeing the black spots of pigmentation on the iris that made Reina's pupils look oblong, almost like a cat's; the caiman-like scutes over the bridge of her nose; the long, pointed tips of her ears. The marks of her nozariel breed, undiscernible from far away but never failing to earn her a scowl or a grimace from most humans. "You actually came."

"Explain yourself, Doña Ursulina," Doña Laurel commanded.

"I sent the badge to Segolita, along with this letter, to my granddaughter."

Doña Laurel's mouth hung open. "As in, Juan Vicente's daughter? He has a daughter?"

The way they said his name, with the familiarity hinting of a past Reina wasn't privy to, reignited the agony in her chest. She chewed the insides of her cheeks, tasting her own blood, and forced the words out despite the pain. "I came to meet you." She tried sitting up again, only to collapse with a moan. A violent spasm shook her, made her want to scream.

"She needs a doctor," Celeste blurted out from her spot by the doorway.

"The tinieblas hungered for her heart, and they have tainted it.

This is dark magic, and it will not be cured by a mere doctor, if at all," Doña Ursulina said.

It was a blow, renewing Reina's fears. She let out a shuddery breath. With an angry hiss and the last of her strength, she said, "I came from Segolita—I traveled this far—to be your family. Not to die!"

And the witch who shared her blood smiled.

"Then it must be fated that you live, child, for if there is one person capable of salving a tiniebla's rot, it will be me."

2

One-Quarter Valco

There wasn't a single instance when Eva enjoyed Don Alberto's company. Their two-decade age difference was too large, their interests too incompatible. And now that she was in his office, enduring his long-winded speech about his profession, she regretted her plan of pretending to visit him at all.

Don Alberto was the keeper of names of Galeno, a dull bureaucratic appointment he tended to with much earnestness and the only thing he had a passion for, really. Presently, it was this proximity to Eva's official family records that interested her. Nothing else.

Eva tugged on the lace of her dress, feeling sweat roll down her back from the lack of air circulating in the stuffy office. Cluttered desks and loaded bookshelves monopolized what little space there was. The only natural light came from the two small windows positioned near the ceiling. Even after so brief a visit, Eva already felt suffocated and longed to leave. Her smile was fake as she said, "I just wanted to see what you have for my family's records—the format and details—I've never properly seen it myself."

He watched her closely, as if she were a hummingbird likely to disappear in the blink of an eye. Maybe from someone else, Eva would have appreciated the attention, but from him it was unnerving. "I'm sure it's a story you're well acquainted with," he said.

Eva nodded.

"The Serranos' book?"

Her smile vanished. The Serranos were her family on her mother's side. And as Eva didn't have a family name given to her by her father, or a paternal family for that matter, the question landed bitterly. She was, after all, Eva Kesaré de Galeno. She was *of* Galeno—of the city. A bastard. And he knew this.

"Yes," she said.

He didn't notice her displeasure and simply beckoned her down a row of bookshelves. He located the heavy tome with the names, likenesses, and recorded histories of every Serrano born in Galeno. The tome was heavy and free of dust as he pulled it out from the most accessible and centralized location on the shelf. The record book saw much use, as the Serranos were a large lot and were the descendants of Don Mateo Serrano, the governor. With his wife, Doña Antonia, he'd had enough children for every finger on Eva's hand, and those children had had almost as many offspring. The women were shipped off to families all over Venazia or in Galeno to spread the blood, and the men were given positions in the capitol building. As Eva's nineteenth birthday drew nearer, she was overdue for her turn. Don Alberto Villarreal was the best consolation prize her grandmother could procure for, in her words, a "fatherless valco girl with an inclination to madness."

Don Alberto stood closely behind Eva as she leafed to the most contemporary records, where her mother's name was inscribed. His proximity incensed her, as did his breath, which often had an insidious scent of onion from all the carne mechada his mother overfed him.

One of the few good things to come out of their courting was that she could get a glimpse of the government records on her father. She wanted—no, *needed*—to know who he was. Without that, a piece of herself would always be a mystery.

"It'd be interesting to see the history of your family," she lied. "I guess the thought of how we'll be uniting them intrigues me."

He cheered up at the suggestion and waddled away to search for said ledger. Eva exhaled gratefully and sought her mother's entry, looking for clues to whatever brought so much grief to her grandmother.

Dulce Concepción Serrano Monteverde, second daughter
of Don Mateo Luis Serrano de Monteverde and Doña Antonia Josefa Monteverde de Serrano. Born in the year 326
of the King's Discovery, on the day of Saint Dulce of the
Provincials. Full-blooded human. Married to Don Federico
Daniel Jáuregui Rangel. Mother of Pura Maria Jáuregui Serrano. Mother of Eva Kesaré de Galeno. Widowed. Died in
the year 357 of the King's Discovery. Cause of death: litio.

Eva chewed on her lip, annoyed. It wasn't anything she didn't
know already. The next page revealed her own record, which was
rather bare:

Eva Kesaré de Galeno, second daughter of Doña Dulce
Concepción Serrano de Jáuregui. Born in the year 348
of the King's Discovery, on the eve of the Virgin's rising.
Three-quarters human, one-quarter valco.

Her mouth opened in disbelief. That was it. Nothing regarding
her father had been logged. She leafed to the next page and only
found records of her younger cousins.

Don Alberto returned, lifting a cloud of dust as he dropped his
family's records on the desk. His lacked the gilded spine, the richly
dyed leather.

Eva slammed the Serranos' tome shut before he could glimpse
what she had been looking for. The two masculine voices coming
from outside the registry office were the sign her time was up, as
was her interest in Don Alberto. "*Oh*, I completely forgot about
Néstor," she said.

Don Alberto watched her with rounded, disappointed eyes.

"We came together—got a ride from my grandmother. But he
didn't want to stay long, and we have errands to run in town."

Eva navigated out of the labyrinthine shelves with Don Alberto
in tow. She swung the door open right as the voices passed the
hall. Luck was on her side. It was true, Néstor was looking for her,
accompanied by another young man of his same age.

"Oi, Eva!" he called out.

He was lanky, had dark brown skin, and was dressed in a velvety tunic—his fine downtown clothes. They were all the rage in Galeno, yet they were more practical for the Segolean imperialists in their cold fortresses than in this city perched in the center of the Llanos. As Doña Antonia's son—her youngest, and the baby of the family—Néstor shared Eva's brown-red eyes.

Don Jerónimo Contador was Néstor's companion. He was the youngest grandson of the Contador patriarch. He had olive skin prone to turning a radiant shade of brown anytime he offered to help the ranchers working for his father, and his pointed nose made him resemble the Segolean statues of saints erected within the cathedral. His eyes, which Néstor raved much about, were chocolate colored and kind.

Eva made a show of grabbing Néstor by the hand and offered Don Alberto a grateful smile that didn't reach her eyes. Don Alberto's enthusiasm to spend time with her almost—*almost*—clenched her heart. After decades of being hindered by his introversion, he was desperate for a partner, or so went the gossip in town. Eva knew of him through her grandfather, but she couldn't fathom ever being excited to spend the rest of her life with someone twice her age, no matter how much she understood his ache for companionship.

Néstor, Don Alberto, and Don Jerónimo exchanged quick and awkward greetings before Néstor turned to her and said, "We're leaving soon." Néstor knew Eva's plan and wouldn't leave without her. "Jerónimo's carriage is ready for us and waiting outside."

Eva opened her embroidered fan and aired her chest dramatically, where the lace concealing her cleavage clung to her from the sweat. "Thank you for the tour, Don Alberto, though I fear I'm not used to the rigors of clerical work. I'm very impressed by what you do," she said, imitating the tone she knew her female cousins used so freely, acting like they were less than capable, hiding behind the men's expectations of what they were supposed to do.

Néstor and Don Jerónimo smiled at Eva, seeing right through her façade. Don Alberto ate it up.

"It's no bother, Señorita Eva," he said, bringing her hand up to his meaty lips. "I'm just grateful my work interests you and that I get to spend time with you."

Eva's smile almost fractured at his honesty. She was rotten—exactly as her grandmother branded her.

Don Jerónimo led the way through the open hallway. The second-story balcony walkway of the capitol building overlooked a courtyard where a team of clerics received lectures on the office's latest procedures. Pampered hedges brimming with hibiscuses created paths within the large courtyard, allowing private spaces where government dignitaries met for their deals. Ahead of her, Don Jerónimo's low ponytail swayed with the tickle of a breeze. Eva closed her eyes, breathing in the freedom of leaving Don Alberto's office behind.

"Did you find the information on your father?" Néstor said softly as he snaked his arm around the bend of her elbow.

Eva's other hand traveled up to her curly bangs as the wind ruffled them out of place. Her fingers stopped, pressing against the pair of stunted antlers hidden within her rowdy light brown hair. Most everyone pretended Eva didn't have them, and they could easily do it, as Eva kept her bangs puffy to conceal them. But the physical reminder was always there.

"There was nothing. He's not even listed under mi mamá," she replied bitterly.

Instead, the ledgers listed her blood with so much certainty. One-quarter valco. Eva didn't personally know other valcos. They were a rare species, on the verge of extinction according to her grandparents, with their antlers crowning them, and red irises. Eva's blood was too diluted for her to have inherited the eye color from her father, but her stunted antlers were her indelible proof that she was unlike her half sister and every other Serrano of Galeno. No other valcos lived in Galeno presently. Her father must have been here at least once. But this idea proved to be yet another dead end.

Néstor watched her curiously as they descended the steps to the ground floor. Before he could ask what was on her mind, Doña Antonia emerged from an adjacent hall. Eva's colossal grandmother strolled alongside the archbishop. Doña Antonia wore a layered dark blue dress that could just as easily be confused for black, including the hat and flaps that covered the back of her neck and braided hair. The blue complemented her umber skin tone, and the shade of plum on her lips was modestly chosen, not much darker than her normal color.

The footsteps of Eva's entourage piqued the archbishop's interest. "Doña Antonia, I didn't know you came with company," he announced with good humor as they intersected in the hallway, the melody of a nearby troupial flitting with the breeze.

"My dear Néstor is finally considering a position in politics," Doña Antonia announced with a raised eyebrow, prompting Néstor to do nothing but agree.

"A family of politicians. I wouldn't expect anything less," the archbishop said, then turned to Eva with thinly veiled distaste.

Doña Antonia didn't miss the cue, so she said, "And Eva Kesaré came because she was meeting with Don Alberto."

Eva said, "We're courting. But Néstor and I are now leaving."

Indeed, Néstor and Don Jerónimo led the walk to the stables, but they practically left her behind to be absorbed into the archbishop and Doña Antonia's stroll. The traitors. The last thing Eva wanted was to be caught in conversation with the holy man. Almost as if in reaction to this very thought, the archbishop became very interested in her. He regarded her with his cloying smile and said, "I have noticed you making yourself scarce after Mass, Señorita Eva."

Eva cleared her throat, counting the steps until the archway to the stables, where a team of workers had set up a scaffolding to repair the red clay tiles of the roof. Why did they have to walk in the same direction?

"Eva Kesaré is one of my quiet ones." Doña Antonia rescued her, likely because every thought and judgment on her children and grandchildren was only a reflection on her as a matriarch. "She makes herself scarce in most social outings."

Heat bloomed in Eva's cheeks, but she kept her gaze fixed on the stables. In truth, Eva would avoid going to the cathedral if she had a choice—which, of course, she didn't. Instead, she swallowed the bitter nausea crawling up her throat anytime she went to Mass.

When she was inside the confining walls of the cathedral, a heaviness always weighed on her, suffocating her. A stifling multiplied by a congregation of people all covered from head to toe in their best attire. She was drowned by a desire to flee the cathedral's wooden doors and never return, because she feared the Virgin saw the truth in her. She saw the icons of saints standing like sentinels on either side of the entrance and altar and couldn't help but feel their judging eyes seeing what she was.

"In my experience, I've always found nozariels and valcos to be the most reluctant in accepting the Virgin into their lives, with their dangerous inclinations to believe in *that geomancia*. But the Virgin is good, and Her answers to this chaotic world are more than enough." He shot a sideways glance at what hid beneath Eva's curly bangs. "I hope it's not because of your *inheritance* that you're so eager to leave, Señorita Eva, for you are most welcome in Her house."

"I don't touch geomancia." Eva's lie came quickly to her lips, rehearsed.

"Is that so?"

"You know how young women are these days: more concerned about their dresses and their gossip than about being devout. But it'll come soon enough," Doña Antonia added in Eva's defense. Though her eyes told a different story—one saying Eva better prepare herself for a swift and much-deserved tongue-lashing as soon as they were back home, for no reason other than sparking doubt in the archbishop. "My family and I are very dedicated to the church. I adore the work you do."

So dedicated, in fact, that Eva felt she had to wear someone else's skin in her own home. She was forced to look away from the rifts of light that banded around trees or antique objects like a heat mirage, to ignore how the air charged with a spark when the rains rolled in. For her family's sake, she had to constantly convince herself the sorrowful calls in the middle of the night were merely fragments of her nightmares and not something that should be called *magic*.

Eva lived in a constant ache for those things humans couldn't see. She survived from morsel to morsel, sneaking attempts at geomancia behind closed doors and seeking answers to her parentage in the city records, even though she knew they would only yield more questions. After all, Doña Antonia kept the identity of Eva's father a secret but not the nature of how her mother, the gentle Doña Dulce, had come to have her. No, Doña Antonia and the biggest gossipers of Galeno never held back in whispering about the ravishing of Doña Dulce. How her father's dark magic had coerced false love in the devout Dulce, steering her from the right path and shattering her sanity. Not only robbing her of her dignity but, as Doña Antonia shamelessly put it, planting the seed of a devil in her.

Finally they reached the shade under the scaffolding where the workmen exchanged roof tiles. A honeysuckle vine hugged the stone archway, sweetening the air.

"Your family may need the church more than any other," the archbishop said. "It is no secret that valcos struggle with a certain inclination..."

He left the words unsaid, but Eva knew he meant to call valcos monsters, lured to darkness. It was the same opinion nearly every human of Galeno had.

"Only the Virgin can protect you from such thoughts."

The afternoon was sweltering, but Eva scorched hotter. He thought he was being magnanimous when, in fact, he only made her nauseous.

Doña Antonia had a nervous look about her at the insolent way Eva's eyes met the archbishop's. Eva's jaw rippled in indignation.

"If you fully accept the Virgin, then you won't have space in your mind for the darkness that inevitably consumes your lot—for you, it is only a matter of time. And you have a lot of praying to do, to atone for the actions of the monster who sired you."

"That makes absolutely no sense!" Eva growled, and the air around her cheeks crackled and sparked. "I am not responsible for what he did."

With a resounding crack, the scaffolding gave beneath the workers' combined weights. The wood groaned, rapidly toppling onto itself. Eva watched with wide eyes as the men screamed, throwing themselves to the adjoined balcony to flee the cave-in. A quick thinker—Néstor—yanked Eva and Doña Antonia by their dresses away from the wood and splinters raining over the cobbles. The yard burst with the sounds of the destruction. Eva could taste the detritus in the air.

Once the dust and the exclamations of concern settled, the archbishop and Doña Antonia watched Eva with shocked expressions. Eva, too, stood speechless as her heart thrummed a dissonant tune. She could see in their eyes that they wanted to accuse her of smiting the scaffolding with her anger. As ridiculous as it sounded, Eva wasn't sure they were entirely wrong.

The rest happened in a blur. Néstor made excuses for her and pulled her to Don Jerónimo's carriage, where Don Jerónimo also watched her with a gaping mouth. Néstor practically shoved her down on the velvet-cushioned seat and barked at the driver to get a move on, securing their escape. For that, Eva was endlessly grateful.

3

The Curandera

Silence reigned between Eva, Néstor, and Don Jerónimo as the carriage passed Galeno's plaza, where at its center stood a statue of a man in military uniform riding a galloping horse. People strolled through the cobbled roads, dodging the few carriages and using embroidered umbrellas for shade. The carriage passed houses painted in alabaster, ocher, cerulean, or any other alternative bright enough to reflect the spicy, unforgiving sunlight that was signature to the Llanos.

It was Néstor who shattered the quiet, saying softly, "That was not your fault."

Eva peeled her eyes from the row of yellow-blooming cassia trees flanking the plaza. Behind them was the cathedral, the tallest structure in the city.

Don Jerónimo raised his eyebrows at him. Their hands were linked over Néstor's lap, their fingers intertwined.

"You are both mad for thinking so," Néstor told Eva and Don Jerónimo.

"So it's a coincidence?" Eva said, her voice breaking. She wasn't sure she believed it. This wasn't the first time something inexplicable happened because of her. This was just the most . . . catastrophic.

Néstor gave her the straight face parents gave their children when hoping to avoid riling emotions. "Eva, please."

She ran her hands over her face, wiping the perspiration gathering at her temples. "Whatever happened back there—it only supports their case."

Néstor looked down at his feet. "You shouldn't have talked back."

"For how long must I put up with people saying I have a darkness in me? He said it was *my* duty to atone for my father!"

"People like to talk, but no one really believes it in their heart. It's only entertainment." Néstor shrugged. "Otherwise you'd be worrying about a trial rather than silly gossip."

Eva grimaced. "Are you trying to console me? That doesn't make me feel better. What if one day...they do it?"

"You are granddaughter to the governor. No one is going to outright accuse you of dark magic," Néstor said with a light wave of his free hand.

Don Jerónimo's gaze traveled up to her bangs. Eva wondered if he saw her like everyone else in Galeno and if he was only civil for Néstor's sake. "Outside of Galeno there are places where geomancia is seen differently," he said.

Eva nodded. Like in the southern mountains, the place valcos used to call home before humans had arrived on the continent. The bits of valco history she knew, she had pieced together from what people said—she never had access to any education on the matter. Again, she was struck by the hunger to play with geomancia.

"I don't want to go home. Take me to Doña Rosa," Eva blurted out.

Doña Rosa was a bastard of the Contador patriarch, a nozariel half-breed the gentry referred to as *the curandera*, after she'd gained infamy for spelling back to life the dead avocado tree in the Contadors' yard and for curing a Contador baby from the illness of mal de ojo.

"Again? Are you obsessed with making your situation worse?" Néstor said, reaching for her.

Eva withdrew from the touch. Yes, Doña Rosa was an outcast, hidden away in the Contador residence while the people of Galeno formulated horrible narratives about her origins and her openness to geomancia. Eva understood Néstor was afraid Doña Rosa gossip would inevitably embroil her. But she was desperate for a change of pace.

"You have no high ground here," Eva said, eyeing Néstor's and Don Jerónimo's intertwined hands. Néstor and Don Jerónimo's relationship was a secret everyone knew yet no one acknowledged, least of all Don Jerónimo's mother and Doña Antonia, who were both fond of the idea of getting grandchildren out of them. On their clandestine visits to the Contador residence, Eva and Néstor were coconspirators.

Don Jerónimo smirked, and Néstor sighed in defeat.

"Doña Rosa understands me," Eva added.

"I understand you."

"No, Néstor, not about this. You don't have the blood of a monster in your veins."

They were silent in the carriage: Don Jerónimo pretending to look out the window, while Néstor's and Eva's gazes met in conflict. Once upon a time, he would have chided her for speaking of herself that way. But everyone who knew her in Galeno thought this behind closed doors. For once in her life, Eva wanted to stop pretending.

Unlike the Serranos, who lived in a hacienda, the Contadors had a downtown house. Wrought iron gates shielded a pampered topiary garden and a red bougainvillea that looped around the house's majestic double doors. The two-story mansion had a façade of white-and-ocher stucco, with window frames and balconies of black-painted iron wrought in filigree designs and curling olive vines, all in a baroque style inherited from Segol. Inside, the house was as stuffy as the capitol building, with polished tiled floors and walls decorated in Pentimiento trinkets—rosaries and icons of the saints and the Virgin.

The main hallway opened to an outdoor kitchen, a courtyard, and another archway leading to a large plot of land, where the infamous avocado tree stood in its center. The yard was big enough to fit a servant house, stables accessible from a different street, and the curandera's house.

Eva headed to the shanty house on her own. The building was made of red clay, unpainted, and shaded by the canopy of a vast mamoncillo tree. A wicker curtain interwoven with the seeds of moriche palm fruits served as a door.

The scent of tobacco hung heavy in the single-room home. Shadows rose behind baskets, chests of drawers, and a cooking counter populated by herbs and utensils. From the ceiling hung garlic bunches and salted meats. A woman sat across the table, facing the door, her skin the same sun-kissed sandy shade as Don Jerónimo's. She wore a dress of undyed cotton that wrapped around one shoulder, the other shoulder exposed and showing her nozariel scutes. Her hair was in long braids, abundant and frizzy with curls.

"I'm never getting rid of you, am I?" Doña Rosa said, her voice low, the result of a lifetime being overly friendly to the pipe. She was a beauty around Don Alberto's age. She had a symmetrical face, plump lips, high cheekbones, and pointed nozariel ears. Her frame was large and well-fed.

"Do you want me not to come back?" Eva ground her teeth at this, stung by the relentless rejections thrown her way.

The woman chuckled. "How can I deny you?"

"I'm not forcing you to see me."

"You entertain this dull life," Doña Rosa said.

Eva sat across from her on the rattan chair. The table was covered in a tablecloth embroidered with an eclipsed sun. The iconography belonged to Rahmagut, god of the Void. Doña Rosa revered him for representing the opposition of what was conventional. Like Ches, god of the sun, Rahmagut was one of the few deities who'd survived the arrival of Pentimiento. Only under this roof was Eva free to talk about Ches and Rahmagut, whom Doña Antonia had forbidden from her grandchildren's lexicon. But Eva didn't engage in it unless absolutely necessary. Speaking of Rahmagut was an assured way of inviting the Virgin's scorn, or Her abandon.

"I went to the governor's office today, to see if there were any mentions of my father in my birth records."

Doña Rosa croaked a laugh at that. "You are naïve for believing you would find anything in the books."

Eva let her mouth fall open to retort, but she knew the woman was right. "I had to try..."

"Your family will never allow the secret to come out."

She spoke with so much surety. Eva arched a brow. "Do you know anything?"

"When I was your age and you were this big"—Doña Rosa lifted her palm up to her hip—"your mother, the gentle Doña Dulce, brought you here with a sickness no human doctor could cure. You were vomiting your guts out, and shitting them out as well. Don't you remember?"

Eva smiled graciously but shook her head.

Doña Rosa squinted an eye at her. "The illness has no proper name, and no human physician has treated it. But I'd seen it before, in other little valcos in Fedria."

Fedria, the sister nation east of Venazia, separated by Río'e Marle and the differences in politics between the Liberator and the caudillos who'd helped him free the land from the Segolean colonists. "You've been to Fedria?" Eva said.

"Oh, dear no, I wish. Then my life would have turned out differently. I was born in El Carmín, as my name can tell you. Living close to the border, you see all sorts of folk. I saw with my own eyes a valco or two, during the revolution." She smiled bitterly at a distant memory.

Eva wondered what life had been like for Doña Rosa, reaching maturity before the Liberator won the war for independence and freed nozariels from slavery. Before the revolution, Venazia and Fedria had been colonies of Segol, and nozariels were bred to serve the human aristocracy, including families like the Serranos. After independence was won and Segol's influence was ousted, nozariels were sent to Fedria under an agreement between the new Venazian king and the Liberator. Doña Rosa was the only exception Eva knew of, kept in Galeno for being the bastard daughter of the Contador patriarch. Had Doña Rosa been enslaved under the oppression of humans in her youth? Eva swallowed the question, for she hadn't earned the kind of trust to ask it.

Instead, she reeled Doña Rosa back to finish the tale. "Did my mom say anything about my father?"

With pursed lips, Doña Rosa shook her head. "I poked and prodded her for a clue of who your father was, but even in her moment of desperation, she wouldn't confide in me."

Eva stared down at her wringing hands. Perhaps Dulce had loathed speaking of the monster who'd beguiled her with dark magic, who had forced her to betray her vows to her then husband, father of Eva's older half sister, Pura.

Disappointment filled her. Eva swallowed down a sigh.

"Doña Antonia has done a fine job of keeping your father's name out of everyone's mouths." Doña Rosa leaned forward, purring, "Besides, didn't you call him *wicked* last I saw you? Why would you want to get to know such a villain?"

Eva scowled, hating the mockery. It made her guard the truth: how she was without a crucial part of her identity. Perhaps she should just drop it and lean on her human side, exactly as her grandmother wanted it.

"So how did you cure me?"

The woman tapped her chin as if in thought. "Well, either one must procure the dance of a virgin, or you can take a tonic of galio." With a chuckle, she added, "I'm afraid we were short on virgins at the time, so I made you the tonic."

"Galio," Eva mouthed, remembering the old rhyme for the major branches of geomancia, which Doña Antonia prohibited Eva from speaking as soon as she learned it:

Bismuto in the sword
Litio for the shield
Galio in the salves
But no matter: to iridio you yield

The prickle Eva often felt in the air stirred, awoken. She rubbed her arms, glancing at the clay icon of Rahmagut sitting cross-legged. It was tucked in one corner of the room, a bowl of black beans and another bowl of midnight-blue powder facing him in offering.

Doña Rosa fished in her drawers for a crystal vial filled with an oily, clear liquid with a fine powder precipitating to the bottom. "Today I mixed a solution of litio. Take it with you, ward your room, just in case. There's a wicked spark in the air these days. Like something nasty is brewing. Don't you feel it?"

Eva wanted to scream that she felt this all the time. But maybe she was the wicked thing.

"Do you feel it because you're half nozariel? The spark?"

"Anyone who doesn't shut themself off to the *spark* will feel it. Magic lives around us," Doña Rosa said plainly, as if Eva was the fool for not believing this already.

"But—the people of Galeno. Someone would have said something."

"And risk being called a curandera? A witch? Risk reducing your social life to desperate mothers who don't know how to treat their half-breed children? How many of the proper ladies in your circle are willing to choose this path? You've met that wolf dressed as an archbishop, always sniffing for people who are different. The world is changing, and the more Penitent humans there are, the less it's 'socially acceptable' to acknowledge the existence of magic."

Eva stared at her lap. Doña Antonia's wrath was the unspoken consequence. A sliver of understanding wormed its way into her. "Even humans can feel it?"

Doña Rosa watched her long and hard. "Dulce had an aptitude for geomancia. And I watched your grandmother beat it out of her, along with what little happiness she managed to build up for herself. Have you inherited that aptitude?"

There it was again, a morsel. Another piece of the truth Eva so longed for. "Yes," Eva said softly, "but I thought it came from my father."

Doña Rosa arched her brows in amusement.

"I'm ready to learn something new, please," Eva said, gripping the edges of the table, her eyes rounding. "It comes easy to me. Maybe something with galio, since we're on the topic."

This drew laughter from the curandera. She searched through her belongings before withdrawing a small flask, a leather-bound journal, and a string holding together a series of colorful paper cutouts.

"Our little sessions—I should be compensated."

"I'll bring you all my escudos," Eva said quickly, and the woman laughed some more. She slid the journal across the tablecloth.

Eva ran her hands along the rough leather cover, feeling the areas where the binding was weak. It was meant to look innocuous, to stave off suspicion. Scribbled within was all the knowledge on geomancia that Doña Rosa had collected throughout her life.

Doña Rosa lent Eva her middle finger ring. "Put this on."

Eva did so, as all galio potions had to be worn on the middle finger. In order for a geomancia spell to be cast, one needed to carry the actual metal on one's body. The geomancers of old solved this by developing recipes to dilute the metals into solutions, which could be worn in capped rings or lockets, to serve as conduits.

"Why is it so hard to come by the ingredients for geomancia?" Eva wondered, for she had only ever seen traders of geomancia metal powders once or twice at the Sunday pop-up market and never in an actual storefront.

"You can blame Penitents for that. People are scared to be seen as practitioners of geomancia nowadays. And with less demand comes scarcer supply. Before the revolution, it wasn't uncommon to hear of miners selling ores to alchemists, who made small fortunes extracting, purifying, and selling mixed solutions to geomancers. But the Pentimiento Church has Galeno by the throat. In other places, there's more freedom."

Eva nodded. She wished she had the courage to leave Galeno, to head south.

Doña Rosa lifted the string with the paper cutouts. They were part of the decorations put up in town during the Saint Jon the Shepherd holiday celebrations. The triangular cutouts were hung crisscrossed from rooftop to rooftop and were often in the tricolors of the revolution: goldenrod for the riches the Segoleans discovered on Venazian shores, cerulean for the Cow Sea and ocean separating their land from Segol, and scarlet for the blood shed by the revolutionaries.

"Every budding geomancer knows that galio is the conduit for healing through magic."

Eva nodded eagerly.

Doña Rosa shot her a mischievous smile. "What I'm going to teach you today is that it can also be used for spells of animation."

Doña Rosa gestured for the journal, then leafed through the pages. Eva's attention was snagged by a page with the illustration of a naked woman with a split-open neck. The woman sat up from a workshop table with tools scattered about, a hooded person behind her. The caption jumped at Eva like the letters were screaming. "Resurrection?" she said, holding the sheet down before Doña Rosa could leaf through to her destination.

The older woman cocked an eyebrow at the interruption. "Oh, yes. Galio can be used for that as well. From what I understand, it was an art developed by desperate witches attempting to heal the helpless or to bring back the dead."

Eva ran her fingers along the hastily scribbled text, her poor fluency in the old tongue revealing a few words that Doña Rosa was kind enough to explain to her: "When attempting resurrection, it recommends using a living person's body as the host, because the dead rot and waste away. These spells call for binding the soul of the person you want to resurrect into the living, breathing host to give them a second life in the body of another."

Eva thought of her mother, then immediately chastised herself.

"Fascinating, no? But I didn't bring this so we could talk about resurrection." Doña Rosa flipped to the next page, pointing her stubby finger at another passage. "I want to show you how galio spells can be extended to animating what has no life to begin with."

Doña Rosa paused, her dark stare seizing Eva. It was a humid day, apparent by the beads of perspiration hugging the older woman's forehead. Eva felt her own sweat rolling down her back.

"I was only ever successful at it once before, years ago, when I was furious at my father for the way he's allowed the family to humiliate me," Doña Rosa said. "I think my anger made it work. I wonder if you can do it now."

It was posed as a challenge. Eva stared at the page and spoke truthfully. "I don't understand the instructions."

Doña Rosa folded one of the paper cutouts until it resembled a butterfly. She handed it to Eva. "Put your hands in the shape of the drawing and blow on the paper." She pointed at the illustration of two joined hands, their fingers locked, the indexes pointed outward and the thumbs propping up the butterfly. The hands were drawn wearing a capped ring on the middle finger.

One thing Doña Rosa failed to mention—which Eva caught at once, for it was undoubtedly part of her challenge—was that she needed to have a vision and intent for the animation at the forefront of her mind.

She took the paper butterfly and pinched it between both thumbs, her fingers entwined according to the illustration. Eva focused on the spell, desperately desiring for the meek paper body to flap once and twice until it didn't need to be propped between her thumbs anymore. She deeply wanted this hot yearning to travel from the depths of her chest, to her finger, through the ring conduit, and out into the material world. She blew on the paper.

As Eva had valco blood, she was capable of seeing the strings of geomancia flitting out of the ring, circling her fingers, and ultimately infecting the paper cutout with Eva's desire for animation. The folded scarlet wings twitched in her grasp. Eva's heartbeat quickened. She let the golden threads twirl around her hand until all of them were spent in animating the paper before she released it. Once she did, the butterfly flapped and flew over the table. Her very own creation.

"You're brimming with power," Doña Rosa murmured in awe.

Eva too felt this awe, deeply, and was overrun by the rush to do it again. To produce many more flapping little creatures of her design.

"I did it," she said, beaming.

Doña Rosa let out one of her deep, hearty laughs. "Well done, child."

"I really did it."

"Now, don't pat yourself in the back too fast. You have valco blood in you."

"And you have nozariel blood," Eva said with a toothy grin, as if to prove she needn't be angry to do it. She didn't need the help of her emotions or blood to accomplish this—and more.

An outside breeze tickled the shells hanging on the door, carrying a call of Eva's name. She recognized Néstor's voice telling her it was time to go. She clicked her tongue in disappointment.

Doña Rosa also understood their time was up. "Take them with you," she said, helping Eva disenchant the flapping butterfly and fold the cutouts into a single pile. "You can pay me for the galio ring later."

Eva nodded, hiding the litio vial, for warding, within the folds of her dress. She grabbed the papers as Néstor entered the small house. He grimaced, either at the smell or at the sight of them.

"Let's go before mi mamá gets home. I don't want her suspecting anything."

Eva could imagine Doña Antonia's outrage: her youngest son getting friendly with someone who wasn't his betrothed and her granddaughter learning from the resident curandera.

Doña Rosa and Eva exchanged a conspiratorial nod before Eva bid her goodbye.

Néstor and Eva snuck out of the Contador house like children up to a scheme. Their driver welcomed them with a blind eye. Just before they ascended into the carriage, Néstor whispered in Eva's ear, "You shouldn't meddle with Rahmagut—that's the devil's magic."

Eva whipped around, cheeks flushing. "I wasn't."

"I saw the little icon she had in her house," Néstor murmured, and entered the carriage.

Eva had, too.

Doña Antonia had shown the images of the sitting man to all her children and grandchildren, as a warning, so that they would know what the devil looked like.

Eva chose to ignore Néstor and his fear. Instead, she clung to the most important piece of information reaffirmed to her today. Geomancia came to her naturally. She'd been born for it. Now she needed to figure out a way to reconcile this hunger with becoming the person her grandmother expected Eva to be.

4

The Benevolent Lady

Her heartache was like the splitting of mountains. It fractured Reina from the inside out, as if a despondent god were raising his fist to the vast sky, only to slam it down on her, with enough force to erupt volcanos and rupture continents. The pain made Reina writhe like no breath was enough to bring her out of Rahmagut's Void. When she finally opened her eyes, attempting to scream, someone shoved her back down by the shoulders on the hard surface where she lay.

Reina screeched, her vision flooded in tears and black spots of agony. The same person who held her down stuffed a rag into her mouth to silence her.

When the tears cleared, Reina saw the tall woman from earlier standing by. *Her grandmother.* The woman regarded Reina without sympathy, even if the screams that made it past the rag were enough to make anyone's hairs stand on end.

Doña Ursulina's gloved hands held a ragged black ore reflecting light like a night sky peppered with stars. A string of fervent whispers violated Reina's thoughts when Doña Ursulina lowered the ore to her chest, as if something foreign were forcing itself into her the moment she laid eyes on it. The woman sighed and said, "Your galio potion wore off." Then she gave Reina a long look, seemingly debating something with herself.

In the end, she spared Reina no mercy. Doña Ursulina shoved the ore right into Reina's chest, which she suddenly realized was wide open and the reason for her agony. Except she didn't know real agony until the edges of the ore contacted the crystal contraption Doña Ursulina had installed in Reina's raw, open chest.

Her nerves exploded. Pain like the scorch of fire licked her spine and blinded her. Reina screamed through the gag. Her ears pressurized, then were deafened. She screeched and writhed as this woman brutalized the area where Reina's heart ought to be. Then Doña Ursulina's whispering lulled Reina into the oblivion of a weighted sleep.

Reina awoke later from the rapidly fading dream of meeting her father again: A tall, lean, umber-skinned man with short curly black hair and tamarind eyes. Her eyes. They were on a jungle path, where he beckoned her to follow him.

She groggily stared at the window, where morning light filtered through gossamer curtains. Somehow she was still alive. She couldn't be sure of how long she had been unconscious or how she lived at all. She tried sitting up, her interest piquing at the memory of being on that hard table, under Doña Ursulina's ministrations.

Beneath the woolen bedcovers, a loose cotton shirt and pants protected her modesty. The fabrics around her were high quality, her pillows of soft down. She lifted the bedsheets and her shirt to look at her chest, where a dull throb emanated. Her torso was bound by bloody bandages, and something pulsed beneath them. A chill struck her, as if whatever was inside her now drained the warmth from her chest. She heard voices, a low susurration growing louder as she fixated on the thing burrowed into her skin. Upon bringing a shaky hand to her chest, she found raggedness where her heart should have been. Her breathing came short and heavy, and it got stuck in her throat, her flesh sweating cold in a panic.

Memories flooded her more vividly than any dream. She remembered feeling like she was drowning in never-ending agony, where no amount of writhing or crying could soothe her. And the dark creatures who'd ambushed her as dusk draped the mountains, their wicked smiles and animal ferocity as they clawed and bit at her.

Reina chewed her lower lip raw. She shut her eyes to force out the memories of the creatures Doña Ursulina and Doña Laurel had called *tinieblas*. Her heart palpitated beneath her palm. At least she still had a heart—or a semblance of it. At least she was alive.

A gasp sounded from the room's door. A human woman carrying bandages froze by the doorway upon seeing her. Reina wiped her tears away. Before she could ask where she was, the woman scurried out. Maybe the sight of a battered nozariel was enough to spook her.

Reina decided she was too weak to get up. And if they hadn't wanted her to sleep in the bed, they wouldn't have placed her in such a lavish setting. She snuggled back under the covers and allowed herself to be swept away by a light sleep.

Later, the clicking of heels on the stone floor roused her again. A woman dressed in an azure gown entered the room. Reina recognized the blueness of her eyes and her full lips.

Doña Laurel carried a bowl sloshing with a steaming soup. The layered scents of broth filled the room, awakening Reina's hunger. She handed Reina the wooden bowl, which swirled with a milky chicken broth, diced potatoes, and small blocks of white cheese topped by a poached egg and a sprinkle of scallions.

"The cook made pisca today. Help yourself," she said, then helped Reina sit up. "I have to say, I'm surprised to see you made it."

Between spoonfuls of broth, Reina said, "Thank you for saving me, and for your hospitality...and for your food." She could go on, really, because she meant it.

Doña Laurel stared out the window as the curtains fluttered with mountain breeze. "I suppose introductions are in order. My name is Doña Laurel Divina Herrón de Águila. My husband is Don Enrique Águila, the caudillo of Sadul Fuerte."

Reina had heard of caudillos. Segolita didn't have one because, as the capital of Fedria, it enjoyed the protection of its centralized government's armament. But other cities and provinces in Fedria had them, as did all the provinces of Venazia, including Sadul Fuerte. They were the warlords who protected the land. The men who profited from farmers and traders to maintain a standing army and serve as the people's sword and shield. As Juan Vicente had once told her: In Venazia, the caudillos wielded all the power.

This meant Doña Laurel was likely the most powerful woman in this city, if not the whole country.

Reina swallowed awkwardly, a cough away from choking on the broth.

Doña Laurel placed a hand on Reina's knee. "Please. Relax. You are healing."

"Mi señora, I am in no state to address you." Reina lowered her head. She couldn't maintain eye contact. Was she supposed to bow?

Doña Laurel squeezed the bedsheets over Reina's knee. "Please, regard me like an equal for now. I command it," she said, her gaze fiery despite the sky-blue color of her eyes.

Reina coughed, then nodded.

"So where are you coming from?"

"Segolita, mi señora." Reina's old home, where her idealistic father had chosen to rear her, expecting the city to become a place of prosperity for nozariels after the revolution. Except Juan Vicente couldn't have been more wrong. As the capital of the colony formerly under Segol's command, which had split into what was now known as Venazia and Fedria, Segolita was owned by humans raised with the colonists' prejudice. Humans who still saw nozariels as filthy, lesser creatures.

"From the Llanos?" Doña Laurel chuckled. "I've traveled there before. Segolita's majestic—if you can ignore the misery hiding in its back alleyways. If you're willing to convince yourself the stink of shit is actually the aroma of roses. Things smell stronger in the heat, did you know that? Maybe that's why people here in Sadul Fuerte can be such good liars." Doña Laurel watched her with a coy smile, gauging Reina's reaction. "I'm sorry, I didn't have a very good time when I went there. It was too hot, and my clothes were more of a sweat-drenched burden than a statement of my good fashion sense," she finished with good humor.

"I have no love for Segolita. That's why I came here."

Doña Laurel's gaze surfed Reina's ridged nose and pointed ears, her lips quivering as if she were reconsidering her questions. "So you are Juan Vicente's daughter, with Beatriz?"

It surprised Reina that the lady knew both of her parents' names. She slurped the last of the bowl, set it on the bedside table, and stared at her hands. They were covered in scars from handling lye and boiling water, along with fresh cuts from her tussle in the mountains.

"He was my father, yes," she said with a nod. "He died when I was just a girl."

Doña Laurel's eyebrows sloped with concern. "So Juan Vicente has passed. I suspected this was the case, but I never wanted the confirmation. Not even from his mother. I suppose the truth cannot be avoided forever."

"You knew my father?"

After a long pause, Doña Laurel licked her lips and rose to stand by the window. Her absence left Reina cold.

"Your father was one of my best friends many years ago," Doña Laurel said. "I say 'one of my best friends' because I only ever had two, and the other is my husband." She turned her fierce gaze on Reina, piercing straight to her soul. "Juan Vicente was the kindest person I've ever met. He was so kind he even had the courage to go live in Segolita, with your mother. He left a life of comfort and riches in Sadul Fuerte behind for her."

"I never knew my mother," Reina said, her nostrils flaring at the bitter truth. "Sometimes I wonder how my life would have turned out differently if my parents were still around. If my father hadn't been so alone in raising me."

Doña Laurel's gaze carried to where Reina's tail was tucked beneath her. "I didn't know her well either. I only met her once, when Juan Vicente was saying his goodbyes. Although I do remember she had her tail cut off, unlike you."

The words took Reina by surprise. They were invasive, and normally she would ignore such remarks because it was too late. She couldn't conform and pass without her tail, as most nozariels born before the revolution did, for it needed to be severed shortly after birth. Her tail was too well-developed now—and a part of her. But Doña Laurel spoke with such fondness of Reina's father, she deserved to know. "Father thought it was barbaric that nozariels were forced to do this."

Doña Laurel looked affronted. "They're not forced anymore."

"No, now it's just easier to do it so that we don't live such a... difficult life. Well, so that *they* don't."

That ship had sailed for Reina. Her skin had become impervious to all the long looks and scowls of disgust she received from humans. Her father had impacted the course of her life forever with one measly decision, and he hadn't even stuck around to help her through it. Reina clenched her jaw and looked down, lest Doña Laurel catch the darkness in her eyes.

The doña picked up on it anyway. "I'm sure Juan Vicente did it with the best intentions. He abhorred the way nozariels were treated. It's what drew him to the cause. I hope he was happy in Segolita. What happened to your mother?"

"Father said she died of a cold when I was just a baby."

"I'm sorry," Doña Laurel said simply. She walked back to Reina and again sat on the bed, closer this time, bringing back her warmth. She tugged a silken handkerchief from the pocket of her dress and extended it to Reina. When Reina didn't immediately accept it—held hostage by her fear of touching a human possession, having had the habit beaten out of her—Doña Laurel gently wiped the cold sweat from Reina's temples, then caressed her cheek. And Reina watched her speechlessly, her new heart flailing uselessly in confusion at the woman's kindness.

It gave Reina the courage to ask the question casting a shadow over her entire life: "Did he say why he left, when he said goodbye? If he had everything here, why did he have to give it all up?"

Doña Laurel didn't answer right away. She wrung her hands and frowned, with her gaze lowered. "Once Segol was ousted after Samón Bravo's and Feleva Águila's final battle, a power vacuum disrupted the order in Sadul Fuerte. There were prosecutions and trials of alleged loyalists and just general chaos. But despite your father's best wishes for the revolution, one thing remained constant: Humans couldn't bring themselves to see nozariels as equals. Shortly after, Enrique and the other caudillos agreed it was best to send nozariels to Fedria, where Samón had garnered more sympathy for your kind, and the politicians who took power agreed to build a country governed by the people. I'm sure he took you there as part of that exodus. Thank the Virgin that Samón and Feleva were valcos, and most humans see them as heroes, otherwise the discrimination would also extend to valcos in the same way."

Also, valcos were never enslaved, the doña failed to mention.

"Did my grandmother—Doña Ursulina—did she disapprove of their union?"

"Perhaps—or perhaps you'll have to get the answers out of her. I'm sure it was a better life for your mother in Fedria. After emancipation, many families in Venazia disposed of their nozariel slaves in ways I'd rather not mention." Doña Laurel paused, picking at the lace of her long sleeves, which was patterned with doves taking flight. She wore three rings on each hand, made of gold and capped, like the ones worn by practicioners of geomancia. One ring per hand for litio, galio, and bismuto each. "I regret not paying attention to what was happening with Juan Vicente. I guess I was caught up in my own fairy-tale ending," Doña Laurel said dreamily, her smile reaching her eyes as she thought back. "Enrique was a war hero, and we were just married. Celeste was only a few months old. I was the luckiest girl in the land. I got what every noble lady west of the Páramo Mountains coveted in that time: marriage to the future caudillo of Sadul Fuerte. So, as you can imagine, I didn't have a lot of room in my mind to understand why Juan Vicente was so keen on leaving. I figured he was fed up with the way his circle mistreated his new mistress. Even the archbishop of Sadul Fuerte refused to marry them."

"They didn't marry in Segolita either." This was a fact Reina had never been able to wrangle out of her father, who'd spoken of his brief time with Beatriz so fondly. It was the gossiping people who knew Juan Vicente who'd told her.

"Juan Vicente deserved to be happy," Doña Laurel said and rose.

"I resent not knowing he was struggling. I resent that I couldn't help him. The people call me *the Benevolent Lady* because I pride myself on using my position to give kindness, which is something this city lacks."

Cold perspiration slicked Reina's hands. She saw the opening and almost didn't seize it, but in the end, desperation drove her to say, "My father's not here anymore, but I still need help. I left everything in Segolita for the opportunity to be a part of my grandmother's life."

Doña Laurel waited for her to finish with a sad look. Reina held her breath.

"Are you aware that nozariels are banished from Venazia?"

Reina's heart announced itself with a throb. Grimacing, she said, "I don't have anywhere else to go." Anytime doubt had assaulted Reina and begged her turn back to Segolita, the hope that there might be somewhere she belonged had kept her going, even to the hostile Venazia. "I know of the decree, but I also heard stories of nozariels who live with humans, if their families allow it. Doña Ursulina sent me a letter—"

Doña Laurel stopped her by raising a palm between them. "I would never hurt Juan Vicente's memory by turning you away. But while I may be the luckiest woman in all Sadul Fuerte, this is not a world where I'm allowed to make all the decisions. Focus on your recovery—once your strength returns, you should discuss your future with your grandmother."

It wasn't a rejection, but it stung nonetheless.

Doña Laurel made to walk away. Before she could exit, a wild side of Reina almost begged her, but she only managed the strength to say, "Th-thank you, Doña Laurel."

From under the doorway, Doña Laurel offered her a beaming grin, all squinted eyes and straight white teeth. "You're welcome, dear."

For the first time in years, Reina thought she might be.

5

Águila Manor

The Águilas' servants changed Reina's bandages and attended to her every need, but the mastermind behind the operation was Doña Ursulina. She made her appearance several days later, when Reina had the strength to sit up on her own and shakily stand with the support of the bedposts. Doña Ursulina coughed loudly from the doorway, arriving in black silk robes with a neck of white feathers, resembling the condors Reina had spotted circling the Páramo. The woman's scowl shook Reina to the bone, and her knees gave, collapsing her on the bed.

"How bold of you to assume your heart is ready to support your body," Doña Ursulina said, sweeping inside and closing the door.

Reina's breaths were weak and shivery, barely enough to supply her newly pounding head. She lowered herself to the plush pillows as steadily as she could manage. "I thought I felt better," she said once Doña Ursulina sat on the bedside chair.

Doña Ursulina didn't wait for Reina's permission before unbuttoning her loose cream shirt. The stink of dried blood emerged from her stained bindings. "Do not squander the miracle of your recovery with your foolishness."

Reina almost grabbed Doña Ursulina by the wrist to stop her, but she hesitated. She had not heard anyone display concern for her life in years, perhaps since Juan Vicente's passing.

"The skin is mostly healed, and your body didn't reject the ore. That is a miracle," Doña Ursulina murmured with her gaze on the bandages. She plucked a vial from the bag she'd brought and handed it to Reina. The small bottle was filled with a liquid the color of nighttime, peppered with glittering dots like the ore from her feverish memories of her operation.

"Drink it. All of it," the witch ordered.

The liquid stung Reina's tongue with bitterness. She erupted in coughs as heat speared through her body, sprouting from her heart to her extremities. A pain exploded in her chest, like she had been sprinting for hours.

Faintly, she heard the older woman's command to open up the bandages. Doña Ursulina didn't wait for consent, reaching to undo the binding. Addled by the potion, Reina seized Doña Ursulina's wrist with the proper strength of a nozariel, stunning the witch.

"Release me, you ignorant creature!" Doña Ursulina snapped, squirming. "If you break my wrist, no one will treat your heart," she hissed. "My only interest is in keeping you alive."

Reina's eyes were teary and her nose snotty when she let go. She winced but swallowed the tears as Doña Ursulina cut and peeled away the bandages.

"What did you make me drink?" Reina asked when she caught her breath.

"A tonic of concentrated iridio."

"Iridio?" she muttered to let it sink in.

A small pouch of iridio powder was easily worth a year of the salary Reina had earned as a criada back in Segolita. She'd once worked in a house where nearly the whole staff was replaced (including her) when a bottle of diluted iridio solution had gone missing. Some people made deals with kilos of iridio instead of gold. The stuff was beyond valuable in Segolita, where it was imported from Sadul Fuerte. She couldn't believe *she* had arrived at the source of it, as Águila Manor sat on top of the only iridio mines on the continent.

She followed her grandmother's gaze down to her chest, afraid to see the mess it had become, and was swamped by the sickly whispering of a hundred voices when she laid eyes on it. Chills ran through her spine and prickled her skin. What little food was in her stomach threatened to resurface as she saw what Doña Ursulina had done.

A pressurized crystal contraption sat above her left breast, on the space formerly taken up by her ribs, with the glittering black ore encrusted at the very center. The skin surrounding the crystal was red and inflamed, flaps of it barely shrouding the tubes connecting the crystal to her body. The sight made Reina's skin itchy, and she felt trapped, for she was forever married to it. She was possessed by the urge to yank the whole thing out, tubes and all, but it would only lead to her excruciating death.

The foreign object was startling enough that Reina didn't have a thought to feel shame or discomfort from her chest being exposed to this woman.

Merely looking at it, or thinking of it, was enough to rekindle the terrible susurration, the words in unintelligible tongues. The part of her that ran on instincts, that could sniff magic and taste the charged air, warned her there was evil in it. "What have you done to me?"

Doña Ursulina didn't look up as she gently poked and prodded at the object of Reina's horror. "I saved your life. If this ore weren't supplying the correct amount of iridio to your transplant, you wouldn't have felt any pain drinking the tonic." From the drawer of the bedside stand, she withdrew a fresh roll of bandages. Reina sat up, wincing, and helped her bind her chest again. "It is only because your new heart works perfectly that you feel this discomfort."

"My new heart?"

Doña Ursulina nodded.

"Why would you do that? Why would I need this?" The panic returned, and Reina had to grip the bedsheets, writhing. "You took out my heart?" Something about saying it aloud made every nerve in her chest flare. She choked down a sudden sob and hugged herself as best she could.

"Are you that ignorant of tinieblas? Don't you know what they do to people?"

She wiped her eyes stubbornly, angry at shedding more tears in this woman's presence. "The things that attacked me—you keep calling them tinieblas, but I thought tinieblas were nothing but a story—just a word for shadows. Tales to scare children into obedience."

Doña Ursulina smirked. "Horror tales are inspired by reality. They are Rahmagut's creations, allowed into this world by a cruel, prideful god. And you nearly became their meal."

Reina ran her hand through her bangs, wiping away the cold sweat. Her gaze skimmed the edges of the black ore poking out of the bindings, spurring the whispering again. How it made her want to scream.

"Why was I attacked in the mountains? I made a long journey from Segolita without a problem."

Doña Ursulina leaned back, giving her a long, hard stare. "The Páramo has been a place of many deaths. Of broken promises. And the mountains are home to the iridio star—the mines that make the Águilas so rich. It's only natural that they would be attracted to the Páramo."

"And why me?" Reina was doing what many wouldn't. She had left the comforts of the familiar for the hope that her luck would change. Sadul Fuerte was supposed to be a fresh beginning. The opportunity to have the family her father had denied her. And just when she was close to making it, the gods had been cruel again. Not even Ches, whom she cherished the most for being the bringer of light and creator of the sun, offered her reprieve. She tried swallowing the despair, but surely Doña Ursulina saw it written all over her face.

Doña Ursulina mirrored Reina's sloped lips and brows. There was supposed to be compassion in her black eyes. And yet Reina was left feeling so cold.

"Tinieblas see no reason," Doña Ursulina said. "They don't pick and choose. They don't have to have a purpose. They're pure malignant energy. Rahmagut dabbles in creation just like every other deity. But he cannot make whole creatures, so his tinieblas are ravenous for hearts."

Reina tugged on the sheets and covered herself up to her nose. "Is Sadul Fuerte overrun by them?"

Doña Ursulina packed her tools back into the bag. "The caudillo and his army keep tinieblas under control. But they can't ensure that the mountains are safe for everyone at all times." Doña Ursulina's thin eyebrows arched. "Just be grateful you landed in the hands of the right people. Celeste, who was raised by Laurel. And me, who's been waiting for someone with your exact condition to attempt this highly theoretical procedure. No one else could have saved you."

She rose to leave, then stopped as if reminded of something. "That ore is veined with iridio, which supplies the spell keeping your transplant heart pumping like your former one. It should be enough iridio for a decade or two. Avoid showing it to anybody. I don't have to remind you how valuable iridio is, even here in Sadul Fuerte. If it is ever taken out of you and you do not replenish the heart, you will die."

"So I'm a slave to it."

Doña Ursulina ignored the remark. "When that happens, let us hope Doña Laurel or Celeste is feeling charitable and can supply you with new ore from their mines. But I'm sure by then, you will have become essential to their lives."

The days in the room passed her by. Reina counted a moon cycle, and her own. Doña Ursulina came and went every other day for brief moments. She prodded Reina's heart and patted herself on the back for her own ingenuity. Sometimes Reina would drift in and out of sleep and find a tray of pastelitos on the bedside table or a hot tealike sugarcane drink that she'd never had before coming to Águila Manor. The person who left her the gifts would spirit away like a shadow shifting in the light, so Reina never had the chance to marvel at their kindness or thank them properly.

One morning, once she was strong enough to walk, Reina decided to see the manor from a different vantage than the bedroom window. She woke up with a renewed sense of hope: She was strong enough to have a second chance, so perhaps Ches had listened to her prayers. For this, she needed to thank him.

She slipped on her old boots and ripped jacket (for the cold), stuffed a pan de bono from the night before into her jacket pocket (for Ches), and snuck out before the scullery maid made her usual rounds. Corridors of polished stone floors and tall ceilings accompanied her brief tour. Reina passed a sunroom, a library, a drawing room with a pianoforte and a harp, noting how every detail was gilded or engraved with rich threads.

The sky was overcast when Reina emerged onto the bustling yard, where men descended the gravel path from the mountains, their mules transporting sacks of moras, cassava, and ocumo. She dodged women carrying laundry of embroidered linens and knitted ruanas, and she hugged herself at the shivery reminder that she was unprepared for the perpetual cold of this region. A forest of non-native firs surrounded the estate, and behind them rose the Páramo Mountains, the closest hills draped in colorful squares of farmland, while the tallest summit was cloaked in snow.

The red-clay-roofed servants' building and adjoined armory were shaded by the imposing height of the manor. With its thick stone walls and corner turrets, it resembled a castle more than anything else. Cabins and homesteads of the common folk loyal to the caudillo sprinkled the hills. Reina circled the yard, avoiding the ruddy children chasing chickens and goats and each other.

She hiked to the forest, searching for a quiet clearing to make her offering to Ches. She wasn't one for praying every day, like Penitents did to their Virgin and saints, but she did recognize when she owed a debt: She'd promised Ches her devotion in exchange for his help in getting out of dark times. Waking up with her needs met in Águila Manor felt like divine intervention. It merited leaving him a prayer and a gift.

The clouds didn't let up as she searched the forest for a sunny clearing, so she merely left the pan de bono by a creek. Juan Vicente had told her how her mother, Beatriz, believed sharing food was the ultimate gesture of hospitality, especially when food was a scarce resource. Sacrificing food created bonds and brought people together. That was why she did it for Ches.

A drizzle kept Reina company as she headed back. The paths twined and twisted, and she lost her way but later emerged into the ascending roads leading to Águila Manor, where it sat on a hill. The wrought iron gates were wide open, the grounds of the estate shielded by a barrier of hedges and orange-flowering coral trees. A path encased in rosebushes led to the entrance, where the dark wood doors were perched at the apex of stone steps. Rippled stone pillars supported a second-story balcony. The terrace was decorated in potted orchids, their blooms so foreign and exquisite Reina imagined they were constantly spoiled by a gardener.

There was a flurry of steps behind her, and someone yanked her by the tail. Reina stopped, yelping.

The jeering face of a valco met her. She recognized the young man instantly, with his silvery-blond hair loosely tied back, his long face and narrow frame, his valco antlers knotting like an ivory-colored crown. He had been one of her rescuers.

"I don't think I've ever seen a nozariel with a tail before," he said with his teeth bared in a sneer.

He was accompanied by Celeste, who said, "Javier! You are so *rude*." She was dressed in a shirt and trousers dirtied by greenery, much like how Reina remembered her after the fateful day of the tinieblas' attack. She wielded a scythe with the handle veined by a red glow. Her hair was up in a braided ponytail, and her cheeks and neck were red from the cold, covered in dirt and sweat.

Reina faced them fully while her tail thrashed behind her. She could still feel the phantom sensation of his touch. Shivers ran up her spine.

"Don't touch my tail."

Javier squared up, smirking. "Why? What are you going to do about it? You dare challenge the caudillo's brother?"

Reina glanced away to her muddy boots at the realization.

He laughed. "Just who does this tailed nozariel think she is?" he added, circling her, tugging the tail again so fast she couldn't step out of his reach in time. "This is my home, my land, and if I feel like grabbing it on a whim, you should just be glad I'm not cutting it off instead—you know, to do you the favor." He tapped his scabbarded blade to make the point.

"You're vile!" Celeste said, and Javier only laughed his way into the manor.

Celeste offered Reina an embarrassed grimace.

Reina didn't need the gesture, for she had grown up having her tail yanked and pulled by the people immediately repelled by its existence. "It's okay. I've endured worse."

"It's best to stay out of his way. He doesn't learn. And no one can shut him up except my parents." Celeste gave her scythe a shake, and Reina watched with wide eyes as the weapon vanished into thin air, the veined glow of its handle disappearing last.

Her shock was obvious, for Celeste revealed the locket hanging beneath her shirt collar. "I summon it with iridio. That way it's more reliable than any real steel, because it'll never break—not if I don't want it to."

Reina blinked, surprised to witness what was said about valcos with her own eyes. How they were so attuned to geomancia that it served their life like an everyday tool. The Águilas owned the source of iridio, so it made sense that Celeste should spend it so carelessly. But the wastefulness was hard to swallow.

Reina followed Celeste into the foyer. There sunlight speared through stained-glass windows and painted the patterned tiles with rainbow light.

"The caudillo's brother. And you are the caudillo's daughter." Saying it made Reina tingly, like she was overreaching and someone would jump out of a corner to beat her for daring to fraternize with the masters of the house. "He is your uncle?"

"By definition only." Celeste rolled her eyes. "But enough about Javier. I'm glad to see you're feeling better." Her gaze flitted down to Reina's chest.

Reina wondered if Celeste could see the spell keeping her heart pumping at this very moment.

"I hope the guarapo and pastelitos worked?"

"The gua...ra...po..." Reina said slowly and beamed as she

realized Celeste was the mysterious benefactor of her favorite snacks while she'd recovered. "You left those for me? Thank you. They kept me motivated to get better, so I could have more," she said. She slowed behind Celeste, unsure of the etiquette. How was she supposed to thank the caudillo's daughter for such a kindness? No one had forbidden her from addressing Celeste, but from experience it would only be a matter of time before they did. She felt so ugly, and inadequate, and *nozariel* beside Celeste's natural-born radiance.

"Is everything all right?"

Reina's transplant heart thrummed out of sync. "You've helped me so much. I owe you my life," she said, referencing the agonized moment when she'd almost perished on the mountain.

Celeste leaned against the arched doorframe to the dining hall and laughed. She carried a deep confidence in that sound. Reina loved hearing it.

"There's no need to thank me," Celeste said. "Your life wouldn't need saving if we didn't have the iridio mines. Wicked things are attracted to the iridio."

Reina gripped the jacket covering her chest. "So they'll be attracted to me."

Celeste's eyes fell on Reina's chest with purpose, confirming what she could see. "Yes."

Reina swallowed thickly. That made her a fool for entering the woods alone.

The soft melody of a four-stringed guitar flitted from the dining room, as did Javier's jeering voice. The reproach of a boy-man. It sobered Reina. "I came here looking for my grandmother—and I've found her," she said.

Celeste waited patiently.

"I didn't expect things would turn out this way—I mean, who can? But from what I've seen so far, I would like to stay."

The words came from her heart. The mountains were a whole new world, but it had Doña Laurel and Celeste. Reina could find purpose here and, if she dared, even friendship and companionship. She could be a granddaughter to her grandmother. Thus, she needed to learn why Doña Ursulina had summoned her in the first place. "I don't know how my father could have this life and leave it."

Celeste nodded and smiled. "The manor is always in need of more help. I'm sure we can find you a job here with the servers."

Reina pressed her lips into a line, neither agreeing nor disagreeing. If this truly was to become a great new beginning, she wanted to strive for something more. She had already lived a life in the shadows in Segolita, scrubbing floors and accepting the abuse of capricious masters. But she could be patient, if that was what it took.

"Where do I find Doña Ursulina?"

"The east wing is Doña Ursulina's domain. She has a townhome in Sadul Fuerte, but it's mostly empty, I think. She spends all her time here."

Celeste beckoned her to another corridor away from the dining hall. Reina followed her as the floors changed from tiles to flagstones, through wallpapered hallways decorated with maps, banners, and the occasional framed paintings. They stopped before a studded door of rotting wood. Celeste pushed it open, revealing a descending staircase shrouded in shadows.

"She has an underground laboratory where she studies iridio. I'm not too fond of going down there—and I have to go wash up to break my fast. But that is where she healed you and where you'll likely find her."

Reina took issue with referring to her transplant as *healing*, but she bit the objection down. She just nodded in thanks.

"I believe it's the first door to the left."

Reina descended the stone steps alone, guided by the dim light pooling from the first landing, and emerged onto a corridor lit by wrought iron sconces. Down here the air was stale, the reek reminiscent of dead frogs, with the slightest hint of incense. Humidity clung to the walls, and grime. The corridor turned into darkness ahead, but the first door to the left, as Celeste had said, was slightly ajar.

Voices flitted out of the room.

"Tonight I have the Virgin's favor." The first was instantly recognizable, kind but commanding: the Benevolent Lady's. "And Enrique will return from his journey by moonrise."

"Your tonic is ready. I know it is time for your cycle. I will always have it ready for when it comes." The second voice was lower, older. Reina's grandmother. "Do not feel like it is your fault. Do not question your womanhood. Valcos and humans are inherently different species—"

"Celeste must have a brother."

Reina clenched her fists. She had stepped into a world where she hadn't been invited.

Doña Ursulina's voice carried on. "The gods didn't intend for this mixing and interbreeding."

Heeled shoes approached the open door. Reina panicked. Where could she hide in this bared corridor? And if she did, unsuccessfully, she would be all the more guilty for attempting it.

"Accept Celeste as the miracle that she is. Should any misfortune befall her, the succession is secured with Javier," said Doña Ursulina.

Reina could almost hear Doña Laurel's outrage in her pause.

"That won't be necessary," Doña Laurel said, "because Celeste will have a brother."

The door swung open with Doña Laurel's exit. She nearly ran into Reina. Instead of withering at Reina's obvious eavesdropping, Doña Laurel's expression warmed. "Reina? Coming to see your grandmother?"

Reina nodded quickly, avoiding glancing at the vial clutched close to Doña Laurel's chest.

"Let me get out of your way, then," the woman said, graciously making an exit.

Reina nodded to herself, squared up, and walked into Doña Ursulina's underground lab.

A smoky incense crawled up Reina's nostrils, the burning scents bordering on sweet. Glittering light from a plethora of candles bounced off crystals and trinkets hanging like chandeliers from the ceiling and the tall bookshelves. There were tables and book-stacks propping up gilded artifacts, which spun and ticked like metronomes, surely alive from the touch of geomancia. Two walls were lined with floor-to-ceiling bookcases, the wood framed by intricate curls and leaves, the details painted in gold. Colors burst from the assortment of bottles and vials on Doña Ursulina's shelves. A large square table served as the center desk, cluttered with more books and maps.

Doña Ursulina stood by her bookcases, contemplating a book. She turned and raised a brow upon seeing Reina, then thrust the book back onto its shelf. "You're finally out and about, I see. Did the head matron kick you out of the room already?"

"No—no, I was just feeling better."

"And you decided to come strolling down to my laboratory?"

"I was looking for you, and Celeste pointed me down here."

A derisive smile split Doña Ursulina's face, but she waited for Reina's cue.

Reina took a deep breath. She gestured with open palms. "I'm feeling much better now, and I wanted to thank you for saving me. I want to offer myself—to you. You called for me, and I came. I left everything I had." The part about her not having much to leave behind in the first place, she omitted.

Doña Ursulina approached. Reina couldn't keep herself from gulping, her nozariel instincts begging her to flee. But she shoved down the fear and merely looked up at the taller woman with her best excuse for courage.

"And I'm glad you did, my granddaughter." The word sounded odd coming from Doña Ursulina's lips. Perhaps Reina just needed to get used to it.

"I just want to know: Why didn't you ask for me sooner? I missed out on knowing you for nineteen years."

Doña Ursulina's expression was like smooth stone, utterly unreadable. "I would have been in your life earlier, were it not for your father. Did he talk about me?"

Reina shook her head. "Never."

The woman furrowed her brows at the admission.

Reina stared down at her hands to avoid the hurt of losing Juan Vicente from creeping back into her chest. She had gotten so good at not missing him. It worked best when she didn't talk about him at all. "Why did you summon me here?"

Doña Ursulina let out a sigh. She ran a hand down the refined braid framing her temple. "You can say I crafted that invitation in a moment when I grew tired of being alone. I did so blindly, because I had no idea what state you would be in; if Juan Vicente raised you to hate me; if you had passed away, like him."

Reina clenched her jaw. Both had indeed been possibilities.

"I did it because I knew I would need a successor for the legacy I'm building here. That was supposed to be Juan Vicente's role, until he denied me."

Reina's eyes rounded, but she hid the hunger for information before it became obvious. "Well, I'm glad I'm here. I would like to stay," she offered. "As your granddaughter, I mean." Her new heart thrummed uncomfortably. She was laying bare all her desires, opening herself up to this stranger.

"It won't be easy. You're half nozariel in a country hostile to your kind."

"I can't go back," she said quickly. "Let me prove to you that I can be worthy of the Duvianos name." Reina didn't know what possessed her to say those words, but as Doña Ursulina's eyebrows rose, she knew they were the right ones. "I don't know what happened between you and my parents. I don't know if I'm like them. I can be a clean slate. I can be whatever you need me to be."

The seconds that passed during Doña Ursulina's deliberation felt endless. It was unsettling to look at her this deeply. To see her unlined countenance and come to terms with the fact that there was no way she could look this young naturally.

Doña Ursulina nodded. "Good. I will vouch for you to the Águilas, but you will have to prove yourself trustworthy."

Reina nodded eagerly.

"We will have to train you—make sure you can read the written word and defend yourself from the creatures thirsting for the iridio in your heart. Turn you into something proper, so the society in Sadul Fuerte can overcome…" Doña Ursulina paused, her eyes landing on Reina's tail switching and turning in anticipation, "The sight."

Doña Ursulina's bejeweled hand took a gentle hold of Reina's braid, running her thumb along the coarse texture of the hair, turning it over. Reina felt the sting of a challenge, of her invasion of space, but she remained frozen, as was her place.

"If you want to cement your position in this house, you must make yourself necessary to its masters. That includes Doña Laurel, Celeste, *and* Javier and Don Enrique."

Reina nodded obediently.

"But most importantly, Reina, I summoned you because the day I finalize my legacy will arrive soon. It will come as a reward from a god." Doña Ursulina's nod was sure, firm. "You're here to be an instrument for that legacy, which you will benefit from if you do exactly as I say."

"Sí, señora."

"Remember that you are a Duvianos before anything else. I was the one who saved your life, and it was Juan Vicente who gave you his name."

Reina curled a fist over her chest, the back of her hand feeling the raggedness beneath her clothes. With the iridio heart, she was a monster. She was everything the humans feared. And perhaps her grandmother wouldn't have accepted her any other way.

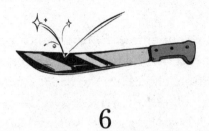

6

Gods for Worship

Ever since coming to Águila Manor, Reina had mornings when she woke up from a recurring dream of following a path to a lagoon. In it, she trekked a canopied trail through the jungle with the radiant sunlight at the end guiding her forward. But despite the path's unfamiliarity, deep in her bones, Reina knew the way. When she woke up, warm as if showered by the light in the dream, she couldn't decide if the journey was a fragment of her dreaming imagination or a childhood memory long since forgotten.

There was magic in Águila Manor, from its proximity to the iridio mines. Perhaps the dreams were spurred by it. And it was magic to be alive after all that pain, with a new heart. Now Reina could walk, could breathe, could put her hands to good use earning the Águilas' trust by working as part of their staff.

She was alive. She had a second chance. She had a family.

Two months into her employment, Reina kneaded the maize dough with all the grateful energy she had to give. When the head cook walked behind her to inspect it, stuck his fingers in the dough to see if it had chunky clumps of corn, and instead found it smooth from her grinding and kneading, Reina beamed in self-satisfaction at his approval.

The staff wasn't particularly friendly to the newcomer, but her ties to Doña Ursulina inspired them to treat her decently. Reina had soon learned they did this out of fear. Doña Ursulina was Don Enrique's left-hand woman, with tales told about her from even before the revolution. Everyone from the Páramo to Sadul Fuerte, except perhaps for the master of the house, cowered before Doña Ursulina. Reina quickly came to see how the servants preferred to swallow their disdain for the nozariel newcomer than to cross the woman rumored to have one foot in this world and the other in the Void.

Around Reina, the kitchen bustled in preparation for breakfast. The head cook was back at his station by the fire pit, leaning over a large cauldron and stirring the thick bean soup inside. A big woman entered the kitchen from the back, carrying a large sack of moras, freshly gathered from the plantings bordering the estate. She scattered the fruits on her workspace and began crushing them in a bowl. Reina watched her curiously, wondering what they did with them.

Reina had been doing that a lot lately: asking questions and studying Don Enrique's staff to learn their strange habits. Like when they dropped a pinch of salt into Don Enrique's, Javier's, and Celeste's wash water, but they didn't do it to Doña Laurel's because they believed it was bad luck for a human to clean with salt water—and conversely that the salt water granted well-meaning wishes on valcos. (It didn't make sense to Reina, because Don Enrique and Javier were half human, and Celeste was even more so.) She'd also learned the recipe for their special kind of arepa, made from wheat, like bread, instead of making it from a mix of maize, milk, and eggs, as she'd grown up seeing it in Segolita. Or how the servants placed wooden bowls with small portions of food in the corners of rooms, tucked behind pieces of furniture to conceal the icons of Ches, even though Doña Laurel and her highborn friends only prayed to the Virgin and the Pentimiento saints.

Once, Reina had tried to join the servants in their offerings to Ches. She saved a portion of her buttered arepa and brought it to the clay sculpture of his head that the laundress kept near the bedsheet storage, as a thanks for her change of fortune. A scullery maid yanked hard on Reina's braid before she could offer it, telling Reina, "Don't soil Don Ches's offerings."

A rush of heat sprouted from Reina's chest to her armpits. She watched in disbelief but didn't utter a word as the maid hammered the lid on the coffin of her absurdity, saying, "This is our offering. Touch his things again, and I'll have the cook beat you bloody, you squalid little duskling."

Duskling was what people in Segolita called nozariels for taking the worst jobs in the shadows of dungeons and cellars. It took her aback to realize the label had traveled to even the farthest reaches of this country.

Actually, what baffled her the most was the maid's attitude and how she had it so utterly wrong. Ches didn't belong to humans. He didn't belong to anyone. Even the human vagrants in Segolita understood this. One could confer with Ches regardless of species. It was a personal relationship, not one set up for pomp and show like the humans had created with their saints. And the way she had called him *Don Ches* felt false. It implied that Ches was like the humans with their titles. But Reina understood Ches to be bigger than that, like how a dawning sky yawned away the darkness of night, unstoppably and irrepressibly.

She couldn't eat the arepa after the experience either, because deciding it was for Ches made it for Ches. Reina had snuck away from her duties to find the sunniest spot near the creek behind the smithy and had left the arepa under the rays of the Páramo sun.

During her break, she went back to her shared room in the servants' quarters to check on her scarring torso. Reina didn't have to touch the ore to hear the whispering as she glanced at the monstrosity protruding from her chest. The mere act of focusing on the ore and tubes surrounded by scar tissue was enough to rouse the voices. Hearing them prickled her skin in goose bumps. She shivered, hesitant to learn where they originated from. If they were demons, how was she supposed to live with the truth? That darkness was the source of her life.

She glanced behind her, fearful of the shadows formed by the beds and cabinets. A straw Pentimiento cross was nailed above the doorway, yet Reina didn't feel its alleged protection. Perhaps... with her wicked heart, the devil in the room was her.

Reina rearranged her garments. She sucked in a deep breath as she stared at the brown face reflected by the murky mirror hanging across the beds. The cold of the Páramo had burned her nose and cheeks a ruddy color. Her full lips were chapped—lips she now knew she had inherited from Doña Ursulina. This was her life now, here in these mountains with her monstrous heart. The least she could do was learn what it meant to have it.

She was on her way to Doña Ursulina's underground lab with the question when a servant cornered and handed her a goblet of mora juice. "Take it to the Benevolent Lady," they told her in passing.

"Wait—"

The servant snapped, "She likes to have it every day at this time. Don't dawdle."

Reina ascended to the third story of the manor, where Doña Laurel's quarters resided on a long corridor overlooking patches of Águila farmland and the Páramo peaks. Past rippling wine-colored curtains, the windows allowed a view of the soaring golden eagle on ivory banners of the Águilas' battalion and of the people who sparred down in the yard. Reina had quickly learned the sight of the soldiers meant Don Enrique was home. Most recently he had returned from a summit held in Puerto Carcosa, the capital of Venazia, where he and his vassals had met with His Majesty Don Rodrigo Silva.

Don Enrique's presence brought an anxious mood to the household staff, which had infected Reina the moment she first laid eyes on him. He was a good head taller than Javier, with broad shoulders made for swinging the greatsword he wielded to the battles of the revolution. His stature was made more impressive still by the pair of ivory antlers that sprouted from the crown of his head, which were thick, with cracks and chips revealing the history of his aggressive youth. His eyes were his most fearsome feature, however, as they were the color of dead blood. They regarded Reina without emotion when Doña Laurel first introduced her as Juan Vicente's daughter. To him, she hadn't even been worth acknowledging.

Was it too bold of her to knock on the doña's door? It didn't matter, because no answer came. Eventually she found herself on the second story. The spiraled staircase opened to a chilly corridor where the stone floors and walls trapped the cold of the region. A large portrait painting of Feleva Águila, Don Enrique's late mother, hung beside the door to Don Enrique's study in a gilded frame. Reina paused in awe, as she always did when she passed by the portrait to bring up food or fetch laundry. With eyes of the deepest red and braided starlight hair, she was said to have been the last full-blooded valco of Sadul Fuerte. The portrait depicted her as a confident maiden, donning a tight-fitting military tunic and a rapier, her antlers gnarling up to the edges of the canvas. The painted woman's beauty made Reina think of Celeste, and Reina's cheeks scorched.

She peeled her eyes from the painting, swallowing to clear her thoughts.

Glass shattering rang out of the study, followed by faint noises. It sparked Reina's curiosity. She found the door slightly ajar, as if whoever had entered it last forgot to close it all the way.

"Perhaps it's for the best if we marry Celeste and Javier," someone said as she approached, immediately piquing her interest—and disgust.

Reina peered into the room and saw Doña Laurel's black hair first, one of her shoulders exposed from her blue gown coming undone. She was sitting on Don Enrique's desk with her back to the door, seals and quills and papers strewn out of her way as if in a careless hurry. Don Enrique stood in front of her, his body hunched, embracing her with his great frame.

Reina's heart skipped a beat.

Doña Laurel pushed him back slightly, angered, her words too soft to leave the room, but the action rooted Reina to the spot with curiosity.

"That boy is my brother and a half valco like me. We are the last of our kind in this land. Me, him, and Celeste," Don Enrique said from the valley of Doña Laurel's collarbone and neck.

He held her with his big hands as if she were the last floating raft in a vast ocean. So mesmerized, Reina couldn't peel her eyes away. She had never once seen someone be worshipped this way. A man so cold and severe with his blood-red stare, holding Doña Laurel like her body was a lifeline and without her proximity he would drown. Reina forgot to breathe.

"He's her uncle," Laurel said, this time louder, her anger rising.

There was a fumble between them, their hands and their proximity getting in the way of shedding their clothes. Don Enrique lifted Doña Laurel's skirt.

Reina watched the forbidden. She didn't move. Instead, she was painfully reminded of her ore as her treacherous heart raced. The fervent whispers returned, chanting something she couldn't understand. They came because she, too, was wicked like *it*.

"It doesn't matter," Don Enrique whispered to his wife. "Mother's parents were cousins. Every surviving valco is a valco because their parents married blood."

Reina savored the information in her mouth, noted how in this rule, he and Laurel were the exception.

His voice went even lower as he added, "You know better than anyone that every valco birth is a gift from the gods. We do not have the luxury to choose."

Doña Laurel unfastened Don Enrique's pants herself.

"Javier is what Mother wanted." His voice shook when he lifted his lips to her ears. "Power still matters in this world, even as humans try to change this to better protect their frailty. But Celeste is beyond human. She doesn't need the protection of the law. She is Mother's legacy."

He thrust into his wife, earning himself her broken exhale.

When he looked up, those dead-blood eyes found Reina.

Reina's heart stopped, and should have stayed still, because she was dead anyway.

But she ran.

She descended as far as the underground, leaving the mora juice atop the first chest of drawers she passed, her skin humming with panic. Her fear took her there, she realized as she stood outside Doña Ursulina's lair, doubling over and gulping down the air of decay infecting the corridor.

If there was anyone who could dissuade Don Enrique from

ripping her bowels open, it would be Doña Ursulina. But Reina couldn't imagine her grandmother ever standing between her and the caudillo. Reina had seen Don Enrique spar against his officers while she carried dirty rags for the laundress or while she minded the goats. She had seen the way he swung his greatsword at lightning-fast speed with a ferocity that should only exist in legends. With her own eyes, she'd witnessed why valcos had evaded enslavement and instead risen to prominence as military leaders. Hidden beneath their immaculate façades were creatures who could rip leather and chains with their bare hands. And now she had meddled in the privacy of the strongest valco in all Venazia.

She knocked on her grandmother's door as the panic flared again. Maybe Doña Ursulina wouldn't stand between them, but surely Don Enrique wouldn't banish Reina if he saw she was essential to his left-hand woman.

Inside, Doña Ursulina leaned over her desk, engrossed in the writings of a large scroll and surrounded by other strewn literature. She looked up to the intruding Reina with the whites of her eyes inundated in black. "I could hear you all the way down the stairs. You have no sense of stealth."

Reina let out a shuddery breath. Don Enrique was valco. He had better ears and eyes than any nozariel or human. He'd probably known she was skulking outside the whole time.

"What do you want? Don Enrique knows he shouldn't be bothering me—I'm hard at work. And if it was that woman Laurel who summoned me, well, then tell her nothing at all. She doesn't deserve explanations."

Every doubt embraced Reina with a wicked, mocking smile. She hesitated, the words sounding silly even before she murmured them. "Does Don Enrique know everything that happens in this manor?"

Her grandmother's raised eyebrow was her answer.

"I saw him and Doña Laurel together, and I wasn't supposed to. And he knows—"

"What does it matter? This is their home."

Reina frowned, relieved. She stepped closer, seeing the scroll was an elaborate star chart.

"I suppose I should ask what you were doing in their private quarters, but, alas, I do not care. You're but a fly on the wall to them. Meek and insignificant."

She met her grandmother's gaze, even if their darkness inspired nothing but fear. But Reina didn't want to be fearful. She wanted to be irreplaceable, otherwise there would be nothing stopping them from expelling her back to where she came from.

"I don't want to be meek and insignificant." She had seen the staff cower in the presence of Doña Ursulina, like they did with the caudillo. It wasn't hard to see why. But Reina wished to know how Don Enrique and Doña Ursulina had come to be that way. She wanted to learn from them. "I want to be respected."

Doña Ursulina croaked a laugh. "Expect it to be an uphill battle. You're not in Fedria anymore. This is a land that's slowly ridding itself of nozariels. Here, soon, your lot will disappear, just like the yares were killed off."

The name was a familiar one, even if Reina had to search deep in the confines of her memories for it. Yares, the horned and winged man-eaters who'd shared the continent with valcos and nozariels before Segol's colonization. They'd been hunted into extinction shortly after the humans had arrived.

"You should consider yourself lucky the Águilas allowed you into their household. There's a ban on nozariels, and most landlords hold the opinion that it's cheaper to slit their throats and bury the bodies than to secure them passage to Fedria. After all, there's no law against slaying animals."

"*I'm not*—" Reina's hands curled into fists. "We're not animals. We're people."

The words weren't new to her ears. She knew her life mattered less than a human's. But it cut deeper uttered by someone who shared her blood.

Doña Ursulina reached for a nearby cup and took a sip. "No. You are daughter to my son, whom I loved, even if he abandoned me." Her lips drew into a line as she stared at the map, drawn into the memory of a life past. "He was supposed to be like a brother to Enrique, did you know that? He was my world. Then that nozariel woman had to come and poison him with radical ideas of a life in Segolita. She took you both to live in misery. So forgive me if I don't exactly have the highest regard for your kind. If I can't help looking at you and seeing *her* in your face."

Anger lanced through Reina. Not because she knew her mother and was indignant about an unfair judgment on her character. But the words were acidic.

"I told him it was a mistake to leave everything, and I was correct—look at us now." Doña Ursulina's black eyes descended on Reina, her upper lip curling bitterly. "You know how I found out about you? Secondhand gossip, which took years to reach me by the way. It's not every day that a mutual acquaintance from Segolita travels to Sadul Fuerte."

Doña Ursulina cleared her throat.

Reina liked to believe she saw sorrow there. "Well, now I'm here."

"Yes, and I'm glad for it. You have his eyes, after all."

Reina held her breath. She didn't want to blink and ruin this sliver of acceptance.

There was a moment of silence between them, a comfort, during which Doña Ursulina resumed her studies without expelling Reina from the room.

"I hear things when I touch my new heart," Reina said uncertainly, praying her concerns weren't misinterpreted as madness.

Doña Ursulina gave her no acknowledgment.

"It's because of this ore, isn't it? Tell me why I feel like I'm never alone now that I have it in me."

Doña Ursulina beckoned Reina to approach the table.

The star map covered most of the dark wood. It was inked in a thousand little dots, some labeled and connected by more lines and charts. Despite her grandmother's beliefs, Juan Vicente had taught Reina how to read the written word, so she knew this chart had been immortalized in a language she couldn't understand. The guttural whispering haunting Reina filled her ears, awoken by whatever secrets were recorded in the map. It reminded Reina of when humans prayed to the Pentimiento rosary at wakes. She grew itchy, hot, and trapped by her new heart, like she was locked in a tight, stuffy closet with no hope of ever getting out. Her hands grasped for the roughness of her apron, touching the bulging ore on the left side of her chest.

"Do you recognize geomancia when you see it?" Doña Ursulina asked.

Reina nodded—a lie.

"And void magic?"

"Magic from the Void is forbidden," Reina said in a little breath, her instincts clawing at her neck with the prickling to run away.

"By those who live in fear, maybe. But down here, no one needs to know what we do. I didn't become who I am by being a coward." Doña Ursulina scoffed. "You're a nozariel. You know of the god Rahmagut."

Reina bared her teeth. Her tail swatted the air behind her restlessly. "He's not a god. He's a demon."

"Look at you, fearing him like the Penitents who pray to the Virgin, thinking She's capable of protecting them. You denounce his godliness."

Unease gripped Reina again. She hated the way Doña Ursulina could hold her prisoner with a mere stare and mock her. "Gods don't hurt people."

Her grandmother's lips curled. "You have so much wisdom, for a duskling."

Reina squashed the urge to sneer.

"Maybe gods don't care for people, but they give us the tools to protect or hurt each other," her grandmother said. "While you join the Penitents in worshipping some virgin who promises miracles, Rahmagut makes miracles happen for those who seek the way. If you ever doubt it, just think of your heart."

Reina crossed her arms, disgust worming up her throat at the ore's ragged sensation.

The older woman laughed. "That is why I want you to recognize spells and curses drawn from the Void." She gestured at Reina's thrumming chest. "What else do you think could have been strong enough to repel the rot of tinieblas and keep you alive?"

"This is void magic?" The voices grew deafening, so much that Reina brought her hands up to her ears. Blocking them didn't arrest the chanting, for they came from within.

She was the darkness. A creature of flesh and iridio, amalgamated by her grandmother.

Doña Ursulina nodded, satisfied. "Just one of all the things we can achieve with void magic. There are far worse spells—even curses that turn people into tinieblas. Let this be your first lesson. I want to hear you say his name without fear. I want you to tell me who he is, in your own nozariel words."

Reina's nostrils flared. Every instinct told her to stop, to flee. Everyone knew that the more his name was uttered, the more he was being invited to perch on their lives and leech off their happiness. She forced herself to ignore the whispering of her heart.

"He's the opposer of Ches. When Ches banished him, he created el Vacío."

"Why?" Doña Ursulina barked, "Say his name."

"Rahmagut, the nozariel conqueror who coveted Ches's power and who ascended to oppose him."

Doña Ursulina nodded for Reina to keep going.

"Rahmagut, who violated the natural order of the world, and for that, Ches cast him out." Reina licked her lips like the name spiced her mouth. "So he created a new domain to rule over: el Vacío."

Doña Ursulina leaned back with a sneer. "Such slanderous tales. Who am I to judge a god? Who are *you*? I believe what I see and what gives me tangible results. Rahmagut became godly because he utilized the iridio that landed on this world lifetimes ago. He harnessed its magic and left its trace behind so that we could harness it as well." She gestured at the star map as if it would enlighten Reina. "Feleva seized the fallen star as her property and used the mines to make herself the richest woman in all Venazia. Now here we are, listening to the whims of her son while his coffers grow fatter. Do you think Don Enrique prays to Ches? Or to the Virgin? His only god is gold and power. And one day, when Rahmagut gives me his favor, Don Enrique will be worshipping me."

The memory of Doña Laurel and Don Enrique joined flesh to flesh pierced through Reina's mind. He definitely worshipped something, and it wasn't Doña Ursulina.

"Do I have to worship Rahmagut like you?" Even as she said it, Reina couldn't stop the words from sounding bitter. "Is that what having this heart means?" If that was the case, then Ches had already forsaken her.

Doña Ursulina regarded her with amusement. And, perhaps, with a tinge of satisfaction. "Don't fret. Your next task is to get close to Laurel and Celeste. They're already predisposed to trust you. Use that, for me."

Reina frowned but kept her mouth shut as expected. She held nothing but warmth in her heart for the ladies of the house. She would do it gladly, while maintaining her loyalties.

"And stop fearing the power of iridio, which is the only thing keeping you alive. Let me worry about Rahmagut. After all, I am the only one in this house worthy of his attention."

Reina followed Doña Ursulina's gaze to the star map. The stars' position in the sky and their labels provided no context, yet her heart's reaction told her this was the center of her grandmother's plans and desires.

"Now go. Tonight's a new moon. When the night is darkest and the stars are brightest, fetch Don Enrique and bring him here."

Ice ran down Reina's spine.

"It is time Rahmagut makes a return to this world."

7

Rahmagut's Legend

Later, once the whirlwind of stars over the estate shone brightest past the curtains of Águila Manor, Reina ascended to the third floor. Darkness draped the corridors tall enough to accommodate the antlers of its inhabitants. Reina watched her own shadows apprehensively, holding a lonesome candle in palms slick with perspiration, as she hesitated outside Doña Laurel's chambers. She had already gone to Don Enrique's quarters and found no reply when she knocked. Missing him in his room had been a relief, for she couldn't fathom how she would look him in the eyes after what she had witnessed. Now she'd have to look at Doña Laurel instead. Reina didn't feel any better about it, but she would swallow her embarrassment if it was what it took to become a crucial element in her grandmother's life.

"Come in." Doña Laurel's voice traveled through the heavy wooden door. She was slipping on a sleeping gown when Reina stepped in. The caudillo was not with her.

"It's Doña Ursulina, mi señora. She says there's something Don Enrique must see tonight."

"There's no need to be so formal, Reina." In the darkness Reina could still see Doña Laurel's smile, her short black hair tousled. "Enrique left a while ago."

"Where to?"

"I think he's gone riding in the mountains. Let us go for him. I'll come with you."

Doña Laurel covered herself in a ruana and lit a candle before sweeping out of her room. Reina trailed behind her.

"The caudillo rides at night?" Reina asked conversationally as their espadrilles slapped the polished floors.

Doña Laurel's cheeks glowed under the candlelight. "He took a gray stallion on a ride through the woods, like the Virgin did in the holy books. Penitents stole that from an old valco custom—valcos believe it is a rite for conception."

"A rite for conception?" Reina parroted.

Doña Laurel faced her just as they arrived at the second-story landing. "We're trying for a boy—we've been trying for ages," she said with gentle humor. "Doña Feleva said she rode both times when she conceived Enrique and Javier. So, if it'll get me with child, I'll accept every superstition valcos cling to."

Reina's heart broke a little. If Celeste was their only child, they must have been trying for nearly two decades.

They passed the archway to the dining hall and slowed at the sight of a lit candle. Javier sat at the head of the table, alone, so engrossed in a book that he didn't look up. Doña Laurel shook her head and led Reina to the backyard.

"I try not to judge him too harshly. I really do," Doña Laurel said. "That boy grew up without his mother, with Enrique's indifference raising him."

"His mother died when he was young?" Reina asked, more because Doña Laurel seemed keen to revisit her memories than out of her own curiosity.

"Soon after Celeste was born. Your grandmother will say Doña Feleva raged her way to an early grave after I married Enrique." Doña Laurel scoffed at the memory. "Anyway, I couldn't raise him myself. He was always latching on inappropriately and jealous of Celeste. After living with valcos for so long, I've learned they like to indulge in their emotions and primal instincts. Javier especially, and he has a natural talent for triggering Enrique's anger. So let's just say he wasn't exactly raised ... gently."

Reina squinted at the dark yard, where the night was cold and undisturbed, her tail twitching with disagreement. After her father had died, she'd also tasted a fair share of cruelty, but she hadn't turned out insufferable.

A shadow broke out of the introduced pine grove near the grounds. Don Enrique zipped along the gravel road with his magnificent steed, detouring to the stables. Reina noticed Doña Laurel beaming. She thought of the fairy tales that highborn girls told themselves, about princes coming to rescue them from the traps of a witch in acts of fated true love. Doña Laurel epitomized what those maidens ought to look like. Reina liked the thought, because Doña Laurel was kind and beautiful. She deserved this home, and her baby boy, and to be worshipped by the richest man of all.

Don Enrique found them within moments, the light from the archway's sconces revealing his disheveled short-cropped hair and flushed cheeks. He paused to allow a petting on the cheek from his wife; then he regarded Reina, again with his monumental indifference.

Reina looked down at her espadrilles as she conveyed Doña Ursulina's message.

Then the three of them descended the spiraling stone steps together and entered her grandmother's lair. A single sconce remained lit, the one closest to her desk. In the dim light, Reina couldn't be sure if the long shadows resembled the pieces of furniture they belonged to or if they were bipedal in shape. Her tail switched and turned uncomfortably, her chest prickling.

Doña Ursulina stood behind her large desk with the star map splayed over it. She wore a black tunic and gloves, and in her palm she held a glittering ore not unlike the one feeding Reina's heart.

"Masters," Doña Ursulina said with a nod.

"What is this that can't wait until dawn?" Don Enrique said. "I could have been asleep."

Doña Ursulina offered him an insolent smile. "Something told me you wouldn't be."

"Iridio is strong here," he said, covering his nose with the back of his hand. "It's suffocating."

Reina had heard many tales about valcos, because that was what people did: talk about what they knew of them, since their numbers were so sparse, regardless of if there was any truth to it. The Liberator was a valco, so the people of Segolita said valcos were handsome beyond belief. Reina had found this to be true the moment her eyes opened after her attack and she saw Celeste. They said they leapt and ran so fast it was like a strike of lightning: Blink, and you'd miss it. This Reina had seen when she witnessed Don Enrique spar in the yard. They even said that valcos could see geomancia at work, as glittering threads looping around whatever a spell was trying to achieve or manipulate. And as Don Enrique's eyes followed something she couldn't see above the star map and the ore, Reina now understood this was true as well.

Doña Ursulina's other hand grappled something over the ore and tugged as she raised it high above her, drawing an invisible substance out of the ore's orifices. The movement spurred the tang in the air, the sourness taking up residence in the back of Reina's throat. It grew strong as Doña Ursulina placed the ore on the table and waved both hands over her star map.

With her arms spread wide, Doña Ursulina used magic to peel the charts and scripts off the map and shove them overhead to the ceiling, tugging along the projection of a hundred different dots and constellations that manifested everywhere in the room. Stars and nebulas pierced Reina's skin like the caress of a breeze. Too many to count, they glowed such bright cyans and oranges that they twinkled white.

The stars looked familiar. Reina understood why her grandmother called them when it was darkest, for they were the arrangements in the sky tonight.

It would have been a beautiful sparkling sight, if the whispers in Reina's heart hadn't erupted in a fervor. They weren't within her anymore. The words slithered and punched and rebounded, a medley of guttural and high-pitched voices filling Doña Ursulina's laboratory. Reina's skin rose in goose bumps. She hugged herself, pressing her back against a wall where there would be no star to pierce through her and no shadow to sneak up on her.

Don Enrique blanched like he understood what the whispers said.

Doña Ursulina brandished her arms and transposed the position of the stars. She waved and waved, nights turning into days turning into nights again, changing the view of the constellations until she arrived at a future moment in time. She paused as a great rock ripped through the night, glowing with cyan and violet light, its long tail tearing the fabric of the black sky and allowing another world to peek through.

"Forty years ago, Rahmagut's Claw tore open the sky for twenty days and twenty nights," Doña Ursulina said, the whites of her eyes again inundated by the blackness. "On the last night, his favor was summoned by one of his disciples."

Reina covered her nostrils and lips with her palm. She stared at her grandmother in awe.

"According to the legend, Rahmagut can grant any wish a person desires. Immortality. Reanimation. The breaking of void curses. Boundless power and riches. Nothing is out of his reach, as long as his will is summoned by an act of great evil, such as spilling the blood of his runaway nine brides—their reincarnations, that is."

Where was the falsehood? For there had to be one. Rahmagut was *the* deceiver. Ches wouldn't have banished him otherwise. The whispering grew feverish, and Reina's fear of the demon god clutched her. She ground her teeth, needing the vision to end just as much as she wanted to understand Doña Ursulina.

Doña Laurel gripped Don Enrique's forearm, also afraid.

"Rahmagut's Claw is returning?" Don Enrique murmured.

With her chin Doña Ursulina pointed at the manifested sky, where the cyan tail of the shooting star left a dent in the safety of their world. "Two years hence, Rahmagut's Claw will tear open the seal between this world and the Void for twenty nights. During that time, anyone bold enough to pursue the legend will be able to ask anything they want from the god del Vacío."

"We will have no part in this," Doña Laurel said with a jerk to her husband's forearm.

Don Enrique humored her for a moment before saying, "I will hear what Doña Ursulina has to say."

Doña Laurel flared her nostrils, but there were no objections from her husband when she swept out of the room. "Get to the point. Why are you bothering me with tales and legends?" Don Enrique said.

Doña Ursulina was unfazed. She pointed at a passage on her star map. "The invocation must be performed in Rahmagut's ancient tomb, in Tierra'e Sol, right where the Liberator erected his home."

All the confidence drained from Don Enrique's visage. His jaw clenched, and his gaze flickered to Reina, noticing her there for the first time. He sized her up while she held her breath, stopping her tail from twitching. A million thoughts rushed through her mind. Primarily: He probably imagined this was a great opportunity to disembowel the pesky fly on the wall.

"Samón is going to invoke Rahmagut?"

The smile softening Doña Ursulina's features told Reina she was getting exactly what she wanted. "Even if he isn't, we can't be sure that he won't. He is already positioned to block anyone else from fulfilling the legend. If he ever wielded that kind of power, you would never be able to measure up to him."

His eyes hardened even more as he spat out, "And he could force my hand with his idiotic ideas of how Venazia should be ruled."

Doña Ursulina's smile widened. "Precisely. We don't need to change how we live for his whims. The governors oversee the city-states, and the caudillos protect them. It is as it has always been— now instead of a king across the ocean, we have a king in Puerto Carcosa."

Reina thought back to the people she had known in Segolita and whether they cared who ruled in the capitol building. Maybe the humans had cared, back when nozariels were still enslaved and earning them fortunes in free labor. Personally, Reina had been too concerned about securing her next meal to care who was in power. Why wasn't Samón Bravo the Liberator the one in power? If he wanted to rule, he certainly deserved it.

"But he hates this," Doña Ursulina added. "He's always been vocal about that."

Don Enrique scoffed. "Him and his senate of Segolita. They

think they can let the people choose how they want to be ruled. It is utter nonsense. If the common folk are to thrive from the protection my wealth and army provides them, then they should bend the knee to my family and let me decide how they shall be ruled."

"You have the strongest army of all the caudillos, but for how long? Until Rahmagut's Claw comes and goes? *Everyone* in the world will be able to look up to the skies and see the opportunity."

Don Enrique drew a step closer to Doña Ursulina, raising his index finger between them.

"Samón succeeded in leading one revolution," he bit out. "He isn't incapable of leading another one, especially if he finds the strength." He nodded, as if reassuring himself. "Find out who the reincarnated brides are. Gather what you need. Even if we don't pursue it, we will be a step ahead and take it away from his hands."

He whirled to leave with his cloak surfing the air behind him. Doña Ursulina gave her arms one final wave, dispersing the projection of the skies. The whispering ceased, and a hush blanketed the laboratory. Doña Ursulina grimaced as she backed away to her chair and collapsed over it with a sigh. Reina thought she could hear the creak of her knees.

She wasn't sure if it was her place to witness her grandmother like this. She was, however, surprised to hear there was someone even Don Enrique feared.

"Would the Liberator really invoke Rahmagut?" she asked, softly and unsure.

"It doesn't matter. We have Don Enrique's blessing."

Reina chewed her lips at the implication. And now she was involved.

Still, Doña Ursulina regarded Reina coldly and said, "I asked you to bring only Don Enrique."

Reina fisted her hands by her sides. "I—I didn't think it would be a problem."

How would she have even begun to peel them apart? The don y doña of the house were inseparable.

"Here, iridio is everywhere." Doña Ursulina gestured to the tall ceilings of her underground study. "Copious amounts of it. And even more came from that ore after I extracted it. Though our eyes cannot see it, iridio is shooting out in every direction, impaling the matter that makes us, us. Going through our skin, our bones. Tiny indiscriminate knives. Except it does discriminate, with a preference for the most vulnerable, such as an unborn babe. Don't you know Laurel's greatest desire is to conceive another Águila valco?"

Reina stuttered a yes. Doña Laurel had stated it plainly, already entrusting Reina with her dreams.

"Babes do not have the same sturdy skin and bones we do. And the unborn can be harmed, and even killed, if enough iridio shoots through them."

"Could she be with child now?" Her question came out high-pitched. If Doña Laurel's babe was harmed, it would all be her fault.

Doña Ursulina chuckled. "I'm merely saying this so you understand that magic cannot be taken lightly." She yanked off her gloves and tossed them over the star map. "Do not worry so much about Laurel. That woman acts so innocent, but don't believe her for an instant. She knows what exists down here. She's quite the capable geomancer."

"Doña Laurel?"

"She plays her role well."

"Why does she need you to make her fertility drafts, then?" Reina approached the star map. Within her, the voices stirred.

Doña Ursulina shot her a satisfied look. "Well done, fly on the wall. Laurel swore off geomancia after the revolution was over. All those crowing highborn ladies in her circle are slowly turning to Pentimiento. The doctrine is sweeping the city and the country. Penitents paint geomancia as an unsavory evil and iridio geomancia, with its largely undiscovered applications, as the equivalent of communing with their devil, whoever that is. Nowadays, geomancers are on the verge of becoming social pariahs. Laurel can't have that. She needs everyone to see her as the Benevolent Lady, after all."

Reina struggled to believe her grandmother. Nothing about Doña Laurel seemed fake. "Why? She can be anyone she wants. She's the caudillo's wife."

"Enrique is too much of a narcissist to bed anyone capable of besting him, and Laurel knows this. She is merely being the wife he wants." For a moment Doña Ursulina was lost to a faraway memory. "Him and his mother, both narcissists who can't stomach the idea of an equal for a partner."

Doña Ursulina noticed Reina's curious gaze, and the faraway look was promptly replaced by annoyance. "Do you see all we have to gain, if you do exactly as I say?"

Reina nodded to avoid appearing daft.

"Many pieces will be moving out of balance in two years with Rahmagut's Claw, both magical and in the natural world. If we invoke Rahmagut, we will also be making ripples in people's lives. It will not matter that the greatest sorceress to ever live has a nozariel for a successor, not here or anywhere in Venazia."

Reina sucked in a breath. The ore's chanting ignited. It punched Reina's blood with the thrumming beat of her heart. Her lips trembled as she stopped a smile, her tail switching like a metronome.

"We will finally be the family Juan Vicente denied us all these years. You and I."

8

Tigra Mariposa

Anytime Néstor snuck out to see Don Jerónimo, Eva snuck out as well.

They fed Doña Antonia half-truths. They claimed the Contadors had hired a foreign tutor from the freed colonies west of Venazia and that Eva and Néstor sought his lessons on history and politics, for personal enrichment.

Rather, once they arrived at the downtown house, Néstor and Don Jerónimo locked themselves away somewhere in the Contadors' large residence, while Eva scurried to the small house flanking the yard. The one shielded by an herb garden brimming with yerba buena and mayaca, under the mamoncillo tree's shade.

Eva nurtured a fickle friendship with Doña Rosa, one she knew wouldn't exist if she didn't bring the three gold escudos for every visit. But Eva didn't begrudge her for it. They occasionally attempted an invocation or two from the scribbled instructions in Doña Rosa's journal, using up her reagents, which weren't abundant, nor cheap.

For several months Eva studied geomancia in this sanctuary she'd created for herself, away from her family's watchful eye. It was her escape.

Heavy rain fell on Eva's latest visit. It weighed the air with the smell of decay, mud coating her espadrilles and clinging to the hems of her araguaney-colored skirt. Eva sat by the table with her chemise still wet from the downpour. She'd come hoping to attempt a barrier of litio, but Doña Rosa was in a mood, and the air felt heady and wrongly sparked. Maybe Eva was uninspired today, because in her rings, the litio solution behaved as nothing more than inert oil.

Doña Rosa crushed herbs in her mortar under the window's dim light, preparing a poultice for her father.

Idly, Eva flipped through the sun-bleached pamphlet Doña Rosa had abandoned on the table. "What's this about?"

Doña Rosa glanced back and said, "It calls for a meeting to discuss the legitimacy of the new king, by El Cónclave Llanero." She chuckled in derision. "Heard of them? I have. But anytime I hear of their chisme, I only think to myself: They don't care about the caudillos crowning a king. They're just angry they've been shut out of lawmaking, without the possibility of having a senate, like in Fedria."

Eva skimmed the page and was impressed by Doña Rosa, as the printed words didn't clearly reveal the true purpose of the conclave. Eva had personally heard the grumblings about the new king because she lived under the same roof as the governor of Galeno. Doña Antonia and Don Mateo often complained about how the bloody war for independence had ended, how instead of freeing them from the yoke of a monarch, the caudillos gave themselves power by crowning Don Rodrigo Silva king. The puppet king, Don Mateo called him.

"How do you know the meeting is about not having a senate?" Eva asked, raising a brow.

Doña Rosa wrapped the poultice in a bundle of dried maize leaves. "You see that I live as an outcast, and you wonder how I know gossip from your grandfather's office?"

Eva shrugged.

"My father's old, and sick, and he long ago stopped caring that I'm supposed to be the bastard curandera. He talks about anything and everything when I go up to his room to treat him. I know many things about the families of this city." She shot Eva a vulpine smirk. "Like I know how the Serranos are loyalists to Segol at heart. Father never gets tired of saying how the Liberator didn't go after them once the war was over because they know a dark, dark truth about him."

Eva's mouth parted. "What truth?"

"And once the truth comes out, the Liberator will wipe the Serranos off the face of Galeno, and then the Contadors will rise to power. It's father's greatest dream."

Eva frowned. Where would she stand in this alleged massacre? Her position in the family was a weak one, without even the Serrano name to bolster it. Either way, it all sounded unlikely. The Liberator was the lionized hero of the revolution because he was an honorable, benevolent victor. He'd freed the colonies and advocated for nozariels. The Serranos weren't actively going against his wishes in lawmaking. As far as Eva was concerned, her grandfather was a good governor.

"What's the truth that they know?" she asked again, impatient for the gossip she wasn't privy to. Whatever it was, it certainly colored her grandparents' opinion on the Liberator. Though they moaned about the new king, Eva's grandparents weren't fond of the Liberator either. Their approval of him always manifested with thinly veiled disgust for his being half valco. For changing their lives, which had once so thoroughly profited from nozariel labor and connections to the Segolean aristocracy.

"Stupid girl, that's the point. Only they know it."

"But I'm a Serrano," Eva muttered, then immediately felt foolish.

Doña Rosa laughed. "You're a Serrano like I'm a Contador."

Eva glared at the back of Doña Rosa's head.

"My father's a nasty old man. Don't take him too seriously." Doña Rosa returned with a small flask and two tiny clay cups. "I hope he dies soon."

"You hate him?" Eva thought of her own father. She supposed she hated him for what he'd done to her mother. But never meeting him in person definitely dampened her rancor.

"How could I not? He keeps me locked up in this house, afraid the world will see how a Contador bedded a nozariel—afraid they would know he's a hypocrite, living with his human superiority while lusting for my mother. And now he uses me as his obedient little galio healer, chasing death away when the Virgin would have claimed his life long ago."

Doña Rosa poured a viscous carmine liquid from the flask into the tiny cups and slid one toward Eva. "Here, some mistela, so you don't feel like you didn't get your money's worth."

Eva sighed loudly; there was so much to unpack there. She merely accepted the drink with an untrusting twist of her lip. The strawberry-juice-and-anise-liqueur concoction was something the Serranos only drank in celebration after a new birth.

"I don't feel like I don't get my money's worth," she grumbled and took the shot. Crinkling her nose at the cloying strawberry flavor, she said, "Why mistela?"

"I spiked it a little bit."

"Really," Eva bit out with sarcasm.

Doña Rosa chuckled. "To open up your spiritual mind."

Eva's eyes flitted to the icon in the room's corner. The clay sculpture was a rude depiction, yet Eva could somehow feel the god's gaze boring into her. She made a point not to think his name and shuddered. "Are there other kinds of geomancia, besides litio, galio, and bismuto?" Eva knew of iridio, but she wanted to hear it from the older woman's lips.

Doña Rosa followed her gaze. "There are, like iridio, which is not understood well yet. We call it *geomancia* because we use metals, and the world has many metals with many properties that lend their uniqueness to each spell. So I'm sure other kinds of magic are possible with the right substance: oro, plata, the list goes on."

Eva looked away from the icon. "Have you tried other kinds? How do you know?"

"Everything I know I learned when I was a young girl, younger than you, before my father stole me from El Carmín. Mi mamá, who taught me, said there was a moment in time when valcos and nozariels and even the extinct yares tried to uncover other kinds of geomancia spells from metals, but the Segoleans and their church put a swift end to that. Everything we know has been passed down from parent to child, when the Penitents weren't looking."

"Why?" Eva couldn't imagine how someone could gaze at the vast unknown of geomancia and decide to shut it out forever.

"I don't know, but I like to think humans recognized the threat in geomancia. I mean, they exterminated yares out of fear. They saw valcos and nozariels as the superior species that we are and cowered at the idea of seeing our strength multiplied by a mere invocation."

The thought brought Eva great satisfaction. She smirked.

"You've heard of Doña Feleva Águila, right?"

Eva nodded. "The valco caudilla. Her fortune came from the iridio mines." She remembered her mother, Dulce, with the sweet smiles of her namesake painted on crimson lips, and how she used to reassure Eva with stories about Feleva. She would say, "See? She is great and admired. There is nothing wrong with her, just like there is nothing wrong with you." Of course, Eva was sure her mom hadn't known what she was talking about, because everyone in Galeno treated her differently than her older sister, Pura, and her cousins. Fear of her lived in their eyes.

"Iridio is a conduit like the others. You can use it for spells that are stronger and more abstract. Iridio is the rarest because no one's found it outside of Feleva Águila's mines."

Eva squinted. "Just because they haven't found more doesn't mean it doesn't exist."

Doña Rosa chuckled. "That's exactly what it means, child. The iridio the Águilas mine is a fallen star that landed when Rahmagut was alive."

Eva straightened out, the back of her neck prickling.

"It came from the sky. It doesn't exist in this world," Doña Rosa added.

"But it's a mine. It's deep in the earth."

Doña Rosa laughed at Eva's wide-eyed look. "It's buried in the earth because it landed thousands and millions of years ago. Do you really think Rahmagut was prancing about with your Serrano ancestors, putting up with nuns and bishops shoving their Penitent ideology down his throat? He is older than this city—older than the Segoleans—arguably older than this land. He found the star, harnessed its power, and used it to ascend." She gestured at the icon behind her. "I keep his image in my house because I know he was real, and I have to respect that he was the discoverer of this magic."

Her grandmother's admonishing warning jumped into Eva's thoughts, calling Rahmagut a demon.

Doña Rosa no doubt knew she had Eva's attention, so she leaned forward and said, "According to the legend of Rahmagut, if you gain his favor, he's capable of giving you the world, if you ask for it."

"How do you gain his favor?" Eva said softly.

"I don't know exactly how, other than it requires an offering of great malice . . . but I do know it's happened before."

Despite the danger in the answer, it was reassuring. It meant Eva couldn't simply accidentally commune with him, like Doña Antonia bemoaned time and time again. It had to be deliberate.

"When? How?"

"Mi mamá told me." Doña Rosa pointed at the icon. "It used to belong to her. She told me that years before I was born, the icon pulsed with magic on the night a star ripped through the sky. How else would you explain that?" Doña Rosa nodded to herself. "If that was him giving his favor, then it means it's only a matter of time before he returns."

Silence engulfed them as Eva held Doña Rosa's dark gaze. Her devotion radiated from her eyes—her belief in Rahmagut.

"So you know how to use iridio?" Eva asked.

Doña Rosa shrugged with a shameless tilt of her head. "Why should I limit myself to the three geomancias?

"Will you teach me?"

She barked a laugh. "I cannot teach it because we don't have iridio. There's a reason why the Águilas are so filthy rich. Iridio is finite, and therefore, it is expensive."

Eva beamed with the new information as she climbed into the carriage behind Néstor. Her tongue was still sweet from the mistela, of which she'd had several more servings. Doña Rosa claimed it opened up the mind, and at this moment, Eva wanted to *feel* magic.

Her uncle was silent, until he said, "Your face says everything."

"What?" Her voice creaked guiltily.

"You look much too satisfied for your own good. They're going to suspect you, at home," he said, pointing at her.

Eva tugged on his index and said with emphasis, "I'm not a fool. I'm not saying a thing about anything."

"If mi mamá finds out what you're up to, she'll never let me come back to the Contadors'." He crossed his arms and turned to the carriage window, where raindrops mercilessly drilled down on the glass.

"And she'll never let *me* go back if she finds out what *you're* up to," she pointed out in return.

Eva followed his gaze to the scenery, watching as the carriage turned from the cobbled roads of Galeno to the bumpy dirt road leading to their family's land. The fields of the Llanos were bare and flat, going on forever until heat mirages blurred out the horizon. Large rain trees stood like lone sentinels, their wide canopies providing the cattle with a reprieve from the downpour. Herds of cows dotted the fields of every landowner in Galeno. They made up the commerce and livelihood of the people in the region.

"So...what did you and Don Jerónimo do?" She had never asked before, which made her a bad friend. "Did you talk about anything?"

He turned to her. Sometimes Néstor looked at Eva in a way that reminded her of her mom, resurfacing the ache of loss. It was unavoidable—Néstor was Dulce's youngest brother. They had the same hair, the same eyes, even the same height. Usually Eva ignored the similarities—it was a necessity all the Serranos had to adopt, to move on in a home that could never be whole again. Until Néstor's brown-red eyes softened. Until he offered her a caress or an embrace, or when he uttered words a little too mature and sensible for his nature. And they caused the memories to flood back and punch Eva across the face.

"Jerónimo and I are talking about leaving Galeno together."

A piece of her heart traveled down to her belly. "Why?" she said.

"Mamá keeps insisting I marry, if I ever want to claim my inheritance. She says it's the only way I'll give her grandchildren. I think I'm going to turn it down. And Jerónimo will, too, even though you know his family's a lot stingier about who gets what. We were talking about starting over on our own, somewhere far from here, like proper partners."

Eva reached forward to squeeze his hands. "You're a Serrano! You don't start over. You take all the escudos under your name, you move to your own hacienda, and you come visit me every once in a while. You two can still be together."

He smiled.

The corners of Eva's vision went hot. "You're my best friend. How can you leave?"

He squeezed her hands in return. His hands were large and warm. They draped over Eva's like a blanket as he said, "I'm not leaving you. I'll always be with you." Then he pointed at her chest. "In your heart—like mi mamá says."

She wanted to snarl at him.

"Besides, we're just talking about it." He shrugged. "It's only *talk*."

Eva wished she could be reassured, but she knew Néstor. He had a free spirit, yet he was also adamant. He shared her same Serrano stubbornness: to follow through with the ideas that enthralled them, no matter who got trampled along the way.

They returned to the hacienda right before suppertime. Past the gates, the long driveway leading into the hacienda was lined by cassia trees heavy with bunches of golden flowers. A two-story façade of adobe walls covered in stucco and red clay roofs welcomed them. The rustic double doors were framed by two pink-flowering bougainvillea trees that wrapped in opposite directions. A servant saw the arriving carriage and darted through the open arched corridors to fetch them umbrellas.

Néstor and Eva climbed the soaked stone steps and entered a tall foyer where a large rosary was nailed to the adobe plaster across the entryway. The walls were decorated with lavish tapestries depicting folktales of the family history: a man overlooking the vast plantation granted to him by the Segolean king; his successor overseeing the establishment of the Galeno township in Venazia. Next to those tapestries were gilded trinkets, family portraits of majestic dark-skinned women in equally majestic ball gowns, and Pentimiento icons.

Eva rushed to change out of her muddied dress and into a white cotton one with short puffy sleeves for the family dinner. The dining hall's arched entryway connected to the open corridors, where rain continued to soak the flagstones. A dark wood table stood at its very center, with enough chairs to seat Eva's plethora of tías, tíos, primos, primas, and their wailing hijas e hijos. Several generations in one room, exactly how Doña Antonia liked it. As dusk settled, the candelabra in the corners washed the room in orange firelight, bolstered by the candles arranged on the table, lighting the feast of rice and pulled capybara meat that they called pisillo.

The governor sat at the head of the table. He was a short man in comparison to Doña Antonia, umber-skinned and potbellied. He wore a white shirt tucked underneath a mahogany-colored vest. Doña Antonia sat at the opposite end of the table, her gown airy and patterned with flowers. Eva took a seat inconspicuously and nibbled the food. Her family broke into cliques to discuss the latest gossip of who was courting whom and who was bringing business or headaches to Don Mateo.

Décima, a cousin two years younger than Eva, sat by her side. Décima was quiet, which meant she was bored. And in no time at all, she turned to Eva with a mocking smile.

"Don Alberto came to call on you today, and you weren't here."

Eva didn't lift her gaze from her pisillo, spearing a chunk of red bell pepper with her fork. "I was in town with Néstor. You know this."

Décima leaned forward in a motion not unlike a slither. "Don Alberto's a bore, but at least he's interested in you. You should be a little more grateful. How else are you going to find someone who'll take you off grandmother's hands? That's all she talks about now, you know."

As the daughter of the governor's first son, Décima was already betrothed to a man from the office of commerce. This was a fact she loved to bring up anytime Eva was around, especially as Eva was older than her and without a proper engagement.

"Mi abuela knows he's going to propose any moment now," Eva said dryly. A truth she wished she could sprint away from. Luckily for her, geomancia kept her too preoccupied to think about her future with Don Alberto.

"Aren't you interested in making him fall in love with you? He'll never propose at this pace. He'll realize you're as uninterested as you look. Why don't you even try to love him back?"

Décima's trap was obvious. She wanted Eva to agree so that she could follow up with some nasty comment about how Eva was afraid no one would want to fall in love with her to begin with.

But Décima needn't any help saying what she'd wanted to from the beginning. "He's probably the last well-bred person in this city with a fetish for bachacas," she said, meaning the mixed-colored children born with dark skin and light hair, "or for horns."

"They're antlers. It's different. Educate yourself, fool."

Décima chewed on her food smugly. "Like you're educating yourself with your visits to the Contadors'?"

Eva's throat went dry. She washed down the food with her guarapo water made from pineapple peels. If only she could have some anise liqueur to spike it, then she'd be able to put up with Décima. "It's important to learn what's going on in the world" was all Eva could say, hoping she didn't have to elaborate on her lies about the tutor.

Décima, too, took a deep sip from her goblet. But her smile was vulpine. "Oh, I definitely hear what's going on in the world. The servants love to exchange gossip, and they've brought an interesting tale from the help at the Contadors'. Something about our bastard fraternizing with their bastard."

Eva faced her cousin, cheeks flushing. The desire to spear

Décima's hand with her fork ran through Eva's mind like a blazing torch. Her grip vibrated with the impulse.

Décima's smile only widened in victory. "You know, the criadas talk a lot," she warned her, "and they take their gossip to every noble house in the city. If I were you, I would avoid this talk of you becoming Doña Rosa's successor in the social hierarchy. At least until Don Alberto weds you—then you can do whatever you want."

Eva grabbed Décima's wrist. "Stop it," Eva hissed. She downed another sip of her guarapo, her gaze flitting to her grandmother for an instant. It would be disastrous if Doña Antonia heard.

"Why? Because it's true? I care about you, you know."

Someone to Eva's right gave the back of her arm a gentle, but painful, pinch. Eva turned, ready to defend herself with venom. But it was just Pura, taking her usual seat next to Eva. Her skin was several shades darker than Eva's, her coily black hair styled in a braided updo more out of convenience than fashion. She, like Eva, had inherited Dulce's brown-red eyes, but hers were circled by dark bags of exhaustion from the long nights with her newborn daughter. Pura's husband sat across from her, but he only bothered with Don Mateo's conversation.

"Stop fighting already," Pura told both Eva and Décima with raised brows. "You don't want Doña Antonia's anger tonight."

"I'll stop fighting Eva when she stops bringing the wrong sort of attention to our family."

Eva straightened up in her chair and tried to put the memory of Décima's taunt behind her.

"Where's your little one?" Eva asked her half sister.

"Asleep, finally." Pura scooped herself servings of supper and attacked the food without ceremony. "What kind of attention is she bringing to the family?"

Décima didn't miss the cue to spill the chisme about Doña Rosa.

"You're doing what?" Pura said.

Eva lied: "I've been having these weird thoughts lately, and I wanted to see if she could give me a remedy."

When Pura's eyes doubled in alarm, she looked a lot like Doña Antonia. "What weird thoughts?"

"About…Don Alberto," Eva whispered as she wrung her hands beneath the table. Pura watched her patiently, waiting for Eva to formulate the words, her concern almost palpable. Eva's sister cared for her. Pura believed her above anyone else, even when Eva lied. For this, Eva felt filthy. "About marrying him. I just wish everyone weren't so obsessed with finding me a match."

Pura frowned. "But having a match is your duty."

The back of Eva's neck grew hot. She loathed this topic, of the children she birthed giving her life value.

Pura shot her husband a glance. "I fulfilled this duty, and I'm bringing love and honor to our family. You marry so you can have cute little babies and more love in your life." She put a deep emphasis on the word *love*, as if insinuating it was something Eva lacked.

"You know, maybe you're right. I clearly don't have enough love in my life, if my own family only sees me as some birth-giver and is offering me up to a man twice my age just to get rid of me."

Décima tittered. "You'd be more desirable if you stopped associating yourself with that curandera. Is it true that she conspires with Rahmagut?"

"Décima!" Pura hissed. They were all afraid of his name.

Décima grimaced. "I'm not the one who's summoning him to our house."

"That is not what I'm doing!" Eva nearly cried out, then lowered herself on her seat when Doña Antonia shot her a brief questioning look. Eva glared at her empty plate while Pura told her one thing through her right ear and, through the left, Décima told her another.

Eva replied in nods or grunts of agreement, even if on the inside, she burned with disagreement. For all her good intentions, nothing Pura said was reassuring. Eva didn't want to be handed off to Don Alberto. She knew his only interest stemmed from the novelty of what she was: the last of a dying bloodline.

The world thundered outside when Doña Antonia finally dismissed the family. Eva and Pura retreated arm in arm to the east wing of the hacienda. Their bedchambers were next to each other, connected to the central courtyard. The rain cooled off the evening, the air wafting in the scent of mud and manure.

Eva left her door to the courtyard open before getting in bed, her mind swirling with too many conflicting ideas. She thought about the icon sitting in the corner of Doña Rosa's house. Doña Rosa wasn't the malevolent witch everyone accused her of being. She healed, and she listened, and most importantly, she didn't judge Eva for being born the way she was.

Eva could never be devout or motherly. The humans lived with ease in a world they'd built for themselves. Perhaps Doña Rosa was correct, seeking solace in a god who didn't bother with prejudice.

Eva tossed and turned in her bed, until the sounds of the rain lulled her into another fitful dream. In this one, she was a snake. Like the great tigra mariposa feared by the ranchers working her grandfather's cattle. She was discolored, because color could only be obtained with magic, and she was cold, curling over the branches of the araguaney in the courtyard as raindrops pattered on her scaly back. She was desperate for warmth and for color, so she slithered down the tree and into the first room with the courtyard door open. The room was warmer than the rain, but still her chill was unbearable. She was a creature of darkness, unable to exist without heat. Eva coiled on the tiled floor, in a corner, as a man rose from a bed made for two. He stumbled. Eva could smell the fermentation of alcohol wafting from his lips. He had the warmth she sought, but the anise smell was repulsive. So she waited until he left the room before slithering to the bed.

Eva found herself beneath the covers. She met a small body first—a babe. It smelled of milk and, faintly, of blood. That scent of milk seduced her. She moved by instinct as she drew closer to the sleeping woman swaddling the baby. She was warmest, with her smell of milk driving Eva over the edge. Eva's mouth closed around the woman's breast, biting, milk and blood squirting into her mouth, heat and color drawn at the same time.

The woman screamed.

Eva awoke suddenly. Around her, the room burst with desperate yells. She found herself facing the thundering courtyard.

"Get it out of here!" Pura screamed behind her.

Eva whirled around, realizing she wasn't in her room but standing under the doorway connecting Pura's bedroom to the courtyard.

Pura's newborn wailed at being roused, and his mother screamed, too, taken by a different kind of terror. Her sister flung the covers off, discovering a sickly white snake hanging from her right breast. It clung to her with its ravenous fangs.

Eva froze as the memory of the dream rammed into her mind. She stared in horror, Pura's screams chilling her very heart.

One by one the rooms along the courtyard came alive with candlelight. Horrified aunts and cousins rushed into Pura's room, while Eva only watched with her mouth hanging open.

Décima arrived after Néstor. She turned to Eva as Néstor beat the snake with a broom. Her brown-red eyes went round and wild, and she yelled with a pointed hand, "You *witch*!"

Eva's hand shot out to grasp her cousin's finger. But it was too late. The Serranos watched her.

"Eva did it!" Décima repeated, "She's bringing demons into the house!"

Doña Antonia burst into the room a second later, her ivory sleeping robes sweeping the floor. She took in the scene: her granddaughter, attacked by an animal reserved only for nightmares, and her other granddaughter standing at the foot of the bed with guilt written all over her face. The matriarch collapsed to her knees and wailed to the Virgin.

Pura looked up once the pale tigra mariposa had been beaten into unlatching. Tears streamed down her face, the betrayal in them shattering Eva's heart. Eva took a deep breath, breaking her stupor. She flung herself to her sister, despite Décima's and Doña Antonia's hysterics. Eva took Pura's hands in hers and begged for forgiveness. She cried, too. Because she knew she had caused this. She'd gone to sleep thinking of Rahmagut, high on the mistela drink, and a milk snake on her sister had been her reward.

"Please, forgive me."

The dream replayed like a wicked reminder of what she was. She didn't need to deny anything. Her dream had shown her all. Eva covered Pura with the sheets and grasped her hands. Her sister was too horrified to object.

Forehead to forehead, Eva told Pura, like the hypocrite that she was, her own tears welling in the corners of her eyes, "Pray with me, please."

Eva understood this was her punishment, for straying from the Virgin. For welcoming a wicked god into her life.

9

Mineral Veins Underfoot

Reina joined the swordsmanship and fencing lessons in the yard behind Águila Manor every day for several months. The sword master who trained Celeste and Javier couldn't deny her without contradicting Doña Ursulina. Instead, he worked Reina twice as hard, giving her a dull sword and putting her in charge of clearing the yard, washing their sweaty rags, and reassembling the training dummies that she smacked at least a hundred times a day to memorize the motions.

Their sword master was a quarter-valco swordsman from Fedria, middle-aged, imported as a gift to the caudillo by one of his vassals. He was an impassive man with the technique to best Javier, who was half valco and was expected to surpass them all. The sword master cut and bruised Reina anytime it was her turn to demonstrate her quickness of foot or the strength in the muscles knotting around her arm. Reina endured it all, even as Javier laughed when she fell and jeered when her blunt sword feigned a strike that made her a victor. She did it despite feeling Celeste's quiet gaze on her, for no matter how Reina tried to ignore it, it was always a distraction.

Steely clouds shrouded Águila Manor after their practice one afternoon. The grounds were enveloped by chilly air smelling of rainwater, which would likely descend from the mountains as soon as nighttime fell. The laundress and her children bustled to and fro, bringing the dried linens back into the manor. A delicious scent of charred meats wafted from the kitchens, and Reina's stomach rumbled in protest, for she knew she wouldn't be allowed to have any of it.

Despite the precarious relationship she had managed to secure with her grandmother, the help still viewed her as one of them, which suited Reina just fine. Except when they expected her to be an assistant to the cook or the laundress or the scullery maid and then denied her food when she didn't perform her tasks, which, with her combat lessons, was nearly every day.

She slumped against the moss-covered walls of the yard. The backs of her heels were chafed, and her wrist throbbed from a blow she'd received earlier. A wayward chicken from a nearby flock scurried past her, shooed by Javier, who approached with his signature scowl.

"Every day I wonder, is this the day Laurel's pet nozariel is going to stop showing up? And every day you prove me wrong."

Reina matched his gaze with equal animosity. "You should stop thinking I'm going to give up."

He kicked a loose pebble at the chicken, who clucked miserably as it ran away. "Why do you need to learn to use a sword? Is your grandmother going to send you to die for Brother's wars?" He pointed at her with his left-handed sword, the tip of the metal getting uncomfortably close to Reina's eyes.

"She can go hunt tinieblas with us," Celeste said, returning from the armory after putting away the sword she used exclusively for training.

"Do you really think I would entrust my life to a nozariel?"

Reina rose to her feet with her dull sword tight in her grip, meeting him face-to-face.

"Why don't you prove you're even worth bringing to a tiniebla raid?" His gaze landed on her chest, his valco eyes seeing the iridio pulsing in her transplant heart. He knew the anger he inspired in her. "Why don't you show me what beating that little dummy over and over has taught you, or are you scared?"

"She's not ready to fight you," Celeste said.

But Reina didn't want Celeste's defense. "No, it's all right—let's do it."

He smirked and lunged at her a split second later. His sword sliced her neck, or at least it would have, if she hadn't ducked and swiveled out of the way, returning a strike of her own. Javier blocked it, the impact sending a vibration down her injured wrist. She hissed but pushed him off. He swung again. Her sword whistled in the air before parrying him. Each of his steps and swings were an invasion on her defenses. All Reina could do was block and step farther back, the yard ringing with the clash of steel. He slashed upward, and she blocked, but the impact pushed her to the wall behind her, where her head banged against the ragged wall, her tail slamming against the stone. She angled her weapon badly, so she couldn't stop the tip of his sword from cutting her thigh. Flames licked her leg. Her blood ran in warm rivulets, then pooled in her boot. Reina bit the insides of her cheeks to stop herself from voicing her pain and giving him the satisfaction. He lifted his sword again, and without her defenses, Reina knew she was at his mercy.

"Enough, Javier!" Celeste said behind them.

He stopped with the blade close to Reina's neck. "If this were a real battle, you'd be dead," he purred. His breath smelled like a stale, dirty rag.

Up close Javier reminded Reina of the dead, with his blueish lips and skin so pale she could see the veins branching down his temples. It was hard to breathe, imprisoned by the blood-red madness in his eyes.

He rammed his pommel against Reina's wrist, making her lose grip, and kicked her useless sword aside. In his proximity he felt the ragged edges of the iridio ore underneath her shirt and flinched.

"*What*—" he said, pushing off her.

It was the opportunity Reina needed to sprint out of his reach, even if it would be a futile escape, for each of his valco strides were twice as fast as hers. But Celeste stepped between them. An undercurrent of emotions sparked the air between the two valcos. Javier's scowl turned into a smirk as he faced his niece. He raised his sword to her instead, a challenge that Celeste accepted.

Celeste slapped her hands together, her bracelet containing an iridio solution jingling from the movement. When she pulled her hands apart in a wide arc, a glowing red scythe materialized between her palms: The handle solidified into ebony etched with flowing rivers of iridio red, and the curved blade manifested from the air, which rippled like a heat mirage.

"Are you done with your theatrics?" Javier asked her. Celeste merely tilted her head, and Javier lunged.

The pain of her bleeding thigh was forgotten as Reina watched Javier and Celeste exchanging blows. One left swipe, one right parry.

"He's...not threatening her, is he?" a gentle voice said beside Reina, emerging from the archway to the manor.

Reina saw Doña Laurel and attempted to straighten up in respect. Instead, she earned herself a lick of lightning from her wounded thigh. She sucked in a breath.

"Oh—Reina." Doña Laurel took her arm to give her support.

Reina pulled herself free. She couldn't be a burden to Doña Laurel, especially as her growing belly attested that she held the most precious thing in the household.

"I'm all right, mi señora. This is part of our training," Reina said, stretching the truth.

"You must have Doña Ursulina tend to you at once."

Reina could only offer her a tight smile in return. As far as Reina was concerned, the sort of spells Doña Ursulina bothered with had nothing to do with healing.

"So...is Javier being gentle?" Doña Laurel asked again. "They—they move too fast for my eyes to see properly," she admitted with a little laugh. "I can't tell if he's being sportsmanlike."

Reina's immediate inclination was to lie a reassurance. Her gaze traveled to the sparring valcos, and her heart jumped in a concerned pirouette as Javier sliced the air over Celeste, each time getting closer to drawing blood. "Y-yeah. He's not being too rough."

She picked up her dull sword in case she needed to intervene, even if she was wounded, and was nozariel, and could never measure up to the speed of a valco.

A pained cry filled the yard when Celeste miscalculated one of Javier's strikes and his sword sliced the side of her arm. Celeste collapsed to her knees, releasing her scythe to nurse her wound. And Reina couldn't understand why she would lower her guard just as Javier spun around to strike a second time.

Heart in her throat, Reina ran to stop him with her sword raised. Even as a wicked inner voice told her she was going to be too late.

"Stop right this moment!" Doña Laurel's voice ruptured the yard, hard and commanding, earning her the attention of all three. Javier's outstretched sword hand stopped in midair.

Doña Laurel stepped closer, pointing at Javier. "You would wound your niece?"

He regarded her with dark, glaring eyes. "We are sparring. It is part of the game."

"A game?" Doña Laurel blurted out, outraged.

Celeste scampered to her feet with one hand shielding her bleeding arm. The blood coated her fingers and spilled onto the cobblestones, joining Reina's splatters.

"You cut her," Doña Laurel said.

Javier shook his sword to get her blood off it, his face scrunched in disgust. "Yes, it's what happens when warriors train. You wouldn't know it, since your role is to breed."

Doña Laurel diminished the space between them, and the air was infected with that same heady energy that filled Doña Ursulina's lair. "You will not disrespect me in my own home," she hissed.

Javier waved at the air around him. "This is also my home."

"For as long as I allow it," Doña Laurel bit back.

"*No?*" Javier grimaced, petulantly.

Reina limped to Celeste, her gaze lingering over Celeste's lips as they parted to allow a huff of pain.

"You cannot cast me out of here!" Javier yelled. "This land belongs to Mother. You did nothing to gain it or grow it. You have no claims to it. Just because you walk around like you own the place doesn't mean you have any real power over it!" He turned to the archway leading back to the manor. His retreat.

"I own this home, and I am this close to banishing you from it, forever," Doña Laurel said, pursuing him into the dark passageways of the manor.

"People only endure you because they fear Enrique—but that's all they do, *endure you*." Javier's voice carried into the yard.

Reina turned to Celeste, even if her chest was achy and apprehensive at the quarreling masters. If it stung Reina to hear it, she couldn't imagine how Celeste could cope with the constant bickering of her blood family. Celeste offered her an uneasy smile and allowed Reina to guide her back to the armory, where they kept the cleaning rags and ointment when training went a little too far.

"This is why I don't like it when mi mamá watches me spar," Celeste admitted as she claimed one of the wooden benches and cleaned her cuts. Reina settled on the bench as well, at the other end. They cleaned their wounds superficially, then wrapped themselves with fresh bandages. Reina stole a glimpse at Celeste, noting her slender neck as she bent down to swab at her ankle. It was dotted in pretty brown moles.

"She doesn't understand that I'm not fragile. How am I supposed to learn anything if I'm constantly coddled because of her?"

"It's not about you. Javier was not being fair."

The apprehension of watching him get closer to Celeste with every swipe resurfaced. It angered Reina, that Javier would treat Celeste with such contempt. For no reason at all. Celeste didn't lash out unfairly at him or anybody. She treated the staff like the friends she had known her entire life. She welcomed Reina, ignoring the differences other people would so easily latch on to.

Celeste made a pout of disagreement. "Javier can't hurt me, even if some instinct deep within him wants to. It's fine—I'm glad he doesn't treat me like a princess. It's suffocating."

"Doña Laurel was worried about you today." Reina, too, had been worried.

Celeste shrugged. She gave Reina a long look, as if debating something with herself. Then she left the bench and offered Reina a hand up. Her fingers were warm and soft, unlike Reina's scarred palm.

"She has no say in the matter. Mi papá knows this is what it takes to be someone in this world." Celeste beckoned Reina to come with her.

"Power?" Reina inquired, following her on the gravel path leading into the surrounding woods.

"Our legacy was forged by spilled blood," Celeste said. "I have a big name to live up to. My grandmother became a legend."

Reina nodded. Even in Segolita, people told tall tales about Feleva Águila. She was the Liberator's ally during the revolution; her iridio and armies played a key role in ousting Segol, an empire with the income of many colonies to quell any uprising.

They entered the grove's shadowed canopy, where moist ferns licked their pants and prickly undergrowth crunched beneath their bootsteps. Reina stopped before the forest could swallow them completely. She was without her sword, even if it was a blunt, useless thing, and the memory of what lived up in the mountains made her hesitate. Creatures hungered for iridio.

"Where are we going?"

Celeste let out a small laugh. When she smirked, Reina saw her resemblance to Don Enrique and to Javier. "I want to show you... a secret. Besides, I think you're ready for a better sword than what they're letting you use. Don't you want a proper weapon to tell Javier to back off?"

Reina was stunned. She tried not to think too hard about the way Celeste's eyes shone in kindness and expectation, with the idea of a secret to be shared. For she was nozariel, and this was the lady of the house.

"Okay," Reina said feebly. They continued.

Dewy ferns and moss crowded their path as they hiked farther up the mountain.

Celeste led the way. "So, back to my grandmother: She was ruthless and ambitious. You know those antlers in mi papá's study?"

Reina knew exactly the ones. They hung next to the boiled-leather map where delicate cursive, along with illustrations of caimans and troupials, demarcated the cities and landmarks of Venazia and Fedria.

"They were the antlers of a valco who fought for Segol during the revolution. Mi papá told me she bested him and scalped him of his antlers. She kept them as a trophy."

Reina swallowed hard, her gaze surfing Celeste's stunted pair. Surely Don Enrique, Javier, and even Celeste had it in them to do the same.

"There's a story about her that started her infamy. Mi papá says the caudillos of the Llanos tell it to their children to stop them from ever thinking they can antagonize us. Maybe you've heard of it." Celeste paused dramatically, giving Reina a hand over the boulder blocking their path.

"I don't know. Tell it to me."

"*Once upon a time*," she said, shooting Reina a coy smile. Giggles bubbled out of Celeste as Reina returned it. "Actually, years ago, on an estate much like ours, a lord was hosting the quinceañera of his firstborn daughter."

Reina nodded for her to go on.

"People from all over the land traveled to the Llanos to see her, because the girl was kind and smart, but most importantly because she was very beautiful. After dancing her vals, the girl fluttered from one group of people to the other, charming all with her beauty and wit."

They continued along the path, their hands brushing due to their proximity. Reina moved hers away, her fingers curling.

"She had particularly charmed two men, who fell head over heels for her honey-colored curls. One was a self-made man, who'd built his fortune by hunting down outlaws and catching runaway enslaved nozariel for the governor. The other was a rancher with a large inheritance and an award-winning bull. Each argued they were better suited to be her husband. And each offered a mighty prize to the lord for his daughter's hand. But the lord was a just man, and he declared she should be the one to choose her future husband."

A few small frailejones began dotting the wilderness as they hiked to higher elevations. The Páramo's crisp air enveloped them, running a draft through Reina. At one point, Celeste detoured from the worn path, and Reina blindly followed.

"So, before the party ended, the rancher and bounty hunter took the matter to the quinceañera. You see, she wasn't interested in being their wife, and she was clever and knew the party would soon end, so she announced they should duel in contrapunteo. Her plan was to sneak away during the middle of the singing to avoid the question altogether. She said the one with the best song should have her hand."

"Contrapunteo?" Reina interjected.

"You've never seen it? The ranchers of the Llanos do it all the time. It's like a verse duel that they improvise to the melody of a cuatro." Celeste clicked her tongue and rolled her eyes. "And it's kind of tradition, in their quinceañeras. I've seen my fair share... Anyway, the rancher and bounty hunter faced off in the best contrapunteo match of the land. The rhymes were so clever and so entertaining, even city folk gathered around the house gates to listen. There were so many people the girl found it impossible to slip away. But in the end, the rancher had the obvious advantage. When his song finished, even the girl's father stood up to clap."

Celeste stopped at a sodden clearing, where the entrance to a large burrow opened for them like a maw.

"His victory was the obvious outcome, because not only did the rancher compete with his bulls, but he also was a renowned singer of contrapunteo, who won many contests in the region. The party attendants said so, and the bounty hunter felt cheated. He whipped out his gun, pointed it at the rancher, and said, 'The quinceañera cannot choose to marry a dead man,' and upon the stipulations of their duel, it wouldn't have been unlawful if his gun put a bullet between the rancher's eyes."

Celeste paused dramatically, and Reina indulged her with wide eyes, because she was curious and because it was enthralling to watch Celeste tell the story with such enthusiasm.

Celeste beckoned Reina to approach the burrow. "He pulled the trigger, and a cloud of smoke filled the patio. But once the smoke cleared, there was a great outcry, because the gun malfunctioned (as guns tend to do) and instead the bullet ricocheted right between the tamarind eyes of the quinceañera."

"*Oh.*" Reina frowned, and Celeste grinned.

"But as it turned out, the quinceañera's lover was within the crowd and had seen the tragedy with her own two eyes."

"*Her* own two eyes?"

Celeste's grin widened.

"She was just a girl, not yet fifteen herself, but she was pure valco and descendant of a great bloodline, and she was furious. She swept through the patio and, with her own clawlike fingers, ripped open the throats of the rancher and the bounty hunter in hot-blooded revenge. Then she lived happily ever after. The end."

Reina yanked on Celeste's sleeve. "Wait—but what happened to the valco girl?"

Celeste shrugged. "Nothing. The father, who was just as grieved that his daughter had been taken away from him, declared that the men had died from their duels, so there was no murder to report to the authorities, and the valco girl went on to live a very infamous life." Then she leaned closer to Reina and whispered, "As the mighty Feleva Águila."

Reina could imagine it so vividly. The beautiful rage. The bloodshed spurred by violent instincts.

"Mi papá told me that story," Celeste said, wiping her sticky bangs from her forehead. "He says everyone in that town still talks about it, how my grandmother was just a girl but had been born brave and ruthless, and it was no wonder she accomplished all she did during her lifetime. All things considered, it was a happy ending...the valco way. Mi mamá hates it when I say that, but it's true. We're different from humans."

Reina nodded. Celeste was only a quarter valco, but Reina could tell the bloodlust existed within her as well.

Celeste began descending into the burrow as if it weren't a pathway to the Void, where nothing but darkness awaited them. From the shadows, she said, "Mi mamá's being foolish by worrying so much for me. Javier would never seriously harm me. If he did—well, he fears mi papá, and he'd never be able to escape his wrath."

Reina imagined Don Enrique's big hands taking hold of Javier's underdeveloped antlers. He had the strength to snap them in two, if he wanted.

Sudden coolness made her shiver, and she stopped at the foot of the burrow, her muddy boot leaning into it while Celeste descended farther into the shadows. "Wait—where are you going?"

Celeste beamed at her. "To get you your new sword. Don't you trust me?"

Reina frowned. "I trust you." Without Celeste, she wouldn't be alive.

The answer satisfied Celeste. She beckoned Reina to the darkness with an arched brow. A challenge to prove that she did.

They descended the muddy tunnel, where even the walls felt unstable and apt to cave in at any moment. The air was stagnant, heavy with the scent of decayed leaves and dirt. The light of the Páramo left them with every step they took, and Celeste produced a wisp of firelight with a spell of iridio. She cast it by snapping it into existence and tossing it into the air. The light enclosed them in a pocket of orange.

A heavy door of dark wood, hugged by roots and slick vines, met them at the end of the tunnel.

Celeste used the entirety of her body weight to tug the door open. It gave a groan, threatening to pull the ceiling down with it, and allowed them into a candlelit chamber of stone walls and flagstones. Reina took in the room, glimpsing the worktables strewn with open tomes and flasks scattered about. A severed caiman arm and the coiled skeleton of a snake sat on a bookshelf. One wall was bordered by shelf cabinets, which were stocked with too many bunches of herbs, teacups, and rosaries to count. Another wall was completely covered in hanging leather maps of more townships and territories than Reina ever imagined could exist. Her eyes fell on the great stone table in the center of the room, which was surrounded by two engraved standing stones on either side. The sight made her scarred chest itch.

Reina followed Celeste to the staircase on the other side of the chamber. It hinted there was more to this place.

"Welcome to Gegania."

"Gegania?" Reina parroted, leading the way up the stairs in curiosity.

The landing gave way to a tiled corridor lined with more doors, a doorway revealing a dining area, and the doorway to an entrance foyer. The air was dusty, cobwebs clinging to portraits of black-haired, white-skinned humans on rotting wooden frames. Bewildered, Reina swung open the front door and met green mountains with a view of a conuco and of the setting afternoon sun. A wind buffeted her, ruffling her bangs and chilling her through the openings of her clothes. Waves of hills marked the landscape where the house sat, barren of the firs that surrounded the manor and the burrow. Rather, these lands were dotted with sturdy wildflowers and the occasional frailejón. When Celeste caught up to her, Reina's mouth hung ajar. This was nowhere near the burrow. "Where are we?"

"It's mi mamá's childhood home."

Reina squinted at her.

"Yes, far from the manor."

Reina's frown only deepened. A headache prodded at her temples. "Are we still in the Páramo?"

Celeste nodded.

"But not on the same side?"

Celeste shook her head. It was impossible. One had to hike up the Páramo to higher peaks to find views like these.

"How?" Reina said, walking back to the corridor and down the staircase. The door to the tunnel was still open, and she chased it back to the entrance burrow. This time she was a lot less careful and uncaring about the lack of light—almost slipping once or twice in the mud. Thankfully, Celeste caught up to her with another flame wisp.

Reina emerged onto the clearing at the other side. Here the air was moist and acidic, with less of that chilly bite. She could taste the forest's decay in her mouth. The sky was hardly visible through the trees, but it was cloudy.

"How are we in both places at the same time?"

Patiently, Celeste tugged Reina's arm back to the underground chamber. "Try not to attract too much attention. The entrance is still connected to Papá's land." She didn't explain until they reached the table surrounded by the standing stones. "The house is connected to both places because of this." Her hand swept over the table's rough surface, where lines glowed dimly in the shape of capillaries, sprouting from the looping symbol at the center.

Celeste met Reina's bewildered gaze with pride in her eyes. "Mi mamá grew up here."

Reina approached the table. The capillaries were lighted in a soft white, pulsing sleepily.

"Mamá's ancestors were miners and cartographers, and her father, my grandfather, studied geomancia here. He spelled this table to create a tether from this house to anywhere that has an underground vein of metal that responds to geomancia. We only walked for a few moments in the connected tunnel, but we crossed a very long distance."

Doña Ursulina's warning about Doña Laurel echoed in the depths of Reina's memory. "The Benevolent Lady also knows geomancia?"

Celeste nodded but worried her lower lip. "Yes, but she doesn't practice it anymore. She says it's unnecessary for her life, which I guess is true."

"So where is it really located? Where are we?"

Celeste strolled to one of the largest maps hanging from the moist stone wall. Her hand hovered around the homestead illustration drawn near the center of the Páramo. She jabbed her finger on the cursive label. "We're very close to Apartaderos, perhaps only a half hour away on foot. I can show you the land and the conuco later."

Reina nodded, very much liking that. She wanted to take it all in, to marvel at the magic embracing every part of Celeste's life. There was such an open use of geomancia in Águila Manor, a wanton expenditure of iridio. Geomancia was something Reina had only acknowledged on the fringes of her desperation in Segolita, but here she had an actual shot at living with it. She inspected the illuminated lines stemming from the looping symbol on the table.

"Is this powered by iridio?"

"Lots of it. That's why I mostly just keep it connected to home. That way I don't have to explain to mi papá why I suddenly need to take so much iridio from the stores. With the proper amount of iridio fuel and the right guidance, we can probably connect it to any place in Venazia, even to your home in Segolita," Celeste said this enthusiastically, as if she wanted the news to impress Reina.

"Segolita's not my home," Reina said without missing a beat.

Celeste quirked her brows.

Reina stared at her dirty fingernails. She hated talking about it. But Celeste was curious, and she had already been so forthcoming. It'd be selfish of Reina to never let her in. "I hated living there, especially after my father died. I was alone."

Celeste reached for her hand, using her index to lift Reina's pinky, asking permission to offer comfort.

"Just surviving, you know? Being hungry and dirty."

"You're here now," Celeste said softly. "Águila Manor can be your home."

Reina nodded. She was already happier than she'd ever been, despite the long days working with the staff and the darkness of her heart. "So does Don Enrique know about this place? Doña Ursulina?" she asked.

"No, and you can't tell them. Mi mamá's kept this secret all these years because she wants to make sure it only goes to me. She doesn't want Javier to think he can use the magic in this house, so she never told Papá." Celeste licked her lips and returned to the wall, with its plethora of illustrated maps. "She brought me here a few years ago and told me to keep it secret and to use it for whatever I need. At first I thought, wow, how selfish of her to never tell Papá, but then it dawned on me how powerful it can be."

Reina pressed her fingertips on the rough surface, feeling its soft pulse of magic like a lap of warm water. Don Enrique was already master of all the iridio in Sadul Fuerte. She couldn't fathom the kind of influence and power he would also have if he could be anywhere he desired at a moment's notice.

What would happen if she attempted to connect the iridio of her heart with the table's? She pushed her palms against the stone and closed her eyes, focusing on the darkness of her transplant heart. The uttering enveloped her, almost gleeful at being acknowledged. The ore and the table connected with a spark. Reina flinched, but she was glad. Perhaps, with some practice, her own iridio could help her control the table itself.

Celeste rummaged through one of the storage chests and retrieved a weapon with an "Aha!" The blade whistled as Celeste drew it from its scabbard. "It's only a machete, but it was forged with iridio."

Heat rioted in Reina's cheeks as she accepted it. Her jaw dropped a little, and she was without words for a moment, that the caudillo's daughter deemed her worthy of receiving any gift, let alone one with such weight and build. The blade needed sharpening, but Reina could see the iridio alloyed to it, as the metal had a gradient of color from its black tip to the steely gray approaching the hilt. Honestly, it reminded Reina of rot.

"It's perfect," she whispered earnestly. It was fitting for someone with her monstrous heart.

Once it was time to recount the day's events to Doña Ursulina, as was her daily duty, Reina kept Celeste's secret. Instead, she drew focus to what had occurred in the yard, and her grandmother ordered her to follow Javier's tracks.

Doña Ursulina gave the instruction haphazardly while drawing angles and tangents on the star map, as she was consumed with unearthing the requirements for fulfilling Rahmagut's legend. "See where his loyalties lie," the witch told her.

At first Reina imagined her grandmother was doing it in service of the caudillo. After all, his younger brother was not harmless, and his status was day in and out threatened by the lady of the house, who could give birth to a boy who would further displace him. But as Reina left her grandmother's study with her orders at the forefront of her mind, she realized Doña Ursulina merely saw Javier as another player in her schemes for power.

The task sounded simpler than it was, for Javier no longer saw Reina as insignificant since she arrived to spar with a machete of iridio. He observed her, perhaps more shrewdly than the rest of the Águilas.

It wasn't easy to walk into a room carrying a platter of bizcochos for the merienda and linger around to hear Don Enrique, having reneged on the plan to betroth Javier to Celeste, bark an order at Javier to find another valco to marry. Or to witness how Doña Laurel urged Javier to "have some compassion" when the family gathered for supper and the topic of an inquisition by the Pentimiento Church on geomancers came up. Reina had to practically tiptoe on the second-story corridor when, one morning, while fetching Javier, she turned a corner and witnessed Don Enrique's fist knocking the air out of him.

"Laurel is the doña of this house, and she will continue to be so for as long as she lives," Don Enrique hissed to Javier, his vein-bulged left hand lifting his brother against the wall by the neck.

Blue in the face, Javier managed to shove him away. Between splutters for air, he said, "I don't understand why I have to live surrounded by women leeching off Mother's legacy—telling me what to do." He snarled, eyes alight with resentment, "I am also her son!"

A cold indifference wiped the anger from Don Enrique's face. "If Mother were alive, she would only see you as a disappointment."

The chill percolated even into Reina, seeing Javier's gaze darkening and falling to the floor in silence. She scurried down the stairs before they noticed her. The interaction was interesting enough that her grandmother would be content, just as Reina took satisfaction in seeing Javier get what he deserved.

In all these instances, she did notice a difference in him: Javier looked sickly and unkempt, with large circles under his eyes. Eventually, he even stopped attending the sparring lessons.

Reina reported the matter to her grandmother. As reward, Doña Ursulina gave her a copper ring crowned with a capped top, to put on her ring finger, and offered to teach her geomancia for the first time.

By the third try of entwining her fingers with her thumbs flicking skyward, Reina was able to manage the bismuto spell for opening the eyes. It let her see the iridio zipping through the air in Doña Ursulina's study and exuding from the ore, like valcos could. It allowed her to see her grandmother surrounded in the faintest glow of blue, which Doña Ursulina told her was the litio protection she kept on her at all times.

"When you see geomancia, it manifests in different hues according to the caster's nature," Doña Ursulina said. "It manifests in the red spectrum for the dominant and assertive, like Don Enrique. In violet colors for the supportive and sympathetic, as you'll see if Laurel ever casts geomancia again. In yellows and golds for the inspiring and persuasive, as is Javier's geomancia—"

"Javier is inspiring?" Reina blurted out in disgust.

Doña Ursulina chuckled. "*And*—" She splayed a slim jeweled hand on the desk to demonstrate her indigo radiance. "Blues are for the cautious and analytical."

Reina's copper bismuto ring glowed blue as well. She placed her hand next to her grandmother's, Reina's lighter by several shades of brown but marred and bruised, the knuckles rippled with scutes. Doña Ursulina noticed the blue color as well and, with a raised brow, offered the most minuscule nod of approval. Reina bit her inner cheek to keep her face straight until she was dismissed; then she beamed all the way through the rest of her chores.

10

Sadul Fuerte

The bleak sunlight of a cloudy morning reflected off the silver cups Reina carried from the kitchens to the manor. The yard she crossed smelled of moist earth, as if those clouds rolling down the mountains were unleashing rain that would inevitably reach the estate. Inside the dining hall, her destination, a lighted chandelier of glittering crystal hung over the dining table, where the masters of the house sat on plush brocade seating, the patterns made of golden eagles for the family's crest. Doña Laurel's harpist kept the family company with a crooning melody, and two servers flitted around the table, clearing porcelain dishes where the grilled trout and arepa breakfast had been left half-eaten.

Reina approached slowly, unnerved about encroaching on the family's privacy while the don and doña discussed Sadul Fuerte politics. She glanced at Celeste, admiring the thick black hair draping her shoulders and the high-necked vest nearly reaching her back hairline, a style Celeste wore relentlessly. Reina didn't understand what it was about Celeste that drew her eyes. It couldn't be jealousy, because she never saw herself in Celeste's shoes. She didn't yearn for this life of being the center of attention, of high expectations and of being so beautiful it was an effort to look away. Rather, Reina's desires inhabited the realm of wanting to demonstrate she had value. And the Águilas were doing that for her—namely Doña

Laurel, who included her in matters beyond her responsibility as a kitchen wench. As she did now, involving Reina in a secret plot to surprise Don Enrique with the amapola juice presently filling the silver goblets. The juice of a fruit Reina had grown up believing was magic. Doña Laurel trusted Reina, and it was this trust that made Reina feel so guilty for glancing at Celeste. It made her feel like she was coveting something Doña Laurel possessed.

"We won the war, Javier." Don Enrique's heated tenor snapped Reina out of her thoughts. "It is the victors who decide how the land shall be split, who shall have what, and what the distribution of power shall look like." His chair scraped the marble floor as he pushed to his feet, ending their breakfast conversation. "And as the victor, I say this land shall have a king, and Rodrigo Silva is the one to play that role. Anyway—I must go. Business awaits me in Sadul Fuerte."

"So Rodrigo is a pawn, not a king?" Javier quipped from his seat on the table. "Mother would have wanted you to crown yourself. We have all the iridio, escudos, and arms to keep that power. We wouldn't need anyone's help, like the Silvas so desperately need ours."

Reina tucked the information away to share with her grandmother later—the endless debate between the caudillo and his younger brother. Eventually, Doña Laurel noticed Reina and waved her closer with a smile, her other hand resting on the roundness of her belly, which was swollen as her forty weeks of gestation fast approached an end.

Reina smiled back. With her thoughts, she sent a brief prayer for the doña. She wished for the Benevolent Lady to get the son she so deeply desired. In fact, she wished for Doña Laurel to get anything she wanted, for she deserved it all.

"Oh, enough of it already," Doña Laurel said. "I grow green listening to your dreams of becoming a prince. We don't have to concern ourselves with Puerto Carcosa's politics. We're in the mountains—anyone trying to get to us will first have to get past the whistlers and the tinieblas. Here we are happy." She struggled to rise, but Don Enrique rushed to help with a nervousness outside of his character, one he'd donned since the moment they'd found out she was with child. "We don't need to be kings and queens to live a fulfilling life. Reina, can you bring it now?"

Reina approached with steps quiet as a cat's. Her heart hammered as all valco eyes landed on her. She presented the first silver goblet to Doña Laurel and the second to her adoring husband. A honeysuckle-colored juice filled it to the brim, smelling sweet like sugarcane.

Don Enrique saw the contents and murmured his wife's name in wonder.

"I had it delivered all the way from Fedria," Doña Laurel clarified for him. "Truthfully, I was waiting for a more special occasion, but I couldn't let the fruit rot."

"Amapola juice?" he said, awestruck.

They, like Reina, knew the tale of the amapola well: The legend of the nozariel princess Marle, who'd also given her name to the river dividing the lands of Fedria and Venazia. A tale of how the princess and a human warrior met in a battle ending in stalemate. After the battle the warrior fell hopelessly in love with the princess, but she refused all his advances. So the warrior consulted with a worshiper of Rahmagut, who gave him the local amapola and bestowed it with an incantation to tie their fates together. No matter how often the princess refused, time and fate would eventually override her stubbornness. Princess Marle's successors were half human, half nozariel, and thus the myth had been born. The story that those who shared the same amapola would have their bands of fate tied for eternity.

"If magic is real, then why can't the tale of the amapola also be?" She petted her husband's freshly shaved cheek. He nodded warmly, a rare display of love Reina knew he reserved only for his doña.

The love of family. The comfort of a partner. Both were things Reina witnessed from the fringes, in other people's lives. The ache in her heart for that unconditional love she'd lost when Juan Vicente perished had dulled. She was numb to its hurt. Though sometimes, when she saw it in other people, so bright and unadulterated, the pain throbbed anew. As she was reminded of how utterly alone she was.

It was a foolish thought, she knew, for more important things needed her attention. But...how she longed to have that. To stare into someone's eyes and see her home in them.

Treacherously, her gaze flitted to Celeste, her transplant heart betraying her with an inkling to the desires she denied. When she did, she found Celeste already looking at her.

"To peacetime," Doña Laurel said, raising the remains of her drink in a toast.

Don Enrique raised his. "To a household full of little valcos."

They drained the goblets, and Reina imagined the bands of amapola magic weaving around them, tying their lifetimes together. Without a bismuto spell, she couldn't see the magic, but she was sure Celeste and Javier, with their valco eyes, could.

This was a life Reina could get behind. She had a future in Águila Manor. While Don Enrique and Doña Laurel toasted to their destiny together, Reina prayed to Ches for the things she'd never had until now: to have a roof over her head, a family, and to be needed by the people around her.

Doña Ursulina's high-heeled boots clicked on the marble as she entered the hall. Her entrance disbanded the breakfast, for she was a reminder of the business she and the caudillo were due to address in the city.

Celeste clung to her father, and Reina mimicked the cue, following Doña Ursulina to the stables and saying, "I want to go, too. Please take me." She had ideas of what Sadul Fuerte ought to look like, but her journey into Venazia had ended before she could glimpse the city for herself. And that had been one of her many turns of good luck, for with her tail, it was impossible to hide what she was. But Reina couldn't live hidden in Águila Manor forever. The people of Sadul Fuerte, those who worked in the governor's office and did business with Doña Ursulina and the caudillo, had to see her as an active member of the household. The sooner she expedited this introduction, the safer she would feel with the promises of a life as a Duvianos successor.

Her grandmother didn't spare her a glance. "*You?* You want to make your entrance to Sadul Fuerte?"

Reina grimaced. Was there some kind of decorum she needed to account for? "Not officially, like a debutante or anything." She had heard of such things in the high society of Segolita, but she'd grown up so far removed she was sure she was missing at least several dozen details.

Laughter cold like the morning breeze bubbled from her grandmother's lips. Those clouds threatening rain opened a slight drizzle on the outdoor walk to the parked carriages.

"If you're going to meet the governor—I can just observe—"

Doña Ursulina whirled on her outside the gilded carriage as the driver held the door open. Don Enrique and his progeny followed a few steps behind. "Reina, you are nozariel, with a *tail*. It will inspire . . . questions I would rather not deal with right now."

"I'm coming as well," Celeste stated with her brows raised high. "Reina's yet to see Sadul Fuerte, and if I am there, they'll think she's my companion. No one will question it."

Reina avoided smiling. She withheld the urge to exchange any conspiratorial glance . . .

"Just hide the tail under your ruana or something," Celeste said with a shrug.

They all looked to Don Enrique for the final say-so. His demeanor still held the smile of sharing the amapola with his wife and the reaffirmation of the future prosperity awaiting them. He gave a noncommittal "Very well."

"I shall come as well." Javier's voice emerged from the doorway.

Don Enrique paused, considering him with a long look. "You will present yourself to the Palace of Commerce in this condition?"

Reina took in Javier's fine navy tunic of embroidered laurels and troupials, his trousers brown and fitted to his lean form. His attire was twice as appropriate as hers, with the richness in material and craftsmanship signaling his rank. Reina squashed the urge to slither behind Celeste, to hide her appearance from the inevitable discussion.

Javier's nostrils flared. His red gaze battled Don Enrique's, his lips drawing into a thin line.

Don Enrique repeated, "You will go to the city in this state and announce to all those sycophants that you, my brother, are not strong and well?"

"How would they know?" Javier said, but even as he said it, Reina knew he wasn't the same young man who'd stumbled upon her mangled body in the mountains nearly a year ago. Or the Javier who'd hardly held back in bruising her with low blows and feigned strikes when they'd trained with their valco sword master. His skin was pale and paper-thin, the veins beneath opaque as if his blood had curdled black. He had circles under his eyes, which didn't fade no matter how long he slept (and Reina knew, from her duties fetching food or laundry, how the caudillo's brother spent his days sleeping away an ailment that wouldn't leave him be).

"Stay today and rest," Don Enrique said, a command hiding behind some pretense of compassion. "There will be other times when your presence is needed. We are merely reviewing trade agreements with a new shipper." He paused and waited for an objection.

Javier had none. He stomped back into the warm confines of the manor, his gaze gliding over Reina a moment before he disappeared, as the shame became all the more apparent: Doña Ursulina's nozariel was receiving the preferential treatment he had not.

Don Enrique and Doña Ursulina entered the gilded carriage, and the driver promptly shut the door in Reina's face. Another driver was summoned. Celeste and Reina were handed knitted ruanas before being ushered to the open cart following as an entourage. It wasn't appropriate that Reina ride with the caudillo, which was just as well, for she couldn't imagine spending the two-hour drive to Sadul Fuerte sitting across from him. Don Enrique's guard joined the convoy, for one of the carriages was transporting iridio to the Palace of Commerce.

"I wish I could say you didn't have to do that," Reina uttered as the choppy ride out of the Águila grounds began.

Celeste tilted her head. "Who knows? Papá seems to be in a good mood. Maybe you didn't need the help at all."

Reina allowed the bumps of the ride to shimmy her closer to Celeste, their shoulders grazing. In such proximity to her, Reina was warm. "Celeste," she said softly, "what does Javier have?"

Celeste frowned at the curving path as their caravan zigzagged down the mountain and entered the shadows cast by the introduced conifers. "He seems odd, doesn't he?"

"He wastes the day away in his chambers. Sometimes I bring him food, and it's left uneaten." Reina only cared for his health as a factor impacting the careful balance she had carved for herself within the household. And because it was a curiosity Doña Ursulina would want to know about.

"I don't know what's the matter with him. He looks like he might be ill, but you can tell he still has his strength."

Reina agreed. It was indeed strange. She thought of the illness of mal de ojo, of the fatigue, loss of appetite, and sleeplessness, which could be the reason for his maladies. But out of all the Águilas, why should Javier be the one receiving someone's envious ill wishes?

"I think he is just angry at my father. Javier wanted us to be betrothed, did you know that? He has this twisted idea that my grandmother somehow wanted it so we could preserve the valco blood."

Reina chewed on the insides of her lip and feigned ignorance. "And you don't agree with that?" The question came with a tightness in her heart, one that loosened as Celeste shook her head.

"I wouldn't do it, even if mi papá wanted it. I think there were just worries about the longevity of our breed. But…"

"But Doña Laurel is going to have more children," Reina finished for her.

"Exactly. And even if my grandmother was the last full-blooded valco in Venazia, there must be others out there, in Fedria, for example. I'm sure of it. There may just be mixed-breeds, like us and like the Liberator. Did you know that when we were little, the Liberator sent us a coffer of presents?"

"Like all the other gifts you get?"

This won her a laugh from Celeste, who went on, "He sent us pearl necklaces from the waters of the Cow Sea, where he lives, and woven little dolls with valco antlers, and rattan baskets, and bocadillos of guava preserved in sugar and wrapped in bijao leaves."

Celeste's face lit up as she recalled the distant childhood memory, and Reina decided she could hear her talk all day long and never grow tired of it.

"He sent us a lovely letter with it. In fact, I think I still have it. He said we were the future of valcos, and so we had to protect each other. Mi mamá reckons the gift was a gesture we should have returned for his daughter, but sometimes I get the impression that mi papá doesn't like him very much."

The cart gave a bump, and Reina gripped the edges of her seat to stop herself from sliding into Celeste. Celeste merely nudged her shoulder against Reina's, unbothered and giggling.

"How could anyone dislike the Liberator?"

"Right?" Celeste chuckled in agreement. "Did you ever see him in Segolita?"

A flush crept to Reina's cheeks. "I only got a small glimpse of him many years ago, at the welcoming parade when he went to marry his new wife at the cathedral," she said, deflated at her inconsequential experience. A *glimpse* was a stretch of the truth, for Reina had been just a child lost in the sea of people who agglomerated outside the palace's studded gates to welcome their war hero into the capital. Amid the shoulders and heads of excited revelers, Reina had scored a look at only the tip of his antlers. Even that had been a morsel, enough to fill her with the shared pride of the independence he'd fought for.

"But he doesn't live in Segolita," Reina added.

"He lives in the Cow Sea, no?"

Reina shrugged, recalling Doña Ursulina attesting the Liberator lived in Tierra'e Sol. "I have no idea why he wouldn't live in Segolita, where everyone loves him."

Celeste held her gaze, unabashedly so, a comfort they had earned in their nearly yearlong friendship. There was no need for words, as Reina could tell they shared the same observation: how the Liberator chose to hide away from his deserved role in Fedria's governance, while the Águila caudillo placed himself and his family at the apex of Venazia's political machinations.

Idle chatter carried them through the next hour as the caravan took them farther down the mountains. The drizzling clouds were left behind, and the sun neared its zenith as the stone walls of Sadul Fuerte loomed at the end of the road.

The city stood on a valley, the conucos and farmland enshrouding the hills like a quilt of colors. The tallest point of the domed cathedral, its golden Pentimiento cross, stood out amid the endless rows of clay-roofed townhomes and beard moss–covered trees. Banners were perched on the city's fortified stone walls, but the highest and most notable of all was the golden eagle on ivory of the Águilas.

The open city gates allowed them into busy cobbled roads where the women dressed in an overabundance of skirt layers and the men wore hats and walking sticks marked with the symbols of their family crests. Greens and wildflowers painted every balcony and terrace, bursting between sidewalk cracks or climbing up brick walls. People yelled from one street to another, advertising their specialized goods or attempting to converse over the ruckus of guitar-playing panhandlers. Don Enrique's convoy was immediately recognized by the people it passed, sparking interest, reverence, and fear. Reina's armpits grew hot as curious gazes surfed from the stunted antlers of the Águila heiress to her before flitting to the rest of the company.

Their destination, the Palace of Commerce, hugged a magnificent plaza, where the bronze statue of a warrioress with large valco antlers was perched at the center of an aesthetic formation of red coral trees. The town square was blocked by other buildings with exquisite architecture in the style of the Segolean imperialists: white-painted spires, golden trim, tall windows, and wrought iron balcony railings wrapped in pampered gardening. The cathedral of Sadul Fuerte faced the plaza, a baroque architectural feat with a brightly blooming garden fenced in by hedges. On the opposite side of the cathedral, across the plaza, was a multistory building with gilded frames—the Governor's Palace. As the party unloaded near the gates of the commerce building, Celeste pointed out the plaza's statue for Reina, calling it the ancient valco Sadul, from whom the city took its name.

Inside the Palace of Commerce, the door attendant cowered before Doña Ursulina, who led the vanguard, while Don Enrique lagged behind as he was approached for greetings. Reina followed like Celeste's shadow, stepping farther back whenever someone nodded a bow to Don Enrique, then delightedly kissed Celeste's hand. Celeste kissed the cheeks of the young people her age, other heirs and heiresses who beamed as they reunited with their social kindred. Reina pretended not to notice when Celeste sought her gaze, likely trying to introduce Reina to her attractive friends.

Reina forced her tail to walk in the same rhythm as her legs, to minimize people's shock at seeing the extra appendage. But the farce evaporated the moment the humans turned around and glimpsed the truth of what she was.

Celeste raised her eyebrows at the first man who opened his mouth to utter an objection. Don Enrique didn't miss the expression, and he watched. But the man's conviction visibly evaporated against the Águilas.

It made Reina want to smile.

They crossed halls supported by pillars carved with the anthem of their new national identity. Images of laurels, rearing stallions, and orchids adorned every dark wood doorframe and love seat–sized bench. The primary tricolor flag of Venazia hung from the doors of meeting rooms and offices.

"G-good day, Doña Ursulina—you're in town," a stout man stuttered as Doña Ursulina strutted into the final waiting room of their journey. He flipped through the ledger of appointments nervously.

Doña Ursulina was a whole head taller than him. She was satisfied with the obvious apprehension in the man's eyes, a look everyone in this building seemed unable to hide at the sight of her. Reina had a feeling it wasn't Doña Ursulina's height or her high-browed condescension sparking their fear but her well-earned reputation as a master geomancer.

"Our appointment is for the morrow, but we decided to come today, as the iridio caskets are freshly excavated," Doña Ursulina said.

The stout man gave up searching through the ledger, bowed, and scurried into his boss's office.

"You two wait here," Doña Ursulina commanded Celeste and Reina. "You have seen Sadul Fuerte like you wanted," she told Reina. "Now stay out of sight. It will be some time before we are finished." Don Enrique nodded his agreement.

The caudillo and his witch entered the trader's office, shutting the door behind them.

"Welcome to Sadul Fuerte," Celeste said moments later with a cheeky smile, pressing an ear to the mahogany door to eavesdrop.

Reina mimicked her with the opposite ear, facing her. "Everyone here loves you," Reina whispered as her nozariel ears picked up small traces of the conversation within—the discussion of an increase in tiniebla activity disrupting iridio transports out of the Páramo.

"Mi papá fought in the revolution. You know that." Celeste shrugged.

So had Reina's, according to her father's tales, but she swallowed down the assertion. The last thing she wanted was to dampen the mood by recounting pieces of her past. "He's the strongest man in Sadul Fuerte." Reina parroted the talk uttered by the help as she worked about the manor. "Because he's valco, and he has all the iridio."

Celeste nodded.

"With the strongest army, due to the mines' income."

Again, Celeste nodded.

"I hate to agree with Javier on anything—"

Celeste saw the comment coming.

"But *why* didn't he crown himself king, instead of crowning Don Rodrigo?" Reina finished.

Celeste stepped closer, her reply soft like a shared secret. "The humans don't love us. They fear us. Sure, a king can rule through fear, but it is always an uphill battle. Papi told me they would smile and bend the knee while clutching a knife at their backs, waiting for the right moment to unseat us and slaughter the last remaining valcos. Most humans only have love for their own kind. Don't you know the only reason we weren't enslaved, too, was because we were a war breed? The humans recognized there was a difference between your kind and mine, and they were careful not to antagonize valcos."

Reina disliked the words, even if the tales of nozariel fighters paled in comparison to the valco legends. But her training with the machete proved she had a predisposition for combat. She dropped her gaze to the ground, discomfited at the implied meaning. How did Celeste see her, then?

"If Don Enrique were king, he could force the humans to be fair to everyone," Reina muttered bitterly, without filter. "The Liberator wanted that change." She'd grown up hearing of the manifestos, of the nozariels' mistreatment spurring the revolutionaries to action. Were it not for their victory, Reina would have been born a slave to the humans, like all other nozariels before her.

Celeste shook her head. "But we don't need them to treat us the same. The crown is in our pocket. King Rodrigo Silva can waste his life dodging those who conspire against him while he holds the crown, but he still has to do everything mi papá says. Besides, most people didn't want a king after the revolution. But it was the caudillos with their soldiers who made that decision. Without influence and strength, you cannot have a say," Celeste finished, with pride in her eyes that she would inherit all of it. "The common folk live safely and comfortably thanks to us."

Reina decided not to press it.

Celeste yawned. "I grow bored of this building. Let's go get almojábanas."

"There's going to be a tiniebla hunt today," Reina added, following her out of the waiting room.

"Is that so?"

The party of Águila soldiers left every fortnight or so, to banish the tinieblas that migrated through the wilderness and crept closer to Águila Manor, seduced by the iridio mines sitting beneath Don Enrique's lands. It had been one such party, almost a year ago, that had saved Reina's life.

"I wanted to see how it is for the first time," Reina said, rolling her eyes to the ceiling. "Not as someone who's been bitten, that is."

Celeste laughed, and Reina loved being the source of it.

"I think I might be able to assist, too."

Celeste's smile was vulpine. "I'm impressed, Reina. Don't think I haven't noticed."

"What?" Reina stared at the marble floor with hot cheeks.

"Coming to Sadul Fuerte and now hunting tinieblas? You are up to something."

They stood in the welcome foyer, with the bright daylight behind Celeste shadowing her features. Reina steeled herself, meeting Celeste's smugness with a fake calm. "It is expected that you do both things."

Celeste swayed her head, considering the limitations of Reina's statement. They both knew: not if Doña Laurel had a say in it. But that was only a technicality.

"And you need someone to keep you out of trouble," Reina added, smiling despite the doubt nestling in her chest, carving space next to the budding dream of one day becoming Celeste's equal. "Besides, you like to have me around. Just admit it."

Celeste laughed as they exited the Palace of Commerce (and she did admit it). Their driver drove them to the bakery. With stomachs full of the cheesy bread, they ordered the ride back to the Águila estate, to make it in time for the tiniebla hunt.

11

The Last Smile

They joined six soldiers on foot through the trails to the mountain. They were accompanied by two hounds and a master of galio healing for their wounds. Reina and Celeste wore boiled leather armor underneath ruanas that were more cloaks than shawls.

The trail carved through the pine forest until the elevation made the terrain too inhospitable for the conifers. Trees were replaced by prickly shrubs and frailejones. The air thinned out as well, making Reina squeeze her ruana around herself as her breaths came like puffy clouds.

Higher up, the path was treacherous, thin in some areas and hugging rocky cliffs, more appropriate for salt-licking goats than for people. They walked in a single file, the unit commander leading the way, with the healer right behind him. The group sang together to pass the time: "Soul of the Llanos," which Reina knew, and aguinaldos, which she didn't. At some point Celeste whipped around, pointing at the sky, where a pair of condors soared through the clouds, their black wings casting shadows thrice their size.

Soon enough, when the sky was streaked in pink, the hounds became agitated and tugged the unit commander into a run. Reina followed Celeste and the soldiers while her heart ached in anticipation.

A putrid stench infected the air as Reina ascended the rocky path. The hounds circled a large frailejón tree, their barks thunderous in the Páramo stillness, where a mass was blocked from view. As Reina and the others approached, the source of the foul odor fell into view. A severed arm and a leg. Bones jutting out from rotting flesh.

"Ugh!" Celeste covered her nose at the sight.

Dread licked Reina's spine. "Tinieblas did this?"

But the unit commander instead pointed at a shadow hiding behind more frailejones, to another corpse's remains. "It was a whistler," he said, gesturing for his party to carry on.

Hand shielding her nostrils, Reina approached the gore. "A whistler?" she murmured. The thing was dressed in the clothes of a shepherd. Even a straw hat lay discarded not too far from it. But its face was wrong, the irises blanched of color and its mouth a deep gash that cut from ear to ear.

Celeste approached for a peek herself. "Never seen a whistler before?"

"No."

"These mountains are cursed and dangerous. You know this. Mi papá told me that when shepherds or travelers perish here, if they're people of bad intentions or people who caused pain to others, the mountain can take them." Celeste gestured at the corpse to make a point. "They become these whistling creatures that warp the sound around you so you can't even hear them. Sometimes they come from the Llanos, lured by the iridio."

Reina stepped away and licked her lips, then immediately regretted it and felt filthy from the decay. "Have you ever seen one alive?"

Celeste shook her head. "According to what the soldiers say, the whistlers can't coexist with each other. They stay in separate territories, and if they ever cross the path of another one, they usually mutilate each other until all that hatred empties them, and they go back to being just...corpses."

Reina pretended the chill running through her was from the breeze carrying the scent of moss and earth and had nothing to do

with Celeste's tale. Was seeing a whistler at all like encountering a
tiniebla?

"So...what about tinieblas?" Reina said, her gaze on the rocky
path to guarantee her sure footing. She shuddered again, for saying
their names aloud felt like a curse by itself. "They're attracted to
the iridio mines, right? Like the whistlers. But where do they come
from?" She wobbled, and Celeste's hand shot out to steady her like
a solid wall. Reina muttered a thanks.

"You know how the Virgin creates life?"

Reina nodded but instead thought of Ches.

"Mi papá says Rahmagut isn't a real god. Not like the Virgin or
the other old gods who have been forgotten. I don't know if you
believe the same or—"

"He's a demon," Reina said quickly, to demonstrate her
agreement.

Celeste smiled in relief. She moistened her lips. "Still, from el
Vacío, Rahmagut deceives himself into believing he can create life
like a god, and he attempts to. He tries to give life to animals
because they're simpler creatures than you and I. Mi papá told
me that the animals he gives life to enter the world as corrupted,
amalgamated monsters."

Reina held her breath. She listened to the stillness of the mountain and watched the bare scree. The terrain was covered in bur-
rows and shrubs—perfect hiding places.

"A mountain lion might give birth, and what rips out of her is a
monster with the smile of a human and the body of a goat," Celeste
added. "And because Rahmagut is not a real god, he cannot give
hearts to his creations."

"So they hunt for them," Reina finished for her.

Celeste watched with her big eyes. She had a query at the tip of
her tongue, but she lacked the confidence to ask it. The thought
warmed Reina's cheeks, how she could read Celeste's face.

Reina cleared her throat and said slowly, "When I was in their
clutches...they had this humanlike laughter and sense of sentience.
Somehow I could tell what they wanted, and I knew they wanted
to eat me." She flexed her right arm, feeling the weakness in the

muscle where the tinieblas had taken a bite out of her. She looked down, fidgeting with her gloves, ashamed. "They got what they wanted in the end. They rotted my heart."

The hounds took off again, and the soldiers followed them up the scree.

Celeste slipped on a loose rock, and it was Reina's turn to catch her wrist and prop her up. Celeste lifted herself so closely that Reina caught a whiff of her breath. It was sweet and not at all unpleasant. "I think the tinieblas are up ahead."

Reina's chest constricted.

"Are you afraid?" Celeste asked.

Maybe it was painted all over her face. Maybe the color had blanched from her as cold perspiration trickled down her temples. She shook her head in a lie, clenching every muscle to stop them from betraying her with tremors. Reina withdrew her grandmother's badge from her pocket. The medal was imbued with the litio ward that chased away the tinieblas and with a bismuto incantation, Doña Ursulina later told her. The bismuto spell was what had allowed Reina to see the tinieblas that night, for they were imperceptible to humans and nozariels without the use of geomancia. She ran her thumbs along the inlaid ridges of her family's crest, for luck. Taking a deep breath, Reina shoved the badge back into her pocket before sprinting after Celeste.

The soldiers disappeared around a rocky elevation skirted by thorny shrubs. An agonized yap erupted from one of the hounds ahead. The soldiers' swords left their sheaths with a keening whistle. Celeste produced her scythe. Reina ran around the cliff just as blood squirted into the air, followed by another howl. She withdrew her machete as she passed the healer, who was crouched behind a frailejón while his hands articulated galio incantations.

One soldier lay across the scree, with one arm draped over his belly while the other held his hound. A big shadow ran at him, all flexible limbs and jutting horns, and was pursued by two other soldiers. Celeste swung at the second tiniebla that crawled out of a burrow in the ground.

The healer yelled her name, and Reina whipped around as the

sounds of crunching twigs muted out the carnage of the battle. Behind her came a tiniebla, pawing at her with caiman claws. Reina raised her machete just before the creature could slice her shoulder. The impact rang down her elbows, shoving her heels against the ground. The tiniebla had the face of a rabid wolf, its mandibles snapping at her and its spittle slapping her across the cheek. Again, she sensed that wicked humanlike laughter that infected the air around her, zeroing in on her and making her taste the metal flavor of fear.

With a grunt, Reina shoved the creature away. Her legs caught on a boulder behind her. She fell out of reach just as the tiniebla pawed at her again. She was lucky or foolish, she couldn't decide. But now she was off her feet. The tiniebla pounced again. Reina lifted the machete between them, shutting her eyes, bracing herself for the white-hot pain of her flesh ripping open.

Someone yelled above her. Reina opened her eyes only to catch the flash of red as Celeste sliced the tiniebla's throat. Reina scrambled to her feet as another shadow went for Celeste—her protector. Reina swung down with all her might, cleaving the second attacking tiniebla in two.

A stillness descended over the mountain. The healer ran to the wounded, waving his hands again, manipulating the galio stored within his rings to bring relief.

Reina cleaned the cold perspiration from under her curly bangs. She shoved her long braid behind her, watching Celeste rearrange her clothes and hair the same way.

"Well done."

"That's it?" Reina asked in bewilderment, scanning the scree for signs of any remaining tinieblas.

The corpses of the ones they'd slain disintegrated into shadow, then into nothingness, fading back to el Vacío where they spawned from. The other Águila soldiers were in similar bloodied and disheveled states, and they waited patiently for a turn with the healer. Even the hound, which Reina had thought would die, was back to wagging its tail in anticipation of another hunt. They had no casualties.

"We were lucky this time," Celeste said, as if reading her mind. "It's more common that the dogs don't make it."

Reina grimaced at that.

"But without them, we'd be scouring the Páramo for days."

Without much fanfare, the unit commander ordered them to get a move on if they hoped to return to Águila Manor before nightfall.

No one welcomed them when they emerged from the body of pines bordering the grounds. The yard was free from its usual comings and goings of the help and their children. Wind buffeted the trees, rising a howl of branches and dead leaves.

Something felt different about the manor, though. Reina didn't have to see it to feel it. A few of the younger maids ran from the corridors to the courtyard, hauling water buckets or bloodied sheets. The goats hadn't been put up yet, despite how late it was getting, and Reina loathed the thought of having to do it herself because ever since her transplant, they didn't like her.

Reina and Celeste spotted Javier sitting on a bench on the courtyard that separated the larder from the main building. He was wrapped in a colorful wool blanket like a geriatric, his eyes darker than usual, but with a certain satisfied tilt to his lips.

"What's going on?" Celeste asked her uncle, likely picking up on the heady apprehension that hung in the air.

Javier coughed but didn't say a word. The corner of his lip twitched upward. Reina shuddered, like a breath had been blown on her neck.

An older maid crossed the yard to the kitchens, her arms tangled in bloody bedding. She noticed Celeste and said, "It's Doña Laurel. She's gone into an early labor."

In that moment, as understanding sank in, Reina felt transported back to the Páramo, when Celeste had illustrated a tiniebla ripping out of an otherwise healthy pregnancy. Reina sucked in a breath for her wicked thoughts, fisting her chest and only meeting the gleeful whispers of her fake heart.

She ran after Celeste as the valco sprinted up the stone steps of the manor, two at a time, with strength and urgency pumping through every stride.

A chilling cry echoed through the third-story corridor leading to Doña Laurel's room. Reina recognized the sound of excruciating, never-ending pain.

Don Enrique stood next to the bedroom door as the maids rushed in and out of the room, bumping each other in the doorway and sloshing warm water from their pails. He stood like a statue, staring at the landscape painting hanging on the opposite wall, the color drained from his face. He didn't even notice when Celeste and Reina ran past him and barged into the room.

Reina froze by the door at the sight. There was so much blood that even the air smelled warm and metallic. Doña Laurel was drenched in it, and in sweat. She gripped the posts of her bed behind her like she was hanging on for dear life, while two women on either side held her legs and massaged her belly. A river of that sticky redness pooled on the sheets between her legs, from where a bald head peeked.

Another keening cry pierced the room. Reina wanted to run to Doña Laurel. She wanted to come to her rescue and cradle her in her arms, for even in agonizing childbirth, the Benevolent Lady was so lovely. But fear kept Reina rooted to the spot: Fear of trespassing into Doña Laurel's space. Fear of the outrage she would incur from the maids for letting her nozariel hands touch the most precious thing in this home.

A moment later Doña Ursulina entered the room and roared at them to leave. Celeste never made it to her mother's side. Someone grabbed her from behind, and she thrashed and clawed and bit to be let go. But from Don Enrique's grip, she never had a chance to break free.

Reina was given an empty pail and ordered to fetch more water. But when she ran back with the pail sloshing and steaming, the old maid prohibited her from even setting foot on the third-story corridor. She said there was no need for it anymore.

Silence and icy rain enveloped the manor that night. The only sounds were Celeste's shrieks reverberating all the way down to the first floor, where Reina sat in a broom cupboard with her fists shielding her eyes. There she prayed to the Virgin, who was the matron of motherhood, even if she didn't believe the Virgin would listen. She prayed to Ches, who had opened the world to the sun and had granted them the gift of life—who gave her solace when she felt the most alone. She even prayed to Rahmagut, though he was likely the one who'd taken away the fleeting happiness of Águila Manor.

Because for a few moments, Reina had been happy.

A hollow like the shadows of twilight settled in the depths of her heart. She remembered how Doña Laurel had touched her face with dignity and tenderness the very moment she'd come into Águila Manor. She hadn't cared that Reina stank of death and writhed like a worm. Doña Laurel's light had been too strong to care about that.

Reina plunged into a suffocating ocean of tears.

She didn't know it yet, but that morning, when Don Enrique and Doña Laurel had renewed their vows to the magic of amapola, would be the last time Reina saw Don Enrique smile.

The baby boy followed his mother into death before dawn broke the next morning.

Their funeral happened in a whirlwind of red-eyed strangers who rode into the estate to pay their respects. Reina worked tirelessly in the kitchens and in the barn for seven days straight, serving people who'd traveled from all over Venazia. People who eyed her curiously upon realizing she was a nozariel living in Sadul Fuerte. People who never shied from demanding "some other wench" serve them rather than let Reina touch their food.

So she scrubbed floors and pots. She milked the goats and kneaded the maize dough. She burned her hands with boiling water and lye washing clothes. She scurried between corridors, avoiding Javier and Don Enrique and Celeste. Because being tired and sore made it easy to forget her heart now throbbed with a different kind of ache.

Mass was held in the cathedral of Sadul Fuerte in Doña Laurel's honor. And again her body was transported back to Águila

Manor, where she was buried in close proximity to Don Enrique's mother. Reina watched the ceremony of candles and prayers to the rosary from the fringes, clutching her chest and choking with heartache. She stopped leaving bits of her food in the sunlight by the creek, because why should she give offerings if Ches was deaf to her prayers?

On the eighth day, when the last guests packed their carriages and set out to warmer lands, Reina decided to stop hiding from Celeste. Her search ended swiftly, as she found Celeste in Gegania's underground chamber—in the place where Reina knew Celeste undoubtedly felt closest to the part of herself she had lost.

Celeste sat on the floor next to a bookshelf, surrounded by her mother's old books, with her back to the open tunnel door. The hem of her black dress was filthy, brown from the slop plaguing the estate after the week's never-ending rain.

Reina stopped, taking a silent, hesitant breath as the fears that had festered in her all these days returned: It was *she* who had driven Celeste to partake in the tiniebla hunt. It was because of her that Celeste hadn't been by her mother's side during the last moments of her life. Her actions had added to the grief, and Reina was sure Celeste saw this as clearly as she did. She tried not to think of her role in bringing Doña Laurel to Doña Ursulina's laboratory—to the brimming iridio ore. She had so many reasons to be ashamed, but she couldn't turn her back forever.

Reina draped her hands over Celeste's shoulders by way of greeting, and Celeste jumped.

"Hey," Reina said.

"Oh—I thought—that you were one of them, again."

"No, they've left," Reina told her gently. All week Celeste had been perpetually fleeing the sobbing women who'd suffocated her with their tears as soon as they saw her, as if Celeste were the one obliged to console them. As if she hadn't been the one to lose a mother.

"Where have you been?" Celeste demanded.

Silence clutched Reina. Silence and fear.

She wasn't worthy of the pain she felt. Doña Laurel had been

Celeste's mother, not Reina's. Reina didn't know what it was like to lose a mother, because she had never had one.

"I was giving you time," she lied.

"Mi mamá is dead, and I am all alone. That's how you take care of me? By giving me time?"

Reina lowered her gaze. She kneaded her leathery hands.

"I'm sorry. I don't understand why this hurts so much."

"You're supposed to take care of me," Celeste bit out, "so do it."

Reina obeyed. She embraced her because it was the only thing to do. Celeste was cold and smaller than Reina. With heaving shoulders, Celeste buried her wet face in the crook of Reina's neck. Celeste squeezed her, and Reina knew there was love there, and that she would do everything in her power to protect it.

For the first time since coming to Águila Manor, Reina devolved into that perpetual state of fearing the unknown. For, without the protection of the Benevolent Lady, anything could—and would—happen.

Soon enough, it did.

12

The Archbishop's Inquisition

The Saint Jon the Shepherd celebrations were back in Galeno again. The annual weeklong revel celebrated the patron of passing time. They always happened right after Eva's birthday, when the buttery araguaneys planted around the city bloomed after the rainy season. The trees took Galeno in a flurry of petals yellow enough to make the sun itself blush. The Serrano hacienda had an araguaney in one of its many courtyards, in the center of a garden populated by a wrought iron breakfast table and matching chairs for two. It was a romantic setting, the seats arranged between two large bushes to protect the privacy of whoever enjoyed its amenities.

Eva couldn't say she enjoyed Don Alberto's company. Especially not when he stared at her during their long awkward pauses, trying to understand the reasons for her introversion. Eva would never speak of it, of course. Because how could she ever explain to him that she had spent nine months without color? How could she name the feeling of muting the impulses inside her—of drowning herself in prayer to the Virgin to repel any thought or desire stirred by her valco side?

After the milk snake had slithered into Pura's bed, Eva decided magic was a fair price to stop demons from latching on to their lives. She stopped speaking of geomancia and visiting Doña Rosa.

To appease the rancor in her grandmother and all the Serranos who witnessed or heard of the tigra mariposa, she pretended she was completely and utterly free of rebellious thought. Eva became Doña Antonia's poster grandchild: devout, dutiful, silent. She'd earned Pura's forgiveness, even if the loving Pura, who'd inherited Dulce's nature, hadn't made it difficult.

Don Alberto took Eva's hand in his big sweaty one. "I have always been very enthusiastic about you, Señorita Eva. But sometimes, when we spend time together like this, I worry this feeling is not reciprocated."

Eva withdrew her hand. Like all their meetings, this one had been arranged by Doña Antonia. Hearing him pretend otherwise annoyed Eva to no end.

Lately, she'd grown resentful of her role, and restless. She swallowed thickly, once again battling the urge to shatter her pious façade.

"It's merely your own hesitation that's stopping you, mi señor," she said dryly. "You already know how I feel about our future together."

She accepted it, begrudgingly. He was smart enough to recognize this; otherwise he wouldn't be taking so long to formally propose.

"My preference is a bride with a little more passion."

This time she did look at him. She frowned at his round face, his cheeks flushed and his temples perspiring from the afternoon heat.

"I understand the rules of this game," he said. "How propriety demands a coy act for the sake of modesty. But this is not coyness anymore. Every time I see you, you make me doubt that you can be the wife I'm looking for—someone with love to give."

The way he regarded her, demanding more when she had already given up so much, evaporated the last ounce of pretense she could spare.

"You know as well as I do, you won't find this passion in any of the other women suitable for your rank." She didn't care about her lack of tact. If he was going to become her husband, why did she have to continue pretending? Eva was already being forced into a life she didn't want. The last thing she needed was to keep on acting like this was a dream of her own design. "We are each other's last options," she added coolly.

Don Alberto stiffened. He folded his hands under the table. "You're incorrect in thinking I don't have choices, señorita." He called her *señorita* anytime he wanted to patronize her. Anytime he wanted to assert he had more wisdom for being two decades her senior. "And you'd do well to be grateful for this. I'm not the one carrying the reputation of causing every curse and misfortune that has befallen the Serranos."

He wasn't wrong. She had been the cause of her mother's sadness and the bringer of discord into the hacienda.

"I'm not the one who befriended the witch the Contadors keep hidden in their house."

The iron chair scrapped the cobblestones as he pushed himself up to his feet. Eva followed suit, insolently so. Their glares clashed for a fraction of a moment before the courtyard door swung open.

Néstor emerged with a relieved sigh. "Eva Kesaré, I was looking all over for you."

Eva smoothed her skirt and offered her uncle a tight smile. The whole interference was staged. She had begged him to interrupt the meeting when Don Alberto had come calling earlier in the afternoon.

"I suppose this is as good a stopping point as any," Don Alberto said without sparing Eva a glance. "I have business to attend to with the governor. I shall see you again soon, Señorita Eva."

Alas, Don Alberto wasn't the type to take assertive rein of his life and look for a better wife. Of course he would be back.

Eva felt a crack in her façade. The desire to act out—to indulge in it. She linked her arm with Néstor's as they watched Don Alberto head to the front foyer.

"Can the man be any more mechanical?" she murmured to her uncle.

Néstor shrugged. "It's rude that we don't walk him out."

"I don't think that'll stop him from coming back."

"By the Virgin, Eva, you have him smitten."

"Whatever he sees in me . . . at least it keeps grandmother off my back."

Her young uncle cackled. With arms still locked with his, Eva accompanied him to the stables. Even though Néstor had saved her from dealing with Don Alberto's accusations, Eva's belly swirled in anger. She was wounded from the comment. Don Alberto was right, and it incensed her into wanting to do something destructive.

Bitterly, Eva noted she must have been born wrong, because being the good granddaughter felt like so much work.

"You're riding to see Don Jerónimo?" she said.

Néstor unlatched himself from her and ordered the stable hand to ready a ride. "I need to comfort him, even if he never really cared for his grandfather."

Just the day before, Doña Antonia had opened the family breakfast by announcing the death of the Contador patriarch, Don Jerónimo's grandfather and Doña Rosa's father. The official account was that he'd passed in his sleep, which no one bothered to question, since the man had already been headed into his eighth decade.

Néstor smiled with a blush. "Well, it's not like I don't miss him."

"Let me come with you," Eva said on impulse.

Néstor's gaze rounded, his lips parting. He knew she had bowed out of geomancia. But Eva was tired. She just wanted a small breath of fresh air. A morsel, to replenish her strength so she could continue faking this role. "I should offer Doña Rosa my condolences."

Néstor eyed Eva suspiciously, but he complied. This was the best part about him: While everyone else was busy judging each other and drowning in someone else's embarrassment, Néstor merely indulged impulses.

The sky east of the Serrano hacienda was covered in black rain clouds, so Néstor arranged for a carriage. The rain started halfway through the ride. When they arrived at the Contadors' town house, they found another gilded carriage parked outside the iron gates. It was a carriage bedecked in art depicting scenes from Pentimiento scripture. Eva and Néstor exchanged a look. The archbishop was also making a house call.

"Maybe they're arranging the funeral," Eva said behind Néstor as he gestured for the house butler to let him in.

Thunder rumbled as Eva followed Néstor through the foyer and into the hallway connecting the innards of the house. Every window-lit room they passed was covered in long shadows, the rain clouds blocking the late afternoon sun and joining the Contadors in their mourning. The air smelled dusty, of dead flowers. The windows hadn't been opened in days. Eva looped her arm in Néstor's and clung to him as they crossed hallways decorated by the framed painted faces of the Contadors who'd come before. She felt rotten, for she had abandoned Doña Rosa for so many months. Surely the woman didn't miss her, but it still marked Eva as nothing more than self-interested.

Néstor paused at the foot of the stairs to the second floor, and Eva nearly crashed into him. Loud voices rang from the adjacent hallway leading to the outdoor kitchen and the house yard. Don Jerónimo descended the stairs in a hurry. Frowning, he offered Néstor and Eva a quick greeting before heading to the kitchen.

"A rot for this city!" One of the loud voices erupted from the yard. Eva would recognize that voice anywhere. After all, she had to listen to it every Sunday morning during Mass. "She's bringing the scorn of the saints by being here. The Virgin will stop protecting us for as long as we continue tolerating this nonsense."

Eva's heart pounded. She understood. She knew the speaker. And she only wished her conclusions were incorrect.

Her answer came quick. Eva, Néstor, and Don Jerónimo emerged into the yard, where the pouring rain drowned the cries of Doña Rosa. A party of acolytes stood outside her dwelling, boots covered in mud and clothes clinging with water, undisturbed by the rain. The archbishop's voice rang from inside the home, joining the sound of crashing glass. Eva imagined him shattering Rahmagut's icon behind that curtain door.

She tried running into the hut, but Néstor's hand stopped her from leaving the roofed safety of the kitchen. She shot her uncle a scowl, but he didn't release her. Eva couldn't believe he lacked the courage to defend Doña Rosa and that he expected the same from her.

Don Jerónimo's mother, a slim, pale woman with a hawkish face, stood under the awning to watch the ransacking. "Now that Don Julio's dead, there's nothing stopping the archbishop. No one in this city's going to risk their neck protecting that nozariel."

"What's her crime?" Eva asked heatedly, even though she already knew the answer.

Don Jerónimo's mother gave Eva an unkind look. "She doesn't need one. The Virgin does things for a reason, and that reason doesn't have to make sense to us."

Panic welled in Eva. She wanted to demand justice. She almost did it, too, until she imagined what her grandmother and Décima would say of the ordeal: how Eva completed the soiling of her own reputation by defending the curandera.

Two acolytes dragged Doña Rosa out of her home while the heavens wept over the yard. Every servant in the Contador house gathered under the awning to watch the spectacle. A few faces were more satisfied than concerned.

"Do not despair, my children," the archbishop told the watching crowd as he crossed the yard with an acolyte shielding him with an umbrella. "This witch will face the justice of the church. The Virgin will be the one to judge, not I."

Doña Rosa writhed in the acolytes' grip. Her hair and clothes were made limp by the rain, but her eyes burned with hatred at everyone who watched. Everyone, including Eva.

With his cloying, omnipotent tone, the archbishop told the crowd, "Please understand this act needed to be done. The saints become unhappy when their own people start worshipping demons. We cannot lose their protection. We cannot have this conflict of beliefs."

At that moment all Eva could think about was the milk snake, slithering from her dream into Pura's bed.

"It weakens the spirit—it makes you vulnerable to be snatched up by a demon. Therefore, I will conduct a public inquisition on all suspected to have communed with false gods." His assisting acolyte handed him an icon of a sitting man—the one Doña Rosa kept in the corner of her home. He waved the icon at all the watching servants, his eyes glowing at their fearful reactions.

Shoulders bumped against Eva, and she was nearly pushed into the rain. There was a wicked spark in the air. It stung like the bite of a mosquito on the back of her neck. But Eva knew it had nothing to do with magic. She glanced at the people surrounding her and only saw fanatical faces.

The mood in the crowd alone was enough to stop her breathing. Eva could imagine them turning their hateful eyes and fingers, pointing directly at her. She needed to get out.

That was when she noticed Néstor's absence. She couldn't spot Don Jerónimo's tall head sticking out of the crowd either. She dove back into the house, pushing herself through a tight crowd, and headed to Don Jerónimo's bedroom on the second floor.

A large trunk was strewn across his bed when Eva burst in. Néstor turned to the doorway like a startled chigüire, then relaxed after seeing her.

"What are you doing?" she asked breathlessly.

Néstor shut the door behind her.

"Ever since my grandfather died, the people in this house have lost their minds," Don Jerónimo said as he tossed clothes into the trunk.

Eva turned to Néstor, her eyes wide and betrayed. "What are you doing?" she repeated.

"You saw how they're acting." Néstor gently grasped her hand. His touch was as icy as hers.

The way he looked at Eva only multiplied the panic brewing inside her. She remembered that conversation they'd had ages ago, in the carriage. Of his dreams with Don Jerónimo.

"My uncles have turned against my father," Don Jerónimo explained. "My mom can't decide if she wants to mourn my grandfather or throw Tía Rosa onto the pyre. I'm going to lose my mind if I stay here a moment longer. I think Tía Rosa cursed this house, in case we ever turned against her."

Néstor squeezed Eva's hand. "We're leaving Galeno."

"*What?*" Eva practically shrieked. She flared her nostrils and shook her head. "No. You can't leave me."

Néstor nodded in an opposite motion to Eva. "I'm sick of that archbishop, Eva, and we've bided our time for long enough." He glanced at his lover, fishing for a glance of reassurance. "I think now's the time to leave forever."

Eva wanted to tug Néstor into her embrace—to cling to him so he had no option but to never let go. "Take me with you, then."

Don Jerónimo coughed like he choked on his spit.

"Eva, we can't," Néstor said with an anguished face.

"Yes, you can—"

"You're going to marry Don Alberto and have a wonderful happily ever after. You just think you won't, but—"

Eva let go of his hands and instead shoved him, petulantly. "If you leave me, they're going to come after me. It's going to be *me* next."

Néstor's cheeks were flushed, but he didn't react to Eva's tantrum. His love for her was the true love of an uncle, patient and unconditional, despite their closeness in age.

"Be courageous, Eva Kesaré."

"No."

"I'm being courageous, too, and I'm pursuing what my heart wants. I can't stay here." He said it with a finality that betrayed his age. Eva angrily swallowed back the tears beginning to form in her eyes. He wrestled her into a hug.

When she finally peeled herself from him, he said, "You should be happy for me. Just like I'm going to be happy for you when you find the thing you really want."

Eva watched him with a stunned, faraway look. What did she want? She wanted to go back to those days when she could visit Doña Rosa while Néstor snuck away with Don Jerónimo. When coming to the Contador house had meant a day full of possibility, of enjoying the idea that she wasn't odd or broken. She wanted to grasp the way it felt to embrace geomancia, obliviously, without the threat of the Virgin's punishment for straying from the scripture. She wanted a family that accepted her for who she was, valco or not. She could not continue feeling like she didn't belong.

The people of Galeno would certainly turn against her the moment they grew tired of abusing Doña Rosa. Eva would be the next easy target for the archbishop's inquisition. All they had to do was ransack her bedroom, like they had done to Doña Rosa, and discover her books on geomancia, her litio powder, and even the paper butterflies Eva hadn't had the heart to discard.

Her chest ached. "Please take me home, Néstor."

He denied her. "We need the carriage to take us to the river harbor."

Eva's face flushed. Her tears inundated the corners of her eyes, ready and available to punish her with their torrent.

"Wait—you're leaving now," she murmured, more to let the words sink in.

He nodded slowly, sorrowfully.

Eva threw her arms around him and hugged him again. The previous embrace had been for him. This one was for her. She squeezed him with all her strength, took a big whiff of the musk of his hair, wiggled when he tickled her sides.

"I can't change your mind?"

In her embrace, he shook his head.

"I'm going to miss you," she whispered. He was her best friend.

"Be courageous," he repeated.

"I hope you write," she said as she pulled away. She waved at Don Jerónimo with a fond smile of goodbye. He was Néstor's special one, and for that, Eva loved him dearly, too.

A somber silence embraced her as she left the room and closed the door behind her. This would be their last goodbye. As much as she wanted to stay with Néstor until the last moment, she needed to head home and rid herself of the incriminating remnants of her studies on geomancia.

Downstairs, Don Jerónimo's mom was gathered in the parlor with other women, praying loudly to the rosary. They were surrounded by flickering candles and the wilting carnations brought in for their deceased patriarch. Their chants pursued Eva until she fled the house. The afternoon rain swallowed her as she stepped out, her espadrilles dunking into muddy puddles and her dress growing heavy and saturated. She ran through the cobbled streets and out to the gravel road toward the Serrano hacienda. In the rain, Eva felt no shame in unleashing the might of her sobs.

13

When the Demon Is You

Eva hated herself for never once standing up for Doña Rosa. She replayed the archbishop's outrage in her mind while the rain slapped her across the face, wishing she'd had the courage to demand mercy from the mob. But she was no different from the Contadors, using Doña Rosa in self-interest and discarding her at the first chance. She wanted to hate Néstor for leaving, too, but all she could find within herself was a deep chasm as she imagined life without him. Dread clawed up her throat, latching there as the images of her future rushed through her mind: when the archbishop accused her of communing with Rahmagut and her grandmother saw her fears materialize before her eyes.

Eva reached the Serrano lands as the rain clouds cleared, leaving in their wake the deep blue of settling dusk. The golden cassia trees welcomed her like sentinels when she crossed the gates to the driveway. She wrung her hair and clothes under the weeping bougainvilleas. Through the windows she spied Pura and Décima sitting in the parlor. Pura had her babe on her lap. Décima caught Eva peeping and got up.

"I'm not in the mood for your harassment," Eva said the moment the double doors opened to allow Décima out.

Décima grimaced at her as if she stank. "When will you stop being such an animal? Did you walk from town?"

Eva ran inside, driven by the need to purge her bedroom before the archbishop and his acolytes turned on her.

"Didn't Néstor go with you?" Décima said in Eva's pursuit.

Eva wiped her wet bangs out of her face, her hands stopping at her antlers. "Don't you have—I don't know—a life? Why are you keeping track of where everyone is going?"

"He took the carriage!" Décima pressed her palm to her chest and pouted in indignation. "I want to go into town because I heard a most delicious rumor about something happening today. Is that why you came in such a hurry?"

"*Chisme!*" Eva cried in utter exasperation, shocked at the speed of the traveling gossip, and sidestepped her cousin.

"Eva Kesaré?" Pura's voice flowed out of the parlor, stopping Eva before she could walk away.

Eva stuck her head under the doorway. "Yes?"

Pura noted Eva's soaked hair and the muddied hem of her dress. "Are you all right?"

Eva silently sucked in a breath. Always one to see the best in her.

"I'm fine. It's just—things happened at the Contadors'—I wanted to come back." She glanced behind her, fully expecting to witness Décima's insult, but her cousin wasn't there anymore.

Eva excused herself. In her room, she had a small coffer hidden inside a trunk of her possessions. It was concealed beneath layers of fabrics and scarves and a bodice that no longer fit her. Her heart pounded as she pulled out the coffer from underneath the mess and opened it. Stored was a flask filled with a litio solution, a titration tube, and a handkerchief embroidered with the eclipsed sun symbol of the god of the Void. Underneath the flask and the handkerchief was a small leather-bound journal where she had poured her adolescent melancholy and where she hid her enchanted paper butterflies.

Eva hesitated. Her hands were clammy and shivery. Somehow, she had to muster the courage to get rid of them.

She supposed it wouldn't hurt to look—to open the journal and meet the wispy scarlet, goldenrod, and cerulean paper cutouts flying out of its pages. Traces of galio sparkled gold as the butterflies fluttered around their master. Eva let out a wounded, shuddery breath. How could she ever extinguish the life of her own creations? She knelt beside her trunk, her fists clenched over her knees and her eyes screwed shut, the suffocation gripping her.

Eva sucked in a loud hiss. Her cheeks scorched. She wanted to scream. Her life—this cage where everyone in Galeno was a jailer—was constantly out of her control. When Dulce had been alive and still had happiness, she had filled Eva's head with legends about valcos. Like Feleva Águila, who'd made the Páramo Mountains her home. They were said to be mighty and independent. Proud, with accomplishments trailing behind them, because when one was born so beautiful and capable, how could everything else not follow naturally? But not Eva. She had nothing.

If she were any less cowardly, she would leave Galeno for those mountains. She would abandon the comforts of the Serranos and forge her own path. But Eva felt shackled. Afraid.

The paper butterflies tickled her cheeks as they flew near her. It was a wretched thing—to see their whimsical possibilities and have to end them forever.

Suddenly her bedroom door swung open. Eva jumped, her knee knocking the flask all over her handkerchief, where the oily litio solution spread. A strong smell saturated the room.

"Eva Kesaré!" Doña Antonia's voice was a crack of thunder.

Eva scampered to her feet as her grandmother and Décima walked in.

"Oh, by the Virgin—it smells of sulfur!" Doña Antonia said, with her thumb tracing a cross over her heart. She took in the sight of Eva, all dripping curls and muddied dress. Then her eyes doubled in size at the sight of the fluttering pieces of paper. "You're summoning demons into this home!" her grandmother said, crossing the distance to the butterflies.

"I told you she was up to no good." Décima smiled behind the matriarch.

"It's not what it looks like—" Eva pleaded, but Doña Antonia didn't care. She swatted at the paper butterflies, which crashed against the wall, falling lifelessly onto the ground.

"No!" Eva cried, tugging on her grandmother's arms as the

big woman stomped on the paper cutouts with as much ardor as if she were squashing well-deserving cockroaches. "Please—" But the word was slapped out of her mouth by Doña Antonia's heavy hand. Fire erupted on Eva's bottom lip. Black dots blurred the image of her grandmother and her smug, snitching cousin. At the sight of her crumpled creations, Eva cried.

"The archbishop warned me not to let you near that woman, and he was right! This is why Pura had a snake come into her bed: You've let yourself be seduced by the devil. And the lesson was not learned then. Here you are summoning creatures into our home! What is the matter with you?"

Even as the taste of iron spread within her mouth, Eva remained on her own two feet and howled back, "I would never do that!"

"There will be an inquisition on the nozariel bastard. She worships demons, and everyone in Galeno knows it. Just like they know you've been going into her home, spending time with her, learning from her?" The last words, her grandmother said with an inflection, making it clear this was Eva's act of betrayal. "You will bring that sort of reputation to our family?"

"It's not bad!" Eva pleaded, uselessly, "You can't summon demons with litio. Litio is for protection!"

Horror rounded Doña Antonia's eyes. In her pause, her disappointment smothered the room. "Your mother used litio to take her own life."

A sharp silence enveloped them. Whatever rebuttal Eva had been formulating dissolved in the blood taste of her split lip. It was true; litio was deadly if digested. The Serranos had learned this when Dulce had swallowed a whole flask.

Doña Antonia fled the room, her disappointment filling the void where she had stood.

Something awful twisted inside Eva. "Wait, Abuela!" she called out.

Eva shoved her cousin as she passed through the doorway, giving her a taste of what Eva yearned to gift her later, once she appeased the mighty Doña Antonia. Unhearing of Eva's calls and always five steps ahead, Doña Antonia entered the governor's study and slammed the door behind her.

Eva stopped, her hand hovering over the door handle. She threw herself against the wall beside the door and ground her teeth as she listened to Doña Antonia's outcries.

"That girl has no morals! It's as if she doesn't care for what we hold dear and holy. Tell me, Mateo, tell me I've failed in giving her a proper education!"

The governor said something too soft for Eva to hear, and her grandmother went on, "How long will our family suffer through that man's crime? How much longer do I have to sleep in fear that Eva Kesaré is going to invite the devil himself through our front doors? I can't control her anymore. You know one day she will! She has the blood of that demon—she can't contain herself. She sought out the curandera for brujería. It's why that snake defiled Pura. Mateo, when will we be rid of her?"

Eva's heart twisted. She sucked on her busted lip, the copper taste thinning as the bleeding stopped. She missed the taste of that blood. It was the only distraction she had from the heartache. How could she make them understand she wasn't a threat? And how could their fear conquer their bond of blood? If they'd ever loved her to begin with. She almost mustered the courage to knock and beg for forgiveness, but her hand refused to rise.

"If Don Alberto won't propose, then you find her a southern man who'll see worth in her. The girl's nineteen and more than old enough to marry. They'll want her over there in the Páramo, won't they? The Águilas, they're all devils like the man who defiled my Dulce, aren't they?"

Eva's nostrils flared. The heartache morphed into anger. This wasn't love.

"I don't care how much you want to get out of her marriage. A coffer of escudos is a fine bride price if it means I won't have to go to sleep every night fearing a demon might slither in and latch on to this home, if it hasn't already."

Eva whirled back to her room. She went back with a burning desire: to find Décima and reward her for what she'd done.

Her geomancia ingredients were shattered and spilled in the corner, where she had left them. The butterflies were crushed and without a droplet of life. A foul acidic smell filled the room, coming from the spilled solution soiling Rahmagut's handkerchief. Besides the mess, the room was empty.

She ran from candlelit room to candlelit room with the heat tingling her armpits, earning curious glances from her aunts and uncles. She took the back doors of the house, which faced the auxiliary kitchen, a garden of pampered topiaries, and the fenced fields of pasture where the governor's cattle grazed freely.

Eva found her cousin in the stables.

Décima's hair was concealed by a shawl. Her eyes widened as Eva cleaved through the long shadows of the back porch, made black and severe by the sun plunging below the horizon. Décima looked shocked and guilty, and it took Eva only a second to realize her cousin intended to slink out of the hacienda. Décima had been sneaking out more and more lately to visit a boy from the plaza—a boy she wouldn't be able to see anymore after her wedding to the councilman's son.

The sight incensed Eva to no end. "You got what you wanted, didn't you?" she snapped.

"I did it for you: You're going down a dangerous path."

Eva took one step after another toward her. "But your path is the right one, isn't? Acting all proper and virtuous while going on your nightly escapades? Should I tell our grandmother for you?"

"This isn't about me. The whole community thinks you're possessed. And all you do is feed the fire. I thought after what happened with the milk snake, you would see reason."

Eva clenched and unclenched her hands, praying the urge to strangle Décima left her.

"Can't you see how people look at you when we go to the market or to Mass? They all know where you came from. They all know what happened with your father."

Eva didn't let her finish. She threw herself at her cousin, slamming her against the wooden doorframe behind her. They rebounded in a wrestle, Décima whirling and slamming Eva back against a wall. Eva grabbed a fistful of her hair, snarling, "You're not helping—you're making everything worse!"

Décima screeched. She scratched Eva's face, leaving hot marks along her cheeks. "Get off me, you rabid creature!"

"You don't lose anything by leaving me alone!"

They tumbled and fell on the dirt path. A tearing sound joined the grunts of their scuffle as Eva yanked at Décima's clothes. Décima kneed Eva in the ribs, and Eva gasped, releasing her.

Décima crawled away from Eva's reach. Her cousin's clothes were disheveled, her shirt torn open on one side. Still, Décima scrambled to her feet, triumphant, and said, "I did it because I care about you! You mad, vile devil!"

Eva scrambled up as well.

"Mi abuela's going to hear about this—I promise you!"

"Not if I kill you first." Eva feinted a lunge, which was enough to spook Décima into sprinting back inside the house.

She wiped the sweat and blood from the side of her lips. Her mouth bled again. Her gaze roamed the fenced pasture behind the Serrano hacienda as she rearranged her grimy dress and pushed back her mass of curls. The night was quieter than it had been when she'd left the house in rage. It was so still that it held Eva's attention—something was out there. That bubbling sensation in her belly flared, her valco instincts stirring.

Movement near the entrance to the bull's corral caught her eye. The governor's prizewinning bull watched her, its pointed horns moving up and down, its hoofs stomping the earth. Like it had witnessed her fight and was satisfied with the outcome. Then the black bull got up on its two hind legs, like a person. Despite the darkness, Eva was sure the creature was smiling in approval.

A chill locked Eva's spine in place.

The bull grinned at her, then climbed over the corral fence with the nimbleness of something that was more human and less bovine.

Eva couldn't order her lungs to take a breath or her legs to move.

Instead of rushing her, the creature climbed the large mango tree beside the corral. The branches rustled loudly with its weight. A bird squawked and flew away. Four mangoes fell to the ground, the overripe ones filling the silence with their bursting.

Night veiled the tree and the bull in black. All the same, Eva knew she would never forget the sound of flapping wings, so large that the air lifted in a gust, slapping her across the face. Only it couldn't be possible because bulls couldn't walk on two feet or climb fences and trees, let alone sprout wings to fly away.

Eva's panic manifested in loud, heavy breaths. Sound returned to the night. Thus, she knew she was alone again.

With her heart threatening to tear out of her chest, Eva had the acidic realization that a part of her wished the bull had snatched her away. Then at least she wouldn't have to carry on with the nightmare of her life. She wouldn't have to go to Mass or sit in the dining hall and face her grandparents, who saw her as an object to be traded away before her corruption rendered her valueless. Eva's fist traveled to her chest, trembling, pressing against the riotous thrums of her heart. A teardrop landed on her raised knuckle.

All the pretending she'd done those months—all the praying— it amounted to nothing. She'd caged her true nature for naught. She had seen a demon and had dreamed herself into a snake because the Virgin had never been with her. The Serranos tried molding her into a shape she could never fit, for they didn't understand her, and they never would. She could see it now. Here she was alone.

Doña Antonia was right, in a way.

In her blood, her valco side had won. Staying in Galeno was a danger. No longer was there a road to winning her grandmother's approval. And deep down, Eva didn't want it anymore. Rather, she wanted a life without disguises. She wanted to live like valcos were supposed to.

For this, she needed to seek answers and to find a path of her own. No valcos but her remained in Galeno, but Eva knew of the Águilas, in their cold mountains. Perhaps they were her solution.

14

Damas del Vacío

The days in Águila Manor without Doña Laurel were the hardest. Silence reigned with an iron fist, as its inhabitants scurried from corridor to corridor performing their roles in the most inconspicuous way possible. There was no laughter, and in the nights, solace only came with darkness.

In her room, Reina festered with hatred. She grew angry at the lies of magic, for giving them hope when Doña Laurel and Don Enrique had shared the amapola. Reina hated how much she had hurt to obtain this life, which for a sliver of an instant had been so perfect, only for it to be turned to ash before her eyes.

She had been wrong to believe in Ches, she decided. She had given him all her reverence, and when she'd needed him most, he'd been silent. Reina dug her fists hard into her eyes, squeezing out the tears. She'd been a fool to surrender pieces of her daily aliment, expecting his grace and protection in exchange. She should have known that with her monstrous heart, Ches had already forsaken her life. She should have followed in Doña Ursulina's steps— channeling her devotion to Rahmagut instead.

Most of all, Reina abhorred herself as the silence allowed her treasonous thoughts to take her back to the night, months ago, when she had guided Doña Laurel to the iridio-ridden underground. To the moment when the iridio pulsating from Doña

Ursulina's ore had impaled Doña Laurel—for she had surely been with child—setting in motion their premature end.

Thus, Reina descended to her grandmother's laboratory with purpose in her heart.

Doña Ursulina lay on her chaise longue when Reina entered, a gloved hand draping her eyelids, but she wasn't asleep.

"You said Rahmagut can grant reanimation," Reina said as she shut the door behind her. There was no time for salutations or niceties. Either way, her grandmother abhorred them.

Doña Ursulina watched her with an arched brow. "It is possible."

"Don Enrique will want to bring Doña Laurel back."

"What about what you want?" Doña Ursulina challenged.

Reina approached with her arms crossed. Her tail thrashed, and her pointed ears grew hot. The despicable thought crept back to her, like the grating of nails on a glass surface.

"I want...to know if it's my fault. Was it because I exposed her to the iridio here?"

She could almost touch the memory, how the chill of that night had felt so meek while in Doña Laurel's company. Her grandmother's silence grabbed Reina by the throat and stopped her from breathing. Anticipation ate her from the inside out, along with her self-hatred.

Doña Ursulina's gaze was hooded, regretful. "Yes."

Reina's lungs expelled a sob. Tears warmed the corners of her eyes.

"I told you what iridio does to expectant mothers. And we all paid the price."

Reina leaned against one of the bookshelves for support. She swallowed thickly. "Why haven't you punished me for it?" She deserved to be flayed and beaten.

A deep frown warped her grandmother's features. "This is your punishment." She nodded and added, "Knowing what you did."

Reina clenched and unclenched her jaw. She wrung her hands at her sides as her mind whirred. Finally, she wiped away the tears. How could she ever face Celeste again while knowing she'd had a hand in Doña Laurel's death? And Don Enrique...

Reina looked to her grandmother, desperate to read her cloaked façade. Would she keep her secret? Or would she bring her to Don Enrique for judgment?

Like she could read her desperation, Doña Ursulina said, "It's a truth you will bear, but you will not burden the Águilas with it. You and I, we are here to serve."

"Even if that means lying to them?"

"You will only worsen their lives by telling them. Instead, you should be thinking of how to set things right."

Reina knew exactly what she needed to do, now more than ever.

Henceforth, every path she took would be guided by a single desire: To undo her impact on Doña Laurel's untimely end. To bring back Celeste's happiness.

"Don Enrique visited me like you have."

Reina held her breath.

"He's a man with all the gold and power in the world, and now he wants what no mortal has ever had: the power to defy death itself. He wants his wife back."

Reina's chest palpitated to the point of discomfort. Doña Laurel was a piece gone from the manor, which left them forever incomplete. There was no balance without her, no happiness.

Reina wanted this as well.

"Rahmagut is capable of resurrection," Reina said, an answer she sought only for reassurance.

"And much more."

"So how do we do it? How do we fulfill Rahmagut's legend?"

Doña Ursulina smirked with satisfaction. "You ought to be glad this is a puzzle I've been working tirelessly to solve, before it is too late."

Reina was, and she nodded eagerly.

"I have all the pieces, barring one single detail: the reincarnated souls of Rahmagut's nine wives." Doña Ursulina strolled to her table, her eyes circling the splayed star map. "I think I know a way we can get the answer."

"How?" Reina stepped closer. She was vaguely reminded of how months ago she would have flinched and protested at the idea of revering Rahmagut. But her grandmother had been right all along. Never again was Reina going to question her.

"I told Don Enrique. He's already bringing me the man who knows: a former member of the cult of Rahmagut, who now lives in Puerto Carcosa. He shall arrive in a few days. I will call for you when he does."

Reina lifted her eyebrows. "There's a cult of Rahmagut? Are we part of it?"

Doña Ursulina's eyes darkened. "No. They're a family descended of the yares. Fanatics, so far lost in their made-up origin story they no longer separate truth from lies. Do not confuse them with us."

The days Reina waited for her grandmother's summons passed without acknowledgment. She performed one motion after another, still dodging Celeste for the guilt over her role in what had transpired. And finally, when a moonless night veiled Águila Manor once again, Reina received the beckon.

The door of the laboratory was cracked slightly open as she descended to the underground. Reina paused outside, hearing the all-too-familiar voices of Don Enrique and her grandmother, along with a third person.

"Answer the caudillo. That is your only purpose here."

The stranger spluttered and stuttered.

Doña Ursulina said, "We know death is only a door, and we need the key to open it. It is not a matter of whether Rahmagut has it—we know he does—it is a matter of compelling him to lend it to us. We will parley with him. So tell us about the damas."

Reina sucked in a breath and entered. Inside, the torches were dim, the air tasting stale and, faintly, of sweat and shit. A skinny robed man in shackles knelt between Doña Ursulina and Don Enrique. Sweat dampened his clothes and hair, and his skin was scratched and bloody from a struggle. He wept with a deep, helpless sorrow when he saw Reina enter, identifying her as another indifferent conspirator.

Don Enrique regarded Reina with the coldness he'd donned since Doña Laurel's final cry. But he didn't kick her out. Like Doña Ursulina, she was part of the house.

The stranger's lips trembled as he said, "Rahmagut's damas: wives in title but prisoners in reality. He took them with him to his Void when Ches banished him. But they conspired against him. They knew he was amassing a will to return to this world, so they took his power, one part each."

Reina's mouth twisted into a sneer as she circled Don Enrique to stand by the wall. She hated the scene, but the curiosity gnawed at her from the inside out.

"What's recorded in written lore about how they came to reincarnate is contradictory. All I know is that their souls are trapped in a cycle, being reborn over and over again until the offering of their blood returns the power they stole, and until Rahmagut has enough of it to break from Ches's seal."

"What does that mean?" Don Enrique said.

The man sobbed harder. "It means—if one is killed, their soul will reincarnate into another newborn. Rahmagut's constellation will connect and become visible on the night a new reincarnation is born. There will always be nine damas reincarnated and alive."

Doña Ursulina grabbed the man by the cheeks, her long-nailed fingers squeezing. "Tell the caudillo how he is invoked."

The man cried and she squeezed harder.

"You must give their blood when his claw rends the fabric separating this world from the Void. How can you be willing to do that?"

"Silence," Don Enrique commanded. "It is not your place to question us."

The chained man sobbed.

"The nine damas are out there, at this very moment," Doña Ursulina concluded.

"So she will be returned to us?" Don Enrique inquired from his witch. "If we unveil their identities and offer Rahmagut some of their blood?"

Reina's heart drummed so hard it ached. The air hummed in anticipation.

"Yes, and much more," Doña Ursulina said.

Reina looked up. Her grandmother's smile reminded her of a similar scene, once when Reina had stood at the entrance of this laboratory, starved and begging for food after the help refused to feed her. When Doña Ursulina's salvation had been an arepa with spoiled meat.

"Did you not hear what I said?" the chained man howled, the last gamble of his courage. "Every time the Void god is invoked, you return him some of his power, and the seal Ches placed on him weakens. He was invoked forty-one years ago. Your witch knows it. Do you really mean to weaken the seal even more?"

The edges of Doña Ursulina's lips curled in a sneer. "Whatever shall we do about him, Don Enrique? He knows too much."

"Have all the pieces been answered? Are you certain of how to proceed?"

Doña Ursulina's smile widened in a gesture Reina fully understood. So did Don Enrique. He shot Reina a sideways glance, finally acknowledging her, to which she offered a nod. He wasn't seeking her approval—this she knew—but this was her admittance of her complicity.

"I will need help collecting them," Doña Ursulina said with her eyes gliding to Reina, her satisfaction feline.

Months ago, Reina had stood in this underground lab pledging her allegiance to her grandmother. Many times, she had descended to learn a new facet of the Águilas' arcane life. She had grown. And their agreement had been clear: She was going to become someone in this life, in exchange for serving Doña Ursulina and helping her cement the legacy Reina was set to inherit. This still held truth, even if there was darkness in the path ahead.

Thus, Doña Ursulina's suggestion was a challenge. Reina saw it and rose to it. "I will do it," she offered. "I will bring them to you."

"It is done, then," Don Enrique said.

His dead-blood eyes lingered on her a second longer before he reached for the sobbing man and opened a line of bursting red along his neck. It splattered the floor, the walls, his clothes and theirs. Then Don Enrique threw the man to the flagstones. The problem of a witness was easily solved.

The whispers of Reina's heart blared as she tried to care for the wasted life but couldn't. Instead, the hope Doña Ursulina offered them intoxicated her. She had come here seeking a cure for the guilt and sadness, and her grandmother had delivered. Reina's fingers shuddered as ignited blood pumped through her extremities. This was the key to returning them that happiness, to undoing her mistake. There was a way. And in that moment, Reina knew she was willing to seize it—to open the proverbial door to death all the way.

Something like rancor scorched Celeste's gaze as Reina and Javier loaded their traveling supplies on a rudimentary carriage. The reason for the trip wasn't a secret to Celeste. Reina could tell she disapproved, from the way Celeste stormed out of rooms with doors slamming behind her, from the sneers twisting her lips whenever Doña Ursulina and Don Enrique were seen striding through Águila Manor in conspiring debate. Celeste loathed the new objective keeping everyone in the manor busy—or at least the help who didn't quit after, in his grief, Don Enrique welcomed Rahmagut into the household.

Despite her bone-deep disapproval, Celeste never said a word to stop them. Her glower merely hollowed as Reina approached her in the yard. "I'm crossing the mountains with Javier. We think we found the first girl," Reina said, squeezing her biceps with crossed arms. She grew cold.

Celeste's quiet scorn was her reply.

"Would you like to come?" Reina invited her, like when there were errands to run in Sadul Fuerte or like with a tiniebla hunt.

"I would never," Celeste growled before whirling indoors.

With a sour taste in her mouth, Reina joined Javier in silence as their driver took them up the switchback roads out of the Páramo.

"The brat gets to weasel out of this, but I can't?" Javier said.

Reina ignored him, focusing on the drizzle-coated landscape.

He scoffed. "Laurel dies, and I'm reduced to the work of a gofer. Brilliant."

"Keep her name out of your mouth," Reina said automatically.

"Make me."

They rode with thinly veiled animosity for two days and nights, begrudgingly united by the command of their masters. A quarter-crescent moon lit the sky when the carriage finished its descent down the other side of the mountain, to wide-open fields dotted by rain trees shrouding snoozing cattle. Reina understood the dry heat, having grown up in the Llanos.

Their destination was the hacienda of a landowner under the protection of another caudillo, who, according to Don Enrique, would have no reason to suspect treachery from his Páramo neighbor.

The stable horses stirred at the sound of Reina and Javier scuttling from shadow to shadow in the home's open corridors. She feigned ignorance as Javier shot her a questioning frown. The animals didn't sense them because they lacked stealth. Rather, they perceived the imbalance in the air from the mere presence of Reina's iridio heart.

The doors of the hacienda were unlocked. They crossed the tiled floors silently, the halls empty as its inhabitants and their help were tucked away in their beds, and reached a room decorated in plush cream upholstery. There the landlord's middle daughter slept.

She woke up in alarm as Reina clamped her mouth shut with a gloved hand. The girl squirmed and fought. Javier waved his hands to cast a sleeping galio incantation, one that drowned the senses and shrouded the mind with darkness.

He slung her unconscious body over his shoulder like a sack of grain. Reina helped him load the girl onto the carriage while her conscience kneaded her chest with discomfort. The utterance of her heart resurfaced, delighted.

Reina turned a deaf ear once the girl woke up and realized she wasn't in the safety of her family's hacienda. Javier's lashing of "Stay put!" was the only response to her begging to be returned home. Frightened, the girl endured the journey across the mountains in silence.

They took her to Doña Ursulina's study, where the witch and Don Enrique awaited.

Reina watched from the fringes of the room as Doña Ursulina circled the girl who was supposed to be the first of Rahmagut's reincarnated wives, seeing how her grandmother's bejeweled fingers lifted the girl's black curls to reveal cheeks mottled in tears, then further lifted her hair to look behind her ear. The girl seemed no older than fifteen.

"We must offer them at the same time. We must keep them safe until we have all nine," Doña Ursulina noted to the room. The girl wept harder.

"Then let us allocate them living quarters." Don Enrique passed Reina and Javier, spared them a brief glance, and swept out of the underground after saying, "Well done, you two."

Javier followed after him.

Reina rubbed her arms through her jacket. She stood behind the girl and faced Doña Ursulina. Regret gnawed at Reina's insides for the indifference she had afforded the girl on the ride here. At the very least, she should have been gentle.

"Are you sure she's one of them?" she asked her grandmother. And she knew she deserved a lashing for doubting her, at this stage, but if the girl's life was to be reduced to being a captive, then she needed to say the words.

Doña Ursulina yanked the girl's hair, earning her a yelp, and rotated her head so the marks behind her ears were visible. Moles dotted her beige skin below the hairline. Doña Ursulina waited until Reina counted all nine of them before approaching her star map and jabbing a bejeweled index at the constellation inked among all the other stars lighting the nights of the Páramo.

"Rahmagut's constellation." She pointed at the same pattern that was marked on the girl's skin. The drawing of a bull was superimposed over the nine stars on the map. " 'A birthmark of the constellation lighting the sky on the night of their birth, branded on the place where Rahmagut handled his wives most adoringly,' " Doña Ursulina added, quoting the lore written in the legend.

The girl's shoulders shuddered like an earthquake, her body overtaken by fear. Her frailty only made Reina think of Celeste, who appeared frail of frame but in reality was quite the opposite. What would she think of Reina, if she saw what she was doing?

It didn't matter. Once the Benevolent Lady was back to warming the corridors of Águila Manor with her light, Celeste would see that it was all worth it.

"It is an imprecise estimation, of course, with all the factors involved," Doña Ursulina said, "but there's a way to test it out."

"How will you do it?"

"Wait outside," her grandmother commanded. Her black skirts swept the flagstones as she walked to a shadowed corner of her laboratory, where a chest of drawers held the weight of a basket full of blankets.

"Why?"

It wasn't until Doña Ursulina dug her hand into the basket that Reina realized something stirred and cooed within. The soft mewling of a baby.

It was the last thing she expected to see in this dungeon. Whose baby was it? And what role could an innocent babe have?

"The person who invoked Rahmagut forty-one years ago tested the powers of the Damas del Vacío by having them bless a newborn babe with their protection," Doña Ursulina explained in a gentle voice, as if she were capable of harnessing the tenderness to handle a newborn.

When Reina frowned, Doña Ursulina pointed at the worn journal filled with the thin, elegant writing for Reina to read the notes herself.

Doña Ursulina said, "If we abandon the babe in the mountains, where whistlers and tinieblas and other creatures haunt the land, the dama's blessing should protect him. He will survive the night, and come the morrow, we will know with utmost certainty that she is the correct one."

An ache throbbed in Reina's belly. She inhaled deeply, her jaw tightening as the girl cried silently to herself in painful anticipation of what her captors had in store for her. In Doña Ursulina's arms, the babe gurgled contentedly, oblivious.

Doña Ursulina's lips thinned to a dangerous line, her eyes hardening. "Do not waste my time, Reina. We must act now, or else we will miss the moment that comes *once every forty-two years*."

This was her last opportunity to parley with the god of the Void. They both knew it.

Reina backed away. The air was slapped in her face when Doña

Ursulina's wordless magic slammed the door of the laboratory in front of Reina. She leaned against the hardwood door, her skull clattering behind her, the pain nothing but a distraction. The weaker part of her begged her to turn away. It moaned how it was not yet too late. She could change course now and save her heart from this stain. Then she remembered how Ches had given her silence and suffering. How all the praying to the Virgin had made no changes to their lives. Only Rahmagut's void magic could offer a second chance, as proven by her new heart.

Besides, it was only a little bit of blood to be taken from the damas, and the girl's blessing would keep the babe safe in the mountains. These were the sacrifices they needed to make, to have the lives they wanted. With Doña Laurel, Celeste's gratitude, and all the power Rahmagut was willing to spare for his devoted disciples.

The laboratory door cawed open sooner than Reina expected. Her grandmother stepped through with the bundled babe in her arms, the infant's rosy lids draped shut in a deep sleep. Without care or decorum, Doña Ursulina handed her the wrapped baby.

"Take him. Leave him high up in the mountains. And note the location so you can fetch him at dawn."

"*Me?*" Reina's voice broke.

"Yes, you. Being my left-hand woman isn't always a glamorous job. Isn't that what you want?"

Reina watched the babe's peaceful sleeping face, his cheeks so velvety and pure.

She was wretched for nodding and for taking him through the shadowed trails leading up the mountain. But there was no use denying her nature. Reina was a creature of the Void, with her whispering, monstrous heart reminding her at every opportunity. She was in the retinue of the Águilas, valco masters of the iridio that drew demons and shadows into this world. And she was going to prove she deserved to be the rightful successor of the greatest sorceress who ever was.

Part 2

*Year 368 of the
King's Discovery*

CELESTE VALENTINA ÁGUILA HERRÓN

JAVIER ARMANDO ÁGUILA

MAIOR DE APARTADEROS

15

Rahmagut's Servants

A bright dusk bled the sky red. It was the kind of sunset rarely seen on mountains prone to evening rains, as clouds tended to roll down those snow-caked peaks on most nights to shower the Águila estate with icy water. Reina descended the tracks to the manor with the red sky as her guide, aware that a dusk this bright only bred starker shadows. She watched the long shapes formed by boulders and trees and the occasional frailejón plaguing the rugged mountainside, tense. Should one such shadow move, it could mean a tiniebla. Her fear was an icy trickle on her spine, a clawlike scraping over the scars from that night.

Reina's muscles ached, and the fabric of her leather and wool clothes itched the cuts and gashes that were constant companions to her body. Her feet were blistered from the long trek, but she kept on going, eager to rid herself of the sack she carried. A simple rough-spun bag hiding terror within its folds.

Her throat closed up as the large hand of shame clutched her neck. She tried not to think of it, but it was impossible to blot out the memory of when she'd arrived at the marked clearing, parting marcescent trees to make way, and was slapped in the face by the sweet decay of the leftover gore. The blood-drenched fabric was the sign the test of the blessing had failed.

The cold remains of a babe without a heart weighed her bag,

staining the fabric red much like the sunset stained that far-off sky. Without a dama's blessing, life didn't prevail in the higher elevations of the Páramo, especially not unprotected, innocent lives. It was clear a tiniebla had gotten to the babe.

She remembered the babe's mother. A girl younger than Reina, banished from her baker father's home once the size of her belly made it hard to conceal the undeniable truth. Reina and Doña Ursulina had heard about the scandal. They were around when the girl was thrown out of her home by a father more concerned about the neighbors' whispers than about his daughter's well-being. Reina loathed witnessing it from the shadows of a nearby alleyway, the urge to console the girl bright in her heart. She hated the father's conviction and how the pious people watched, reminding their own daughters in hushed voices that they would do the same if a child were conceived out of wedlock.

Doña Ursulina took notice of the girl. She had lingered in Sadul Fuerte for several more days, asking about the girl's new home, if any, so that when the nine months were up, she could whisk away the newborn babe in the height of night. For a babe born to a destitute single mother was the perfect candidate for Doña Ursulina's tests.

No. On second thought, what Reina despised most was how she was complicit. She didn't murder the babes—the monsters of the Páramo didn't need any help with this—but she was no better than a murderer for leaving them in the lonesome company of frailejones at her grandmother's command.

The first time she'd done it, there had been the promise of safety, of the ritual succeeding. And it did. But the other times afterward quickly unveiled how imprecise Doña Ursulina's methodology for detecting the Damas del Vacío was.

Doña Ursulina kept the process hushed up, as if the methodology were proprietary and ran the risk of being copied by potential rivals also following Rahmagut's legend. From what Reina glimpsed, lingering after being dismissed from the laboratory, Doña Ursulina used a spell of iridio not unlike what simmered beneath Gegania's foundations. As the reincarnated wives each had a piece of Rahmagut's power, they wielded magic with a certain signature, which was what Doña Ursulina sought in her scouring of geomancia metals coursing through the earth. Doña Ursulina had an instrument she had created for the deed, and she fell into a trance when she used it, with the whites of her eyes stained an inky black. She would skip meals or spend days in deep mediation, searching the land for the damas' signs. Once she found a candidate, she tasked Reina and Javier to deliver her to the manor.

But the process lacked precision. Sometimes the scouring of iridio identified the wrong geomancer. Moles and freckles could easily be confused with the birthmark of a constellation. It was at the final step, when the blessing imparted behind closed doors ought to have protected the innocent babes from the mountain's demons, that Reina discovered Doña Ursulina was often wrong.

There had been terrible moments of doubt on nights not unlike this one. The first time Reina protested abandoning a babe for the ritual, Don Enrique had ordered Javier to do it instead, and he'd handled the babe without any kindness. Then Don Enrique had called Reina a duskling, useless in the assignments he asked of her, and offhandedly pointed out her enslavement to iridio ores, of which he was the master. And Doña Ursulina had offered Reina no comfort, warning that her dissent would achieve nothing outside of proving she wasn't a worthy successor.

The scent of manure tickled Reina's nose as she entered the far-off perimeters of Águila Manor. Beyond the line of pines, she spotted the smithy's smoke curling up to the sky. It was a familiar sight, one she had seen many times when descending these same trails with a similar sack in hand. For there had been other babes— too many to count. And so far only seven of them had survived the night. Reina had carried them down to Águila Manor, the babes bawling and clinging to the folds of her clothes as she cooed with whatever pretense of motherhood she could muster.

When they were alive, Reina brought them to her grandmother, who would then arrange for their return: under the veil of shadows, to families who merely saw it as another act of the Virgin answering their prayers.

When they weren't, Reina brought the bodies down to the small chapel flanking Águila Manor for a burial. For even her heart, with all its wickedness, ached at the idea of abandoning them in the mountains forever.

The stars were out by the time Reina finished patting down the last of the moist, fresh dirt outside the chapel with a shovel. She'd buried the babe's remains beside the small spaces taken up by the others. Then she plucked a wildflower from some nearby weeds and placed it atop the fresh mound. She didn't bother offering a prayer, for Águila Manor was a home with a god who didn't care for prayers.

A servant coursed the corridors lighting candles and giving life to an otherwise empty home when Reina entered the manor. Inside, there was no warmth. All the walls did was block out a howling wind that had picked up during the rising night. In the vast dining hall, Reina found Celeste sitting beside the head of the table. She was barely visible behind candles and gilded centerpieces. Porcelain dishes, crystal goblets, and gold utensils covered the length of the table, as every nook of the manor was populated by some extravagance or another; excuses to spend escudos they simply couldn't fit into their vaults anymore.

Celeste left her seat as Reina crossed the distance to her. Reina threw her arms around her, warming from the slow return of the embrace. She curved around and buried her nose in Celeste's long rivulet-like hair, inhaling the sweaty, oaky musk of home.

Celeste peeled herself away first. "Your grandmother is looking for you." Her voice was incense and smoke. Lustrous and graceful. An amalgamation of a valco's severity and the grace she had inherited from Doña Laurel. "Earlier this morning she said she'd found the eighth dama."

Reina stepped back with her jaw clenched. "Already? There's no way she's found another girl so soon. I just came back from looking for the last baby."

Celeste sneered, baring sharp white teeth underneath the plum lip paint she overused, its pigment so rich the stain persisted even after she wiped it off. She was dressed in sparring clothes, always with that high-necked vest style of hers. The leather straps of her scabbard still hung from her hips. And the baby hairs along her temples clung to her hairline from dried sweat. As she whirled back to her seat, she said, "Was the baby protected? Did the girl turn out to be a wife?"

The hand of shame constricted Reina's throat again. She flexed her jaw and stared at her muddied boots. Celeste could probably see the answer in the worn lines of her eyes.

"No," Reina said softly. "I . . . the baby was dead."

Celeste watched Reina coldly and with disapproval, which Reina thought was unfair. It was easy for her to judge her actions from far away, when she could merely dodge her father's orders and ignore Doña Ursulina's altogether. But Reina knew, once Celeste saw her mother's smile again—once Doña Laurel's return brought life back to this grim manor—she was going to shower Reina in gratitude instead.

Reina reassured herself with this future and all the possibilities this door opened for them. She tainted her hands so Celeste wouldn't have to.

The double doors of the dining hall swung open. The caudillo stormed inside but paused at the sight of Reina and Celeste. Little of him had changed in the last year. His hair remained cropped short. He still had those sharp edges to his cheekbones and jaw, though he had grown a short beard, immaculate as the jackets and tunics he wore.

"Reina, Ursulina has been looking all day for you."

Reina stepped away from the table with her head bowed. "Mi señor, I was searching to see if last night's ritual had been successful."

"It wasn't. We don't need you searching for a corpse to know it. Ursulina says she's discovered the identity of the eighth." He swept to the head of the table and said to his daughter, "Celeste, you couldn't be bothered to wash up before supper?"

Celeste's sneer never eased. "So what?" she said.

"Don't be insolent."

"Don't worry, you won't have to suffer my presence long. I'm done eating." She made to stand up.

"You ate without waiting for us?"

"The arepas were getting cold."

"Do *not* leave this table." Don Enrique's voice thundered in the vast hall. It froze Celeste into obedience. It always did.

Celeste could tug and stretch the bounds of her insolence. She knew she was the precious reminder of the only thing to ever bring Don Enrique happiness, and she abused this knowledge. But in the end, Don Enrique's commands would always reign supreme.

Celeste shoved herself back in her seat. She glared at her father, then at her half-empty plate.

"Reina," Don Enrique said, regarding her, "because you were gone all day, Javier had to be the one bringing the girl. So go and take over so that he may eat and pack for his journey to Galeno."

"Of course, mi señor."

"Why is he going to Galeno?" Celeste said at once.

"The Serranos invited me to the wedding of one of their granddaughters. So instead of insulting them by turning them down, I'm sending Javier."

Celeste huffed. "I want to go to a wedding…"

"It'll be a dangerous journey. Unrest is brewing on the road with this talk of overthrowing King Rodrigo. There have been reports of attacks on merchant caravans from the Llanos all the way to Sadul Fuerte."

"Are you sure it's not the tinieblas?" Celeste asked with an insolent smirk. "If you'd let me go hunt them, the roads would be safer."

Many things about the caudillo were the same since Doña Laurel's passing, but not his relationship with Celeste. He barred her from training with Javier and Reina and from going on the tiniebla hunts. One could speculate his undue protection was his way of preserving his last possible heir. For tinieblas were becoming a growing problem for all who coursed the mountains and the Llanos. Their numbers grew swiftly, like the ticking seconds were delivering them all closer to the coming of Rahmagut's Claw. With each hunting party, fewer Águila soldiers returned unscathed and alive. But the truth was Don Enrique was no longer interested in the legacy Celeste could forge with her strength and his influence.

In fact, he wasn't interested in anything that didn't immediately benefit the return of Doña Laurel.

Don Enrique ignored Celeste. "Reina, I do not want to hear again of Javier picking up your slack on the matter. You're only useful to me if you perform the duties we command of you. It is in your best interest not to fall out of line."

Her transplant heart betrayed her with a shudder. Reina's cheeks went hot from shame, as she knew the iridio spell flowing through her heart was visible to their valco eyes. Even Celeste could see she was terrified of the caudillo. Reina supposed that brought Don Enrique great satisfaction. With her jaw clenched, Reina nodded and whirled out.

Javier waited for her in the courtyard, under the pocket of light from a nearby wall torch. His antlers were slightly bigger, as were his shoulders. But he was still lean, his frame so feminine he was apt to be confused for a woman from behind, especially as he wore his shoulder-length starlight hair tied back in a low ponytail.

Finally he heard her approach and said, "About blood-damned time you arrived. Aren't you supposed to be around when things like this happen? What, were you too busy sniffing Celeste's under-garments to come when you're called?"

Reina's fists curled. "*Don't—*" she blurted out. "Why would you say that?"

"Pace yourself there, duskling. You'll give yourself a heart attack," he said.

Maybe her face was an open book. Maybe it told him everything she felt. But even if there were nothing she should be feeling guilty about, any word or misheard whisper was fuel enough to feed the worst sort of gossip at Águila Manor. The kind that could earn her a whipping from the caudillo.

"Don't spread lies about me," she said in the steadiest voice she could muster.

Javier shot her a side-glance as he entered the larder. "If it really bothers you, then, you know, stop looking at Celeste like she's a fine meal, and the household will move on to better gossip. No one cares if you fancy girls of your breed. But keep off my niece."

"Your mother bedded women."

Reina had even asked her grandmother about it, when she'd heard the rumor one too many times from the help. Doña Ursulina confirmed it with a sneer, and the consequent conversation had revealed she didn't care if Reina, like Doña Feleva, never had eyes for men.

"What did you just say? Did you just compare yourself to Mother?" Javier lunged to push her against the wall, but Reina had been fully expecting the reaction. She was quick-footed and sure of her words, so she stepped out of his way.

"The whole world knows it, and she was still mighty and renowned all the same."

Javier didn't pursue the assault. The red in his eyes glimmered dangerously under the torchlight. "Yes. But she didn't bed animals. And despite her renowned stupidity, Celeste wouldn't either."

Ire blazed through Reina. It made her foolish. It made her want to reach for her machete and demand a duel. But Reina remembered Don Enrique's threat. She swallowed the hatred for this spoiled, hateful man who had a heart worthy of a tiniebla and said, "Show me the girl already. The caudillo wants you to join him for supper."

It was too dark to see him, but Reina could almost feel his smirk; his smugness for her lack of retort.

With a spell of iridio, Javier lighted the wall torches inside the room. He approached the crate perched in the middle, by barrels and dusty crates of armor and other abandoned junk. He shoved the lid open, revealing a sleeping human in a rough-spun dress. She had the milky-light skin typical of the people from the Páramo, and her hair was black and cropped to the jaw.

"Found her in Apartaderos," Javier said.

"Right under our noses?"

Apartaderos was the small village perched on the crossroads on the way out of the Páramo. A place that had started as an outpost until eventually someone opened an inn. Traveling from Sadul Fuerte to the Llanos meant crossing this dingy little settlement.

"You could say that. Living right under our noses and without a clue of what she is. And once again, I have to be the one

dirtying my hands kidnapping them, like some lowborn grunt."
Javier scowled, blatant in his displeasure when the caudillo wasn't
around. He leaned over the crate and broke the galio spell imprisoning her in an endless sleep. "You can take over now."

"Yes. I don't need you."

Javier glared at Reina, probably formulating more toxicity to
spew her way. But the silence in the room grew loud as the young
woman began writhing, rustling the hay beneath her. She sat up,
tufts of short black hair blocking half her face. Awake, she didn't
look younger than twenty. Her eyes found Reina's, then Javier's,
and a muddle of panic and confusion fell over them.

"What—where—where am I?" The woman's voice was broken
and delicate.

"Fantastic." Javier rolled his eyes. "You deal with that," he said,
leaving the courtyard as quietly as a shadow.

16

The Eighth Dama

His antics left Reina digging half-moon nail prints into her palms. She sucked in the anger with a deep breath. She had to be civil, for the woman, if no one else in this household could spare the heart to.

The woman scooted against the far edges of the crate as Reina approached. Her lips, rosy and plump, trembled. Her brown eyes met Reina's tamarind ones. They were intelligent, and steadfast, and pleasant to hold until they realized she was nowhere near home. That was when Reina saw even the terror in her eyes looked soft, like the harshest reality she'd ever faced might have been a whipping from her mother.

Reina took in a deep breath through flared nostrils. Suddenly she hated Javier from waking the woman up so far from Doña Ursulina's laboratory. Of course he'd done it on purpose.

"Follow me, please," Reina said, hating herself for robbing the woman of everything worth smiling for. *Please.* How she was a fool for thinking her manners would matter at all.

The woman stuttered, "Bu-but—"

"Would you rather stay locked up in there?"

Reina offered her a hand, but she wobbled out of the crate without accepting.

The young woman was short and chunky, like she would have had the potential of being curvy if only she were a whole head taller. There was no reason for her to be pretty, with her grimy dress and tousled hair, and yet Reina couldn't shake the word out of her thoughts.

"Where are we?"

Reina stepped back to the doorway, allowing her more room. The woman's face changed as she regarded Reina—as the torch-light unveiled the scutes on the bridge of Reina's nose and the pointed tips of her ears peeking from behind her fishtail braid. As her gaze found Reina's tail switching and turning in anticipation.

Disgust wormed its way into the woman's eyes.

Reina was suddenly self-conscious. She didn't care if she was pleasant to look at or not. It was a fact she didn't bother refuting because she didn't need beauty to serve the caudillo. What she needed was the strength in her muscles and her handiness with her machete. But she didn't deserve to be viewed with *disgust*.

"You—you kidnapped me?"

"Javier," Reina corrected her. "If it were up to me, you wouldn't be here." A mild lie.

"Please let me go," the woman said.

Reina gestured toward the courtyard behind her. "I'm trying to help you. If you listen to me and stay calm, things won't be too bad." Reina didn't believe it herself, but she needed the woman obedient.

It took her a moment, but the woman followed her back into the manor quietly, shivering and hugging herself. That was, until Reina slowed at the entryway to the underground, the rotten steel-banded door the telltale of where they were headed.

Reina slipped off her indigo-and-goldenrod ruana, with the Águila crest stitched at the breast, and gave it as a peace offering.

A half-formed sneer warped the woman's mouth. Instead of taking the woolen warmth, she backed away, her chest rising and falling with one forced breath after another. Reina knew what she was thinking. She had seen it time and time again in the other girls.

The woman brushed her hair away from her eyes and said, "I'm not stupid. You're taking me prisoner—but I haven't done any-thing wrong! Why would the caudillo take me? I haven't served Águila soldiers in months! If I did anything to offend them, please just give me an opportunity to set things right—please—"

Reina pinched her nose, feeling scutes. "What are you talking about?"

"I—I healed your men—at the stone chapel," she said and gulped. "They came after hunting tinieblas, and that was the last time I talked to anyone wearing the Águila bearing. Is that—is that why you're taking me? I offended the caudillo?"

Reina shook her head as her chest wrung itself. It was always the same: their confusion and indignation. They were victims of their destiny—pawns in Don Enrique's plans, and in the manor, they were treated like nothing more. She pulled the heavy door open, revealing stairs shrouded in shadow, and explained, "Javier took you because we suspect you're a Dama del Vacío."

The woman couldn't keep her lip from trembling. She watched Reina for a moment, then frowned deeply. "I—I'd heard the tales— but I figured they were just stories—rumors people were coming up with just because lately the caudillo hasn't been protecting us. But it's true?" She grimaced. "The caudillo worships the god of the Void?"

Reina was impressed. Perhaps the intelligence behind the woman's eyes wasn't unmerited, for she was absolutely correct. But the ends would make it all worth it.

She nodded.

"I've heard tales...of the caudillo's witch snatching babies and kidnapping virgins. Tell me it's not true."

Reina's lips twisted into a smirk. It wasn't the time for humor, but she couldn't help the words, for they were as absurd as their disposition: "So you're a virgin."

The woman scoffed. "The wives of Rahmagut are but children's stories! And that is none of your concern."

Reina's smirk widened.

"A stupid, stupid superstition!"

"Get inside already."

The woman's eyes widened. She whirled and sprinted down the corridor, her bare feet slapping the tiles and leaving marks of condensation in her wake.

Reina lunged as well, but the nozariel blood pumping through her veins propelled her farther, five of the human's strides equaling one of hers. Reina caught up to her, stopping under the doorway at the other end of the corridor and blocking it.

She tried to gently grab her wrist, and the woman fought her.

"Just let me go—please!"

"Calm down."

"You're going to kill me."

"*No*, we won't. You will be protected," Reina spat.

Don Enrique showered the damas with silk and luxuries in their captivity. He had all the escudos in the world to spare, and he did spend them, feeding the damas expensive cuts of meat and all the sugary desserts the baker could come up with. The servants dressed them in embroidered garments, draped them in ruanas spun from fine wool, and scented their bathwater with fuchsia and coral tree flowers. Then, once they were full of contentment, Doña Ursulina made them docile with a never-ending sleep.

The woman clawed at Reina's hand. "If you're mad enough to kidnap me over a stupid tale, then you're mad enough to kill me for it!" Her nails drew blood. "Let go."

"You don't know what the legend is about," Reina said.

"Let me go, you dirty duskling!" Her voice reverberated down the corridor.

Reina let go, but not from the command. Heat bloomed from her belly up, making her ears burn. She reacted without thinking, shoving the woman against the wall and drawing so close she scented the sour fear in her breath. Reina was wicked, this part was true—for abandoning the babes in the mountains, for taking innocent women away from their lives. But hearing the slur from this woman, a human clearly coddled all her life who didn't understand the things Reina had to go through to be here, seared her.

The woman's pulse thrummed with terror beneath Reina's grip.

"Listen to me," Reina hissed. "Your freedom is gone. You're a prisoner and property of the caudillo of Sadul Fuerte. He doesn't care what you have to say about it. Blame your birth or Rahmagut, if you want to blame anything."

The woman's eyes grew glossy. Reina had the gut-wrenching

realization she had terrorized her into silence. To the woman, Reina was probably a monster, well deserving of any insult.

She took a deep inhale and shoved off her. Regret draped her shoulders, weighing her down with shame as she took in the tremulous expression in the woman's face. When this all had started, Reina had made an oath to give them kindness and patience, and in a single stroke, she had shattered her promise to herself.

The silence was thick and painful.

"Despite what you believe, I don't enjoy this," Reina admitted with a side-glance. She shoved her bangs away, feeling how oily her hair was.

Dirty duskling.

"Is that supposed to be a reassurance? Because it's not working," the woman said, squaring on her two feet as if she honestly believed she could stand up to Reina.

"I'm not asking you to expect roses."

The woman's glare deepened.

"Whatever happens, I'll be the one to take you to your new bedroom. And if you need anything—anything at all—you can ask me. I'll try my best." Never mind explaining how little sway she had over Doña Ursulina's whims.

"My *new bedroom*? How generous of you. What's your name?"

"Reina. Reina Duvianos."

"You're related to the Duvianos?"

Reina grunted. One day, she would be able to answer what her heart ached to see true: that she was the future of the Duvianos name, that she had a place and home in Sadul Fuerte, and that she *belonged*.

The woman snorted. "I didn't know the Duvianos bedded nozariels."

They don't, Reina thought bitterly. She motioned to the dark staircase, where the air clung to her skin like wet ice. The smell always reminded her of dead frogs.

"And yours?" Reina said, descending.

"Maior."

"Maior what?"

"Maior de Apartaderos."

De Apartaderos. The woman was a bastard, unclaimed by a parent and forced to use her birthplace as a surname.

They descended the steps in pitch-blackness until the soft orange of the torches on the underground level spilled onto the steps. The narrow antechamber was lined in heavy doors. They were the rooms of the other damas and Don Enrique's treasures. The first door led to Doña Ursulina's laboratory.

Maior sensed Reina's hesitation. "What's going to happen to me?"

Reina's keen hearing picked up Maior's terrified heartbeat—the *tha-thump* in her neck.

"Doña Ursulina's going to verify you are who we want." Reina paused, considering whether to divulge the details of the test. "She does other things, sometimes."

Maior's question came out as a croak. "What things?"

Before Reina could answer, Doña Ursulina's door creaked, tugged open by the strings of iridio she maintained so abundantly in her laboratory.

"Come on in, darling," came Doña Ursulina's satisfied voice.

A slim bed was perched in the corner of the room, by the potion desk. It was where Doña Ursulina put the women for their examination. And beside it was a small crib, a mound of blankets tucking in another innocent babe her grandmother had procured for the occasion.

All paled in comparison to Doña Ursulina. Today she was dressed in a luxurious white gown embroidered with mother-of-pearl, her hair hidden beneath a silky head wrapping. It was the kind of outfit she would wear when visiting the gentry of Sadul Fuerte.

Doña Ursulina offered them a smile Reina knew didn't reach her heart. "So Javier delivers—unlike yourself," she quipped.

"I was searching for the other babe." Reina's eyes were on the crib, her thoughts imagining the mother's horror upon realizing the person she loved most was gone.

"Oh, that? As soon as I found the sign for this girl, I knew the other one was to be disposed of. Waste of our time, really. You, too, can stop wasting our time with your sentimental antics. Nature is perfectly capable of removing the evidence. Honestly, Reina, you're slipping."

Reina clenched her jaw to stop herself from reacting. She had been doing this a lot lately—pretending to be all right with the awful things they did.

Doña Ursulina beckoned Maior with a slender hand, saying, "Come on now, you'll be fine."

"No," Maior said.

"Sweetheart, being a Dama del Vacío is the most fascinating thing that will ever happen in your life. Reina, allow the girl some privacy, will you? And don't go too far. Today I have something different I want to try—something that won't take very long. She might need extra attention afterward."

Maior clamped a clammy hand over Reina's wrist. "Don't leave me! Please."

Reina stared at the spot where their skins touched. Her heart fluttered unexpectedly, the urge to reassure sharper than ever. Maior's eyes rounded with pleading expectation, as if she understood Reina was the lesser of two evils.

She was wrong.

Reina peeled Maior's hand off. And Maior pleaded again, Reina's name rolling from wet lips, that desperate gaze begging for an ally. Reina yanked her toward Doña Ursulina; no matter how much Maior squirmed and tugged, she was just a soft human under Reina's steellike grip.

Reina pretended not to hear Maior while shutting the laboratory door behind her. She pretended the twisting and wringing in her chest was nothing more than pity. The memory of all the other instances when she had brought the suspected girls lanced through her, mocking her. She had done it over a dozen times, with the seven they had found and all the others who had been mistakes. So why, today, was she plagued with so much regret?

Her feet carried her to the kitchens to grab some cold almojábanas while she waited. The anticipation worsened her aches. She didn't want to wait outside the laboratory door, right where she could still hear Maior's protests to Doña Ursulina's examinations. But she didn't want to walk away either and forget to fetch Maior once her grandmother was finished, especially not as both Doña Ursulina and Don Enrique kept throwing jabs at her, calling her useless.

Reina had worked hard this past year, enduring Don Enrique's disdain and Doña Ursulina's ambition, avoiding Javier at every turn, because she wanted them to see she belonged in the household. She had tended to Celeste's fevers and sadness. She had fought off a specter or two who'd threatened the iridio mines. She had kidnapped innocents and had stumbled upon the bone and sinew and guts that were the product of this cursed mission. Her hands were dirty, but she couldn't waver now, when they were so close, when the coming of Rahmagut's Claw would make it all worth it.

Through a sooty window, Reina caught Javier climbing into the traveling carriage while she chewed on the cheesy almojábana. He was accompanied by a small escort of armored soldiers, hurrying them to pack their supplies. Reina didn't like him any more than she had when she'd joined the household, but at least now she trusted he acted in favor of their purpose.

She tried to image her life afterward, and her thoughts flitted back to Celeste. To those Páramo-sky eyes and moonlight face that were so exquisite to stare at for hours at a time. What would Celeste feel for the person who brought her mom back?

Reina found the laboratory in cold darkness when she finally descended for Maior. The room was devoid of lights and smells and whirling sounds in Doña Ursulina's absence. Reina brought in a torch from the outside, its light caressing every crevice and revealing Maior shivering against a wall. She cowered at the sight of the firelight, so Reina left the torch propped against an empty holder near the door.

Blood stained the insides of Maior's bare legs and arms, originating from a slit in her wrists and from the depths of her thighs, underneath the rough-spun dress. Reina frowned. This was unusual. Her grandmother never harmed the women. But there was no nearby knife that Maior could have used to harm herself.

Slowly, she knelt by the shivering Maior. "Are you all right?" Reina said, though her voice and hands ran cold.

"You left me," Maior whispered. A remnant tear rolled down her cheek, plopping over her collarbone. Her bob was short enough that Reina could easily see six of the nine birthmark dots behind her ear.

"We have a room set apart for you. I'll take you there," Reina said. "The caudillo will shower you in luxury to make this easier—"

"Like I'd ever forget what you've made of me!" Maior cried, burying her face on the inside of her elbow. "I'm not some dog that can be appeased with a thrown bone."

"You'll have your own room. A servant will come and take care of you—pamper you. You can have a warm bath and sugary cakes and soft, silky dresses," Reina said, hoping Maior cared about such luxuries at all. "No one will come for you here, though, only Doña Ursulina's cruelty."

For lately, she had grown crueler.

Reina tugged Maior's wrist and brought her to her feet, the threat turning her malleable. She led her out to the icy corridor, then walked her down to one of the farthest doors. She forced a tight smile and opened the room. It was a comely chamber with a small bed, a dark wood dresser, a dining table, and a loaded bookshelf. The girls received the hospitality of a guest in the confines of the underground until the test of the babe confirmed or denied their identity. If they turned out to be a true dama, there was another room down the corridor where Doña Ursulina laid them in an endless sleep to await their fate.

"And I'm supposed to be happy staying here?" Maior asked as she walked to the center, gesturing at the brightly patterned wool blankets, the tapestries of wildflowers and alpacas dressing the wall, the cushioned espadrilles peeking from beneath the bed. "Just let me go home. That's all you have to do—let me *go*."

"One thing is what the donkey thinks and another what the rider wants," Reina said automatically.

Maior's nostrils flared. "Spare me your nozariel sayings!"

"What I mean to say is it's not my call."

"I'll do anything in return."

Maior's despair—Reina knew what it was like. She knew what it felt like to hang by the mercy of a stranger, when a small act of kindness was enough for her to carry on hoping. And her heart ached at the memory of Doña Laurel doing exactly that to her life. So she took off the rings on her index fingers. They each encapsulated a litio potion, which served as the conduit for protection magic.

"I can't do anything to help you," she said, offering them to Maior, "but I want you to know that I'm your ally. Take them."

As far as Reina was concerned, litio was the simplest and most harmless type of geomancia. It was only good for barriers and wards. In Maior's hands, they wouldn't harm anybody.

Maior's shoulders tensed. "What am I supposed to do with this?"

"See it as a loan. I have to come back for them, eventually, and I will have to come to you."

As Maior took the rings, her cold fingertips grazing Reina's in the exchange, her touch lingered. Then she snatched them to her chest as if they were a prized treasure.

A smile threatened Reina's lips. She was no good at using litio anyway. "Would you like me to come by tomorrow before high noon?"

Maior accepted the invitation for company with a nod.

Reina hurried out. At the final step out of the underground staircase, she ran into her grandmother, who held a stirring baby boy. Reina sucked in a breath, the sight paralyzing her.

"Where have you been? I went looking for you to hand you this," Doña Ursulina said, depositing the bundle in Reina's arms. "Take him to the mountains now."

"She's one of them," Reina said. She couldn't explain how she knew it. But the presage had latched on to her heart and wouldn't go away.

"I do not need your reassurance. Don Enrique wants to be absolutely certain."

Reina's gaze fell on the babe's rosy cheeks. He seemed so alive and healthy.

Her jaw rippled, tense.

"Don't despair, Reina. If you're right, then there's nothing to be afraid of."

17

A Hidden Constellation

Reina didn't linger near the mountain clearing where she deposited the babe. She wasn't supposed to, lest she get in the way of the demons drawn to the site or was tempted to strike them down with her machete. Interfering would only yield the test moot. And she wasn't motivated by the possibility of doubt. Rahmagut's Claw was going to stain the sky for only twenty days, and then it would be gone for another forty-two years. They needed to have all the preparations sorted and ready for when the star's cyan tail weakened the fabric separating el Vacío from their world. According to Doña Ursulina, at any moment now they would gaze up to the inky velvet and see the beginnings of its journey across the night skies.

Reina descended the trails again for a brief bath and a dinner of leftovers. Sleep comforted her only for so long, before her anxieties spat her out of her dreams when dawn was a few hours away. She reasoned, as she groggily peered at the grandfather clock in the dining hall ticking past the witching hour, that it had been long enough for the test to count.

Reina hiked up those known and worn trails of the Páramo beneath the stars' watchful eyes. Marcescent leaves tugged her trousers and dead shrubs snapped under her weight. A lone breeze sang past the sparse trees, then chilled her to the bone. Her hand found the hilt of her machete on its own, the feel of it a reassurance, despite the perspiration clinging to her palms. And as she walked, as the air grew colder and she hiked higher still, Reina couldn't shake the feeling of being followed.

She clutched the hilt tightly as she paused to listen, taking in the hummocky landscape. She listened to the wind whistling between tall grass and frailejón trees. Crickets committing to their chorale around her. Some fox-like animal yapping in the far distance.

Suddenly a shadow shifted from the corner of her eyes, falling beneath the view of the knoll. A movement a human would have missed.

The tall grass stopped breathing. Or maybe she did.

Reina leapt away from the pursuer, scrambling over stumps and slippery, mossy rocks.

With a bold arc, she swung the machete around. She parried out of instinct. Then her breath died at the depths of her throat as she realized who hunted her.

Her attacker froze, recognition washing over their face. A scythe clanged against Reina's machete, stopping but a hair away from the tender flesh of her neck. Celeste gasped a cloud of condensation. "*Por la Virgen.*"

"Celeste," Reina said, "you nearly killed me."

Crescent moonlight bathed her and turned her stunted antlers into a silver crown. Celeste shoved her scythe away. "No, *you* gave me a fright! I thought you were . . . something."

Reina took a shaky step back, her heartbeats calming. "I should be telling you the same." She sheathed her machete. Her gaze lingered on Celeste a little too long, so she looked away. But no matter how often Reina was entangled in this dance, in this realization of her staring, Celeste's face always drew her back.

Reina said, "Just the other day, I think I saw the madwoman Luz Caraballos."

"It's but a tale."

"She looked real to me."

Celeste pursed her lips. A cloud covered the moon, so Reina couldn't tell if she was smiling, but her voice sounded like she was. "We're a little too old to be scared of ghosts."

"I think I've surpassed you with the things I've seen in these mountains."

Celeste chuckled.

"So why are you here?" Reina asked, withholding the urge to remind her of how the caudillo had banned her from trekking up the Páramo. Celeste should be tucked in her bed right now, warm and dreaming in the safety of Águila Manor. This was Reina's job, not hers.

"I came to intervene," Celeste said.

"Intervene?"

Celeste sidestepped Reina up the scree-side path. "I'm sick of this...ritual or whatever. I'm sick of living in a house of kidnappers and murderers. Father has lost his mind and all honor—all for this...this *insane* legend."

Reina followed her like the puppy she was. "Wait—you can't. Maior is the eighth, I know it."

"Maior?"

"The woman Javier brought tonight." Reina hiked behind her, climbing on a slippery rock and extending a hand to Celeste. Thunder rumbled in the distance, despite the glow of the crescent moon and her shimmering companions.

"If you're already on a first-name basis, shouldn't you be a little more concerned that she's a prisoner?"

Something about her tone made Reina clench her jaw. "I don't decide how they're kept. Doña Ursulina does."

"Spoken like a true lapdog."

Reina stopped, gave her a look. It wasn't the first time she'd heard the words, and it never hurt any less.

Celeste sighed loudly. She reached out to squeeze Reina's arm. "I'm sorry. I didn't mean that. But she's not an object for keeping. None of them are. They're people. Look, don't fight me on this. Go back to the manor, and pretend you never saw me."

"Doña Ursulina will want to know the results."

"She's not getting her results," Celeste snapped.

Coldly, like the wind enveloping them, Reina said, "If she can't prove Maior is a Dama del Vacío tonight, then she will steal another unbaptized babe, and she will repeat the ritual until she does. Someone else will lose their child, Celeste." *Don't be naïve*, she thought. Besides, they were running out of time.

"Head back to the manor. I command it."

The words were icy water. Heartless, like her uncle. Tyrannical, like her father. They reminded Reina that she could never be an equal. For if Reina ever disagreed, a command could simply wipe her opinions away. But she didn't move, because she already carried someone else's command. She had chosen this path, and her hands were too dirtied for her not to see it through.

"You should have tried to change the caudillo's mind sooner," Reina said bitterly, "but you didn't. You also want to see your mother alive."

"Don't talk about my mom."

Reina's chest tightened. She'd regretted it as soon as she had said it. "Celeste, we're so close."

Celeste whirled up the path, hissing, "Not if I have something to do with the matter."

Nightly silence enveloped them as Celeste rushed up, her boots crunching on rocks that Reina later stepped on. Part of her wanted to toss Celeste over her shoulders and haul her all the way back down to the manor—to lock her in her room so she couldn't play at this game where so much of the future was at stake. It was so easy for Celeste to wake up one day and decide she wanted something completely unattainable, to demand the people around her provide it to her, and actually get it. Celeste had never learned the disappointment of a no, and Reina feared even their friendship wasn't strong enough to change her mind.

A soft whistling brought Reina back to reality. The breeze stopped and the night became truly quiet. It was the melody of climbing notes, one over the other, coming from far away like they were being whistled by an unsuspecting traveler. But she knew this melody—had heard it once before.

Reina and Celeste paused beside a tall, lanky frailejón.

"Did you hear that?" Celeste whispered.

Reina glanced to her left and right. They stood on a path with a slopping scree to one side and plentiful frailejones to the other. Standing in the shadow of a moon hidden behind clouds, the trees were an easy place for a creature to hide in plain sight.

Moments passed and the whistling faded. Stopped. Then it started again, faint and broken as if coming from very far away. A *swoosh* cut the air behind them, and Celeste gasped, yanking Reina forward and out of the way.

The sound was sucked out of the night as Reina whirled around to face the bipedal fiend. A tall whistler emerged from behind a crooked tree, hunched, claws outstretched and ready for a second strike. Its eyes were shrouded in the shade of a straw hat, the bottom half of its face gnawed bloody, probably by another whistler it had encountered. Caked blood stained the sides of its lipless mouth, trailing down to the tattered clothes of a farmer.

Reina forgot to breathe as the whistler regarded them with a gaping grin. Her gaze found Celeste, who said something, but Reina couldn't hear a thing. She couldn't hear the crickets, the wind's howls. She couldn't hear her own thrumming heart.

It was what whistlers did, jumbling sound to confuse those they hunted, their whistling loud when they were far and faint when they were close to their prey.

The whistler slashed a second time. In forgetting how to breathe, Reina also forgot how to move.

Celeste wrenched her out of the way. They hurled to the ground, slamming on a rock and dead brambles as the whistler shredded the air where Reina had stood.

"Reina!" Celeste's voice snapped her back to reality. "Remember your training."

Reina sprang to her feet. Her machete whizzed out of its scabbard to become an extension of her arm. With a machetazo she swung at the whistler's slashing claw, severing it in a clean swipe. Celeste swung her scythe at the other arm, hacking through sinew and bone and nearly getting stuck along the way.

The whistler let out a deafening high-pitched whistle as Celeste rammed her way through the cut. Without its arm, it ran at Reina, snapping bloodied teeth for a desperate victory. But this time Reina didn't hesitate. She swerved out of the way, her legs acting on muscle memory, and muted the whistler with a thrust right through the heart.

The smell of sweet yet rancid flesh slapped her across the face.

Reina let the body fall to the ground and yanked her machete out. She was wet with foreign blood and tendrils that smelled of corpses. A smell she knew well.

Despite the stickiness, Celeste took her in an embrace that grounded her. Reina shuddered in her arms. Celeste's touch made her remember she was safe and not in the clutches of the tinieblas who'd left her heartless.

Together they took a deep breath that seemed to return the sounds of the mountain.

Celeste let go. She watched Reina, eyes surfing her curly braid and tawny face.

"You didn't have to do that," Reina said to regain whatever pride she could muster. "I could have handled it."

"You froze."

Reina was supposed to be the one saving Celeste. She was supposed to be the better warrior. If she wasn't worthy to humans, and if she didn't have a fortune to her name or a proper family, the least she could do was be self-sufficient. And not freeze.

So she offered Celeste a very reluctant "I mean—thank you."

They turned to the fallen body. Sores and cuts oozed with black-red blood all along the whistler's pale skin.

Reina wiped the blood from her hands on her trousers—her good pair. Thankfully none was theirs. "I struggle killing whistlers," she confessed. "I rely too much on my hearing."

Celeste's eyes fell on Reina's chest. She said, "Are you using an iridio spell? Your chest is pulsing so much."

"You know I don't cast iridio." She hated to, in fact. With the ore keeping her alive, iridio was part of who she was. Casting a spell of it and depleting her own supply left her feeling like a breath was being sucked out of her lungs.

Celeste gave her a smug look that made the heat rise to Reina's cheeks. She needed to stop staring so much.

"It's all right, you know," Celeste said. "I'm here for you, even if you infuriate me sometimes. The Virgin made me run into you so I could save your life because she knows I'll be the one needing saving someday."

"I'm not useless." *And gods don't look out for me*, Reina thought.

"I'm not saying you are."

Still, even if she pretended, Reina didn't miss the meaning: *I'm here for you.* The night wasn't dark enough to shroud the brightness in Celeste's eyes. She smiled, her plum lips slightly parted. A flutter awoke in Reina's belly.

Everyone else in the manor only had critiques of her role. But the good things in her life, her machete and her sense of home, came from Celeste. Reina's skin hummed. She could be anywhere in the world, soiling her hands facing any foe, and it wouldn't matter as long as she was with Celeste. And she wanted to be with her. Her bones ached with the suggestion of what it would feel like, to take Celeste's slender neck in her hand and bring her close so their lips were but a breath apart. Would Celeste object, if Reina's lips trailed soft worship down to her collarbone?

Reina stepped closer. Without the whistler, the night was loud again in its orchestra of nocturnal sounds, yet it felt like privacy had blanketed them. A hush, and Reina's wildly beating heart.

Celeste's eyes widened. She wasn't blind to the heady bubble.

Reina swallowed thickly. The daring to turn her fantasy into reality was right there, her fingertips ready, until the sound of an anxious coo dissolved the impulse. A babe's cry; it was loud enough that it couldn't be too far.

Reina and Celeste looked around, then their eyes met.

The cries intensified.

"The baby—" Reina said, her pulse blazing with disappointment. It had robbed her of the moment.

Celeste took off toward the sound. They climbed the rocky slope and reached an elevated clearing. There a barricade of frailejones circled a small pond. And right on the banks was a bundle of hemp blankets, stirring and spilling with the cries of the abandoned infant.

Reina ran to the baby first. But before she could fully reach to scoop him up, a shock of electrifying energy stopped her. Her hand reached again, and the energy lapped her like fire.

She hissed and stepped away. "¿Qué diablos?"

Celeste stopped beside her, staring at thin air.

"Well?"

Celeste extended a hand, touching something invisible, her palm molding around the shape of a dome. "There's a litio barrier."

Of course, Reina thought. Celeste could perceive geomancia.

"Is this what the damas' blessing is supposed to look like?" Celeste gave breath to the same question flooding Reina's thoughts.

The babe's cries became wails.

Celeste dissolved her scythe incantation and picked up the babe up in one smooth, unhesitant motion. She lifted him to her chest, the barrier never once inhibiting her.

"Why isn't it stopping you?" Reina was suddenly reminded of her breed. Of all the things she couldn't do as a nozariel.

The clouds parted, allowing moonlight to reveal the babe's teary eyes and ruddy cheeks. He was distressed but unscathed. Celeste squeezed him closer, cooing and squeezing his mottled blanket, and calmed him.

"I don't know. I just had a feeling I could do it," she said. When she looked up at Reina, triumphant, it wasn't her eyes or smile that earned Reina's attention.

Speechless, Reina reached out to dislodge Celeste's jacket and vest collar from her neck, moving her black hair aside. She wasn't thinking about whether it was proper or not, and if Celeste objected, she never expressed it. Reina's attention zeroed in on the marks sprinkled behind Celeste's left ear. Dots she had marveled at and interpreted as beauty marks in the past, before acquiring the damas had sucked up all her time and mental energy. But now, as she gazed at the pattern she had observed in the other women time and time again, she knew with utmost certainty that they weren't just moles. Reina ran her thumb along the marks, caressing the soft, unmarred skin protected from the elements by Celeste's hair.

Beneath her touch she could feel Celeste's shiver. "Reina?" she said, pulling away.

Reina sobered up. This touch was improper.

"What's going on?" Celeste's voice held the same panicked edge as the babe's cries.

"You have...the birthmark."

Reina felt like a fool. All those days when they had frolicked in the pine grove with Celeste's hair in a high ponytail. All the times they had sparred and Reina marveled at the slick length of Celeste's neck. She had been too blind by her own desire to see the truth tattooed across Celeste's skin.

"The birthmark?"

The babe sensed her distress and began stirring unhappily.

"What birthmark?"

Eight times Reina had confirmed the pattern in the other women. And only one remained to be found.

"Well?" Celeste snapped, startling the babe.

Reina didn't want to say it. Her heart began to pound, dread licking its way up her spine.

"You have the birthmark of Rahmagut's constellation behind your ear, 'on the place where Rahmagut handled his wives most adoringly,'" Reina said, quoting the journal writing. By now, she was an expert on the matter.

She had seen Celeste's moles and freckles in the past. Her shoulders and back were dotted in them, just like they had dotted the Benevolent Lady's. But the possibility of Celeste being one of them had never even registered in the furthest confines of her mind. Reina couldn't have found something she hadn't been looking for. But the ability to cross through Maior's blessing was a second sign Reina would be a fool to disregard.

"But—" Real alarm filled Celeste's voice. "I'm not like them. I *am not*."

Despite the emphasis—the self-assuredness—it was futile to argue it. The signs didn't lie. And they wouldn't lie to Doña Ursulina, when she decided to risk the life of a babe on the ritual proving what Celeste was or was not.

Reina shook the tension from her arms and shoulders, her hands navigating to the hilt of her machete. She met those blue eyes.

For months, Reina had looked up to the skies hoping for her luck to change. Hoping that Don Enrique would acknowledge her strength and stop seeing her as a worthless half-breed. She yearned for her grandmother's kindness, which Reina knew existed deep down, buried underneath layers built from a life of prejudice and lessons learned the hard way. She ached for a future with Doña Laurel back, with Celeste by her side. To see it unfold this way... It only filled Reina with apprehension. Because she was duty bound to her grandmother, who'd saved her life and offered her a future. But she had also made an oath to herself: to protect Celeste at all costs, and to be the person Celeste saw home in when they looked into each other's eyes. But if this discovery unraveled them both at opposite ends, Reina wasn't sure where she was supposed to stand.

18

A Convent or a Prince

S picy sunlight stung Eva's exposed shoulders as she waited outside the post for the postman to hand her the letter. An aristocrat, he was closing up early to attend the most talked-about wedding of the season, so he'd prohibited her from entering his office, lest other customers also get the idea of delaying his departure. As she dallied, a breeze lifted her frizzy curls, displacing the beads of sweat already gathering behind her neck. She took a big inhale to taper her growing anticipation, scenting the all-too-familiar river harbor smell of turtle water. Behind her the cobbled streets bustled with carriages and hollering drivers transporting the influx of wedding guests arriving by ship into Galeno. There was traffic on the main road leading to the center of town, a backup of donkeys and mules herded by the hired hands of the Serranos, Contadors, Villarreals, and other noble families welcoming their relatives.

If Eva stood out on the rotting stilts of the harbor, she didn't acknowledge it. Every day that month, she had visited the post with the same query: Did she have any new correspondence? Thankfully, the postman was a dry man lacking any interest in small talk, so he kept to himself and didn't bother spreading the gossip far and wide to the society of Galeno, of the governor's granddaughter receiving letters with the wax seal of a soaring eagle.

Finally the postman emerged from the shade of the office and handed

Eva a wrinkled envelope. She accepted it greedily, uncaring of the stains and dust that were a guaranteed embellishment. It was unavoidable, for a letter making the cross-country journey to reach her.

Of course, she didn't open it right away. She navigated a few short blocks to the plaza with the sculpture of Saint Jon the Shepherd shaded by a tamarind tree, where she had commanded her driver to wait. She didn't open it even as she sat on the carriage's velvety cushion, her chest and thighs gathering sweat beneath her dress. Life with her family had taught her to be careful—or paranoid—of what even the help might see or hear. She couldn't risk her final correspondence with the Águila heir being confiscated by a nosy cousin or aunt. Not when her plan was this close to fruition.

A traffic jam of carriages slowed their arrival to the hacienda. Eva told the driver to drop her off near the gates, by the golden cassia trees, as the Valderrama carriages clogged the driveway with their army of attendants coming to serve at the wedding of their son to Eva's cousin. They'd been there since the morning, when Eva had headed to the post, bringing enough bodies to fill up every guest room in the Serrano hacienda. And it wasn't just them. It was also the Castañedas and the Silvas (only the lowly cousins, not the king himself, for this wedding wasn't *that* important), and many more families with names and fortunes inherited from the era of Segol's rule. Eva approached inconspicuously, avoiding the kind of glances that could snare her in unwanted pleasantries.

An army of proper girls, severe grandmothers, boastful heirs, and their lord fathers emptied the gilded carriages parked on the driveway. Doña Antonia greeted the women with a kiss on the cheek and extended a hand to be kissed by the men. She ushered them to the doorway, where a servant was stationed to offer them papaya or mango juice and escort them to their rooms. Mules followed them, hauling sacks and coffers down the back doors to the outdoor kitchen and servants' quarters. Eva could only imagine the treasures hidden within: fine silks and emeralds mined from the jungle and even more mother-of-pearl encrusted rosaries. A hundred treasures brought to the family as wedding gifts. There were goats and thoroughbred palfreys and so many chubby piglets Eva couldn't keep count; sacks of plantain, papaya, and cassava; and stacks of anise bottles and wine.

She watched the arriving guests with a tightness in her chest, perking up anytime she glanced upon a particular body frame, at the hope of seeing Néstor jumping out of one of those carriages. Néstor with his husband. Néstor with his optimism and endless love for Eva. It was a daydream she'd been nurturing since the moment she'd drafted his invitation letter. Even Doña Antonia hadn't complained when Eva's own calligraphy had begged for his return, if only for the wedding.

Pura cornered her before Eva could disappear inside. Her sister had emerged from behind the porch's bougainvillea with her newborn. She wore a vibrant apricot and poppy-red dress embroidered with flying macaws. A large leather hat hung from her neck. Her hair was half-braided up, her kinky coils bouncing over her bared shoulders.

"The guests have all arrived, and you still look like this," Pura said.

Eva couldn't tell if this was a question or an accusation. She shrugged. She wore the same dress from her morning ride, and the hems of her skirt were muddied from the harbor's detritus.

"I have *time*. I just had an errand to run," she lied with a whine.

Pura clicked her tongue and grabbed Eva by the arm, then herded her back into the house. It bustled with servants running this way and that, frantically carrying platters of food and overfilled goblets. Tradition dictated the guests ate as much as their bellies could handle before the wedding ceremony in the cathedral so that they could drink as much as they could handle during the evening reception. The urge to weasel out of Pura's grip was bright in Eva's chest, but she played along to avoid any interest being drawn to her letter.

"What are we doing here?" Eva asked, gesturing to their grandfather's study, which was several hallways away from her room. "Shouldn't I be, you know, getting ready?"

"Because I told her to bring you here," a deep voice said from behind her.

Doña Antonia carried a heavy perfume of honeysuckle as she entered the governor's study, gesturing for Eva to follow her. Eva complied, her grip on the envelope growing slick, even as the thought of making a run for it nearly electrified her soles. *Don't bring attention to it*, she had to remind herself.

Pura closed the door behind her, and the sounds of the hacienda were forgotten in the dark stuffiness of the room, save for the gentle rustling and mewling of the babe in Pura's bundle.

Her grandmother wore a rich indigo dress, and her hair was braided up in an intricate hairdo adorned with pearls and tiny gems. "Eva, I realize this is last-minute," Doña Antonia said, "but a marvelous opportunity just came up."

Eva's belly clenched. Her opportunity was in the letter. In the future she was carving for herself.

"I was just chatting with the queen mother, Doña Orsalide Silva; she's the guest of honor tonight, aside from the bride and groom— but you know what I mean. We've been sharing correspondence for a while, and in the past, she's mentioned how she's got this grandson who, to put it bluntly, is without much purpose and who's at risk of wasting away his life to vices, like Néstor did," Doña Antonia said with tight lips, and Eva stared at her feet. Her boots were muddy, and her soles were on the verge of divorcing from the leather. "She just told me she brought that grandson to the wedding. So I told her I have a granddaughter who is wasting away with daydreams and who's apt to be spirited away by some demon or another any night now."

Eva pressed on her worn boot hard, drawing a sharp pain to her toe. Doña Antonia was not wrong.

"She wasn't intrigued, of course—young women without an interest in motherhood are useless to a person of her stature. That was until I told her this granddaughter of mine is valco."

With her nostrils flared, Eva met her grandmother's eyes. Her valco blood was the only reason her life was miserable and why she had an escape to begin with...

"And now she's extremely interested. The Silvas are close business partners with the Águilas from Sadul Fuerte, who are all valcos. They see your blood as a boon."

Pura squealed in delight.

Eva couldn't bring herself to breathe. She merely listened.

"Can you imagine, marrying a prince? A far-off prince with absolutely no chance at the throne, but a prince all the same!" Her grandmother's eyes twinkled. "Oh—like I always say, the Virgin does things for a reason. This could be the opportunity I've been praying for since your engagement to Don Alberto fell through. You would bring so much honor to this family, tying our name to the Silvas. If they're able to solidify their reign, this could mean many more unions between our families. Picture it: a king with Serrano blood."

Doña Antonia crossed herself, while Pura squealed again. Both with a joyfulness Eva couldn't even fathom tasting.

"I knew all this hard work we put into raising you as a proper lady would pay off someday, despite your breed. Oh, don't give me that look. You know we can never ignore or forget what you are, and your tendencies to this witchery certainly don't make it any easier. Blame your monster of a father, if there is anyone to be blamed here."

Eva's belly tightened and twisted. But she couldn't grow angry at her grandmother. If anything, mirth blossomed and brought a smile to lips. Eva humored it, actually, and allowed Doña Antonia to believe her happiness came from the matchmaking.

No, Eva's delight crawled out of a dark place, all claws and sneering teeth. For she was going to rob the Serranos of this future. Eva wasn't a piglet to be sold off to the highest bidder. As her grandmother often said, she was a monster like her father, bringing milk snakes and flying bulls to their home. And she was going to take away their say on her future, their anticipated bride price, and this frivolous dream of a Serrano monarch.

Her grandmother went on, oblivious. "Or, like I said before, maybe this was the Virgin's plan all along as well, if it positions us to become equals to the Silvas. This also comes with great timing to what I've been discussing with the governor about your future."

"Discussing what?"

Doña Antonia hesitated, gulped. She averted her gaze like she was unsure of the words she wanted to say. "Mateo and I talked. We agreed to send you to a sisters' convent. But this changes everything. Besides, I know a convent would be very harsh on someone such as yourself."

Eva forced out one croaky breath of disbelief. "Someone such as myself?"

"A valco with an affinity for magic," Pura said gently as she rocked her stirring baby, like she was trying to steer the conversation somewhere positive.

But Doña Antonia would have none of it. After all, her unforgiving honesty was her greatest weapon: "A spoiled young lady with a demon inside her." Her eyes bulged, her nostrils flaring. "When you hear the river, it's because it carries stones. I was right about you all those years. But it will not be our problem anymore."

A hush draped the room, heavy and caustic, daring Pura and Eva to have any objections. Eva supposed her grandmother was tired of pretending. She allowed it, even as her chest ached for a do-over, wounded from the love she carried for her family. But Doña Antonia was right. She had been born different, and soon it would never again be their concern.

Pura glanced at Eva with that rueful gentleness she'd inherited from Dulce. A soft, but weak, heart. She didn't have the courage to contradict the matriarch, not even when her face was clearly painted with regret.

Finally Doña Antonia said, "So you can have that choice. And when you're older and you mature some more and you realize how I've only done my best to look out for you, then you can thank your grandmother."

"A convent or a prince," Eva repeated with a bitter smile.

"See how good I am, giving you such an impossibly good alternative? I trust you will choose the path that will bring honor to your family name—that will redeem the crimes of your father and make me overcome my grief for Dulce."

The jab didn't touch her. Eva had grown a mineral armor to it.

When she looked up with a smile as fake as her acceptance of the Silvas, her grandmother and Pura beamed, and the mood changed entirely. They squeezed Eva's hands and herded her back into her room, coaching her on how to approach the queen mother and how to charm the royal family's youngest son, to make the whole transaction pleasant for all parties. All the while Eva brimmed with satisfaction. They never questioned her letter.

Doña Antonia left them, tittering about how she had to convey the marvelous news to the Silva matriarch. And Pura lingered for only so long. Her babe began to stink, so she scurried away to clean him up. They left Eva alone in the company of her reflection in her mirror, her hands clutching the wrinkled envelope. Maybe she did look like a witch, with her bachaco hair frizzy and growing out of control, her curly bangs concealing the stunted antlers sprouting from the crown of her head.

Her fingers trembled as she ripped open the golden seal of the soaring eagle. Her chest pounded, aching in anticipation for the crossroads holding her future prisoner. When she finally read the message within, she collapsed on the folds of her dress skirt with a sob of relief.

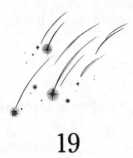

19

To Plot with a Valco

After the ceremony in Galeno's cathedral, the glowing bride and her husband rode on horseback to the Serrano hacienda for the wedding party, as was the tradition in the Llanos. Waiting for them in the Serranos' vast patio was a large crowd of people dressed in what was probably a significant fraction of the country's wealth. There were so many guests: Friends of the Serranos, and the sons and daughters and cousins of those friends, and the friends and neighbors of those sons and daughters and cousins. People who ruled over capitals and towns and haciendas too small to exist on the map. Eva didn't think there was a single person capable of naming every guest. Not even Doña Antonia herself.

The wedding was the event of the year, and with the queen mother attending, the Serranos had spared no expense. Eva and the family were already gathered in their tables when the bride and groom arrived on mares wearing fuchsia and araguaney flowers in their braided manes. The guests sat on chairs dressed in colorful woven skirts. Laurels and wildflowers wrapped around the gates and supporting patio columns. Trained macaws and toucans flew freely over their heads. The birds perched on posts strategically placed around the patio, where they ate off platters loaded with chopped mango, guava, and topocho. The large centerpieces brightened the space with their saturated sunflower-and-pepper arrangements.

Eva did some drinking herself; otherwise she would have no patience for the crowd. Pura and her babies sat beside Eva on one side, and another niece, daughter of Doña Antonia's second son, sat to her other side. In short, Eva had been assigned to the youngin table, which was a slight she didn't overlook. They were served multiple courses of grilled quail swimming in honeyed pineapple sauce, lamb stew, fine cuts of beef raised on Serrano pastures, and if that wasn't enough, the spit-roasted pigs were being cut up to be served as the heavy final course.

The upbeat melodies of a harp, drums, maracas, and a four-stringed guitar carried the guests to the dance floor, where the men stomped the flagstones and twirled the women so the ruffles of their dresses surfed the air. Eva forked the last cold tendrils of her lamb to the bone as she watched the guests dancing joropo. Her gaze followed the crowd of people who left their family tables and began the joyful crisscross walk across the dance floor to meet with old friends or acquaintances from the war, or to meet new people. She grew anxious, but not at the throngs of people.

"By the grace of the Virgin, Eva, go enjoy yourself already!" Pura said as she rocked her youngest back and forth on her seat. The baby was fussy, likely because the music was so loud it was impossible he would ever have a rest tonight.

"Take my wine if you must," Pura said, sliding her filled goblet to Eva's side. She was breastfeeding.

Eva stirred the goblet and nursed it for a while. In truth, she was biding her time. So she gave her sister a mild lie. "But I don't know anyone."

"No one knows anyone until they go out and talk to each other. That's what weddings are for."

"They all think I'm a witch."

Pura clicked her tongue. "And they'll think it even more if you stay brooding here all night."

Eva's gaze surfed the heads of people, from left to right, until a peculiar sight gave her pause. Far at the end of the patio stood a slim man kissing the hand of a lady thrice his age. He had blond hair so light it looked like starlight and the palest skin Eva had ever seen.

Like most other men in the party, he wore the high-necked and long-sleeved liqui liqui jacket worn by Llaneros for special occasions. His was black and tight-fitting and made of a thick fabric, with a small gold chain hooking his collar together. But the most striking feature of all, which sent Eva's heart into a frenzy, were the two antlers curling from the crown of his head, thick and strong and much more developed than hers.

"Who is that?" Eva's voice broke. She had a guess, but she wanted to be surer than sure.

Pura followed Eva's gaze and said, "Oh—that's—uh...Don Enrique Águila's youngest brother. He's an Águila, from Sadul Fuerte."

Eva took a long drink of her wine.

"Mi abuela invited him, don't you remember?"

"Pura, I made hundreds of invitations. Do you really think I was paying attention?"

Pura giggled. "Yes, well, of course they had to be invited. They might've been revolutionaries, but they're still the richest family in the country. All that geomancia you obsess over? They own the iridio mines for it."

Eva watched the young man go from one table to the next, smiling, kissing hands or cheeks, introducing himself to strangers and reacquainting himself with old faces. The thought of him eventually making his way to her table made her chest flutter.

But she couldn't let it happen. They couldn't be seen together. Not yet.

"Is he married?" Eva said as the curiosity sparked in her, for she genuinely didn't know.

Pura laughed, long and hearty. "Who cares? Grandmother *hates* revolutionaries. She hates that they took away all the plantations under our name and that they cut off all our influences in Segol. She said we were earning *thrice* as much as we're earning now when we could keep nozariels working in the plantations. Our grandmother would never, ever let us fraternize with an Águila." Pura leaned closer to Eva conspiratorially. "They're friends with Samón the Liberator, who's also a valco. Didn't you hear the tale of how our grandfather banished Samón from Galeno? It was the juiciest gossip of the time. Trust me, if Segol had beaten Samón Bravo and Feleva Águila during the war, the king of Segol would have granted those iridio mines to our family. It might have happened before you were born, but that kind of bad blood doesn't just go away in one generation."

"Then why was he invited?" It was too perfect. The Serranos had handed her this opportunity on a silver platter.

"We invited the family out of formality. The country's supposed to be united now. We lose more by angering them with bad manners. And don't you worry for them, Eva. They don't like us either."

"Why?"

Pura shrugged, nodding in the direction of the young man. "Don Enrique couldn't even be bothered to attend. He sent his brother. I've heard tales that he's ill, and weird."

Eva watched the young man, inspecting his mannerisms, how he gently tipped his head and smiled so politely at the people who greeted him and marveled at his antlers. People said Eva was weird, too, but that didn't make it true. She listened to the wind and to the earth, and she noticed when darkness slithered. She could see iridio and could summon litio as naturally as she could work her calligraphy. For this, people called her weird. But he was valco, and she was valco. So maybe what humans saw as weird was normal in them.

As much as she wanted, she couldn't cross the patio and introduce herself. For as soon as she attempted to, every pair of eyes would turn to them, including her grandmother's.

Thankfully for Eva, Doña Antonia had been too busy butterflying around the patio and greeting families to care much about her. At the present moment, Doña Antonia was at the Silva table, exchanging gossip with the queen mother that got juicier by the moment, if her exaggerated eyebrow raising was an indication at all. Then the big-boned queen said something that made Doña Antonia shoot a glance at her granddaughter, nodding, and Eva knew her peace was about to be over.

Beside Doña Antonia sat two young men dressed in beige

high-necked liqui liqui jackets. One sat whispering to the young woman sitting next to him, and the other young man shot Eva furtive glances, which she only interpreted as him already knowing about the matriarchs' arrangements. He glanced at her; she looked away; she looked back and caught Doña Antonia's raised-eyebrow gaze on her. It wasn't a choice anymore. It was a command. She downed the last two gulps of her mora wine and straightened her skirts before heading to their table.

The staring man stood up at once, as if he were meeting someone important, and dragged up his companion, who reluctantly peeled himself from the beautiful young woman by his side. He had striking tamarind eyes and a head of pretty black curls. A golden tooth shone beyond his companion's smile, though he was just as handsome as the one with tamarind eyes. Doña Antonia and Queen Mother Doña Orsalide pretended to be delighted by Eva's approach and stood up as well.

Eva's chest thrummed uncomfortably as she curtsied and said, "It is my greatest pleasure to finally meet you, Your Majesty."

"The pleasure is all mine, young lady," the queen mother said, watching her with shrewd eyes. Her skin was brown and leathery like the trunk of a palm tree, the rouge of her cheeks gracing her smile with youth. She wore a layered violet-and-indigo dress with many frills and lace. She boldly reached out and petted Eva's antlers. It was a violation of space that sent shivers shooting through Eva.

"It's such a rare sight to see a valco these days," Queen Orsalide said.

"So she really is valco," Tamarind Eyes said in mild surprise, watching Eva with admiration. It was a look that made Eva a little hot in the cheeks. A look she decided she quite liked.

Why couldn't anyone in Galeno appreciate her like this?

"Aside from the Águilas, I thought valcos were fully extinct from Venazia," Tamarind Eyes said.

"Sometimes it feels that way to me," Eva confessed.

"You must feel terribly lonely."

But before the conversation could derail to territories she was uncertain to embark on while under the watchful eye of her grandmother, Doña Antonia interceded.

"Loneliness isn't the life of this valco, young man. She's surrounded by her family, and you saw how many we are. Eva, why don't you tell them of your other capabilities?" Doña Antonia wore the joyful pride she only showed about her progeny around people she thought were important. As if their success and virtuosity reflected her hard work at leading the family. "Eva has a talent for calligraphy," her grandmother said with an uncharacteristic beam. "Did you know she inked each and every one of your invitations?"

"Oh, bless her! You must have the patience of a saint," Queen Orsalide said, though the furtive glances she shot at Eva's antlers were easy to catch. It wasn't for her calligraphy or education that Queen Orsalide wanted her.

"It's just a lot of practice and dedication to the task, really," Eva said. What would they say if she also shared her accomplishments in litio wards? Would Doña Antonia still appear to be this proud of her?

"Eva, meet Don Marcelino. Her Majesty tells me he's quite the writer himself," Doña Antonia said meaningfully, gesturing to the man with the golden tooth. Not Tamarind Eyes. Not the young man who had made her blush with his attentiveness.

Don Marcelino had been mouthing something at the beautiful young woman who still sat at the table, likely both waiting for the formalities to pass so they could return to each other, so he missed Doña Antonia's cue for the introduction. Tamarind Eyes nudged him in the ribs, and Don Marcelino straightened up rather comically.

"Oh, yes, it's a pleasure, Señorita Eva," he said, while the queen mother's lips thinned in disapproval.

Eva tried to smile. She tried to force her eyes to keep this humble, grateful façade. But she already understood the situation. She had foolishly failed to notice the ring on Tamarind Eyes's fingers. He wasn't the grandson lacking direction, whom Queen Orsalide was hastily trying to pair up with a valco who could bolster his stature. Don Marcelino, the man spellbound by the full-lipped, straight-haired, voluptuous young woman at his side, was the bachelor Doña Antonia wanted to sell her off to.

It made no matter. Not after tonight.

They struggled with a brief exchange under the watchful supervision of their grandmothers, of Don Marcelino uselessly asking Eva how difficult it was to create the calligraphy she had mastered for the wedding invitations while explaining how his muse for writing was a maiden shy like a fleeing doe. Tamarind Eyes saved the day by asking them if they fancied drinks. At once Don Marcelino, his beautiful companion, and Tamarind Eyes slipped away from the Silva table. Eva's gaze flitted across the patio, meeting the crimson pair of the other antlered person in the party, recognition and meaning heavy in their eyes. But with a nod, Doña Antonia commanded Eva to follow Don Marcelino's posse. She couldn't make her move yet.

Eva sidestepped a dangerous dance floor, avoiding the long ruffling skirts of women who slapped the floor with a zeal inspired by the band's joropo. She dodged waiters and a little girl who was chasing after a barn cat. When she finally made it to the bar, Don Marcelino already had a goblet filled with wine.

"So, is there anything interesting in this city, or is heat all it has to offer?" Don Marcelino told her with an air of indifference, as his beautiful companion was caught up in conversation with one of the other guests.

Eva hesitated. "I'm afraid the heat will always be the main attraction. Unless you enjoy counterpointing."

He laughed. "Wow. I was only asking ironically. You don't actually believe I want to get to know what's interesting in this land, do you?"

Eva was at a loss.

He sipped his wine and leaned on the bar, sliding closer with a charming look that in no way matched what he said. "Every Serrano I talk to is so excited to tell me how beautiful their Llanos are and how lucky I am to be here. Sure, it's beautiful, if you only care about reedbeds and mosquitos, and this disgusting heat."

Her opinion of him solidified into stone. "Why speak to me if you're just going to insult my family?"

"I figured you would enjoy a few jabs at them. Don't tell me you're actually excited about the plans they've got for you."

"And for you," she said, accepting the refilled goblet the bartender slid her way.

"Indeed," he said, as his eyes surfed the curves of his companion. "That is why I insult them. I'm only pretending to make conversation with you because my grandmother expects it of me. She wants you to be charmed and forget about the fact that I have five uncles who have at least three sons each, so I'll be lucky if I inherit a house or even a coffer of escudos. She wants you to feel like the luckiest maiden in the world for being invited to join our family, even though I have as much chance as this bartender of ever becoming heir. But... I feel quite the opposite. As you can tell, I have good taste, so I can't be in any way excited about ending up with a bachaca like you."

Eva chucked her wine at his liqui liqui without thinking. The joropo music was loud enough that nobody noticed Don Marcelino's outrage at first. And Eva didn't linger long enough to witness it either.

Heat crawled up her cleavage and neck as she whirled on her espadrilles. "*Shit, shit, shit, shit*" was her mantra as she took to the dance floor, dodging the dancing guests. She rushed to the gardens beyond the patio, far from the music and the lights, near the solitude of an avocado tree decorated with hanging paper banners of the country's tricolor. There she leaned against the trunk, hugging herself with trembling fingers as the implications of her aggression fully unraveled in her mind. *She'd chucked her wine at a prince!* Eva gripped the fabrics of her dress hard as she imagined Doña Antonia's outrage. Despite her plans for the night, Eva couldn't shake the apprehension at the guaranteed consequences: a whipping, likely.

A shiver ran through her. Maybe they were right. She was mad, for how could the whole world say it and be wrong? She could run away from home and still carry that madness everywhere she went. In the stillness it was easy to take notice of the shadows. How they seemed to be watching her; how they waited for the moment to seize her attention.

One such shadow on the patio moved. Eva stilled. She watched the darkness in front of her as an orchestra of cicadas and crickets masked the sound of whoever or *what*ever stood before her.

"Who's there?" Eva said loudly. The spell for a protective ward came to her mind. It was a small, silly one, but it was better than nothing. She hoped she wasn't about to witness another bull fly away.

The shadow moved again, stepping into the dim light cast from the party behind them. She froze as her eyes made out a frame of average height and sharp shoulders, made tall because of the two twisting shapes sticking out of the head. *Antlers.*

Her breath hitched. The moment she had been waiting for. She exhaled in relief.

The young man took two steps forward, where he became real.

"Eva Kesaré de Galeno, pleasure to finally make your acquaintance, *in person*," he said, his voice a velvety chocolate melting at the last emphasis. Like he knew he was making her heart flutter.

Eva couldn't conjure a reply.

He filled the silence for her. "I'm sorry you had to suffer through the idiocy of a Silva." He was younger than he'd looked from the far distance of the patio. A fistful of years older than her, perhaps.

"You . . . saw that?"

"I was watching you, waiting for the moment to approach. I'm sorry it couldn't be done sooner. But I fear the mighty Doña Antonia wouldn't take too kindly to an Águila taking interest in her granddaughter."

He lifted a hand, palm side up, and produced a wisp of fire. *Geomancia*, Eva realized with a flutter in her heart, watching the golden strings twirling in and out of his pale skin. She took in his eyes as the firelight kissed him. They were the color of recently spilled blood, glossy and terrible, in a face of hollow cheeks and a pointed nose.

"Don Javier," Eva said in a weak, girlish voice. She couldn't help it. She had dreamed of this moment for too long.

Their meeting was predetermined, agreed upon in the letters they'd exchanged for nearly a year since she had initiated the connection.

Her pulse shuddered, and sweat licked the back of her neck.

"Please, call me Javier. You are no stranger to me," he said, lifting a slim hand between them, the gesture an invitation. Firelight danced in his eyes. They were unlike any she had seen before, red and rare.

Finally she took the hand of Javier Águila, son of the last fullblooded valco, and her heart was ready to drill straight through her ribs. His touch was cold and ragged. He lifted her hand to brush his lips against the back of it.

She followed him farther away from the sounds of the party. Behind the avocado tree was a carved bench, just the right length to accommodate two people. They sat together.

"So we meet," he said. "Is that disappointment I sense in your silence?"

Eva shook her head furiously. "No—no, I just can't believe it finally happened. That we made it real."

Once upon a time, she had been too scared and small-minded to imagine she would get to meet another living valco. But after witnessing the bull soar into the night, she'd written a short, desperate plea addressed to the Águilas and sent it in secret. She figured it was luck it had landed in Javier's hands.

"Thanks for coming." She tried tapering her voice so he wouldn't hear it shaking.

He smirked. "There's no need to thank me." His gaze surfed her crown, where her antlers had been oiled to appear lustrous for the party, her curls braided tightly and pinned back with a fuchsia barrette to match her dress. "I couldn't ignore the pleas of another valco. We are few and far between, and I was raised to put our kind first. I'm more than happy to take you away, as you've so eloquently pleaded in your letters."

He smiled and she blushed.

"But there is another detail I couldn't mention in our correspondence, in case it was intercepted. The matter is too delicate."

"What is it?" Eva liked the sound of his voice, the way it was raspy and androgynous. She wished to never stop hearing it.

"There are many changes occurring in my family. We're standing on a house of cards ready to collapse, and it will happen soon. This wedding and your family's invitation came at the right moment."

She nodded eagerly, for he couldn't come without his brother's blessing, and it would be impossible for an Águila to openly arrive in the city without the governor's approval. Their families were allies on paper only. The thought delighted Eva; how it would anger the mighty Doña Antonia to hear her granddaughter ran away with the valcos of the Páramo.

"It was lucky for me, too. I don't have very much time," she said. "My grandmother wants to marry me to Marcelino Silva, the swine that he is."

"All the Silvas are."

She smiled at that; how he understood her perfectly.

"What you said in your letters—you are prepared to do whatever it takes not to follow your family's command, correct?" he said.

"Yes."

Eva had initiated the correspondence by asking him if it was normal to live a life of visions. She offered to enter his service, as an apprentice or calligrapher or anything else he could find of value, as long as he freed her from this prison. When she wrote she hoped her proposition would be viable. But she never expected to see it unfold so easily. Javier reciprocated the exchange with earnestness, never missing a reply and always escalating their friendship. In his letters he had talked about what it had been like to grow up in the shadow of the strongest valco in Venazia as his brother and guardian. In turn, she'd shared lines of how it had hurt to lose her mom, the only true protector she'd had in Galeno, and her resentment for the father who'd bewitched her mother.

"What price would you pay?" he said.

"I would...not join a convent." It sounded so silly that they chuckled.

"Humor me here."

"All right."

"Wouldn't it be grand if Eva Kesaré de Galeno married a future caudillo? What if you became a caudilla?"

The humid air of the Llanos closed around her. Clouds rumbled somewhere in the distance, the breeze carrying the slightest scent of rainwater, but the night remained clear.

The question bristled her skin. She sought to flee exactly that. "You speak so lowly of my future husband, and here you are proposing to buy me just the same?"

"It is not purchasing if you do it willingly. If nothing else is exchanged. I would be a partner you already know and trust, unlike the Silva."

Eva's chest grew tight in the painful confines of her sweaty dress. She was so afraid to turn him away with the wrong answer. Javier was her only escape. "I want a new life, away from here. I want to freely be myself, the valco that I am."

"Free to practice geomancia?" he said, quoting one of her letters.

She looked down at her hands, her cheeks warming. "Yes."

"Well, Eva Kesaré, if what I propose is the price of freedom..." He shrugged. "And you are willing to pay it, aren't you? What are the alternatives? If the ascended god Rahmagut himself offered you this exit, in exchange for your hand, wouldn't you take it?"

She stood up, her heart hammering. He followed. "Please don't mock me. My whole family already does that enough." A wild thought wormed its way into her, and the words were out of her mouth before she could stop them. "How do I know you're truly Javier the valco and not some demon trying to steal me away? How do I know you're even real?" Her voice broke at the notion.

His face hardened. "So what if I'm a demon? Isn't that how the world sees us?"

The melody of a harp filled the pause between them. It was a rueful song, the kind that told stories of loss and unrequited love. The kind you were supposed to dance in the embrace of the person you loved most.

"I agree, you deserve more than Marcelino Silva. But I will leave, and tomorrow you will go back to your life. Marcelino will pretend none of it happened because he wants his grandmother's approval, which only comes with you. But that will be it. He will wed you, impregnate you, and have you as his breeder. The royal family are allies to my brother—they value valco blood. You can feel important with them—have it be your purpose. That is a choice you can make."

Eva would be offended, if what he said weren't exactly what would happen. Her gaze couldn't compete with his violent red one. "Turn the flame off," she said, and he did so, without a flicker of hesitation.

In the darkness, he said, "As I agreed in my letter, you also have the choice of coming with me."

A cuatro joined the harp in a flurry of notes, taking Eva's soul by the hand and lifting her up, up, and up.

"But if you will, I must have this guarantee."

"Why do you need me?"

"You've heard of Rahmagut's legend."

Eva blinked and grimaced. Why was he bringing that up? "Every child has. But it's just a tale—"

"The legend is true. Soon, Brother will fulfill it. He's already captured eight of the wives."

Eva covered her mouth.

"It is only a matter of time before he discovers the ninth. When that happens, I need the support of a second valco to seize Rahmagut's reward from him." He searched her eyes. "This is the matter I couldn't write about in our letters. If we succeed, Enrique will have no choice but to bow to *me*. It won't matter that it's his daughter's name and not mine in the succession papers. I will be caudillo and protector of Sadul Fuerte. And Eva Kesaré, that second valco must be you."

She frowned, for he was sharing so much, as if he knew her deepest desires. Like he was assured she was going to accept, aware her alternative was too unsavory.

"I didn't come here for your cousin's wedding. Our families think they can play us like puppets, command us here and there. Brother had no idea how much I had to gain by coming here— because *you* are here. And if I'm going to risk the wrath of my brother, the Silvas, and your family by taking you away, then I must have the guarantee of gaining something *worth it*. For ages, Brother has hounded me about forging my own legacy. Well, this is me doing it. I will need allies and a worthy partner."

Javier spoke of her as if she could supply equal influence. He saw her as worthy for her natural affinity to the arcane, the same thing earning her the scorn of her people. Maybe he had even seen the hunger in her writings and her eyes and realized she wielded the potential for more. Her chest fluttered with satisfaction. She chewed on the inside of her cheek to stop herself from smiling. This man, beautiful and valco, needed her for his conquest.

"I am not like Marcelino. I know where my worth lies. With me, you'll have the freedom to do whatever you desire, even if that is to become a caudilla as powerful as Mother—if you're willing to do what it takes."

As she clenched her jaw, Eva realized she was very willing. It didn't sound so bad, when he laid out the cards for her to truly understand.

"And in return for coming with me, for being my valco bride, I will teach you everything I know. I will give you the key to unlocking the magic in your blood." Again, quoting the letters.

Eva allowed herself a breath.

"You will be my greatest ally. Not a wife or a breeder. A woman of power, as my mother was. So, Eva Kesaré, now that I've laid out my terms, what is your choice?"

"I can't stay anywhere near Galeno if I go with you. My grandparents would hunt us down."

He held her eyes captive. "We cannot stay in Venazia for this. The place of the invocation is in Fedria."

Fedria, the sister land east of Venazia. Eva could feel her heartbeat at her throat, at her fingertips, tingling every vein and vessel in her body. Images of everything she'd ever imagined about Fedria flashed through her mind: The sun bronzing her skin as she beheld the enormity of the Fedrian jungles. Feasting on snappers freshly caught off the aquamarine waters of the Cow Sea.

"This is a dream, right? I'll wake up at any moment now."

His smile was small but comforting. He seized her hands, and this time they were warm. "Don't vacillate, Eva Kesaré. I won't stand for it. I'm not your savior—merely a partner in business. What is your answer?"

Where their skin touched, his energy coursed to her veins, heightening Eva's senses. She was seeing unlike she had seen before, the darkness of the yard becoming less black. It allowed her to take in his face again, edged and determined and femininely handsome.

Behind him, a bright blotch streaked the inkiness of night, more dazzling than any star to have ever crossed the skies. It was a ball of blazing cyan barely surfing the horizon. A rising celestial body—and her sign, Eva decided, giving her the courage to mirror his determination.

"I will come with you. With your terms," she whispered in awe.

Javier caught her eyes and turned around to see the line ripping the night. The corners of his lips curved upward. "It has begun," he said.

"What has?"

His gaze caressed her like she was more stunning than the sun, the moon, and even that cyan star combined. "Our new life."

20

The Caudillo's Loyal Servant

Reina never imagined, when she left Celeste after seeing the sign, that it would be the last time she saw her in Águila Manor.

Her hands had tingled in foreboding, and her shoulders were heavy with dread all the way down the mountain. They parted ways at Celeste's bedroom, Celeste in denial. Reina ran to her grandmother's laboratory to scour the constellations in the star map, her belly wringing for the possibility of a misplaced star or dot, for the slightest deviation signaling their discovery was merely a false alarm. What she found only had the opposite effect.

Before Reina could bring the confirmation to Celeste, though, Doña Ursulina snared her with an assignment to Sadul Fuerte, which she dutifully accepted like any other to avoid raising suspicion. She didn't have a reason to hide Celeste's truth from Doña Ursulina, not a logical one at least. Reina withheld the information on a gut reaction, or maybe because she simply wasn't ready to accept it herself.

She would have stayed in denial, too, if on the fourth night of her stay in Sadul Fuerte she hadn't stumbled upon a crowd of people on the plaza facing the cathedral and seen them pointing upward, marveling at the cyan ball streaking the inky sky. The sight sucked the breath out of her, along with her vacillation. Rahmagut's Claw. That night, in the cold room of the nondescript inn where she had stayed all those days for the assignment, she dreamed again of following the canopied jungle path to the lagoon.

She was held up in Sadul Fuerte for her task of guarding an iridio shipment until it was transferred to its buyer, who didn't show up until the afternoon. The day was nearly over when Reina finally made it back into the manor, and by then the whole staff was buzzing with the gossip of Celeste's vanishing.

A cook and a chambermaid crossed the cobbled path, exchanging whispers and glancing at Reina as she unloaded her mule in the yard, which at first wasn't out of the ordinary, with the amount of prejudice tossed her way daily. But Reina was high on a bismuto incantation she had cast while fighting off a Páramo ghoul near the estate. Her enhanced ears picked up their gossip, of how Celeste hadn't been seen for several days. Then a stable boy cornered Reina as she refilled a pail of water for the mule, and he told her, "You better put on your espadrilles, 'cause what's coming is joropo," which was the overly complicated way for people from the Llanos to say that Reina better get ready for what was coming, because Don Enrique was summoning her to his study and he was in a mood.

The second story of the manor was an empty place, the quiet shattered by rain pattering against the windows. Reina paused in front of Doña Feleva's portrait to brace herself.

Between Don Enrique's door and his mother's portrait was a painting of Doña Laurel. Don Enrique had commissioned the painting in a more modest frame because nothing else could suit the Benevolent Lady. In it, she was surrounded by the rosebushes she maintained around the entryway steps to Águila Manor, and she was dressed in a blue dress and ruana, her signature color.

Reina sucked in a breath through her nose. How she missed Doña Laurel and the happiness she had brought to their lives. But now that the moment had arrived, Reina hated the way Celeste was involved.

A vast room of intricate crimson tiles and stone walls welcomed her. Don Enrique awaited her behind a desk of cherry, where he was surrounded by bookshelves, the leather map of Venazia and Fedria, and a plaque engraved with his family's crest. On the lounging love chair at the center sat Doña Ursulina. And next to her sat the last person Reina ever imagined seeing here.

A young woman of pale, freckled skin. A blue gown hugging a plump figure.

Maior.

Only Reina couldn't be sure it was Maior. She blinked, and she saw the striking eyes of the late Doña Laurel. She blinked again, and there was Maior. One image superimposed over another, as if alien thoughts were forcing her to believe this was the Benevolent Lady. Only this vision was realer than even the most realistic of paintings, as if Doña Laurel were truly back.

Reina shut her gaping mouth and bowed. "Don Enrique. Doña Ursulina."

Doña Ursulina watched her with not a care in the world, her hand petting the woman's knee. Yet there was no life in the woman's eyes. They were open, yes, but without gleam or recognition. A doll to advertise. Reina's belly knotted as understanding wormed itself into her like spoiled food. They were so close to their objective, and this was nothing more than a flaunt of all the caudillo had to gain, Doña Ursulina taunting them with a taste of their reward. After all, to reanimate the Benevolent Lady, they needed a living body.

"Señor, you summoned me," Reina said.

Don Enrique beckoned her closer, so she took the seat across from his desk. He stared Reina down with an impervious gaze of the deepest red. "Where is Celeste?"

Reina's jaw locked. Her brows pinched, and perhaps it was the sign she was clutching a secret.

When he repeated, "Where is my daughter?" Reina knew it would be trouble if she didn't answer.

"I don't know. I just got back from Sadul Fuerte—"

The desk tremored as Don Enrique brought a lightning-fast fist down to it. The ink bottle to his right swiveled dangerously, a minuscule motion away from tipping over. "You'd best have an answer for me, Duvianos, or I'll make you rue the day you ever set foot in my home."

Reina's heart shuddered and shriveled as she realized the caudillo didn't know where Celeste was either. But the way he talked to Reina—she didn't deserve this. "I've been away. I—I thought she was here."

Don Enrique's jaw tightened, the line sharp as a polished blade. "Celeste is nowhere to be found. A servant saw her with you on the night she disappeared."

"Don Enrique, we were just following Doña Ursulina's test of the eighth dama—"

"Don't interrupt the caudillo," her grandmother said.

"I know she didn't go with you to Sadul Fuerte," Don Enrique snapped. "I have informants in the city and in my forts. Celeste is not easy to miss. But you...she tells you everything. You visit her room, at *inappropriate hours* even, and you mean to tell me she didn't trust you with her childish plan to disappear?"

The assertion was like a knife to the back. Celeste couldn't have run away. She would have told Reina.

"Speak! Or are you a mute?" Don Enrique said.

"There was no plan," Reina said. "If Celeste is gone, then she didn't plan it. What if she's in danger? What if—"

Doña Ursulina snorted.

Don Enrique turned to her. "What is it?"

Doña Ursulina waved a languid hand, tittering. "Look at her, deflecting with talk of Celeste being in danger. Danger of what, exactly? Pray tell, who sees those valco antlers and decides they want to cross the daughter of the most powerful man in Venazia?" Her shrewd eyes fell on Reina. "Don Enrique, it's obvious she doesn't know. True, she's like a puppy to Celeste, but she would tell us if she were keeping secrets for her. Let us end this charade."

Reina's fists were clenched and blood-drained, her nails threatening to bite through her skin. She focused on that pain. She squeezed hard so she wouldn't have to feel the disgust radiating off the caudillo's gaze.

Don Enrique rose to tower over the desk. "Your purpose in my home has always been a precarious one. Lately I have wondered why I'm keeping you at all. And if you can't even be bothered to protect my daughter—to stop her from whatever ridiculous game she's playing—then I have no use for you."

Reina's gaze glued to the desk. She couldn't look the caudillo in the eye. She wasn't useless. She wasn't like the kitchen slaves of Segolita, never daring to pursue a better life just because their blood was nozariel. She had trained and bled and endured Doña Ursulina's tutelage. She had kidnapped women and deposited innocent babes on the mountain.

She was not useless.

Don Enrique went on. "If you can't even be useful to me now, then your employment in my household is obviously nothing but a waste of resources."

"Don Enrique," Doña Ursulina purred, conversationally, as if seeing Reina berated were as interesting a sight as the frailejones, "the Benevolent Lady Laurel trusted her, and Celeste still does. There is use for her."

"And you expect me to care for your opinion?" Don Enrique snapped. "She's daughter of your son! And from what I hear, with tastes that clearly must run in your blood."

Reina frowned and extended a glance at her grandmother. What was that supposed to mean?

"Señor—"

"Silence, Ursulina."

Reina's eyes fell on Maior. With her hands folded over each other and her eyes vacant, Maior was a pretty but wretched imitation of Doña Laurel. Disgust flooded her as she imagined the use the caudillo was planning for Maior.

"I allowed her here under the assumption of her strength—that she would be capable like Juan Vicente—but I've yet to see any of it."

"I'm not useless," Reina muttered, the sight of Maior feeding her nerve.

"What did you say to me?"

Reina welcomed the anger like an old friend. She rose to her feet. "I am not weak. I kidnapped those girls. I brought them to your dungeon. I left innocent babes on the mountain. You should see me as worthy."

It stunned Don Enrique and Doña Ursulina into silence.

"I've earned my keep and devoted myself to your cause and to Celeste. Not only because Doña Laurel and Doña Ursulina wanted it of me, but because Celeste's my friend." The words rushed out of her, fast and hot. "If she's gone, then she didn't plan it. It must have been against her will."

She almost spilled Celeste's secret to reaffirm her conviction. Or the truth about Doña Laurel's hidden mountain home, in the hope that they might find Celeste hiding there after all. But seeing Maior like a puppet by Doña Ursulina's side made Reina realize she didn't trust Don Enrique's intentions. Did the pursuit of Rahmagut's legend twist his mind? Or had his heart already been rotten, even when Doña Laurel had been alive?

Her heart pumped so hard it ached, but Reina couldn't back down.

"If you don't believe me—that I'm more than a duskling and that my loyalty is to you—then let me prove myself. I will gladly find her. I don't know where she is, but Celeste wouldn't just leave without telling anyone. She's not...she's not selfish. She would at least tell me. And I would do anything to protect her."

Don Enrique stared her down, but this time Reina didn't look away. Even if the seconds were nothing but pallbearers, escorting time to Reina's undoing under the caudillo's wrath. She couldn't look away.

"If I say you are weak, it is because I see you and know it," Don Enrique said in a low, dangerous tone. "I could snap your neck here and now to end your misery if I so desired. Your insecurities reek, and that fake heart of yours betrays you." He smiled, but there was no mirth in his eyes. "Because I value loyalty, I will give you this opportunity you cry for. I will let you show us if your words are true."

"All we need are her whereabouts," Doña Ursulina said as she stroked the thick locks of the doll beside her.

"Do not make me silence you again, Ursulina," the caudillo snarled, never once peeling his gaze from Reina's.

Reina didn't see it, but she could feel her grandmother's outrage.

With one swift movement, he cleared the clutter from his desk. Scrolls, quills, and seals rolled to the ground, ink spilling and documents flying. He uncapped the fat ring on his thumb and emptied bits of iridio potion over the desk. It was but a sliver of sparkly black fluid, the viscosity like milk. With his left index finger, he spread it into the shape of a sigil, tracing a pattern to trigger an incantation of iridio. He gestured at Reina with his gaze and said, "Do it. Swear those words to the stars that watch us."

Reina's blood pumped hot and fast, tingling her ears and stinging her underarms. She slapped her dominant hand against the sigil, her bared palm burning from the lick of corrosion. Don Enrique did the same.

With Don Enrique's left palm and Reina's right splayed against the moist wood, Reina said, "I will bring Celeste back—"

"You vow not to return without her."

"I'll find her and help her return, unscathed—"

"Unscathed and unspoiled, for she left as a maiden, and as a maiden she will return."

"It'll be the proof of my loyalty, and in return—"

"And only with Celeste at your side will you be allowed to course these corridors again. For without her, you are banished."

Reina stared at the caudillo, speechless. In her shocked pause, the incantation sealed into place.

The air was sucked from the room and into a parallel plane with a whirlwind, then thrust back in. The sigil glimmered red under their palms—the color of his dominant personality trait, brightly visible thanks to the bismuto spell still burning through her—and the agreement sealed into a pact.

"Now, hold on—" But before Reina could muster a full sentence, jabs of iridio shot at her chest, flowing around her heart like scalding water. "*No*," she sucked in the air, the chair saving her from recoiling against the ground.

"You no longer belong in this manor," Don Enrique said. "Even your grandmother can attest to it."

The incantation had been a trick, mocking her for all the scars she had earned under the Águila banner. Reina wanted to howl. To curse him with every droplet of anger boiling in her. Instead, once she was able to suck a breath into her lungs, she glared at him with her lips trembling in indignation. Against the caudillo, there was nothing she could do.

Finally Don Enrique said, "You want to earn your place in my army? Bring me my daughter. Or else be gone and never return."

Reina didn't grant him a nod of reply. She whirled on the spot and left.

21

The Duvianos Heir

Reina's boots took her out of his study in a stomping rage. She didn't care for the servants' eyes that followed her in curiosity. Nor if her scowl or her slamming of doors seeded the gossip of her banishing. A weight settled in her heart, like Don Enrique's incantation truly was kicking her out of the manor. It was a thought Reina refused to accept. That was, until she reached the building of the servants' quarters, where she found the final gift from the caudillo in her bedchamber.

Everything she owned had been searched and carelessly upturned. Her bed and sheets, her clothes, her chest of possessions, even her sparring clothes and potions were broken and strewn across the floor. Like they'd been hoping to find the truth about Celeste's disappearance within her things, in the process showing how little regard they had for her.

Reina slammed her fist against the doorframe. *"No."*

She leapt to the dresser across the room, where one door was smashed and the other hung meekly by the hinges. There the coffer of her gold savings sat open and empty, with nothing in it but dust.

All of it, gone.

The gold she had saved up during her two-year employment with the Águilas. The escudos that were supposed to be her pathway to establishing herself in this new home.

She slammed the coffer lid shut, then slammed the dresser door until it gave. Instead of taking careful steps to her bed, she kicked everything to the wall. The books, the accessories, the mementos Celeste had gifted her. In her rage she punched and kicked and broke the pieces until all were trash. *Trash*, she thought vehemently, as Don Enrique saw her.

She forced a deep breath.

Her torso knotted with a foreign jab. Reina slipped out of her vest, unbuttoned her shirt, and unwrapped the cotton bindings that flattened her breasts. When she faced the silver plate nailed to the wall, she saw a brown-skinned woman with a piece of ore protruding above her left breast. Flesh and sinew grew over the tubes and edges of the black ore, a chorus of fervent whispering electrifying the air as Reina's hand neared its epicenter. A thousand rushed, guttural voices, like the sudden pitter-patter of demons scuttling through corridors. Months ago, during a lesson on void magic, Doña Ursulina had confirmed Reina's suspicions of the chattering voices being the manifestation of every iridio spell ever invoked. The good and, obviously, the wicked ones.

Her hand hesitated, not because of the susurration but due to the crimson stain advancing upward from the bottommost corner, like a rot. She touched the spreading red, and a searing fire shot through her.

It was the incantation she had agreed to, to bring Celeste back at all costs.

Celeste, who was a Dama del Vacío. Who was simultaneously missing *and* the only person standing in the way of bringing Doña Laurel back from the dead. The heaviness in Reina's chest constricted her even more. She backed up against the bed, surrendering to it as exhaustion squeezed the air out of her.

She couldn't accept that Celeste had been taken. She didn't believe it. Likely she was hiding in Gegania, away from Don Enrique's madness and Doña Ursulina's ambition, in the place only Reina knew of. Celeste hated their pursuit of the legend, but what she didn't understand was that the coldness in her life could so easily be fixed by Doña Laurel's return. Celeste didn't see it, but Reina was doing this for her.

Reina wrapped her chest and buttoned up her shirt. Her shoulders shuddered from her sobering up. How foolish she was acting, breaking trinkets as if losing some escudos was the end of the world. It wasn't. She didn't know where Celeste was or if she was in the danger Don Enrique professed. What she did know was the ache in her very core, gnawing and cold and straining her bones, which told her losing Celeste *would* be the end of her world. Reina needed to make sure she was safe. She needed to earn her welcome back into the manor and shatter Don Enrique's curse, so that she might resume her future as it was meant to be. As Doña Ursulina's successor and the protector of Celeste's heart. She had to make Celeste realize all there was to gain from having Rahmagut's favor. They had to finish what they had started. Otherwise all those deaths she'd witnessed and been complicit in would be for nothing. If Celeste cared for her, then she would see how much Reina needed this.

In her chest, her transplant flapped like a useless, dying trout. Celeste cared. Reina was sure of it.

Reina rummaged for the few items that remained unbroken and stuffed them into her traveling knapsack. Her potion flasks were shattered, but she still had the pair of bismuto rings on her fingers. She spared the room one last glance, hoisted her knapsack, turned to the doorway, and froze.

Doña Ursulina was standing right outside her door.

The scars on Reina's chest itched and screamed.

"Take a walk with me."

Reina did so, following her until they were well beyond the damp darkness of the gardens, past patches of mud and under a tree still weeping with leftover rainwater. Doña Ursulina turned to her, the evening lights of the manor glowing behind her at a distance. She had changed into a tight-fitting jacket and pants, black as the night.

"I never imagined you would be this stupid, when I brought you into my life," Doña Ursulina growled. "When you find Celeste, you bring her to me. Do you understand? You forget about Enrique."

"But I have to prove to the caudillo—I'm banished—"

"Your fealty is to me, not to him, you fool. Your little spew about loyalty, it was inspiring—a little touching, even—but see where it got you. You're a fool for promising Enrique anything—and now you've gone and made a pact with iridio? Iridio keeps you alive, or have you forgotten?"

"He was treating me like a traitor!" Reina said and flinched, already imagining the sting of Doña Ursulina's backhand for her insolence.

Instead, Doña Ursulina grazed the side of Reina's jaw with her fingers—a tender threat. "Enrique's never cared about you, and he's not about to start, regardless of whether or not you return his beloved brat."

"His men ransacked my room! They took my escudos." Reina didn't know what made her say it or if Doña Ursulina would care at all.

"They wanted to see what you knew, under Enrique's orders. See? And you would pledge your loyalty to someone who treats you like that? I might have been stern with you, but it was for your own education. If it were up to Enrique alone, you wouldn't be welcome in this manor at all. Your time here wouldn't have expired if you hadn't decided to air out the dirty laundry—if you had just kept your mouth shut. Do you think he doesn't know what you have done for him? Enrique hardly acknowledges the things that benefit him. He never gives credit where it is due."

Blood flushed Reina's face. In hindsight she should have controlled her emotions.

"Without his blessing, you'll have no choice but to return to the cockroach nest that is Segolita." Despite the darkness, the glint of Doña Ursulina's smiling teeth was unmissable. "Unless, of course, you become my successor."

Reina forgot to breathe in the silence. But she'd heard correctly. "Now?" she said in a weak voice.

The skies clamored around them, the air smelling like the rains weren't through with the night.

"Yes, now. When else?" Doña Ursulina said, her long pointed nail lifting Reina's chin to better gaze into her eyes. "My blood ends with you. Why else would I waste my time saving you, educating you?"

When her nail let go, she made a grasping gesture in the air between them. A sharp tang filled Reina's lungs. Something clutched her heart, reeling it in, as if Doña Ursulina had the power to crush it in her half-open palm.

"Why else impart the capability to control the very thing keeping you alive?" She yanked Reina's shirt open, revealing her chest to the bite of the Páramo air. "I wanted a useful, obedient heir." She yanked Reina's bindings down, then dug her talon-like fingernails around the iridio ore latched to Reina's artificial heart. "Not one who would abandon me like Juan Vicente did."

Reina couldn't move. She lost her breath and for a second was sure she'd never get it back.

"So, as a guarantee that you will be obedient—that you will return to me—I shall be taking this," Doña Ursulina said, dislodging the ore from its socket. It disconnected with a click, exposing the crystal cladding beneath, which protected the pump feeding life into Reina's body.

Reina's breath returned with a painful gasp. Her knees went buttery, but Doña Ursulina's influence kept her rooted to the spot. Unable to move or fall.

Her grandmother held the ore in front of her, like hanging a bone over a hound's head. It hissed with a thousand devilish iridio spells, mocking Reina. Her transplant heart still pumped as frantically as it could, for it still had iridio *solution* surging through its tubes and chambers. Only, without the ore to replenish that iridio solution, every passing second truly was a pallbearer escorting her to the end.

A fat droplet of rainwater landed on the bridge of Reina's nose. The freedom to move returned to her. "Why?" she croaked out, steadying on her feet and fighting the dizziness, the panic, and the *tears* as she fumbled to button her shirt up. "Why take it from me?"

"I have invested so much in you, and my trust has been thoroughly shattered in the past. I cannot afford to lose another one."

Another one. Another son; another heir.

Reina's gaze held her grandmother's. She wanted to reach out, to reassure her that she would be true and return, for she had so much to thank Doña Ursulina for. This was the family they had, all tatters and tainted edges, but it was still their relationship and their shared blood. Yet the deed had been done, the ore unlatched. If anything, it only felt like a knife rending their bond as Rahmagut's Claw tore the sky.

"Find Celeste. Make her understand it is only a draw of blood. You bring her to me, and I shall give this back to you, along with much, much more."

Reina frowned as the truth opened between them, at the shock. She was a fool for feeling surprised. For not assuming Doña Ursulina would be a step ahead in knowing.

Her hand shot out to grip Doña Ursulina's wrist, to stop her. This time she didn't care if she crossed a line. "But I'll die without the ore."

Doña Ursulina's toothy smirk flashed white in the darkness. "Indeed. These ores are as rare as they come. From the great fallen star. You will either become enslaved to iridio potions, or you will bring me Celeste and become the obedient heir I'm asking you to be."

Heir. Reina didn't miss the bone thrown her way, even as she understood her grandmother was merely exercising her cunning by tossing it. Though the promise was true enough. Doña Ursulina, like Reina, had no one else, both of them drawn from the same stock.

There was a rustle as Doña Ursulina fished under her jacket, then pulled out the pendant hanging from her neck. "Here's enough iridio potion to carry you through, once whatever's left in your heart runs out." She withdrew a velvet pouch jingling with escudos. "And some gold, in case you need it."

Reina accepted it, her jaw rippling as their hands touched in the exchange.

"Do not look so grim. We have less than twenty days."

Twenty days to find and bring her Celeste, or perish from her starved heart. How she felt a fool, thinking she could have kept Celeste's truth a secret from her grandmother.

"How long have you known? Did you always intend to leave her for last?" Reina had lost so much, she might as well take a shovel and dig her own grave.

There was no answer, but she could *feel* her grandmother's smile. "Does Don Enrique know?"

Doña Ursulina lifted her chin once again. At that instant, the sky split in lightning that revealed her hungry eyes. "Even if he did, do you doubt he would force Celeste to give her blood? For the return of his beloved wife?"

"I'm not going to force Celeste into anything."

Doña Ursulina's silence warned Reina of her outrage. "No, you will not." She pointed to the night, where black-shrouding rain clouds blocked the view to the traveling star. "You will bring her to the tomb in Tierra'e Sol before Rahmagut's Claw finishes its journey through our skies. There you will meet me, and I will bring you your ore."

Reina took in a heady breath, letting her grandmother's plan steady her. Despite her monumental stupidity with the caudillo, they had a way forward.

"You'll bring the other damas?"

"Yes." Doña Ursulina paused. She was ready to leave, as if their exchange were nothing but a trifle. Reina could taste it in the air. Suddenly Doña Ursulina squeezed Reina's wrist, yanking her closer so Reina wouldn't miss it. "Reina, with Rahmagut's favor, you can ask for a brand-new heart." She raised the ore between them, which was as black as the night enveloping them. "You can make iridio irrelevant to your life. Do not miss the chance."

Her grandmother didn't care for a goodbye. She simply turned and disappeared into the damp darkness of the estate. Reina watched her go as her chest throbbed and begged for sustenance, each gulp of air feeling inadequate and leaving her starved. Hot tears burned the corners of her eyes as she glared up at the sky—at the vast domain of Rahmagut's Claw. With all the strength her lungs had to offer, she shouted a curse that was drowned out by thunder and answered in rain.

22

A Contract of Iridio

Eva wasn't sure what to expect when she gathered her geomancia rings and, with just the clothes on her person, allowed Javier to spirit her away. They traveled with his guard, a party of six armored men wearing high-necked jackets embroidered with laurels and the ivory-and-gold eagle crest of the Águilas. They covered as much distance as they could in their gilded carriage at nighttime. Then the guards dropped them off at the river docks of a fishing village on the banks of Río'e Marle (as a gilded carriage made for a conspicuous traveling party) at dawn, and Javier paid a boatman who escorted them for another full day and night by river. As twilight unveiled the following morning, the boat left them near a swampy lowland dominated by moriche palm trees. The road hugged the edges of the morichal and, as Javier assured her, would take them to a port by the Fedrian border.

Just two days' travel meant they weren't too far off from Galeno. Yet it was the farthest Eva had ever been from home. As farmers and traders joined the hard-packed road with their horses or mules hauling produce, Eva couldn't help stealing glances over her shoulder, expecting to see a familiar face who would yank her back to Galeno by the hair. Surely her grandmother would send a search party after her or put a bounty on her return. Eva couldn't imagine Doña Antonia ever forgetting this slight or admitting to the Galeno gentry that her granddaughter was courageous enough to abandon them of her own accord.

Eva stole secret glances at Javier as the long dirt road opened to the fringes of the port town, where a white chapel stood with its golden cross reflecting morning sunlight. He was a real person. Not a savior born out of her fantasies. A tangible, handsome valco man dressed in a vest of midnight blue and carrying a knapsack twinkling with flasks of geomancia reagents, he later told her.

The respect with which he regarded her was an assurance, even though every inch of her skin screamed that she had reached new levels of madness. Because it had been mad, to abandon the Serranos like this. Yet Eva felt so sure of her path.

The chapel was the first building on a cobbled street where other colorfully painted adobe houses welcomed them. The morning air was hot, smelling of fresh bread and, faintly, of roasted pork. A Pentimiento preacher beckoned all passersby toward the chapel, his booming voice announcing the beginning of the Saint Jon the Shepherd celebrations.

"Hopefully we'll be out of town before the procession starts, and we won't get stuck in them," Javier said with a tinge of annoyance.

She understood his meaning. In Galeno the whole city amassed to follow the Saint Jon the Shepherd statuette. The celebrations were a revel of singing and dancing to the beat of drums. Eva was delighted to see other places partook in it.

"Where are we?" she asked him.

"In El Carmín."

"We're already at the border? Heading straight to Fedria?" she said, hoping her knowledge of the world would make him forget everything inadequate about her.

He nodded. "First we marry. Then we seek Rahmagut's reward."

The way he said it—like it was written in the laws of fate, with its inevitability—made her chest soar.

He led her to a three-story inn near the town square, with clay-tiled roofing and orange paint chipping off the adobe walls. By the entryway was a cluster of gambling men. They sat in a circle and placed painted cards on a wheel, which was attached to a wound figurine that spun its pointed hand to choose the winning card.

"Calamity," Eva said as she watched the game master, also called the arbiter, who kept the winning prize in a bucket by his side. "Look how many escudos they've got."

"Oh, yes—but don't get too excited. They would never let you place a bet," Javier said.

To humans and nozariels, Calamity was a game of luck. But playing against a valco, who could see the workings of its magic, was a fool's bargain.

Eva glanced up at Javier's curving antlers as he held the door open for her. They were the most majestic thing she had ever seen. She touched her bangs, which she kept layered at the crown to hide her stunted ones.

The scent of roasted corn jumped out of every crevice inside the inn. Groups of people were scattered across mismatched tables, some drinking the hangover away, some enjoying a coffee to break their fast.

Eva and Javier settled on a table near an abandoned corner, away from curious eyes, and were approached moments later by a strange man. Strange because Eva never imagined seeing the tips of his ears pointing up at a stark angle or the scaly skin draping the bridge of his nose.

"What do my masters fancy?" the middle-aged man said, his fast-paced Fedrian accent stomping every *t* with vigor.

Javier waved him off. "Whatever's the special. And three cups of your house coffee."

Eva waited until the man walked away, then leaned forward on the table and said, "He's nozariel."

"Indeed."

"I thought...they are banished from this land." Her grandfather had once told her how, before she was born, he had given the order to round up all nozariels in Galeno in many great cages to transport them to Fedria, where the Liberator was offering them asylum. That was before she'd met Doña Rosa.

"Oh, they are. But it is more work for the politicians in the capital to enforce their banishing than it is to look the other way.

Besides, this is El Carmín. You can't do anything in this town without having some wretch serve you. I suppose it helps. Their labor is cheaper than dirt."

Eva frowned. She tried not to think too much of the memory of Doña Rosa, of imagining her agonized screams when she'd been burned alive by the archbishop. Eva hadn't been around to witness the brutal scene, but her heart ached and she cried for several nights after Décima shared the news with a veneer hardly shrouding her glee. Sometimes when she woke up from nightmares of Doña Rosa, where Eva was the one being burned alive for rejecting the conventions of Galeno, Eva welcomed the sorrow and the fear. For she had been a coward, and she deserved them.

"You should probably get used to it. We *are* traveling to Fedria."

Eva cleared her throat, shooting furtive glances at the two servers walking between tables and carrying coffees and food. All were missing their tails, likely cut off soon after birth. If one didn't look too hard, they could pass as regular humans.

"But how can they live so openly here? Couldn't a caudillo's army come and deport them—or worse, jail them?" They would have no recourse should a madman decide to murder them, like the archbishop had immolated Doña Rosa.

"I suppose the measly escudos they earn are worth the risk. You see them all over El Carmín because it's more trouble than it's worth to hunt them out, especially as we're right at the crossing. They're like cockroaches. They always find a way in."

Eva wrung her hands under the table. She hated hearing the words, especially with how they were in perfect dissonance with the gentle tenor of his voice. "Have you met many nozariels?"

He shrugged. "I've had to travel all over Venazia for the family business of dealing iridio, and I've seen them everywhere. After a while you start realizing they take the labor no one else will do. Humans are hypocrites in that way, shunning them while profiting off their work." He smirked. "Didn't your family own more than a hundred nozariel slaves before the revolution?"

"Before I was born," she emphasized. "It's a part of my family history I'm not proud about."

"Don't fret. You will not be paying reparations in your lifetime."

Eva faked a smile, which he saw right through.

He laughed. "Eva, you and I are going to be profiting off the humans. It's the natural pecking order."

The server returned with a dish of cachapas and queso de mano. Melting between the folded flat bread made of sweet, chunky corn dough was the thick slab of cheese. As Eva finished her dish, strings of cheese spilling onto her plate, a third person joined them.

He grabbed a chair from a neighboring table and took a side of theirs, as if he'd meant to meet them all along. The man wore the velvety red-and-black robes of a Pentimiento cleric and introduced himself as Javier's servant. Then, after some pleasantries, he produced a scroll, which he unfurled on the table.

"Blessed by the archbishop of Sadul Fuerte and approved by the governor. No one will be questioning their legitimacy."

Eva inched forward to catch a glimpse of the writing. The ink was the color of soot, but she could see its magic in the way golden words superimposed the text. "What are these?"

"Marriage papers," Javier explained.

"Marriage papers," she repeated with butterflies in her belly.

It all seemed so perfectly planned, and fast. Only nights ago, Javier had approached her in the darkness of Galeno with his proposition. But as Eva read the scroll, she realized he had fully expected her to accept all along.

The cleric gave Eva a cold look, his gaze surfing over her messy hair. "Sí, señorita, it's improper for a highborn lady like yourself to travel alone or escorted by a male companion who isn't your husband."

Javier nodded and said, "Imagine the sort of gossip, if someone were to recognize either you or me along the way. They would question your virtue. Of all people, you understand the sort of weight that is placed on a woman's honor and name."

Eva stiffened. She wondered if he knew of her mother, then felt a fool for thinking he wouldn't. How juicy the gossip would be, if Dulce Serrano's ill-begotten daughter became a wild runaway, indulging in the company of men without a husband to protect her virtue. Eva enjoyed the thought, in a spiteful way, as she imagined the headache the rumors would cause her grandmother.

"I didn't think it would be so soon," she said.

Javier's pale hand slid forward, palm side up, beckoning her hand to drape over his. "As we discussed, I will need this guarantee. You are important to the success of my legacy, Eva Kesaré."

Her hand inched to his. His touch was cold when their palms came into contact, but energy pulsed there. It bit her skin as it flowed from his hand to hers.

"Soon, Brother will wonder why I haven't returned from your cousin's wedding. He'll realize his daughter is gone and will start creating imaginary scenarios in his head—for he never had any love for me. I am risking much, and should anything go wrong, I will lose a lot, if not all. So, yes, it would be false of me not to admit that I have high expectations of what we can accomplish together."

"You were prepared for this," she said softly, hoping the intruding cleric would leave their table so they could have this conversation in private.

His gaze surfed up to her crown, where her valco mark was hidden beneath her curls. "Do you deny you have the ambition I'm asking of you? The hunger for more?"

Eva's jaw clenched tight.

"Your choice spoke volumes to me. And who else would give you what you want?"

Her ears burned at his truth. There was no better companion for her chosen path.

"So, before we proceed, I ask that you fulfill your part of the bargain. We can't continue to hesitate. Rahmagut's Claw has begun its journey through the skies."

Indeed it had, the majestic traveling star.

"You and I are valco," Javier said, and she again marveled at the height of his antlers.

"It's the best match I could have hoped for," Eva said with her chin raised high, meaning it. His mother had become legend. His name was worth all the iridio in the world. If anything, she should be the one begging him.

To that, he smiled the slightest bit.

She glanced at the golden ink. A marriage signed in magic. Enchantments in marriage papers were entirely unheard of in Galeno. But coming from a valco of Sadul Fuerte, it made sense.

The cleric went on. "After signing, you will be the luckiest woman for marrying Don Javier, who is the future of the Águilas."

Eva forced herself not to indulge the thought or blush from it. After all the stories her mother, Dulce, had told her of Feleva Águila, Eva had never imagined she would end up marrying *her son*.

"I'll do it. But I'd like a moment first," she said.

The way the red in Javier's eyes flared made the tiny hairs along Eva's spine stand on end.

Something in her gut, built solely on intuition and keeping generations of her ancestors alive, screamed at her that this was dangerous. It told her to *run*.

But he just nodded. His gaze on her was mild, his left eye hiding behind strands of that luxurious starlight hair. "Of course. We have until nightfall to get this sorted out. But don't forget, our time is short."

Eva walked past the town plaza, where the great stone bridge connecting Venazia and Fedria began. Morning light glistened over Río'e Marle's tranquil brown-green surface, interrupted only by the beady eyes of hiding caimans and turtles poking their heads out. Moriche palm trees lined the river to both sides, their centers heavy with fruit and their palms dancing in the humid breeze of the Llanos. If beyond the river was the land of nozariels, who worshipped other deities with Ches and Rahmagut among them, did that make it the epicenter of Rahmagut's legend? Ahead of her was a land of magic and a frontier Eva had acknowledged only in the maps hanging in the governor's office, and never as a place she could visit.

A delightful shiver lifted her arm hairs at the promise of her future with Javier. He was going to teach her how to be a proper valco, with all the knowledge of geomancia he had inherited from the legendary Feleva. He wasn't demanding the typical duties of a wife, of getting sons or rooting her in a house in Sadul Fuerte as a trophy. Instead, he sweetened her with the potential of her breed and as a conspirator in building a legacy. All the things she wanted. Eva smiled. It felt good, to be desired this way. And to know that for as long as he needed her, they stood on equal ground.

All she had to do was accept, sign her freedom away in a binding magical document. She snorted at the thought. She'd never had freedom. Leaving had been the first leap of trust to take control over her life.

Javier had talked about his conquest. But what Eva had failed to disclose was this act would be part of *her* conquest. She was tired of being meek, of others forcing her to satisfy their expectations of her. Now she would do whatever it took to become the person she'd been born to be.

Eva walked back to the inn with a strange lightness in her chest. She stalled near the entrance, where a small but thriving crowd gathered around the Calamity game. At the center of the crowd was the arbiter, who was nudging a bucket of escudos with one hand while beckoning bystanders with the other.

"Wagers! Place your wagers! Test Rahmagut's influence over your life!"

Eva allowed herself to be sucked into the hubbub, curious. The game was about Ches and Rahmagut's ancient war. The event that supposedly rent the world, shaping oceans and upsurging mountains. Pentimiento preachers rejected the story as well as the existence of Ches and Rahmagut. They rejected the idea of a world created by a conflict of gods, of a world not gifted to humans by the Virgin, as perfect and balanced as it was. It was a game Doña Antonia forbade her progeny to play. In a pious city like Galeno, Calamity was only played in underground scenes, spurred by travelers not completely enthralled by the Pentimiento beliefs deeming Rahmagut a demon of darkness and Ches a charlatan.

"Ches and Rahmagut are here to answer your pleas for riches," the arbiter went on. "Give yourself the test of faith. Will the gods

intervene in your wager? The sure way to lose is not to try at all!"
He patted the edges of his bucket, which was brimming.

Eva's fingers dug into her curly bangs, as a reminder that the antlers were hidden beneath her mane. With the ability to see the game's
magic, she would have an unfair advantage if she dared play. Had she
any escudos, she would join. So, for now, she just watched, taking
note of how the nozariel who had served them the cachapas was part
of the throng. On his break, perhaps, gambling away his earnings.

Flanked by the crowd, six gamblers faced the arbiter's table,
where he had a wheel and a spinning figurine. The Calamity wheel
was split into seven equally sized pie pieces, each painted with an
illustration, now faded, depicting the disasters Ches inflicted on the
land after Rahmagut dared call himself a god. Every player chose
from one of seven cards: the earthquake, the flood, the plague, the
horde, the day of shrouded sun, the star fall, and the legion of valcos. And the final card would go to the arbiter.

The figurine was in the likeness of Ches, who was a robed man
with a drawn blade pointed at the sky, and it had a winding crank at
the back. The arbiter inserted each card into the free wooden hand
of the figurine, and a sliver of gold geomancia wormed its way into
the plague card, marking it as the winning card.

The players each began calling cards, and as they did, the geomancia thread slithered into another free card, eventually ending
up in the arbiter's card, the horde, which no one else chose. Eva
saw the truth unfold with her jaw lowering, just as she noticed
his hands beneath the table, working the spell manipulating the
winning thread to move into his card. Then the arbiter wound and
spun the figurine.

"Ches wrecked the world with his ire, slaughtering nozariels
and valcos in his pursuit of punishing the defiant Rahmagut! How
will the world end this time? Are the gods on your side?"

When the thing stopped on the horde card, the gamblers threw
their hands in the air, bemoaning their loss. And the arbiter only
smiled. His pockets already brimmed with escudos, but he pretended to be magnanimous and dumped the winnings back on the
table, for the men to keep gambling on the promise of a future win.

He was a cheat and a thief.

Eva could play; she could use her innate ability to see the glittering thread and choose the winning card. If the arbiter lost all his money to her, he would only deserve it. But the plan would be too simple, with too many variables to control. Instead, Eva allowed herself to spectate another round and waited for the nozariel man to choose his card, the day of shrouded sun, which coincidently already had the winning thread. If the arbiter were a just man, and this were a just world, he would be the winner.

The nozariel was worthy of winning, Eva decided, for having to live in a world where humans only saw him as wicked and lesser. At that moment she could only think of Doña Rosa. Of the fear in her eyes when they'd met Eva's as she was dragged away. At the realization that Eva was as cowardly and corrupt as the people of Galeno, who used her only to later judge her and condemn her to death.

Within the crowd, Eva clamped her hands and twisted her fingers. A simple litio ward came to her, bright and purposeful, and she used it to stop the glittering thread from being forced to leaving the nozariel's card by the arbiter's cheating magic.

Her lips curled to a smile as she beheld the arbiter. His look of concentration intensified while he tried forcing the winning thread to move. But Eva was stronger. The fact made her brim her with surprise, then satisfaction. She shouldn't feel astounded. She'd always had an aptitude for casting. Against her litio protection, the arbiter had no choice but to despair as the figurine stopped on the card with the day of shrouded sun, and the crowd witnessed the nozariel become the winner. A roar exploded within the throng. Maybe there was satisfaction in it, that the arbiter hadn't won this time.

Eva's cheeks burned with delight. She hoped Doña Rosa could witness this, how Eva had the courage and the capability to set things right. She returned to the inn with her heart still soaring afterward. Javier watched her return with wide eyes. He looked even handsomer when he was surprised. It melted any last doubts she might have had.

23

The Fair Demon

Eva had always imagined her wedding as an event loaded with strong emotions. Love. Hate. It all depended on whom she'd be marrying, really. Ages ago, when she'd been just a girl, she saw herself falling in love with a Galeno boy of base birth. In that fantasy, she was happy for her wedding because her family had conditioned her into believing she didn't deserve better. Later, while courting Don Alberto, all she could think was of how much she would hate the moment of signatures and of vows—and the revel afterward where everyone was merry but her.

Neither was to be her destiny, and for this she couldn't be happier. With just three signatures, she was bound to Feleva Águila's valco son. There had been no room for hate or love as Eva signed her name onto the document spelled with iridio. Only the smug satisfaction of knowing she was taking ownership of her life and that the son of the legendary valco actually wanted *her*. It was like she was breaking out of the cage bridling her hunger, and now her magic ached to bloom.

They celebrated with a bottle of cheap rum and a roasted chicken. Eva drank until giddy, as Javier didn't pause in replenishing her goblet. By midday she was so disoriented that he paid for two rooms at the inn and walked her to hers, where she collapsed on a damp mattress that cried loudly under her weight. He left her there, murmuring something about being next door. But by then Eva was drowning in sleep.

Eva woke hours later at sunset. Her mouth tasted vile; her temple throbbed. She left the bed wondering why she was alone and if Javier had left her behind.

The room was outfitted with a grimy mirror, reflecting a brown-skinned young woman who looked as nasty as she felt. Her eyes were puffy, her mane matted to the side she had slept on. Eva took the time to wash the sleepiness off and braid her hair, despite its very obvious need for a combing.

Her traveling sack had been carried up to the room somehow, comforting her that she hadn't been abandoned. Javier was already a man worthy of her trust—letting her have her space, allowing her to sleep off the hangover without tricking her or demanding they consummate their union.

She walked out to the hallway, where the faint buzz of conversation from the downstairs common area trailed up. She went to the room next door, the one Javier had talked about paying for, and knocked. The door clicked and was nudged open slightly, until he realized it was her.

Eva met a sight she didn't expect. Javier's chest was uncovered by the shirt hanging loosely from his shoulders. His skin was hairless and pale, free from sunspots or scars, the muscles beneath angled like rippling ropes. A slim silver pendant hung from his neck, the crystal sloshing with a dark liquid Eva assumed was iridio. He needed to eat more, she thought vaguely, then immediately felt her cheeks growing warm.

She averted her gaze to the rudimentary room behind him, with its unmade bed and desk cluttered with his traveling assortments.

With a hand lazily pushing back his silky hair, he said, "You're awake? Feeling better now?"

A witty reply eluded her. Thankfully, he allowed her into the room so she wouldn't feel awkward standing under the doorway marveling like a fool.

"I was feeling bad?" she murmured as her weight made his bed creak underneath her.

He combed through his hair with his hands, and Eva's eyes betrayed her by flitting to his abs. The sculpted quality of them.

"You don't remember? How often do you drink rum, anyway?"

Eva cleared her throat. The room steamed, or maybe it was just her. "My family prefers anise. But—I've never been a heavy drinker."

Javier smiled as he buttoned his shirt up, then slipped on his vest. "Just as well. Alcohol addles the mind. I apologize if I forced too much on you."

"It wasn't forced," she said honestly. At that moment, all Eva sought was the belly-deep pleasure of making her own choices (or mistakes) and living her own moment without a care for what her family could do or think. In her mouth the bitter rum had tasted of freedom.

She wished she had the nerve to hold his gaze and inquire why he'd gotten them two rooms. For during their drinking, she had distinctly noted how it could only be the buttering up for what would come after. A wicked doubt had stung her then, hinting he also needed the rum to endure her. But she liked that they hadn't done anything more. It only deepened the puzzle that he was.

"You drank quite a lot, too." She remembered how his laughter had been additive. The words spurred some of it again.

"Of course. I had to celebrate the beginning of something great."

Them.

It was a wonder, how she'd felt so ugly and heavy and inconsequential before him, yet he managed to wash all of it away with a simple notion. She left the bed, and it creaked again. "So what's next?"

"Rahmagut's Claw will finish ripping the sky three weeks from now. Before that happens, we have to collect the ninth dama and bring her to the site of the offering: Tierra'e Sol."

"That is a lot—to take in."

He flashed her a smile. In the dimness of twilight, Javier's eyes looked black, narrowed and cunning.

"Who is the ninth dama? Where do we find her?"

"We have the advantage of knowing exactly where she is going because she told me. That's how we find her."

"You know a lot about her." Eva allowed her gaze to surf his defined nose and thin lips. It didn't feel out of place to take him in, and maybe she was silly for thinking so. She had a right to, as his wife.

"The ninth dama is Brother's daughter."

There was distance in his choice of words. Was this the way he coped with using his niece as a moving piece of his conquest?

"We got in a row the last I saw her, the morning I left for the wedding. She's convinced she'll be able to stop the invocation." His hand drifted up to take gentle hold of a brown curl hanging by Eva's jaw. The side of his palm grazed her skin for fractions of a moment. "Actually, I owe so much to you. Your letters and interest in me. It was the jolt I needed to seize this opportunity."

"You wouldn't have done it otherwise?"

He paced the room, his hands finding his hair again. "I deserve better than to be Brother's errand boy," he hissed. "I brought in the damas—*me* and that nozariel pet his witch keeps in the house. I should be the one reaping the benefits of having Rahmagut's favor. But I can't do it alone and without certain guarantees."

Eva only frowned. She couldn't fathom what she would have to offer.

"Let us go for supper," he said, vetoing the opportunity for more questions, and headed out the door.

Following like a puppy, she said, "I'm ready to learn more. I need to be ready for the things ahead. You said it yourself: There are expectations I have to meet. And I want to know what it's like to be a true valco, without feeling like I have to hold back because of what my family would think or say." She could only imagine his magical prowess as the son of Feleva Águila and as a nobleman of Sadul Fuerte. He had a lifetime of experience ahead of her.

The sound of someone calling for the inn's attention came up to the hallway. Eva ignored it as she said, "I know we don't have a lot of time. I'll do my best." She followed him to the stairs. "I'm behind, but I'm a quick learner. It was my grandmother—she forbade me from being any good at geomancia, but I learned a couple of things behind her back." Of this, Eva was mighty proud.

Javier was half listening to her, his attention on the floor below. "How idiotic. Geomancia is what valcos are best at."

"Can we start tonight?"

He was too distracted watching the men waltzing through the inn to reply.

A ball of lead weighed on Eva's belly when she recognized the faces downstairs. The Calamity arbiter fussed at the nozariel attendants, demanding to see "the cheater."

Something horrible and rotten unfurled in Eva's belly. She couldn't believe they were talking about her. How could they know what she had done?

"Come out, you filthy half-breed! Or my men will beat you bloody before handing you to the authorities!" the arbiter called out, zigzagging through tables while the three heavy men from the game trailed him.

"What authorities?" A potbellied man emerged from one of the back doors, chest and belly shielded by a greased apron. "Pray tell, what authorities does El Carmín have?"

With that sly smile, the arbiter said, "Aye, I guess we'll just have to pretend *we* are the authorities. Hand that cheating valco over, and we'll deal with her swiftly—no one needs to get hurt. See it as our doing the town a service."

The inn broke out in murmurs of confusion and people asking for answers. A cowardly voice took residence in the back of Eva's mind. It told her to run up the stairs—to hide behind the door of her room. She fought it as she took one steady step after another behind Javier. She wasn't the valco to run away from belligerent humans, not anymore.

The arbiter's eyes fell on the antlers crowning Javier. He saw Eva, and his face turned red. "Look who it is: the cheaters."

"What right does a Calamity arbiter have in calling anyone a cheater? The word was created to suit people like you," Javier said, his voice demanding the attention of the inn patrons.

Every step down the stairs felt heavy, like Eva was suddenly the weight of a cow. She pushed through, thinking of her grandmother and of how all Galeno cowered before her. Eva needed to be like that—not weak like her mom.

"You were looking for me, and you've found me. Now, what do you want?" Eva asked coolly as she stood beside Javier, shoulder to shoulder, antler to antler. She brushed her curly bangs back, arching an eyebrow mockingly.

"You manipulated my game with a spell." The arbiter thrust his cane in her direction accusingly. "Where's the duskling wretch you were in cahoots with?" His cane surfed the tense inn, scouring for the server who had won all the escudos. The man was smart, for taking the gold and never returning.

"Where's your proof? My only companion here is my husband." The label was like honey on her tongue: heavy and sticky, new and sweet for the future. She avoided glancing at Javier, not ready to see his reaction to it.

The arbiter's face twitched in poorly contained rage. He pointed at one of his men. "I have a watcher in the crowd who spots cheaters." The man had a glow of red about his skin, the sign of a spell enhancing his body. "With bismuto he can see when there's a cheat in the crowd."

"So he could see you manipulating the game." Eva didn't miss a beat.

"As you could as a valco! Cheat!" the man roared.

Javier placed his left hand over the hilt of his sword, lazily. "You don't get many valcos around here, do you?"

The arbiter spat on the floor between them.

"Perhaps you need to be schooled in respect," Javier said.

"Not here, he doesn't!" the potbellied inn owner bellowed across the inn. "You can school each other all you want outside. Just take it outside," he hissed.

"Yes," Javier said with his lazy charm, "why don't we deal with this without a spectacle. Or are performances all you know?"

"You shut up, you wretch!"

Javier's scabbard clicked as he dislodged the sword, revealing polished steel. His jaw tightened.

"We will leave as soon as I have my escudos back!" The arbiter pointed at her, riling the beefy men who trailed him. "And if you can't find them, then you will repay them."

"You will leave now!" roared the inn owner.

"We want our gold back!" one of the arbiter's followers said.

"That duskling robbed the whole town. Anyone who ever bet on Calamity lost their gold thanks to that half-breed," the other one added, pointing a sausage finger straight at her.

The motion was close to Eva, close enough she would barely get a moment's breath to sprint away should he try to hurt her. But Eva had already made her choice. She stood up, holding her head high. A proper valco, afraid of no one. "It's called gambling—but you cheated."

"Gambling with your life, you bitch." The arbiter hollered to the three men, "Grab her!"

Eva gasped, and the whole world took an inhale with her.

The tallest gambler lunged at Javier, who stepped back with ease, like a bamboo leaf carried by a river current. In the same fluid motion, he rounded on the man, and the pommel of his sword met the man's temple with a fleshy *thud*.

The impact sent the big man hurling across the room before crashing against two occupied tables. Patrons roared and jumped away, mugs spilling and food flying everywhere.

"Out of my establishment! *Out!*" the owner cried.

Javier's hand clamped over Eva's shoulder. He yanked her behind him. She crashed hard against a chair, the backrest bashing into her hip bone. Pain lanced up her side. She sucked in a furious hiss, her valco blood coming alive as the arbiter's cane sliced the air right where she had stood.

The arbiter reeled back, composing himself with a mien of confidence as he prepared to meet Javier. Like he was prepared to walk away victorious. Eva's stomach lurched as her husband straightened his lithe stance, ready for the next blow.

The arbiter swung. Javier stepped to the side, avoiding the sure shredding of his perfectly tailored garments. Then he whirled, swinging his left-handed sword to the arbiter's undefended side. Steel hit flesh with a wet *thwack*.

Eva's gaze jerked away as footsteps stormed at her. A member of the arbiter's entourage, the man with the bismuto spell, ran to tackle her. She sidestepped him, but his swinging fist was made faster by the enhancement and caught her arm, making waves of pain shoot up her shoulder. She croaked, flinging the chair behind her to slow him down, and scurried out of reach. But his heavy hand clamped down on the leg of the chair. He took a massive stride forward with a vicious grin on his face. Instead of pausing, he grabbed the chair and grinned.

"I was hoping you could fight, if you had the nerve to steal from us," he said before hoisting the chair high over his head and slamming it down at her with a roar.

Eva jumped to her left and knocked her shoulder on a wall as the chair whistled through the air beside her. A leg of the chair caught her on the side, ripping through clothes or skin—with her spiking adrenaline, she couldn't tell which. Then the wall cornered her.

Ahead, the inn owner and another man wrestled, pummeling each other's sides while knocking fleeing patrons and furniture everywhere. Javier's and the arbiter's steel rang from a parry. Javier leapt onto a chair as the arbiter swung for his calves. She didn't have to worry for his safety—he stood so perfectly balanced, unfazed and without a single crease marring his clothes.

Rotting teeth grinned at her as the bismuto user raised the chair in the air in front of her, the threat of striking clear in his eyes. Eva's heart migrated to her throat.

Then he swung.

She threw herself to the side, slapping her chest against the stone floor. Then she scampered away on her hands and knees, lashing out with her foot to kick her pursuer in the shin. The hit bought her just a few seconds to scramble to her feet and bolt to Javier.

Her pursuer followed, unsheathing a knife. Eva toppled chairs and tables behind her as she ran, her flitting eyes catching Javier slashing at the arbiter's side. Blood spurting from the gash. The arbiter screaming like a butchered pig.

There was a *swoosh* behind her. Eva spun to see the man standing at arm's length.

She was going to die tonight.

Eyes manic with adrenaline, the bismuto man swung a second

time. In a flash of silver and blue, Javier materialized in front of Eva, his weapon raised like an afterthought, as if the motion were not for her but for the benefit of their attacker.

"Javier." Eva's whimper unmasked all the pretending she had done since she left her home.

The bismuto man eased back. He glanced at the bleeding arbiter, then at the other man wrestling the inn owner and at his fainted ally. They looked defeated.

He stepped back, raising his knife to yield.

Eva dragged in a sharp a breath of relief. They had won. It was over.

But Javier didn't care. With a swift slash, his sword sliced the man's hand holding the knife. Both bounced to the floor, detached.

The man doubled over in howls as hot blood hissed and squirted from the divorced wrist.

"Javier!" Eva cried, her eyes taking in the terrible bloody sight of the man. Her body shook. She tugged at Javier's arm, begging, "He's done! Leave him!"

Javier turned to her, glaring at her with eyes wholly infected by tendrils of black.

He shook her off and barked, his voice morphed to that of a demon, two superimposed voices in one, *"Eva Kesaré*—know your place."

Fear rooted her to the spot. Strings of black magic invisible to human eyes snaked in and out of his eyes and skin, like a disease.

Javier's lip curled at her hesitation. He approached the howling man, who cradled his fallen hand in a pool of his own blood. When he saw Javier, he whimpered and kicked back, but it was in vain.

With his fingernails pointed and sharp like steel, Javier lunged, impaling the man in the throat.

All who witnessed sucked in their breaths.

In a single sickening motion, Javier ripped through the man's flesh and vessels, pulling out tendrils of once-living matter. The man gurgled noisily. Around them, people screamed. And Eva dug fingernails into her belly, the squeezing easing her shock, telling her it wasn't a nightmare. This was real.

"You lunatic!" cried the inn owner, forgetting all about wrestling the arbiter's second cohort. "Get him out of here!" he ordered his nozariel servers, who only watched, petrified.

Blood still dripping from his fingers, Javier straightened up to watch them in delight. "Get me out of here? I paid for my rooms. Did I not?" he barked, his corrupted voice bouncing off the walls as if a hundred Javiers filled the room. The sound lifted Eva's skin in goose bumps.

The man who had wrestled the inn owner made a run for it, following the last patron to the door.

Javier's fist knocked blood into the man's teeth before he could reach the exit. The impact sent him hurling into a wall, the crash of his shoulder and skull on bricks imprinting in Eva's memory.

Guilt bubbled in her belly like food gone spoiled. This was her fault.

Javier leapt at the man, who stumbled up and used the wall as support.

For a second Eva imagined the same flash of fingers, the same sickening ripping of sinew. She couldn't stomach it. She called Javier's name and stumbled past the mess of furniture to reach him.

Javier grabbed the man by the head; then he slammed him against the brick wall. Once. Twice. When the man's knees gave in underneath him, Javier let him fall into a bloody heap.

Eva tried to steady her breathing but couldn't.

Her husband shook the blood off his hand in disgust as the stain of black magic rippled in and out of him. When his eyes met Eva, they froze her. This person was a demon, not the graceful youth she had met at her cousin's wedding.

She murmured his name, as if her imploring had the power of bringing normalcy back to him. But she was a whimpering fool for thinking it could.

Fear gripped her as Javier walked past her, his shoulders rolling in a swagger, turning to the inn owner. He had everyone's attention, and he held it unapologetically, like a fistful of crushed flowers.

"I expect no more interruptions tonight," Javier told the inn owner with his voice still corrupted, "unless you're interested in sharing a similar fate as . . . this scum." He smiled toothlessly. "Close the inn for the night. You have a lot of cleaning up to do."

The inn owner's throat bobbed, and he nodded.

Those hellish eyes snapped to Eva, who stood amid the broken furniture.

"Let's go, Eva Kesaré."

The length of her arms prickled with the cry of panic running along her skin. She was paralyzed under the gaze of a man capable of awful things. And the papers with golden iridio ink upstairs could attest that she had no other choice but to obey. If he could do this to these men, what could he do to her, the person he now owned under the stipulations of their marriage? Eva hesitated with her heart thrumming loudly in her chest. In the end, every step forward was a battle with herself. The threads of black lapped in and out of him as Javier led the ascent to her room. Eva watched the corruption with a held breath. They were like hungry snakes, taking bites of his flesh.

Javier held the door of her room open for her and watched her walk in with a face that looked changed. This wasn't the beautiful man she'd married.

He shut the door, the motion forcing what was left of pure air out of the room. When Eva turned to look at him, she choked, her throat closing up.

She squeezed whatever courage she had in her and said, "I'm sorry—"

"It's hard not to leave an impression, everywhere I go." He absentmindedly stroked his antlers, leaving a smeared trail of blood. "The antlers—they're impossible to hide."

She stepped back as he stepped forward, though it didn't take long for her legs to meet the edge of the bed.

Eva's heart became a dying troupial.

"I can only hope people forget me when they see me outside Sadul Fuerte. But . . . here in El Carmín . . . how can they, when there's a scene at the inn?"

"You didn't have to kill them—"

Eva's words were smacked out of her mouth by his backhand.

It sent her plummeting against the creaking straw bed. Fire and lightning spread over her cheek, and she shrieked.

"I didn't have to kill them?" he growled, pacing the edges of her bedroom like a caged beast. "After they talked to us—to our *species*—like they did? Should I have let them demand escudos from us? Filthy, entitled humans—"

Eva trembled, the pain of her cheek spreading to her head. She clamped her hands over her face and tasted blood on the inside of her mouth.

Javier leaned over her, his eyes wide. "Do you think we could have *talked it out*, Eva Kesaré? After you acted like you wanted to fight them yourself? Do you think that arbiter was going to let you walk away?"

"Don't—don't—" Eva began, her voice broken by sobs. "Don't call me *Eva Kesaré*."

When said together, her first and middle names were supposed to be endearing, used lovingly by her grandmother and late mother. Eva had allowed the handsome, gentle Javier to use them because hearing him say them had filled her with warmth. But coming from this beast, it sounded spoiled.

"Oh, no? How about *wife*?"

He wrenched one of her hands away, and Eva yelped, but he wouldn't give it back.

"I hope it scars," he said of the cut on her lip, "so every time you look at yourself, you remember where you stand." He threw her hand back at her.

With two thunderous steps, Javier marched to the door. He paused with his hand on the knob for so long that Eva forced herself to look up.

The black corruption was gone. The ripples, the threads, the terrible aura of decay. He gave her a sidelong glance, one that made Eva wish she could turn back time. When he spoke, his voice was handsome again. "Rest. We leave for Fedria at dawn."

Eva watched the door close behind him with tears brimming in her eyes. Sleep never came to her—not out of defiance but out of terror for what she had done.

24

The Whistling Crossroads

After leaving Águila Manor, Reina spent the night at the iridio mining camp, where the Águila miners saw her as nothing more than another familiar face, unaware of her banishing. The next morning she sought the trails leading to Gegania's burrow and wasted the whole day only to discover the entrance was gone. She recalled the location; they had carved their initials on a nearby tree during one of their hikes, just for the fun of it. Reina came upon the marked bark and saw the tunnel was nowhere to be seen. If anything, a mess of sediment and crushed bramble made the area look caved in. The hollow expanding within Reina made her jittery and breathless, as the truth became realer with every moment she circled the tree with the *C* and *R* initials and found no underground entrance.

Celeste had broken the connection to Gegania. This made sense, if she was hiding from the people employed under her father. Only it stung Reina to realize it. She held Celeste's secret—more than one of them. Celeste could trust her. There was no need to take such a radical route and cut Reina out of the house.

Reina had no other choice but to make for Apartaderos the following day. Gegania was perched near the mountainous settlement, through a trail she vaguely remembered from when Celeste had shown her the house for the first time. Reina would have to find the house via the village and meet Celeste through its front door. It was the best lead she had.

Her body ached and chills shuddered through her by the time Reina first glimpsed the smoke from the farthest house on the edges of Apartaderos. She squeezed her ruana about her, her condensing breaths reminding her of the cold descending with the dying sun. She felt ill, her muscles weakening like butter from the travel and the shock of losing the core nourishment to her heart.

A thick fog draped the mountainside dotted in frailejones, brought on by the ending day. The trail to Gegania was on the other side of the village, which sat on the crossroads to the only road out of the Páramo. If Reina couldn't reach Gegania before dusk, she would have to spend the night in Apartaderos. She could make a stop in the town for food or at least to pick up talk of an antlered woman passing through, if there were any.

As she descended the gravel path, dread licked its way up Reina's spine upon seeing the tents circling the town, marked by Águila banners. Don Enrique's soldiers in Apartaderos meant nothing more than trouble. They'd never mistreated Reina, but she had seen the intent in their eyes. She had seen their disgust and had even heard the whispers of confusion, of "How could the brutal Ursulina Duvianos have a duskling half-breed for a granddaughter?"

A soft whistling broke through the fog, curling the hairs along her arms. The climbing melody was unmistakable. She was reminded of tattered clothes and bloody grins. Likely, with their overabundance of iridio, Don Enrique's soldiers were attracting a whistler.

The whistling grew fainter as she neared the first homestead, where she could only see up to an arm's length away due to the fog. Reina was so exhausted and fog blinded that casting a spell of bismuto became necessary.

She slapped her hands together, then pulled her palms just enough so her opposing fingertips never disconnected. Fingertips still touching, she flicked her wrists to opposite sides, finalizing the incantation. The surge of bismuto power filled her. From her rings, to her fingers, up her arms, and into the rest of her body.

At once the world took a sharper form. The cloudy brightness became blinding. Crisp Páramo air bit her, carrying the scents of moss and earth and, faintly, of rotted whistler blood. A tingle of electricity shot through her muscles, through strong calves and trained biceps, and swelled her with the strength she had lacked. She unsheathed her machete.

The air went still, heavy, devoid of all sounds save for the crunching of her bootsteps on rocks and dried ferns. Reina's transplant pounded, the memory of her previous clash against a whistler beating furiously against her rib cage. Her gloved hand squeezed the hilt of her machete, sweat slicking her palm.

She couldn't hear the whistling anymore.

Reina came upon the town square, where the stone statue of three women from the revolution welcomed all travelers with determined faces and pointing arms. The familiar sight, which ought to offer reprieve to anyone making the long trek across the mountains, only filled Reina with apprehension. The streets were silent, every door closed and every curtain drawn. Then a bloodcurdling scream ripped through the fog. She vaulted in the direction of it, toward the center of town, as the screams gurgled and then choked.

Reina swiveled this way and that, breathlessly seeking the screaming woman, but the mist felt impenetrable. She spotted a crouching figure in the distance and approached it. A pool of blood bloomed around the figure like a crimson halo. The figure heard Reina and turned, regarding her with a grin dripping with freshly spilled blood. Underneath it was a rent-open woman, her eyes and mouth gaping with her incomplete scream.

Enraged, Reina flushed with boiling-hot blood. She lunged at the whistler just as it drew up to its full height, all long limbs and tattered shepherd's clothes. Sweet decay filled her nostrils as the creature swung. But this time Reina was ready, and she was furious. She dodged the whistler's blow and replied with a machetazo that sundered the whistler's arm, the smell of putrid flesh slapping her on the nose.

The whistler screeched, nearly deafening her in her bismuto high. Its other claw caught her, tearing through clothes and skin.

Fire erupted from her side. Reina was hurled to the ground, knees and elbows scraping and streaking blood on the cobblestones. She dodged a slash that would have shredded her face, her mind razor focused on the battle and not on the sharp stings of her injuries. It was either that or lose her life to this petty fight.

She sprang up and rounded on the creature, slashing its neck from ear to ear. A shower of blood caught her right in the chest, the splatter coating her lips and besmirching her mouth with a bitter taste. Then the whistler collapsed to the ground as she stepped away.

Reina's breathing was the loudest thing in the town square while the whistler's decayed blood pooled on the cobblestones around her. She sheathed her machete. Her gaze gravitated to the fallen woman. Reina didn't have to hope for a pulse. Even from where she stood, it was clear the life had left the body.

The inn across the street burst open with a party of Águila soldiers, shattering the town's silence. A good dozen of them approached her. Their smirks made her pulse pound, overwhelming her with the instinct to run away.

The man with the captain's insignia eyed Reina and said, "And here we hoped the whistler would finish you off."

"You were watching?" she said. Seeing them, with their shiny armor and unscathed leather, flared every bruise and gash the whistler had given her. The pain made it hard to speak, but she said it anyway: "Why didn't you help? Protecting these lands is your job." Her tail thrashed behind her, whipping the air with leftover adrenaline.

"You dare tell us what to do, *duskling*?" one of the men spat. "That woman was dead before anyone could do anything about it. Some homeless whore meandering around even after hearing the whistling. Too bad the beast didn't take you on a trip back to where you came from. To save us the work and all."

Reina swallowed the slight. The lie humans loved to scoff at her face, of nozariels originating from Rahmagut's Vacío.

"The whistler was attracted by your iridio, and they're going to keep on harming innocents while you're here." Reina gestured at the corpse.

The leader laughed at her. "We'll leave, but you're coming with us." To his men he called out, "Take the Duvianos bastard!"

"What?" Her voice came out like a squeal. She stepped back once, sensing the men behind her.

"You stole a Dama del Vacío from the caudillo." He rallied his men, announcing loudly to anyone who would listen, "The little bitch thought she could leverage her return to Águila Manor by betraying Don Enrique."

One of the men swung at Reina with a battle cry.

Reina leapt out of reach, her panicked heart reaching as high as her throat. "That's a lie! I haven't taken anybody!"

"Seize her!" the leader repeated, and the closest four charged.

The sound of the sword slicing the air behind her sent Reina into motion before she could think. She dodged, a blade whistling past her and narrowly missing her. Her fear was a metallic tang in her mouth.

Her fist crashed against the jaw of the closest lunging man, sending pain like impaling icicles up her wrist. The soldier staggered far, buying her a second. She dodged another's reach with an instinctual, though awkward pirouette. Then she swerved out of a sword's slice, so close that she heard it whistling through the air. And when the whole group crowded her, her feet reacted for her, the bismuto electrifying her soles. Reina sprang up and landed on the inn's tiled roof with a painful roll that almost sent her slipping off the other side.

Their leader was the only one fast enough to cast bismuto on himself to pursue her. He leapt up as well. But before he could steady himself, Reina kicked him square on the stomach and off the roof.

Reina fled as his body thumped on the ground. She vaulted onto another roof, landed, then sprinted to another, her body blurring out of sight in the fog. Finally, she stopped when the distances between homes prevented her from leaping any farther.

Reina crawled on all fours to the roof's edge, listening for the Águila men. She heard faraway grunts of complaint and the leader's orders to "search every home for that bitch duskling and the dama she stole."

Her blood boiled. How could Don Enrique assume she had stolen one of the damas? They couldn't mean Celeste... Reina gripped the ledge hard as she imagined jumping down and dueling them one by one—taking their swords and humiliating them just as they undoubtedly wanted to humiliate her.

She squeezed the scutes on her nose bridge as the implications settled on her throat like bile. She couldn't stay in Apartaderos, but she was so fucking exhausted.

The notes of a faint whistle made her still. She squinted and watched the streets, which were so cold and solitary that not a stray cat nor a drunk dared to step out. The houses, with their moss-covered stone façades and clay flowerpots hanging from balconies, were silent. The cobbled roads usually trodden by mules and shepherds now empty. As if time itself had yawned and paused on the town.

Then Reina heard the whistling a second time. A whistler was still around.

She jumped off the roof and landed gracefully on a graveled road.

The blood spilling from that woman. The way the whistler ripped raw sinew and innards. Reina's belly threatened to retch at the memory. She had to find it—she couldn't leave it prowling about to harm another innocent. So she took off jogging toward the small stone chapel flanking the town's burial grounds, apexed by a rusted Pentimiento cross. The whistling grew fainter as she went, reassuring her she was heading in the right direction.

A thick mist settled low, draping over headstones and wilted flowers. Reina took out her machete, the squelching of her boots on wet grass hardly audible. A feminine gasp made her stop. She listened. Then came a scream.

She sprang in the direction of the cry and ran around the chapel. There a cowering figure crouched beside a statue of the Virgin. A woman. And separating the crouching person from a whistler that slashed and snarled and bashed was a litio barrier shimmering with violet light. Reina could see it, like valcos could, because of the bismuto still pumping through her veins.

She sprinted to them, her past failure incensing her strides. The fiend saw her and slashed at her, overwhelming her with its reek. Reina ducked beneath its reaching arm. She swerved around behind it, then returned a doublehanded decapitating swing. Headless, the whistler hit the ground with a squelch.

Silence descended on the graveyard once it was over, save for the woman's sniffling.

Reina kicked the whistler body far away, then kneeled in front of the young woman, ready to tell her it was going to be all right. To beg her not to fear the scutes of her nose and pointed ears. Even as she imagined herself a disgusting sight with whistler blood splattered all over her jacket and face.

She extended a hand as the barrier disintegrated.

The light left. Her eyes adjusted. And she saw the litio rings, the moles on milk skin, the afterimage of a noblewoman with blue eyes, and she froze.

"Ma-Maior?"

Maior pressed herself harder against the Virgin statue, her legs kicking dirt between them. She pointed a litio ring at Reina—the one *she* had given her—and said, "Get away!"

"What are you doing…here?" The last word came out a whisper as realization dawned on Reina. Maior was the runaway dama. "How did you escape?"

Maior wasn't listening. She murmured some incantation and pointed the ring at Reina, sparks of magic uselessly hitting her on the chest. Litio geomancia was only meant for protection, never offense.

"You can't take me!" she said.

Reina seized her wrist, and Maior thrashed so much Reina had to let her go. "All right—all right—stop or you'll hurt yourself. Did you use my ring to escape from Águila Manor?"

If there were any traces of Reina's geomancia left in the dungeons, then it was no wonder Don Enrique was pointing fingers at her.

"Well?"

"You can't force me to go back to that—to that place!" Maior was disrupted by sobs that seemed like beasts of their own. She bowed her head and let her hand fall to the ground, where one litio ring slipped off, the cap opening and spilling the last of the potion. "*Please*," she begged.

Reina stuck her machete in the ground and sat across from her. They were close enough that the fog didn't dampen Maior's features. Her cheeks were pink from the cold but missing the glow of health. Her wavy black bob was knotted with muck.

Reina picked up the fallen ring. If Don Enrique thought she had helped Maior escape, it complicated everything...And of course he would think so. Taking Maior could only be interpreted as a play to secure more influence in their united, twisted goal, for even as Celeste was the ninth dama, she was still missing.

"Why did you return to Apartaderos?"

"It's where I'm from!" Maior said, still not meeting her gaze.

Reina rolled her eyes. "I know. Don't you think this is the first place they'd come looking for you?"

When Maior looked up, Reina saw eyes that made her nervous for a second. That made her want to look away same as when Celeste caught her staring.

"I don't have anywhere else to go," Maior said. "Do you know what it's like to cross the Páramo with this stupid dress?" She yanked on the blue dress meant to mimic the Benevolent Lady's style. Maior was too short and fat to fit into Doña Laurel's old clothes, so it looked like Doña Ursulina had given her something *similar* to what the Benevolent Lady would wear. But the mountains had turned it into a muddied and frayed mess.

"Speaking of the Páramo—how did you do it?" Reina said.

"Do what?"

"How did you cross the Páramo by yourself?"

Maior huffed. "I was born and raised in Apartaderos, and I've had to come down to the markets in Sadul Fuerte every year. I know these trails."

"But you escaped Doña Ursulina's wards."

A glimmer of satisfaction brightened Maior's eyes. "That was your mistake, giving me geomancia to use."

Reina's jaw rippled. She was paying dearly for it.

Maior extended her open palm. The inside of her arm was scarred where Doña Ursulina had hurt her, a line still red and crusted with scabs. "Can I have it back?"

Reina hesitated. In Maior's expectant gaze, she could see Maior desperately needed the rings if she was going to have a chance at evading the Águila men. But this would not be an issue because Reina knew exactly what she needed to do now. So she plopped it on Maior's opened palm—watched the delight pinken her cheeks as she now had the pair once again.

In their silence, it was easy to pick up on the hushed conversations beyond the chapel, as neighbors discussed the recent happenings. The Águila soldiers were still around, shouting angrily and accusing townsfolk of hiding Reina.

It was almost as if Maior could feel the inevitable coming, for she asked, "Do you have to take me back?"

Reina sighed. She ran a hand over her bangs, smoothing the frizz. "No."

Maior let out an audible breath of relief, a cloud of condensation forming between them. She pushed herself to her feet.

Reina did the same, positioning herself so Maior was blocked between her and the statue. "But you're coming with me," Reina said.

"Wait—what?"

Reina pulled her machete off the ground and slid it back into its sheath. "The caudillo calls me a traitor even after everything I've done for his household. He'll still think I'm a traitor if his men catch you," she said, swiping the blood from her cheeks and temples, dusting the grime off her pants. She could hear Maior's heartbeat, panicked and rushed, the implications probably unfolding like a bad dream.

"Well—you gave me the rings, so you were planning to help me—so, in a way, he is right."

Reina couldn't see why Maior would make this point at all, so she stopped Maior before she dug herself deeper into a hole. "If I let you go, they'll still blame me, only you'll most likely be caught and sent back to Don Enrique." Which was counterproductive to where they needed to be. Reina's future awaited her in Tierra'e Sol.

Maior paled.

"Don Enrique sent a whole party searching for you. We're running out of time, and you better believe he'll be spending all the resources he has to secure the damas who used to belong to him."

"I don't belong to anybody," Maior said, sneering. She pressed herself against the statue of the Virgin, perking her chest up. Reina hated being distracted by it.

"You've got a ninth of Rahmagut's power," Reina said dryly.

Maior's lower lip trembled. It reminded Reina of her own weakness against Don Enrique. All this time she had been banking on her strength being the pathway to a better life. And in the moment when she had needed it most, this "strength" had failed her.

Reina paced away, her jaw tight. Maybe she had no strength. Maybe she had always been a pawn in their games, and she wouldn't stop being one until she started making moves herself.

"I'm searching for Celeste, the caudillo's daughter who is a Dama del Vacío just like you. While you're with me, you'll be safe." The words were a shiny apple poisoned with a lie, but she needed Maior docile. Trust was a better tool than fear. This she'd learned from her grandmother.

Maior hugged her trembling arms, her gaze on the graveyard's emptiness. "And if they never give me up?"

"Rahmagut's Claw will finish its journey in less than twenty days. You'll be a free woman afterward."

Reina could nearly taste her grandmother's delight in her mouth when she saw Reina arrive in Tierra'e Sol with both Celeste and Maior. The last two pieces of Rahmagut's puzzle. No one would be questioning her usefulness then.

Disbelief clouded Maior's eyes, but there was no time to address it. Reina picked up on the voices of three Águila soldiers who were headed to the chapel.

"They're coming," she whispered at once.

"Who—"

"The Águila soldiers. If they see us, they'll assume I really took you."

"But you are taking me!"

Reina shushed her and crouched in front of her. "Get on."

"Wh-what?"

"Are you only capable of stuttering?" she whispered. "Get on my back, and I'll take us out of here. *Now*."

As soon as Maior's legs hooked around her torso, Reina leapt. There was little time to ease her into balancing her soft roundness around Reina. And when she tipped over to one side, Reina's prehensile tail propped her up by the waist. Maior squeezed Reina's chest and whimpered in shock at the hard edges of the protruding transplant beneath her clothes. Reina hissed at her to be quiet, propelling them up to the same roofs she'd come from before the bismuto high could run out. They reached the farthest house in leaping distance, where Reina brought them to solid ground.

Reina didn't let Maior down until the valley was far behind them. Then she tugged the human into a brisk hike, breaking out of the mist blanketing Apartaderos. Relief flooded Reina as she recognized the hummocky landscape. The footpath was not easy to find.

"You can let go of me now, right?" Maior said with her gaze on the tug of her wrist. She glanced behind them. "No one is pursuing."

Reina regarded her with thinned lips and a tight jaw. "I can't let you run away."

"You're a nozariel. We both know how that worked out last time."

Reina hated the implied meaning. At least Maior wasn't stooping low enough to call her a duskling again. "Just be glad I'm taking you away from the caudillo" was all she said. Her lie.

"Where are we going, anyway?"

"To a place only a few people know of, where no one will be able to reach you. You'll be truly hidden there."

A yawning silence stretched out between them as the hike delivered them to dusk. The temperature dropped further, and the wind sparked with the stir of unnatural creatures. Reina sobered up from her bismuto spell, and the warmth of her muscles left her, replaced by weakness. She almost lost hope, glaring at the mark of

Rahmagut's Claw becoming visible in the darkening sky. Would Doña Ursulina save Reina's dying heart again, abandoning her threat, if Reina didn't deliver the damas before the days were up?

Before Reina could ruminate on her grandmother's possible bluffing, the clay tiles of a roof became visible beyond the hill. They arrived through the back of Gegania, which hugged the descending mountainside. Moss and lush vines hugged its walls where the yellow-and-white paint was visibly peeling off. A path of stone steps, flanked by overgrown yellow and lilac wildflowers, led them down to the house's entrance.

The front door was not locked; Reina swung it open with her chest hammering in anticipation. It could only be an invitation from Celeste, who surely awaited her, who knew that Reina recognized their sticky circumstances and would want to come to be her support.

Behind her, Maior crossed herself and said, "Cuídame Virgen," before following her in.

Reina ran through the kitchen and all the upstairs bedrooms, coughed through the dusty attic, then whirled down to the underground with a hopeful smile. Yet once she reached its cold depths, she found books and papers strewn all over the iridio table, the tunnel door shut, and the room empty.

In her disappointment Reina approached the iridio table and felt the sting of its activation as her fingertips fell over its edges. Gegania was connected to a new location. That was why the tether to Águila Manor had caved in. The filigree branches of mineral veins superimposed on the map of Venazia and Fedria on the table were nearly all inactive, save for a single lighted path. The house was connected to a town beyond the Río'e Marle border.

Reina traced the lines with a burning question, and no matter how she spun it, she couldn't arrive at an answer. Why, out of all places, would Celeste go to La Cochinilla?

25

Fleeing with the Red Sea

Eva had never understood what it meant when the wise and decrepit talked about their regrets. When her great-aunts and her grandmother shared a coffee in the sunroom in midafternoon and bemoaned the wrong paths they'd taken in life. For, if faced with the wrong or right choice, how could they have made the wrong one? Well, now she knew: Sometimes the garden path lined by rosebushes could lead to a thicket of thorns.

Eva didn't have a demon in her, despite everything her grandmother had drilled into her head. She was sure if she took Javier's hand and led him into a church, he would be the one going up in flames, not her. Néstor had always called her impetuous, and maybe at one point or another, she had been in agreement. But now Eva knew she was taking the blood-damned crown. She'd run away with a demon and was now his bride.

The morning after the massacre at the inn, Eva went through the motions like she was little more than a pet. Darting eyes avoiding his. Noncommittal grunts of yes and no becoming her only form of communication. Her ire growing as she watched him play this game as well. They left El Carmín with him pretending nothing had ever happened.

Javier paid for a boat that took them southbound on Río'e Marle, where Eva spent two days avoiding him, and they touched Fedrian soil in the early morning of the third day. Then they walked a dirt road flanked by palms and plantain trees, by greenery blooming in violent oranges and fuchsias and smelling of sweet fruits. The sights were a distraction from the anger boiling up inside Eva. Hatred at being deceived. Resentment for being struck. Nevertheless she followed Javier, plotting her escape as her only consolation. She didn't care if she had no clue where to go without him or if it put a hitch in her plans to master geomancia. Leaving Galeno was supposed to be her act of taking control of her life. She wasn't going to stop now.

As the sun was finishing its descent, they came into a village possibly a quarter the size of El Carmín, with houses of colorfully painted adobe walls and clay-tiled roofs, most falling apart from neglect. Despite the dilapidation, the roads were decorated with ropes strung between the roofs of opposite-facing houses, crisscrossing in the air. Hanging from the ropes were paper cutouts, like tiny fluttering butterflies. Some white; some dyed in goldenrod, scarlet, and cerulean. It looked like the village, too, celebrated Saint Jon the Shepherd.

Here the nozariels were in equal quantity to the humans.

Eva saw adults and children with hair and eyes the same color as those of humans, only their irises were stained by a slit of black, giving their pupils a feline impression. They had pointy ears, and the bridges of their noses were scaled, as well as the tops of their shoulders, their kneecaps, and elbows. She thought she would see them with their tails switching behind them. Eva imagined the short fur along their lengths in the same color as their head of hair, their tips hairy, long, full, and braided like when she'd braided the tails of her family's horses, banded by ribbons. Yet she couldn't spot a single person with their tail intact—not even in this land where their existence wasn't forbidden.

She followed Javier past a fruit stand of bursting papayas and golden mangoes, where a gaggle of girls feasted on their pulp. Eva saw their pointed, glistening fangs like the canines of a jaguar. Small differences, minor enough to make them close cousins to humans (were they truly demons escaped from el Vacío, like the superstition told?) yet weirdly unsettling to see—at least for someone who didn't grow up around them.

At the center of the village was a town square peppered with equal amounts of wildflowers and weeds, where a bronze statue of Ches stood. Here he was depicted as a robed nozariel man, with a blade pointing up where the high noon sun ought to be. If so many tales of Ches and Rahmagut were still passed on from nozariel parent to child, it wasn't surprising to see this statue as the most interesting landmark of the village. It made Eva think of her grandmother, who held a fierce grudge against Fedria, where nozariels worshipped other gods besides the Virgin. What surprised Eva the most, however, were the waves of light exuding from the statue—minuscule pulsing threads, visible with sunlight one moment and gone the next. A spell alive and woven with care, flowing outward through the nozariels and even through her, disappearing as glittering stars toward the edges of the village.

"You're noticing it?" Javier said, catching her staring.

It was iridio, enchanted there by someone very powerful. Whatever its purpose was, Eva would rather not learn than have to rely on Javier as her source of information. She held her nose high and instead watched a group of men on the road. They argued about transporting a large statuette of Ches on a cart, as its affixed mule was refusing to cooperate.

"The tale of Rahmagut bringing demons from el Vacío isn't just human hate talk," Javier told her, like he expected to pique her interest. As if he was trying to say something so enthralling she would have no choice but to grace him with the privilege of her attention.

The group was joined by musicians hauling drums and a blowing horn out of one of the homes. They were regular folk, different from humans in only the slightest of features, living lives undeserving of the mistreatment and hatred they received in Venazia.

Eva shook her head to herself, feeling foolish for trusting her family's view of the world. The only demon here was Javier.

"I don't care for tales," she said flatly, incensed by the afternoon sun and by the injustices she'd had to face for being different.

"Yet you believe in me. You believe in Rahmagut."

One of the men in the group began slapping the leather top of his drum.

Javier grabbed Eva by the back of the elbow to herd her away. Once, in El Carmín, his touch had made her weak in the knees. Now she just wanted to yank free.

"I can walk by myself, thank you."

Another man joined with his own drum. Eva recognized this beat. It was the same rhythm of the song played for the Saint Jon the Shepherd revel.

"Let's get going before we get stuck in their crowd," Javier said.

"Didn't you have a great speech to make? About el Vacío? Can't make it in front of them?"

With poorly masked annoyance, he glanced at the nozariels, then at Eva. As he did so, angled sunlight caught his eyes, turning them into brilliant garnets. She looked away, forcing herself to ignore his looks. Hate was what she was supposed to be feeling, not this puppy-eyed amazement.

He tugged her around a corner, away from the musicians. "All day, you have been acting like an obstinate mule, and I don't have time for it, Eva Kesaré. We need to get going and purchase supplies before the day ends."

She frowned at the use of her name, wary of once again forbidding him from it. She jerked her arm free.

Javier towered over her, surprised by her reaction, and she stepped back until she bumped against a wall. Half of her cowered, yet the other half didn't care. He had deceived her, poisoning her dreams with a false journey.

He grabbed her by the arm and pinned her to the wall, her shoulders and head scraping against hard, ragged clay.

"Did you not learn your lesson last time?" he growled. "What did I tell you about pretending to be something you're not?"

He was so close Eva could inspect his blemishes. His chapped lips and his silvery fuzz of unshaven facial hair. The bead of sweat rolling down his temple. The proximity made it hard to breathe.

"I am not a mule to be tugged around," she said in the bravest voice she could muster.

"We have to get a move on before the parade begins. Otherwise we will be stuck here. Haven't you seen it in your hometown? The great dancing parties of Saint Jon the Shepherd?"

She opened her mouth, but no reply came. It was her favorite time of the year, when Galeno became alight in the revel and all pious inhibitions were thrown out the door. Her gaze found the nozariel men around the corner, their drums and red-stained garments, the stitched bunches of dyed yarn hanging from their ankles and waists. She had seen those clothes before on the acolytes and volunteers serving the archbishop during the holiday. The outfits were designed to flutter in the air with their rhythmic dances and stomping feet. But the statuette the nozariel men carried was of Ches, and not at all like Saint Jon's.

Were their parties like their resemblance to humans, a close cousin that appeared the same when one didn't look too hard? Or was Saint Jon's celebration a bastardized version of the nozariels' traditions? Once, Doña Rosa had told Eva how so many Penitent beliefs were stolen from nozariels, renamed as to appease the enslaved workforce in a land where the human colonizers were the minority. Eva was glad to see it with her own eyes, after living so long under the lies of her family.

"We're here to get you geomancia rings. It's what you wanted, no? To become great and feared?" he prodded in a poor attempt at persuasion.

She only flexed her jaw, holding back the intention to correct him. He had misinterpreted her desires so thoroughly, but she wasn't interested in educating him.

"All right," she said.

He let her go. "I liked you better when you didn't fight everything I asked of you."

As he walked away, Eva glared at the back of his fair hair. She was squeezed by a deep disappointment. Her dream of freedom with the valco man who treated her as an equal was turning bitter in her mouth. She braced herself and tried not to dwell. Just as she had gotten into this, she would find a way out.

They went into a trading post as the cloud-blotched sky turned stark with the shadows of the dying sun. A shopkeeper sat on a rocking chair on the porch, his bloated child playing with twigs and rocks by his side. They were shaded by eaves heavy with plantain bunches and sacks of cassava and the occasional pork rinds.

They walked through a screen door woven from leaves and seeds, which rattled as Javier opened it for her. The shack was hot and smelled of sweat, like a dirty rag overdue for washing. The trader gestured at the pots and bags filled with trinkets and stones and spices to either side. Among the goods was a tray of sliced fried plantains and queso de mano. At once Eva's gaze fell on the plantains. She was so hungry she could have eaten the whole dozen of them. Javier bought them for her.

"I'm looking for conduit jewelry," he told the shopkeeper.

Eva was too hungry to listen to them. The plantains were cold—probably cooked early in the morning—but the edges were still crunchy, the center sweet from a properly ripened plantain. She stared at the street through the screen door, daydreaming herself into the celebrations, even if here they worshipped Ches. From the thrum of the faraway drums, it sounded like it had already started.

Moments later Javier turned to her, showing her a necklace with a crystal container.

"Did you eat them all?" he asked, amused.

Eva was in the process of chewing the last one, so it was no use lying about it. She shrugged.

"Not that I wanted any."

She sucked the gunk off her teeth and said, "You don't care for nozariel food, remember?"

"Right."

He showed her the necklace and said, "It's not the prettiest, but it's got the biggest crystal container."

Her eyes went from the necklace to the shopkeeper, who had a display of jewelry laid out on a velvety cloth across from him.

"To hold your iridio," Javier said as he wrapped his arms around her (she flinched, expecting something else entirely) and latched the necklace to her neck. "You're also getting rings for geomancia."

This close he looked young, boyish, like the highborn boys who'd come to visit her grandfather's court and ignored her for being bastard born and ugly. Heat radiated in waves off him, making it even harder to breathe in the already sweltering day.

He gestured to the rings. "Try them and see which one fits you. Not the silver ones, though. Gold complements your color."

Eva did her best to disregard the compliment. Eventually they left the shop and walked straight into a sea of people.

The parade for Ches—or Saint Jon the Shepherd. Eva couldn't tell if there was a difference. The crowd was as big as the village population. Everyone had taken to the streets, all dressed in clothes dyed a pigmented red. With their torches burning bright in the darkness of early dusk, they were an ocean of crimson.

The people's singing bordered on shouts. They danced, and sang, and followed the Ches statuette, which was now far from view.

"Le le le lo, time that pass don' come back!" the leader of the procession sang the same lyrics Eva had heard all her life.

Then the voice of a woman near the front of the procession rang out. "Evil time!"

And the crowd sang, "Don' return!"

Eva let the sound of drums percolate to her bones, mouthing the lyrics.

Dancing women stomped past her, their breasts bouncing and their eyes on her.

"Wretched time!"

The men followed them, also stomping.

"Don' return!"

As they passed, one, two, three people stepped between Eva and Javier. It was a fleeting moment of separation, of darkness and confusion and loud voices, and at once Eva recognized it for what it was. A distraction.

Her opportunity to slip away.

She delved into the crowd, one hand warming her new iridio pendant and her fingers heavy with the new rings of geomancia. She didn't know how to use iridio and could hardly consider herself adept at geomancia, but it didn't matter.

Her grandmother had once told her that people didn't get to choose their time. That opportunity simply came and went, whenever the Virgin willed it. It was up to her to recognize the chance. Eva had followed the principle when she'd allowed herself to be enthralled by Javier's coaxing letters, which had massaged her into leaving everything behind. It had been her opportunity to take rein over her life. Just like now was her opportunity to right her mistake of tying herself to him. She'd left Galeno to be free, and free she was going to be.

She ducked her head low and zigzagged from person to person, falling in pace with the procession leaving the village.

If she lost herself within, then she could make her escape.

Thirsty for her independence, Eva slipped away.

The buzz of excitement filled her lungs. Eva's heart joined the chorus, beating hard and fast at the prospect of what was ahead. The distance between her and Javier doubled, then tripled as she walked with the crowd. She even dared herself to join the chanting, to feel included. They exited the boundaries of the village, parading down the road.

She had seconds before Javier discovered she had left, and he was going to come looking in the most obvious place. So she squeezed out of the crowd and jumped into a thicket that led straight into the jungle. Those glittering threads of magic tickled her goodbye as she went, and the chanting faded behind her, replaced by a vibrant nightly cacophony: the chirping of insects and the distant caress of wind on leaves.

If only she knew how to summon flame wisps on command.

"But maybe it's for the better," she told herself, basking in the freedom of giving breath to her thoughts without fear of being judged. "He'd find me if I used fire."

She sped farther into the thicket, even if all that welcomed her was darkness. Distance from Javier was what mattered. She would deal with the issue of direction after dawn.

Eva stumbled on roots and stubbed her feet on protruding rocks yet didn't slow. The darkness smelled damp and sweet, like she was passing bushes or trees blooming with flowers. Branches scratched her limbs and tugged at the hems of her skirt. Thorns pricked her arms. Moist leaves caressed her face. A gnarled root impeded her path, and she tripped and landed painfully on a bent ankle. She cursed, curling on the ground to nurse her joint.

There was a certain crispness to her breathing as she waited for the throb to soothe. Her nose got cold. Then the hairs along her arms and legs prickled from a chill. Eva touched her forehead. Were these the cold sweats of a fever? A sweltering, humid heat had kept most of the afternoon company. She thought of Javier—of how his proximity had suffocated her. So why was it cold all of a sudden?

She stood up, watching the blackness of the jungle and listening. The cacophony had ceased, as if every critter had fallen into a deep sleep. She suddenly hated the idea of being alone. Not even the wind breathed in and out of the trees anymore. Eva slapped at the prickle of a mosquito bite on her arm.

That's when she realized: She wasn't alone in this jungle.

The rustle of a faraway bush caught her attention, the movement loud in her expectant silence.

Eva's heart jumped. She couldn't see anything, but she trusted her intuition. There *was* something lurking behind the trees. Her instincts again begged her to run.

This time she listened.

Eva sprang back to where she'd come from, tripping over the same root a second time. She shoved the pain to the confines of her mind and ran.

A creature jolted out behind her. It snarled, as if in satisfaction, stomping over the underbrush with feet that sounded like hoofs. Like the terrible stomps of a bull.

Leaves slapped her across the face. Dim starlight filtered through the jungle's canopy, showering its density in shadows. She could barely see where she was going.

Behind her, the footsteps grew louder, manic and determined. She could hear it behind her, its snarls laced with laughter. In a fleeting moment, Eva glanced back and saw the terrible black silhouette of a creature at least a head taller than her, with a torso covered in ragged fur, like a wolf's, and the curled horns of a bull. The starlight reflected wide eyes.

It was catching up to her, and it was going to shred her to ribbons.

She stubbed her foot on a large boulder. She flew forward, crashing hard against a tree. A coppery wetness filled her mouth as her teeth split her lip from the impact.

She didn't give herself the luxury of acknowledging the pain. She crawled around and pressed her hands together in a litio incantation. The protection came out sharp and determined.

The creature's slash crashed against a sparkling barrier of gold. The blow was a terrible sound, like nails against crystal. The demon faltered for an instant, surprised, then resumed with one relentless strike after another.

Every slash chipped away a bit of the litio. The barrier cracked with sparks of gold that lighted the velvety black face of a bovine, a scarred muzzle with salivating fangs, and the clawed hands of an eagle. As a large fissure streaked the length of the barrier, the beast grinned down at her with a hundred pointed teeth.

She created a different incantation a second before her barrier shattered—a wall. It reconstructed in a bright flash, blinding them. She seized the reprieve to run away from the creature.

Behind her, the wall held for a second longer before bursting.

The creature tore through the jungle as if growing bigger from her panic.

Finally the thicket opened to a clearing of tall grass. The sounds of her pursuer multiplied, like there were more than one. She heard a second pair of hoofs, then a third.

Eva's lungs burned. She leapt over rocks and air roots until her knees gave from the abuse. She glanced back again, foolishly, and saw three creatures possessed by slithering black smoke. Like Javier's corruption.

The nearest one lunged. It caught Eva on the side with a single slash, drawing hot blood. Eva screamed in agony. The monster attempted to grab her, and in the struggle she was hurled far. She rolled onto her back and pressed her trembling hands together, willing a barrier into existence.

The creature's second slash was stopped by glittering magic, which materialized as a dome of golden threads.

The other two joined the onslaught. They snarled and laughed all at the same time, like superimposed sounds. Like those of something half beast, half person.

Fire and acid ate at her open wound. Eva curled up in a ball and cried, the relentless slashing on the barrier a shrill torture to her ears. Bit by bit, she could see the flakes of protection coming undone. The fissures multiplying like branching rivers.

Rivulets of tears blurred her sight. Her trembling hands were drenched, pressed against her gash that wouldn't stop bleeding.

Blinded by pain, Eva let go of the wound to recast the protection, imagining an even thicker wall—of steel or obsidian. It didn't happen. The rings Javier had gifted her had run out of litio potion.

With a vicious snarl, one of the creatures punched through, its leathery skin tearing as the hand broke in. This one had the hands of a decayed human corpse and reeked like one.

Eva scooted to the other side of the dome, only to hear the slashing behind her. A fourth had joined the assault.

The creature pulled its hand back, then fervently tugged on the breach. Tug by tug, the barrier gave. It stretched it out until it was deformed enough to allow for a wide cavity. They yanked her out by the foot.

The world was black and red and searing like fire as the creatures pulled her between each other. They bit and slashed and ripped. Blood bloomed in her mouth. Their putrid stench blocked her nostrils. Then they pinned her against the ground and raised their amalgamated hands to the air, intent on striking her chest.

A whirlwind stopped them midway. They screeched, and Eva had the briefest relief from the agony. She was a bloody rag. Every inch of her body burned in never-ending pain. She didn't care to open her eyes. All she wanted was for it to end.

In a way, her wish was granted. While the creatures fought and screeched around her, Eva allowed the darkness to numb her.

The black was like a blanket, cold and without kindness.

Mercilessly, it claimed her.

26

The Galio Healer

For two years Reina had lived with the whispers of the iridio ore as the only reminder of her abnormality. Thanks to the transplant and its iridio, she had thrived on the stability of this good health, her nozariel strength swelling with the sparring lessons and her grandmother's coaching in the arts of geomancia. So used to these comforts, she didn't understand why the air emptied her lungs as a great ache shook her shoulders. She hadn't imagined it would feel this way to be starved for nourishment, to have her emptying iridio reserves feel like a punch to the gut, leaving her writhing like a dying earthworm.

It was hard for Reina to recall exactly how it happened. One moment she marveled at the magic of the iridio table, wondering why Celeste chose to go to La Cochinilla, and the next the cold flagstones were pressing against her cheeks, sucking out her heat like the slick damp of her palms. The pain was like a splitting of slabs, sudden and thunderous, but she recognized it after having lived through it once. Reina gulped for air and cried until soft hands cradled her shoulders. Maior. Reina's name was called several times, she recalled that. And the concern in the human's voice was enough to spur Reina into lifting herself off the ground. Somehow, Maior herded her up the stairs and toward the first bedroom they could find, where Reina collapsed on a hard bed packed with hay.

Reina buried her head in the dusty pillow for many moments before Maior's voice was finally discernible. "What is the matter with you? Are you all right?"

Even in her dizzy delirium, Reina knew what was wrong with her. "My heart," she croaked.

She was a docile doll under Maior's ministrations, letting her unbutton her jacket and unwind the binds over her chest. Maior's gasp at the sight was as sharp as Reina's pain.

"Are you dying?" Maior asked.

She was, but there was a way to prevent it. "I just need this—the iridio."

With a shaky hand, Reina lifted between them the iridio pendant Doña Ursulina had given her. She forced herself to sit up. Her chest pounded and ached, and Reina bit on the insides of her cheeks until she tasted sharp iron to distract from the pain. She slapped Maior's hand away when the human tried to help, for she couldn't trust her with this: the delicate moment of unclasping one of the two tubes sticking out from the crystal contraption, for the other one was a pressurized connection, which would truly kill her if it came undone. With the steadiest hand she could muster, Reina titrated two drops of iridio from the pendant directly over the opening. Then she screwed the tube back in place. The effects were delayed but a few seconds before the iridio showered Reina with shivery relief. She collapsed on the pillow again, eyes lulled back and breaths panting. The throbbing heartbeats calmed.

Maior shook her shoulder. "Please tell me you won't die?"

There was no joy in the moment, yet Reina couldn't help the bitter smile. With eyes still closed, she said, "I thought that would bring you satisfaction."

"Why?"

"Because I took you away from your home?"

"I do not want to see you die."

"I will live," Reina said flatly.

Maior had no reply, which was just as well, for Reina had no more words left in her.

Reina allowed the darkness of sleep to lull her away.

In her sleep, Reina was transported to that tunnel through the jungle, where the prisms of sunlight filtering through the canopy kissed her skin and graced her with warmth. She awoke later to the wetness of fresh water on her lips and, in her addled state, concluded she must have reached the lagoon at last. She swallowed it on instinct, then coughed and spluttered as someone helped steady her on the bed. It was Maior, who handed her a cup sloshing with chilly water. Reina gulped it down as she realized her thirst.

Maior sat on the bed's edge. She brushed her hair behind her ears, watching Reina intently until Reina got ahold of herself. "You slept for a whole day."

Reina sucked in a startled breath and tried to sit up, but collapsed dizzily back on the bed.

"Easy now. You needed it."

Reina grimaced, ashamed of her weakness—disappointed at her inability to get a move on with her task.

"There are supplies in this house. Cassava and purple potatoes in the stores. Corn to be ground in the shed. Everything halfway done. Does someone live here?"

The thought of Celeste made Reina smile. Those were Celeste's antics, trying to make the house livable but giving up before it was done. She was too used to the comforts of a fully staffed home, of someone taking out the chamber pot and dusting the sheets. Cooks meticulously grinding and seasoning legumes and meat cuts to deliver extravagant meals to her table. Gegania was a functional house; it just lacked the labor of the Águilas' staff.

Maior helped Reina wrap herself up again, in the binds and the shirt and under the blanket. Outside, dusk deepened into nighttime, draping the room with its cool shadows. It made it easier to accept Maior's help, for if they were shrouded in its darkness, then Maior's inquisitive gaze wouldn't be able to detail the abnormality bursting from Reina's chest, the darkened scar tissue, and the rot of the caudillo's curse.

"This is the Benevolent Lady's house. Her daughter inherited it."

Maior's voice shook as she said, "If this is the Benevolent Lady's house, why did you bring me here? You said I would be safe from the caudillo. I thought she had died."

"You will be." The lie came steady and sure. "Don Enrique doesn't know about this house, for reasons that are none of your concern. The house has a great power, which I'm going to need in the next few days."

Rahmagut's Claw was the countdown to the end of her life. If she didn't procure more iridio, and she didn't bring Maior and Celeste to Tierra'e Sol, there was no future left for her. She needed the house to slice the length of her journey, or else she wouldn't make it.

Reina tried sitting up again—ignited into action by her own panic—but Maior shoved her back down on the bed.

"You are weak. You need to sleep."

Reina tried again. "What do you know?" But she was stopped.

Maior pressed the back of her hand to Reina's forehead. "You have cold sweats, and for a mighty nozariel, you sure can't stop me from keeping you on this bed."

It was too dark to see her eyes, but Reina could imagine the raised eyebrow. The pointed look.

"Don't worry, your weakness can be cured with a meal and another full night's sleep. When was the last time you had those?"

"My occupation doesn't always allow me those comforts."

"And what is your occupation?"

"I serve the Águilas." The assertion left Reina before she could weigh its truth. Maybe this had been true once, but without Celeste, Reina was banished by the caudillo himself. She decided against correcting herself.

The air was heavy with Maior's outrage.

Reina took a deep breath. "What do you know about my weakness? And why are you so concerned? Normal people would have taken this chance to make a run for it."

"Make a run for it where, exactly? The caudillo's men have overrun my home. If you're a woman of the Águilas, then you know as well as I do that the mountains are dangerous. My only options are Apartaderos or Sadul Fuerte. You can imagine how that will go for me."

A deep weariness embraced Reina. She hugged the wool blanket closer around her shoulders, cozying up as the prospect of resting seduced her. She was running out of time, but maybe she could afford one night's sleep at the least. And Maior didn't seem likely to run away...yet.

"So you are smart," Reina muttered sleepily, one foot in this room and another tugging her into her dreams.

Maior scoffed. "You never wondered how I made it to Apartaderos with your shitty rings, did you?"

"I thought you liked my litio rings."

"I do. But they are shitty."

Reina chuckled. "So how did you?"

Maior took a deep breath. She leaned back, better settling over the bed for her tale. "Apartaderos is a haven for travelers. All sorts of people from the Llanos think they can cross the Páramo to Sadul Fuerte without issue, but they don't have any idea of what truly lives here. We get many injured and weary travelers, and we receive them in the stone chapel where you found me—us, Las Hermanas de Piedra."

Reina spluttered the name. "The sisters of stone?"

The human looked away. "It's what we call our order. It was founded when I was just a girl. I grew up with them. We take our name from the chapel, since it's the only notable thing about Apartaderos."

Reina waited, listening to the orchestra of nightly critters surrounding the house, the crickets and the awakening amphibians. She squinted in an attempt to keep herself from surrendering to sleep. She couldn't pretend she had heard of the order before, but a lot of things from these mountains were new to her. Every day she was learning.

"We take care of the tired and injured. Our founder has experimented with the powers of healing through galio, how it's related to our faith for the Virgin. She taught me how to use it."

"Pentimiento and geomancia are in contradiction with each

other," Reina muttered. She'd learned it from Doña Ursulina and seen it with her own eyes. "Penitents are the first to deny magic." In fact, Penitents were the first to decry anything that didn't fit into their arbitrary mold: how a human woman should look and act; what their role and profession should be. Under these molds, Reina was undesirable and abnormal, for her senses, her tail, her muscles, and her capabilities.

"The Virgin created this world with geomancia in it. How can something that exists under Her watch be a contradiction with Her teachings?"

This sobered Reina. Anger stormed within her, sloshing in her weak stomach and sharpening the edges of every object in the shadowed room. Her nozariel blood gave her an acuter vision than humans, and with it she took in the sight of Maior, with her round cheeks and naïve eyes. How she wanted to shut her up for her ignorant view of the world. "My existence is contradictory to Her teachings," she hissed.

Maior paused, and Reina could imagine her jaw tightening as she wound herself up for the typical sermon all Penitents engaged in, to justify their hatred for her kind.

"You exist in Her world; therefore you belong in it. You aren't *wrong*."

The meaning was clear in her intonation: She was wrong for her opinions but not for existing under Maior's version of the Virgin's world. Reina glared at the human, who likely couldn't even see her expression in the darkness.

The silence stretched on, ragged and cold. As Reina waited, she realized Maior had no intentions to further patronize her with her beliefs.

"So Las Hermanas de Piedra dabble in galio healing," Reina said, reeling them back to the query that led them down this path. Geomancia was a stoppered skill. One needed to unlock only one school, and the rest could easily follow like toppling dominoes. Or perhaps Maior's prowess was due to Rahmagut's power, since she held a fraction of it within her.

"Not only galio. We study the body, tend its wounds. I have

seen many sick travelers and have tended to the caudillo's soldiers as well. That's how I can tell on the surface that your shivers are from a lack of rest and not because your blood is spoiled."

"Spoiled blood?"

"An inner bruise or a curse."

Reina snorted. Then Maior didn't know anything at all, because Reina was sick from a deficit of iridio in her heart. Her ailment couldn't merely be cured with a hot meal.

"My mentor, she taught me a galio spell to ease the mind and put people to sleep. We use it when the pain of treatment turns the procedure into torture, like when you have to saw off a limb. With your litio, I tried it on the servant who came to bring me supper. It didn't put her to sleep, but she was paralyzed beyond remedy. She fell like a rock, and I used the moment to escape. I regret what I did to her, but my freedom came first. Anyway—you have the strongest geomancer of Sadul Fuerte in your manor to set her right."

A bitter smirk warped Reina's lips at how wrong Maior was, but she kept her silence on the matter. "So, this order of yours, are you duty bound to cure me?"

"Not at all."

"Then why?"

Maior rose suddenly. "I do what I want, especially with a duskling."

Reina wanted to spit at her feet.

"You will need your health to teach me how to properly live here, while that star journeys through our sky. They won't want me after that, right?"

Reina let out a noncommittal grunt.

"Tomorrow you can show me." Maior maneuvered out of the room.

She was a human with many pretenses, Reina noted with a scowl, used to reaching for and getting what she wanted under the guise of exchanging kindnesses. Obtaining comforts during her time of captivity as a trade for getting on Reina's good side.

No other human had attempted this tactic on her. Perhaps

because Reina had never before been in a position of power over their lives. Faintly, Reina decided she liked it.

The next day, after boiling creek water for a bath and raking the tangles out of her curly hair, Reina showed Maior around Gegania. The house was bordered by a garden of herbs now overrun by weeds, a stable without a donkey or mule, a shed with tools to process grains, and a conuco where purple potatoes, cassava, corn, and malanga grew freely. The fresh water came from a nearby sparkling creek, which fed seven small lakes at the base of the valley farther east. The bushel of corn and bundles of cheese in the stores were the telltale that Celeste had planned to make an extended stay before disappearing.

Maior didn't need much more instruction to make herself at home. She ground the corn and made them arepas on the dusty budare and inquired about the potatoes to later cook a pisca without a chicken or an egg.

Reina ate the shared meal and laughed when Maior grew flustered at the insinuation that she always had to keep her hands busy. The human had a talent for cooking, but this compliment Reina withheld.

They spent the day in friendly cohabitation. Maior pretended there were no hurt feelings between them, or maybe she was just easy to talk to. Mostly, Maior kept to herself while Reina cataloged Gegania's curiosities and inspected any traces left behind, seeking to understand why Celeste chose to travel to La Cochinilla at all.

As nighttime fell and Reina's belly was full from Maior's arepas, the healer again coerced Reina into sleeping for a full night. And Reina humored it, to prove her ailment was due to the caudillo's rot and the deterioration of her starved heart, nothing else. Indeed, the next day her exhaustion became an insidious thing, resurfacing when she needed to take the steps up and down the house and the surrounding conuco. The iridio her grandmother had given her was a salve. It refreshed her ache anytime she applied another drop-let or two, until the haunting pain returned with the reminder that she was no longer complete.

Iridio was the catalyst to change the course of Gegania's con-nection, and so Reina dared not touch the iridio table, afraid it would consume what little fuel she had in her. As she stood at the entrance to the underground storage, she saw that a ransacking or a whirl-wind hadn't been the cause of the mess. Everything stood right where she expected it to be, with the exception of open books sur-rounding the table, a trail of crumbs leading to the tunnel's heavy doors to the outside world. She knelt by each book and found their commonality: All were accounts and publications on the folklore and legends arisen from the lands of Fedria and Venazia before Pentimiento's arrival. Ancient tongues and fairy tales and tradi-tions of worship. The native valcos, nozariels, and even the extinct yares had believed in as many gods as there were facets of life: gods for blacksmithing; gods for mixing herbs into salves; gods to over-see funeral rites; gods for growing bountiful harvests. Few names escaped obscurity through the passing of generations, like Ches and Rahmagut did for being protagonists in many surviving tales. Perhaps it was because their magic was the realest. Or at least Rah-magut's was. (The susurration in her heart stirred in agreement.)

As Reina leafed through the pages across the multiple books, she saw they were all recounting Rahmagut's legend, the changes his claw exerted on the world, and his reign of el Vacío. Celeste had taken a deep dive into the pursuit she had abjured from the very beginning. It made sense she sought a solution, now that she knew she was a Dama del Vacío. And she'd always had the resources to do so: first with the wealth of knowledge Doña Ursulina and her laboratory held, and now with the collective books and maps of Doña Laurel's cartographer ancestors.

One of the open books had a page ripped out, and beside it on the remaining page was the tale of Ches's Blade. Reina barely spared it a second look, for it was one of those fables she had known from rhymes and superstitions since she'd been a child: Ches leav-ing signs and tools for those he deemed worthy. The honorable and righteous warrior reaching the summit of the Plume and encountering Ches's Blade, a weapon that could tear nighttime from the sky to create a full day of perpetual daylight if swung from the highest peak of the highest mountain. Reina chuckled. If one such place ought to exist, it would probably be in the Páramo.

Her chest shook her with pain again. She fell to her knees, the fall scraping the skin beneath her pants. Black dots cluttered her vision, and her temples throbbed, deafening her. She realized she wasn't alone when her name flitted out of Maior's lips as Reina's body contacted the ground a second time.

An ache like two boulders colliding sprouted from the left side of her chest. "I need more iridio," she said breathlessly. For she was *so* tired of continually collapsing. Of being so utterly weak, like some trout out of water. What Doña Ursulina had given her wasn't enough sustenance, especially as she dared not use it all in one go.

Maior's brown eyes fixated on Reina. They were arched with worry, and her rosy lips were slightly parted. It filled Reina with anger, that Maior was acting this concerned for the fate of her heart, after all the angry side-glances and the speciesist quips about her nozariel blood. But mainly, it angered Reina to notice how comely she was, with her smooth freckled cheeks and thick lashes curled up.

"I can try a galio spell—if it can ease the pain," Maior said with her gaze hinting at Reina's galio rings.

"I can't be cured with galio," Reina muttered. She would have howled it, but her belly was full from the meal Maior had cooked her.

"I'm not trying to cure you. But galio can make you forget you're suffering this much."

"So that I can ignore the pain and walk myself straight into my grave?"

Maior opened and closed those lips of hers like a fish. Finally she blew away at her own hair in exasperation. She sat across from Reina but shoved some distance between them. "Do you have to be this difficult? I'm trying to be grateful."

"Grateful?" Reina's voice was brittle.

Maior waved at the vastness of the underground room, gesturing all about her. "I'm trying to force myself to believe this is the best thing for me. I'm trying to show gratitude to you, for not taking me back to that witch. You know—you spend so much time thinking about how I'm going to hate you that you can't even recognize kindness when I'm obviously trying to offer it."

It left Reina without anything to say because...Maior was right. So Reina stubbornly retreated to the facts. "A spell of galio can numb me, but I will still be weak. I will need to buff myself with bismuto, to make it anywhere before I can find more iridio."

"And where can we get more?"

"Anywhere with geomancers. The richer, the better."

They had Gegania's connection to La Cochinilla as an option. Reina had never visited the town before, but the name wasn't unknown to the travelers of Venazia; hence it had to be more than a mere dilapidated mark on the map.

"Someone should sell it in La Cochinilla," Reina added.

"Do you have escudos? Or something we can barter for it?"

Reina nodded, thinking of the velvet pouch given to her by her grandmother.

"All right, give it to me, and I'll go fetch you more iridio."

Reina choked on her own spit. She spluttered until tears gathered in her eyes. Meanwhile, an indignant glare manifested in Maior's expression, at the mockery of her offer. But even as she tried, she couldn't manage looking menacing, for she was soft and plump, with the face of someone who had never attempted malice before.

"You will not," Reina said, though she was in disbelief to have to say it at all.

"You need help."

"And you are forgetting what you are." She lacked the finality she needed, but she was weak and grimacing and clutching her chest again.

"Well, I am not your prisoner!" Maior said like a child, stretching the truth. For beneath the surface of her attempted self-preservation existed an irrefutable fact: what Reina would do if Maior ever did try to leave on her own. She muttered, "I just don't want to be left behind in this house. I think you are my only ally in this."

Reina nodded with a pointed eyebrow.

"You might die if I let you out of my sight."

"Maybe so." What she didn't know, which Reina didn't bother to attest, was that until she had ensured Celeste's safety, she would fight tooth and nail before she let herself perish.

Maior's brows bunched up. A plea.

Shivers rocked Reina, so she surrendered to the offer. She leaned toward the human and said, "All right, soothe me with a spell, and you may come."

Reina handed Maior her galio rings for the incantation. Reina carried them for the most basic first aid, a superficial cut or a sprained ankle.

Maior wore the rings up to her middle knuckles, as the bands were too small for her fingers. They fit snuggly as she intertwined her fingers and massaged her hands. Then she spread both palms as if tugging threads of candied sugar between them. Her warm hands surfed over Reina's frame, hovering over her frizz and shoulders and chest before ferrying along the length of her arms. The soothing effects were instantaneous. Reina's heartache disappeared, her breathing calming to that of a pleasant resting state.

Reina closed her eyes, more to ignore Maior's proximity, her warmth, and the fullness of her chest. A pang of betrayal hit Reina then, for the desire worming itself within her. She forced Celeste into her thoughts, as if by conjuring her into her mind, she could remember just how rudimentarily plain Maior was in comparison.

They leaned away from each other when it was over.

"Better?" Maior asked.

Reina nodded and got to her feet, wiping her palms free of floor dust. She fetched her machete from where it stood against the staircase doorway. "We must go immediately," she said. "The gold is in the kitchen upstairs."

Maior looked eager and ready when she returned with the velvet pouch in hand. She was a sweet, expectant thing.

"I never imagined myself adventuring with a nozariel."

"Adventuring," Reina parroted in mockery. Her tail slapped the air behind her as she approached the tunnel's door, to make a point of what she was.

"It'll make me hate you a little less for forcing me to live here," Maior said lightly, following.

"Of course!" Reina made a fist in the air. "I've always wanted to be a good kidnapper! A dream come true."

The human woman threw her smile to the ceiling and laughed.

27

Heart of Iridio

Gegania's canal opened next to a lone rain tree standing on a vast flatland. Reina didn't have to question the tunnel's magic, for she could immediately tell they had emerged far from the mountains. She understood this heat and found she'd missed it; stepping into it felt like reuniting with a long-lost family member. It was the same suffocating humidity she'd grown up with in Segolita, with a sun mercilessly beating down on her shoulders and drenching her body with perspiration. Not even the breezes were a reprieve, blowing hot air through the trees, their rustling of parched grasses joining the cicadas' shrill. Heat mirages twisted and bent the moriche palm trees in the far distance, where the horizon merged with an enamel-blue sky.

Río'e Marle wasn't far off. The burrow had the convenience of opening near a reedbed. Thus, with Reina's memory of the iridio table's superimposed map, she led them upstream toward La Cochinilla.

The journey's brevity was a mercy under the sun. Silence kept them company like a third traveler, as Maior wasn't one for useless small talk. The only times she spoke were to point out in wonder or surprise a baby caiman hidden beneath the river's surface or a startled capybara swimming in the opposite direction of their passing.

Reina endured it thanks to her own spell of bismuto, one she'd cast before leaving the burrow in case they encountered tinieblas. With the enchantment, her swelling body felt the same as it had back when all was right in Águila Manor. But this stability was a lie, hinging on magic masking her unraveling health. The biggest surprise, however, was turning to Maior under the influence of bismuto and seeing Doña Laurel's taller ghost as an afterimage on her body, planted there by Doña Ursulina to be the reminder of all they would gain.

Reina didn't allow herself to feel guilty or conflicted about it. She had a goal and a life to look forward to after fulfilling Rahmagut's legend, and any pity for Maior was nothing but a distraction.

"Something I can't piece together," Reina said, "is how you made it to Apartaderos before me."

Maior wiped the sweat from her forehead and glanced at the taller Reina with her rosy mouth agape. Her eyes glossed with confusion.

"I saw you in the caudillo's office, when he tricked me into an iridio pact. Don't you remember that?"

Their footsteps crunched on the tall grass as she waited for Maior's memory to piece together. A bird or a monkey hooted in the distance.

"Yes, I remember."

Reina tried reading Maior's expression, but Maior looked away in avoidance. Reina gave Maior the space to speak, and eventually she did. "I couldn't move myself."

"I saw that."

"But that doesn't mean I wasn't aware."

Reina hated the admission.

"So you saw everything? You heard how he called me a traitor and accused me of being worthless to the family?"

Maior chewed her lower lip, as if it would somehow excuse her from telling Reina the truth. "I didn't care so much about what was happening to you, if I'm being honest. And I lacked a lot of context to understand it, really."

This perked Reina's brows. She let her gaze surf the softness of Maior's cheek and took notice of the constellation of moles climbing up her neck.

Maior hugged herself, despite the heat. Finally she ceased gnawing on her lip and said, "When I'm under Doña Ursulina's control, it's like I'm in a nightmare. I can kind of see everything that's happening around me, but I can't do anything about it. It's like a spiraling panic. Knowing that I can't control what's happening around me makes it worse. It compounds, you know?"

Reina nodded, even if she understood in only the vaguest terms.

"I saw you, and I could tell the caudillo was berating you, but I was more focused on what was happening to me—not being able to get out of that. Then you and Doña Ursulina left."

"She left you with the caudillo?" Immediately the implications made Reina feel filthy.

"It's not like it was the first time."

Reina had no words.

"But this time she didn't keep me under her control when she left. I came to myself." Maior shook her shoulders, unloading a shiver. She frowned to the heat mirages on the horizon.

Reina wanted to prod further for the tale. But to what end? Likely, she was only going to discover more horrible things for which she had been an instrument.

"He didn't like that I was myself again," Maior added. "That I wasn't his wife. So he dismissed me."

Reina could already imagine the rest without being told. Her lips battled a smile of admiration. Escaping Águila Manor was no small feat.

"A maid escorted me back to the dungeon room, and I knew that galio spell of putting people to sleep, like I told you. But I did it wrong, I guess, with the litio."

"This wasn't just that maid's mistake," Reina said, with a swell of contentment, because it meant Doña Ursulina herself wasn't as infallible as Reina had always imagined. "My grandmother let you out of her control."

"Yes, she underestimated me. All of you underestimated me," Maior concluded with a raised chin.

"Well, up until you, none of the other women put up much of

a fight." Now she doubly understood why Doña Ursulina had left Celeste for last—she thought she was the only one who could foil their plans.

Maior grimaced, her glimpse of Reina full of disgust.

Perhaps Reina deserved it, and the look was already directed at her, the first stone thrown, so she went on. "It was easy to collect the ones before you. What was not easy was confirming that they were truly damas." Reina tried not to think too much about the endless trek to deposit or retrieve the babes. "The country is supposed to be at peace. Most people don't expect to be taken away in the middle of the night by a witch, or a valco, or me. I mean, there are fireside stories warning against ghosts and such, but mostly everyone feels protected, with their Virgin." The last she added with a derisive chuckle.

"Keep Her out of this."

Reina rolled her eyes. "Where was your Virgin when Javier took you from your home?" Where had Ches been when Reina was being devoured by tinieblas? Or when the emptiness of Doña Laurel's death had filled the manor? Only Rahmagut was capable of giving answers.

"She gave me the courage to flee Águila Manor at the right time."

Reina could not refute it. Finding Maior had been one of her few strokes of luck.

"Just like She put you in my path when the Águila soldiers came to Apartaderos."

Reina glanced at her in surprise, and Maior only stared ahead, sucking on her lower lip in an attempt to hide her amusement.

"*I* was *your* stroke of luck?" Reina said.

Maior didn't reply right away. She merely watched the vast Llanos with a look of satisfaction. "Are all nozariels as strong as you?" she asked.

Reina's right hand rested lazily on the hilt of her machete, the ragged texture as familiar as her own body. "Strong?" she parroted with an inflection, surprised. She knew she was strong—it was where her value lay. But this was the first time hearing the acknowledgment from someone else. "I guess they could be," she said, unsure, "if they trained like I did or learned geomancia."

Maior huffed in disbelief.

"What?"

"You dragged me around like I was a twig, in Águila Manor and in Apartaderos."

Reina snickered. "More like a bollo."

Maior opened her mouth in feigned offense.

Reina didn't bother clarifying her thoughts on the matter, and she only jested. She liked Maior's roundness, she decided. "Yes, we're stronger and faster than humans. But I also use bismuto a lot."

"You'll take me back to Apartaderos after this is over, right?"

The sincerity in the question took Reina aback.

"You promised me I would be safe. That's your part of the bargain."

Reina shrugged and muttered a noncommittal, "You'll be fine."

With a toothless smile, Maior sized her up.

"What is it now?"

"I suppose I should consider myself lucky, to have you as protector."

Reina rolled her eyes and added dryly, "I'm all you've got."

Maior nodded and said, "But yes, to answer your question, I probably made it back to Apartaderos before you because I know the mountains better. They've been my home all my life." She arched a brow, waiting for Reina to fight the declaration.

Ego wounded, Reina almost blurted that she'd nearly wasted a whole day of hiking searching for Gegania's burrow. But she caught herself and swallowed it down. Why did it matter what Maior thought of her? This moment was nothing but an inconsequential detour on her path of reconciling with Celeste.

Soon enough the riverbed met a footpath, and they walked until the crumbling remains of a fort came into view.

"This must be it," Reina muttered, wiping trickles of sweat out of her brows and temples. "La Cochinilla."

They took in the entirety of the town from the highest point of a mild knoll. La Cochinilla was nothing more than a walled stone fort with rusted cannons spiking out of the highest turrets like a thorny crown. From their elevation, they had a view of the dilapidated houses of clay and stone within, as parts of the walls were caved in or had holes where they'd been breached by a siege. Beyond the fortress, and visible from their vantage point, were raised rectangular fields growing produce, kept humid and prosperous by the flooded canals surrounding them. And even farther behind those fields was a colossal mountain in the shape of a table, jutting out of the earth as if forced by a willful god, a blot of dark brown against a blue horizon. The Plume.

Maior had a look of silent determination as they entered the town. She took rein of their mission once Reina shrugged upon being asked if she knew the way around. And Maior didn't flinch or cower, as Reina had expected her to, after encountering one nozariel after another.

"Why don't they have tails, like you do?" Maior asked as she watched a chiding mother drag a boy by the pointed ear back into their home.

Reina clenched her jaw at the question, though she knew it came from a place of innocence. "You recoiled at the sight of mine."

"You're the first nozariel I've ever met. Don't tell me only *you* have it?"

It certainly felt like it. "I just told you why they cut it off: Because humans treat it with disgust. Because you already don't accept us when you realize what we are, and having a tail just makes it even more difficult."

When she'd been just a child, a gang of boys from her street had even tried to chop it off her. The kids in Segolita mocked her endlessly in church and school and in the streets, when Juan Vicente wasn't looking. And one day, they actually caught her—by the tail, no less. Reina had nozariel strength, but she was skinny and always hungry, and she was against six boys who dragged her by the tail into the shadows and pinned her to the muddy ground. They brought with them a sheep's shears, claiming they were doing her a favor. She would have lost it, and likely her life from the blood loss or infection, if one of the chapel nuns hadn't heard her cries through the alley at the right moment in time.

"In Segolita the nozariels who aren't poor or homeless wear their hair long to hide their ears," Reina explained. "They wear long-sleeved clothes even though it's always hot like today. There's a powder to be worn over the nose. And it's preferable not to smile, to avoid showing the teeth. A tail has no purpose for people who want to live in a world of humans."

"So they're cut off?" Maior asked softly. It was a wonder, how she made her face as tender as her voice. Reina couldn't even look away.

"Most mothers do it to their newborns, because the bone is soft and the body heals quickly."

"And what about you?"

"My father was a fool. He thought the world would change after the revolution, so he made the decision for me. Don't give me that pitying look. You treated me with disgust like all the rest."

Maior glanced down, jabbing her boot on the dusty path. "I'm sorry for that."

Reina could only bring herself to shrug.

They continued their search, and most townsfolk eyed them curiously, pointing here and pointing there when asked about the alleged trader of geomancia reagents. The town had a curandera, a smoking grandfather with a straw hat told them in exchange for an escudo (but not without laughing at their accents, which he called odd), his leathery finger gesturing to the derelict citadel that had once belonged to the Segolean loyalists who'd founded La Cochinilla.

As they passed the citadel's splintered and dislocated double doors, they found that it had been repurposed as a trading market, its vast hall conveniently providing shade and protection from the elements to the farmers and herders who made La Cochinilla their home. The stone walls concentrated the heat, soaking the air with the stink of manure, spices, leather, and sweat. The outdoor hall-ways and adjoined courtyards were a hub for meetings, gossiping, and even gambling on Calamity. A cuatro's melody was a constant companion to the citadel's chatter, played by a beggar sitting under the shade of a bougainvillea.

Maior lingered over a round of Calamity, watching, until Reina was racked by coughs and they were reminded of their urgency.

"Let me ease the pain," she offered, to which Reina swiped her hand away.

"Don't waste the galio—I'm fine," she said, earning her Maior's scowl.

Finally, after bribing a group of gossiping abuelas for directions, they found the curandera on a higher floor of the citadel, in a wide chamber that had likely once belonged to the former masters of the town. Cracked colorful marbles decorated the floor. The wooden double doors had delicate carvings of moriche palms, herons, and caimans, but now their edges were dull and rounded, swelling with the humid heat of the Llanos.

A man in worn military uniform bid his goodbyes to the curandera as Reina and Maior entered the room. The air was pungent with a mixture of incense and tobacco, and the contents of the room reminded Reina of the caudillo's office, with its maps, dark wood furniture, and plush brocade seating. The crests and family portraits hanging from the walls. The inkwells and pens of exotic plumage.

A wrinkled woman sat behind the counter, filling in a ledger. She was large and dark-skinned and irrefutably nozariel. Her tail switched behind her, like a cat's. A crimson satin ribbon looped around its silky, curly end. Reina watched the tail in awe, as she did on the rare occasions of meeting another like her.

"Well, well, well." The woman cackled when they entered. "I haven't seen such a pretty face around these parts since the Liberator himself kicked them humans out of this fortress."

"We're looking for geomancia metals—iridio, to be precise," Maior said, bravely leading the conversation.

The woman produced a pouch and a stoppered bottle from beneath the counter. "Trying your luck with Ches's Blade, like all the other travelers who've come by my door since the coming of Rahmagut's Claw? I have it in powder form and in solution."

"Excuse me?" Maior uttered uselessly.

"Since its arrival, that star has been the best thing to happen to my business in many years." The woman chuckled.

It wasn't every day that an ancient legend was brought to Reina's attention twice, especially not by two independent sources. Her heart was weak, but her mind was razor-sharp, and it whirred as she connected the crumbs of the books Celeste had left behind. She said in a flurry before she could stop herself, "Did a valco woman come by seeking your iridio? A noblewoman."

The chair creaked as the woman leaned back with a satisfied, vulpine smile. "Why, indeed. Valcos are not easy to miss."

"Light-skinned and black of hair? Was she seeking Ches's Blade?"

The memory of the open books and ripped pages came rushing back to Reina. If only she had spent more time deciphering what Celeste was trying to get out of them.

"The look of most Segoleans. And yes, like most of the strangers coming by my shop these days. La Cochinilla isn't known for much. It's not like travelers are pouring down for our cassava and maize. But we are at the foot of the Plume. This is the last place you'll find geomancia reagents if the lure of adventure is telling you to look for the weapon."

Maior looked from the woman to Reina as if they were speaking in another dialect.

The heat suffocated Reina, as did her own desperation. She approached the counter, where in the candlelight, she had a better view of the curandera, and she of Reina.

"The valco woman, did you see her wear the ivory eagle crest of the Águilas? Did she wield a scythe?"

"She was the daughter of the caudillo of Sadul Fuerte, yes."

"You recognized her?"

"Not immediately, but I know of her father. Who do you think supplies my iridio? Águila is a famous name for anyone who makes a living out of trading geomancia materials."

"That's why Celeste connected the house to La Cochinilla. She's after the blade, at the Plume," Reina said, thinking aloud and turning to Maior with a crazed, distant look. But as she regarded the shorter woman, she thought only of Celeste, imagining her standing under this same roof seeking the iridio powering her scythe and Gegania. Reina asked the curandera. "You said there were other travelers going to the Plume as well. Why?"

Like a perched feline enjoying the attention, the woman laughed. "I suppose, for many, seeing Rahmagut's Claw in the sky is proof of the old gods, despite how hard the Penitents try to erase this truth. If Rahmagut's Claw makes his legend real, then Ches's legend must be real as well."

Maior's warm hand circled Reina's elbow. The gesture was familiar, intimate, and it grounded Reina. "What is Ches's legend?" asked Maior.

"His blade, girl." The curandera's words were a lash. "Rahmagut and Ches are gods at odds. Ches, the creator of the sun, and Rahmagut, his greedy opposer. Rahmagut gives boons to his followers, a promise of power to those who weaken the seal Ches forced on him. Ches does the same, but his blessings fall on those who seek the light." She snorted wetly. "All of you coming to me for iridio before heading to the Plume, your heads are filled with nothing but hot air, thinking you are Ches's chosen one, destined to find his blade. Only tinieblas and death await. Mark my words."

Maior's eyes continued to be clouded in confusion, so Reina explained the crux of the matter. "In the stories, Ches's Blade ends nighttime. It cuts through it and brings back the day."

According to Doña Ursulina, Rahmagut's Claw needed to be visible for the offer of the damas; thus they could only do it during the twenty days it took the star to travel through their skies. Though now, from Celeste's actions, Reina understood it also needed to happen during nighttime. But not if the night itself was prevented by the blade. And every part of Reina knew without a droplet of doubt that Celeste was worthy to be blessed by Ches, to wield his blade.

The realization paralyzed her, tugging her with equal force in opposite directions. Celeste was relying on a nozariel legend to deny her father and Doña Ursulina. If Reina cared for her (and she did, deeply), how could she act against her wishes? How could she reconcile the promises of her grandmother with her dreams of Celeste?

Her heart, too, protested, whispering devilishly and summoning the pain Reina and Maior had numbed with their spells. Her vision muddied with dots of black. She supported herself on a nearby chest of drawers, which gave under her weight and squeaked loudly as it slid over the marble. Reina had known it was coming—knew the bismuto and galio had worn off—yet it didn't make it any easier when the air was knocked out of her.

Maior called her name, rushing to her.

Reina's body betrayed her as she collapsed like a rag to the floor. Searing pain erupted from her chest, constricting her throat, ringing in her ears, and blurring her sight into blackness. She curled into a ball, grasping herself. She was crying or moaning—she couldn't be sure. And someone screamed above her. Maior. Her voice was shrill and obnoxious, and Reina couldn't understand why this woman couldn't just let her writhe *in peace*.

Maior gathered her in an embrace, but her touch was also fire, until it wasn't. The agony in Reina's chest turned to a warm, comforting water. She smelled moras, and in that moment, the image of Celeste smiling crossed her mind. Like when they'd built castles of pebbles and dirt in the courtyard after sparring lessons or shared the freshly picked overripe moras from the Águila finca.

Was this going to be her end?

Clarity yanked her back to consciousness. Maior and the curandera crowded her, moved her so she lay on someone's lap.

Reina glanced directly overhead and met Maior's wide doe eyes as she massaged Reina with soothing galio magic. Maior unbuttoned Reina's vest and yanked her shirt up, her hands working with purpose to move her bindings and unclasp a tube from her heart's contraption.

"Don't," Reina moaned, panicking at the prospect of Maior undressing her. If she handled the wrong tube, it truly would be the end.

"I know what to do." Maior's voice trembled, like she cared.

She told the curandera, "*Please* let us have the iridio—we'll pay for it later."

"I have no guarantees you will pay for it once it's all consumed," the woman said. "Humans betray my trust at every opportunity they can."

"She is nozariel like you!" Maior hissed with a fire Reina had never imagined she could wield. "And her death will be on your hands if you don't give it to us now. It's not for me! You have a solution of it right there on your counter. Bring it over, and if our gold isn't enough, I will personally be indebted to you until it can be paid back in full." She had conviction, even if it came brittle and broken. "If you call yourself a curandera, then you must give it. Please."

Reina was blinded and deafened by the pain. She didn't see or hear what they did. All she knew was that, in a moment, it was over. The world came into focus. Her headache and heartache calmed to a mild throb. She sucked in a fat breath, and when agency returned to her, she reconnected the tube and scampered away from Maior's lap.

Maior's face split into a relieved smile, beads of sweat rolling down her temples. The flask of iridio still hung from her hands. "Are you all right? Is it better?"

Reina's fingers were clumsy sticks fumbling to rearrange her bindings and smoothen her shirt. She didn't want to imagine what Maior thought of her, after seeing her naked and squirming pathetically. She forced a stoic face and just muttered a thanks.

Maior helped her to her feet.

"Well, that was quite the spectacle," the curandera said, settling back behind the counter.

"We came here for iridio because we need it." Maior spoke for Reina, shooting a meaningful look her way.

The curandera ignored Maior. She said, "And to think that witch was right: a nozariel with a heart of iridio."

"What witch?" Reina blurted out.

"You're not the first Parameña to come by my shop today. I can tell where you come from by the way she speaks," the curandera said, pointing a sausage finger at Maior. "And, of course, from the spectacle of your heart."

When Reina grimaced in confusion, the curandera elaborated. "Like I said, Rahmagut's Claw stirred the hive. First came the valco half-breed, and second came that witch from Sadul Fuerte. Ursulina. She talked about you, her granddaughter."

"What?"

"She came demanding to know if a nozariel half-breed had come by already in the company of the caudillo's daughter. She expected you to have an...urgent need for my iridio, and I can clearly see why now."

"Doña Ursulina was here," Reina said, to let it sink in.

The curandera chuckled. "Indeed. Came like a tyrant, demanding I sell her all my iridio. I gave her a good amount for an inflated price—not like she'll have much luck finding it anywhere else in these parts. Though, for someone who works under the employ of the master of all iridio, she sure has a demand for it. Why is she buying it from other sources if she can get it directly from the caudillo? Something stinks there." Her eyebrows curved shrewdly as she added, "And she offered me a mighty prize for holding her granddaughter when she inevitably came by."

As Reina made sense of the tale, she realized it sounded like a trap. But why would Doña Ursulina bother with snaring her before reaching Tierra'e Sol? They had agreed on her objective, which Reina desperately needed to complete in order to live. Unless Doña Ursulina distrusted Reina's intentions after Maior's disappearance.

"Mentioned you were fetching something for her—Rahmagut's reincarnated wife?"

Reina's eyes found Maior, who was paralyzed by the news, backing away against a crate near the door. Doña Ursulina expected Reina to come to La Cochinilla with Celeste, not Maior. Even if the curandera had her facts befuddled, they were true, and they lifted the veil Reina had spun all this time to keep Maior docile.

"How can you tell I'm the one Doña Ursulina speaks of?" Reina asked in a last attempt at self-preservation.

"How many nozariels with hearts of iridio do you think exist?" the curandera said.

Maior looked to Reina in disbelief or betrayal—a gaze Reina couldn't hold for long. She knew the human was on the verge of bolting. And she knew once she did, Reina would have no other choice but to hold her back, by force if necessary.

"Either way, I'm not in the business of helping humans with their schemes. They always involve the wrong crowd, and a nozariel always ends up getting hurt."

Reina shoved the bag of escudos her way, plopping it over the counter. "Sell me your iridio. In powder and solution—all of it."

The curandera's eyes glinted at the gold. "Now wait a moment. First we must weigh it and count your gold. And you must pay for the solution the human used on you. I'll sell you half of it, for *all* your escudos. But only because we both know it's that nozariel blood in you that's stopping them from treating you fair." She put an emphasis on *them* and gestured behind Reina.

With a sinking stomach, she saw Maior taking off. She had to squash the instinct to dart after her. Purchasing the iridio was her priority.

"Some galio healer, that girl is," the woman muttered as she walked to her cabinets to scoop half the powder into a sack. "Never trust humans. *Or valcos.*" She gave Reina a meaningful look as she added, "Learn from this bitter old woman, and don't repeat my mistakes. We're separate creatures for a reason. Just say enough is enough and refuse their schemes. It's the only way to end the abuse. I mean, look at what happened to the yares. Killed to extinction."

Reina bolted the moment she had the sack of iridio powder in her hands. She caught up to Maior at the crowded entrance of the citadel marketplace and yanked her by the arm.

"Hey!" Maior yelped.

"You can't run away," Reina growled.

Maior towered over her with all the shortness of her stature. Her glare fixated on Reina, glossy. "You've been playing me for a fool. This whole time—it's always been a lie."

Reina's cheeks burned, at her pretenses and the open-ended meaning. As if whatever existed between them hadn't been born exclusively from self-interest. So she leaned on the irrefutable facts. "I helped you escape Don Enrique's men, and Gegania is the only place where you'll be safe. Has that been a lie?"

"Safe." Maior spat the word between them. She yanked herself free again but headed in the direction of Gegania's burrow.

Reina fell into pace with her. "You heard the curandera: We have to go to the Plume. That's where Celeste went. She's the Dama del Vacío the curandera was talking about, not you."

Maior jerked away as Reina tried steering her by the elbow. "You just said I would be safe in Gegania."

Reina had no patience for her protests. She was too hot and wired from the fresh iridio. In the shade of La Cochinilla's walls, Reina wrenched Maior by the arm to stop her from heading in the wrong direction. She trapped Maior against the crumbling stone.

The surprise was bright in Maior's eyes. Her cheeks and lips were red and flushed, from the heat or from her anger, and Reina swallowed heavily to clear her mind of the distraction. She didn't think on the words; she just spoke from her chest, still raw from the humiliation of having her cavities opened and exposed.

"I don't trust you. I don't trust you won't run off if I leave you alone in the house. You'll be found by the caudillo's men. Or worse, you'll be killed by tinieblas." Reina couldn't be sure Maior wasn't going to do something reckless after learning Reina's true purpose.

Maior's scorn came with her silence. There was betrayal written on her face. The sting of it angered Reina. Because why should she feel weighed down by Maior's expectations? Nothing and no one mattered besides her singular goal. Her heart ached for the stability of health and family, for the companionship she knew only Celeste could give her. For this to happen, their life needed to be back to normal, with Doña Laurel in it. And Rahmagut was going to give it to them.

"Your whole speech in Apartaderos, about helping me stay free from the caudillo and that—that *hag*, was all a lie, wasn't it?"

Maior's voice was soft but not without her relenting determination. "You saw me as a naïve fool and used that to get me to follow you while you looked for the other dama to collect us all."

"What we're doing is bigger than you. It is a year in the making."

"You will continue to do that witch's bidding?"

"You wouldn't understand. She saved my life."

Reina's breath shuddered. After nearly a decade of loneliness, of being regarded with disdain, Doña Ursulina and Doña Laurel were the only ones who had given her a home. Despite her unconventional methods, Doña Ursulina was all Reina had. She had left Segolita for this. Her home was back in Águila Manor, awaiting her triumphant return.

"Well, back there, so did I," Maior countered.

Reina clicked her tongue at that.

"So you will drag me along in search of this Celeste."

Reina hated the tone and implication, the flippant way she referred to Celeste. "I don't care what you think about this. I'm going to the Plume for her, and if I have to bring you along, so be it. Nothing changes. Celeste's capable of taking care of herself, but as long as she's away, I won't know if she needs my help. She's my best friend, and I would do anything for her."

Maybe she'd said too much. Maybe it was unnecessary or a confession. But it felt cathartic to say the words, even if to the wrong person.

Maior sucked in a breath. Then, she whispered, so softly that it was almost lost to the surrounding town chatter, "Why do you talk about her that way? Like you love her?"

The racing of Reina's heart had nothing to do with its adjustment to this new method of using iridio. She stepped back, glancing about them, afraid someone had overheard. But no one cared about the nozariel and the human tucked into the shadows of the fort.

Maybe all this time, while Reina was noticing the dimples and the pouting lips and the flush on her cheeks, Maior had been watching her back. A pang bloomed in her chest, making it hard to breathe while they were this close. All this time, the concern this human had felt for her had been genuine.

The realization infuriated Reina—especially as a part of her *enjoyed* the discovery. It was anger she clung to as she reminded herself now wasn't the time to have doubts or unnecessary feelings for the wrong person. Celeste was her priority and her future. Her grandmother and the Águilas would always be the priority. So she calculated her statement to sting as much as possible, to squash any hope Maior would otherwise have. "What exists between me and Celeste—it's none of your concern. So now you know the truth about me. My grandmother instructed me to bring her the damas to invoke Rahmagut, and that is what I will do. Even if it validates your speciesism. Even if you hate me for every moment of it. You think you're not a prisoner, but these are freedoms I have given you, and right now, if you don't come willingly, I will take them away."

28

The Fallen Star

Eva's eyes snapped open to darkness. She curled forward, gasping. She sat up suddenly and smacked her skull against a forehead.

The person moaned and moved away.

Eva, too, hissed from the impact, screwing her eyes. She grappled at her clothes, feeling for blood or for gashes but finding none. The fire-lick pain she had felt before losing consciousness was utterly gone. She was in one piece.

As her eyes adjusted, the darkness became less absolute. In fact, the sky was lit by the swirls and waves and clusters of stars. Millions of them. And the star with the streaking tail of cyan was the brightest of them all.

She was in a clearing, at the foot of a great cliff, wrapped in a hemp blanket and lying across from a burned-out campfire. Bordering the clearing was the dense blackness of a jungle bursting with the sounds of night. A mild, hot breeze lifted the sour, moist smell of the surrounding greenery.

Javier sat across from her, perhaps too closely. With a grimace he massaged his forehead where they'd collided.

The memories of the night came down on her, like one of her grandmother's backhands, heavy and deserving.

"I...I thought I died."

Javier let out a deep breath. "You would have, if I hadn't found you," he said. "How could you be so stupid?"

Eva looked away. She gripped her clothes tight, ashamed and repulsed that she had one more item to add to the list of things she was indebted to him for.

He pressed both hands to his face and sighed.

Eva lifted the hemp blanket tighter around her. It was comforting to do so, to feel her chest and skin unexposed to those flesh eaters. Her stomach felt feeble, like one wrong thought or memory would be enough to make her retch out what little was stored in there.

"You're incredible. Somehow your litio wards were strong enough to protect you from the tinieblas' rot. Otherwise you'd be alive right now, but your heart would...be rotting away." Javier reached forward, almost like he had any kindness in him. His great farce. "You're fine—just disoriented—it happens. Galio healing will do that if the wound is severe—"

She swatted his hand away. "Don't touch me."

Silence descended over their campground.

"Just tell me what happened," she said.

His shoulders stiffened. He leaned away. "Fine. You want me to tell you? You're an idiot, that's what happened. Suicidal. Stupid. Reckless. I get the running away part. You must be regretting leaving your comfortable home—homesick—"

"It's disappointment. I was tricked," she said. His assumptions angered her. He couldn't be more wrong. "Did you forget about what happened in El Carmín?" she asked him.

Javier only stared, which was more of an insult. He couldn't even give her the decency of an apology. But perhaps she was the fool for expecting one. "What else do you want me to tell you? You left the town and its wards, and you walked right into a tiniebla nest."

Eva ran her hands down her forearms, the memory of the attack lifting her skin in goose bumps. Their eyes. Their manic greed. How the light of her spells barely touched them and yet Eva could sense their hunger.

"I don't understand," she said slowly, and it was once again the painful reminder of the imbalances between them. His wealth of knowledge and her sheltered ignorance. "I—I don't understand what that means. My heart rotting. The town's wards. Tinieblas." A second shiver ran through her, like a pointed icicle scratching down her spine. The name sounded fitting, for the darkness they exuded. "Is that...what they are—those creatures?"

Javier nodded. "Didn't they ever teach you about tinieblas in Galeno?"

Images of the hacienda returned to her, the fire-red sunsets and the lonesome rain trees standing guard on flatlands that went on forever. How she missed her cousins' laughter, their silly games across the courtyards, and the admonishing call of an aunt telling them to settle down. The smell of black bean soup with coconut, when the cook wanted to spoil her.

"My grandmother never concerned herself with talk of Fedria."

Javier chuckled. "Tinieblas exist everywhere, even in Galeno, I'm sure."

Eva clenched her jaw as she recalled the night when she'd fought Décima. The bull standing on two feet and climbing a mango tree with the dexterity of a capuchin.

He got to his feet and moved away to sit over another hemp blanket he used for his bedding. More traveling supplies surrounded them. Blankets, a kettle on the burned-out campfire, and firewood. There was even a tied mule facing the jungle, snoozing, perhaps. All necessities Javier had been forced to procure while Eva had been unconscious.

"Well," she said, "what are they?"

"Rahmagut's spawn from el Vacío. Broken creatures he makes in his pretense for godhood. They don't serve a purpose in this world. They just hunger."

He gazed up at the million stars dotting the sky, so serene and infinite. And Eva followed his gaze, which lingered on the cyan star guiding their journey. Underneath it all, she was so small. A mere sigh of time in the breadth of the expansive universe.

"They're what I would consider true evil," he explained. "Every person they touch, they rot. They're not like a jaguar, serving a purpose to the world by killing. They're born incomplete, and they spend their lives searching for hearts to devour." He pointed at the star. "I can't prove it, but it feels like the tinieblas have gotten worse since the arrival of Rahmagut's Claw. Alborotadas. Like they can sense Rahmagut's influence is stronger."

"You speak of Rahmagut as if he's really real." Even now Eva still shuddered at the mention of the name. Such a habit wasn't easy to overcome, like her fear of leaving her family.

He scoffed. "You better get used to the idea that he is. How else would you explain the monsters that nearly killed you?"

Eva crossed her arms and looked away, indignant. "I always thought of him as real like...the Virgin is. People believe in Her, and She's only watching and listening to prayers." Acting in ways Eva didn't understand, as Doña Antonia used to say. "She doesn't actually interfere in people's lives."

"So when I told you I wanted to parley with Rahmagut, what did you think then?"

Eva had thought he was beautiful, not only for the grace of his valco blood but because he had crossed the country to rescue her. She would have gladly agreed to go anywhere with him, figurative god or not. She'd never admit this now, of course. "You were getting me out of Galeno. I wasn't hung up on the details."

At this, he laughed. "You know the tale of Ches and Rahmagut. I mean, with Calamity, every child grows up knowing at least a bastardized version of it. Where do you think the tale came from? The Pentimiento Church tries to erase it, and they deny the gods' existence, but their influence over our world is real. Rahmagut is the key to our future, Eva."

"How come this is the first time I've heard of tinieblas?"

"How much did they spoil and pamper you in that household, exactly?"

"My family kept me sheltered and ignorant, not spoiled."

Javier clicked his tongue. "Tinieblas only prowl places of great evil. A few exist in the countryside. In Venazia, caudillos task their armies to hunt them down. But Fedria doesn't have many caudillos—most landlords can't even afford the armies to call themselves caudillos. So town chiefs and pastors or curanderos rely on wards to keep their filthy nozariels safe, like the warded statue you saw where you escaped me."

Despite the hemp blanket, Eva couldn't bring herself to feel warm. She was so uncomfortable and alone. She had taken for granted the small comforts of her home. The dry clothes. The exquisite meals. The plush hugs of her grandmother.

"So the geomancia coming off the Ches statue was a protection," she muttered, regretting choosing to ignore him when he had wanted to explain back in the town.

Javier stood up and dusted his clothes. "It's normal to see a statue or chapel with wards made of iridio. Otherwise tinieblas would be pouring in to shred the people of Fedria to ribbons," he said airily, the idea amusing him. "Geomancers bless the sites every so often. And guess where they get all that iridio from?"

His smirk made something deep inside Eva's stomach flutter, but she squashed the feeling.

He approached her. "There are those who say we profit from tinieblas, that we should be giving the iridio freely. But I spit on that notion. Mother discovered iridio. We are the owners of it."

"So what did they do before that? Before the iridio was discovered?"

Javier shrugged. "More resources were spent on the military. Towns couldn't exist without it. But this wasn't that big of a problem when the Segoleans were in power. They had all that gold they've been siphoning from colonies all over the world for generations."

He gave her a long look, taking in the whole length of her, her sweaty face and disheveled hair, probably fascinated at the sheltered life she'd lived. Eva, too, felt cheated by her family. Geomancia and the tinieblas. Fedria and its nozariels. There was so much out there, and they willingly lived blindly and decadently. They were no better than the cattle they raised. Well, Eva wouldn't be like them.

"You said they were supposed to rot my heart, but I stopped them with my magic." It was a reminder that she was already on the right track.

"You saved yourself with litio," he said, extending a hand for her, which Eva avoided. "Get up."

Eva pursed her lips, knowing any objection would only sound like a prissy complaint.

"Despite your lack of training in geomancia, you used up all the litio in your rings and protected yourself against the tinieblas. It was the strength of your geomancia that lured me to you. I could see it all the way from the road."

Eva got to her feet before he demanded it of her again. "Why are you impressed? Wasn't that why you took me out of Galeno? Because I had some potential?"

She let the blanket pool down around her shoulders and onto the ground. As she did so, Eva realized her clothes were different from the ones shredded by the tinieblas. Her skirt had been swapped for pants. Her shirt, a loose cream linen. Was she wearing his clothes that he'd brought for the journey? Shame burned her cheeks.

As she met his impervious gaze, she wished she had the nerve to slap him away. For tricking her out of her life. For changing her clothes without her consent.

"Your use of litio was clumsy," he said, "but it got the job done. Now, let's try to reach a similar level with galio and bismuto, and maybe even iridio."

He summoned a flame wisp between them, letting it shower them in warmth and light.

"When she left home, my niece said she was heading to the Plume. She was so sure she would find the answer to all her problems there." The disdain was clear in his eyes and tone, even as he pointed to the top of the cliff behind them, where the earth jutted toward the sky. "We'll catch up to her at the summit. But she's a willful creature, and she's going to protest everything I say. So I'd like you to be somewhat competent at geomancia before then. You will give me backup."

"Rich of you to assume I'd assist you."

He didn't bother hiding his sneer this time. "If I fail, Eva, you fail with me."

"I didn't run away from you just for the fun of it." Eva wasn't sure she had the mettle to argue with him more or fight him off if he forced her to anything. She merely wanted to maintain an ounce of pride—all she could afford before him.

"Correct me if I'm wrong, but isn't this exactly what you want? To learn geomancia?"

Eva ground her teeth, but in the end, she nodded.

With a slap to the air, he sent the flame wisp hurtling onto the logs and ashes of their campfire. The embers took the fire slowly, creating just enough light to encompass them. Eva watched him cautiously, straining to see if the snaking slivers of black were back. She didn't see them this time.

"So," he said, "geomancia." He nodded at the bands on her fingers. "Litio for protection, bismuto for enhancement, and galio for healing."

From his bedding he grabbed his pocket-sized journal. He opened it somewhere in the middle, then showed it to her.

"Iridio for destruction?" Eva asked.

"No. Iridio's versatile. The key is in the concoction of the solution and the cunning of the caster. It's only ever used for destruction because most humans are so unoriginal they don't care to find out what they can do with it. They just care to blow things up."

"And you don't?" Eva asked, uncaring to hide the insolence. She was going to treat him as bitterly as she felt because he'd earned it, and because being disagreeable was all she had left.

"I like iridio. Only a fool wouldn't. But I have my blade and my blood. In most cases I don't need anything else. The real masters of iridio figure out ways to use it creatively. For example, I know a nozariel half-breed who is alive only because she has a heart of iridio."

"A nozariel half-breed..." Eva parroted, her jaw slightly hanging open. "Is she a master of it?"

At this, Javier let out a mean laugh. "In her dreams maybe."

A small leather knapsack was part of his supplies. He fetched it and opened it for Eva, showing her the velvet pouches and glass potion vials stored within. His slim hand brushed the cork tops of the bottles, clattering the crystals against each other so that Eva could see the solutions glinting in different hues of chartreuse and azure as the liquids caught the campfire light. Glimmering gingers and blacks so dark all the light was sucked in.

"I bought the metals as powders from the trader. We'll do the lesson of mixing them into solution later. The mixing has to be done carefully, and we need proper light to do it. If the potions come out wrong, they won't channel our spells correctly, and they'll go to waste. For now, I want us to go over casting. I want to see what you can do."

"I know a bit of litio," she offered, and he nodded.

"Sure. Litio's the simplest to cast and the hardest to master. Those who master litio, of all three geomancia metals, are untouchable. Your skill with litio is strong. Though you still need to learn how to conserve the potion and minimize its usage. Here, let me refill your rings."

He unstoppered one of the vials as Eva flipped open the crystal cap of her index finger ring. His hand was steady like steel when he ferried to her the dropper replete with a clear liquid. Javier squeezed three droplets of it into the ring's capsule, and she flicked the cap shut. Then they refilled the others.

"Thanks," she said.

"Now try to cast with bismuto." He placed the trunk near the safety of his bedding and brought out the journal once again. The open page had the illustrations as a series of steps: slapping the hands together, then pulling them apart without separating the digits, and finally flicking the wrists to opposite sides. "It's supposed to strengthen your muscles, to give you the strength to move faster, to hit harder. Try it," he commanded.

Eva's eyes lifted to meet his blood-red gaze. Finally, they were doing what she had wanted for so long.

She pressed her hands together like in the illustration, but nothing happened.

"Harder," he said, and there was a tremor to his voice, like a stir of the demon.

"Harder? What's that supposed to mean?"

"You know—you need intention." At her blank stare, he said, "You don't know how to cast body armor with litio."

Eva shook her head.

"And you're too slow anyway. So, if I wanted to strike you, you wouldn't be able to shield yourself from me." Javier took one step closer, then another, his boots crunching loudly on crisp twigs. His eyes were changing. They were still red, but they were cruel and old, as if he had centuries of life behind him.

The terrible dark magic began seeping in and out of his cheeks.

"You can only run away," he purred.

Eva's breath caught in her throat. She tried stepping back but only bumped the back of her calf against a boulder and nearly tripped.

She remembered the way he had flashed from one side of the inn to another, his sword an extension of his left arm. Strides as fast as an afterthought.

"I won't learn like this," she breathed. "I—I need more time."

Javier slapped her on the cheek. It wasn't painful, just a mocking feathery pat.

"So slow and soft," he teased. "If only there were something you could use to run away from me?"

Eva was a sheep awaiting a wolf to pounce. A rodent paralyzed by a slithering snake. She was at the inn, when the putrid magic marred his beauty and turned him into something that wanted to hurt her.

Like now.

Eva leapt back. She ducked away from his second strike and performed the bismuto incantation as described in the journal. At once her essence multiplied into existence in a million different planes and realities, fragmented like the unlimited reflections in opposing shattered mirrors, days and nights whooshing past her, animals and people cutting through the spot where she stood like a ghost. In all of them, her spirit brimmed with glittering magic, a million versions all holding a tiny piece, summing to a colossal well. All at her disposal, to be plucked if she willed it so. And she did. Eva channeled the strength through her rings and hands.

At once, everything flared into cognizance. The warm air became spikes to her lungs. The light of the campfire, a blinding flare of orange. Javier's fist flying toward her, sharp ringing in her ears. She jumped out of the way with strength alien to her muscles and realized: *She* had evaded *him*. Finally, that smile did peek through.

Then he pursued her.

Eva skidded around the campfire and dodged his punch. She leapt again without direction, fear rippling through her at the very real possibility of his strike. The demon was back, and it was enjoying every second of the pursuit.

She ran from the fire, for it was so bright she couldn't see him. She could only hear his breaths, the grass, and his footsteps as loud as shattering glass.

He reappeared in front of her, and Eva screamed.

His laugh was like thunder to her eardrums. "Not bad," he said with the blackness gone. "Bismuto is simple. You just have to learn to conserve your supplies. Are you almost out?"

Eva could feel how much liquid each ring cap had the same way she could feel how empty a jar was by simply lifting it.

"I have enough," she said, her heart still racing.

"Your incantation worked, but it was weak."

She lifted her chin in defiance. "I managed to get away, didn't I?"

"I was going easy on you."

Her jaw clenched. He had been, with the darkness barely at bay. What was he doing that made it consume him? Could it be that it was unintentional, or was it the real him?

If only she had the strength to punch him back—to shove her fist into his face and break that perfect nose of his. But one day, if she kept this up, she would.

"You're going to have to practice—"

"Don't lay a hand on me again. You have no rights to touch me."

As nonchalantly as someone might ask the price of a coffee, he told her, "Oh, Eva Kesaré, I'm not about to stop. Not unless you make me."

He was older, and half valco, and a man. Besting him would be satisfying indeed.

"Until then, you're little more than my minion."

She cursed him.

"Didn't you see this coming? You left your home with a complete stranger," he said, clicking his tongue derisively. "You're only remarkable in your own head, Eva Kesaré—"

"Don't call me that—"

"But to me you are naïve—"

"Don't soil my name—"

"A little bit foolish—"

"Just shut up—"

"And soft, like a rotting banana."

Eva glared at the smile that didn't touch his eyes. Behind them the fire spat, the crackling a soothing companion to nighttime now that her brief bismuto high had faded.

He stepped closer, asking, "So, ready for galio?"

"What—"

But before Eva could finish her sentence, he reached for her forearm and slashed her across the wrist in the same motion with which he had slashed the man at the inn, as if his fingernails were made of steel.

Eva cried as hot blood spilled out in all directions. Fire sprouted from her wrist. She collapsed to her knees, then onto her ass. Javier was back moments later, waving the journal in her face. It was open to the illustration of a different incantation.

"Do it, and quick. Your blood is already scarce from the tiniebla attack."

She thrashed her feet in his direction as her gash pulsed. She cursed his name and his mother's and even his grandmother's, well aware that each word took her closer to her expiration. Eva clamped her hand over her wrist, and still the blood poured out, angry and burning.

"If you lose enough blood, you'll faint again," he told her in his infuriatingly offhanded way.

Eva tried to seize the journal, but he moved it out of her reach.

"Don't touch it with your filthy hands. Just do the hand motion already, and heal the cut. It's not that complicated."

"*Malparido*," she snarled.

He laughed. "What would Doña Antonia say, to hear one of her own have such a potty mouth?"

Hot tears pooled at the corners of her eyes, but she swallowed them down. Hatred was the only thing he deserved.

Eva let go of her wound and slapped her hands together for the incantation. The fingers of her sliced hand were like sticks. She forced them to obey her. In the heat of her pain, it was easy to transpose herself onto the millions of outer planes, to force the will of geomancia into her fingertips like a docile servant.

Threads of gold flitted from her middle finger rings to her pouring wrist, where they took hold of her skin. The glittering threads tugged the opened flesh, and Eva doubled over with a moan. She shut her eyes as the galio sewed the edges together. Then the pain was gone.

She took a heavy gulp of air when it was all over. Blood smeared the length of her wrist and forearm, but it was done fleeing her. A line of scarred skin was the only evidence of Javier's abuse. It looked faded, like it had long since disappeared into the history of her skin.

"Regenerating blood matter is a far more complicated spell," Javier said, standing over her all smug. "I know it, but it requires more galio than you have left. And I already spent too much of mine healing you from the attack. Try to preserve what little blood you have left, in case you decide to run into tinieblas again."

Eva stood up, rancor burning through her nostrils, and immediately regretted it as dots of black blurred her gaze. She almost collapsed on her ass a second time, but Javier's hand shot out and caught her.

"Steady now. Remember the blood."

She shoved him away once her two feet found balance.

"You animal," she spat. "*You* cut me, and all you can do is mock me? *I'm sorry* for suddenly realizing I don't want anything to do with you."

He didn't seem fazed. "Were it not for the bleeding, you would have moaned and complained about learning geomancia. You may be a quarter valco, but you strike me as the type to need that extra push. Let's just say...the traditional methods take too long."

Eva reeled. This was the first time she'd heard him mention the extent of her valco heritage. Like he personally knew her more than she knew herself.

She bit down the questions, which would be better asked when she wasn't fuming.

"Are you ready to learn iridio?"

"What, are you going to let a tiniebla loose on me? 'Oh, what better way to learn iridio than to have a starving demon rip your bowels open!'" she mocked in a crude impression of him.

Javier smirked. Again, he moved so fast Eva barely registered him slamming the heel of his palm to her chest, where the iridio pendant hung from a chain.

The blow dislocated her soul, her essence. She was shoved into the vastness of the open universe, thrust into a darkness disrupted only by the faraway swirls of galaxies, hundreds and millions of them.

Every star and every planet was bursting with light energy. Vivid and hot and bright, boiling through clusters to suffocate her. The energy went into Eva. It impaled every inch of her body, filling her with starlight. Slowly the darkness and the vastness faded away. Eva was transposed in all those different realities again.

Meanwhile Javier was still talking. Though his voice was muffled, the tone was crystal clear. Condescending.

"Shut up," she muttered. She was capsuled in a sack of hot air. Or energy. And beyond it, Javier went on and on.

"Just shut up," she repeated, his stupid, condescending smirk clearer than ever.

The energy bottled into Eva as the black vastness faded. She was left in that bland campground, with nothing but Javier and the power inside her, yearning for an outlet.

He reached forward, like he was going to hurt her or force her into something against her will again. It didn't matter; it rubbed Eva the wrong way.

"Come on, now. Don't you want to do something with it?"

"Don't touch me!" she roared. Despite her warning, his hand grazed her wrist, right where he had slashed her, on flesh that itched from the memory of his cut. "*Don't!*"

She shoved him off with both hands, the motion bringing a

burst of fire that sent him hurling across the campground. It was his turn to land on his ass.

The fireball roared right over him, missing him by slivers and incinerating a hole through the greenery behind him. It set the jungle ablaze.

Eva stared at Javier in awe, then at her hands.

He stared back in equal wonder, his face and clothes stained with char.

She hadn't fantasized the eruption. It had been real. She had burned him.

Eventually Javier gathered himself, the nonchalant arrogance dissolving from his façade.

Eva stepped back, heart thrumming at all the inevitable scenarios. The energy was still in her. She hadn't used the entirety of her supply. Just like she could tell how much potion her rings had, she could feel the iridio stored in the pendant. If he came at her, with or without his corruption, she was ready to unleash the fire on him a second time.

"You burned me," he said, fingers grazing his sizzling eyebrows.

"Stay back," she warned, though he didn't look like he wanted to pounce.

"How did— Have you cast iridio before?"

"Don't come any closer."

"Oh, for Rahmagut's sake, Eva. Just answer my question."

"I can't trust you."

"I'm not interested in hurting you. I'm interested in knowing how you almost blew me up."

Eva didn't have a special equation for it, or an answer. It was annoyance that had fed the fire, so she shrugged.

Javier ran a hand over his face, then his hair. "Fine. Well—can you do it again?"

Eva nodded. She couldn't name it. The attack had come so effortlessly, like knowing how to breathe. "I . . . always had the lock, and the iridio was just the key."

He gave her a face of utter disbelief. "Did the fireball burn your wits?"

In a growl she said, "I did it because I could. I didn't have to learn it. I just did it, and I'd do it again."

"And did you use up all the iridio?"

"No."

The look Javier gave her reminded Eva of her first impression of him, back at her cousin's wedding.

"A huge burst for a fraction of the cost..." he muttered, staring at her chest, then at the fire rampaging through the jungle, threatening to surround them, spooking the poor mule. "Did you just break every iridio principle?"

Eva grimaced. "Wasn't that what was supposed to happen?"

Javier shook his head, teeth glinting behind a hungry smile. "No. Unless you're a falling star."

29

The Plume

Reina and Maior headed to the tabletop mountain behind La Cochinilla while the day bled into dusk and the smear of Rahmagut's Claw resurfaced in the darkening sky. There was no need for a map, as the Llanos were easily crossable, all knolls and short grasses and half-dried reeds. The Plume was their guide, an indomitable blot on the horizon feeding Reina with the anticipation of seeing Celeste again. She had a good feeling about it, the intuition that she was on the right path singeing her shoulders. Or maybe it was just the heat.

The trail to the summit ascended in zigzags, with visible footsteps made by the adventurers the curandera had mentioned, foolishly following a legend and journeying to their demise. The night shrouded Reina and Maior, and the breezes ended, abandoning them to silence as if time itself had ceased passing. Up above, a million stars took the heavens in a whirl of white and blue and magenta, lighting their path. As Reina glanced up at those faraway worlds, panting from the hike, she couldn't shake the hope out of her bones. Would Celeste be looking up now, wondering if they were sharing the same never-ending sky? Reina clung to that.

Maior followed in furious indignation, building a robust wall between them. In the silence, Reina replayed their conversation over, turning it this way and that, massaging it and imagining what she should have said instead. She had thought it would be easy to wrangle Maior into following her, to treat her like a prisoner. But despite what she had absorbed from the caudillo and Doña Ursulina, Reina couldn't bring herself to be completely devoid of warmth. And Maior was in the right. She had cared for Reina, saved her. She didn't deserve this treatment.

Regret gnawed at Reina until she had no choice but attempt to make it right.

Conversationally, and because she couldn't handle Maior's silence anymore, she said, "Have you heard the tales of the Plume?" When Maior didn't immediately answer, she went on. "The final battle for independence was won here."

"I was just a babe when that happened," Maior said curtly.

"Didn't anyone tell it to you? Teach you the history?"

Maior gave her a long look. "I spent most of my life worrying about having a roof over my head. I didn't have time for history or books."

"Can you read?"

Maior shrugged noncommittally. "I can read the scripture."

Reina almost laughed. She knew the sort, who had the holy books memorized but could hardly hold their own against the most basic signage. She was privileged in this way, that Juan Vicente had taught her many things before passing.

Maior gave her a sour look, as if she knew exactly what Reina was thinking. "It was Las Hermanas who saved me from the streets. The scripture is all they have."

Reina couldn't blame her, so she nodded. "The Liberator had his final battle for independence here." She told the tale because it was better than withstanding Maior's quiet reproach. "According to the stories, Segol's last standing general was holed up in La Cochinilla. There was a long siege, and the emperor's reinforcements arrived from the north, through the Cow Sea." Reina pointed in the general direction, where Rahmagut's constellation was tattooed among the clusters of stars. "But the Liberator predicted the move, and he used the mountain's elevation to smite the Segolean army with geomancers, with Feleva's iridio."

"It sounds like cheating," Maior muttered.

"Not if you consider that for every day of siege, the Segolean general was flaying enslaved nozariels and hanging them from the turrets to taunt the Liberator. In war, anything goes."

Juan Vicente had told her that tale. He had been at the Battle of the Plume, as advisor in geomancia to Don Enrique, who led the vanguard. Did Doña Ursulina also play a role? As Don Enrique's left-hand woman, it sounded unlikely that she wouldn't. Everyone who was anyone likely had been involved. As Don Enrique had once said, the victors were the writers of history. For such an infamous witch, Doña Ursulina seemed oddly absent from this chapter of history.

Reina rubbed her hands, noticing a chill as they left behind the sounds of night from the lower altitudes. Sweat coated the back of her neck from the switchback hike, yet the cold felt unnatural, enveloping her.

"Well, that's not the worst part," Reina went on. "The Segoleans caught on, and they sent their infantry up to the summit. Apparently they emerged from the other side of the battle with the rising dawn, and they gained the advantage and slaughtered most of the geomancers."

Reina awaited Maior's reaction. Her wonder or disgust. But Maior stood behind that wall of hers, unfazed.

She tried again. "According to the tale, there was so much iridio used up in the battle that even to this day, the corpses of all the fallen soldiers are stuck in perpetual decay."

Maior didn't even grunt in acknowledgment.

Reina clicked her tongue. She grazed the back of Maior's elbow, casually, and Maior yanked her arm out of reach.

"Come on, you're ignoring me," Reina said.

"I don't have anything to say."

Their boots crunched on a path littered with dead matter, all brittle undergrowth and dust, loud in the silence between the two women. Reina rubbed her shoulders again as a strange chill percolated through her.

"Listen, Maior—"

And Maior snapped. "Why are you trying so hard to get my attention now? All this time you've treated me like a bother, so I'm doing what you want. Just going where you tell me to go. Your prisoner."

"That's not fair."

"*I'm* the unfair one?"

Without the right rebuttal, Reina worried her lower lip and focused on the hike ahead. The slim pathway hugged the rocky mountain, with sparse tress growing from the lower elevations and serving as make-believe fences, saving their nerves from the possibility of the sharp cliff drops. It was a blessing that there was no wind, for a wrong step or the pushback of a gust could send them over the cliff's side, plummeting to a sure death.

"You're not a prisoner," Reina said and was met with silence.

Maior glanced behind them. Reina mimicked the motion, shooting a look at the sloping trail, the rocks and shrubs in shapes that a wild imagination could easily confuse for people.

Maior shuddered visibly, the *tha-thumps* in her veins loud to Reina's ears. The human hugged herself, and that was when it hit Reina. She wasn't imagining the contours. It wasn't only her body noticing the strange drop in temperature, which shouldn't happen in these llanos. Reina's jaw tightened as she tried to keep her composure, to not incite unnecessary alarm.

The path flattened out, kissing a vertical drop as tall as the Pentimiento cathedral in Sadul Fuerte. In the far distance was the glow of La Cochinilla, burning against the night like the final embers of a dying hearth.

A dead twig snapped in half. The sound was so real and so close that they whipped around to look. Reina didn't hesitate in summoning enhancing bismuto. Her spell flared everything about the night. Her own cold-slicked palms. The frantic beats of Maior's heart. The dry dust in the air scraping Reina's nostrils. And most importantly, the two bipedal beasts of solid shadow, with the hind legs of a horse and the slitted eyes of a black goat, stalking them and ready to pounce.

She hadn't been wrong. They were being hunted.

The tinieblas lunged.

They went for Maior first, who stood closest to them and was the meeker prey. Time slowed to a crawl as Reina watched their eagle-like claws swiping for Maior. Reina yanked Maior by the back of the clothes, tossing her to the other side with more force than she intended. The dehydrated tree Maior toppled against couldn't withstand her weight. A loud crack whipped through the night, Maior's wet scream echoing. Reina's panic doused her like a bucket of icy water, but she couldn't spare a look.

She sucked in a sharp breath as the second tiniebla struck her side. She swiveled out of reach, barely, the claw shredding her shirt and slicing a line on her belly. Blood burst from the tender flesh, burning her like acid. She chewed the insides of her cheeks and swung her machete at the aggressor. It struck the tiniebla's coiled horn, its armor. The reactive force reverberated down her arm, shaking her elbow and creaking her shoulder. Reina bit down the pain and swung again, this time cleaving the creature from the shoulder down to the opposite armpit.

Maior screamed Reina's name, the fear in her voice a high-pitched lance spearing Reina right through the chest. She whipped around to look, and her stomach plummeted to the nether regions of the Void.

Maior was hanging from the cliffside, her fingernails lifting with blood and her palms clinging to the crumbly earth the only things stopping her inevitable fall.

The second tiniebla snarled—a deadly reminder. Reina withdrew a split second before its mandibles chomped on her arm.

Panic rent her in two. To save Maior, and risk getting bitten and contaminated by the tiniebla's darkness, or to leave Maior to her own devices.

Her instincts chose for her. The fear of withstanding another ravaging.

Reina leapt behind the tiniebla. A grunt surged out of her as she swung again, decapitating the shadow in one clean motion. Its head bounced into the air before disintegrating with the rest of its body.

Another scream, more urgent than the last.

Reina hurled herself to the path's edge as Maior's last hand surrendered to the pull of her weight. Reina threw her torso and arm over the ledge, grappling for Maior's upper arm. She caught her, and a heave and groan later, Maior safely collapsed into Reina's arms.

Their breaths came desperate and broken. Reina's heart drilled against her ribs. Fear continued blooming in her mouth, sour like bile, but this time Maior was safe.

It might have been an eternity before they let go.

In miraculous unison, Maior said "thank you" as Reina uttered an "I'm sorry."

Maior's glossy brown eyes widened. The apology was open-ended, and Reina let it be so, for there were many things she regretted. This human had received the brunt of her indifference and petulance. Reina had treated her like an afterthought to her goals, a bridge to be crossed for where she needed to go, and not as the person she was, with her overly nosey and caring nature. This Reina deeply regretted. She knew she didn't deserve for Maior's walls to come down if she didn't apologize first. Yet she lacked the proper words and the courage.

Maior threw herself on her for another shuddery embrace, still reeling. And Reina allowed her that. She didn't even push away when she felt the wetness of Maior's tears on her clothes. The poor woman had almost died.

"Were those tinieblas? I couldn't see anything," Maior said after they had parted and calmed, as the stars continued to move in the sky, taking them closer to the dawn. "I just felt like something was there."

"They're not visible to the human eye. You need bismuto to see them."

Maior gave her an idolizing look. "Can nozariels see them?"

"Only valcos. I also use bismuto."

As they got back up to resume the hike, Reina's body complained from exhaustion, and understandably so. They had walked for hours without rest—ascended most of the Plume in the span of the night. Her muscles ached, and she hissed as the slightest movement brought back the acidic bite of the cut on her abs.

Maior noticed. She cast a galio spell that stitched Reina's skin shut. Then Reina had to remind her to also mend her own rent fingernails.

Reina couldn't help the brightness in her own eyes—the surprise that Maior would prioritize Reina's comfort over her own. Maybe it was the leftover adrenaline, or maybe Maior inspired the truth of how Reina felt to spill out of her. "I'm sorry for the way I treated you. For everything I said."

Maior paused, astonished.

"You didn't deserve that," Reina said. "You were trying to help me, and I couldn't even see it. I'm sorry this is the way things are."

Their gazes met, and Maior's softened after a moment. Reina thought she saw a comfort there. The acceptance of their odd allyship.

"I guess...I forgive you," Maior said gently.

Reina turned to the star-blotched sky ahead. The stars were shying away, dimmed by a grand light awakening from slumber as dawn prepared to meet them. She didn't stop the smile creeping onto her lips.

"I would rather be with you here than be trapped in Doña Ursulina's dungeon or forced to play a part as the caudillo's wife."

Anger spiked in Reina as she imagined the scenario. She ground her teeth. Reina loathed how Maior was necessary for Doña Ursulina's plot to bring back the Benevolent Lady. She wasn't sure she could go along with that anymore. But there were too many pieces dislodged now, and she desperately needed her ore back.

Maior's warm fingers curled around Reina's. She gave Reina's hand a squeeze. "Thanks for protecting me against the tinieblas."

Why wasn't she saying the obvious thing, that she wouldn't need saving if Reina hadn't dragged her along to a place known to be cursed?

Reina was too busy biting back the words, turning them over in her head and seeking the right thing to say, to pay much heed to the rotten smell meeting them as the ascending trail evened out.

Maior's grip softened and let go. In the absence of her touch, Reina curled her fist, missing it.

Obliviously, Maior went on, "I was thinking...if we keep the connection to La Cochinilla, can we buy a chicken? So I can make a proper pisca. I haven't had a good meal in so long. We could really use one. And I'm so hungry—" Then she tripped on something protruding from the uneven terrain and let out a squeak. Reina caught her and reeled her back to her feet. As she did so, the stench on the air flared. Like wet, rancid meat slapping their nostrils.

Maior clamped a hand over her nose.

The smell was alarming enough that Reina snapped her index and thumb together, producing fire to see by. Her transplant heart clenched, protesting being squeezed of precious iridio to fuel the flame that showered the vicinity in soft yellow light.

Maior gasped and jumped away at the revelation. A body lay across the ground, skin blue and military uniform in tatters. Its limbs were rolled at awkward angles, moved into further disarray by Maior's stumble. It was a man, his facial features gnawed off so there was little more left than exposed flesh wrapped around an empty mouth and eye sockets. A reddish-brown crevice had been carved where his heart would have been.

Nausea snaked its way up Reina's stomach. She stepped away, forcing a gulp. Swallowing left her feeling filthy, like somehow the stench had percolated into her belly. She yanked Maior closer to her side, preemptively, in case another tiniebla prowled about.

"A body?" Maior said, gagging.

Daybreak approached in the horizon, the constellations bidding their goodbyes and Rahmagut's Claw fading in the dawning sapphire-pink sky. As dawn light draped over the summit and reached the vastness of the Plume, legions of corpses came into view. Reina stepped back, her body rocking with repulsion.

They were at the site of the Liberator's battle for independence. Bodies spread across the crag, broken and cleaved and drained of blood, all blue-and-purple flesh. There were no bugs, no carrion, just corpses and the promise of tinieblas.

"Reina?" Maior said in a quivering voice.

Every word of the tales had been true.

A flaring light went off in the horizon, near the center of the summit. It wasn't the inevitable sunrise. It was an outburst of energy, red and loud like the flares of a volcano. The light dimmed, meeting a second one. They danced and fought like clashing stars against the predawn sky. Then a great guttural snarl rocked the summit.

Reina's hand fell before Maior could take it.

"Celeste," she murmured, ears deaf to whatever Maior said— senses ignoring everything except for the sight.

It *had* to be her.

A second roar shattered her stupor. Reina took off, nimble feet jumping and dodging the bodies strewn on her path. Her pulse tingled at her fingertips.

At the center of the summit were two figures.

Reina's heart imploded as she recognized Celeste's outline shadowed against the rising sun. A high ponytail, with bangs barely hiding stunted antlers. Slender legs and tight-fitting armor that didn't shy away from her curves.

Celeste.

Though lithe, Celeste's form was ferocious in battle, her iridio scythe a sharp crescent moon against the dawn sky.

The sight electrified Reina's legs to pump faster, obliterating the distance between them. Her cheeks reddened from a wide-eyed smile. Finally, her search was over.

Facing Celeste was the last creature Reina expected to see in a place like this. A large feline spotted with black rosette patterns and glowing eyes the same color as Rahmagut's Claw. The jaguar roared again before pouncing on Celeste. Celeste's scythe blocked the strike, the force throwing her on her back, the jaguar's rabidly snapping mandibles above her.

Reina boiled with adrenaline as she sprinted faster, desperately.

She needn't, for Celeste shoved pounds of feline muscle off her with a grunt. The ghostly creature skidded to a stop, but Celeste pursued it, attacking as the best defense. She slashed the base of its neck like she was breaking butter. In its wake, the scythe left a gash where blood like smoke sizzled out.

Celeste's iridio scythe disintegrated at the same time as the jaguar. And she waited, staring at the emptiness left behind by the apparition, expectant of something it would leave behind.

"Celeste!" Reina called out, her burning legs steadily bringing her one breath closer.

In the end, Celeste hadn't needed her.

"Celeste."

The dawn behind Celeste made it impossible to see the expression on her face. But she eased as she recognized Reina. She tilted her head, ribbons of hair falling over her shoulder. When she spoke, it was with the same throaty voice that always sent Reina's chest fluttering. "You came," she said.

"Of course."

For her, she'd go anywhere.

Reina approached until she was close enough to take Celeste's gloved hand, which was hot from the fight. And trembling. How Reina had missed the vibrancy of her eyes, the plum shade of her lips.

"It's supposed to be here, the blade." Her voice came like smoke, blackened by chagrin. She glanced at the spot where the jaguar's corpse would have been, had it not vanished like tinieblas did.

Reina didn't understand the disappointment. A sword, yellow like the dawn, rested on the uneven ground before her. The blade was sharp on one side, made for cleaving, with an engraved handle of the same material and a circular pommel taunting her with ideas of the sun. Her mouth hung open at the sight.

She expected Celeste to pick it up. To hold it up against the light of the rising sun, where they would inspect the metal and marvel that the legend was real.

Instead, Celeste just watched it with her eyebrows bunching up. She exhaled, exhausted and devastated. "It's supposed to be there!"

Reina, too, frowned. "But it is," she said, picking up the blade.

The handle was the perfect size for her grip, the metal warm like her own palm. At first glance the blade could pass for bronze or gold or an alloy of both. But it reflected the dawn light without a hint of green rust, and she doubted it exhibited the malleable nature of pure gold. Its length was like her machete, a natural extension to her reach. With the blade in her hands, her shoulders ached to give it a testing swing. But she held back, knowing it was Celeste's prize. *She* had climbed the summit first. *She* had slain the jaguar, now so obviously a watchbeast placed there by Rahmagut himself.

In Reina's grip, the blade became visible to the physical world. Celeste's blue gaze doubled in size at the sight. Her jaw dropped; then she wavered, surrendering to the exhaustion. She collapsed right into Reina's arms.

Reina supported her, welcoming her in an embrace.

Celeste *had* needed her after all.

Reina turned to the breaking dawn, her heart stronger than it had been since leaving Don Enrique's study. Far in the distance, between her and the rising sun, were two figures rushing up the eastern side of the summit. One was crowned in two great valco antlers, and the other was short, wild hair swirling out in all directions, like a burning star.

30

Ambitions Converge

With her breaths coming hard and constricted as she ran after Javier, Eva twisted her hands in the incantation to swell her muscles with the strength of bismuto. The spell coursed through her, doubling the push of every stride, and she managed to match his pace hiking up the butte.

"She's going to take her," Javier had hissed before taking off after the women in the center of the summit, which Eva interpreted to mean that they had finally found Celeste. Despite the distance, the dawn light made it easy to see them. One had skin the color of sand dunes and braided hair with waves like obsidian eddies. She held a blade, golden and reflective like a mirror under the sun. By her feet was the fainted young woman she had lowered to the ground, who was dressed in richly dyed clothes, the antlers protruding from her tied hair testament that she was the one they sought.

Eva squeezed the pendant hanging from her neck, the iridio concoction swishing within as she moved it. Its power sloshed, abundant.

Javier unsheathed his left-handed sword and pointed it at the brown woman. He didn't bother with introductions. He went straight for the kill. "How appropriate: the thieving duskling stealing Ches's Blade from my niece's hands."

The woman's face darkened. "Javier? What are you doing *here*?"

she said. She was dressed in a vest, shirt, and pants, her boots muddied. The way she stood, with her shoulders rolled back and her grip on the sword sure, warned Eva of her strength. "This is hers, but she's in no state to use it."

"All I see is you wielding it," Javier said as he drew closer without lowering his own sword. The woman watched its sharp edge apprehensively. She fell into a fighting stance when she saw he had no intention of easing. "Well? Don't you want to give it a try?"

Javier didn't waste a breath before diving into a flurry of attacks, and the woman parried with the golden blade. Trading one hit after another, they looked like performers in a choreographed dance, like it wasn't their first time.

Javier stepped away, swiping locks of silver hair and beads of sweat out of his face. He regarded the woman with jealously bared teeth. "I see your absence from Águila Manor hasn't made you sloppy."

"I see *your* absence hasn't made you bearable."

"Why don't we trade swords to see if you can still hold your own against me? Or are you afraid I'll best you if I wield it? How do I know all your strength isn't coming from it?"

Was he going to wrench the blade away from the woman? He had talked about the legend of Ches's Blade nonchalantly, without going into details, for Eva also knew the story. But that was as far as she had seen it: as nothing more than a tale. Witnessing the golden blade as a tangible truth in the woman's hands, however, filled Eva with a rush of heat, for it was yet another confirmation that everything Javier attested was true. Rahmagut's legend and his star in the sky. The legitimacy of Ches's existence as ancient god of the sun. It meant that there was certainty to the future he promised her, despite the deceit about his real nature.

The woman didn't humor his question. Instead, she asked, "Why are you here?"

To await his niece, he had told Eva, for Ches presented his blessed blade only at the moment of sunrise. So they had abandoned their traveling supplies and mule and had waited all night hiding in a crevice for the sun to rise. Celeste had come, only he hadn't said anything about this other woman arriving as well.

Javier gave the woman a long look, then offered her a contemptuous bow. "Thank you for finding my niece. Now allow me take her where she belongs."

"I—I'm planning on taking her back to Sadul Fuerte, eventually," the woman said quickly. Eva didn't know anything about her, but at that moment, she knew she wasn't a good liar. "She's just injured."

"Is that so? Did Ursulina put you up to this?"

"Your brother."

As Eva drew closer, the woman's attention landed on her.

"Oh, her?" Javier said, "Reina, meet the newest addition to the Águila name, Eva Kesaré."

"What?" Reina said, easing her fighting stance. Perhaps she was well acquainted with Javier's fickle aggression. Or perhaps her hidden strengths gave her the courage not to be afraid.

"I'm his wife," Eva said loudly, owning her stupid mistake.

The news evaporated Reina's unease. "So...you've been busy?" she told Javier, and Eva grimaced.

Javier had a smug air about him. "And you haven't been?" he said, his satisfaction growing as a short, plump woman caught up to Reina and waited in the periphery. Though there was something off about the woman, a ghostly afterimage Eva couldn't shake off even as she blinked and squeezed her eyes. "Why did you bring the dama from Apartaderos? What are you plotting? You're taking the damas, aren't you?"

Reina didn't answer. Glaring at Javier, she moved her free hand in the elaborate motion of an incantation. Slivers of bismuto wrapped around her hand and slithered into Ches's Blade, a blue glow enveloping her body and weapon.

Eva massaged her hands, cataloging the soft slosh of geomancia potions stored in her capped rings. She knew the counter to bismuto enhancement. With galio she could cure Reina of the high, reverting her to her natural state, should she prove to be too much for Javier. But first Eva wanted to see how she would feel about it, seeing him suffer.

"Are you betraying Brother? Is that what this is?" Javier asked, unconcerned. "And what, you're going to fight me? Kill Enrique's heir?"

"Celeste is the caudillo's rightful heir."

"Are you sure you mean that? Because if so, you know a nozariel like yourself doesn't belong with a woman of her rank. You wouldn't be more than a bedroom distraction."

"I am not a doormat to be made fun of anymore," Reina said between gritted teeth. "Especially not by a leech living in his brother's shadow!"

"If I'm such a leech, then what does that make you, who can so easily be defeated by my sword?" Javier closed the distance between them. He sliced at her where she stood.

The film of blue surrounding Reina flared. Her golden blade blocked him in a blink, the metals ringing and shattering the summit silence.

"I'm tired of your jokes!" Reina growled, giving her blade a slash with the intent to cleave him in half. "Stop pretending that's all I care about! Just *stop*."

They reeled away from each other, one step back and two steps to the side, parrying as if each knew the other's choreography.

This nozariel was as strong as Javier. She had no reason to fear him. Just as Eva had no problem admitting she wished to witness Reina striking Javier down.

"Celeste is injured, and she wouldn't want anyone but me to take care of her."

Javier backed away, lowering his sword. His red gaze settled on the fallen valco woman, pensive. "What she has is beyond physical. You can't help her."

"She's better off with me than with you," Reina spat.

He slid his sword back into its scabbard, the blade hissing in retreat. "Then let us help her, you and I," he said.

Eva and Reina stared at him in surprise.

"We both serve Brother's goal. We have been the ones capturing the women since Laurel died. We are not friends, yes, but we share a common objective, and this has been *our* work for over a year." He raised his eyebrows, basking in this void left in the atmosphere. A silence maintained by the holding of their breaths. "You know you'll need someone with my expertise in galio to cure what she has."

"You'll…help me?" Reina asked. "But you do know what Celeste is, right?"

He exhaled deeply, his stance easing. "Do you think I crossed the Páramo and Llanos just so I could marvel at your nozariel scowl?"

"We came here to see the truths of the legend," Eva said, surprising them both. But she wasn't voiceless or a minion, and it was best if she established this sooner rather than later. "There are rewards to be had, no?" She raised her eyebrows at the blade in Reina's grip, which reflected the blinding light of the sun, as if it were made for exactly that reason.

It was her turn to earn Reina's frown. Eva turned the iridio pendant over in her fingers, thirsting to use it. Craving the sensation of raw starlight fleeting through her muscles and veins. Of it accumulating at her fingertips until the burst of release. Whatever happened next, Eva was never again going to rely on Javier to keep her safe. She had never seen anyone else use geomancia like she could, not even Doña Rosa, with her wealth of knowledge on the ancient arts. And this was just the beginning of her journey.

"The caudillo sent you?"

Javier gave her a slow nod, and Eva bit down the truth. It wasn't her place to give it. First, she needed to understand all the players in this new game of theirs.

Reina assessed them with a tight jaw, the muscles rippling. But something about Javier's answer convinced her. Finally, she looped the leather straps of her scabbard around the blade's golden pommel, haphazardly affixing the blade to her waist. "Very well. We'll have to use a shortcut to get to Tierra'e Sol in time," she said, taking the fallen valco woman in her arms as if Celeste were her bride. "Come with me."

They followed, just as Eva caught the subtle victorious curling of Javier's smirk. He was getting exactly what he wanted. And in Eva's experience, this was never a good thing.

31

Ches's Blade

After more awkward introductions, Reina carried Celeste in her arms all the way back to the burrow, without help, because no one else would have the kind of tenderness Celeste deserved. As she walked, Reina angled Celeste's face close to her chest, so her soft breaths tickled the hairs along her forearm. It eased her anxieties— her fears of Celeste's breathing coming to a stop, even after Reina had found her in one piece.

They had to pass La Cochinilla on the trip back; thus Maior got her wish. The market bustled at high noon. She found the chicken she wanted, and tomatoes and onions and chickpeas, and as the group maneuvered out of the citadel market with the clucking chicken in Maior's grip, a butcher announced a price drop in the offal of his cow. Maior pounced on the opportunity and haggled for a satchel of tripe. She was going to cook it right away, she announced to the weary and annoyed Reina.

The day was bright when they came upon the burrow nestled into that lone tree in the Llanos. Reina had made the decision to show Gegania to Javier before they'd even arrived at its tunnel. She didn't know with utmost surety how long it would take to travel to Tierra'e Sol on foot, but she didn't doubt it would eat up what few remaining days they had with Rahmagut's Claw in the sky.

The thought pummeled her with the truth: She was a wretched

thing for betraying Celeste's secret this way. Yet there was so much chaos around their journey that Gegania gave her a grounding point, oddly enough. With it, they could reach Tierra'e Sol. With it, Celeste could rest and recuperate.

Behind her lead, Eva and Javier walked the stone staircase ascending to the house perched on the hills of the Páramo. Eva watched the change in heat and scenery with wide-eyed wonder. Even Javier couldn't hide his amazement as he realized the whole house was magic.

Without pausing, Reina took Celeste up the rackety stairs to the highest floor, where Doña Laurel's former bedroom door stood ajar. She gently lay her on the bed and tucked a wool blanket tightly around her. Javier's and Eva's footsteps followed, and they entered the room without invitation. But this time Reina was glad for the intrusion, for Javier was a master of galio healing, better than Maior. Celeste needed his expertise in the arcane branch of healing related to the soul. Reina just hoped she wouldn't have to beg him . . . too much.

She sat at the edge of the bed and brushed stray locks of black hair out of Celeste's eyes. "This isn't just normal exhaustion."

"Her spirit's drained," Javier said, parting the gossamer curtains to peek out the window. "She's been summoning geomancia nonstop for days, by the looks of it."

Reina could tell he was studying the hills and the flora and the colors in the sky, trying to discern Gegania's location. She clenched her fists tight. It was risky bringing him here. Still, if he could help Celeste, this was a risk Reina would gladly take.

"You mastered galio. You can help her," she said, drawing his attention back from the frailejón-dotted landscape.

"Look at you, barking orders. Don't let this situation get to your head."

"I just want her to wake up."

Javier crossed his arms. "Will you at least provide me some galio? Or are you going to force me to deplete my own supply?"

"We don't have much left," Eva piped in, earning Reina's attention. The woman had pretty curls. They were of a light brown color, stubbornly coiled and lighter near the bangs, as if the sun were doing her the favor of crowning her in gold.

Reina dusted off her pants and headed for the door. "I'll get you some. *Do not* touch Celeste."

Her gaze wrestled Javier's, to make a point, and she rushed down the stairs to the underground chamber. Gegania had stores of geomancia reagents, except for the one it needed the most. Their new iridio hung from her scabbarded belt in a pouch, along with her machete *and* Ches's golden blade. In a way, Reina felt like a keeper of treasures.

She fetched the galio potion, panting the whole way down and then up the stairs, and ran into Maior on the second-story landing. She would have kept going in her whirlwind of strides, but Maior grabbed her wrist.

The human tugged her into a broom closet. "*Reina*, he's the man who stole me from Apartaderos."

Reina licked her lips and stepped back, unsettled by their proximity. "Get some supper started. Celeste's going to be hungry when she wakes up. And bring us some warm water," she commanded.

"I don't like that he's here. Do you trust him?"

Reina couldn't tolerate the doubt—not now. "Javier listens to his brother, and if the caudillo wants Celeste to be safe, then that's what Javier will do." Of this, Reina was positive. Still, Maior's disappointment radiated in waves. There was reproach in her eyes, that her worries were considered inconsequential.

Reina hated seeing it, so she grasped Maior's hands, reassuring. "He won't lay a hand on you or Celeste."

Maior's eyes wrinkled, unsure.

"Remember? I'm your protector."

Maior nodded and returned the squeeze. "You're going to take me to Apartaderos when this is over," she said with authority, which Reina interpreted as her appeasement.

"I promise."

Maior's eyebrows ascended farther.

Reina nodded, humoring her by doubling down on the reassurance. A warmth embraced her upon realizing Maior trusted her so. And a small part of her craved more.

"I'm hungry," she said to lighten the mood. "Aren't you going to make that tripe thing?"

"Mondongo," Maior corrected pointedly, but smiled.

Upstairs, Javier greedily took Reina's bowl, quipping about her being in his debt after this. He dipped his index and middle finger in the green galio solution. Then he waved his hand, tracing a two-dimensional diagram in the air above Celeste. Reina was sure if her veins still pumped with that bismuto high, she would be seeing the circular diagram he transposed over Celeste's chest as a manifestation of light. For a fleeting second, Reina's curious gaze fell on Eva, who was pressed against the opposite wall, watching Javier with her brows crunched up in horror. But before Reina could make sense of it, Javier lifted his hand away from Celeste, drawing out a ghostly apparition in her likeness, which glanced about the room awake and very much confused.

The magic in her, Reina thought.

Javier slammed the heel of his palm onto Celeste's chest, hard, forcing the spirit back into her body. And Celeste took a sharp intake of air, coming awake.

"Reina," Celeste uttered in her throaty voice, drawing tingles in Reina's belly.

At once, Reina knelt by her bedside, taking her clammy hand.

Celeste's eyes traveled to Eva, then to Javier. "Javier?"

"It's a magical reunion," he drawled.

Celeste sat up. "Does that mean...you've brought me back to Sadul Fuerte?"

"No," Reina said before any doubt could seed in Celeste. "We're in Gegania."

The white of Celeste's eyes doubled in size. Confusion, then anger, warped her face. "You brought him here?"

"What, she wasn't supposed to?"

"Celeste, please." Reina had braced herself for this moment and for all the others they would have if Celeste didn't agree to come to Tierra'e Sol of her own accord. "He doesn't know anything. I just needed him to get you back to normal."

The tension in her elbows eased, her lips a thin line of

disappointment not thorough enough to voice. She leaned back on the plush down pillows.

"What's wrong? I'm hurt you're not happy to see me." Javier chortled.

Celeste's eyes were two cold stones in the Páramo light.

"I only came to help you cope with homesickness," Javier continued, his teeth showing beneath a wicked smile. "Didn't you once tell me you could see Brother in my eyes?"

She rolled her eyes. "Trust me, it's not a pretty sight."

He laughed, which in turn loosened Celeste's lips into a small smile that told Reina she was all right.

Maior entered the room at that moment. She carried a basin with steaming water and a moist cloth. Except... when Celeste saw her, Celeste's eyes doubled in size. Reina recognized the dangerous intent in them a second before Celeste flung the wool blanket off her.

"You!" She sprang out of the bed, and Reina was quick enough to block her before she could pounce on Maior.

Restrained by Reina's grip, Celeste said furiously, "What have you done to mi mamá?"

Collectively, the room held its breath, a silence that was broken by Maior's shocked question. "What are you talking about?"

"Look at her!" Celeste beckoned the whole room to look at Maior. "She has her. *My mom*. Why is she mocking me with her?"

"Hey." Reina shushed her. She draped her arms around Celeste, knowing exactly what she was referring to. Reina squeezed her reassuringly, hoping some of her warmth could serve as an anchor for Celeste. For she could only imagine what a torture it must be. She wasn't blessed—or cursed—with valco eyes. If she got sick of seeing the ghost of Doña Laurel, all she had to do was let the bismuto run its course until her body was cleansed of it. Without it, nothing about Maior looked extraordinary. But Celeste didn't have that luxury.

"You're talking about the woman haunting Maior," Eva said, breaking her silence for Maior's benefit.

"How could you disrupt her rest like that?" Celeste jabbed an accusing finger at Maior as Reina helped her down to the bed and sat beside her.

"You all can see her right now?" Maior's eyes burned with self-preservation. Some of the basin water dipped and splashed as she backed away.

Javier kicked off the wall. He flicked a careless finger above Eva's bangs, flicking away the curls concealing the stunted valco antlers crowning her. "We're valco. We can see geomancia, be it good or bad."

"Don't touch me!" Eva swatted his hand away. She stormed away to linger by the doorway instead.

"And we can clearly see the shade clinging to you."

Reina's gaze followed Eva, and she understood. Javier hadn't married just anybody. He went and found himself a valco bride.

Meanwhile, Celeste was fixated on the poor human, clutching her blanket like she was reeling herself in from pouncing a second time. "I buried my mother, and you're telling me you bound her soul so you could—you could take it for—for what, exactly?"

"Celeste—listen." Reina took Celeste by the shoulders, forcing her to face her. This close, Reina could detail the speckles of silver drowning in the blueness of her eyes, the blemishes that weren't there before, the exhausted rings under her eyes. "This wasn't her doing. Doña Ursulina forced her into it. I know because I took Maior to her. When I saw her again—" Reina shook her head. "Doña Ursulina said she was a gift for Don Enrique."

Shock was red in Celeste's face.

"A brilliant move played by the most terrifying sorceress of Sadul Fuerte," Javier said, more interested in inspecting his fingernails than in Celeste's distress. "We've all heard of this kind of geomancia, or should I say 'void magic.'"

Celeste's fury erupted, a vein bulging in her neck as she screamed at her uncle, "They're just tales!"

"Oh, like Rahmagut's Claw and the legend of Ches's Blade? Were you not at the Plume for precisely that?"

Celeste covered her face with her hand, turning away. Reina fought the urge to reach out. She was reminded of a similar

moment, when they'd been barely adjusting to life without Doña
Laurel. Her heart ached.

With courage Reina didn't know she possessed, Maior said,
"Why did the witch bind that woman to me?"

"To remind Father of what he will gain if he parleys with Rahmagut," Celeste said.

And not just him, but you, too, Reina wanted to howl at her.
She bit the inside of her lower lip until the tender flesh cried and
swelled from the abuse. Doña Laurel's return would be the end of
all their pain. Not just that—Doña Ursulina was going to welcome
Reina, officially, as her successor in the eyes of the governor and the
king's court. When they parleyed, Rahmagut would grant Reina a
new heart. She grew giddy at the thought of having the freedom of
health once again.

"Doña Ursulina plans to bring back his dead wife, the Benevolent Lady," Javier told Maior, who recoiled at being addressed by
the man who'd kidnapped her from her life.

"I didn't ask for it," Maior said, her nostrils flaring. "I didn't
ask for any of it."

A heavy silence stifled the room. What would be of Maior,
after the caudillo achieved his goal? Reina wasn't prepared for the
answer. Not yet.

"I…am sorry," Celeste said in a whisper. "I shouldn't have
acted so cruelly. You have to understand. I lost my mother at a time
when I thought we were invincible. My father has gone mad. And
seeing you with her only reminds me of how everything has gone
so horribly." She clenched and unclenched a palm in frustration. "I
wasn't being honest, when I insinuated that I didn't believe these
legends were true. I went through the trouble of climbing all the
way up to the Plume's summit after Ches's Blade, and it wasn't
there for me. I wasn't worthy, or it's not true."

Reina was almost ashamed to reach for it where she'd hung it
on her belt, inconspicuously, like a second machete. Though the
moment she unhooked the engraved handle and lifted it up to the
room's dim light, it became impossible to ignore. The blade's edge
was sharp like a line of parchment, and pure light reflected off its

surface when she angled it toward the window. A mirror. It was light, yet sturdy enough to feel trustworthy under her grip, capable of cleaving tinieblas and saving lives.

Reina didn't know the appropriate way to present the trophy. Should she kneel, like knights did in the stories? Everyone's eyes fell on her, so she simply carried the blade to Celeste's lap and presented it to her with both hands, clumsily.

Celeste's brows fell in a deep frown. "It's real?"

"It was right there. It's just that the sun made it hard to see," Reina said in her best attempts to reassure her. She angled the blade so Celeste could take it.

But when Celeste's slender hand curled around the handle, it closed in on itself, grasping at air. Once, twice, Celeste tried, and the outcome was the same. Her furious surprise silenced the room, the tension thick and suffocating.

Then Javier let out a bellow. A deep belly laugh with which he doubled over, wiping the corners of his eyes. "Don't tell me—" he said.

Celeste tried again, and her cheeks grew redder.

Reina felt like a paralyzed fool. Her mouth opened, yet there was nothing she could possibly say.

Javier's laughs made it worse or spared her. He approached, saying, "Don't tell me it can only be wielded by the duskling."

Reina allowed him to try. The room witnessed how the effect was the same. Celeste's furious gaze landed on Maior, and Reina understood her desires. Two valcos failed, and a nozariel succeeded. Now it was time for them to see the human's attempt.

Maior's face was a grimace as she circled Javier, keeping a wide berth, and grabbed for the blade. Her hand cut through it as if the golden metal were nothing more than light and shadows.

And Javier laughed even harder. "What, is this going to be a contest of who can lift the blade? We all know it only works for Reina."

Reina had seen the shroud of anger darken Celeste's eyes before, many times, when facing off against her father or when she fumed about Doña Ursulina's ambition. But Reina had never seen the brunt of it, so naked and raw, directed straight at her. It was a fleeting moment, in which Celeste's beauty vanished in one blink and was back the next, an unveiling of a viperous desire. There was a question in that look, and envy.

"So you are Ches's chosen warrior?" she said. "*You?*"

Reina let the blade catch the light again, her chest fluttery, her heart's whispers awakening at the blooming of her self-doubt, for she knew she wasn't worthy of it. Ches had abandoned her since the day she'd woken up with a new heart. She shook her head. "It's wrong. It's only reacting to my nozariel blood," she said without any certainty.

When she glanced up, it was Maior's gaze she met. A warmth filled her. At least she wasn't hated by all. Not yet.

"I went to the Plume hoping to use that blade to stop the night, like it's meant to be used in the stories, to prevent my father from communing with that god, and Ches's reply is to grant it to you?" Celeste added acidly, "So, will you stop the night?"

Reina's reply was to draw her lips into a thin line. On the contrary, Rahmagut was going to give her a new life, and she was going to make sure of it.

Celeste snorted, shaking her head. "Lovely. Well, I don't need your help anyway. Never did. I have a backup plan. I knew I couldn't just rely on a legend."

"And what is that?" Reina asked, pretending like it hadn't stung her.

Their eyes met again, and they held each other's gazes as time slowed, each second endless like the decay on the Plume. Despite Celeste's disappointment over the blade, and their clashing objectives, the bands of friendship still connected them. They were frayed, sure, but the elasticity was not gone, and they could stretch and bend to accommodate the changes in their lives. Reina would never act to Celeste's detriment; she had to see that.

"I'm going to seek asylum from the one person Father wouldn't defy. The person he knows can best him and who it will irk him the most to see me with: the Liberator."

Reina's jaw tightened. She stopped herself from sucking in a breath, from reacting. The Liberator resided on the same island where they needed to go—the symbolic location of Rahmagut's tomb. How could Celeste not know this, after all the searching for a counter to the legend in her books?

"He used to send me gifts when I was little, did you know that?" Celeste continued. "He believes we're the future of the valco species, and he wanted to protect that. I sent him a letter before I left the manor. I told him what I am."

Reina simply couldn't believe her good luck. She wasn't going to have to force Celeste to go anywhere after all.

"How do you plan to make it to the Liberator?" Eva said from the doorway, earning her the startled attention of everyone in the room. "Doesn't he live worlds away?"

"I have my methods, which are none of your concern," Celeste snapped.

Eva's glare was a fiery lash. "Why don't you just wait it out here?" She snapped with equal ardor.

"Because Reina knew about this house, and now all of you know as well. I don't trust you won't go running to Father to tell him about me and Maior."

At one point, Reina had considered that exact plan.

"I'll be in Tierra'e Sol until Father's ready to apologize and I'm ready to forgive him for forcing this on his only daughter."

Reina crossed her arms like an armor about her, the circumstances tasting bitter in her mouth. Celeste was a willful creature. Her ignorance about Tierra'e Sol was nothing more than a stroke of luck—or perhaps she was right to trust the Liberator with her safety even if he lived so close to the tomb. For now, Reina would hold her tongue, especially in this room where everyone was ready to judge her.

Truth was, she desperately ached for the promise of a new heart. Her enslavement to iridio potions was the worst turn in a series of one crisis after another. Ches's golden blade only proved Rahmagut's favor was possible, and with Maior and Celeste, it was nearly at their fingertips.

Still, she could only hold this truth for so long. Once they arrived in Tierra'e Sol, Reina pledged to lay all the cards on the table. She would beg Celeste to reconsider, to give the few ounces of blood needed to invoke Rahmagut. Celeste was stubborn, true, but she would see how much Reina needed this. Their friendship should be strong enough to overcome the return of Rahmagut's Claw.

32

The Dreaming Lady

Rather begrudgingly, Celeste and Reina explained the purpose of the house and its secret treasure: the iridio table that carved tunnels to anywhere in the continent, as long as it was a connection made through the mineral veins beneath the earth. Gegania was a marvel of geomancia. A relic built with care and bolstered by every passing generation of Celeste's maternal line. It needed time to create said tether to the coast of the Cow Sea, Celeste announced, for there was no direct vein to Tierra'e Sol; thus it was to become their roof and haven for the next few days.

As Eva took it all in, she understood it was the reason why the corridors of Gegania shuddered with the spark of an enchantment, why every wallpapered wall breathed and every windowsill glimmered under the Páramo sun. The house was magic. And with its multitude of rooms and hallways, it was easy to get lost in it. Past broom cupboards and closets of dusty china. Past every shadowed staircase and corridor lined by tarnished frames. The home was full of wonders, and as the moments blurred into hours, Eva found she needed the distraction.

She wandered until she came upon a doorknob that shocked her with leftover magic. When she tried it, the room opened like it was meant to be hers.

She stepped in and discovered bookshelves hugging every wall, save for the tiny space where a window allowed for afternoon light to spill onto a desk. A large book lay on it, the title *The Power of Suns* inlaid in gold on the spine. Fingertips had lifted dust from its cover, as if it had been recently used. The title made her think of Javier, of what he was calling her as of late: his fallen star.

A soft cough stopped her from opening the book. Eva turned, quickly, which made her look all the more guilty of snooping.

Reina was standing under the doorframe. "Brought you mondongo," she said as she extended two wooden bowls to Eva. They sloshed with a thick and steaming ocher stew.

Eva watched the bowls with suspicion before taking them. "Thank you," she said.

"Maior made it with the tripe she was losing her mind about. She was too shy to bring it herself. She—uh—doesn't like Javier."

When she didn't turn to leave right away, Eva wondered if she was expecting her to appreciate the food in her presence. Reina's chest pulsed with wisps of a blue hue.

"Sorry about earlier," Reina said.

It was not what Eva had been expecting.

"I was...rude...to you."

Eva's lips opened in understanding. "It's all right. You probably thought, with how despicable Javier is, that I would be awful, too."

The jab at Javier brought a small curl to Reina's lips. She had scars on her lips and chin, severe lines telling of a violent past. Still, everything else about her was in perfect agreement: Lush eyebrows and evenly pigmented skin made for the sun. Curly baby hairs disobeying her braid and framing her face. Tight muscles pulling her posture erect. Tamarind eyes. Without any effort at all, she was pleasant to look at.

"Do you know him well?" Reina said. "I never saw you in Sadul Fuerte."

Eva was ashamed of the answer. "It doesn't take long to understand why people hate him."

"I couldn't have said it better." Reina chuckled and made to leave.

"Did you know you have iridio in your heart?" Eva blurted out her guess.

Reina paused and spared her a fleeting glance of tamarind. "It's kind of a big deal, isn't it? It's the kind of stuff I would know, you know?"

So Reina was the nozariel with the heart of iridio that Javier had talked about. "Why do you have iridio in your chest? Are you a master of it?" Eva's mind churned with a million ideas. Of the possibility of a mentor. Of a teacher she could lean on instead of needing Javier's guidance.

The question was the wrong one. Reina's expression shriveled into a look of distrust. But instead of lashing out like Javier always did, she said, "I need iridio. I don't want it. So no."

"What about Ches's Blade? You wield a gift from a god."

Reina rested her hand on the golden hilt. "I don't trust it—but I also don't want to leave it for anyone else to take. It feels wrong not to use it, you know, since it's been given only to me?"

"Why don't you trust it?"

Reina's lip curled, more to a sneer. "If it's given by Ches, then it's probably a tool against Rahmagut."

"And you are Rahmagut's follower?" Eva forced the name out without flinching.

Reina's jaw muscles rippled before she said, "I used to pray to Ches every day. I would split my meals with him, like he expects. I would take note of his days of celebration. I thought he was *my* god. Not the Virgin or any of the others." Her brows descended, and there was a wound in the look she gave to the floor between them. "Yet he was never present when I needed him. If this blade proves his existence, then it hurts even more to know he ignored me all this time."

She pointed to the window, where the dying day was clear and cloudless, the streak of Rahmagut's Claw emerging on the steely canvas. "Rahmagut is real, too. His star showed up exactly when my grandmother said it would. The damas exhibit all the signs. They have power that wouldn't be there otherwise. Rahmagut's void magic is the reason I'm alive. He is not absent to me. Even my iridio heart is a piece of his puzzle. He may be the god of the Void, but how do I know everything said about him isn't half-truths and lies? Everyone in Sadul Fuerte fears my grandmother, yet she saved my life when she didn't have to. Understanding magic, even void magic, doesn't make you evil."

Eva nodded in complete agreement. She remembered Doña Rosa, who'd taught her the same.

"If what I'm doing makes me a follower of Rahmagut, then so be it. I've lived my whole life as an outcast. This isn't going to make or break me."

Eva exhaled a huff of delight, her chest light as a feather. All this time she had blindly sought acceptance from people who were nothing like her, believing herself broken, a bringer of discord for her blood and the strange occurrences she attracted, when she should have been looking for someone like Reina.

"That's exactly how I feel," Eva said in an airy breath.

"What are you looking for with Javier?"

Inspired by Reina's honesty, the truth came easily to Eva. "My family's ignorance was like a prison. Javier got me out of that life, and he's opening my eyes to a lot of things."

Reina scoffed.

"But I don't need him. If I can learn from...you or Celeste," Eva said quickly.

"I'm still learning myself. But I'm sure one day you'll meet my grandmother. People call her the most terrifying geomancer in Sadul Fuerte. There's plenty to learn from her."

Eva nodded with bright eyes. Reina laughed at her eagerness before turning on her heel and leaving.

As Reina disappeared down the corridor, a smirk tugged the corners of Eva's mouth. So Javier's strength wasn't unique. One needn't become corrupted or vile to be as strong as him. No—this woman was proof. And the longer Eva lingered around her, the more she would absorb those capabilities.

The mondongo was gone before she realized she was scraping the bottom of the bowl. Javier's wasn't steaming anymore, and Eva's tongue curled with guilt. She glanced at the plethora of books. All titled with words like *hermetics* and *dynamics* and *phenomenological alchemy*. This was where she wanted to be, not bringing lunch to Javier—who didn't deserve any kindness.

She opened *The Power of Suns* to a page bookmarked by its folded corner, skimming the flurry of ink until one paragraph in particular caught her eye.

> Geomancia has been observed to manifest in different light frequencies according to the caster's predominant trait. Further experimentation confirmed the appearance of the observable geomancia in hues of red for the dominant conductors, hues of blue for the logical thinkers, hues of violet for the supportive caregivers, and hues of gold for the inspiring promoters.

Eva tugged her pendant. Anytime she cast iridio, it came out gold, but how could she be inspiring? Javier's geomancia was also gold. And whatever spell weaved in and out of Reina's chest was blue.

The realization brought a smile to Eva's lips.

She flipped through the pages and stopped near the end, on a terrible illustration made in fervent inky scribbles. A black goatlike creature with horns and talons and a wicked toothy grin.

A ripple ran through Eva's back, and she shivered.

It was a crude drawing of a tiniebla pointing at the block of text.

> No branch of iridio sorcery is as little understood as void magic. It is believed mortals can attune to el Vacío with the use of iridio. Alas, it comes with a hefty price, with some scholars attesting such spells can cause a fracturing of one's soul. Those foolhardy enough to try either let the thirst for iridio consume them or successfully manage to take control of those we call *tinieblas*.

Underneath the paragraph was the scribbled phrase to rule tinieblas: *Tiempo que pasa no vuelve.*

Eva dared not say it, not while she was alone in this strange room with all the books as witness. So she tucked the spell book under her arm and went to look for Javier. She found him in their bedroom on the third floor, facing a dirty standing mirror. He didn't move despite her bursting in. He just watched her through the reflection with eyes that were two pools of black spoiled magic, dripping tendrils of it oozing in and out of his cheeks, neck, and torso.

How did he end up like this? The instinct to flee bloomed from her belly, almost making her bolt. She swallowed the sensation and settled for reminding herself that she could wield the power of stars.

"Maior made mondongo. Eat it before it gets cold." She thrust the bowl at him, the thick stew sloshing on the verge of spilling out, the fat congealing on the top.

"Eva Kesaré," he said, though his usually handsome voice came out murky.

"You're soiling my name." Her lip tingled where he had struck her. "I told you not to use it."

He turned from the mirror and stepped into the sunset light. Feminine lips and eyes met her, without the rot. "How would you like it if I told you what you could and couldn't say?" he asked.

"You already do that."

He ignored her and went on. "Besides, it's such a pretty name. So, do you prefer *fallen star* for your magic? Or *cosita rica* from your adoring husband?"

"I prefer that you stop mocking me." Eva stepped fully inside the room, though she didn't dare shut the door. "No one else uses my whole name," she went on, "so why should you?"

His eyes softened. He took the bowl and slurped a spoonful. He didn't say anything, but his face brightened at the rich flavor profile. The garlic and onions and broth-absorbing potatoes. The corn that grew on Gegania's surrounding land.

"What are you plotting?" she said.

Between spoonfuls, he glanced at her with brows furrowed in confusion.

"You've found Maior and Celeste, who are reincarnations of Rahmagut's wives. What are we going to do next?"

He set the empty bowl down on a nearby desk, licked the edges of his lips, and said, "My brother's witch, Ursulina, will be bringing the other damas to the tomb. We bring Maior and Celeste. When the time comes, I will make sure I'm the one Rahmagut speaks to."

"How?"

"Big picture? By distracting Doña Ursulina. But why don't you let *me* worry about the details, and you just do your job of blowing things up? I'll walk you through it when it's relevant."

Eva jabbed her index finger at him, stopping short of touching his chest. "We agreed on being equal partners. You said so in Galeno."

He stepped forward so her finger came into contact with his chest. Eva withdrew to the wall.

"Yes, and as your equal, I don't owe you anything. As equals, you will have to learn to extract information out of me. As equals, it's in your best interest to stay on my good side."

"No."

"Why not? I am your husband. You signed the papers." He waved his hand at the small bed and said, "And we are, after all, about to share the same bed tonight."

She tried shoving him and sidestepping away, but the motion had no effect on him. He simply blocked her escape with his arm.

"Seeing as we haven't even consummated our marriage yet, you should *want* me on your side," he said.

Eva's heart faltered. It was as weak as her knees. "We married for convenience. Not for—"

"Not for the pleasures of the bed?"

Warmth bloomed in her belly. She inwardly cursed her treacherous body for physically responding to him when hate was all she should be feeling.

"Not for the pleasures of conception? What about the valco bloodline?"

"I'll sleep on the kitchen floor before I let you try anything," she said between gritted teeth. "I'll—I'll burn this whole house to the ground."

Javier laughed and moved his arm away. She had freedom.

"Celeste and Reina wouldn't very much like that."

"What is the matter with you?" She wanted to yell but instead hissed, lest everyone in the house hear their quarrel.

"Nothing and everything, depending on how you look at it."

She seethed. "You were joking about having your way with me!"

"And frankly, there's nothing to stop me. Look at yourself; you're softer than a plantain—"

"Every time you use geomancia, you become someone else," she said, her curveball catching him by surprise.

"We all do."

"No." This time she mustered the courage to shut the door. All in the hope of honesty. "I'm still me when I summon iridio. I can *see* geomancia, Javier, don't forget. And I can see you're not yourself." Her voice trembled. The place where he'd struck her itched again. "You became that monster when you were healing Celeste."

He closed the gap between them, fast like a fleeting thought.

Eva gasped and nearly crumpled to the floor. He held her up by the arms, his grip squeezing so tight she imagined it would bruise come the morrow.

"Have you considered the possibility that maybe *I am* myself with spells? That what you see now—none of it is real?"

She whispered, "You're a demon?"

His nostrils flared. The black ooze began to fill the white of his eyes. He blinked and swallowed hard to clear it away.

"Are you?" Eva asked. "You tricked me out of my home. The least you can do is tell me. I didn't want to hate you when I left Galeno. You did this all by yourself."

"You hate me." It wasn't a question. He spoke as if he was realizing it for the first time.

"You're delusional to think I wouldn't. Maybe if you treat me like an equal—like you promised—and less like I'm some minion, then maybe I can begin to forgive you."

"Forgive me?"

"Yes! For hitting me. For—for acting like an ass, *always*."

He let her go. His red eyes blazed against her brown ones for a second. Then he had to look away.

Eva took one gulp of air after another. She waited. And waited. "Don't you have anything to say?"

Javier's gaze fell on the mark on the corner of her lip. "I'm sorry," he finally said.

It drenched Eva in disappointment. He couldn't have given her a more inadequate, hollow apology. "*Sorry* isn't going to make the scar go away," Eva said in a low voice. Her jaw worked itself into knots, until she realized how futile it was to expect decency out of him. He was as rotten as the magic possessing him.

She whirled to the door. He tried reaching out to stop her, but this time she was quicker. She descended the stairs in a mad dash. As she passed the first-floor hallway, she snuck a look of the kitchen and of Reina and Celeste at the dining table. They leaned close in quiet privacy, unaware of her passing. Eva didn't stop until she reached the entrance foyer. There she took a deep breath.

How she hated him, and how she wanted him out of her thoughts. But how could she when they were bound by law and magic?

She took another deep breath.

Eva knew one thing for sure, though. She had to put up with it. Just by osmosis, she was learning. And she was going to use him—to feed her magical prowess—until she could blast him back into the depths of Rahmagut's Vacío. Surely, it was where he belonged.

The last lick of dusk light spilled onto the foyer from the open door. Eva walked out to Gegania's cobbled entryway, then to the sloped gravel steps leading into the vegetable garden, where Maior sat on a boulder with her hands entwined in prayer. Eva clutched her borrowed woolen ruana closer around her shoulders, the spell book still tucked under her arm. She thought of all the pious women in Galeno and of her hatred for Mass, but instead of repulsion, Eva felt the urge to smile. After all, it was Maior's ruana warming her shoulders unused to this cold, and Maior's mondongo that filled her belly.

Eva approached, and they exchanged some pleasantries, with Maior scooting to the side so Eva could sit beside her.

Ahead, the conuco and the hills remained quiet, unconcerned by the existence of people. The sky above the mountain peaks was streaked in pinks as the afternoon prepared to bid goodbye.

"I was just wondering if I should forget my old home," Maior explained after a while. "If I want to go back at all."

Eva perked up from leafing through the spell book. Memories of Galeno came to her, of the heat and the youngins and the scent of cattle seeping from every crevice. "Where is your home?"

"I grew up not far from here—I think. But I doubt I would ever be able to go back."

Up close it was hard to ignore the ghostly woman in Maior. Eva could see the resemblance to Celeste. Blue eyes. Pointed nose. She forced herself to stare at her own dangling legs instead. "I don't ever want to go back home," Eva said.

Maior watched her with an arched eyebrow.

Maybe it was the fact they'd just met or the way Maior's eyes watched Eva without judgment or expectation. It made the honesty come easily to her lips. "It was so stifling there. And my grandmother never let me forget about my mom. Or what I am."

Maior's gaze gravitated to the antlers peeking out of Eva's curls. "Why do you want to forget your mom?"

"I don't want to forget her. I just want to stop remembering her sadness so much. It's not fair that they made it my fault."

"What did you do that made her sad?"

Maior did this thing where she gave Eva her undivided attention, earnestly, without a hidden agenda. It was so different from how her family treated her, from how Javier schemed, that Eva allowed herself to be completely open. She sucked her lower lip and said, "I think...my mom loved so much she couldn't take it anymore." A sigh left her lips, but it was no relief.

"She loved you too much?" Maior said.

My father, Eva thought.

She remembered the days Dulce had spent watching the rain in silence, pining for someone else, when Eva's and Pura's love was just an arm's length away. The truth of what ailed Dulce was no secret. Doña Antonia had attested it to anyone who asked: Eva's father had used darkness to addle Dulce's mind, to seduce her and put a child in her.

But Eva didn't want Maior to know her as the people of Galeno knew her. That was past Eva. The new Eva had no mamá y papá.

"No. She was tricked to love someone else—put under a spell,"

Eva said with finality, hoping Maior would abandon the prying subject altogether.

Maior's eyebrows bunched up. She had more questions, Eva could tell, but she graciously swallowed them down. "To love so much it hurts? Wow," she said with a small frown. "I used to think I wasn't capable of liking anybody."

Eva waited for her to go on.

Maior smiled at the pink sky. "There was this man, in Apartaderos. He treated me nice. And there were so many other pretty girls—petite with long hair—rich daughters with horses and good fashion. He had green eyes like a cat, and he could've had any girl he wanted. Yet he went to the chapel every day, not for prayer or salves but for *me*. And it scared me, because I couldn't understand the words he said. I used to wonder: What's wrong with me? He's perfect in every way, and I still can't feel anything. Except pity, for us." Maior hugged herself and made a weird, pained smile, stealing a fleeting glance at the weed-grown path leading back to the front door. "But...I've realized now that it's not that I'm not capable of liking anyone. It's just that I was looking at the wrong people, and the right person hadn't come by." She picked at her nails. "If your mom loved too much, it must have been torturous. I'm sorry she didn't have a happy ending."

Eva nodded, understanding every word left unsaid. She didn't know what made her utter, "Reina's with Celeste right now." But maybe she did it as a warning, to safeguard Maior's feelings. After seeing how Celeste had treated her, Eva decided the human needed the protection.

A chilly breeze swept through them, and Maior's dark hair rode it like froth on waves as she stared out at the rolling hills, where a single line of sunlight surfed the mounds of the Páramo Mountains. She had a tiredness to her countenance, accentuated by the dark rings under her eyes. "Yes. Doña Celeste being here changes everything. She's important and...I'm not."

Eva felt it, too. Celeste was beautiful, and valco, *and free.*

Maior's gaze surfed the points of Eva's antlers. "Valcos can see magic."

Eva nodded.

"You're valco."

Eva nodded again.

"You can see what that witch did to me, can't you?" Maior gripped her belly, stricken by a sudden ache. "You can see the Benevolent Lady?"

She couldn't lie, even if it was uncomfortable to answer. Her voice shrunk. "She's bound to you somehow. I don't...know how."

Maior turned her forearms and rolled up her sleeves, revealing two long vertical scars, the skin hardly healed. "It's the bindings. Does she talk? Is she saying something right now?"

"She seems...dead." Eva tried being as kind as she could. But nothing about the truth could ever sound kind. "She's just there, like a guest that never leaves."

"Does it bother you?"

Eva licked her lips. "Yes."

There was no privacy with the woman around—or her remnant.

Maior crossed her hands to squeeze her scars, fingernails tearing the scabs. She doubled over and winced.

Eva struggled to hold her back—to stop her. "What are you doing?"

"I want her out of me—I can't stand it!"

The scab on her right arm ruptured, the small trickle of blood smearing their wrangling fingers with crimson. At that moment Eva realized Maior's wounds should have long since healed.

"Stop. Whatever you're doing won't make you better."

"Every night I dream of this valco—of this man," Maior told her, her eyes shinier and wetter. "Doña Ursulina brought me to him, through *her* eyes. Now I dream and dream and *dream* of him, like I love him, but I don't! I'm so tired of him. *I loathe him.* I hate seeing him!"

"A valco man?" Eva said.

"Don Enrique Águila, the caudillo of Sadul Fuerte—her husband."

"You have her dreams?"

Maior went still. She gave her head the slightest shake and said, "No. In my dreams, I'm her. I have...her *memories* when I sleep."

Every cell in Eva's body screamed at her to reach out, to warm Maior in an embrace. But a voice reeled Eva back, telling her, *You've only just met*. Instead, she flipped the spell book open.

"Void magic bound her to you, so void magic must be the way to break the bond."

Maior watched with wide eyes as Eva skimmed page after page, her finger underlining every line, eyes furiously absorbing every word despite the dying light.

The tome was thick, every page filled with tight paragraphs and diagrams requiring patience and time to absorb. Knowledge and foundations she didn't have. Eva sucked in a breath. It was like she was staring at the depths of an ocean, arrogantly thinking she could dive in and pluck the right shell from its endless floor.

Maior placed a hand on her wrist. She offered her a small smile to stop her. She shook her head, wordlessly freeing Eva from the weight of the commitment.

Eva's jaw clenched. She was useless now, but one day she would know the answer. One day *she* would be the one known as the greatest geomancer.

Two things happened in close succession at that moment: First a loud crack erupted from behind them, coming directly from the depths of the house. No—from beneath it. Then Eva's core, the part of her deeply attuned to the workings of geomancia, which could never be deafened, felt the plunging pull of an inky void, a suction so strong that the air squeezed out of her lungs and left her empty.

There was a lot Eva didn't know, but this time she understood the source without an inkling of doubt: a burst of geomancia, the kind that pertained to the wonders and horrors of iridio.

33

Tinieblas

Eva reeled as Maior squeezed her by the shoulder. The dusk was darker than light, yet she could still see Maior's wordless inquiry and surprise.

"What happened to you?"

Eva blinked to ground herself. She took in the garden's umbra, the immobile vegetal shapes, and the smells of wet moss. The air temperature dropped. Without them noticing, clouds had shrouded the skies, hiding them from Rahmagut's Claw...and the possibility of light from its neighbors, the moon and stars. The night crackled with far-off thunder.

Her chest and extremities pulsated with unease.

As a vein of lightning streaked the sky, Eva could swear she saw one of them shaped like a grinning devil.

They whipped around at the sound of footsteps. Celeste, Reina, and Javier emerged onto the garden.

Eva craned her neck to get a better glimpse up the slope to the house. "Did something collapse?"

"We gave the house a load of iridio to speed up the connection," Celeste said without her usual confidence.

Javier unsheathed his sword. "Something's not right. You feel it?" he asked Eva, and she nodded.

"The house took up the iridio kind of violently. I don't think it has attempted a connection with somewhere so far before. We might have overloaded it," Celeste added by way of explaining.

The moments dragged in thick apprehension. They waited in silence, the mountain's chill leaking past Eva's ruana and clothes.

"Did you attempt to troubleshoot it?" Javier asked exactly what Eva was thinking.

Celeste's cheeks glowed red. "Do you take me for a fool? The problem is not what's inside the house...I think the problem will be what's coming."

Something like thunder rumbled in the distance again. Eva didn't want to think of it, but her instincts yanked her back to the night with the tinieblas, when everything had seemed well one instant, and the next they were upon her, all teeth and claws.

"Let me guess, it just announced to the whole mountain the iridio it has in its stores?" Javier said.

"What does that have to do with anything?" Eva asked as she twirled her iridio pendant, the touch a reassurance.

"Tinieblas are attracted to iridio," Reina said dryly.

At that moment the darkness over the hills took defined shapes, shadows becoming masses of galloping creatures, all headed in Gegania's direction, proof her words were true.

"Stand back," Javier ordered Eva and Maior.

Reina unhooked Ches's Blade from her belt, but without the sun to bounce off its gleam, it was nothing more than an ordinary sword.

"We must protect the house," Celeste commanded. She pressed her palms together, then spread them in a wide sweeping gesture. A tall ornate scythe materialized in her hands, with a handle of ebony and a curved blade shimmering in crimson iridio.

Eva and Maior retreated closer to the front steps. Eva tugged on her pendant, shuddery from the fear tugging her in one direction and the thrill of using her geomancia pulling her in the other.

"We won't fail," Celeste said fiercely before running down the hilly path toward the approaching horde. When neither Javier nor Reina objected to splitting up, Eva assumed she was doing it to gain ground.

Reina gripped Maior by the shoulders and told her, "Stay near the house. If they invade the grounds, run up to the highest room and hide. Do *not* let them bite you."

With glistening eyes and red cheeks, Maior nodded.

"Until then, please use galio to support us from afar."

Maior clutched Reina's wrist before she could follow Celeste. "But how?"

"Just numb us if we get hit, like you did to me in La Cochinilla— as long as we don't feel the pain, we'll be fine."

"And take comfort in knowing there's no better way to learn than in battle," Javier added, always with his amused condescension, even in times like these. "Because if Reina dies, it'll be me you'll have to deal with. Eva—"

Eva made a point not to let her terror show. She chewed on the insides of her lips and nodded. "I know what to do."

Javier and Reina followed Celeste, plunging into darkness. The mass of tinieblas swelled with every heartbeat. They were amalgamated animals snarling and snapping in a mad sprint, all horns and grins.

Eva's insides vibrated, the panic molding into excitement. Javier had saved her from them. And there were Reina and Celeste. *We can handle this*, she told herself. *I can handle this.*

She pressed her hands together and shoved her spirit into that vast universe. There everything was safe and endless and unbound. A warmth like Galeno's lapped her forearms. The thrumming hoof steps were hushed by the energy flowing into Eva, sloshing like the soft waves on a lake. The starlight came to her. She was born to seduce it, and when it was in her, she nestled herself into reality.

A ball of light grew in the space between her palms. She stretched the distance, letting the ball grow bigger and wilder.

Maior gaped at her. "I can't see the tinieblas."

"It's all right," Eva told her. "I won't let them touch you." She released the energy in the direction of the horde, a fallen star illuminating the hills. The blast took out a good dozen.

Ahead, Javier unleashed a flurry of blows as he dueled at least five. They leapt and slashed at him, their elongated claws dangerously close to ripping through clothes and flesh. The other side of the field flashed in flurries of red as Celeste twirled the scythe all around her. She whirled to her left and parried a slash, slicing an attacking tiniebla in two. To her right, an opportunistic tiniebla leapt out of the horde, mandibles wide for a bite.

In that split second, Eva knew Celeste wouldn't have time to evade.

The starlight came to her hands instinctively, heat licking her palms and flushing her fingertips. She screamed as she shot it, and luck was on her side, the ball blasting the tiniebla in the chest before it could strike Celeste.

Celeste's stunned gaze met with Eva's. She nodded once, her thanks, then continued her onslaught.

Near the conuco entrance and closer than ever before, Reina screamed as a tiniebla's talon sliced her side. She collapsed to her knees, blood trickling past her hand.

"Reina!" Maior's panic was thick and cloying. She foolishly ran to the conuco, tripping on a gnarling brush but catching herself from falling. Gesturing her hands in a circle, she muttered an incantation that sent threads of amethyst light shooting at Reina. They wrapped around Reina's torso, easing the expression of pain.

Eva ran after Maior, screaming for her to stop. A throaty cackle seized her attention. Eva whipped around to see crazed eyes and flared fangs hiding within the cornstalks. Then the tiniebla lunged at Maior.

The incantation for a litio barrier came to Eva's mind like a godsend, and she flattened her palms together.

Maior screamed as the tiniebla crashed against the glittering dome with a thud. Clumsy and disoriented, the creature rolled off to the ground. But when it got up, it was joined by a second attacker.

Eva summoned the power of starlight a third time, producing a ball with flames that licked and spat in the space between her hands. She willed the litio barrier to disintegrate a second before she shot the fireball. The tinieblas caught the attack head-on, exuding the stench of charred meat before disintegrating into darkness.

Maior sent the healing power of galio at Celeste and Reina and Javier, who inched closer to the house with each kill as the tinieblas encroached around them. A great crash came from behind Eva as Reina hurled a tiniebla into the larder with a strike, the splintered door impaling its black body. With a grunt, Eva willed a protection around Celeste just as a tiniebla's talon swiped for her neck. The talon didn't split her skin, hindered by the litio coating her, but it sent her crashing against the front door window, shattered glass shooting in all directions.

A stray group of three tinieblas turned their attention to Maior, who twirled her hands like a baker kneading dough as she supported the others. Heart hammering, Eva wrenched Maior's forearm and jerked her to the front door. "Run!" Eva's mind whirred for the right spell to use in this moment. Should it be a barrier or a fire? Should she pump their calves with bismuto to make the getaway swifter?

Treacherous like an uncoiling viper came the void spell, of winding iridio to reach into el Vacío with the leash that could rein tinieblas to do her bidding. As Javier had advised, now was as a good a time as any.

Eva tugged her pendant with the words clear and bright. *"Tiempo que pasa no vuelve!"*

Time flashed and stopped. Her spirit split into two. One version of her was tethered to the mountains, and another was plunged into a vast space of inky black. Light-sucking black. Never-ending black.

El Vacío.

Despite the darkness, she could see the horde of tinieblas as outlines of shadow and light, some near, some far away, all horns and limbs. They were as static as her, waiting. And the intent purled around her, the uttered spell inviting her to command the tinieblas to her whim. Telling her she could make them her marionettes.

Eva thrust herself back to the present plane. The passing of time resumed. With her return came the knowledge that the tinieblas were under her thrall.

She commanded her pursuers to fight each other until their own killing blows disintegrated them into nothingness. Commanding the three tinieblas burned the last of her iridio.

All at once the remaining tinieblas noticed her, angered at her nerve. They rerouted toward her like a flock of crows. Snarling and enraged that she'd dared control them.

"Oh—*no*," Eva muttered a second before bolting toward the house, pulling Maior along with her.

The creatures stomped the vegetable garden muddy. They were faster, and the closest caught up to her, a four-legged capuchin-and-jaguar amalgamation with bulging muscles that yanked her by the leg. Eva fell screaming. Maior grabbed her arm and tugged with all her might as Eva desperately kicked and cried. Its mottled capuchin hand closed around her ankle, its jaguar fangs snapping foamy spittle as every tug brought her leg closer to its mouth. Eva sucked in a fat breath as she stomped on the head with her other boot, and the skull caved in with a sickening crack.

Another tiniebla zipped out of the conuco, razor-sharp claws outstretched, followed by another one. With her hands and elbows sunken in mud, Eva saw Javier, Reina, and Celeste struggling to catch up to the rushing horde, too far away or distracted to realize she and Maior were breaths away from death.

The tinieblas leapt. Eva screwed her eyes shut, already imagining the belly-tearing agony, the demonic laughter as their teeth unraveled her inner tendrils in the darkness. She hugged herself and closed her eyes, screaming like a child.

The pain never came.

She opened her eyes to a dazzling light of the purest blue. It encapsulated them, turning the air sweet with the aroma of a wildflower field. Standing with them beneath the barrier was a tall woman. With her short locks of black and robes of midday blue, she stared at the tinieblas, unflinching as they slashed and tackled the barrier.

The woman's brightness blinded Eva to what happened next. She heard the tinieblas' screeches, shuddered as their talons shrilled against the crystal barrier. When she turned to Maior, she saw her sprawled on the ground, unconscious.

"No!" Eva shook her and called her name until her throat felt like bleeding.

The weight of the ghostly woman's stare fell on her. Eva met eyes that were blue against dark lashes. In them, she saw sadness. A gaze that understood they were nothing but pawns in someone else's game.

Slowly the woman faded. Then Maior gave a great inhale, and with it the barrier evaporated into nothing. A great hush fell over the conuco once the protection dissipated. The chaos that had once engulfed them was done.

Javier, Celeste, and Reina circled them with their weapons raised after routing the last tiniebla. And they watched Eva and Maior with a mixture of confusion, exhaustion, and disbelief.

Reina was the first to rush to Maior. She cradled Maior with such gentleness, Eva couldn't help but recall Maior's quiet longing when they'd talked about love.

"Mi mamá was here," Celeste murmured, her face stained in sweat and smears of her own blood. "How is that possible? Did you summon her somehow—" she demanded of the teary Maior.

Panting, Javier said, "Come off it already. Do you really think she wants to keep Laurel in her?"

"She came out just now!" Celeste snapped back. "Mi mamá was here!"

"Clearly. She's the reason they're alive! Now let's make a sweep to make sure no tinieblas are still lurking on the grounds. *You and I*," Javier said with emphasis. He gave Eva a long look, then gave up on whatever lingered on the tip of his tongue.

Eva retreated with Reina and Maior back into the house, their boots crunching on the shattered glass littering the foyer. The structure of Gegania itself wasn't compromised, but it was clear the façade was battered and scratched, the floor muddied and the frames splintered. Eva followed them to the kitchen and set up a kettle on the hearth. Reina helped Maior sit by the kitchen table, then stood against a wall. Though she pretended to stand firm, her crossed arms shielded a wound, her knuckles pale and bloodstained.

Celeste and Javier were in a similarly stained state when they walked into the kitchen as Eva fumbled through serving the teas. And with a hand swiping her sweaty face, Celeste confirmed they had banished all tinieblas for now, and no traces remained.

Javier pointed a thumb at the foyer, where the front door was too dislocated to properly close. "That, out there, was caused by the iridio table?"

Celeste's cheeks turned a bright red. "Like I said, I've never attempted a connection to somewhere so far before."

"I felt it in my bones," Eva said. Had Celeste and Javier reeled from the sensation as well? Was it an innate affinity of their blood or her own attunement that she had nurtured these past few days? But instead of an answer, all she got from them were grimacing looks.

Reina let out a pained cough. "If the house uses iridio, then tinieblas will be drawn to it. It's a fact."

Javier pointed again with arched brows. "Just like that? So what's to say that we won't have another attack while we sleep through the night? I have seen more tinieblas in the past fortnight than in my entire life. They are *spawning* out of control ever since the arrival of Rahmagut's Claw."

"There are wards I can activate. My mom's family had this house for years. They had safeguards."

He humphed.

"And Reina can keep watch, no?" Celeste shrugged as she shot Reina a glance.

It didn't sit right with Eva, especially not in Reina's visible condition. But perhaps there was more to her capabilities than what Eva had witnessed today.

"We just need a few more days. The connection will be ready soon. Then we'll head to Tierra'e Sol," Celeste added.

"Very well," Javier said before any more interjections could be thrown their way. He took Eva's hand and said, "Let me help you to the room."

Celeste looked up. "Javier."

"What?"

Eva's blood rushed through her, pumping violently as she

imagined the inevitable accusation, of how she had manipulated the tinieblas, igniting their wrath. Would they think less of her for being stupid enough to attempt void magic?

Celeste watched Javier coolly and surprised Eva when she said, "Heal us."

"I beg your pardon?"

"Use your galio and heal us." Her tone was a command, like it came naturally to her.

Eva walked to the arched doorway, taking full advantage of Javier distracting them with his disdain.

"I'm not interested in being your nurse," he said.

"Why not? You're the only one here who's mastered galio."

"You're forgetting about Maior," he retorted.

There wasn't hatred in the look Celeste gave Maior. But there wasn't anything positive in it either.

"Maior needs proper galio training," Reina pointed out, exhaustion blurring the edges of her voice. "You're the only one who can teach her."

"Fantastic," Javier drawled. Then, to Maior, he said, "Lesson number one: Heal them all. Think you can handle it?"

She nodded. "I'll need more solution."

"It's not that easy," Celeste protested. "Otherwise we'd all be masters of galio."

"And what are you afraid of, exactly?" Javier shot back. "That you'll be forced to ask her for help? Stop complaining. You're both Damas del Vacío, so start cooperating. You're in it together."

With that, he extended his hand to Eva, the invitation a command more than anything else. Eva took it and exited the kitchen, her ankle screaming where the tiniebla's grip had sprained her. As soon as Eva and Javier entered their bedroom, he closed the door behind them and said, "I felt it."

Eva's eyebrows crunched up.

"Whatever you did to anger the tinieblas. I felt it."

She freed her hand and slipped on an aloof mask. "I have no idea what you're talking about."

He watched her long and hard. "Don't do that again."

Eva eased into the room smugly, turning away from him. "You sounded like quite the uncle back there," she said to put the subject behind them.

His expression simmered to something like amusement. "Celeste only listens to me sometimes. What you witnessed there was a rare moment."

Eva settled on the bed. The feel of the mattress on her aching bones was a relief she hadn't indulged in a while. *Melt into me*, the bed told her.

"I don't blame her. You're not that much older than her," she said and yawned.

"No." He ran a hand across his sweaty forehead.

"You're...young enough to be her cousin."

"Yes."

"Why is that?"

Javier's lips became a thin line, and for a second, Eva imagined he was going to spew something vile.

"I mean," she said, feeling silly, "your brother's so much older than you, right?"

He tossed his sword to the ground and unbuttoned his doublet. "Do you know why valcos are on the verge of extinction?"

Eva wasn't listening. She stared at the stained satin he shook off, her mind racing, grappling for what he meant to do.

He pushed his slick hair back out of his face and continued. "Valcos are a dozen times stronger than humans. You could say the gods balanced this out by making us notoriously infertile. The conception of a new valco child is so rare, it is a gift from the gods."

Eva frowned. She refused to believe an ounce of it, for the implications of what her father had done to her mom.

Javier folded his doublet. He loosened the strings of his shirt, then slipped off his rings, save for the galio pair. Eva watched him get comfortable in his clothes as the sleep dried out of her like left-over rain under the Llanos sun.

"Once, we were many—or so the stories say. Some couples didn't conceive at all, while others only raised a single child. After the humans settled and overcame us in numbers, the last pure-blooded valcos had no choice but to marry each other, cousins and siblings. Mother's parents were cousins, as were their parents before them. Your ancestors and mine could even be of the same blood. I wouldn't be surprised."

He shook one boot off, then another. Eva's muscles transmuted to stiff marble. She inched farther and farther back onto the bed.

She asked him, to keep him busy talking—instead of whatever he was doing... "Did your father have valco blood?"

He shook his head. "Mother was an only child and the youngest of her cousins by a good generation. Her cousins were loyalists; they fought on Segol's side and were killed for it. So, no. She bred with humans, and her valco line dies with us."

Finally, once he stripped to his loose long-sleeved shirt and trousers, he meticulously stacked his doublet, accessories, boots, and weapon into a neat pile, which he placed atop the corner chest.

"Soon enough you'll hear the hateful rumors that our age gap was because Mother was too busy indulging in her affection for women to conceive another child. But the truth is that Enrique's father was a charlatan, and he abandoned her. Eventually Mother had to try again with another human, hoping for sons and daughters who could marry each other and pass on the blood. I was the only one."

Eva swallowed uncomfortably.

He spread his arms, showcasing the whole of him. "Obviously it didn't work out. I was born male, and our valco blood is doomed to be further diluted. Only, now that I've found you, not so much."

He kneeled on the bed and took off her left boot.

Eva pulled away at once, her belly in a swirl of panic. "But—there's Celeste. She's valco. If it's the family tradition to inbreed, why not marry her?"

His eyes hardened. Her question opened a terrible box, but it was too late to take it back.

"Celeste was the only good thing Laurel gave Mother. And yes, she was supposed to be my bride. But Enrique doesn't value Mother's legacy anymore. He became a tool under Laurel, thinking with his prick rather than with his head. Stop squirming, and give me your foot!"

This close, her throat itched with the tang of his sweat and their blood. "No—you can't undress me." Eva's chest pounded with a flurry different to when the tinieblas threatened her. No, this panic was compounded with delight at the thought that this beautiful monster could desire her. He was talking about consummating his marriage to try for heirs.

"*Undress* you? I'm trying to heal you, you half-wit."

Her mouth went dry.

"You were limping all the way up. I saw what that tiniebla did to you."

With a puff of relief, Eva eased to the ministration of him removing the other boot. Shivers bloomed in her stomach as his fingers took her foot gently. "But you refuse to be a healer."

"I mastered galio to be undefeatable in battle. Not to make anyone else undefeatable. Besides, you very well know Celeste can see spells of geomancia," he said, avoiding her gaze. "And during the battle, Reina was flaring bismuto—I couldn't risk it."

Understanding dawned on Eva.

Black, putrid magic began to slither in and out of his cheeks, then his arms, as he summoned the galio from his rings. A smoky blackness overtook the white of his eyes. He tensed, the monster taking over.

She watched, petrified, well aware he was restraining whatever terrible thought or action the demon in him itched to perform. Then she felt it—waves of pleasure from the healing. She closed her eyes, sucking in air as the pulled ligaments of her ankle shrunk and rearranged themselves. Relief like a splash of water on hot days in Galeno.

When she opened her eyes, she saw a young man demoralized by a curse.

He hadn't wanted to heal anyone in the kitchen because he knew Celeste could see him for what he was. And he wasn't just half valco, half human anymore. Slowly but surely, he was turning into something else.

34

The Liberator

Excitement charged the kitchen on the morning Celeste announced that the iridio table had finished mapping the mineral vein network. The house was now connected to the Cow Sea coast, where they could charter a boat to the Liberator's residence in Tierra'e Sol. The news was highly anticipated, for they had spent days anxiously making repairs to Gegania while seeing the cyan smear in the night as the countdown to their journey's end. With Celeste, Reina had patched up the fractured plaster around the front door and windows. Eva and Maior had replanted the vegetable garden and the conuco. And Javier kept the grounds safe from the trickle of tinieblas, whistlers, and other unnamed ghouls attracted to the iridio churning underneath the house.

The party broke fast on Maior's pisca, exchanging pleasantries with giddy anticipation about the travels ahead. Mostly, Eva and Maior did all the talking, and for that, Reina was grateful. She was worn, and her head throbbed, and it wasn't until she ascended back to the room she'd claimed and almost collapsed on the unmade bed that she realized she needed another refill of iridio.

There was only a small amount left. Three beads or so of liquid that she kept for an emergency, which a moment like this did not qualify as. She could delay the refill and risk collapsing in front of Celeste and Javier on the way to Tierra'e Sol. Or she could give herself one last boost, hastening her reconnection with Doña Ursulina, who would give her the ore back as soon as she saw that Reina had fulfilled her objective. Either alternative carried its plethora of risks, with Reina's death as the only sure outcome. So she just unbound her chest with her teeth grinding in self-hatred and her hands shaking from exhaustion to do the blood-damned refill.

"Hey, I think they're waiting for you," a soft voice said behind her, the person entering the bedroom.

Reina startled, a droplet of iridio flinging out of the dropper and landing on the ground, lost. She cursed.

"Oh—I'm sorry." Maior hurried to her.

Reina scoffed. "Really? I can't afford a mistake."

Maior's cheeks reddened, her gentle warmth morphing into hot indignation. "Then let *me* do it. My hands are sure, and yours are shaking." She raised an eyebrow pointedly.

Reina nodded, making a point for her eyes not to linger on Maior's lips. She allowed the human to herd her to the bed, where they sat under the cool rays of the morning sun.

Reina turned to Maior stiffly, a flush rushing to her face. She was without a shirt, and her cloth bindings were loose and parted, allowing access to the scarred flesh and tubes. If she wasn't careful, the slightest movement in the wrong direction could slide the bindings farther down, revealing the pigmentation of her areola, or worse, her nipple.

Maior had seen her, she was sure, when she'd blacked out in La Cochinilla. But that was then, and this was different. She wasn't in desperate need of iridio. She still could hold on to her dignity.

Those brown eyes glanced up, rounding with a question. Perhaps asking for the consent to begin. Reina nodded, and Maior's palm gently planted against her skin, positioning the dropper over the tube opening. Her touch seared Reina, or maybe Reina was already scorching.

"Try to relax," Maior murmured.

Reina didn't obey. Couldn't.

She wondered how Maior saw her, with her atrophied skin and

the hollow crystal where the ore used to fit into, all ragged edges. Incomplete. Monstrous. Reina certainly felt like all of the above.

The sunlight kissed Maior's cheeks, and they were so close Reina imagined she could count every one of those soft peach fuzz hairs tracing her jaw. What would it feel like to run the back of her fingers against them? Her belly fluttered and warmed suddenly. Her tail coiled. The sudden treacherous question sobered her. An aching to get closer and find out. Reina stiffened up even more, holding her breath, forcing the moment not to feel so utterly relaxed. So comforting and private. Because she wasn't supposed to be feeling this now, not with Maior.

She forced Celeste into her thoughts. Imagined the blue fire of her eyes. How her face was in perfect symmetry, carved by a master of the arts. The image muddied whatever traitorous desire misconstrued this moment with Maior. She let out a shuddery exhale just as Maior dropped a tiny amount of iridio into her transplant heart. The timing was perfect, masking the true reason for her relief.

And indeed, the refresh of iridio was delicious. Like the first gushing bite of a ripe mango. Reina closed her eyes and took another hard swallow. "Thanks," she said.

Maior smiled. She didn't waste a second before screwing the tube back in place, and again her palm came in close contact with Reina's breast, almost igniting the same treachery.

When Reina opened her eyes again, she found herself trapped in Maior's gaze. It held her, steadily and unafraid, and the minute distance made it impossible for Reina to hide her emotions.

"You'll still take us to your grandmother?" Maior asked, as if Reina's answer were going to change.

"I have no choice."

Maior frowned a little. "Sure you do." But she saw the anger it sparked in Reina, and she backed away.

"Do you not see how I'm enslaved to iridio? Unless I change this, I will not be able to live without a constant supply."

A furious silence paused between them, and Reina refused to look away. Maior was asking the impossible from her. She would never be able to afford the iridio to stay alive, especially not if Doña

Ursulina or the caudillo himself decided to make her life a misery for disobeying their commands.

Finally Maior said, "You can force me. You know I'm weak compared to you. But you can't force Celeste."

"I'm not going to," Reina said, tightening the bindings around herself and twisting away from the human. Even if she physically could, and it was doubtful, Reina would never force anything on Celeste. "She's coming willingly, and once we're there, I'll tell her everything." She fished her shirt and jacket from a rackety shelf and covered herself back up.

"Why don't you tell her now?"

Reina dared not turn to face her. She didn't want to see whatever smug victory Maior donned. Because they both knew Celeste was willful and mercurial if given the opportunity. Reina couldn't know with any certainty that Celeste would come to Tierra'e Sol if she understood it was the place of communion. Reina was rotten for misleading Celeste, for not divulging the truth—this she knew. But she also needed to fix her heart, desperately, and Doña Ursulina was the only one offering her a solution. Surely, once Reina explained in Tierra'e Sol, Celeste would understand that.

She took a deep breath to reply with a half-truth, but the will evaporated as the door opened again.

Eva paused under the doorway, taking in the scene awkwardly, likely realizing she should have knocked. She cleared her throat and said, "Listen, I don't want to come here pretending I'm anybody's pigeon—"

"A pigeon?" Reina asked.

"Delivering messages," Eva said. "But Javier is getting impatient."

Reina rolled her eyes.

Celeste appeared behind Eva. "All ready to go?" she said, and the smile in her eyes clouded at the sight of Maior in Reina's room. No one else saw it, because no one else noticed Celeste like Reina did.

Reina stiffened, quickly strapping the scabbard around her body and nodding with a grinding jaw. It was time they ended the journey.

The passage out of Gegania took them to a jungle of slick verdant leaves the size of banners. A profusion of sea grapes and elephant ears, vines looping on every trunk or branch, desperately reached for sunlight through a dense canopy. The floor was crowded by unfurling ferns and palms dripping beads of moisture. Humidity exuded from every plant, clinging to Reina's cheeks and nostrils as the group climbed up the muddy path. She regretted bringing her ruana. She pulled it off and hooked it from the scabbard as beads of sweat began their track down her back. Walking behind her, Celeste, Eva, Javier, and Maior imitated her shedding of clothes, the heat a stark contrast to the comfortable chill of the mountains.

They followed the cry of seagulls and the soft sound of waves to emerge out of the jungle and into a sprawling beach of powdery white sand. Maior and Eva ran up to the aquamarine shallows, gasping with delight, tossing their espadrilles aside, and splashing their toes in the water. The waves were nothing more than a small breath, serene and quiet. Teeming within the crystal clear waters were tiny unafraid fish, schools glimmering in pinks and rainbow teals, and the occasional shimmering clam, likely heavy with pearls. Palm trees stood along the verdant edges of the beach.

They walked for a good hour under the bite of the sun in search of a marina, their foreheads drenching and noses burning red. At one point, Eva tugged Maior with her into the water, entering the shallows up to their knees and drenching their clothes in salt and sand. Eventually they came upon a fishing village of bungalows painted white like the sand in the tropical backyard, where Javier managed to convince the village chief to grant them a boat ride to the island Samón Bravo had made his residence. He did most of the talking, and Reina suspected it was his antlers and not Celeste's stamped correspondence that earned them the legitimacy for the request.

They were herded to the docks, to a small boat painted in rich blues and reds, the wood ornately carved with the symbols of the revolution. A stallion standing on hind legs. The red spilled blood of the revolutionaries. The white dove whose delivered message saved the Liberator's life. It was manned by a human captain and two nozariel rowers. And once they were all aboard, they took off.

Tierra'e Sol was the name of the cays and archipelagos stretching along the Cow Sea. It was a band wrapped around the Fedrian coast, of small islands and pools made shallow by the coral formation bursting in all hues of the rainbow. A land of sunlight and sparse seasons of rain, it had been given an obvious name by the human pilgrims of Segol when they'd found its shores after an arduous voyage.

Far in the distance, on the biggest island, sitting at the foot of a mountain and shielded from the beachfront by a forest of sea grapes and palms, were the clay-tiled rooftops of several buildings, including the peeking windows of a watchtower. A chapel's bell caught the light of the sun and glinted a blinding gold. A great black bird soared over the island and disappeared behind the mountain. Distantly, Reina thought of a condor and how her grandmother owned a black jacket with a white collar that made her resemble one.

"What's that?" Maior gasped, leaning forward in the boat and pointing at something below the surface, right under the reflection of the sun.

Celeste also leaned over, the ends of her long hair dipping into the water like a brush into an inkwell.

"It's a sea cow," the captain told them, galvanized by their delight.

The boat tipped in one direction with their collective weight as they caught a glimpse of the mammal. There was no need to strain. It swam closer curiously, joined by a companion. They were each the size of a calf, round and gray, with two stunted front paws and a large flat hind fin. A layer of moss covered their backs, spotting them in green. They remained submerged right below the surface, tentatively sticking out their muzzles while considering Celeste's and Maior's outstretched hands.

"Are they dangerous?" Eva asked.

"Not at all," one boatman said. "Sirenas share these waters with us. They're not our game, so they have no reason to fear us."

Maior giggled as she managed to graze one with the tip of her fingers.

"They like to say hello." He chuckled.

The second one spluttered Eva with salty water when she leaned forward for a petting. She gasped, jumping back, and the group laughed.

Maior moved over so Celeste and Reina could get a chance to touch the nearest one. "So wait," she told Reina, "is that why the Cow Sea is named...?"

Javier chuckled. "Sea cow, Cow Sea. Clearly the Segoleans weren't creative with their names."

"Aye. But here we call them sirenas," said the boatman.

The sea cows kept them so entertained they were surprised when the boat reached the island's small docks, which were shaded in the jutting shadows of a red-and-indigo-painted galleon. The ship was devoid of attendants, yawning with the gentle rise and fall of the tide, a perch spot for the gulls and occasional pelican.

"All right, my lord and ladies, we've arrived. Please take care hopping off, though if you do fall, you couldn't possibly drown." The captain chuckled, gesturing to the shallow waters.

Two pretty nozariel girls descended to the beach, carrying a tray of refreshments. "Welcome to Tierra'e Sol!" they said in unison, their intact tails swishing.

"Look, Reina, they're just like you," Javier said with cheery sarcasm.

The server handed Reina a copper goblet rimmed with chunks of coconut. Reina's cheeks grew warm from the attention, but she denied him the reaction he wanted.

"The Liberator eagerly awaits your arrival," they said after divulging about the watchman on the tower who saw their approach. Then they led the group through a canopied trail carved through the jungle's innards.

There the day was alive with the hooting and chirping of native critters. A high noon breeze ran through the trail, flowing to a far-away outlet and carrying the crunchy leaves strewn on the ground. Every tree breathed and sang and rustled. The sides of the trail were naturally decorated with sprouting flowers of too many hues to count. And within them were tiny lizards and colorful little bugs that scurried away as Reina and the others passed.

"Oh!" Eva gasped, pointing at the iguana that skittered from one side of the path to the other.

"I hope Don Samón agrees to protect me," Celeste said with her eyes to the canopy. "I could live here forever."

In reply, Javier yawned.

They chatted until the canopy opened up to the twisting wrought iron and gold-plated gates of Don Samón's manse, which were nearly buried in an exuberant growth of fragrant jasmine. The grounds hummed with the chatter and presence of people. Folks with sharp posture who Reina immediately recognized as soldiers out of uniform. They huddled in different cliques, some wrestling, and others sharing stories with sloshing goblets in hand. The sight was a surprise and matched in earnest by those who noticed the arrival of the antlered valcos. Reina felt eyes on her as well, the looks that paused on the tail swaying with her strides.

A girl around the age of ten or twelve dodged the crowd to meet them, escorted by another pair of servants. She was a pretty thing, donning a tunic the color of sunlight. Ringlets of sun-bleached hair framed her brown eyes, crowned by two marble-white antlers. They were short and inconspicuous, like Eva's and Celeste's.

She bowed stiffly, as if unused to the gesture, and said, "Doña Celeste Águila of Sadul Fuerte, we have been waiting for you for so many days. And you brought friends!"

Celeste smiled, eyes on the girl's antlers. "I take it you are Don Samón's daughter."

With a toothy smile, the girl nodded.

She was little more than skin and bones—not emaciated, but with a thinness too thin for a girl of her status. She introduced herself as Ludivina Bravo.

They followed her into a large courtyard, where the melody of a faraway guitar lazily joined the birdsong of the surrounding greenery. A man-made pond sat in the very center, populated by fat fish of saturated colors and curious little plants Reina had never seen anywhere else before. The pond was square in shape and lined by a dozen handsome palm trees, all heavy with coconuts.

The guitar stopped, and Ludivina gestured to the courtyard, where people dressed in bright clothes that hung loosely around their bodies milled about in mild conversation. "We don't usually have this many visitors over, but this is a special time, because of Rahmagut's Claw. Are you familiar with the legend?" she said with innocent brightness.

"Yeah, we know of it," Celeste muttered.

Reina wondered if the people were here to commune with Rahmagut, or to prevent it. But she decided against asking now, not to rouse Celeste's suspicions.

Ludivina giggled contentedly. Her smiling eyes reminded Reina of someone, though she couldn't pinpoint the resemblance. "I'm excited that you've arrived. Papi said he would host a big party to welcome you. You will love it."

"Are our guests here?" a middle-aged man boomed from the entry steps of the building across the pond, briefly earning him the attention of everyone in the courtyard. He approached, unfazed. "Welcome to Tierra'e Sol!"

"Oh," Celeste whispered, her cheeks turning pink. "That's the Liberator."

Javier chuckled and said, "Indeed it is."

Perhaps it was the way he carried himself, capturing the attention of everything and everyone. Or his charming confidence, setting trusting eyes on the group like he'd been born to inspire them. Reina's pulse went jittery, her own gaze struggling to hold his when it landed on her.

Don Samón was tall, with sturdy antlers and handsome angles. He was all tanned skin and sun-bleached ash hair, his red valco eyes shining with a warmth Reina had never seen in Don Enrique or Javier before. Eyebrows thick like his ash beard. He wore his long hair in a low ponytail, golden-ash strands lazily framing his face and quite complementing the casual look of his cream linen shirt and dark trousers.

After a polite nod, he said, "Doña Celeste, Don Javier, I see you both traveled here together."

"We found each other halfway through the journey," Celeste explained.

"Of course. Family should always stick close," he said. "And these are your companions?"

Javier gestured to Eva, saying, "Don Samón, meet Eva Kesaré de Galeno."

The sunshine left Don Samón's eyes.

"Who's now Eva Kesaré de *Águila*, my lawfully wedded wife." Javier took Eva's hand away from Maior.

Eva didn't look too happy about it, but she stepped forward all the same, smiling a bit awkwardly.

"You've wed her," Don Samón said.

"It's a pleasure to meet you, Don Libertador," Eva said, reminding Reina of the highborn ladies who'd visited Doña Laurel in Águila Manor. She came from that world—she'd been trained in it. "I never imagined I would get to meet you. I've heard many great tales about you."

"Yes, Doña Eva..." he said thoughtfully. "And you have met my daughter, Ludivina?"

Eva exchanged a smile with Ludivina. "She's been a great hostess so far."

"Indeed—now, dearest Doña Eva, Don Javier informed me you're a valco?"

Eva nodded and in their pause realized he wanted to see her antlers. A ruddy red touched her cheeks as she pushed back her ringlets of light brown to reveal them. The sight left Don Samón in awe.

"Daughter of Doña Dulce Serrano of Galeno?" Don Samón prodded.

Eva frowned.

The expression seemed to have been enough for Don Samón, for he quickly said, "It's wonderful to see there are still some of us left alive. Well, my guests, please be welcomed to my residence. I shall have the servants show you to the guest quarters. Anything you find there shall be yours to use and take." He nodded at the nozariel girls, who quickly darted into the manse to ready their

things. He gestured for the group to follow him through the two
giant doors of the main building. Tall doorways for his sturdy
antlers.

Celeste walked beside him, saying, "Don Samón, we came here
in haste because I'm in need of asylum. My father has lost his mind.
And his witch has, too."

Reina worried the inside of her lower lip, again conflicted at the
way Celeste referred to Doña Ursulina after growing up with her
under the same roof. What would she call Reina after Reina told
her the truth?

They stepped into a vast antechamber of veined marble floors
and tiled mosaics on the walls. It was stuffy inside, despite the small
windows near the ceiling that were designed to give a reprieve to
the heat with a flow of breeze.

"And I'm glad you sought me out, Celeste," he said, his voice
bouncing off walls decorated in intricate tile work. The antechamber opened to a bright hall with richly pigmented mosaics of sea
cows, dolphins, and jellyfish. Across the hall, a floor-to-ceiling
stained-glass window flanked a dais, a design of sea turtles surrounded by hibiscuses refracting rainbows over two chairs. The
doorway to the right was open, allowing a view into the open corridor hugging another courtyard that brimmed with the lush, vivid
colors of tropical flowers and caged birds.

"As I said in my message, here you shall be safe for as long as you
need it." He turned with a little flourish, and it wasn't dramatic—
more like everything about his regular mannerisms was grand, a
magnet for the eyes. "The people you see out there?" He gestured
slender fingers to the courtyard behind them. "They are my most
trusted officers. The retired and those who are still active in Fedrian politics. I invited them here since the arrival of the claw to help
me guard Rahmagut's tomb. Your father is a great man, but he
does not intimidate me."

"Rahmagut's tomb?" Celeste said slowly, and Reina's heart
jolted.

Don Samón stepped onto the dais, entering the shower of rainbows. "Yes, Rahmagut's Claw ends its journey through our skies

in one week, and we will safeguard the tomb until the threat has passed. Afterward, we shall be safe again from Rahmagut's influence for another forty-two years. Since I likely won't be alive for the next one, I believe I've fulfilled my purpose."

He offered them a handsome, carefree smile. Reina didn't share any of his mirth. In fact, the idea of standing in opposition to the Liberator made her want to be sick.

"As for tonight, allow me to welcome you with a dinner party of sorts. It's not every day we get someone from the Páramo in these parts."

"You promised it would be grand," Ludivina piped up.

"Yes, but don't spook the guests, Ludivina. They are tired."

"Who's invited?" Javier asked.

"Be reassured in knowing that my home is a place of neutrality, where I forbid violence. I cannot interfere with cross-border matters that could hurt the delicate balance between Venazia and Fedria. But since you are kin—valcos—I shall make the exception of letting you stay however long you desire. I cannot antagonize Don Enrique, but he cannot arrive uninvited." His words told them very little, but there was an uncontestable finality to them.

He spread out his arms, his smile toothy. "Dearest guests, make yourselves at home. See you tonight, and come looking your best." He took the guitar resting on one of the chairs and extended his other hand to Ludivina. To his daughter he said, "Let us give them a chance to recuperate. The Páramo is a long way from here."

"Sí, papi," Ludivina replied, and the two left the hall.

The yaps of a faraway parrot shattered the silence of his departure. Reina looked to Celeste, who looked to Javier; so on and so forth.

Maior was the one who spoke first. "I've...never felt so welcomed anywhere before."

Reina understood the apprehension, even if she was no stranger to the attention and hospitality often afforded to the Águilas for the mere virtue of their name.

"He's so nice," Eva said, "but...why did he seem so familiar with me?"

To this, Javier seemed ignorant.

Celeste told Reina, "Something's not right. What does he mean about protecting against Rahmagut's influence? And the whole thing about diplomacy? Does that mean Doña Ursulina will be here?"

Reina's throat closed. Now was not the time to give the whole truth, especially not in the presence of Eva and Javier.

"And it's clearly smart to be talking about it now," Javier hissed, saving Reina. "In an unfamiliar palace, where the walls could have eyes and ears."

Before anyone could escalate his concerns, they were interrupted by four servant girls. They were nozariel, all with skin the color of umber and wearing sheer linen dresses with cutouts to allow for their intact tails.

Reina had to force herself not to react in delight.

"My lord and ladies, follow us to your rooms."

They did, down the open corridor, taking in the adjacent courtyard with its romantic benches shaded by magenta bougainvilleas. Finally, they were separated at a long corridor, each of the maidens stopping outside engraved doors and first motioning to Maior, then to Reina, then to Celeste, and at the fourth door, to Eva and Javier.

As soon as Reina walked through the doorway, she had the incredible urge to turn it down. The bedroom was too big for her, with a plush bed made for two, lavish decorations, walls of terracotta red, and verdant upholstery. It was a room for someone important. Surely not for a grunt under Doña Ursulina's employ.

The maiden gestured to the dress sprawled across the bed, then to the wardrobe to the left.

"A dress for your daytime enjoyment," she said, her words laced with Don Samón's same flowing accent. "You'll find your dinner clothes in the wardrobe. If you'd like, you're welcome to try them on before the evening. Don Samón's tailor has orders to fix it to your exact measurements."

Reina watched her speechlessly.

The girl lingered at the door a second longer and said, "Don Samón likes it when his guests indulge in the refreshments of his beach. Please do visit. And enjoy." Then she bowed and left.

Reina stood there like a fool for many more minutes, fully expecting someone to barge through those doors and, with violence, announce that this was a mistake and none of it was for her. But...silence was all she received.

So she buried her face in her hands and indulged in an ear-to-ear grin of pure, unadulterated joy.

35

Tierra'e Sol Amapolas

The alcove breeze stopped with the closing of the door. Reina was left in the stillness of paradise, her ears perking to a faraway birdsong. Beyond the alcove was another garden, then descending cobbled steps lined in palm trees leading to a beach.

From her vantage, the beach looked empty. Clean and untouched, the waters were a crystalline aqua. The pool seduced her with the promise of its refreshments. What had she done to deserve such a good turn of luck? Of course, she saw it for what it was: life tempting her with relaxation, right as the last of her iridio was on the verge of running out, wooing her to docility so she could die on the beach with a smile on her face.

A wicked part of her wondered if such a fate was really all that bad.

She left the room. Celeste welcomed her into hers after a few knocks. She had a coy smile as she showed Reina the dress she had changed into. It was of white linen, like the dress Reina had been lent, sleeveless. The hems of the neck and ends of the skirt were adorned with wide ruffles in the color of fuchsia and goldenrod. The fabric fit her like a second skin, molding around the curves of her breasts, leaving little to the imagination.

"They didn't leave you clothes?" Celeste asked, reaching up to undo her ponytail. Her hair cascaded down her back, all black silk and waves.

"A dress."

"Put it on."

Reina made a joking cringing face.

"You'll melt in those clothes. I'm thinking of going to the beach. It's wonderful, it really is."

"It looks it." Reina approached Celeste's alcove, which was connected to a path descending to the beach. From there they had a view of the servants setting up a tent over the gypsum-white sand. Under the shade they sprawled out a mat of woven leaves and a tray of fruit.

She glanced at Celeste and realized she had been staring at her back. "Your shirt is all bloodstained," Celeste said in a small concerned voice.

"Sometimes my cuts reopen," Reina said lamely. Her injuries weren't healing fast enough, and the sweat didn't help with keeping the stain from her shirt. She came to the sad conclusion that it was her body struggling from the lack of iridio.

"Does it hurt?"

Reina tried not to get hung up on her concern. After all, Celeste was no stranger to the injuries of battle.

She shrugged and said, "You know when something hurts for so long you stop acknowledging it's there?"

Celeste's cracked lips stretched in a smile. "I know exactly what you mean. Honestly, Javier is such a prick. He should have just healed us instead of having that human do it."

"*Maior*," Reina corrected her.

"She means well, I can tell, but she's still got a long way to go to be useful in battle as a healer."

Reina wrung her hands and noticed her nails were filthy. She made fists to hide them. "Hopefully we'll never have a need for a master healer."

Celeste considered her, but her mirth fell after a while. "Then we'd be too lucky." She looked down and gave breath to the words Reina had been too afraid to acknowledge, "Do you think this is a trap?"

She mistook Reina's rippling jaw for her agreeing.

"Like they want us to strip off our armor and our weapons and our rings so we can get drunk and stupid on Cow Sea water and pineapples?"

Reina nodded and added, "Like a lechón for a New Year's Eve butchering."

Celeste seemed to deflate. "Is it bad that I want to play right into the trap? I'm so tired of running and being angry. I just want to rest."

Reina's heart did a little pirouette then. The truth almost spilled from her lips because she wanted to say it. She wanted to come clean and be welcomed in Celeste's embrace, hear the sound of Celeste's heartbeats as she confided the horrible conflict of this path they all took, how everything would have been so much easier if they hadn't decided to pursue Rahmagut's favor. If Reina had had the courage or the strength to stand up to the caudillo once the first of the babies had started dying. Well, now she didn't have a working heart, and her grandmother had found the other seven damas. She would be a fool if she didn't at least attempt the solution they all knew Rahmagut could grant her.

A new heart.

Doña Laurel's return.

Her grandmother's fulfillment.

A brand-new life.

She took a heavy gulp and decided to keep the truth clutched to her chest for just a few more moments. First, she needed to see if Doña Ursulina was somewhere on the island, despite the Liberator's heightened security.

"Just keep your rings and wits about you," Reina added. "I'll keep you safe...you know I will." And something rushed to Reina's belly, because she meant it more than anything.

"Oh—Reina," Celeste moaned, then gave her a half embrace, probably to avoid hurting her wounds. "I'm so glad you're here with me. Come to think of it, you have always been there..." She trailed off, and they both marveled at how lucky it was that Reina had fallen into this life where Celeste needed her friendship so desperately. And where Reina needed this belonging.

"What does your grandmother say about all this? Does she know what I am?" Celeste's breath was warm and humid against her shirt, smelling of the coconut water the server had given them.

Reina knew she could return the embrace. As friends, their boundaries were as thin as the fabric of Celeste's dress. Yet as Celeste held her, a rush that had nothing to do with being friends bloomed in Reina's belly.

It was a lapping fire asking for more.

"Of course she knows."

Her tail coiled, aching for what it would feel like to be touched as well.

"And she dares use me as a pawn anyway?"

Reina quickly stepped back, eyes avoiding Celeste's. "She's only following the caudillo's desires." There lay the true reason behind the complications in their lives. The caudillo's whims and ambitions. His longing for his dead wife.

"What's the matter?" Celeste asked.

The voices from the corridor spared Reina from more half-truths and lies. Someone knocked on Reina's bedroom door. She could make out the voices of Eva and Maior, then Eva saying, "We don't have to wait for her. Just leave her." Their footsteps receded seconds later.

Maior had been looking for her.

Maior, with her never-ending concern.

Reina wondered if she should be leaving her unprotected and alone.

Then Celeste licked her lips, and the thought flitted away. "Shall we join them at the beach?" Celeste said.

"We wouldn't want to offend the Liberator by declining his offer."

Celeste toyed with the end of Reina's braid. "Change into your dress," she commanded.

"Fine. But I'm bringing Ches's Blade."

Celeste's room was locked and empty when Reina came back moments later. A wave of relief flooded her. She nervously smoothed out the folds of the linen dress over her abs and the disfigurement around her chest, where her crystal contraption was all hollow, ragged edges. At least she could postpone the inevitable—Celeste seeing her in this dress that clearly disagreed with her skin—for a little longer. She followed the corridor until meeting a door to the beach. The garden path was decorated with bushes of saturated hibiscuses, violets and fuchsias and reds, made lively by the occasional chirps of domesticated parrots and toucans. The cobbled path opened to the mouth of the beach, where the sand was a fine powder of hot coral, blistering beneath Reina's borrowed espadrilles.

There Javier stood under the shade, looming over Celeste, who rested on a mat. The serene coming and going of the shallow waves was only a few paces away. Under the sun the water glimmered the lightest blue, unable to conceal the fishes and clams that lived beneath its surface. Ahead, more cays stood against the horizon line.

"Would you look at that monstrosity," Javier said as he saw Reina approach. He hadn't changed out of his traveling clothes.

Reina tugged the fabric around her chest, which was tight around her bindings. "I don't do dresses," she said, flushing.

"And I'm glad for it. You look terrifying," Javier added, and Celeste promptly told him to shut up. "Now I finally see the resemblance to your grandmother."

The dress truly didn't fit her body type. Her shoulders were too broad, her biceps all muscle. It didn't help that she had tightened the scabbard straps around her hips, arming herself with the blade for peace of mind. She tugged at the sleeves, desperate for a readjustment, and stared bitterly at the serene waves lapping the beach. She looked, and felt, hideous in it.

"I'm only doing this for you," she muttered to Celeste, who giggled.

"Anyway, like I was saying," Javier said, regarding Celeste with a sneer, "I can't believe their audacity, that they would leave amapolas here like this. Do they take us for a commune?"

"Maybe they don't know their magic," Celeste said while munching on a pineapple.

"Why are you talking about sharing amapolas?" A pang came with the memories of the first time she'd witnessed amapolas. Reina frowned. She remembered the day so vividly, when the Benevolent Lady and caudillo had shared the juice. An aching crept into her chest. How she wanted it all back.

"We are not," Javier drawled. "Why tie my fate with someone when I can live alone just fine? Learn to love yourself before you start ruining your life with useless declarations of love."

Celeste rolled her eyes and gestured at the fruit tray. Chunks of pineapple, coconut, tamarind, and soursop were arranged around four whole amapolas, the sweet aroma of the pineapple overpowering the other fruits. The amapolas were small and spherical like limes, with thin green skins and the tops flaring up like red flowers. Inside, amapolas were a fleshy red that turned creamy white when it contacted the air.

Reina's frown deepened. "They left us amapolas?"

"They have them growing everywhere here," Celeste said. She stood up and dusted the sand off her ruffled dress.

Suddenly Reina realized she had no idea of where Maior had gone off to. "Where are Maior and Eva?"

Javier gestured to the canopied path leading away from the manse and toward the mountain.

"And you just let them go?"

He shrugged. "Eva's too greedy to abandon me. She was glowing with the idea of Rahmagut's tomb being down that way—apparently a servant told her something."

The workings of Reina's transplant heart hiccupped. "And that doesn't alarm you for a second? What about Maior?"

"She's your responsibility." Javier shrugged and turned to path back to the manse. "Now, if you'll excuse me, I'm going to go take up that servant's offer of a massage."

Celeste scoffed. "Hey—you're married to Eva, or are you forgetting?"

Javier paused and considered her. "While what I do in my

private time is none of your concern, I simply do not desire *that* with strangers."

Celeste's cheeks flushed red.

"And you, my niece, have a monstrous imagination."

Reina just watched him retreat, still frowning. Maybe she was making a mistake by idling. Maybe it was high time she sought her grandmother.

A mild breeze tickled them, lifting the baby curls framing Reina's face.

Celeste reached out and with a smile stole the moments to unbraid Reina's hair. She let loose the curls, which bounced down almost to Reina's waist. Then she held her prisoner with those blue eyes while she finger combed the springy, lithe black hairs that hung near Reina's cheeks.

"There. Try to relax. You seem so tense."

Reina held her breath. "I have to go find Maior," she lied.

"I'll come with you, then."

"What— But Don Samón wants you to stay here—"

"And enjoy this paradise by myself?"

Reina sucked in a deep breath and nodded.

Side by side, they left the shade and the fruits behind, taking the same path Maior and Eva had allegedly walked to. There the sun was reduced to spotting their skins, its rays barely filtering through the canopy. A strange peace bloomed in Reina, as if she were entering a place she understood, a moment from a far-off memory. Or maybe it was the sound of the waves they left behind, lulling her as the jungle of sea grapes welcomed her into its innards.

The foot trail was narrow, the lush trees brimming with eloquent little bugs and reptiles that darted away at the disruption of their tranquility. In their proximity the back of Reina's fingers brushed against Celeste's as they walked, idly and without intent. And when it happened thrice, she had to fight a powerful urge to take Celeste's hand.

Celeste spared her a glance, just as a passing sunray caught her eyes. "Can you imagine if we actually find the tomb? Do you think he's there, Rahmagut?"

"If he is, I'm going to beg him to fix my heart," Reina said with a straight face.

Celeste giggled.

"I'm serious. I'll do anything. He can do it. He can fix me—"

"But you're not broken."

Reina watched Celeste as her belly wrung itself. If only she knew the truth.

"Besides, how can you sell your soul in exchange for your heart? Look at everything you have to do for Ursulina. Now imagine you're indebted to a heartless god."

Then, at least in this lifetime, they could be together. "I wouldn't be enslaved to iridio. We could go anywhere." The thought was exhilarating. She was so close. After this week, they would start afresh.

"But Reina," Celeste cooed and raised her arms to the canopy, "we're already going anywhere we want. Look at us, in Tierra'e Sol!"

Reina nodded, listening to the breathing of the jungle as they walked. The wind carried a gentle breeze smelling of humidity, of moist leaves and saline earth. The sound of water trickling over stones told them a creek was nearby. Again, there it was, the pang of familiarity. The unshakable feeling that she was doing exactly what she needed to.

From somewhere in the distance came the faint voices of Eva and Maior. They talked about Eva's short antlers, about what it would be like at the dinner party. The voices died as they walked farther away. They sounded content with each other's friendship, and safe. "They're ahead," Reina said.

"Yes," Celeste said, nodding. Her valco senses were sharper than Reina's.

"Maybe we should let them be," Reina said, to divert Celeste from her bogus objective. It was Doña Ursulina she needed to find.

"She likes you, you know," Celeste said.

Reina's eyes rounded in alarm. The butterflies in her belly returned, warm and right, like when Maior's hand had pressed against her skin this morning. "Really?" The indulgent question escaped her before she could stop herself. She disliked thinking of

Maior now, when Celeste was right here. When her true fate was days away from being realized.

Celeste chuckled. "Can you really be that blind to it? It's almost like the woman's desperate to have someone."

Reina was nozariel, and poor, and dying, and Maior had witnessed it all. Maybe that was it: desperation.

"I find it funny that Maior likes women—she's such a Virgin worshiper," Celeste said with a smile. "Sometimes I wonder how much happier the world would be, if people allowed themselves to be who they truly are."

Reina watched her cautiously. A spark of hope ignited in her chest. Was Celeste trying to imply that Reina should be her true self?

"Do you like her back?" Celeste asked.

Reina hated the question. She could come clean: About her feelings for Celeste. About her hopes for their future. How they were so perfect for each other. Then a monkey hooted loudly in the near distance, evaporating her courage. "That has nothing to do with why she's here."

Celeste laughed.

The path opened to a clearing along the banks of a creek. Feeding the creek was a shallow lagoon of the clearest green. And behind the lagoon was a great cavern, its shadow slicing the water in half. Its center gaped with a massive opening, rocky and jagged, like the ravenous mouth of a shark.

Celeste rushed to the glistening water, then stopped when she noticed the cavern.

A great sucking sensation imploded in Reina's chest. Like she was falling—like her throat, heart, and belly plummeted to the deepest regions of el Vacío. She almost stumbled, but she grounded herself, realizing the sensation was her iridio heart reacting to the cavern. To its call.

"This is it," she said without a droplet of doubt.

"Rahmagut's tomb?" Celeste whispered.

Reina was half expecting a tiniebla or a jaguar to pounce from the darkness. Pulse tingling, she extended her hands to Celeste, and when Celeste took them, she reeled her back to the safety of her proximity.

"You don't want to go in, right?" Celeste said. "We have no armor—and Don Samón is expecting us tonight."

"We've actually found it," Reina said again—a whisper of awe and apprehension. Doña Ursulina could be awaiting her in those depths.

Her gaze locked with Celeste's. The lagoon's reflected light danced along the velvety smoothness of Celeste's cheeks and lips, so full and perfect in Reina's eyes.

It hit Reina at that moment, why she felt so comfortable seeking out the lagoon, which was an extension of the tomb. She had traveled this path time and time again in her dreams. The canopied path to the lagoon. She was an agent of Rahmagut, and he'd been beckoning her since the moment the iridio heart had saved her. Her new life was but moments away from being realized.

"We should get back," Celeste said, a little panicky. "There will be that party tonight. All those people are protecting the tomb from Doña Ursulina and my father."

The truth almost burst out of Reina. But Celeste was right. She ought to bide her time.

Celeste's brows bunched up at Reina's expression. "Is something the matter?"

"I've seen this place in my dreams," Reina said automatically. "Like I was always meant to come here."

Celeste licked her lips.

Reina's thumb found itself on the pinnacle of Celeste's shoulder, lifting the silk of her hair to allow a view at the birthmark behind her ear. "I was meant to be there that night when we realized what you are, just like we're meant to be here."

She thought she felt Celeste shudder under her touch. Or maybe it was her own mad mind playing games on her.

"As if we already shared amapolas?" Celeste said.

"What do you mean?"

Their dress had pockets, Reina realized as Celeste pulled out the green-skinned fruit from the folds of hers. "Like, our fates are already bound together?"

Something turned in Reina's stomach. It rendered her knees weak.

"I...I wanted to offer it to you. Not like...how my parents took them, but as a thank-you for our friendship." Celeste tore the amapola open, its milky-white juices dribbling down her fingers. "I fled from Sadul Fuerte, and you're the only one who cared about me. You proved it by coming all the way to the Plume—probably pissing off your grandmother and ruining what little you had built with Father."

Celeste ripped out a small chunk and brought the glistening pulp to her lips.

The jungle rustled, a hundred little creatures witnessing their oath within the vines and the trees and the bushes.

Celeste asking for permission came as a nod, which Reina mimicked as her reply for consent. Celeste then plucked a meaty piece off the fruit and ferried it to Reina's lips.

Reina stiffened. She had to. Otherwise Celeste was going to see the tremors that rippled through her arms.

What if this was the beginning to *their* love story? Epic and fated, like the Benevolent Lady and the caudillo of Sadul Fuerte.

Somewhere far away, the fallen leaves of the jungle rustled—crushed. But Reina didn't have eyes or ears for that. She was busy accepting the fruit, Celeste's fingers grazing against Reina's lips. In her mouth the amapola was milky and sweetly tart, the juices exploding with the same texture as a pineapple. It made Reina realize how hungry she was. For food. For Celeste. For *life*.

Celeste lifted the remainder of the fruit between them. This time, Reina took it from her hands before taking a bite that exposed the seed at the center. Then she handed it back. And Celeste ate the rest of the pulp until nothing was left but a smooth brown seed.

They stared at each other, the distance between them receding like the hours between midday and dusk. Reina smiled; Celeste grinned.

"How are you feeling?" Celeste asked.

"Hungry," Reina said. "Do you see magic?"

"There's nothing."

"Nothing?"

They shared an uncertain laugh.

"You looked like you were ready to see rainbows sprout out of my ears," Reina teased, watching Celeste blush. "What if it's just a story?"

Celeste licked her fingers clean. "I guess...it doesn't matter?" Her breath smelled of sweetness as she said, "Anything could happen, and I want to share it while we're still here. If friendships can withstand the bands of fate, then I want ours to be the one to make it—"

Reina gave up on stopping herself. This was a risk she couldn't not take.

Her hands dove behind Celeste's neck, bringing Celeste's lips to hers. She did it gently at first, waiting for the inevitable shove, but none came. Celeste molded to Reina's body like the waters molded to the shores of the lagoon. And Reina took a deep inhale through her nose, taking in the scents of salty sweat and Cow Sea water and a million feelings, reaching—*burning* for more.

But it was just a sweet thing, without the exploding warmth Reina had imagined in her wildest fantasies.

Reina pulled away and saw Celeste's eyes were crystalline. They glistened—from happiness, Reina hoped. Then she looked beyond Celeste, to the trees bordering the clearing and to the source of the crunching of leaves. The two figures standing before them weren't trees. They weren't even part of the jungle.

They were Eva and Maior.

36

The True Legend

Eva spent the evening in Maior's bedroom, the two readying each other for dinner. She took every second with optimism, working twice as hard to bring Maior's mood back to the high of the morning, before the sight of Reina with Celeste had shriveled Maior's already fragile heart. Eva smiled broadly and directed every conversation away from Reina. She did it gladly, reminding herself that Maior deserved this kindness. Maior was a true friend, one who filled an emptiness Eva hadn't known she had. In the short time they'd had together, Maior had been a source of joy and comradery, their friendship genuine and unadulterated by the darkness surrounding their lives.

"Put your arm through here. No. Lift it here. All right, now suck your breath in." Eva stood behind Maior, tying the silk ribbons so the soft fabric was flush to Maior's chest.

In a small voice, Maior said, "This is a waste of time. It's not like I'm a guest."

"You're as much of a guest as I am. Here, help me with the knot." Eva grabbed Maior's hand and directed her to press a finger against the base of the ribbon.

"Doña Celeste is the guest."

"Exactly," Eva said cheekily, to which Maior frowned through the reflection on the mirror. "And we are with Doña Celeste."

Tonight's dresses were a formal version of their flowery, ruffly, daytime beach-frolicking outfits. Maior's was the color of a dawn's sky: a little pink, a little blue, and with the ruffles around the neck and around the ends of the skirt a bright coral. Eva's was a warm butter, the ruffles goldenrod. Each quite complemented its wearer's skin tone. Like whoever picked them out had taken great care in the decision.

Everything in Tierra'e Sol was like that, carefully considered. From the refreshments to the dresses, to the tent at the beach. Not even back home had anyone taken so much care to make Eva feel included.

She smiled at Maior through the mirror. "I like it."

Maior nodded in meek agreement.

It wasn't just the dress. Their skins glowed from the sun, the slight sunburns on their cheeks making them look like they wore rouge. And something about the salty water worked wonders on Eva's hair. Tonight her curls weren't matted or frizzy or sticking out unevenly. Eva dared to admit, for the first time in a long while, that she looked...pretty.

"I don't know why they expect me to join for dinner. I'll be like a cockroach in a chicken dance," Maior said.

Eva chuckled. Her grandmother often murmured the same saying whenever she was chiding someone for being wildly out of place. Eva used her finger to coil the ends of Maior's hair, which held the curl shape if it was twirled strand by strand in its dampness. Maior didn't care for the curls, even though they made her look rather comely.

"We'll both be out of place," Eva said. Normally she'd be the one decrying a party filled with aristocrats. But something made her want this for Maior. After so much indifference and abuse, the poor woman deserved it. "And it'll be...kind of hilarious."

Maior swatted her hand away. "I'm just a nurse from Apartaderos."

Eva moved from their reflection and faced her evenly. With some effort she ignored the afterimage of Celeste's mom. It wasn't an intrusive distraction anymore. Thankfully, the only other valcos she had seen in Tierra'e Sol so far were Ludivina and the Liberator.

And she had a feeling they were unlikely to bring up Maior's peculiar condition.

"You're *my* friend. That's what's important. And I don't want to be out there all by myself."

Saying it felt good. It felt just right, like the sweetness of the island's fruits.

Maior smiled for the first time this evening. She reached out and rearranged the curls atop Eva's head, parting them for her antlers.

"Eva Kesaré!" Javier's voice came from outside, his fist pounding the door. "You best be here, and you best be ready."

Eva rolled her eyes and walked to the door, flinging it open to match Javier's attitude.

Javier was dressed in a tunic of dark blue, the tall neck and the hems of his long sleeves embroidered in the pattern of bay leaves. A golden stallion was stitched near the chest, right over his heart. His hair was brushed back to a neat high ponytail, his jaw clean-shaven. And despite him not enjoying much of the beach, his cheeks had the unmistakable redness of a suntan.

There was surprise in his eyes when he saw her. Perhaps she had stolen the words from his mouth.

Finally, he said, "You look beautiful. The Liberator will love it."

Eva's lips became a thin line. She refused to acknowledge the compliment.

"Come, it's time to meet with Don Samón."

"But dinner's not until later," Eva protested. Mingling with the gentry in Galeno, dealing with their fake pleasantries, had always been a source of discomfort.

"Yes, but his friends started gathering earlier, and now everyone's out there eagerly waiting for us."

"Eager to meet Doña Celeste, more like," Eva mumbled, sparing Maior's bedroom a hopeless glance before following him through the candlelit corridor.

He gently took her wrist and maneuvered her to the shadows of the courtyard closest to the dining hall. Eva's curiosity made her docile, and she followed him to the darkness.

"Listen, tonight, just act your best at the dinner, all right?"

Eva rolled her eyes, even if it was too dark for him to see it. "I thought we already agreed—"

"Yes, but, *also*: Remember our bargain? How when I took you out of Galeno, I told you I was going to need your power?"

Eva straightened up, her pride bloating. "Of course."

"Tonight is the night. After the party, we have to be ready to invoke Rahmagut."

"*What?*" she blurted out, and he shushed her, tugging her farther into the courtyard's dark. They had talked about this moment, but recognizing that the day had arrived was different. Eva always assumed it would happen *on the claw's last day.*

She tripped on the cobbles with the sudden pull, unaccustomed to her borrowed espadrilles, and stumbled into his chest. Javier caught her without decorum before she could face-plant on his tunic, his grip on her arms firmly propping her up. As Eva glanced up, she realized they were but a breath away, his touch a furnace to the perpetual warmth of the island. She wished she had brought the iridio pendant, for without it she was powerless against him. But with her cleavage exposed in this dress, she'd made the decision to leave it in the room. She didn't know what these people were like, if they were like the gentry of Galeno, quick to condemn her for geomancia.

"What did you expect? We're here. Why would we procrastinate it?"

His breath was a tickle on her nose, feathery like the treacherous flutters in her belly. She wrangled herself free before her body could betray her further. "You can't just suddenly say that. What's the plan? And what will I have to do?"

"Yes, I tried getting a moment alone with you today," he hissed (and her chest palpitated at the double meaning), "but you spent the whole day fucking around with Maior, so what was I supposed to do?"

Eva's eyebrows bunched up. "Tell me now?"

"Don Samón is waiting for us to make his toast. And he's not exactly open to the idea of communing with Rahmagut. So I say we do it as soon as we can, without his noticing, if possible." He straightened his tunic where their tumble had rustled it and circled Eva to head back inside. "Doña Ursulina should be arriving soon, if she's not here already somehow. She is motivated—by what, I don't know—but she will be bringing everything she needs to get it done. That's our moment. And you should be ready." He stepped closer, his slender fingers lifting her chin to bring her eyes to his. He was bold like that, as if he had every right to the proximity. They had a magical binding, Eva supposed, one she'd signed agreeing to be his. "We don't want her or Enrique to say their words to Rahmagut before we get our chance. You'll be the one to stall them."

Eva let out a shuddery breath. "How?"

"Remember how you nearly scorched me in the Plume? And how you reached into the Void and angered all those tinieblas? It's likely there will be tinieblas in Rahmagut's tomb. If that's the case, manipulate them to our advantage."

She pulled her chin away. "But she's the strongest geomancer in Sadul Fuerte."

He chuckled. "Sadul Fuerte is just a city. Someone needs to take the title of strongest in all Fedria."

In their rawest form, the words were meant to compliment, but Eva couldn't shake off his flippancy. The way he pulled her here and there like his personal flamethrower, giving her as little information as possible.

"Why do you treat me like what I say doesn't matter? Everything's a joke to you," Eva said with a small voice of defeat, fatigued by it.

He took her hand as if she were wrong. Eva pulled free.

"I don't know the details yet, that's why. Doña Ursulina has conveniently made herself unavailable. I suppose it's smart of her, since the Liberator has a whole company of seasoned warriors ready to stop her if she shows up. But he doesn't want to antagonize *you*."

Eva clenched her jaw and followed him toward the corridor's candlelight. "Yeah…about that—he was acting weird this morning," she muttered. "Like he recognized my name."

To this, Javier let out a noncommittal grunt.

"So you're just going to throw me blindly to the jaguars again?"

"There aren't any jaguars in Tierra'e Sol."

"Great. More riddles."

"All I'm asking of you is to act like a well-mannered lady. Like how Doña Antonia raised you. You'll find out soon enough."

"When? When it's too late?"

"Eva Kesaré, I haven't plotted against you."

"Such a filthy lie," she said. "And don't call me Eva Kesaré."

Maybe he didn't want to make a scene, or maybe she had gained respect in his eyes. He only sighed and said, "This will be good for you. Don't ruin it."

He herded her along into the main hall, where a long dining table had been set up to cleave through the center. The yellow, blue, and red banners of Fedria's new republic hung near the three entryways. Yellow lanterns hovered near the ceiling, tied up by threads of iridio that were obvious to Eva, giving the hall an agreeable warm glow.

The people from earlier were already seated at the table. The women wore ruffled dresses in the Fedrian fashion, much like Eva's, the dresses an ivory or cream cotton and the ruffles of richly pigmented colors. The men wore liqui liquis in variations of their choice of dark blue, black, or cream.

Ludivina spotted them and waved Eva to her side, where two chairs had been left empty. Eva shot Javier a suspicious glance but walked to the girl anyway. Their closeness to Don Samón and his daughter meant they were guests of honor of some kind. Celeste and Reina were already seated at the table, to Don Samón's other side and next to a single empty chair, which was surely Maior's.

In no time at all, they were served a grouper-and-mackerel stew, and when Don Samón made a point to introduce his new guests to the surrounding people—whom he called his closest friends and supporters—the food made it easy for Eva to smile and utter all the pleasantries Doña Antonia had taught her. As much as Eva wanted to hate the moment, his open smile made it easy to surrender to it. No one had cold looks to shoot at her antlers or cared that her new husband was a valco from Sadul Fuerte. It didn't take long for Eva to see why everyone's eyes held genuine love for their former commander. She supposed that made her lucky to sup so close to him like an honored guest.

"See the lanterns?" Ludivina told Eva, gesturing to the ceiling, "I enchanted them myself."

"You know how to use iridio?" Eva asked. It wasn't uncommon for children to display outbursts of magic. Though it *was* uncommon to see them exhibit the self-control needed for complex spells, like levitating a dozen lanterns. Inwardly, she beamed at the open use here.

Ludivina grinned. She hadn't been served the stew. Instead, she had a plate of peeled and cut fruits. "Papi says I'm a natural," she said. "Do you use it?"

Eva thought of her own ease in accessing the star power. "I... I'm the best at iridio."

"Amazing," the girl cooed with wide eyes. "And Don Javier is set to inherit all the iridio in Sadul Fuerte. You'll have so much of it you'll never have a need for anything else."

Eva frowned. *Celeste* was supposed to inherit it.

Celeste sat across from them; her hand was hidden beneath the table, as was Reina's. They were probably basking in each other's attention, pretending to care about the dinner. Don Samón raised a glass in a toast, his jolly gaze set on Celeste. It reminded Eva of the times when Javier had been so sweet and perfect.

Ludivina sighed dreamily and said, "You'll be such a powerful couple. Do you think I'll ever find a valco my age?"

All the valcos Eva had ever met were selfish. Why should she assume Don Samón and Ludivina were any different?

"Hopefully—I don't know," she murmured and pretended the food was too good to say more.

A wave of servants came moments later to exchange their stews with fried snapper, fried plantains, and a medley of fresh vegetables. By then, Eva had given up hope of Maior joining.

Halfway through the dinner, a band of liqui liqui–wearing musicians joined the hall. They set up against a corner near Don Samón's throne, with guitars, drums, a harp, and maracas.

Don Samón's companions raised their goblets and hollered to their host, "Play us el cuatro!"

It only took a few more cheers for Don Samón to leave the table, saying, "All right! All right! But only if you dance."

One of the musicians gave him a four-stringed guitar. Don Samón handled it like the instrument was another appendage. He sat with the musicians, positioned slender fingers on the strings, and led a lively melody on cue with the rest of the band.

His guests didn't waste a second before leaving their chairs to dance.

Eva glanced at Javier questioningly.

He whispered in her ear, " 'Heart of the Llanos.' "

The melody was familiar. A hymn she'd heard from the retired soldiers who'd moved to Galeno after the revolution. Maybe the song had united them during those dark moments of war.

"Do you dance?" Ludivina asked her. The girl had hardly finished half her fruit plate.

"Yes," Eva said, thinking of the Saint Jon the Shepherd parades. Of the electrifying joy the stomping and twirling had brought to her heart. How she could have easily gotten sucked into the parade when she'd fled Javier. "But I only dance alone," she lied.

The ruffled dresses were suited for the joropo dance. The fashion was made for it. The people in pairs danced with one hand grasping their partner's in the air above their heads and the other hand placed flush against their partner's back. They moved in loose circles, their espadrilles slapping the tiled floor in unison. Then they each dropped their hands from their partner's back and twirled each other, the women's ruffled skirts surfing the air like stormy waves.

Eva startled when Javier left his seat and for a second panicked at the thought of him asking her to dance.

"You just got to let the rhythm del cuatro guide you," Ludivina said. "Would you like me to teach you?"

Eva gaped at her. She could only imagine what Don Samón's guests would think: two clumsy girls tearing through the floor and stepping on each other's espadrilles. "No."

Ludivina giggled. "Don't panic! How about we leave, then? Before someone asks for a dance."

She pushed off her seat and tugged Eva to stand up. Eva stole a glance across the table at Javier, who was inviting Celeste to dance. His expression was clean of malice, probably because he was gaining something. *But what?* Eva wondered.

Eva and Ludivina dodged through the dancers before emerging into a small elevated courtyard. There the garden split into hedged passageways leading to several balconies with a view of the beach. The night was bright from the moon, its reflection a giant blurred ball over the Cow Sea, and from Rahmagut's Claw, which smeared the sky to the other side.

Eva figured she could extract information out of the girl.

"Ludivina," she said, "have you met Javier before?"

The girl considered it. "Maybe when I was too young to remember? If not, then no," she said with a shrug.

"What kind of business does he have with Don Samón?" Eva said.

Ludivina was swaying from side to side to the rhythm as the music changed to a new song. Like the dancing was inescapable. "Are you sure you don't want me to teach you to dance?"

Eva offered her a kind smile of rejection.

"*Fine.* But you wouldn't be bad! No Fedrian would ever be deaf to those guitars."

"But...I'm from Venazia."

Ludivina just raised an eyebrow. Don Samón joined them before Eva could ask more. He chuckled as Ludivina told him of Eva's refusal to dance.

"Oh, is that so?" he said, treating them like children, which Eva quite liked. "It's all right, not everyone has to enjoy dancing. Although you shouldn't feel shy about dancing with Ludivina. Reina and Celeste are setting fire to the dance floor back there. It's not the most graceful sight, but my guests are like family. They do not mind."

"My grandmother would be outraged," Eva said without thinking, a breeze of jasmine wafting over the balcony.

"Is Reina Doña Celeste's lover?" Don Samón asked quite plainly, and Eva didn't know how to respond.

"Don't worry, I'm not your grandmother. I won't be outraged by the answer." When Eva took too long to reply, he went on: "It used to not be frowned upon, before the colonists came over and forced us to adopt Penitent customs."

"Was it different before?" Eva said in a small voice.

He glanced up to the moon, caught up in his own musings. "Yes, many things were different before the humans came. Valcos lived in the Páramo, isolated from the nozariel tribes of the coast and the yare kingdom in Las Garras that was the first to fall. This was long before I was born, of course, but I have studied what historians and folklore say on the matter. Our people, the valcos, we stayed isolated for as long as we could, ignoring the enslavement of nozariels and the butchering of the yares. The humans saw we were a war breed, and instead of enslaving us or killing us, they manipulated us into believing their culture was worth trading for and eventually adopting."

Eva was quiet, remembering every instance when her cousins or aunts used her mere existence against her, making her believe she was wrong for indulging in the desires innate to her blood.

He took her silence as an opportunity to continue, and Eva was grateful for it. She ate it all up. "You see, in olden valco communities, disputes were resolved by strength, as valcos are physical creatures. What humans do—involving civilians and family and the weak in disputes—we saw as dishonorable. Disagreements were resolved one-to-one, and the victor was the last one standing—*and* in possession of the loser's antlers."

A brutal scalping. Eva shuddered, then thought of herself and Javier. "Were there ever disputes between males and females?"

"There were, but don't pity the female sex. A battle between two properly trained valcos would have been a sight to behold."

Eva's fists curled at her sides, following his gaze to the moon. This was what she had wanted from Javier when she'd fled with him. It was what had been promised her: knowledge of her people and of a past she'd never had the opportunity to learn from. "But what if there was a dispute between a weaker person and a stronger one?"

"Valco society wasn't perfect, I admit. Valcos are creatures of the sword and of honor to the self. However, you must forget human concepts of pride. Insults weren't enough to cause wars. Pure valcos have high self-esteem, the kind that goes beyond the surface. An insult cannot harm you if you see yourself as superior to it. But humans came along, and although they recognized valcos as mighty creatures, they involved us in their wars for conquest, conning future generations into petty conflicts. So valco families realized the need to adjust. To discourage unions that wouldn't immediately yield offspring, to prevent the extinction we are seeing now. That is how we arrived at a society with people like your grandmother becoming outraged over what a relationship should and shouldn't look like. It was a change of mentality in the high society that happened through generations. But people who are courageous enough to break these human Penitent molds exist, like Doña Feleva Águila, for example. She had two sons to continue her legacy, but all her life, she only loved women. She once told me of the lover she lost and the act of vengeance that turned her into a killer at a young age. The first deaths she regretted, she called them."

Eva nodded in silence, marveling at the kind of life Don Samón must have had as a confidant of Feleva Águila.

"I'm telling you this about Doña Feleva because I know you have heard of her. Your new mother, were she not dead. She is the truest example of how valcos used to be."

A warm breeze enveloped them, caressing her curls, while the merriness of the joropo in the dining hall lifted her in mirth. "Javier mentioned they were harmful rumors."

"What were?"

"Feleva's lovers."

Don Samón scoffed. "Don Javier was raised with human ideals, Doña Eva, under the influence of a human king and a human governor and a human court. Just like yourself. When you do not have valco parents raising you with our teachings, then you default to the human way of life. Doña Feleva was a caudilla; she had no time for raising children, and she didn't live long enough to raise Javier. But Enrique had the coin to hire wet nurses. And humans brought their Pentimiento teachings with them. They colonized our lands, enslaved all they could—"

"Nozariels."

Don Samón nodded. "And spread their beliefs. So, of course, Don Javier and Don Enrique behave like humans. Of course, they involve the weak in their strife and see their mother as a glorified queen—of the human kind. But Doña Feleva was deeply valco. It is why she didn't seek to conquer all Venazia. She could have. She had enough gold and iridio to oust Segol and crown herself queen. That is why she was such a valuable ally to my movement for independence."

Even as Don Samón said it, Eva knew the same applied to him. He could have crowned himself and profited from slavery after securing independence. Instead, he let both valcos and nozariels have their freedom. Now, *that* she admired.

"But valcos are going extinct anyway," she prodded, thirsty for this well of knowledge he gifted her.

"Indeed, now we have our freedom from human yoke, at the cost of many valco lives. So we must cherish what we have left. You, Javier, Enrique, Celeste, Ludivina, and a few others are the future. Carry it with pride, and never forget that."

"So what was the point, then, to achieve this independence if it cost you your people?"

"Our people," he corrected her, and Eva grinned. "Well, halfway through my campaign, I asked myself the same thing. I came to terms with the fact that war is bloodier than I could have ever imagined. And by partaking in it, I was no better than the valcos siding with the colonists. But I also realized that the land has changed. No longer can we be divided by what species we are. Humans and nozariels aren't worth less than valcos. They feel just as much as I feel. They reason just as much as I reason. Did you know I was raised by a nozariel?"

"Really? Why?"

"My mother was a weak human. Rearing me put a large toll on her. So I was breastfed by an enslaved nozariel. My mother died when I was nine, and it was Xarima and my father who raised me, who told me stories of our past before the humans. I began my campaign thinking about the people born on this land, who farmed and built cities and made it prosper, yet had to send nearly half their earnings to a king across the ocean, who thought of us as nothing more than a teat to be milked. I did it for the nozariels who were brutalized by the Segolean Crown. I decided to be a champion for us all. It's not possible to go back to the valco way of life. It is too late for that, and this land is too changed. One day we won't be valcos and humans and nozariels. We will just be Fedrians."

Eva met his gaze and felt the spark of a fire deep in her belly. Now she didn't have to wonder how he'd done it, how he'd rallied thousands into following his cause. It was so easy to hear him and see what he saw.

"I was lucky that I understood my purpose from a young age, and I was able to shape my life around that. But enough about me, Doña Eva. I am curious to know what you believe your purpose is."

She let out a broken laugh because she couldn't shake Javier's words from earlier. *The strongest geomancer in all Fedria.* They were foolish and best left to be carried away by the wind.

"You've put me on the spot. That's not an easy question to answer."

Ludivina giggled, not with derision but with the warmth of genuine interest.

"I apologize," Don Samón said.

"I think it's spells." She thought of the rush, of the *craving.* "Of iridio, particularly."

Don Samón chuckled as he leaned over the balcony railing, his gaze on the cyan comet in the sky. He was a handsome man, untouched by his age, save for the lines of ample smiles. Was this otherworldly beauty normal in valcos? Her blood certainly failed her in that regard.

"It reminds me of Rahmagut," he said, "and you will not be happy to hear what I think of iridio."

"What do you think of it?"

"Did you know he was sole owner of the iridio rock, millennia ago?" he deflected. "I'm sure you know that as a new member of the Águilas you will have access to that much power as well. But don't let it consume you like it did him. Legend says Rahmagut was just a regular man who craved iridio until it drove him mad enough to consider himself a god. Some claim he succeeded in ascending. I suppose, with his legacy, he *can* be called a god—a treacherous, greedy one. We should thank the heroes of our past that his presence is forever gone from this world."

Eva allowed herself a deep frown, as it was too dark for the Liberator to see the disagreement on her face. "He is...really gone?"

Don Samón tipped his head. "Unfortunately, those who pray to Rahmagut pray to deaf ears. Ches sealed him ages ago with the last of his power. He did it for the good of this world, for Rahmagut was prepared to rend this land apart with his ambition. Can you imagine that degree of selfishness?"

Eva remembered the yearning in her heart anytime she dabbled with iridio. It was true. It could consume her if she let it. And part of her very much wanted that surrender.

"But the claw..." Eva muttered, "The legend is real." Even Reina's new golden blade, manifesting only for her. It was more proof.

"It is. And there are people who want a piece of that sealed power." He gestured at the smearing comet with his bearded chin. "People who would use this opportunity to invoke him when the seal is at its weakest and Rahmagut's influence is at its strongest. Thankfully, soon the opportunity will be gone."

"You must know a great deal about it," she said, more to humor him and because of the comfort he exuded. Hearing him talk was an entertainment itself.

"We are the guardians, to stop that from happening," Ludivina said with enthusiasm.

He chuckled. "It is not that simple, but yes."

"Why is it so important that you guard the tomb? What is so bad about invoking Rahmagut?" This time, she said the name with confidence. The lick of apprehension she had grown up with, for uttering a name forbidden in the Serrano hacienda, had dulled. It satisfied her to see she was a step freer from her grandmother.

Making her own path was what she had strived for in leaving Galeno. "What's so bad about iridio?"

"Papi, why don't we show her?"

Eva perked up, making it quite clear she did want to be shown.

He conceded with a smile blurred by the night and led the way through one of the balcony paths. Eva and Ludivina followed, giggling about receiving special treatment unbeknownst to the other partygoers. The music faded behind them as the sounds of night embraced them, joined by the ever-present faraway sound of waves. Finally the cobbled walkway met a beautifully engraved wooden door lighted by sconces. The air was sweet from the overabundance of jasmines clinging to the columns at either side of the door. He opened it without a need for keys and welcomed them into a large workshop.

He shot a quick spell of gold iridio to the indoor sconces, and the room came alight in a sparkly flurry. Books and trophies inhabited the bookshelves lining three of the six hexagonal walls. Several rectangular tables were arranged on one side of the room, populated by instruments like the ones Javier used to mix geomancia reagents, along with tools and half-constructed novelties. Minerals and glistening geodes. At the center of the workshop stood a wide table, carved with a map of the continent. It was a resting spot for a curious globe-like artifact of wrought-gold legs with an illusioned projection of many stars resembling the night sky. The painting of a great bloody battle hung sentinel behind a lion-legged desk. And next to it was a large stone slab carved in the shape of agonized people, bent limbs and gaping mouths pointing up at the ceiling as if they were caught in a half scream while being sucked into the depths of the earth.

"This is my workspace," Don Samón said, trailing his fingers over the brocade backrest of a plush love seat. "It's where I spend most of my time nowadays. Not outside with swords and drills as in my youth, but here, with books, because I am looking for a way to stop the power Rahmagut has bestowed upon this land, through iridio."

Eva blinked. She had heard him clearly, but her mind refused to comprehend the meaning.

From the drawer on the lion-legged desk, he produced a scroll that unfurled to reveal a star map. He also withdrew a stack of correspondence, the opened seals in all colors of wax. He pointed at the star illustration clearly resembling the cyan tail of Rahmagut's Claw.

"Forty-two years ago, Rahmagut was invoked successfully."

"What happened then?" Eva asked, watching Ludivina idly spin the globe, causing the stars' position to change. The illusioned sky changed from the movement, days turning to nights turning to days again.

"I suppose the person got exactly what they wanted. They communed with Rahmagut and irreparably weakened the seal, once again, because there have surely been other invocations in generations past. Coincidently enough, you can scour all the old and contemporary literature on the matter of geomancia and find no mentions of iridio ever being used prior to Rahmagut's Claw's appearance forty-two years ago." He rifled through the stack of correspondence, inviting Eva to look for herself. "Ches sealed iridio when he sealed Rahmagut. But I believe that last invocation gave Rahmagut enough power to put iridio back into this world."

Eva opened and closed her mouth, for no appropriate reply came to her. Doña Rosa had called it a new school of geomancia. An undiscovered frontier. Eva had just never imagined it would be so thoroughly connected to the god of el Vacío.

"His influence—his capability to shape this world—it's not a fable. It's real, but it is weak. Just like the seal Ches placed on him is, and I'm afraid it will finally break if Rahmagut is invoked one more time while that comet is still visible."

Eva turned to the carving of the agonized people, noting how it looked so out of place in an otherwise warm room. She pretended to be enthralled by it so they couldn't see her knowledge of Javier's plans in her eyes. Beside it was a board covered in pinned journal entries and ripped-out book pages. Her cursory look told her they were on the subject of tinieblas.

"Would that be so bad, if he is unsealed?" she said, glancing back.

Fear electrified her spine when his carmine eyes met hers. A reaction based on instinct, taking her back to the horrible moment when Javier had hit her. Because she'd never expected it, and it had been unsettling to see his indomitable ferocity come out of nowhere. But Eva felt foolish, for she could tell there was no universe or world where this man would ever raise his hand to her.

"I received a prophecy soon after Segol withdrew from these lands," Don Samón said, tossing the stack of letters over his desk in anger, "from a man I mistook for a charlatan, claiming all my work for independence would be undone. In my rash youth, I did horrible things to him, but I could never silence his belief that if Rahmagut were to be unsealed, the resulting chaos would weaken our nations, allowing for a second rule of the Segolean Empire. The loss of our independence." He pointed at the slab of the anguished people behind him. "We extracted that carving from the tomb years ago when I constructed this residence. It is only a small piece of the horror filled in that tomb. And it's both a warning and a guarantee of what will happen if the ires of Ches and Rahmagut are stirred. Is it really such a stretch to want to prevent the death of innocents?"

The silence was uncomfortable but brief, for Ludivina said, "It won't happen, Papi. This is the last week. You're here." She beckoned Eva to play with the globe, to spin it and admire the stars orbiting the tiny sphere suspended at its very center.

"Indeed. So it was a natural decision to make Tierra'e Sol my home," Don Samón added, his tone mild again. "Everything I need to know to end the magic of iridio is within that tomb, and it has been my dedication all these years since. If there is no invocation, the seal will not break. And if there is no iridio, there will be no opportunity for chaos and the dissolution of everything I fought and bled for."

"How can you want to end iridio?" Eva blurted out suddenly, the query at the tip of her tongue since he'd first mentioned it. For how could he seek to end something so incredible?

He was unfazed by the reaction. Rather, he smiled at her passion. "The bad far outweighs the good."

Eva vehemently disagreed. It was not iridio's fault that humans were uncreative and backward about their perception and use of it. *Everyone* in Galeno had assumed Eva was possessed by a demon, when they were just ignorant. She shot a look at Ludivina, who had boasted earlier about her own prowess with the dining hall lanterns. Ludivina shriveled, perhaps afraid to contradict her father on the matter.

The girl faked a yawn and stretched her thin arms. "I should go back and find me a dancing partner," she said.

Don Samón smiled at his daughter, nodding. "You do that. Don't forget, hosts are supposed to win over their guests."

"I learned from the best," Ludivina said, winking at Eva before exiting to the darkness of the garden passageway.

Eva nearly sucked in a breath, missing her opportunity to make an exit. On one hand, she felt thoroughly charmed by the Liberator. On the other, she wasn't sure for how long she could keep her knowledge of Javier's and Reina's intentions secret, if he prodded her enough.

Don Samón plopped himself on his seat behind the desk, his ash-blond lashes shading his gaze. "I am glad the claw's journey will be over soon, and with it the threat will pass, at least for another forty-two years, or until I figure out a counter or a cancellation to iridio."

Eva hated the conviction, even if she couldn't hate the man. Sooner or later he would be successful, and it saddened her. "I wish I could change your mind on it," she muttered with her gaze to the illustrations of the tinieblas pinned to the board.

"Are you sure that's not just Rahmagut's influence talking?" he said, and she joined in on his small chuckling laugh.

"So what's needed to invoke Rahmagut, besides, you know, the nine wives? I'm assuming you know everything on the matter," Eva said. Her conniving husband was planning to betray Don Samón's trust, using her to achieve his goals. It would be better if she knew what she was getting into beforehand rather than blindly trust his command.

Don Samón's reply was a finger pointed at the board.

"There *are* plots to make it happen," he said. "I have endless correspondence and accounts from my colleagues in Segolita who have heard talk of Enrique and his witch, Ursulina Duvianos, kidnapping women. When Celeste sent me her letter, I knew those two were pursuing Rahmagut's legend. This was confirmed when a sentry spotted a small host flying Águila colors crossing Río'e Marle just south of El Carmín. If they were en route to Segolita, why wouldn't they just cross near La Cochinilla?"

He said something about spending his nights in fear of having to face Don Enrique, who was once an ally. Eva just muttered a noncommittal reply, for her attention was locked on the journal passage beneath the illustration.

"I know your marriage to Javier is new, but I'm curious if you know of any rifts between the brothers? Have you met Enrique? Is it true that he has been consumed by madness?"

The passage spoke of bringing the damas to the final chamber in the tomb while Rahmagut's Claw still marked the sky.

"I just can't fathom how a father—let alone a *valco*—would be willing to offer up his own daughter as sacrifice. Because that is what Celeste is, no, a Dama del Vacío?"

Eva squinted at the fading calligraphy of the journal entry. The instructions to split open the women's throats as the quickest and most dignified way of offering, drawing their stored power through their blood, letting it all pool at the center of the chamber.

Her breath left her then. She whipped around to face Don Samón, who watched her curiously with that red gaze loaded with meaning she couldn't understand.

"This is not real, right?" she said, hoping for another lecture on the nuances of the legend. Perhaps for the possibility of a workaround.

"We just talked about it. It's all real. Rahmagut's seal will break if he's invoked one more time. And to do so, the lives of all nine women must be sacrificed."

37

Love of Friendship

Reina knew she was the luckiest woman alive.

She watched Celeste laugh, marveling at eyes that were glossy from the touch of wine. Celeste looked like the girl she had been before the death of her mother, at the pinnacle of her father's power. Like she was back to wearing the skin of someone with good fortune calligraphied all over her destiny.

The music carried them to one of the many interconnected gardens, where hedges brimming with jasmine or hibiscus created pockets of privacy for Don Samón's guests. They passed one section where a small group had settled on benches near the ground to bet on Calamity, and another where two bulky men had snuck away to whisper sweet nothings into each other's ears under the moonlight.

Reina beckoned Celeste farther into the garden maze, and Celeste followed, smiling with lips moist from the amapolas. She'd had three. They'd *shared* three. One at the mouth of the tomb and two from Don Samón's dessert platters where they were abundantly offered, as if all his guests would inevitably end up becoming pieces of each other's fates.

Reina's belly burned from the possibilities of this game they played. She didn't have the strength to end it. The wine had banished that ounce of self-restraint. And Celeste's eyes were content, finally, after spending so many days in a state of constant flight.

This was a game every inch of Reina's core screamed at her not to end.

Earlier, soon after returning from the tomb, Don Samón had graciously gifted the group some geomancia reagents, including iridio, allowing Eva to refill her pendant and Reina her heart. But the solution felt watered-down, weak. Reina could tell she'd burned through most of it just from the dancing. Her chest fluttered meekly, yet she ignored the sensation. Nothing else mattered but this moment with Celeste.

Their strides lingered near an elevated balcony-like perch devoid of any activity. The music was far and mild, the harp dominating a song best danced to in close proximity. Far in the distance, a lone heron sliced the sky, and Celeste rushed to the railing to watch it fly. Reina followed her. There a full moon made her acquaintance, then kept them company. Rahmagut's Claw was hidden behind the manse's roofs and palms across the opposite side, making it easy to forget what had brought them here in the first place.

"I didn't know you could dance joropo," Celeste said, fanning her chest.

"I didn't know it either." All that watching others dance it had actually taught her a thing or two.

There was no bench or seating on the balcony, but the wine lessened their inhibitions. Celeste crumpled to the floor like a waterfall of silks, pressing her back against the balcony railing. The ring of faraway laughter came from the level below. Reina joined her, but without the silks. She'd been lucky Don Samón's tailor was a sensible man who didn't mind her requesting an outfit of pants and a fitted liqui liqui jacket for the dinner party.

"It's so hot in here," Celeste said as she pulled the folds of her dress, revealing two slender legs. "It's like . . . there's nowhere to run from the heat."

A bead of salty sweat rolled down Reina's temple. "We're too used to the Páramo."

Celeste let out a little sigh, humming to the tune of the music they'd left behind. Her lips were plump and stained darker by the endlessly refilled wine. With the darkness, her eyes were two deep sapphires, and Reina took them in, even when she needn't, for she had every flicker and variation in color firmly committed to memory.

"You're beautiful, you know that?" Reina said without fear.

Celeste paused her humming to giggle.

Reina's hand slithered over to Celeste's lap, curling around hers, hoping for a grip in return.

Reina waited, but Celeste's fingers remained limp. Reina worried her lower lip, and her gaze fell to the space between them. She had permission to cross the bridge, she'd taken that step earlier at the foot of Rahmagut's tomb, but there was a stiffness to the air. A tension, perhaps of her own making—for the truth she was still too cowardly to give.

Reina took a deep inhale through the nose and decided it was due time she did it. "Celeste, I have something I must tell you."

Celeste's gaze was fixed on the rising moon, unflinching. Reina waited to meet those sapphires, for the acknowledgment, but the tension only coagulated.

Celeste withdrew her hand from her lap. "Don't tell me you want to talk about Rahmagut."

Reina's breathing hitched.

Finally Celeste faced her completely, and her face was hard, like her father's.

"Don Enrique banished me. He said I couldn't return unless I found you."

"Because he knows I'm a Dama del Vacío," Celeste said slowly. "And you did."

"I'm supposed to take you to my grandmother."

Celeste's brows descended farther in disappointment. Perhaps this whole time she had been betting Reina would have the courage to act against the darkness tearing her family to pieces. Reina saw it and knew she deserved every ounce of scorn.

Celeste's spine straightened, her eyes narrowing, the gloss of wine gone. "Well, you can't. Or are you going to force me against my will?" Then she snorted. "Like you could."

Reina tried grasping for her hand again, but the gesture was evaded. "I don't want to force you."

Celeste rose to her feet. "Then what's your plan?"

Reina followed. "Celeste."

"Reina."

A shudder shook Reina's shoulders. There was a mountain between them, one she had hiked merely hours ago but that now felt impossible to climb. "My grandmother took the iridio ore from my heart."

"Father owns all the iridio in the world. I can find you a new one."

This time Reina took a bold step to her and grasped her hands with her own sweaty palms. Celeste didn't fight her. She didn't need to say anything when her entire body recoiled with betrayal.

"It's not about getting more iridio. Doña Ursulina said Rahmagut has the power to give me a brand-new heart. You saw the blade and the claw. We know the legend is real."

A scowl was her reply.

"He can bring your mom back."

Celeste wrenched free. She snarled, "And you think I care about that?"

"You haven't been the same since she died." Reina didn't get on two knees, but she might as well have. "Think of how happy our lives will be afterward."

Acid laughter exploded from Celeste's lips. "You came all the way to the Plume to find me just so you can force the ghost of my mother into Maior—and for what? So my father can pretend he's not a vile monster when he's having his way with that human?"

Reina flinched as if she had been whipped across the face.

"How can you even believe that she would be back? We buried her a year ago!" Her words were a lash in the wind, a loud crack disrupting the peace of the adjacent gardens. "She is bones and worms now, if anything." Celeste whirled, burying her face in her hands and giving Reina her back. "I already mourn her every day, and I've accepted she's gone. Why would I want to tarnish her memory like that?"

"It won't be like you're thinking. Rahmagut has the power to change anything! I have seen the signs—in my *dreams* he showed me the way. She will be normal and alive and *real*. And it's not up to me." Reina knew she was just a pawn in the caudillo's plots. Without the purpose Doña Ursulina gave her, she had little else. When the Benevolent Lady had been alive, all was well. She had been their home and their beacon. Reina ached to taste that happiness again. "Please, Celeste. Your father's going to get his way whether we like it or not. The least you can do is think about me."

Celeste whipped around again, shoving Reina hard by the shoulders as tears sprinkled the air around her face. "Think about you?" she roared.

"Yes! Ever since I came to Águila Manor, I have bent over backward for the desires of your family—to be the person you needed. I never asked for anything. And all I've ever wanted has been some acknowledgment. Yes, you are the heir of the house. You are smart and strong and beautiful, and you deserve *everything*. But for once, I would like to have something." Reina didn't know there were tears in her eyes until the wetness pooled near her collarbone. "I have two droplets of iridio in my chest, and once that runs out, my life will also end." Celeste hadn't seen her collapsing to the ground when no breath was ever enough. "But if there's a possibility that all this will be behind us, why wouldn't we want to try? So what if he's the god of the Void? He can give us a brand-new life." Reina paused as her heart thrummed in a race to consume the last of its fuel. "It would make all those deaths mean something," she added, her voice breaking.

Celeste shook her head, her eyes wide and glossy. "You're a monster like your grandmother."

Reina stepped closer, and her heart shattered when Celeste stepped back. "No—I love you."

Celeste's lips trembled as she sharpened her reply. "In another world, maybe I would have loved you, too. But you're warped by your desperation, scraping for the worst because you know you don't deserve better. It's true what they say about your kind. I lost every ounce of respect for you when I watched you drag innocent women into that witch's laboratory."

A pressure built in Reina's temples. She swiped her sweaty palms on her pants. "But...we kissed, at the tomb. You let me hold your hand all night."

Celeste grimaced.

Reina's voice deflated little by little as she said, "We shared the amapolas."

"*But I told you*," Celeste hissed, "I wanted to share it as friends, not like my parents shared it. Yet you turned my gesture of thanks into your declaration of love."

Reina remembered this tension that was cramping up her core. The same geysering anger she hadn't had the courage to express when the caudillo had accused her of disloyalty. "Then why did you let me kiss you? Why didn't you ever push me away?"

"I let you kiss me because you're my best friend—or *were*. All this time I've known how you feel. Only a fool wouldn't see it. I let you have that—I let you have tonight." Clarity dawned in her eyes. "And I also allowed myself to toy with the possibility, but it's not what I want. I can't help how I feel."

"Can't help but feel that my life is secondary to yours?" The words salted the open sores Reina had wistfully licked and tended to, over and over again, dreaming her destiny went beyond what their births dictated.

Celeste's countenance came alight with malicious spite. She looked like Javier. "Well, isn't it? Aren't you collecting me and Maior so you can claw your way to a better station? Didn't you cross the Páramo to have me as your damsel in distress, playing the role of savior before handing me over to your grandmother for butchering?" Celeste faced her with the full weight of her anger. "You want to end my life to get a new life. How am I supposed to be included in that equation?"

Reina paused, her brows knitting in confusion.

And Celeste saw it written all across her face. "You don't know, do you?" she said on a shuddery laugh. "Rahmagut's nine wives, the Damas del Vacío, they must give their lives. There is a sacrifice that must be given—a complete blood sacrifice."

"It's—it's just a—a bit of blood. I would never—"

Celeste's laughter rang cold like the buffeting winds of the mountains where she'd grown up. "You're nothing but a tool to your grandmother. You believed every lie that witch fed you, and you never considered finding out for yourself if any of it was real."

There was no rebuttal. Reina was empty. The same whimpering, unintelligent fool she had always been. Ches's golden blade didn't change that. Slaying tinieblas and making it to Tierra'e Sol didn't change that.

"Did you really think I wasn't aware the tomb was here? I came despite it, because the Liberator is the last person my father would cross. He knows the tomb intimately. He wants to end iridio—the thing you need to live." Her lips curled in animosity. "I did think you would come as my friend to help me piece together my life after this mess, not as this *fool* who wants to hand me over to Doña Ursulina. Either way, it doesn't matter. Soon that comet will finish traveling the skies and all this will be behind me."

Celeste didn't spare her a final look before storming down the garden's labyrinthine paths, back to the safety of Don Samón's party.

Reina watched the moon alone, paralyzed, accepting the mockery of its bright shine reserved for lovers. She curled both fists and pressed them against the throb in her chest.

She was a fool. For loving Celeste so much that every moment without her was an ache in her bones. For adoring her since the very first day they'd met and *dreaming* it had to have been fate, this crossing of their paths.

But most importantly, she'd always been a fool for trusting her grandmother, when she'd never hidden her true nature from Reina. The conditional approach to saving her life. The rotten food she'd given her. Her methods of finding solutions in darkness. Her advice that was a double-edged blade.

If Reina were smarter—more capable—*better*, she would have seen it from the moment the ore was wrenched from her chest. For Doña Ursulina wasn't asinine like her spawn. She'd noticed Reina's gaze as it lingered over the last precious thing in the manor. She'd caught the signs and left Celeste for last, for she knew Reina would never go so far if she'd known the truth of the end.

All this time, she had been the pawn to the scheming masters of the manor. A game piece to be manipulated and used. The whispers, which had conveniently quieted from the moment she'd set foot on the island, stirred in delight and agreement. She dug into her chest and wished she could rip out her heart. Of course, she was too weak to even do that.

She straightened, pushing her curly bangs out of her eyes, feeling naked without the ever-present straps of her new blade. So what came next?

Traitorously, her thoughts flitted to Maior. The woman who worried about keeping her fed and healed, who fussed about replenishing her iridio. She had been absent all throughout the party, even as Don Samón had the courtesy of reserving a seat for her to Reina's right.

Reina let out a shuddery breath, worried. All this time she hadn't spared Maior a thought, too distracted with Celeste.

Maior's absence wasn't just because she'd seen Reina kiss Celeste, as Reina had assumed. She was gone because Doña Ursulina was on the island—somewhere—preparing to spill the blood of all nine wives. "In the tomb," Reina mouthed.

Perhaps the thing she needed to do was to confront her grandmother herself.

38

Master of Tinieblas

Don Samón pushed himself off the seat as if he could taste the change in Eva's demeanor.

Eva stuttered, unable to conjure the right words. "A-are you sure? That's how it must be done?"

He approached her with warm eyes. "Positive. I mean—there are some words to be said, reaching into el Vacío and conjuring void magic, but nothing beyond Ursulina's capabilities. I just can't believe Enrique would go to such lengths. I wonder what they think they will gain from it."

"I—I don't know them," Eva lied, turning to the door, swallowing a panic rising like salivation.

"Back in the day, Ursulina was Feleva's pillar, I remember that. She is not someone to be underestimated."

And yet that was exactly what Javier wanted Eva to do. She ground her teeth.

"She's mighty, like the mighty Doña Antonia," he said, pointing between them as if sharing an inside joke. He followed Eva to the door, the sconces snuffing behind him. "I've met your grandmother, did you know?"

"You have?" she said in the high pitch of surprise, "How?"

They walked into the garden paths, reentering a world where the air smelled sweet as it carried the sounds of the faraway harp and cuatro. Eva caught the pointed trajectory of a slim heron as it sliced through a moonlit night. She was glad Don Samón could take her cues of wanting to leave. She needed to see where Maior had gone. It was a wretched thing to hope a broken heart was the only reason the human had skipped on the dinner...

"I visited Galeno when I was young and naïve—at the height of my campaign," Don Samón continued.

"Did you ask her for support?"

He chuckled. They reemerged on the same balcony they'd met on. "Your grandmother didn't hate me as much back then. She was quite diplomatic, throwing me a banquet before kindly showing me the door. When I was there, I met the sweetest woman in the world."

Something fragile shook in Eva's chest as she recognized the moniker.

"Would you believe me if I said it?" he said, intuitively offering her a hand.

Eva glanced at it and debated whether it was impolite to reject it. "Say what?"

"That I met your mother, Dulce? That she was witty, and beautiful, and made of sugarcane?"

Her heart went from fluttering to pounding. Eva bit the insides of her lips. She wanted to flee with a lied pleasantry. She despised the implied meaning, his familiarity. He lowered his hand, but there was no judgment or inquisition in his façade. He merely regarded her with those infuriatingly knowing eyes.

She refused to jump to conclusions, especially as she felt alone and vulnerable under the moonlight. "What does Ludivina's mother have to say about this?" she said, deflecting away from Dulce.

"Ludivina's mother was a woman I married to solidify my position in Fedrian politics. Do not worry about her opinion of me. Her absence should tell you everything you need to know. Besides, she would only expect honesty from me. I don't know if you've noticed, Doña Eva, but I've lived a life of hurtful truths. I was put into this world to open the eyes of my brothers and sisters, even if it was to a truth they didn't want to see."

"The truths of equality, regardless of our breed?" Eva muttered, desperate to make an escape. She felt equally tugged in opposite directions: her worry for Maior, and her fear of offending this man if his declaration meant what she thought it did.

"Indeed, though when I showed up at the Serrano hacienda, not even my handsome wiles could make your grandmother see that."

Eva shot a glance at the hall, from where warm yellow light spilled to the cobbles. The servers who ferried trays of wine and amapola. The few dancing pairs that remained. Javier laughing beside a man twice his size while clinking sloshing goblets. A merriment devoid of Maior.

"Doña Eva," he said, seizing her attention, "in my youth, I went to Galeno expecting to leave with an army and coffers of support. Instead, I left without my heart."

He paused, perhaps for the drama of it.

"When I met your mother, she was all skin of cocoa and eyes like dates."

Eva looked away to the floor. She didn't catch her tongue before saying, "And I'm a bachaca. I'm sorry to disappoint you, Don Samón, but I'm nothing like Dulce. And I don't want to be."

His lips thinned.

"My mother might have been sweet like her name," she said, heart hammering, "but she was the weakest woman I've ever know."

"Doña Eva," he growled.

"Forgive me if I speak a hurtful truth." In a way, saying it felt cathartic. "She let a man destroy her happiness. But instead of fighting on, she abandoned me."

"It wasn't a man who destroyed your mother's life—"

Finally she seized the courage to make the exit she'd wanted to all along. "Excuse me, Don Samón, I have a feeling Javier might be looking for me."

Her lie was stupid and transparent, but she had better things to do than pretend for Don Samón's sake. She didn't want to look into his kind face and see that it belonged to a man worthy of such actions.

"It was your grandmother who stole her freedom and her happiness with lies."

Eva heard his voice behind her and was glad he didn't follow her.

The music sickened her when she stepped into the hall. She spotted Celeste listening to one of Don Samón's friends, nursing a goblet while shooting glances at the doorway to the gardens. Across the room, Javier did the same. His gaze fell on Eva as she stalked from one door to the other in a hurry. He glared as if she didn't have any right to retreat, to ruin the plans he had made for her tonight. The heat of heartache flooded her face. It stuffed her nose and threatened moisture in the corners of her eyes. With an equally scathing glare, she dared him to follow her, because she had many reasons to let him savor a slice of her wrath.

A shadow ran into her in the open corridor to the dormitories. Eva jumped, startled, only to see the ruddy cheeks and glossy tamarind eyes of Reina. Something about the fluster of her, appearing just as Eva's own ruminations had spun her conversation with Don Samón round and round, made the ire boil over.

Eva got in her way to stop her, then cornered her against a pillar.

"This has been your plan all along?" she hissed, pointing a finger with the threat of prodding Reina across the chest with it. "You were planning to kill Maior?" Eva's voice came out broken and shrill. In her chest her heart thrummed.

Reina flushed even more. She was paralyzed with a fearful resignation. "No—*no*."

Eva tried discerning any guilt in her eyes but couldn't. "To invoke Rahmagut you have to kill Celeste and Maior. I thought you loved Celeste?"

Fury flashed in Reina. She seized Eva's wrist, yanking her this way and that before shoving her back. And through it all Eva was nothing but a doll to the strength in Reina's grip.

Eva sucked in a breath, a sharp fear shooting up her spine. She didn't have her iridio pendant with her...

"My relationship with Celeste is none of your concern," Reina said with her tail lashing behind her. She was amped for a fight.

Eva couldn't shake the deep disapproval, despite Reina's aggression. "Right now, you are everything to Maior. How could you plot to betray her like this? You're as fucked up as the rest of them."

Footsteps echoed down the corner. The last thing Eva wanted was to see Javier make an entrance to patronize her, so she whirled toward her room, leaving Reina, stunned, against the same pillar.

Eva needed to get rid of the dress and fetch her geomancia jewelry before looking for Maior. She entered her and Javier's room. The newlywed suite, as the nozariel maid had said with a giggle when she'd welcomed them inside. The chamber was twice the size of Maior's, with a massive four-poster bed and an alcove furnished with a luxurious breakfast table. Windowless, the room had only one natural light source: the wide-paned doors to the alcove.

She paced the room to calm herself, her heart racing itself bloody. She refused to replay the conversation with Don Samón. She *refused* to draw a conclusion. He had sounded so familiar and kind, like he had loved the late Dulce. Which could mean many things...but in truth, most likely meant one.

Eva flung one of the decorative pillows across the room. She didn't want to accept it! Don Samón had been so nice. And he was the face—the leader—of the independence movement. *He was a hero.* She didn't want to see him as a—

Her train of thought shattered as Javier stormed into the room, slamming the door behind him.

"Eva Kesaré," he said.

Eva met his anger in earnest. "Look who the tide brought in," she said. "You're exactly who I need right now."

Her response gave him pause. "How could you walk away from Don Samón like that?"

Eva squeezed her lips shut. She wanted to summon that starlight fire. She wanted to burn a hole right through his chest.

"When someone as rich and famous as him wants your attention, you bloody well give it."

She snorted. "From day one you've been scheming with my

life—bringing me here just so you can suck up to Don Samón. How much are you getting for bringing me, exactly?"

He took a step to her, his expression concerned. The decreasing distance terrified her. Eva skidded around the bed. Just three steps, and she could be out in the alcove—if Javier didn't propel himself to stop her, as she knew he could.

"You married me and brought me here like a prize because you knew Don Samón is my monster father."

There. She'd said it.

"What? Eva—you're misinterpreting this."

He approached. So she leapt to the bedside table, where she had left her crystal pendant—the one with the refilled iridio—and seized it.

Arm outstretched and crystal vial in hand, she whirled around, saying, "Not another step, or I'll blow this whole room to el Vacío!"

Javier tensed, a bead of sweat rolling down his temple. "Eva, think about what you're doing."

"Blowing you up, like I should have done the moment I found out I could?"

His throat bobbed. "You've got it all wrong."

"On the contrary. *Now* I know why I'm in Fedria. Now I know why you were so amiable when showing up at my home to trick me into running away." Something cruel unraveled the strings of her heart, like she had a monster lodged in her chest. She could feel it, tendril by tendril. She had thought herself so clever, seeking Javier with her letters as if she were an equal player in the plots they played. "You were lucky I was so stupid and gullible. I left my home to be handed to that man?"

"Eva."

"When were you planning on telling me? Why not just hand me off the moment we came to Tierra'e Sol?"

"Eva."

"I know!" she snarled. "Because you knew I'd never be all right with meeting him. He put a spell on my mother! She never recovered from what he did. And my whole family thinks I'm a monster like him!"

If the Serranos could be called a family at all.

"*Eva*," he said again, and this time she sensed his intention of extinguishing their distance.

"Not one move, or I'll blow you up!" She scoffed. "Like I have anything to lose."

She preemptively tugged on those threads of starlight, summoning the rawness of the cosmic plane. She saw the universe superimposed on the room—on Javier. The power was right at her fingertips. All she had to do was let go.

He took a deep breath. "Yes," he said in the exhaling air. "I brought you here because Don Samón Bravo the Liberator is your father."

Despite her suspicions, the confirmation made it hard to breathe. She had liked the idea of denying it. If no one gave breath to the words, they could all pretend it wasn't true...

"I married you and brought you here and introduced you and asked you to be agreeable because Don Samón has been yearning for this moment for *years*. And I was the one who gave it to him. I'm the one who brought him his daughter—his estranged, beautiful, mighty valco of a daughter. With Ludivina's failing health, your hand in marriage is worth all the gold this wretched country has to give. Literally."

Her lips trembled as the memories of the day overwhelmed her. "He bewitched and broke my mother," she said in a tattered voice.

"Now, Eva, there are two sides to every story. That's not what he says—"

"Of course he wouldn't say that! *He's a rapist!*"

The air around her hand crackled. Wisps of golden iridio began unraveling around the pendant. It was energy on the verge of rupture.

"*Eva*." Her name came out of his lips as a plea. "The stories were fabricated by your grandparents! To stop your mother from running off with a rebel and an enemy of the Segolean Empire! To give a justification for why she, a married woman with a child, would give birth to a valco. They forced her and the whole world into repeating their fabricated narrative—the lie."

The bands of magic grew thicker.

"Liar!" Eva snapped.

One such band popped, bursting with sparks of fire. The flames unraveled before ever hitting the ground.

"Why don't you go ask him yourself?" Javier said.

She could see the restraint in him as he pushed back the demon from coming through. The black tendrils oozed, in and out of his cheeks.

"If he's innocent, why didn't you tell me sooner?" She thought of letting go. She could imagine the destruction. Then her heart descended further. She was stopped by the irrefutable truth that, despite her threat, she didn't *want* to see Javier burn.

His voice was small when he said, "I didn't want to tell you sooner because I knew you would react this way. I wanted you not to hate me, at least not just yet—"

"Why?" she barked.

"Because, like I said, I need you against Doña Ursulina," he said so softly. "Because I'm turning into a tiniebla."

Her hand lost the spark of iridio. A weight plummeted to her belly. Her mouth sagged, for she could see it so clearly.

He spread his palms, surrendering to the truth. "Because I need to be there during the invocation to beg Rahmagut to cleanse *me*. Because my strength alone is not enough to take the damas from Doña Ursulina. Yes, you were perfect for me. When you sent me your letter, I recognized that you could be the wife I needed for the legacy I will build. Then I dug around, and I discovered Don Samón had a daughter with a Serrano, and that daughter was you."

Eva's lips quivered, her vision blurring with an overflow of tears. She squinted, and they streamed down her cheeks. She lowered the pendant altogether.

"He didn't come for you because more and more families in Venazia are antagonistic to his ideals, even if they were allies in the revolution. Back then, they had a mutual enemy. But now, there's supposed to be peace, and he doesn't get to say what happens to the granddaughter of Galeno's governor."

"Neither do my grandparents!" Eva cried.

He took another step, nodding, and the darkness left him. This time, seeing him approach didn't make her afraid.

"No—you decide what happens to you. And I helped you leave them. I gave you all the tools so you could blossom into this flaming, terrifying"—a laugh escaped him—"amazing valco." His gaze fell, and he looked younger, hopeless. He wrung his palms until they turned pink. "And now I just hope that you can help me. I'm turning, Eva. Every day, every spell I cast brings me closer to losing my mind."

He stopped at arm's reach.

Her own step halved the distance between them.

"You're turning into a tiniebla," she whispered. He looked so pitiful, she couldn't deny her urge to comfort him. As her fingertips grazed his chin, a small spark of remnant iridio shocked both their skins. All his anger, his abuse . . . was it *Javier* treating her so cruelly? Or something else altogether?

Eva tried to imagine what it would be like but couldn't. She couldn't fathom what went through a tiniebla's mind. Or if they even had any sapience to begin with . . . One thing was for sure, though: If she ever shared a similar fate, she'd do anything in her power to stop it.

She was so wrapped up in the thought she hardly registered his hands working to unlatch the pendant from her fingers.

"Yes," he said, his breath sweet from the tang of wine.

"How?"

The question brought the black back into the whites of his eyes. Javier stepped away. For Eva's sake, or his.

"Laurel. That woman—" His voice shook. "To everyone she was a saint. But to me? She hated me for trying to convince Enrique to betroth me to Celeste." He chucked the pendant to the bedside table, where it clanked on the verge of shattering. "She hated Celeste's burden of passing on the blood. And what did she care about valcos? She was just a lucky human who'd somehow managed to enthrall my brother. She had access to void magic, did you know that? And when I went to Gegania, I finally saw it for myself. Everyone spits on Doña Ursulina's name for practicing void magic, but

Laurel was doing it behind closed doors—the *hypocrite*. And she cursed me—she thought herself *so* clever. But she went too far. She turned me into this!" He fiercely pounded his chest and continued. "*That's* when she suddenly started feeling bad for me."

Eva watched him pace the room.

"For that, I was glad to see her die."

Despite the terrible connotation, Eva couldn't shake off the fascination. "Did you kill her?"

He faced her. "No. It must have been divine justice. Or Doña Ursulina, the conniving snake that she is. I didn't have to lift a finger."

He closed the distance again. "Please, Eva. Afterward, I'll do anything. After I'm cleansed, I can be a true husband to you. I know I could...I would try." His approach was one seeking tenderness, so she allowed him the embrace.

She liked his small frame, she decided—how her arms could wrap around his chest and feel the muscled leanness beneath the liqui liqui. His hair was soft silk against her cheek, smelling of salt and, faintly, of the island's jasmines. He rested his head on the crook of her neck, his antlers angled in the opposite direction and his breath a tickle igniting a warmth in her belly—of the good kind. Eva held him as those muscles spasmed. Even as some of that darkness slithered from his body to hers. It couldn't hurt her, she knew. Outside Javier they were nothing but shadows.

There was one last thing marring this moment, and it wouldn't be perfect until she got the truth.

Eva squeezed his liqui liqui shirt and shoved him away.

"Eva?"

"Rahmagut's invocation—I have to know. Are you planning to kill Maior and Celeste to cleanse yourself?"

She wanted to hear it from his lips. She wanted to see his crimson gaze shift and narrow when he lied, for she knew his expressions now, after being in his company all these days and nights.

A grimace was all he gave her. "No—it's just a blood offering."

Her face hardened. She inspected him. The lines from his frown. The confusion in his red eyes. His jaw muscles working and unworking into knots. This bewilderment was not a lie.

"They must give their lives," she said with a steady voice, for there was no time or opportunity for vacillation. She told him everything she'd seen and talked about in Don Samón's study.

Javier stepped back with his lips parted. The hope he had gained from her embrace withered, the determination of his eyes dulling. He shook his head, disbelieving. "Doña Ursulina and Brother—they had us do this." He stared at his open palms. "But how could he? I don't believe he knows," he said, meeting Eva's gaze with clarity. "Or if he does—I suppose it's not beyond the realm of possibility that he would offer up Celeste for sacrifice."

"It can't be," Eva said in a whiny voice she regretted. But in truth she didn't fully trust the Águilas. She didn't know them. And Don Samón, the only *sane* person in all of this, was convinced.

Javier's lips rippled, holding back a barrage of thoughts. "It doesn't matter what Enrique believes. What matters is that we've all been working toward this, on Doña Ursulina's counsel. *I thought I was so fucking clever—that I had a solution.*" His words were shuddery with panic, and there were tears in the corners of his eyes. He folded his arms over his chest like it ached him.

"So you won't do it?"

"*How?*" he howled. "Yes, I hate her mother, but this wasn't the plan!"

Eva let out an exhale as if a whole mountain were offloaded from her shoulders. "Do you think Reina will go through with it?"

His face twisted. It was clear he'd never considered Reina's actions in his pile of worries from the inevitability of turning into a tiniebla. He shook his head and threw a palm in the air. "Reina loves Celeste."

Eva sucked a big breath in agreement. Even if she could give Reina the benefit of the doubt, she didn't want to risk anything. Maior was her friend. Without special conditions or concessions. Maior's intentions were pure.

This time Eva was the one to close the distance and take his hand. "We can find another way for you. There has to be one. I won't let you murder more people for this."

His lips were a thin line, his eyes dark, as if imagining two conflicting paths. In the end he nodded, docile like never before. It bloated Eva with self-satisfaction. Past Javier would have never trusted her capabilities, but she had now proven herself. They had resources and allies. An exchange for Celeste's and Maior's lives was not the way.

Soft Tierra'e Sol breeze tickled the curtains of the open alcove doors. Outside, just like inside, the world had quieted. They changed into their traveling clothes, backs facing each other, because Eva wasn't yet ready for that step. Despite his arrogance and occasional wickedness, he still allowed her the choice of intimacy.

Eva buttoned her shirt, thinking of Feleva Águila's purpose for him. Perhaps it had impacted the way he turned out. *Desperate and broken*, she thought. *Una tiniebla.*

She remembered the battle in Gegania, the moment when she'd slipped into el Vacío with that spell. The iridio book had said it was the spell for controlling them, warning such an act could fracture her soul. But as she pressed her fist to her chest, where she'd hung her iridio pendant, she felt whole.

Wicked and treacherous, the thought wormed into her—the idea of being able to control him. It seduced her. What if one day, while he was spouting his usual obscenities, she snagged his voice and commanded him to shut up? It would make for a wonderful surprise.

She could be the master, and he, the minion.

Of course, he'd never let her attempt it. Knowing Javier, he'd see it as an affront of the highest degree. Would he be able to tell if she attempted it, only a little bit? She stole a peek over her shoulder, catching him with his shoulders bare, his skin moonlight white with the faintest scars from sparring.

She turned completely to face him. Her heart was a steady drum as she thrust herself into el Vacío. The darkness swallowed her. She was at the bottom of an ocean. It was a terrible weight. It pressed on her shoulders, on her ears, on her vision. It stopped her from breathing.

Beside her, in the vast blackness, stood a figure. It turned around like her, to face her, its face leathery and wicked.

Tiempo que pasa no vuelve.

She didn't even have to say the words to seize control over it. The connection came so easily. The darkness purred with so much satisfaction it terrified her. She sucked in a breath and thrust herself back into reality.

Waiting for her was a smiling face of eyes turned putrid black.

"Hello, Eva," said Javier in the deep, devilish voice of his tiniebla.

Eva stepped back, but he lunged, shoving her to the bed and pinning her beneath him.

"No!" she cried.

The darkness curled in and out of him, smoke smelling of rotten flesh. He watched with a grin, like she had fulfilled his deepest desire.

"I would like to thank you, Eva Kesaré," he said. "My host—he was doing a mighty fine job keeping me restrained—"

"No!" she cried again. Her belly turned to acid at the implications.

Tiniebla Javier just watched her with that wide spoiled-to-the-core grin.

"The fool thought he could keep my influence and consciousness bottled up forever. I suppose he was good at it, until *you came along*," he said, lifting her chin with one hand.

Eva gagged at the touch.

"Thank you, my dearest."

"Stop it! Let me go!" Eva bellowed with the might of her iridio, hoping to seize some control.

The air crackled, but her resolve was too weak.

"Now it's time to fulfill my calling."

She tried pushing free of his bind with all her might, but to his strength, she was an ant. "No!"

"It's time to spill the blood of the damas, to give them the reward they deserve for fleeing my master." He took a deep inhale of pleasure, then said, "Can you feel it? The gates to His tomb have been opened. It must be fated—Don Rahmagut's return."

He sprang from her and landed on all fours before getting to his feet. The grace and beauty Javier carried like a banner disintegrated. This creature seized his body and turned him into something else.

"Thank you, Eva Kesaré. For this, I'm sure Don Rahmagut will shower you in rewards," he said, sparing her one last corrupted glance. Then he sprinted out of the alcove and into the darkness of night.

Tears swelled at the corners of Eva's eyes. She took one massive gulp of air after another, and it still didn't feel like enough. This was her fault. His eyes, putrid and vile, were imprinted on her memory. She had been but a feather against the steel of his grip. Above her, the ceiling spun and blurred. She covered her face with her hands, and still she drowned.

A scream pierced the quiet of night.

Maior, Eva thought.

He was going to sacrifice the damas to unseal his god. There was no time for useless tears or dallying. Eva sprinted out of the room. Outside, the corridor was shrouded in shadow and silence, as it ought to be when the moon was highest.

She tried Maior's room and found it locked. "Maior!"

She pounded on the door, loud enough to surely wake the manse. Reina's and Celeste's rooms were in similar silent and locked states. The lack of answer was the most terrifying part.

Eva decided to enter the rooms from their doors to the garden, where the path connected the manse to the beach. She found the door to Celeste's dormitory kicked open, the frame splintered and battered. There was no sign of any of the women.

She stood on the steps of Celeste's room, with its view to the serene beach where the water was an endless lagoon of black, rippling the moon's reflection. To the left were the jungle paths. A maze to the tomb's entrance. Eva didn't have the luxury of cowardice any longer. *She* had caused this, so she had to figure out the way through, stitch the path together from the memories of her walk with Maior. She had to find Maior and Celeste. She had to warn Reina.

Mostly, she had to undo her foolishness and reel tiniebla Javier back into the darkness where he belonged.

39

The Sacrifice

Reina wasn't unfamiliar with aches of the heart, but this pain was unlike anything she'd experienced before. Panic choked her, a desperation she couldn't outrun or escape or breathe through. She ripped through the jungle's overgrowth, not blindly—for the bismuto pumping through her sharpened Reina's already heightened eyes—but like a cannonball, tearing everything in her path while the jungle fought back with its own cuts and gashes. Spiking brambles and protruding knotted roots. Vines catching her arms and a muddy soil collapsing beneath her weight, sucking her in.

Still, despite obstacles and the tears clouding her eyes, Reina endured. She was a fool, but she wasn't going to sit idly and lose the people who mattered most. Celeste, in spite of the canyon between them, and Maior, who'd never asked for any of the things Reina had put her through.

Finally, she found the tomb's gaping mouth. Her heart ached from a deficit of iridio, the last droplet keeping her standing. She supposed that when she died tonight, she would deserve it.

A shadow moved within the overgrowth's darkness. A tiniebla, perhaps, so Reina unsheathed Ches's Blade with a holler. Then her eyes adjusted, and she saw it was Maior tiptoeing around the lagoon, Doña Laurel's ghost hovering like an ever-present sentinel.

Reina shuddered a cry and, in her exhaustion, fell to her knees before the woman, the blade falling beside her. Maior mimicked her, saying her name in warm relief. They threw their arms around each other, and Reina squeezed like she needed the proximity to breathe.

Maior's cheeks glistened from that mocking, relentless moonlight when they pulled away.

"Why weren't you in your room? I was looking for you—why are you here?"

Out of all the places, Maior was at the threshold of the most dangerous one.

"Can you get up?" Maior said, eyes on Reina's chest, keenly aware that Reina was operating on borrowed time.

Reina nodded a lie.

Maior helped Reina to her feet. "I felt her, Reina, that witch," she said as she massaged Reina with a numbing spell of galio. Reina closed her eyes, wishing she could lean into it, grateful. "I slipped in and out—"

"Slipped in and out?" Reina picked up the fallen blade and sheathed it.

"I blacked out, for a little bit, like I used to do in Águila Manor when she took me to see the caudillo."

Reina surveyed the greenery surrounding them. Her ears were sharp and alert for any unwanted presence, yet she heard nothing. Then Maior's meaning nestled in her belly like rotten food.

"I blacked out, and when I regained control of myself, I realized I was walking away from my room...like I was going to her. I—I was somewhere on the path when I came to, and I sort of recognized the way, but it was so dark. I didn't know which way was back to the mansion, so I just kept going forward. I ended up here." Maior dug her hands into her hair, her eyes terrified. She was scared.

As was Reina.

"So I hid behind the lagoon, where—" Her gaze shifted away from Reina, in a shame Reina didn't understand. She settled with pointing to the other side and said, "In those bushes over there. That's where I saw them."

Reina could hear the shudder of Maior's pulse. She reached for Maior's arm, then squeezed gently in case she needed the grounding.

It got the words out of her. "I saw Javier dragging Celeste inside."

The air left Reina as if she'd been punched in the gut. Her heart jolted, and she turned to the void-sucking blackness of the cavern.

Maior looked up with a grimace in her face, apprehensive. "So you're going to take me to your grandmother? And I don't have a have a say, again—"

"What? *No.*"

They watched each other in confusion. That was when it dawned on Reina: Maior didn't know the whole truth. Reina sucked in a deep breath. She shoved her bangs out of her face and gave Maior her back.

A hand grazed Reina's shoulder blade gingerly. "You're not taking me to your grandmother?"

"No!" Reina roared to the canopy. She was immediately ashamed of herself—for the outburst, for the lack of foresight delivering her exactly where her grandmother wanted her, for the tears uglifying her face. "Doña Ursulina lied to me! She said it was just an offering of blood—just a little bit: a cut on the hand, and it was done. But it's not the truth! She lied to get me to go along with all this. To invoke Rahmagut, the damas must die."

The shaking of her shoulders—she couldn't stop it. Fury bubbled up her throat, for playing as the pawn her grandmother always wanted. She wanted to scream it out, howl at the betrayal.

Maior's arms circled her waist. Reina stilled as the woman embraced her, squeezing from behind. It gave her the permission to breathe. She surrendered to the gesture. How Maior was a compass to her turbulence. How it grounded her.

"I would never do that to you," Reina admitted. "If I knew, I wouldn't have done this."

"I believe you."

They let go, and Reina fully faced her. She'd had her shame; now she needed to act.

"We have to go in, though," she said in a steady voice, even if she was all earthquakes and fissures on the inside.

"But that's what Doña Ursulina wants," Maior cried, pressing a palm to her heart.

Reina reduced the distance between them, towering over her so Maior would have no doubt of her conviction. Her gaze flickered to Maior's open lips, a treacherous desire for them assaulting her. But Reina quelled the urge by tightening her jaw, for it was the last thing she needed to be thinking about right now.

"I will not leave you alone. And I will not abandon Celeste. This is not negotiable."

The corners of Maior's eyes grew teary, her brows descending. Her lips moved like she had words in her but even she knew the futility.

"There's no time to take you back. And I don't know who else on this island she's roped into this. You are only safe with me." It was a truth Reina clung to like her life depended on it. Because this was all she had: to mend the mistake she'd made by trusting her grandmother. What life did she have after tonight? All that lay forward was Celeste's and Maior's. So she might as well die fighting.

Reina extended her palm. "Do you trust me?"

A breeze tickled the vegetation, loud in Maior's hesitation. Reina's veins thrummed, counting every passing second they wasted waiting on her decision. If the answer was a no, well, Reina also deserved that.

Maior sucked in a breath and exhaled, "I'll support you," before taking the hand Reina offered. "I'm here. I will help."

Her touch was cold and clammy, and Reina squeezed it as she allowed herself a smile hidden by the darkness.

She swiftly summoned a flame wisp and led the way into the cave. The incantation used up a fraction of her iridio with a sucking sensation, a ghost of the pain from when she ran low. But it was necessary. Iridio was going to be her guide forward. Reina could feel it, a tug beckoning her to the depths of the cavern.

The light revealed a tunnel carved within the mountain by artful hands. Fine, sculpted designs had been incised along the walls of nozariels, valcos, and winged yares in rudimentary activities: fishing, sewing, harvesting crops, throwing clay, conquering territories. There was also carved symbology of suns, moons, antlers, bat wings, bull horns, and snake ouroboroses spiraling into a void. Some images depicted people turning into bovines turning into tinieblas. Now faded and crumbling from generations of abandonment, the limestone was ragged where it ought not to be, smooth where there used to be definition. The air was stagnant and pungent with decay, the Tierra'e Sol humidity keeping the walls moist. As the flame wisp lapped the tunnel in orange light, encasing them, it revealed a twisting, descending path of black.

The tunnel groaned, as if the mountain stirred above them. Spooked, Maior clutched Reina by the arm in a cold grip, drawing closer. The flame wisp guided them as they crossed the entryway to a vast chamber decorated in statues of stone. They were carved in the shape of people and furniture. A throne room, with no exit or path forward, or at least not one they could immediately see.

"What's that?" Maior said as she walked to the wall across the chamber, where she ran her hands along the roughness of the stone.

Upon closer look Reina realized the walls were embedded with faint shimmering veins. Not with gems in form or contexture but lines carved in and around the wall, with the faintest trail of iridio encrusted to the wall, twinkling like stars. A tether formed between it and her heart as her palm grazed the rough surface. Underneath her touch, the wall breathed. For a moment she could visualize every pathway and chamber carved underneath this very mountain.

"Turn off the fire?" Maior suggested.

"I don't need the light to see. I was only keeping it on for you. Chicken."

Maior gave her a look, and Reina complied, chuckling.

The darkness ate them a second time. Nothing happened at first. Not until Reina listened to her instincts and pushed the magic of her chest forward. Through veins of pumping blood. Through her bones to flesh. Then, like a servant, the chamber reacted to her command.

Veins of blue iridio became the light that revealed the chamber to them. It flowed from her palm to the walls and ceiling, hissing with the whispers of every iridio spell ever cast.

Reina flinched when Maior reached for her chest. "Your iridio—" the human said, her hand finishing the journey and pressing against the fabric over Reina's heart. "Are you all right to do this?"

Maior knew the consequences as painfully as Reina did.

"It wants us to follow it."

Maior followed her around the statues, the blue lines directing them to an opening in the chamber, hidden behind the statue of the throne and its caudillo. The doorway was open, the stone door shoved to the side, left ajar by those who'd come before them.

"Down there," Reina said.

Beyond the door, the lines wrapped around the walls and down a spiraling stone staircase.

They rushed down the stairs, emerging at a pitch-black opening where the blue geomancia abandoned them entirely. Reina summoned another flame, a weak thing bright enough to light only a small perimeter of this new chamber. Ahead was an arched pathway made by two rows of pillars, the history of the chamber recorded in the pictographs and ancient writing carved onto its stone, moss crawling up the base. From beneath the bridge came the soft trickling sound of spring water.

Carved sarcophagi sat on elevated pedestals near the entryway, and Reina circled them to get a sense of the hall's size. She froze at the sound of a kicked pebble, then hoofed footsteps, followed by a guttural growl; her heart sank at the realization. This chamber had tinieblas.

Maior heard it, too, and gasped aloud, alerting them to her.

Reina shoved Maior out of the way just as a limber grinning goat rushed them with a swiping claw. She met the tiniebla with Ches's Blade, which was dull in the chamber's darkness. The shrill clash rang in Reina's ear, and she shoved forward with a grunt, cleaving the tiniebla in two. In two seconds, it was over, but the sounds stirred the dozen other tinieblas prowling the vicinity.

Maior ran behind the sarcophagi, shaking Reina's concentration, and the meek flame snuffed out. Reina didn't have a chance to summon another one. One breath later she had to jump out of the way as another ravenous tiniebla came slashing at her, fangs snapping and foamy spittle sprinkling her boots and arms. Fear screamed in her veins as the creature swung with its curved talons. She slashed back, screaming with the weight of her body to banish the tiniebla.

Her heart fractured at the sound of Maior's screams.

"Maior!"

Reina summoned a second light as Maior's footsteps alerted more tinieblas to the sarcophagi. A bipedal monster pursued Maior to the other side of the bridge, which she crossed without realizing more awaited her on the other side. Two tinieblas, to be exact, grinning at the prospect of easy prey.

Reina leapt after her, calling her name, and landed badly on her ankle.

Her flame unveiled the dark just as a tiniebla was about to shred through Maior's abdomen. Reina threw herself at it. Both stumbled to the ground, her forearms skinning against the stone floor and her blade sliding out of her grip. Ancient dust stuffed her nostrils.

Instead of her belly, the tiniebla slit Maior's arm open, and Maior shrieked.

Fear like acid filled Reina's throat.

She desperately punched the tiniebla, which wrestled her, claws tearing through both her shirt and shoulder. Swallowing the pain, she fumbled for the fallen blade. Once she caught a grip of it, she hacked the snapping tiniebla into nothingness.

Maior fled from the second tiniebla, leaving a river of blood in her wake.

Reina howled in utter frustration. She vaulted to the stupid human, snatching her up before she could run any farther away. And Maior fought her, confusing her for the enemy. She kicked and bit and nearly deafened Reina with her screams.

Reina pressed her to her chest with one arm, whirling the blade with the other, slicing left and right to stop the tinieblas from having a go at them. Then she seized the first opportunity to leap atop one of the many elevated sarcophagi, out of reach.

"*Stop!*" Reina screamed at her.

Maior did stop, but she shook like a branch at the mercy of a hurricane, realizing she wasn't in immediate danger anymore. The sticky hotness of her blood trickled between them, drenching their clothes.

"Use the galio to close yourself." Reina's voice trembled.

"What?" Maior whimpered.

"Now! This is what being a healer means. *Use the galio on yourself*," Reina commanded.

Maior shakily stepped back, almost tripping off the sarcophagus. Of course Reina caught her. What she didn't foresee was a tiniebla lunging up just as Maior summoned the healing spell.

Time snailed to a stop. With a gasp, Reina predicted it before it happened: the tiniebla's talons ripping through the infuriatingly tender flesh of Maior's neck.

Except a white light sprang out of Maior's chest, blinding them. The light flew forward, creating a barrier between them and the lunging demon. The Benevolent Lady materialized inside the barrier. She stood unflinching, right at the barrier's threshold, staring out at the vast chamber and its tinieblas like she had stood that night at Gegania.

Reina's mouth hung open at the sight. She swung around, about to chastise Maior for not doing this sooner, and saw her as an unconscious crumpled heap over the sarcophagus.

"Maior!" Reina crouched, gathering her in her arms. Had Maior lost that much blood? She ran the back of her fingers against Maior's cheek, feeling her warmth. Then Doña Laurel's apparition drew her gaze.

This was exactly how Maior had fainted on Gegania's grounds, when Doña Laurel had manifested to protect her.

Doña Laurel's potent light skinned the blackness from the chamber, revealing it to be a vast hollow in the earth. The ceiling was at the very least fifty feet high, erupted in stalactites. Ahead, past cobbled steps and a multitude of elevated sarcophagi, was an arched doorway.

It was the only way forward and the only way to Celeste.

Reina gathered Maior's body like a bundle of fragile glass. She shoved herself into the air, leaping away from the tinieblas, which were stunned by the Benevolent Lady's light. Reina sprinted to the doorway, meeting yet another tunnel.

Suddenly the chamber behind her shook in a thunderous explosion. Reina whipped around in time to see Doña Laurel's light incinerating every last tiniebla.

Reina bowed her head in gratitude—her sight spotted in flares from the light—then turned into the tunnel, allowing its darkness to swallow them whole. Soon after, Maior began stirring in her arms.

"Reina?" Her voice came out groggy and broken.

"You're all right," Reina reassured her, her heart still thrumming in her chest.

Maior moaned about her arm. About the pain. So Reina gently let her down before summoning the light of a flame. It filled the tunnel, revealing Maior alert and bloodstained but *safe*.

Reina sighed in relief. "Don't ever run away from me like that again," she said as Maior cast the stitching galio incantation.

"That wasn't my intention. I just couldn't see anything—including the tinieblas."

"If I ever make it out of here, I will teach you bismuto," Reina said with a nod. At this point, it was a necessity. She helped her up and allowed her to keep her arm as support.

"Are you able to control what you did back there, with the Benevolent Lady?"

The question only drew a deep frown from Maior.

"Fine," Reina replied stiffly.

Voices drifted from the other end of the tunnel, faint and inaudible if not for Reina's burning bismuto: a guttural one, and Doña Ursulina's.

Reina armored her heart in steel.

"Maybe it's best if you stay here. I'll go in there and bring Celeste out," she told Maior, who moaned something about tinieblas. But they both knew it was a moot point, in the wake of Doña Laurel's ghost.

Reina walked alone to the end of the tunnel, where dim firelight pooled from the large passageway. The tunnel spat her out into a grand circular sanctum of carved stone. Its walls were rippled, as if layers of lava had descended the walls to meet the ground. But at a second glance, it became clear: The rippled stone was actually sculpted shapes of people. Bent heads and limbs, agonizing and reaching for salvation as the ground sucked them into the Void. A gruesome depiction of what had happened or what would. Lining those walls were the brutally wrought candelabra giving the sanctum its orange light. A stone bridge connected the entrance to the large elevated dais in the middle, where Doña Ursulina stood before two opposing statues. The first was an upright man with billowing robes and a clean-shaven head. He aimed a blade not unlike Reina's to the ceiling, where the design of a sun had been carved onto the smooth domed stone. The second statue, the one Doña Ursulina faced, was of a man sitting on a throne, his face resting lazily upon his fist and his eyes shut. The statues of Ches and Rahmagut.

Surrounding the statues and Doña Ursulina were seven squirming women gagged and pinned to the ground by gnarling roots shooting out from the earth circling the dais. The roots radiated in the signature blue of Doña Ursulina's geomancia. Finally, seven amalgamated tinieblas stood like jailers behind the women, frozen on standby. Doña Ursulina's puppets.

Reina bared her teeth in a sneer, even if it didn't surprise her to see what Doña Ursulina was capable of. Controlling tinieblas was but a natural progression to all the lines she'd crossed with void magic.

Reina entered the sanctum just as Javier threw a thrashing Celeste on the ground beside one of the pinned damas. Reina watched, with her breath held, as he climbed on top of Celeste to hold her down, on all fours like a feline, overcoming her strength in a way Reina never imagined possible for him. He was shirtless, his body oozing with a black smoke that wormed in and out of him.

Doña Ursulina heard Reina's footsteps and turned to the entryway, the sight opening up her face with delight. "There you are. I was beginning to wonder if you were going to make it in time." She was dressed in a tight-fitting jacket and trousers, all midnight black save for the puffy white collar around her neck. Her sable hair was tightly wrapped in a braided bun. She was a condor in human form, long fingernails resembling talons. "You came with the girl from Apartaderos, I hope?" she asked with a minuscule tilt of her head.

"Reina!" Celeste screamed, her eyes dilating in what could easily be confused for betrayal. But Reina knew her, and distantly, she could see the relief in that look.

"Did you really have to slay my tinieblas out there? I was having them guard the sanctum, in case the Liberator decided to meddle."

They assumed she was here for the invocation.

An acrid anger sprouted in Reina's belly. It made her want to retch at their feet. "Where's Don Enrique?"

Doña Ursulina raised a flippant hand. "On the mainland. Let's just say I managed to convince him that an unwanted valco's a lot more conspicuous than a condor."

The black bird she had seen on the boat ride to the island. Doña Ursulina had awaited them all along.

"He trusts you to get what he wants?"

"He may. But we are only doing this for ourselves."

Reina swallowed the bitter fact, letting it pile on the list of things her grandmother had planned. All moves in her elaborate scheme.

Reina approached under the guise of her allyship, her heart fracturing with every one of Celeste's pleads and cries.

"Well? Bring the girl already so I can begin this!" Doña Ursulina barked as she approached the dama to her left with a small ornate dagger. "The god and master of the Void is waiting."

The chamber breathed in anticipation. Reina could feel it in the quivering iridio solution of her transplant heart, like someone or something was indeed listening.

Reina waited for the moment when Doña Ursulina knelt by the first crying dama before leaping on Javier. She threw the entirety of her weight into tackling him away from Celeste, who followed her cue, reading her mind and rising.

Javier snarled, his voice warped and wrong as his shoulder left a streak of blood on the stone. He gathered himself up, retrieving his sword, but Reina was quicker, yanking Celeste by the arm and leading the escape out of the sanctum.

Behind them, Doña Ursulina exclaimed in annoyance just as her knife sliced a line of bursting red on the first dama.

Reina dared not look back. She dared not give herself the luxury of worrying for the other women, for every part of her knew that if she ever hesitated in her objective, in saving Celeste and Maior, she was going to end up with no one alive.

Dusty, stale air rushed her lungs as she pushed herself farther, every stride searing her legs. Celeste squeezed her hand in return. And when Reina looked back to meet her gaze, soaring at the possibility of getting away, she saw Javier in focused pursuit. His eyes were inundated with black, his grin wicked in a way it had never been before. Reina's instincts screamed at her, like a chill grabbing her by the neck and yanking her spine. It stirred a fear she had long learned how to ignore—an irrational reaction that had no place awakening from the mere sight of him. Her fear for tinieblas.

He sprinted in mad pursuit with his sword in hand, unlocking and utilizing every ounce of muscle in his body. A focused, perverse hunter. He caught up to them just as they neared the other end of the tunnel where Maior awaited.

Reina withdrew the golden blade as he passed them. But he kept going, stopping in front of them and blocking their exit. Reina and Celeste had no choice but to stop as well, side by side, Reina's chest imploding at all the awful possibilities as this man stood between her and Maior.

"Javier, you monster!" Celeste said between splutters for breath. To Reina she said, "You see that, right? He looks like a tiniebla."

So that was where her fear came from. His face was wrong because Javier was wrong.

"Who knows what he did to himself," Celeste spat, giving him her back as she arched her hands to summon her iridio scythe. "Unfortunately for him, if there's one thing we know how to do, it's to banish tinieblas."

Javier never uttered a word in reply. Still smiling, he flashed toward her, obliterating the distance between them. He drove the tip of his sword through her lower back, shoving it all the way through in a burst of red like the hibiscuses around the Liberator's manse.

In that fragment of a second, the world froze. Javier's ear-to-ear smile; Celeste's gaping mouth; the sharp scent of iron erupting from her core. Reina took it all in with a half-formed gasp, her hands reaching for thin air, coming a second too late to stop Javier.

She was trapped in a dream—in a terrible nightmare. It couldn't be real...

"I'm tired of you running," he said in that warped voice. "Your blood *will* spill with the other ones' tonight." Then he yanked the length of the sword out, and the burst of blood—of Celeste's life—made it a reality.

Celeste fell to the floor with a muted exhale, her scythe disintegrating in her hand. Reina flew to her.

"You bastard!" she bellowed as she cradled Celeste's trembling form in her arms, both their hands fumbling against gushing red to keep the bleeding contained.

Javier's wicked chuckles were his only regard. "Thank you for bringing them here," he said, turning to Maior, who was frozen in shock. "Now let us take them to the sanctum to complete the offering."

Reina's heart fissured and opened like the gaping hole in Celeste's core, torn at the two equally terrible options before her:

She could toss aside Celeste—and her life—and rush to Maior's rescue.

Or she could idly watch as Javier carved a hole through Maior's belly, spilling her blood for his god.

In the end, Reina's hesitation made the choice for her.

Javier swiveled for Maior with his red-stained sword in a determined two-handed grip. A thrust, and it would be over—

"*STOP!*" said a fourth voice, feminine and determined. "I command it!"

And like a puppet listening to its master, Javier stopped.

40

Hand to Hand

Javier's face screwed in agonized concentration—in a fight with himself—but he was an immobile, catatonic object.

Reina glanced at the tunnel's entryway, bewildered, and saw a disheveled Eva doubled over, her body heaving with shaking pants. Like she had sprinted across universes to stop Javier in this moment. Only she had come a second too late.

Panicked, Reina focused on Celeste, her entire *core* wishing this to be a nightmare. All she had to do was wake up and see Celeste safe, healthy, and whole. But the reality was that no matter how hard she pressed on the opening or how much she spread her hands to drape over the wound, the blood never stopped flowing. She was a useless tourniquet. A useless friend. A useless protector.

Hot, blind panic swelled within her, growing in waves and clogging any chance of her ever breathing again. Reina trembled as Celeste's warm blood soaked her hands and trousers, so warm and once alive, the smell so strong she tasted it in her mouth.

Someone skidded to a stop next to her, tried shoving her away from Celeste. Yet Reina fought them. Tears blurred her vision, and confusion welled around her, but the last thing Reina wanted to do was let go. That was when her name registered, screamed by Maior's lips.

Reina wiped the tears away, smearing her face with Celeste's blood, and realized the person pushing her was Maior, hands twisting and turning, Reina's bismuto revealing the lilac of her geomancia.

"Heal her!" Reina barked, raising Celeste's frame as she understood Maior's intentions. "Now!" Without Rahmagut, there was no spell or incantation to bring someone back from the dead.

The dead.

Reina sobbed again.

It was now or never.

"Save Celeste." Her swelling tears blurred her vision, and Reina hated herself all the more. She was going to miss these last few moments with Celeste.

"I—I think—I don't know—I don't know if it'll work—"

Reina cursed Maior. "Save her! Use your galio—do something!"

Maior's hands spread and kneaded, her brows knitting in deep concentration. The magic slithered into Celeste's clothes, but there was no visible change in her. If anything, her face dulled.

Reina wanted to scream at Maior. "Please, be useful for once—"

"Reina." Celeste's soft voice cut through her climbing rage. Her blue eyes glistened, not in pain, but a bit sleepy, a bit gone.

Reina's own tears threatened to blur the image of her in this final moment. "Please hold on," she whimpered. "You'll be all right." It was a lie Reina was willing to believe and live by, if it meant it would give Celeste the slimmest chance to make it through. "Just hold on. We—we have galio. The bleeding—it stopped."

"I'm so sleepy."

"Celeste."

"I just want to close my eyes."

"No!"

Celeste took a big inhale and carried on. "I'm so glad...I'm so glad we shared the amapolas. I'm so glad our fates were bound, even for a little bit."

Everything she said sounded like a goodbye. Reina didn't want to hear it. This wasn't it. It couldn't be it.

"If it meant being in your arms now," Celeste said in the softest of voices.

"Maior, *save her*."

Reina sobbed. But to Celeste, it didn't matter. She smiled while her lids closed. Then even the smile faded.

Reina pressed her bloody fingers against Celeste's neck, praying for a pulse. But her hands were too shuddery—too shaken. She dropped her head to Celeste's wet chest, which was still so warm.

Maior's arms wrapped around Reina, trying to ground her. This time it did nothing.

Reina couldn't breathe. The heat and shame clogged her throat. Everything was so wrong, so wrong, so wrong—*it hurt*.

Eventually Javier's and Eva's voices yanked Reina from that suffocating ocean. In fact, the *reminder* of Javier was what pulled her out. White-hot anger invaded her chest, flaring from her belly up.

Reina took in a big inhale. She peeled Maior's arms off her and laid Celeste down, gently, because she deserved the treatment of a petal.

Across the tunnel, Eva called Javier a monster, but his mien had changed. He was on his knees, pleading, like he was someone other than the devil who'd impaled Celeste. To Reina, it didn't matter.

Maior also rose, backing away. But Reina hardly noticed when she began walking to the sanctum.

Eva screamed something at Reina—which never registered in her mind—and went after Maior.

Reina let the touch of the blade's hilt fill her senses. She let it tether to her being like an extension of her appendage. She had no sense or inkling of how much iridio was left in her heart. What she knew, much like how she knew hunger or pain, was that the iridio was flooding every inch of her being. She was the iridio, and the iridio was her. Reina basked in the throb of the geomancia, embraced the swell of muscle mass, uncaring of whether this would be her last.

With one swift slash, she cleaved the air where Javier had stood a split second prior. The bastard had reacted—heard her midswipe—quick enough to whirl away.

But when there was nothing but hatred in Reina's core, it was easy for her to become as fast as Javier.

It was easy to turn into that same monster.

"Wait—listen to me!" Javier said, with such nerve that Reina swung at him again, howling, the entirety of her weight on the strike.

Javier swiveled away, reaching for his fallen sword to shield himself at the last moment.

"You killed her. Your niece. *Your blood.*"

"It wasn't me. I wasn't me." Javier's voice shook, his eyes glistening.

Reina swung at him again, backing Javier against the tunnel wall.

"Please understand: All this time I've been battling a curse."

"Save your filthy lies!" Reina couldn't wait for the moment when she got to slice off his tongue. When she could rob him of his good looks and of his life.

"And I still am!" Javier went on. "Because of Laurel, I'm doomed to become a tiniebla."

Red swamped her eyes. "Don't you do dare soil Doña Laurel's name," Reina spat. "You're a scheming rat. And you deserve to be brutalized like you brutalized Celeste." She leapt again, swinging the blade down in a vertical line, and hissed when Javier rolled away.

"You can't kill me—I'm on your side—" Finally, Javier began countering with his own swings. "Doña Ursulina is killing the other ones."

One, two, three slashes, the clang of steel echoing through the tunnel.

"Without my help, you won't be able to stop her from taking Maior. You want to save her, don't you?"

The clear, distilled rage gave Reina the quickness of feet, of arm, to deflect each strike with Ches's weapon.

Javier reduced his reach, tricking her into lunging for a close slice to his kidneys, and brought down the hilt of his sword on her wrist before her blade could even graze his clothes. She huffed, pain exploding from her wrist, and was stunned as Javier used the close proximity to knee her hand.

Reina lost grip of the blade. It flew into the air, swiveling once, twice, then clanging against the ground.

"Please stop," Javier begged.

Reina pivoted to him with a snarl. She didn't care. She had nothing else to lose. She had the memory of Celeste, of her smiles, and of her fast-escaping blood.

And she had her rage.

Reina charged. When Javier thrust at her to keep her at a distance, Reina seized the blade with her left hand. Acid shot up her arm as the sharp-edged steel slit her palm.

She ground her teeth from the agony. With a roar she yanked Javier by the sword. She brought him close enough that her right fist contacted his sword-wielding left wrist. And the impact sang with the crack of bones.

Javier bellowed as he lost grip of the hilt. It was an opportunity Reina seized to send the blade flying away from his reach.

Javier tried leaping after it, but Reina tackled him down. They fell hard onto stone, wrestling, punching, her tail slapping him in the face, their limbs skinning against the ground as both rolled farther away from either blade.

Reina punched him on the temple. Javier's knee met her gut and knocked the air out of her—a blazing eruption at her very core. Reina doubled over, vision going black. For a split second, she imagined Javier striking her, but when the blow never came, she opened her eyes and saw him crawling for his blade.

Reina grabbed him by the legs, grappling him desperately. She used her weight as a pivot and swung him to the opposite wall, screaming.

Javier crashed against it. And Reina scrambled to him, dominant hand fisted, and she *punched*.

The world ruptured and split around her, pain bursting from her knuckles to her wrist and up her elbow as Javier moved away at the very last instant. Instead of his skull, Reina's fist dented the wall behind him.

"You backstabbing snake," Reina hissed.

Javier's forehead smashing against Reina's was his reply.

Reina climbed on him and pinned her forearm to his neck.

The rat kicked and pulled her braid and raked clawlike finger-nails along Reina's arm, his cheeks becoming blue. All to no avail.

"You don't deserve mercy," Reina said close to Javier's ears, her voice wet from tears, spit, and blood. Her tail thrashed from side to side—a whip on his legs.

"Please—I didn't mean to."

Reina compressing on his trachea was his reward.

"Please," he spluttered.

"That's why you came with us!" Reina barked. "To do away with her the moment you had the chance!" She let the rage swallow her. She let it burn through her lungs until the ire charred her good sense.

Celeste was gone. It was all for nothing.

"Please—" Javier spouted, "I was cursed—it took over—I—I woke up, and I had her blood on my hands."

Shut up, Reina thought.

"This—this wasn't how it was meant to happen. Your grandmother—"

Shut up.

"Doña Ursulina lied to all of us—"

"Stop talking!"

Javier dug his nails into the bleeding opening of Reina's left palm. Fire licked the length of her arm. She screamed and sprang to her feet but never gave Javier the chance to recover. Her boot thudded into his side. Over and over and over, even after the sound of a crunch. Even after he sucked in a breath and his eyes closed, shedding bloody tears.

Reina fetched Ches's golden blade, his coughs and splutters and wheezes for air guiding her back like a waltz. She raised it above him, hatred blurring the corners of her eyes as she watched the mangle of limbs that he was. Still, his chest rose and fell, life ebbing inside him.

Her own breathing was wild, panicked, but she couldn't make her shaking hands bring the blade down. Her muscles screamed, as did her heart.

She found it pointless, to take his sniveling, worthless life.

Or maybe she was a coward, both useless in protecting Celeste and in avenging—

"Reina!"

A voice cleaved right through her self-loathing.

Exhausted, she turned and saw Eva.

Eva trembled. Perhaps she saw Reina for what she was: a monster.

Eva took in the bodies strewn across the tunnel. Both valco. Both covered in blood. "Maior," she said.

Reina paused, the shrill of panic coursing through her once again. Reina turned this way and that, desperately searching the shadowed tunnel. Her heart fractured. "Where is she?"

"She walked to the sanctum—I literally could not stop her. Doña Ursulina can take control of the woman in Maior—of Celeste's mother. I tried to keep her here, but—it was like she was possessed. She kept on going."

"And you just let her go by herself?"

"Please help," Eva begged.

41

The Choice of Family

Reina and Eva sprang back to the sanctum, leaving the mangled Javier and Celeste in the tunnel. All the while Reina's heart was a rupturing star, its every thump a sear of fire. Maior was out there, enthralled, and entirely alone.

Reina couldn't be this useless, to also fail Maior.

She flared her iridio—every last droplet of what she had to give. She was so close to running out, but she was also so done being afraid. The strength of each stride doubled, her muscles tired but thrumming, her lungs aching but determined. To her surprise, Eva caught up to her paces a moment later, like she was burning through enhancing bismuto herself.

Doña Ursulina's voice flowed from the entryway. "There's my girl," she said. "Now, you, we must keep your body intact so the caudillo can shut up about his wife once and for all."

Reina lunged out of the passageway in a spurt of panic. As soon as she emerged into the chamber, she saw Maior about to cross the stone bridge to the dais with Doña Ursulina and her small legion of tinieblas. Staining her grandmother's black boots was a lagoon of blood—the combined lives of the seven women she'd slaughtered.

The sanctum resonated with a hundred hushed voices murmuring in fervent tongues. The whisperings of Reina's heart, only this time they weren't coming from within her. The gleeful prayers and disagreeable conversations. The hissing and hemming. They drowned the domed chamber, and Reina could only assume they were the proof of the invocation.

Only one life remained.

Maior stepped onto the bridge, her steps sluggish and unnatural, as if each was a battle of wills. One she lost every time.

"Maior!" Reina's scream was a thunder, echoing back to her. It was a gamble she had to take. And to her immense relief, Maior stopped.

The whispering paused, as if witnessing the unfolding events, amused. The silence was a brief thing, engulfing the sanctum as Reina met Doña Ursulina's unfazed gaze. Reina hoped her grandmother could see the disgust contorting her face. There was no hiding anymore. She needn't Doña Ursulina's approval or anyone else's. For she carried no fear—and how could she, after failing Celeste?

Doña Ursulina pocketed a hand and produced a glittering ore from her jacket, which she raised in offering between them. The shape was familiar, designed to fit perfectly in the crevice sitting between Reina's lungs. "Come, Reina, you have earned this."

"I don't want it," Reina spat.

Doña Ursulina tilted her head and went on. "Now bring Maior over, and Celeste. Where is she? Her blood was spilled already—I felt it. Bring her here in case her body needs to be on the dais. I've already started the invocation." She took a deep breath through the nostrils, loudly, making a show of it. "Feel the gods and how they listen. Feel Rahmagut's anticipation."

Indeed, the heady energy, it was suffocating. Reina didn't pretend to rejoice. She didn't react to the static lifting her arm hairs or the way the last sliver of iridio in her heart shuddered in sick expectation. This was a reward she didn't want, for the lives it had cost.

"There will be no more deaths tonight," Reina said, curling one hand and stretching the other holding the blade. Her muscles cramped and creaked. Her skin itched from an abundance of gashes. She was a sluggish creature, the last of her iridio enfeebling her. Yet she welcomed every ache and discomfort. Compared to what she'd allowed Celeste and Maior to go through, she deserved it.

Doña Ursulina's smug satisfaction amalgamated with doubt, then turned into disdain. "Oh? On what authority?"

Reina crossed the bridge to Maior. She grabbed her by the wrist roughly, to shake some sense into her. And it worked. Maior sucked in a big draft of air, snapping out of the trance.

"What are you doing?" Doña Ursulina hissed.

"Reina, *help*," Maior said in a voice that made Reina's insides weak.

Maior grabbed her by the sides, as if Reina were her pillar and Reina squeezed her back. She took in a sniff of her hair, the earthy musk reminding her of all those moments in Gegania, when Maior had been safe and Reina had believed she deserved betterment for her life. There was no time for the embrace, and the fury at her disobedience only built in Doña Ursulina's eyes, but Reina allowed it for herself. Even if she didn't say the words, it was her form of goodbye.

"Go to Eva," Reina whispered close to Maior's ear.

The human shuddered, but the time for objections had long passed.

"Oh, no, you won't," Doña Ursulina snarled. "You will bring her to me." She raised a hand like a talon, and the seven tinieblas guarding the corpses behind her awoke from their stupor. Intention gleamed in their black eyes. They laughed, a hundred superimposed voices, then stampeded toward Reina.

Reina grabbed her blade in a white-knuckled two-handed grip, her heart thrumming to a frenzied beat, bracing herself against all seven shadows. But the tinieblas rerouted before they even touched the bridge. They turned on each other and on Doña Ursulina, disobeying her command.

No—obeying Eva.

Apprehension quaked through Reina as she glanced to the sanctum's entryway and saw Eva standing much like the statues of Ches and Rahmagut, with her arm outstretched, her fingers curved liked talons and her eyes flooded in inky black.

Doña Ursulina had no choice but to banish the tinieblas herself.

Either way, it bought enough time for Maior to reach Eva and the semblance of safety.

Maior called for Reina to follow, which Reina ignored.

"The invocation has begun. Rahmagut's power is flooding this tomb. Finish the job you were tasked to do," Doña Ursulina said icily, her brows raised and the lines of her mouth in a deep bend. "Did you forget our conditions?"

"No."

"You will die without your ore." When Reina gave no answer, Doña Ursulina went on. "Maybe you think you will find the iridio to refill today or tomorrow. But it will run out eventually. You need iridio, and you need the Águilas; therefore you need me."

The witch took one leisurely step after another toward the bridge, leaving the imprint of blood on the flagstones. Reina's mouth tasted of copper and exhaustion, but she was going to hold on. She needed to, for however long it took for Eva to escort Maior out of the tomb, to safety.

"You have been using me since the moment I came to Águila Manor," Reina said, shaking her head. "You don't care if I live or die. I'm just another nobody in your eyes."

Doña Ursulina rose an index finger between them, her other hand armed with the knife. "Yes, you came to me as a useless nobody, but I trained you to be something more. I saved your life!"

She marched up to the bridge, and Reina lifted her blade higher, her breaths coming in shallow. Doña Ursulina stopped halfway with a confused frown, meeting resistance. She cupped a palm to press against the empty air, revealing the rippling golden light of a litio barrier with Eva's signature written all over it. Doña Ursulina pushed, but the protection was impervious to her. With this distraction, Eva had bought them a sliver longer of time.

"You didn't need to spell my heart like you spelled Maior to turn us into your puppets!" The moment under the Páramo rain when Doña Ursulina had wrenched the ore from her chest blazed through Reina's memories. She had experienced that same loss of free will—the impotence of an unresponsive body under that woman's command. "You invited me to cross the Páramo even though you *knew* the risks of me coming to you by myself."

"Please—"

"But yes, I suppose I can't blame that one on you. That was on me, for not trusting my father's hatred for you."

Darkness shrouded Doña Ursulina's gaze.

"He never wanted anything to do with you, and I should have followed his lead. But I was foolish in coming to you and thinking I deserved to have a family—" Reina's voice shattered as the urge to cry returned. She pointed a finger at her grandmother, howling, "You saved my life, but it was always conditional! You always planned to keep me as a tool and not as the person I am."

"I am doing this for Juan Vicente—*for* the family we used to be—to have everything we were denied. I only saved you because you are my granddaughter. Do you really think I would bother with a pitiful little duskling otherwise?"

"I may be your granddaughter, but I am nothing like you. I never would have done any of this if I knew the truth—"

"But you were perfectly fine doing it when you believed it was only a trickle of blood," Doña Ursulina said, the derision blurring the edges of her words into laughter. "You were perfectly fine kidnapping the women and imprisoning them in Enrique's dungeons."

"I did it because I thought your approval was worth it!" Reina didn't care if her cheeks were streaked with tears. She didn't care if her transplant threatened to drill her chest open. "I thought everyone else was wrong about you—I thought they were just afraid of the geomancia you craft from iridio." She waved a hand at the corpses growing cold over the dais. "But for you there's no line." She was Doña Ursulina's descendant. She was nozariel. But she was not wicked, and she was not going to stand for this any longer.

"*And you think there's a line for the Águilas?*" Doña Ursulina's voice thundered across the chamber and bounced off the smooth ceiling. "Do you really value the life of their beloved brat so much you would rather defy me and die with your pitiful, deficient heart? I told you Rahmagut could solve this for you!"

"Celeste didn't deserve this—"

"And you believe she deserved everything else she had? The manor, the gold, the fame of her name? Where do you think that iridio came from?"

"The mine—"

"*The mine?*" This time her laughter came unrestrained. No—her cackles. "Feleva got all she did because she slaughtered nine women in this same blood-damned tomb forty-two years ago!"

There was no worthy reply, just apprehension as Doña Ursulina's shoulders shook as if the pillar keeping her together all these years was finally crumbling. "How did I know this sacrifice would be true? That Rahmagut would listen and give me exactly what I asked of him? Because *I* helped Feleva drag nine women into this tomb, *all* kicking and biting and fighting, when we were just your age. She slit their necks and spilled their blood to invoke Rahmagut. And he replied. He thanked her for the weakening of his seal, and he granted her exactly what she asked for in the form of all that iridio: wealth, fame, power. She was ambitious, yes, but it all fell in her lap, *thanks to my help*."

"Feleva?" Reina breathed.

Her expression brought Doña Ursulina great amusement. "We grew up together, did you know?" She ran a hand along the dusty smooth stone railing of the bridge. "We were friends—rivals—*lovers*. We were light and darkness; beauty and strength; the pioneering conqueresses of our generation." The glow in her eyes was unmissable. A blue afterimage of power brimming for an outlet. "She promised it would be ours—all of it. We were going to be together. We were going to have children."

Reina almost uttered her father's name, but she needn't. Doña Ursulina saw the intention in her eyes and nodded.

"Enrique and Juan Vicente, half brothers. But she forbade me from speaking the truth. She inscribed her name in the history books as the sole discoverer of the iridio. And I let her. I loved her." Her voice broke, and Reina understood the pure, distilled indignation. The scorn of never being good enough. "And that was my folly, believing it wouldn't have an impact on the way people treated me. Because of our blood, she always saw us differently, and she raised her despicable valco son to believe he was the sole heir of her fortune. Enrique never treated your father as equal. He never gave us our due. Not even after the revolution ousted Segol's government. He didn't even acknowledge how we'd helped him build a healthy distribution of iridio all over Venazia and Fedria, hooking every geomancer on its power. The Águilas grew richer, and Juan Vicente was so fed up that he left." She took a deep breath, her curling palm raised as she summoned that terrible void magic.

Reina's grip on the blade—it weakened. She stared at her feet as her chest wrung itself into knots. "So Celeste and I...?" she muttered.

"You share human blood."

"Did she know?"

Doña Ursulina shook her head. "Enrique never took the word *brother* for its literal meaning. And Feleva wasn't happy with how it came to be. But that is not a tale I owe you." She could have spat the answer, and it wouldn't have made a difference. "And all this time, Enrique has had the nerve to see me as his subordinate, the fool. My power goes beyond Feleva's, for I am alive, and she is not. I evolved and perfected. Now, tell me, do you ever hear the Duvianos name in the tales and histories of the revolution? Do you ever hear my name mentioned with the same regard as Feleva's? No, you hear it spat out, calling me a witch of void magic while they glorify her as a heroine for *those antlers* and the iridio Rahmagut granted her when she was a killer all along!" She pressed a palm to her chest, mocking. "So *I'm* the one supposed to be deterred by arbitrary lines? I don't think so."

She sheathed her knife and dug her hands into Eva's barrier, grappling, her gloves tearing and taking flesh and blood along with them. "I waited all these years for the return of Rahmagut's Claw. Now it's my turn to claim the reward. *I* shall become a witch of the Void. *I* shall unseal Rahmagut and smite Enrique for all his transgressions when the time comes. His daughter becoming a Dama del Vacío? It's nothing more than a joke from the gods."

With a howl, Doña Ursulina tugged the barrier's framework, her body flaring black and blue as she pulled Eva's litio barrier apart. The indomitable energy around Doña Ursulina became a prism of violent blues, swirling like a black plume. The stench of decay filled the chamber as the barrier opened. It was like Reina was staring death in the eyes.

"I don't care how much you think you deserve this. You won't kill Maior," Reina said. Otherwise she was going to lose her nerve.

Having disintegrated the barrier, Doña Ursulina extended a hand as a gust eddied around it.

The bite of her magic infected the air. Reina almost recoiled. She was back in Águila Manor, tense and powerless, Doña Ursulina's influence threatening her for obedience. It wrapped around her transplant heart, squeezing, to command her.

"You're going to stop me?" Doña Ursulina took in the length of Reina, all cuts and bruises and torn clothes. "*You?* The creature I groomed to serve *me*?" Doña Ursulina snarled, corrupted and beastly. The spells of her beauty and youth rippled and faltered, for the briefest seconds revealing a wrinkled woman in her sixth decade, with a face marred by evil magic. As quickly as it wavered, the glamour snapped back into place.

"I don't belong to you!" Reina yelled back, fighting, her limbs becoming unresponsive and catatonic.

"We shall see about that," Doña Ursulina said, squeezing the space between them, constricting the organ she'd fabricated and replaced in Reina's chest.

Reina screamed. Her lungs compressed; the air left her as if a boulder were crushing her against the floor. Her vision went blank. Her grip on the blade was loosening upon Doña Ursulina's command. Her body betrayed her.

The agony was too much. Reina closed her eyes, drowning.

Faintly, her grandmother's laughter echoed, worlds away. Then Reina lost grip on her life.

A breeze enveloped her. The relieving, warming comfort of shade during an all-too-sunny day. Reina stared down at her hands, their calluses and scars; they were obedient and wholly hers. She pressed a palm to her chest on instinct, feeling for her heart, finding the ragged texture beneath her shirt. She was still her, standing on a jungle path she recognized immediately, for it was one she took almost every night.

Reina followed it, diving into the jungle's innards, seeking the tomb's entrance. She needed to get back. She was a moribund nozariel, but if she had an ounce of life left, she was going to spend it saving Maior and Eva.

She knew her grandmother thought she had won. But Reina wasn't ready to give up just yet.

The path went on endlessly. Reina ran so much her bangs and shirt were drenched in sweat when she reached the lagoon.

There was no gaping cave flanking the crystalline waters. Just a person sitting on a boulder with their back to her. A lean frame and a high ponytail of black hair like silk.

Celeste.

Reina's heart fluttered. She placed a hand on her shoulder, rousing her.

As the person turned, Reina realized she'd been wrong. They were simultaneously Celeste, and Doña Laurel, and Maior, and even her father, Juan Vicente, with his dark brown skin and black eddies for hair. The person was also a bald man in billowing robes, a golden blade on his lap.

Neither and all, at once.

They turned around and handed Reina the blade as gold as the sunlight filtering through the canopy. It was an offering like the food she used to leave under the sun before she rejected Ches from her life.

Laughter bubbled out of her. She was a fool. She had never been Rahmagut's agent. She should have known this from the moment the blade became hers.

She had always been Ches's.

With a gasp she was yanked back to the tomb, which she'd never left.

Reina was in the sanctum's entryway, hunched in front of a golden filament, her shoulder searing with the stench of burnt fiber and flesh. The scene materialized instantly: Eva cornered to a crouch against a wall, her litio barrier held up with both hands and separating her from Reina. Maior screaming as Doña Ursulina dragged her across the bridge by the hair.

"Reina?" Eva said in a shivery, fragmented voice, inspecting the changes in her face. "You're back?"

That's when Reina realized the scorching pain of her shoulder—

the skin bubbling from its fresh burn—had been self-inflicted against Eva's glittering curtain. Fury and panic boiled out of her throat. Her grandmother had used her against Eva, like some mindless ram. And now Doña Ursulina had Maior.

Reina thrust herself up, wobbling from side to side, snorting out blood from an injury she couldn't recall. She nearly retched.

She sprinted to the bridge. Her nerves on edge, she tackled Doña Ursulina around the middle, shoving her against the railing so she'd release Maior.

The three toppled to the ground, rolling toward the dais, limbs skinning against the stone. Behind them were the statues of the two gods, surrounded in the drying blood of the damas.

Reina's nose itched, the air putrefactive. She scampered to her feet, tugging Maior up with her. She stood between the human and her grandmother, a barrier, and this time she was not going to be struck down. Maior took her cue to flee to Eva again.

Doña Ursulina gathered herself up to her feet, her face contorted from the insolence. She slid a hand over her hair, flattening the curls breaking free from her updo; she smoothed out the wrinkles on her jacket. "What are you doing? You should be dealing with the other valco."

Reina's breaths were broken, her heartbeats frenzied and irregular, but this fear eating her from the inside was not for her own life. "I am not your tool!"

It gave Doña Ursulina pause. She stepped back, raising her hand to the air in that gesture for control.

There it was again, the tug.

"You will not use me *ever again*." Reina's voice was thunder, strong as the roars in her chest. The memory of the abuse fueled her, even when her iridio reserve was so dangerously low.

Doña Ursulina's influence existed within her, but the control was weak and easily sundered. For Reina had Ches. All along, that was what the dreams had been about. It had been his way of telling her. Reina had simply been too deaf to listen. But now, even though her heart was fractured, forever incomplete from all the people she had lost, knowing he was with her filled the emptiness instead.

It made it easy to take a deep breath. To flare whatever iridio she had left in her. And the iridio ran through her brutally, burning every inch of muscle and bone. Damaging her, probably, but she was unafraid.

"Obey."

Reina broke free. "No."

She was met with a scowl. "I groomed you to be useful to me. This strength of yours—of my son—was meant to serve me. Not be squandered against me. *I saved your life.*"

Reina pounded her chest. "You did, and you did it to use me, knowing all I ever wanted was family." She pointed a hand behind her, where Eva and Maior stood—where Celeste *lay*. Her tears were not of sadness but of anger. "They are more family than you'll ever be. As long as I live, you're not taking that away from me."

Doña Ursulina raised her hands again, this time stirring the roots keeping the damas in place. "You would choose death rather than a brand-new heart? After everything I offered you? You were supposed to be my successor!"

There was no dignity in it. To Reina, it sounded like her grandmother was preparing to beg.

"I will never be your successor, and I regret everything I have done for you." Reina almost smiled. There was a fullness in her chest she hadn't realized had been missing since the night of that fateful attack. Whatever the tinieblas had taken from her, Ches had given it back.

"Then you will die with the rest of them."

Doña Ursulina thrust her hands forward, shooting the gnarling roots at Reina and Maior—her final gamble to restrain them. The seconds slowed to a crawl as Reina watched dozens—hundreds—of them crawling out of the earth, reaching for her.

Her golden blade materialized in her hands then, coming to her like an afterthought. There was no sun in the tunnel, yet it was blinding. A gift from the only other divine presence in the tomb. Light skinned the darkness from walls rippled in agonized faces. It revealed the fear that burned bright in Doña Ursulina's eyes.

Reina lunged for the roots, even as she knew there were too

many to prevent them from seizing Maior. But as long as Reina was breathing, she was going to try.

Then a fireball blasted past her, a star, so incendiary that it caught the roots and spread through their network in fragments of a moment. The fire roared through the sanctum, lighting every nook and cranny, cooking the blood, suffocating them with its heat and smoke. It had Eva's name written all over it.

The air turning to smoke meant there was a countdown to the end. Reina didn't waste a moment of it. Screaming, she rushed her grandmother with her golden blade and swung, slashing from shoulder to hip.

Doña Ursulina's cry joined the roar of the fire. It etched into Reina's heart. And Reina didn't spare a look. She couldn't, or else she would end up adding another regret to the night.

She circled the dais, guided by a final resolution that she knew Ches himself had planted in her. The instructions were clear as day.

She vaulted like she was reaching for the ceiling and used the pull of gravity to bring herself down. She swung her blade toward the center of the dais, right in between the statues, where Doña Ursulina had stirred Rahmagut's power. The blade's radiance dueled with Eva's fire, blinding everything and everyone. With it, Reina was like a comet headed for the earth.

She made impact. Her blade shattered the dais, cratering the stone with a great quake that sent Doña Ursulina and the fallen damas slinging against the walls. The sanctum shuddered, a storm of dust and fire raging through it. The two statues finally toppled, raining debris, threatening to crush Reina beneath the rubble.

She dashed out of the way, meeting a collapsing bridge. To her immense relief, Maior and Eva weren't in the sanctum anymore.

The chamber shook behind her. The ceiling and the walls caved in, the tomb's pillared foundations surrendering to the chaos. The whole room collapsed with a great bellow that hurled Reina to the outlet tunnel, where her body crashed to the wall and her temples clattered against the stone.

42

Two Warring Gods

Everything about Eva's body ached: her temples, her joints, her wildly fluttering heart. She took a big gulp of air and nearly drowned in the dust covering her nose and mouth.

A tremor rippled through the tunnel. The sanctum behind it groaned. Eva opened her eyes to utter darkness.

She sat up as bits of rubble and dust descended from a ceiling on the verge of collapsing. When she invoked galio to numb her pain, it came with ease and soothing relief, healing her beyond what she had intended. She summoned a flame and nearly blinded herself from the potency.

After her eyes adjusted, her gaze fell on her hands. They pulsed. Not just from the rush of what they'd endured, but with a tingling, the beginning sensations of hives breaking out on her skin. It was magic that throbbed fiercely, capriciously, on the verge of turning black and seizing control from her.

She shook her hands, unsettled. But the confusion was pushed to the back of her mind as noises stirred across the chamber. Maior beside her, Reina farther down the tunnel near the collapsed entryway, and Javier and Celeste at the other entrance. All were covered in dust and debris.

Eva scrambled to Reina first. The memory of her ferocity when she had been under Doña Ursulina's thrall chilled Eva. She was too strong to be left unchecked, so Eva needed to be sure whose side she would wake up on.

Eva brushed the dust and pebbles off Reina, then turned her over carefully. Reina was inflamed and bloody, her eyes closed and her face glistening with fresh cuts. Her eyes fluttered open without the help of galio. They were confused and groggy, but she looked like herself. For this, Eva huffed in relief.

She then rushed to Maior, who was pale and blood-stained. Eva gave her a soothing spell, to wake her up and numb her ache. The magic rushed through her in capricious waves, stronger than she intended. Startled, she shoved it down.

What was happening to her?

"We have to get out of here," Eva muttered as another tremor shook the tunnel, pebbles and dust descending on her brows and making it impossible to breathe right.

Reina limped to Maior before kneeling and running the back of a filthy hand against her cheek. "I think it's over," she told her.

Maior grabbed her hand and offered her one of those adoring looks.

Eva looked away. She was ashamed to be there as a witness to their intimacy. There was a weight on her chest, one she couldn't shake even as they helped each other to their feet. Perhaps it was her conscience, for her role in this whole mess.

She led the way to the other end of the tunnel, where Celeste lay in a puddle of her own blood. Eva sucked in a breath, ashamed. Just hours ago Celeste had been twirling in her Tierra'e Sol dress, laughing heartily at Don Samón's charm.

Eva avoided where the ground was soaked with her blood and knelt close. How were they going to take her body out of here? And how cruel that it would fall on Reina, merely for having the strength to do it. No, Eva was just as capable of wielding bismuto's enhancement. The least she could do, for the hand she'd had in all this, was carry Celeste's body.

Eva pressed her grimy palms together, summoning the strength from her bismuto rings, but paused halfway. She watched, stunned, at the slightest movement of Celeste's diaphragm pushing up her chest. Eva gasped.

She threw her ear over Celeste's mouth, confirming the slightest tingle of her breaths surging in and out. She felt the airflow, faintly, like the insignificant flutter of a butterfly's wing.

Eva barely registered her scream.

Reina rushed forth, Maior at her heels. The nozariel woman cradled Celeste's face, her own cheeks streaked with tears of relief. And Eva backed away as her heart imploded, her knees buttery, because Celeste *lived*.

Maior met her gaze as Eva retreated with a hand draped over her lips. She was surprised, her smile quivery with the disbelief in herself. And Eva squeezed her until Maior yelped from her own wounds. But what she really deserved was to be lifted up into the air in worshipping thanks. This was a gift, impossible had it not been for Maior—for the skill everyone had underestimated.

"You saved her," Eva whispered, and Maior burst into tears of relief.

Finally, when the tremors of the tomb couldn't be ignored a second longer, Reina lifted Celeste in her arms. She regarded Eva and Maior with a clenched jaw and hardened eyes. "We have to go."

Eva nodded in agreement. But there was one more thing she needed to do.

A stirring in the corner caught Eva's eye—a body within the rubble. Eva's chest fluttered foolishly. She saw locks of starlight, and her breath dislodged.

Javier.

Maior tried tugging Eva along, but she broke free, scrambling through rocks and stones to the caved-in debris. Her heart squeezed, like a lemon for juicing—like it cared.

He still lived. And of course he did. Reina wasn't a murderer.

She ran to him, nearly losing balance as the world rocked beneath them.

"Eva!" Reina called out. She said something else, but it was lost in the groaning of the tomb.

Eva skidded to a stop beside him. How she hated him. How she relished the sight of his beating. But...how the possibility of not seeing him alive again made her heart ache.

She cradled his face, her fingers slicking with his blood.

His eyes opened. They were inundated in black, yet she could see the crimson of his irises. He was possessed but also half in control.

"Eva Kesaré," he whispered. "You're here. Look—look at you, so beautiful and powerful," he said between coughs. He reached out and managed to graze her curls. "A true valco."

Flecks of dust fell on her face. She rubbed her eyes, smudging the dirt with her sweat and tears. "You're a monster. I—I should leave you to die."

He wept. He believed her. It made her feel even more wretched to have the choice in her hands.

"All I wanted was to be cleansed," he said with difficulty, the very motion of drawing a breath paining him.

"But you weren't cleansed!" she said, and the earth clamored, on cue, like she had forced it herself. "And you almost killed Celeste."

Eva gulped to blot out the memories—of witnessing Reina's despair.

"But that wasn't my intention—you did this to me!" He coughed. "*You.*"

All around her the tomb rumbled in a threat. If she didn't act now, she was going to be buried forever.

And he was right. She had toyed with his life and his curse. If anyone was to blame, it *was* her.

"I should leave you to die," she told him again. If she did, no one would ever know the truth.

Tears brimmed his eyes. His brows bunched up, despairing.

With a simple choice, she could undo every wrong turn she'd taken ever since leaving Galeno: her marriage; her culpability in Javier's turning and Celeste's wound.

But how could she be so cowardly and despicable? If she were a great valco, she would face what came after with her head held high.

"But I won't. You're my husband," she said, pressing her hands together and performing a lackluster galio incantation. Just enough to ease his pain. She knew she could close some of the wounds. The power swirling within her was overflowing. And galio was nothing compared to when she conjured the power of the stars.

Javier clung to her desperately as the walls shifted inward, the debris falling from the ceiling growing painful and incessant.

"More!" he demanded as the threads of galio wrapped around his limbs, his face, and his swollen eyes.

"No!" She yanked him by the arm and commanded, "Now get up!"

Like the tiniebla in him had obeyed her, so did he.

"Go," she said, watching his frail body step over uneven rock. The thought to test him crossed her mind.

"Stop," she said sharply.

His body yanked to a halt. He turned to her with a sneer.

A whirlwind of satisfaction filled her from the inside out. "Now go," she said, and he did.

It was all the confirmation she needed.

They darted to the vast chamber with the sarcophagi as the tunnel imploded behind them.

Tierra'e Sol was a land of cloudy gray as the bellowing maw of the tomb spat them out. The arrival of morning unveiled the dark, bringing with it rain clouds streaked in lightning. Rain pelted the jungle canopy, deafening, soaking them to the bone and washing away the grime. Don Samón's companions awaited them within the overgrowth, flanked by the handsome Liberator with the gnarling antlers. "A useless display," Reina spat out as she carried Celeste. Eva, too, watched them with annoyance. So many warriors, and none had bothered to go into the tomb to help them when they'd needed it most.

The cave roared like a great jaguar behind them, exhaling a cloud of dust and pebbles that sealed its entrance forever. Finally they were free from the legend.

"Let us go to the safety of my home," Don Samón offered, a hand shielding his eyes from the rain. "I brought my reinforcements with the intention of protecting you from Doña Ursulina."

"She's dead," Reina and Eva said in unison, shushing the jungle clearing, for there had been an otherworldly quality to their words. A finality not allowing a challenge. A power.

Don Samón bowed a nod from the reprimand and begged them to rest and recuperate in the comfort of his manse.

The wind buffeted through and past them. Eva's joints protested. She was so tired—even the simplest act of breathing was a chore. Her heart was a wildly pumping thing, struggling to keep up with the million tiny aches throbbing within her. Just this once she didn't care that returning to the Liberator's residence meant dealing with the truth of their bond. She just wanted to be dry, to lie in a bed, and to have a meal.

"I am not trying to capitalize on your weakness," he told them, gaze lingering on hers. "I merely know what it feels like to have a helping hand when you need it most."

Water flooded the corners of Eva's eyes. Maybe it was relief.

"You can trust me."

Then the tears of exhaustion broke through.

The rains lulled Don Samón's manse to sleep. Every plant and every flower curled with moisture, the caged birds puffing up in proximity to keep dry while the heavens wept. Life in the manse went on undisturbed by Doña Ursulina's ambition. And it was an odd sight, after spending a night of terror in that tomb.

A bespectacled man still in sleepwear was summoned as they arrived, and he guided Reina back to Celeste's room, along with a small entourage of assistants. When Reina rejoined Eva in the dining hall moments later, her eyes were fearful, and she shuddered, as if, without Celeste, her body were hollow.

The servants fed them cassava crackers, queso de mano, and mango preserve. Then they were ushered past the mosaics of legendary sea creatures and glass-panel refractions made dull by a gray sky, then through the labyrinthine garden paths overrun by jasmine. Until they entered the Liberator's workshop, where in the daytime, a wide window east of the lion-legged desk washed the room with the colors of rain.

Eva slumped herself on the nearest chair. Despite Javier's obvious exhaustion, she ordered him to stand behind her. She had a feeling her companions wouldn't take kindly to him enjoying the comforts of Don Samón's hospitalities. With the power brimming in her, his obedience came easily.

Reina never took a chair and instead stood by Maior, who was slumped on one with a hand over her brows.

"What happened in that tomb?" Don Samón finally asked.

"Javier tried to sacrifice Celeste." Reina spoke the truth, her fists clenched. Eva watched them going pale from constricted rage.

"You would murder your own blood?" Don Samón said. Not a question—an accusation incensed with the severity of his crimson eyes.

"I was possessed," Javier bit out, "by the tiniebla in me."

"Which is so conveniently not possessing you at this moment." Reina's gaze burned into him. Maior laid a hand over Reina's, easing her clenched fist.

Eva could have attested to the truth. She could have spoken up and declared her own guilt in the matter. Instead, her courage left her, and she let their wrath and judgment fester over Javier. But even if she said the truth, how would it change the fact that it had been Javier wielding the sword that impaled Celeste's back?

"He has a tiniebla in him—I've seen it," Eva said. She watched Reina, gaze surfing her sand-dune skin and midnight hair. Reina's comeliness had been dampened by the sharp angles and ragged edges. The cuts and bruises of her skin and the thick muscles taut beneath her clothes.

One day Eva would muster the heart to tell her the truth. Once they were all comforted by Celeste's waking up. But now was too soon. Rather, Eva directed Reina's passions to the Liberator.

"You said it was your purpose to protect the tomb from anyone seeking to make the invocation, but you were never there when we needed help. It's great that you came afterward but—it was done."

Don Samón accepted the criticism with a nod. "Our sentry spotted Águila banners on the mainland, over the shore. I don't know if Don Enrique has a ship, but likely he doesn't, otherwise he could have easily overrun us with his people. I think he might have done it as a distraction—a successful one at that. Nothing seemed out of the ordinary when I went to inspect the tomb." He sighed and stared at his hands. "I always figured, if something were to happen, it would be closer to the final day, not now. Though I'll admit the party wasn't a good idea. It made me comfortable and complacent."

"Doña Ursulina snuck into the island long before the dinner," Reina said, and they all turned to her with gaping mouths. "I saw it. I just didn't say anything because my intention was to help her."

Don Samón's face soured. "You, too?" He rose. "So you are a band of murderers and liars? I thought you were Celeste's lover."

Reina's lashes shrouded her eyes. Her jaw undulated with tension. She crossed her arms over her chest. "I am not. And I didn't know the damas were going to be killed."

"None of us knew," Eva added, giving him a meaningful look, assigning blame where it was due. "We all made mistakes."

Her belly fluttered as his attention landed on her.

This valco who was her father.

"Was Doña Ursulina attempting to lift Rahmagut's seal?" Don Samón said.

"That's not what she cared about," Reina said. "My grandmother wanted Rahmagut to grant her power—"

"But she already had so much—"

"She wanted to receive the same rewards and advantages as Feleva Águila did."

Don Samón frowned. Then, as realization dawned on him, he nodded. "Did she invoke him?"

"She sacrificed seven damas. Celeste and I were next." When Maior spoke, all eyes landed on her in surprise, reminded she had always been there. Doña Laurel's shade resided in her still, an unwelcome, ever-present guest.

Eva smiled at her, to give her reassurance under their scrutiny. In a way, Maior had prevented the worst just as much as Reina.

It was a selfish thought, to value Maior's and Celeste's lives over the others. But Eva was tired of dwelling on things she couldn't control. She had spent her whole life living with guilt. She'd left Galeno because she wasn't going to shrivel for the sake of others ever again.

"What happened in there that the tomb collapsed?"

Reina told him. She unsheathed her golden blade, which didn't need sunlight anymore to glow.

The sight drew Don Samón's frown. "How could you have single-handedly caused the destruction of the tomb, unless something else went awry?"

No one had an answer.

"What are you implying?" Eva stepped forward.

"That kind of destruction—was some kind of power unleashed?"

"Wouldn't we know by now, if her invocation weakened the seal enough to free Rahmagut?"

She liked saying the name, how the *r* rolled in her mouth like a bite of sweetbread. How nothing horrible happened, despite her grandmother's foolish warnings. She wanted to keep saying his name over and over again.

"What about all the horrible things you said would happen?" Eva challenged. She had expected thunder and brimstone, not this calm aftermath, where she brimmed with power from skills learned the hard way. "Wouldn't we notice something?"

"I don't exactly know *how* it would happen. It would be unprecedented." He turned to his monolith with the carvings of agonized people, the one he'd extracted from the sanctum. "Historians and folklorists tell us of Ches's and Rahmagut's ancient conflict, which occurred when this land was still young. A war of gods. Ches succeeded in banishing Rahmagut to the Void and used the last of his power to seal him away, in the process losing his grip on this world. Ever since, both have been absent. You *can* pray to them and pretend they listen. And yes, the veil separating our reality from theirs weakens occasionally, especially during events like when Rahmagut's Claw journeys through our skies. But they are still absent. Their return, as physical living entities, could damage the balance of our world."

He returned to his desk, fetching a blank scroll and a fresh bottle of ink. "A war of gods is not something I wish to witness in this lifetime, and neither should you."

Anger flooded Eva, like his words were a slight. She wanted to say something to stop him. But instead she hugged herself and looked away, bewildered by the irrational idea.

Don Samón went on. "For the meantime, we will have to wait and see. I will reach out to some trusted geomancers and scholars, get their opinion if anything out of the ordinary is noticed." He sighed. "I sent a messenger to the mainland, to inform Don Enrique that I have his daughter, *as a guest*, and I plan on seeing her recuperated before sending her back."

"You will give her to the caudillo?" Reina asked.

He draped one hand over another. "Not doing so could be seen as hostile. Do you even know if he was willing to sacrifice her? I mean, it sounds to me like all of you were in the dark."

Reina lowered her gaze in shame. "Doña Ursulina hated the caudillo. Everything was a lie."

Don Samón's gaze surfed every person in the room in silent judgment. Eva was glad he didn't press the matter. They had already paid for their stupidity—she hoped.

"I want you to know that I understand your plight, and I have nothing against you. You can continue to be my guests, and once you've rested and recuperated, you are welcome to choose your path. As for you"—Don Samón shot Javier a glare—"you will have to answer to your brother when he demands to know what happened to his firstborn." He gestured to the servant who waited by the doorway and said, "Take him to the cells."

Eva's stomach was a stormy ocean. Javier had done what he did because of her.

Still, she never said a word as the man dragged him out of the room. Not even as his eyes settled on hers, tired and resigned, aware she had the power to make him comply if he ever resisted the escort.

She looked away, to Reina, and saw hatred in her glare. Then Javier was gone.

43

A New Valco

The lull of rain on the roof made the silence short and welcoming as Javier departed. Their business was finished, at least for the time being, so Reina helped Maior up and headed for the door. Eva stood to leave as well, trailing behind her friends, but stopped as the Liberator said, "Eva Kesaré."

Her neck heated at the way he enunciated her name. Eva paused with her nails digging into the chair's backrest. She knew what he was going to say.

Reina slowed under the doorway, giving Eva the option to tell them to wait for her or to go on ahead. With a brave nod, Eva let them go.

"We never finished last night's conversation," Don Samón said once the silence was their only witness.

Eva's gaze caressed the spines of the books on his shelves, the exquisite ancient items he stored in his cabinets and on his furniture, the jewels and paintings that adorned the room. She knew he'd let her have it all, desperate for her approval. The idea tugged the edges of her lip.

With a side-glance, she said, "What else was left to be said?"

Don Samón circled his desk to face her. "I didn't bring up the name of your mother just for the sake of pleasantry."

His increased proximity alarmed her—not because she distrusted him but because of the wounded feelings it nuzzled.

"Did Dulce ever talk of your father?"

Dulce. Not *Doña Dulce*, like he was so familiar with her mom he could bypass honorifics.

His eyes weren't the ruby of a heroic valco anymore. They were soft and wounded. "Did she say anything about him at all?"

Eva shook her head, her nose growing hot and stuffy, then said, "My grandmother had many things to say about him, though."

His lips became a thin line.

The silence grew bolder as the rains turned to a drizzle, then stopped.

"And you believed all those things?"

Eva shielded herself with her anger at her upbringing—at the side-glances and cruel gossip she'd received thanks to her father's "crime." "If they weren't true, then why did she take her life?"

Why, if he hadn't addled her mind, filled her with an obsession of fake love so that even the love her daughters had to give was inadequate? Eva's belly twisted. She half wanted to spit at him. But she was held back by the gentle cooing voice telling her it had all been a lie. If so, Doña Antonia was the one to blame.

He looked away. "She wouldn't have taken her life if I had been allowed to save her. I wanted to take her out of that prison, but in the end, the mighty Doña Antonia got her way. When I found out about your existence—that Dulce had birthed a beautiful valco girl—it was too late. I was in the middle of my campaign."

Tears blurred the soft daylight beginning to fill the room. The strength to face him fled her. She coddled her face in her hands and gave him her back.

With his soft, pleading tone, he said, "It was either rescue her and you, or finish the fight for independence. It was a choice between what I loved most and turning my back on our people. I was young, and foolish, and ambitious..." His voice weakened, and he paused. "I knew that if I took you and Dulce out, I would lose the flimsy alliance the Serranos gave me, and I needed Galeno to join me willingly. The city was—and is—too important to the foundations of Venazia's economy to be destroyed in a war. If Venazia is destabilized, then Fedria follows suit. And I didn't think

I deserved this kind of happiness—I didn't know how empty my life was going to be without you and your mom."

She shuddered, and her sob betrayed the holding back of her tears.

"What about afterward? My family—they treated me horribly for being valco. I grew up believing you were a monster." She knew she was a coward for not facing him. A coward for not speaking Javier's truth. "I thought *I* was a monster, until Javier allowed me to be a valco for real."

She could only imagine how different her life would have been if she'd had a valco father to guide her. She would be glowing, like Ludivina and Celeste.

Eva's chest burned with envy.

"New governments are fickle and weak. There's a lot of work to be done to inspire patriotism for a nation. During those years, if I hadn't dedicated myself to the work, then Segol could have taken over again. Everything would have been undone. And when I found out about Dulce's death, I feared it was too late. I was too ashamed of the consequences of my inaction."

The clock on his wall chimed, like an umpire pacing this game they played.

"Afterward, I decided it would only be appropriate if you came of your own accord. The choice was not mine alone anymore."

She flinched as he draped his hand over her shoulder.

"I'm sorry that I failed Dulce, and you. I understand this is a lot to take in, and you've been through so much already. But I want to have this conversation when you feel ready."

His hand left her, and Eva turned around, surprised.

"I have been waiting nineteen years for this moment." He smiled, his eyes sunny and his cheeks tanned, the late-morning sunlight gilding his antlers. "I can wait a few more days, for when you're ready to talk. For when you're ready to hear my side of the story. Because, Eva Kesaré, I wholeheartedly believe you should stay where you belong, with your father."

Eva's chest did a little flutter. His eyes shimmered with the caress of tears, as surely hers did.

She wiped them away and whirled. "Thank you" was all she said under the doorway; then she fled.

Eva returned to a room too big for her alone, to a bed made for lovers and a wardrobe housing the tailored high-necked outfits of a man. She shed her dirty clothes, then drowned herself in the lukewarm tub that had been brought up and filled with water scented in jasmine and hibiscus. There she slept until her skin shriveled like a prune.

Don Samón was true to his word, as a nurse and a maid later invaded her privacy to mend her wounds and feed her boiled plantains and grouper stew. Then, hours later, when the Tierra'e Sol sun was a descending fiery ball, bleeding the horizon in reds and mulberries, Maior came to her door.

She was dressed in loose linen robes, her torso and arms wrapped in bandages and her face swollen and glistening with ointments.

They stared at each other for several long moments, until the caw of a faraway parrot shattered their spell. When Eva extended her hands, Maior melted into her embrace.

"Can I sleep with you?" Maior's whisper tickled the fine curly hairs around Eva's neck.

The request was a surprise. All this time Eva had imagined Maior wouldn't want to peel herself from Reina. "Of course," she whispered back, brushing away Maior's soft locks.

They held hands and walked to the bed after shutting the door behind them. "Why doesn't Don Samón's medic mend your wounds?" Eva said as Maior curled into a ball on Javier's side of the bed.

Between a stifled yawn, Maior said, "He seems tired from all he had to do for Celeste. Maybe I'll go to him tomorrow." She patted the cotton beside her and said, "I don't want to be alone tonight, though."

Eva bit her lip. Her heart was tight—the memory of the tomb stomping it into a dried mush. Maior had come *so close* to dying, and it was all her fault. She swallowed a thick breath and rushed to Maior's side.

Maior frowned as she noticed something on Eva's hair. She crept closer to brush back Eva's curly bangs. "Your antlers are black," she murmured.

Eva's hand shot up to touch them. The texture felt more ragged than before, rippled.

She crawled out of the bed to stare in shock at herself in the standing mirror. All that remained of the alabaster color were lines branching like lightning. The rest was colored in black.

Maior stood behind her to stare at their reflection. "What do you think it means?"

"Trauma," Eva joked, and grinned at Maior's bubbling giggles.

Though the more Eva inspected the twists and ragged edges, the more satisfaction stirred inside her. What if she had come out of that tomb as something more than valco? Javier's compliment drifted back to her again, taunting, because no one had yet claimed the title of strongest geomancer in Fedria.

They crept back to the bed, under the covers. Eva held Maior in a loose embrace as the moon rose through the open alcove. Rahmagut's Claw was not visible from this angle. She brushed the black hair from Maior's temple and watched her lashes flutter and close. She supposed she ought to be thankful. Rahmagut's tomb had collapsed, and Maior was safe.

When sleep found Eva, it was soothing and light. Then it left her, like a coy maiden running away. Eva watched the star-speckled sky for a while, listening to Maior's gentle breathing, and knew her night of sleep was ended.

That was why, after she slipped out of Maior's limp embrace, she scurried through the halls of Don Samón's manse. She knew, from chatting with the servants ealier, that the prisoner cells were detached from the manse, inside a stone fortress accessible through the beach.

Eva crossed the sandy path with the moonlight as guide, her nightgown fluttering from the tropical breeze. She reached the cobbled steps to the fortress and glanced back, guiltily searching for watching eyes, then stepped inside.

Every door she opened was loud and rusted with humidity, every step through the flagstones a thunder. It was no wonder Javier was sitting up by the cells, waiting, when she entered the room with a flaming wisp as a companion.

Despite the obvious trembling of his body, he had the hint of a smirk on his lips.

"You can't live without me, can you?" he said as she fetched the heavy iron key and opened his cell. She allowed herself in.

Don Samón's cells were so seldom used they only smelled of brine.

"You'd think being a prisoner would take away that arrogance," she said, her hands itching to reach forward.

In the end, Eva settled for kneeling in front of him, keeping a safe distance.

His face was purple and battered, his beauty stripped by the beating Reina had given him.

"Why did you come?" he asked after the seconds brought a silence better fit for breaking.

In truth, Eva didn't know. "I'm going to tell your brother everything. And Reina."

"You're going to tell them how you sped up my turning? How my days as a sane valco are numbered?"

She sucked in air. "If you turn, I can still control you."

He let out a little chuckle, then moist coughs.

"You're going to tell Enrique how your magic drove me into shoving a sword through his daughter's belly?"

Eva's lips pursed. She slapped him.

It was a meek one, and he sneered.

"Have some respect—some *decency*. You almost killed her."

"Because of you," he said angrily. "What's to stop me from telling him how your hand was behind it all?"

"The same thing that's stopping me from commanding you to slit your throat. Or from having you walk to the bottom of the sea until you drown."

There was true fear in his eyes. His throat bobbed.

It brought the tears back to hers.

How wretched it was—that this arrogant, self-centered, treacherous half valco man was so close to her heart. From the endless nights under the same sky. From the dawns they'd shared and the sunsets they'd left behind.

Eva couldn't stop herself from reaching forward and taking him in her arms.

There he wept.

"I'm going to figure out a cure for you. I know I can do it."

He squeezed her, and a heat blossomed in her lower belly.

"You won't turn. I promise."

After a while, once his tears had stopped and Eva's heart had calmed, the light of her flame wisp gave out. She never renewed it. This time, the darkness was their protector.

"Can you feel his power?" Javier's voice came gently, like that of a lover.

Was this how it felt, to have a husband with tenderness in his heart? Eva swallowed hard. "Whose?"

"Rahmagut's."

It was as if the mention was enough of a summons. Just the reminder, the name, sent her fingertips tingling. Yes. She did, though she didn't have the courage to say it.

"Do you want to know how I know?" he said.

Again, Eva dared not give breath to the words.

"Because the tiniebla in me is rejoicing. He's raving. As long as we're together, he gets to be with his master. He says Rahmagut couldn't have asked for a better host."

The reaffirmation didn't even shake her. It was true; her body had changed since the collapse of the tomb. Her fingertips were charged, and her curls didn't just hang from her scalp—they floated inconspicuously, also electrified. Her tether to iridio had never felt so strong before.

But she knew, even if Rahmagut was in her, feeding her with power and morphing her thoughts with his, Eva was also there. She was aware and steadfast.

So no, Rahmagut wouldn't use her as a puppet. For as long as he was in her body, nourishing her with his strength and perhaps even his malice, she would only let him be her tool.

She ran her hand over Javier's forehead, swiping his thin hair away, marveling at the softness of it, and said, "Then tell your tiniebla he's got another think coming. Tell him in this body, his god serves *me*."

44

The Sun Comes Out

There was a moment when Reina thought she was going to be perceived as a vulture for lingering outside Celeste's door. She had no intention of leaving until the medic assured her that all would be well (and he had assured her—telling her the worst had passed—but Reina wouldn't trust it until she saw those sky-blue eyes opening again). Don Samón had his beach and gardens and private lounging areas, but with her nerves, none of it interested Reina.

She ended up not waiting for long. The next morning, as a steely sky welcomed the fresh pink of dawn, Don Samón's bespectacled physician exited the dormitory with the news.

The scent of blood weighed the room, coating the roof of Reina's mouth as she entered quiet like a cat. The smell surprised her, if all was well like the medic had claimed, until her gaze flitted to the bucket of bandages a servant carried out after cleaning Celeste's wound.

Celeste wore a cream linen gown, something light and airy, easily swappable and given only to maintain modesty. She didn't notice Reina enter, the valco's gaze on the streaks of pink reflected on the sky visible beyond the alcove.

Reina watched her for a long time, delighted at the rise and fall of her chest, forcing down any breath that could lead to tears.

There was nothing else to cry for, she reminded herself; the threat had passed, and Celeste endured.

Reina gathered the courage and sat on the bed. Celeste was slow in responding. Maybe Reina was her first visit aside from the emotionally indifferent help.

Celeste smiled and extended a hand but came up short in reaching for Reina's, so Reina finished the journey for her.

"I—I'm so glad to see you awake." Even if she couldn't muster any steadiness, she decided to speak honestly.

"Reina." Celeste's voice was meek, like the smoke of a freshly extinguished candle. "You saved me."

"Maior," Reina corrected, giving credit where it was due.

Celeste frowned. "I was impaled by a sword."

Reina understood her confusion. It was the kind of wound one didn't simply live through.

"Don Samón's medic, he says your skin was closed by her galio. That you would have certainly died from the blood loss otherwise." Reina waved her hand as she recalled the lengthy but painful assessment of Celeste's condition, when the medic had warned her that Celeste would only make it if her body could endure. "It was a clean cut. And he had some experience mending innards. He says he learned it in the war."

Celeste nodded.

Reina thought she was going to have many things to say in this moment, but the silence stretched on, heady. There was the truth she had to share, of their singular grandfather, and a word for what they were: cousins.

Reina hated the implications, not for how their familial ties muddied her right to feel what she felt but because of the differences in their lives. So what if they had a blood relative in common? To everyone else Reina would always be the duskling and Celeste the Águila heir. If anything, the truth was nothing more than a sick joke.

And it was best saved for later.

"I'm happy you're awake and that you're going to be okay. I just wanted to see it for myself." She squeezed her hand one last time and made to leave, but Celeste didn't free her.

"Wait—Reina."

Reina paused with her gaze to the closed door. She pressed her lips into a thin line, her heart fearful.

"You say you're happy I'm okay, but you don't look it. You seem cold."

On the contrary, her chest burned with shame, scorn, rejection. But the important bit was Celeste retained her life. Everything else would have a solution in due time.

Reina met Celeste's rounded, expectant gaze. It annoyed her, for it dangled a notion like a bone beyond reach: the idea of rekindling everything she had dreamed for her future before the dinner party had gone to shit.

"What else can I say?"

Celeste was displeased by the answer. "I want you to admit that I was right. You brought Doña Ursulina to me."

Reina deserved the blame and wouldn't deny it. She was just caught in disbelief that Celeste couldn't pick a better time to throw the first stone.

Celeste stared at her hands, which she wrung until white. She exhaled. "I'm sorry—I just feel like my autonomy was taken away from me. Like one moment everything seemed okay, and the next I was closing my eyes because I fully believed I was about to die. And I want you to acknowledge that. My concerns were not without reason."

Reina nodded feverishly. The memory was an incendiary one for her as well. "It was my fault. I take full responsibility, and I know saying sorry is not enough. Just trust that I'm always going to carry this—what I did." She reached for Celeste's wrist and squeezed it to prove she meant it. "How can I make it up to you?"

"Don't leave me."

"I'm not going anywhere."

Celeste shook her head. "I want things to go back to the way they were. We'll go back home and have a new life like none of this happened."

But that was the one thing Reina couldn't grant her. "I can't do that."

"You said you were my best friend. We shared the amapolas."

It struck Reina as odd, how suddenly Celeste had this desire for her to stay.

She considered her reply carefully.

Yes, she was terrified of the uncertainties of what was to come. She was orphaned, without a grandmother, because *she* had killed her. Without a home. Without the future she'd thought guaranteed. But she knew one thing with utmost certainty. "I meant everything I said to you that night. My feelings. My hopes. That I loved you. I meant it all. And so did you."

She tried not to remember how Celeste's reaction had hurt. How it had been like a knife twisting in her gut. Even as Celeste's brows bunched up, confused, Reina didn't let it deter her. She had to be true for their sakes.

"Everything you said, it came from your chest. You meant every word of it."

"Yes, but things were different then. I was mad because I felt like I couldn't trust you. I couldn't believe you were working for that witch."

Even hearing it now felt like salt in the wound. "And now?" Reina asked.

"Well, I wouldn't be alive if you weren't to be trusted," Celeste said airily, as if her answer had to be obvious. It was her turn to grip Reina's hand. "But not knowing if I was going to make it or not—it's had an effect on what I want."

Reina hated the answer. How it reminded her of Doña Ursulina, who'd always leaned on the idea that Reina ought to be happy for how little she got. She shook her fingers free and rose from the edge of the bed. "No, Celeste. I'm tired of never being enough."

"That's not it—Reina, come on."

"And it'll always be that way between us. I came because I care about you. I want to see you well. But nothing will ever be the same."

She headed out of the room, but not before Celeste's last words caught up to her. "What else do you have?" Another knife.

Reina fled to the labyrinthine garden paths and found an empty nook where she surrendered to the hollow pain. She cried for her grandmother, finally, and the twisted future she had offered Reina. She wept, for she hadn't bothered to build anything else outside of her devotion to Doña Ursulina and Celeste.

Hope wormed into her chest then, reminding her of the friendships she'd gained along the way. Maior. And Eva, who had helped her against the tinieblas and Doña Ursulina more than once.

Once the tears dried, Reina wandered aimlessly to the dining hall, swallowing down the hurt and building a wall of ice around her.

A small team of servants bustled about the hall as she entered, moving the main table and chairs and arranging dinnerware, perhaps for an early lunch. One of them caught Reina's eye and quickly scurried to her, telling her the Liberator had summoned her to his workshop. Telling Reina to go see him, when she was ready.

Reina had a moment of remembrance. She stood there thinking of the day another valco had summoned her to his study. How terribly everything had gone from that day on.

The Liberator's office glowed orange from the candles placed around the room; it was warm, unlike Enrique's cold den. The candles stood on shelves and over the desk, casting shadows like flickering dancers, dim in the window's natural light.

Don Samón was engrossed in drafting a letter when Reina welcomed herself in. He wiped the tiredness from his eyes and beckoned her to sit across from him. Then, as Reina hesitated, he said, "Or not. It's all right. I can keep this brief."

Reina recognized pity as what touched Don Samón's eyes.

"I'm not sure what you intend to do in the future or if you've thought about it at all."

Reina paused, her chest constricting. Everything he said threatened to fissure the ice molded around her. The structure keeping her composed—but also numb.

"I know it's much too soon to bring this up, but I must get something off my chest. I just finished speaking with my generals— the men who inspected the tomb and assessed if there was any hint of the gods left. The things they told me, of what must have transpired—it's impressive. What you and Eva did back there was impressive."

Reina's mouth dried.

"I believe you would make quite the capable soldier, and I would loathe for you to leave my home without at least considering the opportunity to work under me."

Hope simmered inside her, thinning the wall of ice until it fissured.

"Every day, good diplomacy and luck is all that remains between Fedria and another bloody war. The neighboring colonies haven't yet reached their independence, so Segol's influence is still right at our borders. Not only that, but now we've got the awakening of the gods of the sun and the Void to contend with. I don't know what will happen. What I do know is that I will accept all the help I can get, to maintain this fragile balance."

Reina gripped the chair's backrest, her wounded hands protesting the strain. There was no balance in *her* life.

"My wealth is not as great as the wealth of the caudillo of Sadul Fuerte. My coffers feed his; it's the only way I can replenish all and any iridio my men need. This country is poorer than Venazia, our people humbler, but I can promise you a breadth of opportunities—"

"I accept, but I will need to be paid in iridio."

Don Samón faltered. For the first time, he was caught without a reply.

Reina spared him, saying, "Don Enrique banished me. I have no reason to go back."

Once, Segolita had been like a hell. Now this hell was Sadul Fuerte, with the memory of her grandmother and Don Enrique's ambition. With Celeste treating her like a minion.

Don Samón did little to veil his smile. "Yes, we can certainly procure the iridio if you prefer that to gold."

She did very much. She needed it to live. Though ever since coming out of the tomb, a lot less so, it seemed.

"You're an impressive woman, Reina, tougher than some of my strongest. You'll accomplish great things, and I want to be there to see it."

Reina fought with all her might not to let that fissure spread—not to shatter the wall she had built and crumble in the presence of the Liberator. She gripped the handle of the blade Ches had gifted her. It had to be one of the reasons why Don Samón was welcoming her like this.

It surprised Reina that Maior would linger outside her door after knocking, waiting for a reply.

"It's never been a problem for you before: bursting into my room," Reina said with a smile as she opened the door for the short human. She chuckled at the red blush of Maior's cheeks and her surprise.

She was glad to see Maior's injuries from before had finally been treated by the medic. For a while Reina had been meaning to reassure her that the delay had nothing to do with Maior and everything to do with how the whole world regarded Celeste: as first for everything.

Maior mocked a laugh. "Very funny. At least I learn from the things people tell me."

"What's that supposed to mean?"

"That I'm not made of stubbornness," the woman said, welcoming herself to Reina's room.

Maior carried a small potion vial in hand, the glass coated in the syrupy black of an iridio potion. She caught Reina's gaze and raised the vial between them after shutting the door behind her. "Oh, this? I got it for you."

Reina's eyebrows ascended.

"You better be thankful for it. I had to haggle a week's worth of medical assisting with the physician to get it, and that was only for a low-grade potion. I don't know how we're going to afford better quality—" Something piqued Maior's interest behind Reina. "Oh, Reina, is that your tail *wagging*?"

Reina backed away as her face flushed to the heat of the earth's core. Her calves met the bed, and she allowed herself to collapse on her bottom, making sure the tail curled out of view. She just stared at anything but Maior, who sat beside her with that expectant gaze. "Okay, so what? My tail moves sometimes." Her tail was a servant to her subconscious and instincts. And it felt good when she indulged in the movements, like a fidgeting leg.

Maior's hand was slow in traveling to the hairy tip, where the tail's end had the same coarse coiling texture of Reina's hair. She waited for Reina's rejection. "May I?"

Reina was a creature robbed of words. She just nodded and pursed her lips, lest she be caught biting them as Maior reached for the tail itself, uncoiling it toward her lap one vertebra at a time. She ran her hand from half the length to the tip, touching the transition of soft fur to bouncing curls, inspecting.

A shiver crawled through Reina, not just because no one before had deemed it worthy of being stroked so gently but because that person was *Maior.*

The tail twitched despite her best efforts for catatonia, traitorously.

"Dogs wag their tail when they're happy. Are you a dog?" Maior teased, leaning forward with her trembling fingers leaning against the black fur. There was no malice in her eyes, just pure, unadulterated curiosity.

Reina smirked. "Who knows? Maybe it's in my blood."

Maior curled her finger on the ends, and Reina was glad she was freshly washed after the night at the tomb.

"Well, are you going to share why you're happy?"

Reina considered the question. She had good news to share. A brand-new life to celebrate, she supposed. But only one answer seemed appropriate, and Maior deserved the honesty. "I guess because I saw you bringing me iridio."

Maior's cheeks glowed bright red. "You haven't refilled in a while. I figured you must be running low."

Reina looked down at her hands to avoid being scrutinized. It was too much. "I should be. But something in me changed at the tomb." She pressed a hand to her chest, over the uneven texture beneath her shirt. They were in complete privacy, in comfort, yet her heart felt agitated, expectant. "I don't feel like I need it as much." What she actually thought she should say was that she didn't need it at all, but that wasn't the sort of statement to be made flippantly. Reina couldn't afford the shattered hope. She needed empirical proof.

"All right, then. It's here if you need it." Maior stretched out to place the vial on the bedside table, like she didn't want to lose the proximity for the menial reason of setting the iridio aside.

When Maior returned, Reina found herself closer. This time she did taste her own lips. She did allow herself the indulgence. Like the way her tail moved without permission.

Reina pulled Maior's hand from touching the tail, found it scorching. "I never thanked you properly for saving Celeste's life," she said. They were so close they spoke softly.

Maior smiled. "I didn't think I was capable."

"But you were." Reina squeezed her hand. "That's a big deal. You're going to be saving so many lives in Apartaderos."

Maior seemed to deflate at that. She hunched and looked away.

"You can go with Celeste after she's healed," Reina went on, hoping she could offer some reassurance. "Don Samón's going to send her to the caudillo sooner or later. I don't think she'd mind you taking Gegania to Apartaderos. And Celeste's grateful for what you've done." Reina said the words before thinking if they were true, but they had to be. "She can be discreet about you using Gegania to go home—her father doesn't know about the house."

Maior grabbed Reina by the biceps, pinching. "You're not going back to Sadul Fuerte?" Her voice was shrill, stressed.

Reina hesitated with her mouth open. To Maior's eyes she probably looked like a grouper. Her chest wrung painfully, reminded of all she had lost. She had thought the Páramo was home.

"Don Samón offered me a place in his army." She tried smiling. "I'll be working here now. I'm never going back to the Águilas."

She could say her ties were officially severed. First Doña Laurel, then Doña Ursulina, and finally Celeste.

Reina ran a hand through her hair. It was for the better, she decided, the more she thought of it. She had always been a blind fool for thinking she belonged with Celeste.

Maior looked away.

Reina couldn't ignore her displeasure. "Maior?"

Maior's throat bobbed. "You're staying here, and you're sending me back?" Reina could hear the frantic pace of blood in Maior's neck. "I guess there's no reason for me to be around you now that the tomb has caved." Her voice trembled, her long lashes hooding the darkness from her eyes.

Reina went for her wrist. She tried turning Maior's hand over to take it yet met resistance. "No. I—I figured you would want to go back to your life. I have been awful to you, keeping you as a prisoner. Putting you in harm's way all the time." She let her voice break—she no longer had the strength to maintain it.

This time Maior did look up. "You always protected me."

A birdsong melody journeyed into the room as their gazes met; then came a breeze carrying the scent of salt and sand. The seconds drew them closer, until Reina finally surrendered to an embrace. She curled her arms around Maior's middle, her shoulders trembling and her heart in a mad race. She buried her nose between the thick softness of Maior's hair and her neck, and Maior squeezed her back.

Reina swallowed thickly and said, "I don't think I would have anything left if I had lost you, too." The confession came easily when she wasn't under the scrutiny of Maior's gaze. When she could immerse herself in the warmth that was Maior and everything else disappeared.

Maior squeezed so hard it was a wonder they didn't merge into each other. Reina realized she wanted more of it, like she had a hunger that could only be satiated a certain way. A sharp longing bloomed in her belly. An ache.

"I don't want to go," Maior said from Reina's chest, her voice muffled by the shirt. "I don't want to go back to Apartaderos and regret leaving behind the one thing that felt real." Her nails dug into Reina's back, digging, drawing a broken exhale from Reina. "I can't think about returning to the chapel without remembering how I was taken and how through it all I felt so alone. They're bad memories, except for Eva and you. You're right, I'm done doing things against my will. And what I want to do is stay." Maior pulled away and feigned a goofy smile. "Besides, I already offered to work for Don Samón's medic—I owe him for the iridio."

Reina's gaze flitted to Maior's plump smiling lips, finding the peach fuzz hairs of her jaw and journeying to the moles of her neck. She had so many, along with the mark of the constellation, which sent them into a colliding path. Her skin was so smooth, if a little bit hairy, the same color as the insides of a freshly baked roll.

Without thinking, she reached for Maior's neck, cradling the smoothness of it. Reina's heart raced. But even as Maior watched her with wide eyes, her lips parted in invitation, Reina was paralyzed by fear. She had already been rejected once. She had already been granted a kiss in pity—

Maior plunged for her lips.

Reina kissed her back, closing her eyes as her heart put the tempo of any joropo to shame. They kissed, ravenous, Reina taking in a scent she had always thought was from the Páramo but now realized was wholly Maior's.

Maior molded the roundness of her body into Reina, who had shoulders enough for both of them. Her breasts pressed against the flatness of Reina's. And Reina exhaled—trembled—as a wicked charge sent shivers down her spine. She was sure she was going to drown. She was sure her heart would give out at any moment now. For how could someone she held in her hands, tangible, feel so *good*?

They fumbled with each other, fingers trembling, delving into clothes and worshipping whatever length of skin they could find. Reina's tail coiled, both of its own accord and with dexterous delight, helping Maior's hands along wherever they willed to go. Every caress and every kiss was irreplicable because it sparked with the magic of newness. Of the marvel that a touch could sear as it traveled along the span of Maior's neck or the curves of her breasts.

When Maior held Reina, it was like having a home, a roof, without fear of being asked to leave. Maior's kisses were not spoiled by the half-truths Reina withheld. There was no magic of amapola. No fear that what she did wasn't enough or that she was wrong for what she felt.

Reina was drunk on it, so she stopped before she could spoil it.

Maior nuzzled her face, blindly searching for her lips, until she noticed the hesitation. Her eyes were dizzy and glossy. "Reina?" She blinked away the confusion.

In her dreams she had always pictured herself as the pillar to Celeste's splendid future, taking a supportive role, merely working in the shadows. For she would always be nozariel, inferior to valcos, and enslaved to iridio.

But ever since their truths had come out at the tomb—ever since she'd realized all she had to do was embrace Ches—she'd known her path had diverged.

And Maior had always been there for Reina.

They were equals. Reina dared believe the thing bringing them together was this feeling. Nothing else. But if she ever had any doubt, all she had to do was see it in Maior's eyes.

Reina caressed her cheek, easing her worries.

"It's too fast?" Maior said and Reina nodded.

"I don't want to ruin it."

Maior leaned into her again, hugging. "You wouldn't." She buried her face in Reina's chest, her breaths close to the ragged transplant, tickling. "But I understand."

Through the alcove, Reina watched the sun rise higher against the enamel-blue sky. A foreign sort of passion bloomed in her then, surging through her veins like a fresh shot of iridio, as if sunlight itself were the new fuel to her heart.

"This time I want to do things right." She stared at her hands, at the calluses and nails chipped from violence, noting how they were rough and battered compared to Maior's soft pair. "All this time I thought earning my grandmother's approval was how I would make it. I was blinded by the idea that Celeste and I belonged together, for no reason other than the friendship we built after I came to her manor. All I wanted was a family and to belong."

It wasn't pity but sympathy bunching up Maior's brows. She squeezed Reina again.

"But I went about it all wrong. This time I want to do things carefully. If I'm going to be with you, I want to do it right, and for the right reasons. I want to build my own home through honest work." Her gaze found the sky again. "Ches gave me another chance. I want to make sure it's not wasted."

She didn't have proof. But it was like one of those true facts about the world: how the sun made the day and nourished everything that was alive. She knew it with the same certainty that had guided her to destroy the tomb.

Ches had never left her. He was real. And ever since the dais had imploded, he had been in her.

Even if she had no other choice but to rebuild, she was stronger and better prepared. With Ches, Reina was no longer alone.

The story continues in ...

The Warring Gods: Book Two

Geomancia

Known Branches of Geomancia

Litio: Branch for spells of protection. Litio is extracted
from petalites and spodumenes. Rings of litio are worn
on the index finger. Proper solutions of litio are clear
in color. Litio can block the healing of galio spells by
creating a barrier around the body.

Galio: Branch for spells of healing. Rings of galio are worn on
the middle finger. Proper solutions of galio are chartreuse
in color. Galio can inhibit the alchemical changes in the
body that come from bismuto enhancement.

Bismuto: Branch for spells of physical enhancement. Rings
of bismuto are worn on the ring finger. Proper solutions
of bismuto are azure in color. Bismuto can shatter the
barriers cast by litio spells.

Iridio: Branch in active development. Iridio is extracted
from a meteor in the Páramo Mountains. Solutions
of iridio can be worn anywhere on the body. Proper
solutions of iridio are black in color.

Visual Manifestation of Geomancia

- Red for the assertive conductors
- Blue for the analytical thinkers
- Purple for the supportive caretakers
- Gold for the persuasive promoters

Glossary of Terms

aguinaldo—verses sung to the melody of four-string guitars and maracas, typical of the Páramo region.

amapola—a fruit endemic to coastal Fedria, spherical in shape, with thin green skin and the stem area flaring upward like a red flower. The insides are a fleshy red that turns white upon contact with air. It is believed those who share the same amapola are forever bound by the bands of fate.

arbiter—the game master of Calamity.

Calamity—a gambling card game retelling the disasters Ches's and Rahmagut's strife brought upon the land: an earthquake, a flood, a plague, a horde, a day of shrouded sun, a star fall, and a legion of valcos.

caudillo—a military commander and protector of lands.

Ches—believed to be the god of the sun by the indigenous societies of Venazia and Fedria.

El Cónclave Llanero—a clandestine group stirring dissent over the appointment of a Venazian king.

contrapunteo—a subgenre of joropo, in which two or more singers improvise a verse duel to the melody of a four-string guitar and maracas.

cuatro—a four-string guitar.

escudo—a gold coin, currency of the Viceroyalty of Venazia and adopted in Venazia and Fedria.

Fedria—a sovereign republic east of Río'e Marle, first established in 344 KD upon the declaration of independence. Segolita is its capital city.

frailejón—a tree endemic to the Páramo, with marcescent succulent leaves.

Las Hermanas de Piedra—a Penitent order of nurses and nuns founded in Apartaderos, who strive for convergence between Pentimiento teachings and geomancia.

La Junta de Puerto Carcosa—a yearly summit of the caudillos of Venazia, in which all matters of public policy are debated.

liqui liqui—a ceremonial outfit of a high-collared and long-sleeved shirt and straight pants, worn for revels and special occasions.

the Llanos—an area of tropical grasslands and savannas.

llanero—a rancher and landowner from the Llanos.

mal de ojo—an illness characterized by weakness, fever, and loose bowels, imparted by envious eyes, most notably on babes.

mora—a fruit endemic to the Páramo range, similar to a blackberry but sweeter and juicier.

nozariel—an intelligent bipedal species native to the Llanos and the Cow Sea coast. They are similar to humans in appearance, distinguishable by their pointed ears, sharp canines, prehensile tails, and scutes on skin—predominantly on the nose bridge, shoulders, elbows, and knees.

Pentimiento—the monotheistic religion of the humans of Segol.

Penitent—one who practices Pentimiento.

Princess Marle—a nozariel princess said to have been raised by a jaguar. She discovered the length of Río'e Marle astride the jaguar who'd reared her.

Rahmagut—a nozariel conqueror who ascended to godliness. He is believed to be master of the Void by the indigenous societies of Venazia and Fedria.

Sadul—a legendary valco warrior after whom Sadul Fuerte is named.

sea cow—a manatee.

Segol—the human empire across the ocean.

tigra mariposa—a speckled viper endemic to the Llanos.

tiniebla—chimeralike creatures spawned by Rahmagut's attempts to create life. They are typically born from animals, corrupted and amalgamated, without a heart.

el Vacío—the Void, Rahmagut's domain.

valco—an intelligent bipedal species native to the Páramo range. They are similar to humans in appearance, distinguishable by their antlers, the absence of hair melanin, and red-pigmented irises. They are of dense bone structure and muscle.

vals—a waltz, traditionally danced during quinceañeras.

Venazia—sovereign stratocracy west of Río'e Marle, first established in 344 KD upon the declaration of independence. Puerto Carcosa is its capital city.

the Virgin—the goddess of Pentimiento.

yares—an intelligent bipedal species native to the coast of the Mar Calavera. They are similar to humans in appearance, distinguishable by horns and lizard-like wings. Known as man-eaters, they were eradicated by Segol shortly after the humans' arrival.

Acknowledgments

The Sun and the Void has gone through an incredibly long journey and would not be here without the support of so many people.

To Naomi Davis, my fierce yet kind agent, without whom this story would be gathering dust in a trunk, abandoned: Thank you for believing in this story and for always believing in me. You are a beacon of positivity and your kindness inspires me every day. Thank you for advocating for *The Sun and the Void* during both the exciting and sticky moments. Words alone cannot express my gratitude.

To Angeline Rodriguez, who brought *The Sun and the Void* to the Orbit family: You saw exactly what I was trying to do with this story. You were its first ideal reader. Thank you for your sharp editorial eye and for helping me elevate it to what it is now. Thank you for your advice and friendship. You were my first editor and I will always miss you!

To Nivia Evans, who adopted *The Sun and the Void* and shepherded it through the publishing machine: Thank you for putting up with me and for giving this book so much care and attention. I am so lucky *The Sun and the Void* landed in your hands, and I am so honored to get to work with you. You are amazing.

To Daphne Tonge, who opened up new avenues for readers to access this story: Thank you for believing in *The Sun and the Void* and for taking a chance on me. Thank you for liking and supporting my art. I am so delighted, honored, and lucky to work with you.

To Manu Velasco and Rachel Goldstein, who had to put up with my horrible English: Thank you so much for your patience and for editing *The Sun and the Void* with so much care and tenderness. I appreciate all the work and attention you put into this story and how you helped me elevate it even further. I'm sorry about all the prepositions. I still don't get it . . .

Special thanks to Lisa Marie Pompilio for the beautiful Orbit US cover and to Jane Tibbetts for the stunning Daphne Press counterpart.

To Lauren Panepinto, Angelica Chong, Paola Crespo, Ellen Wright, Tim Holman, and the entire Orbit US team: Thank you for giving *The Sun and the Void* a warm home and for allowing me to share this story with the world.

To Caitlin Lomas, Davi Lancett, and the rest of the Daphne Press team: Thank you for publishing such a beautiful edition and for all the time and care you have put into this project.

To Maria José Morillo, who copyedited for Spanish: Thank you for easing my concerns and helping me seamlessly integrate Spanish into an English text. Also thank you for reading and critiquing an earlier version of *The Sun and the Void*, and for your enthusiasm!

To Isaiah Womble and Sana Qazi, who inspired this story in its earliest days: *The Sun and the Void* and its characters wouldn't be the same without you. I'm so glad you came into my life. Thank you for inspiring me with your friendship.

To Rachel Fikes and Nemo Xū, who helped me through a dark time in my creative career: Thank you for your friendship, for your encouragement, and for steering me away from impostor syndrome.

I want to thank Dannielle Wicks, Edgar Robledo, Ashley Martinez, Circe Moskowitz, Carolina Flórez Cerchiaro, Lillie Vale, Bethan Rumsey, Jenna Goldsmith, Brett Linley, and Ana-Ilia Jackson for reading and critiquing *The Sun and the Void* during its various phases. Thank you to the Llama Squad for being my crew during the difficult querying times and for your support, camaraderie, and wisdom. Special thanks to Rachel Greenlaw, Sarah Jane Pounds, Cyla Panin, Susan Wallach, Nicole Aronis, Catherine Bakewell, Trisha Kelly, and Lyndall Clipstone for their advice and friendship. Thank you to Kristyn Merbeth and Sandy Roffey for their query-writing expertise.

To my writing siblings, Hannah M. Long, Essa Hansen, Chelsea

Mueller, Kritika H. Rao, Melissa Caruso, Sunyi Dean, Sara M. Harvey, and Sue Lynn Tan: Thank you for your wise career counsel, enthusiasm, friendship, and support.

Special thanks to Zabé Ellor and Morgan Robles, whose ideas impacted the course of this story for the better.

Thanks to the people who supported me and gave me encouragement during this debut journey: the McWeeney family, Aggie, Paty Romero, Tomina, Chelsea Vuncannon, Jade Raven, Gyozados, Sunjuicy, Masamune "Jaiyah," Phil Rogers, Aaron T., Erin D., Kelsey, Regi, Starr, and Jen Elrod. Thanks to my former colleagues Ogechi Chima, Jose Salgado, Sebastian Meza, Tobi Dipeolu, Assem Mahmoud, and Lauren Berlin, who put up with me while I drafted and edited this book.

To my patrons, who support me through this uncertain artistic journey: Thank you for your enthusiasm, and please know I wish I could name each and every one of you.

To Lisbeth and Pedro: Thank you for opening doors for me and giving me the foundation that allowed me to write this story. Thank you for working so hard to maintain our Venezuelan roots and for inspiring me to always seek greater heights. I love you with all my heart.

To my family—los Romero, los Cardona, los Lacruz, the Sefidrous, y los pollitos: Thank you for inspiring me with your tenacity, your endurance, and your stories. There's a piece of each one of you in this tale. I hope one day you will see it.

To Hassan: You were my first fan and you continue to be my biggest. Thank you for helping me untangle all the threads in *The Sun and the Void* and for stopping me from writing myself into plot holes. Thank you for being this story's first reader and for viewing it with a critical eye. *The Sun and the Void* would not be the same without you. Thank you for giving me the best times of my life. I love you.

And finally, to you, the reader: Thank you for choosing this adventure, and for making it this far. I hope it was an enjoyable one.

extras

orbit

meet the author

Hassan Sefidrou

Born and raised in Venezuela, GABRIELA ROMERO LACRUZ now lives two thousand miles from home, in the land of bayous and astronauts. She graduated with a BS in chemical engineering from the University of Houston and, after a stint in oil and gas, decided to dedicate herself to the arts. She writes young adult and adult fantasy stories set in places that remind her of home, so in her mind, she's never too far from the beaches and mountains of Venezuela. She also scratches that ChemE itch with a science fiction story or two. She illustrates as The Moonborn.

Find out more about Gabriela Romero Lacruz and other Orbit authors by registering for the free monthly newsletter at orbitbooks.net.

interview

What was the first book that made you fall in love with the fantasy genre?

I think I loved the fantasy genre since I first started reading with the Harry Potter and Chronicles of Narnia series, but the book that really opened up my ravenous appetite for secondary world fantasy was *A Game of Thrones*. The vast world and huge cast of A Song of Ice and Fire sparked my inspiration, and it made me realize how much I enjoyed worldbuilding above all else. Because of that series, I've now become the kind of writer who will spend a huge chunk of time "prewriting" an encyclopedia about my made-up worlds.

Where did the initial idea for The Sun and the Void *come from and how did the story begin to take shape?*

The Sun and the Void was born from this initial sentence: "Legend tells that the god Rahmagut will reward any ambitious mortal with immortality, if they collect and sacrifice the reincarnations of his nine wives." Once I had this, I began building the story by using the collection of my favorite ideas, characters, and snippets that I kept saved for a later time, once I "became a better writer." I was also thinking that in all my favorite books, video games, and anime, there didn't seem to be any stories that used Venezuelan folklore and history. I grew up in Venezuela and learned about its heroes and war for independence in school, from our history books; and my upbringing is defined by Venezuelan culture, so I already knew there was so much rich folklore to use as inspiration. My favorite media used Japanese, Roman, British, etc. history, folklore, and mythology as the foundation for their magic systems and secondary fantasy worlds. I wondered why no one was doing this for Venezuela. So I decided to do it myself, for the nerds like me, who grew up loving worlds like those of Final Fantasy yet had our existence largely ignored by mainstream media. I never read Tolkien's works, but I knew of their influence in the SFF genre and how his races have inspired those of so many fantasy worlds. I am mixed-race and had a biracial upbringing, and I wanted to create characters who experienced this otherness as well. So I created nozariels, valcos, and yares to populate the world of *The Sun and the Void* alongside humans, and I made my POV characters mixed, so they could explore their world through a similar lens to mine. Finally, I wanted to tell a story with a large cast and morally gray characters, much like A Song of Ice and Fire, so I created the two points of view: Reina with her desperate journey to save Celeste, who I knew needed to be a reincarnated wife, and Eva to become a companion to the antagonist, who at the time was Javier.

What was the most challenging moment of writing The Sun and the Void?

My favorite part of writing this book was building the world, and it was also the hardest. I was not new to writing, but I was new to fitting a vast secondary world to an engaging narrative. I definitely banged my head against many walls in frustration over not knowing how to balance showing and telling worldbuilding and exposition while making it make sense for the plot and characters.

The Sun and the Void's world is inspired by South America's history and folklore. What was your approach to creating this setting? Did you do any specific research to build the world?

My research has been very light. I have done it mostly to reinforce what I knew about Venezuela, Colombia, Gran Colombia, and their histories and culture. My mom is from the Andes and my dad is Afro-Caribbean from the coast, and I spent equal amounts of time immersed in both cultures. Because our large families are scattered all over Venezuela, we also spent a lot of time driving from the páramo to the coast, crossing the Llanos; thus I had the privilege of experiencing many cities and geographies for myself. I immersed myself in música llanera and drew a lot of thematic inspiration from the tales told in the lyrics of Simón Díaz, Juan Harvey Caycedo, Reynaldo Armas, and many others. I'm also very lucky to have a visual encyclopedia and a history book that my mom compiled from weekly issues of one of Venezuela's biggest newspapers, *El Nacional*, published through C. A. Editora El Nacional y Fundación Bigott and Fundación Empresas Polar. I consulted my family and friends for their beliefs in the folklore, and for idioms and foods. I have also visited Colombia multiple times and was delighted to discover there is so much overlap in the culture, geographies, and history, which is not a surprise, thanks to our shared root as Gran Colombia.

The characters in The Sun and the Void *are fascinating and constantly striving to prove their worth. If you had to pick, who would you say is your favorite? Who did you find the most difficult to write?*

My favorite character has always been Javier. I indulged myself when creating his aesthetics and background. And I think we have a shared spoiled, vicious nature, so writing his lines was always a good time. The most difficult to write was Reina, because I was always worried about straddling the line between not ruining her likability for the readers, making her an active pursuer of what she wanted, and ensuring her love for Celeste didn't come across as a misguided obsession.

Who are some of your favorite authors and how have they influenced your writing?

I am constantly blown away by the way Naomi Novik plots her books. I look up to the way she crafts complex worlds and

if you enjoyed
THE SUN AND THE VOID

look out for

THE JASAD HEIR
The Scorched Throne: Book One

by

Sara Hashem

At ten years old, the Heir of Jasad fled a massacre that took her entire family. At fifteen, she buried her first body. At twenty, the clock is ticking on Sylvia's third attempt at home. Nizahl's armies have laid waste to Jasad and banned magic across the four remaining kingdoms. Fortunately, Sylvia's magic is as good at playing dead as she is.

When the Nizahl Heir tracks a group of Jasadis to Sylvia's village, the quiet life she's crafted unravels. Calculating and cold, Arin has a tactical brilliance surpassed only by his hatred for magic. When a mistake exposes Sylvia's magic, Arin offers her an escape: compete as Nizahl's champion in the Alcalah tournament and win immunity from persecution.

To win the deadly Alcalah, Sylvia must work with Arin to free her trapped magic, all while staying a step ahead of his efforts to uncover her identity. But as the two grow closer, Sylvia realizes winning her freedom means destroying any chance of reuniting Jasad under her banner. The scorched kingdom is rising again, and Sylvia will have to choose between the life she's earned and the one she left behind.

CHAPTER ONE

Two things stood between me and a good night's sleep, and I was allowed to kill only one of them.

I tromped through Hirun River's mossy banks, squinting for movement. The grime, the late hours—I had expected those. Every apprentice in the village dealt with them. I just hadn't expected the frogs.

"Say your farewells, you pointless pests," I called. The frogs had developed a defensive strategy they put into action any time I came close. First, the watch guard belched an alarm. The others would fling themselves into the river. Finally, the brave watch guard hopped for his life. An effort as admirable as it was futile.

Dirt was caked deep beneath my fingernails. Moonlight filtered through a canopy of skeletal trees, and for a moment, my hand looked like a different one. A hand much more manicured, a little weaker. Niphran's hands. Hands that could wield an axe alongside the burliest woodcutter, weave a storm of curls into delicate braids, drive spears into the maws of monsters. For the first few years of my life, before grief over my father's assassination spread through Niphran like rot, before her sanity collapsed on itself, there wasn't anything my mother's hands could not do.

Oh, if she could see me now. Covered in filth and outwitted by croaking river roaches.

Hirun exhaled its opaque mist, breathing life into the winter bones of Essam Woods. I cleaned my hands in the river and firmly cast aside thoughts of the dead.

A frenzied croak sounded behind a tree root. I darted forward, scooping up the kicking watch guard. Ah, but it was never the brave who escaped. I brought him close to my face. "Your friends are chasing crickets, and you're here. Were they worth it?"

I dropped the limp frog into the bucket and sighed. Ten more to go, which meant another round of running in circles and hoping mud wouldn't spill through the hole in my right boot. The fact that Rory was a renowned chemist didn't impress me, nor did this coveted apprenticeship. What kept me from tossing the bucket and going to Raya's keep, where a warm meal and a comfortable bed awaited me, was a debt of convenience.

Rory didn't ask questions. When I appeared on his doorstep five years ago, drenched in blood and shaking, Rory had tended to my wounds and taken me to Raya's. He rescued a fifteen-year-old orphan with no history or background from a life of vagrancy.

The sudden snap of a branch drew my muscles tight. I reached into my pocket and wrapped my fingers around the hilt of my dagger. Given the Nizahl soldiers' predilection for randomly searching us, I usually carried my blade strapped in my boot, but I'd used it to cut my foot out of a family of tangled ferns and left it in my pocket.

A quick scan of the shivering branches revealed nothing. I tried not to let my eyes linger in the empty pockets of black between the trees. I had seen too much horror manifest out of the dark to ever trust its stillness.

My gaze moved to the place it dreaded most—the row of trees behind me, each scored with identical, chillingly precise black marks. The symbol of a raven spreading its wings had been carved into the trees circling Mahair's border. In the muck of the woods, these ravens remained pristine. Crossing the raven-marked trees without permission was an offense punishable by imprisonment or worse. In the lower villages, where the kingdom's leaders were already primed to turn a blind eye to the liberties taken by Nizahl soldiers, worse was usually just the beginning.

I tucked my dagger into my pocket and walked right to the edge of the perimeter. I traced one raven's outstretched wing with my thumbnail. I would have traded all the frogs in my bucket to be brave enough to scrape my nails over the symbol, to gouge it off.

Maybe that same burst of bravery would see my dagger cutting a line in the bark, disfiguring the symbols of Nizahl's power. It wasn't walls or swords keeping us penned in like animals, but a simple carving. Another kingdom's power billowing over us like poisoned air, controlling everything it touched.

I glanced at the watch guard in my bucket and lowered my hand. Bravery wasn't worth the cost. Or the splinters.

A thick layer of frost coated the road leading back to Mahair. I pulled my hood nearly to my nose as soon as I crossed the wall separating Mahair from Essam Woods. I veered into an alley, winding my way to Rory's shop instead of risking the exposed—and regularly patrolled—main road. Darkness cloaked me as soon as I stepped into the alley. I placed a stabilizing hand on the wall and let the pungent odor of manure guide my feet forward. A cat hissed from beneath a stack of crates, hunching protectively over the half-eaten carcass of a rat.

"I already had supper, but thank you for the offer," I whispered, leaping out of reach of her claws.

Twenty minutes later, I clunked the full bucket at Rory's feet. "I demand a renegotiation of my wages."

Rory didn't look up from his list. "Demand away. I'll be over there."

He disappeared into the back room. I scowled, contemplating following him past the curtain and maiming him with frog corpses. The smell of mud and mildew had permanently seeped into my skin. The least he could do was pay extra for the soap I needed to mask it.

I arranged the poultices, sealing each jar carefully before placing it inside the basket. One of the rare times I'd found myself on the wrong side of Rory's temper was after I had forgotten to seal the ointments before sending them off with Yuli's boy. I learned as much about the spread of disease that day as I did about Rory's staunch ethics.

Rory returned. "Off with you already. Get some sleep. I do not want the sight of your face to scare off my patrons tomorrow." He prodded in the bucket, turning over a few of the frogs. Age weathered Rory's narrow brown face. His long fingers were constantly stained in the color of his latest tonic, and a permanent groove sat between his bushy brows. I called it his "rage stage," because I could always gauge his level of fury by the number of furrows forming above his nose. Despite an old injury to his hip, his slenderness was not a sign of fragility. On the rare occasions when Rory smiled, it was clear he had been handsome in his youth. "If I find that you've layered the bottom with dirt again, I'm poisoning your tea."

He pushed a haphazardly wrapped bundle into my arms. "Here."

Bewildered, I turned the package over. "For me?"

He waved his cane around the empty shop. "Are you touched in the head, child?"

I carefully peeled the fabric back, half expecting it to explode in my face, and exposed a pair of beautiful golden gloves. Softer than a dove's wing, they probably cost more than anything I could buy for myself. I lifted one reverently. "Rory, this is too much."

I only barely stopped myself from putting them on. I laid them gingerly on the counter and hurried to scrub off my stained hands. There were no clean cloths left, so I wiped my hands on Rory's tunic and earned a swat to the ear.

The fit of the gloves was perfect. Soft and supple, yielding with the flex of my fingers.

I lifted my hands to the lantern for closer inspection. These would certainly fetch a pretty price at market. Not that I'd sell them right away, of course. Rory liked pretending he had the emotional depth of a spoon, but he would be hurt if I bartered his gift a mere day later. Markets weren't hard to find in Omal. The lower villages were always in need of food and supplies. Trading among themselves was easier than begging for scraps from the palace.

The old man smiled briefly. "Happy birthday, Sylvia."

Sylvia. My first and favorite lie. I pressed my hands together. "A consolation gift for the spinster?" Not once in five years had Rory failed to remember my fabricated birth date.

"I should hardly think spinsterhood's threshold as low as twenty years."

In truth, I was halfway to twenty-one. Another lie.

"You are as old as time itself. The ages below one hundred must all look the same to you."

He jabbed me with his cane. "It is past the hour for spinsters to be about."

I left the shop in higher spirits. I pulled my cloak tight around my shoulders, knotting the hood beneath my chin. I had one more task to complete before I could finally reunite with my bed, and it meant delving deeper into the silent village. These were the hours when the mind ran free, when hollow masonry became the whispers of hungry shaiateen and the scratch of scuttling vermin the sounds of the restless dead.

I knew how sinuously fear cobbled shadows into gruesome shapes. I hadn't slept a full night's length in long years, and there were days when I trusted nothing beyond the breath in my chest and the earth beneath my feet. The difference between the villagers and me was that I knew the names of my monsters. I knew what they would look like if they found me, and I didn't have to imagine what kind of fate I would meet.

Mahair was a tiny village, but its history was long. Its children would know the tales shared from their mothers and fathers and grandparents. Superstition kept Mahair alive, long after time had turned a new page on its inhabitants.

It also kept me in business.

Instead of turning right toward Raya's keep, I ducked into the vagrant road. Bits of honey-soaked dough and grease marked the spot where the halawany's daughters snacked between errands, sitting on the concrete stoop of their parents' dessert shop. Dodging the dogs nosing at the grease, I checked for anyone who might report my movements back to Rory.

We had made a tradition of forgiving each other, Rory and me. Should he find out I was treating Omalians under his name, peddling pointless concoctions to those superstitious enough to buy them—well, I doubted Rory could forgive such a transgression. The "cures" I mucked together for my patrons were harmless. Crushed herbs and altered liquors. Most of the time, the ailments they were intended to ward off were more ridiculous than anything I could fit in a bottle.

The home I sought was ten minutes' walk past Raya's keep. Too close for comfort. Water dripped from the edge of the sagging roof, where a bare clothesline stretched from hook to hook. A pair of undergarments had fluttered to the ground. I kicked them out of sight. Raya taught me years ago how to hide undergarments on the clothesline by clipping them behind a larger piece of clothing. I hadn't understood the need for so much stealth. I still didn't. But time was a limited resource tonight, and I wouldn't waste it soothing an Omalian's embarrassment that I now had definitive proof they wore undergarments.

The door flew open. "Sylvia, thank goodness," Zeinab said. "She's worse today."

I tapped my mud-encrusted boots against the lip of the door and stepped inside.

"Where is she?"

I followed Zeinab to the last room in the short hall. A wave of incense wafted over us when she opened the door. I fanned the white haze hanging in the air. A wizened old woman rocked back and forth on the floor, and bloody tracks lined her arms where nails had gouged deep. Zeinab closed the door, maintaining a safe distance. Tears swam in her large hazel eyes. "I tried to give her a bath, and she did *this*." Zeinab pushed up the sleeve of her abaya, exposing a myriad of red scratch marks.

"Right." I laid my bag down on the table. "I will call you when I've finished."

Subduing the old woman with a tonic took little effort. I moved behind her and hooked an arm around her neck. She tore at my sleeve, mouth falling open to gasp. I dumped the tonic down her throat and loosened my stranglehold enough for her to swallow. Once certain she wouldn't spit it out, I let her go and adjusted my sleeve. She spat at my heels and bared teeth bloody from where she'd torn her lip.

It took minutes. My talents, dubious as they were, lay in efficient and fleeting deception. At the door, I let Zeinab slip a few coins into my cloak's pocket and pretended to be surprised. I would never understand Omalians and their feigned modesty. "Remember—"

Zeinab bobbed her head impatiently. "Yes, yes, I won't speak a word of this. It has been years, Sylvia. If the chemist ever finds out, it will not be from me."

She was quite self-assured for a woman who never bothered to ask what was in the tonic I regularly poured down her mother's throat. I returned Zeinab's wave distractedly and moved my dagger into the same pocket as the coins. Puddles of foul-smelling rain rippled in the pocked dirt road. Most of the homes on the street could more accurately be described as hovels, their thatched roofs shivering above walls joined together with mud and uneven patches of brick. I dodged a line of green mule manure, its waterlogged, grassy smell stinging my nose.

Did Omal's upper towns have excrement in their streets?

Zeinab's neighbor had scattered chicken feathers outside her door to showcase their good fortune to their neighbors. Their daughter had married a merchant from Dawar, and her dowry had earned them enough to eat chicken all month. From now on, the finest clothes would furnish her body. The choicest meats and hardest-grown vegetables for her plate. She'd never need to dodge mule droppings in Mahair again.

I turned the corner, absently counting the coins in my pocket, and rammed into a body.

I stumbled, catching myself against a pile of cracked clay bricks. The Nizahl soldier didn't budge beyond a tightening of his frown.

"Identify yourself."

Heavy wings of panic unfurled in my throat. Though our movements around town weren't constrained by an official curfew, not many risked a late-night stroll. The Nizahl soldiers usually patrolled in pairs, which meant this man's partner was probably harassing someone else on the other side of the village.

I smothered the panic, snapping its fluttering limbs. Panic was a plague. Its sole purpose was to spread until it tore through every thought, every instinct.

I immediately lowered my eyes. Holding a Nizahl soldier's gaze invited nothing but trouble. "My name is Sylvia. I live in Raya's keep and apprentice for the chemist Rory. I apologize for startling you. An elderly woman urgently needed care, and my employer is indisposed."

From the lines on his face, the soldier was somewhere in his late forties. If he had been an Omalian patrolman, his age would have signified little. But Nizahl soldiers tended to die young and bloody. For this man to survive long enough to see the lines of his forehead wrinkle, he was either a deadly adversary or a coward.

"What is your father's name?"

"I am a ward in Raya's keep," I repeated. He must be new to Mahair. Everyone knew Raya's house of orphans on the hill. "I have no mother or father."

He didn't belabor the issue. "Have you witnessed activity that might lead to the capture of a Jasadi?" Even though it was a standard question from the soldiers, intended to encourage vigilance toward any signs of magic, I inwardly flinched. The most recent arrest of a Jasadi had happened in our neighboring village a mere month ago. From the whispers, I'd surmised a girl reported seeing her friend fix a crack in her floorboard with a wave of her hand. I had overheard all manner of praise showered on the girl for her bravery in turning in the fifteen-year-old. Praise and jealousy—they couldn't wait for their own opportunities to be heroes.

"I have not." I hadn't seen another Jasadi in five years.

He pursed his lips. "The name of the elderly woman?"

"Aya, but her daughter Zeinab is her caretaker. I could direct you to them if you'd like." Zeinab was crafty. She would have a lie prepared for a moment like this.

"No need." He waved a hand over his shoulder. "On your way. Stay off the vagrant road."

One benefit of the older Nizahl soldiers—they had less inclination for the bluster and interrogation tactics of their younger counterparts. I tipped my head in gratitude and sped past him.

A few minutes later, I slid into Raya's keep. By the scent of cooling wax, it had not been long since the last girl went to bed. Relieved to find my birthday forgotten, I kicked my boots off at the door. Raya had met with the cloth merchants today. Bartering always left her in a foul mood. The only acknowledgment of my birthday would be a breakfast of flaky, buttery fiteer and molasses in the morning.

When I pushed open my door, a blast of warmth swept over me. Baira's blessed hair, not *again*. "Raya will have your hides. The waleema is in a week."

Marek appeared engrossed in the firepit, poking the coals with a thin rod. His golden hair shone under the glow. A mess of fabric and the beginnings of what might be a dress sat beneath Sefa's sewing tools. "Precisely," Sefa said, dipping a chunk of charred beef into her broth. "I am drowning my sorrows in stolen broth because of the damned waleema. Look at this dress! This is a dress all the other dresses laugh at."

"What is he doing with the fire?" I asked, electing to ignore her garment-related woes. Come morning, Sefa would hand Raya a perfect dress with a winning smile and bloodshot eyes. An apprenticeship under the best seamstress in Omal wasn't a role given to those who folded under pressure.

"He's trying to roast his damned seeds." Sefa sniffed. "We made your room smell like a tavern kitchen. Sorry. In our defense, we gathered to mourn a terrible passing."

"A passing?" I took a seat beside the stone pit, rubbing my hands over the crackling flames.

Marek handed me one of Raya's private chalices. The woman was going to skin us like deer. "Ignore her. We just wanted to abuse your hearth," he said. "I am convinced Yuli is teaching his herd how to kill me. They almost ran me right into a canal today."

"Did you do something to make Yuli or the oxen angry?"

"No," Marek said mournfully.

I rolled the chalice between my palms and narrowed my eyes. "Marek."

"I may have used the horse's stalls to . . . entertain . . ." He released a long-suffering sigh. "His daughter."

Sefa and I released twin groans. This was hardly the first time

Marek had gotten himself in trouble chasing a coy smile or kind word. He was absurdly pretty, fair-haired and green-eyed, lean in a way that undersold his strength. To counter his looks, he'd chosen to apprentice with Yuli, Mahair's most demanding farmer. By spending his days loading wagons and herding oxen, Marek made himself indispensable to every tradesperson in the village. He worked to earn their respect, because there were few things Mahair valued more than calloused palms and sweat on a brow.

It was also why they tolerated the string of broken hearts he'd left in his wake.

Not one to be ignored for long, Sefa continued, "Your youth, Sylvia, we mourn your youth! At twenty, you're having fewer adventures than the village brats."

I drained the water, passing the chalice to Marek for more. "I have plenty of adventure."

"I'm not talking about how many times you can kill your fig plant before it stays dead," Sefa scoffed. "If you had simply accompanied me last week to release the roosters in Nadia's den—"

"Nadia has permanently barred you from her shop," Marek interjected. Brave one, cutting Sefa off in the middle of a tirade. He scooped up a blackened seed, throwing it from palm to palm to cool. "Leave Sylvia be. Adventure does not fit into a single mold."

Sefa's nostrils flared wide, but Marek didn't flinch. They communicated in that strange, silent way of people who were bound together by something thicker than blood and stronger than a shared upbringing. I knew because I had witnessed hundreds of their unspoken conversations over the last five years.

"I am not killing my fig plant." I pushed to my feet. "I'm cultivating its fighter's spirit."

"Stop glaring at me," Marek said to Sefa with a sigh. "I'm sorry for interrupting." He held out a cracked seed.

Sefa let his hand dangle in the air for forty seconds before taking the seed. "Help me hem this sleeve?"

With a sheepish grin, Marek offered his soot-covered palms. Sefa rolled her eyes.

I observed this latest exchange with bewilderment. It never failed to astound me how easily they existed around one another. Their unusual devotion had led to questions from the other wards at the keep. Marek laughed himself into stitches the first time a younger girl asked if he and Sefa planned to wed. "Sefa isn't going to marry anyone. We love each other in a different way."

The ward had batted her lashes, because Marek was the only boy in the keep, and he was in possession of a face consigning him to a life of wistful sighs following in his wake.

"What about you?" the ward had asked.

Sefa, who had been smiling as she knit in the corner, sobered. Only Raya and I saw the sorrowful look she shot Marek, the guilt in her brown eyes.

"I am tied to Sefa in spirit, if not in wedlock." Marek ruffled the ward's hair. The girl squealed, slapping at Marek. "I follow where she goes."

To underscore their insanity, the pair had taken an instant liking to me the moment Rory dropped me off at Raya's doorstep. I was almost feral, hardly fit for friendship, but it hadn't deterred them. I adjusted poorly to this Omalian village, perplexed by their simplest customs. Rub the spot between your shoulders and you'll die early. Eat with your left hand on the first day of the month; don't cross your legs in the presence of elders; be the last person to sit at the dinner table and the first one to leave it. It didn't help that my bronze skin was several shades darker than their typical olive. I blended in with Orbanians better, since the kingdom in the north spent most of its days under the sun. When Sefa noticed how I avoided wearing white, she'd held her darker hand next to mine and said, "They're jealous we soaked up all their color."

Matters weren't much easier at home. Everyone in the keep had an ugly history haunting their sleep. I didn't help myself any by almost slamming another ward's nose clean off her face when she tried to hug me. Despite the two-hour lecture I endured from Raya, the incident had firmly established my aversion to touch.

For some inconceivable reason, Sefa and Marek weren't scared off. Sefa was quite upset about her nose, though.

I hung my cloak neatly inside the wardrobe and thumbed the moth-eaten collar. It wouldn't survive another winter, but the thought of throwing it away brought a lump to my throat. Someone in my position could afford few emotional attachments. At any moment, a sword could be pointed at me, a cry of "*Jasadi*" ending this identity and the life I'd built around it. I recoiled from the cloak, curling my fingers into a fist. I promptly tore out the roots of sadness before it could spread. A regular orphan from Mahair could cling to this tired cloak, the first thing she'd ever purchased with her own hard-earned coin.

A fugitive of the scorched kingdom could not.

I turned my palms up, testing the silver cuffs around my wrists. Though the cuffs were invisible to any eye but mine, it had taken a long time for my paranoia to ease whenever someone's idle gaze lingered on my wrists. They flexed with my movement, a second skin over my own. Only my trapped magic could stir them, tightening the cuffs as it pleased.

Magic marked me as a Jasadi. As the reason Nizahl created perimeters in the woods and sent their soldiers prowling through the kingdoms. I had spent most of my life resenting my cuffs. How was it fair that Jasadis were condemned because of their magic but I couldn't even access the thing that doomed me? My magic had been trapped behind these cuffs since my childhood. I suppose my grandparents couldn't have anticipated dying and leaving the cuffs stuck on me forever.

I hid Rory's gift in the wardrobe, beneath the folds of my longest gown. The girls rarely risked Raya's wrath by stealing, but a desperate winter could make a thief of anyone. I stroked one of the gloves, fondness curling hot in my chest. How much had Rory spent, knowing I'd have limited opportunities to wear them?

"We wanted to show you something," Marek said. His voice hurtled me back to reality, and I slammed the wardrobe doors shut, scowling at myself. What did it matter how much Rory spent?

Anything I didn't need to survive would be discarded or sold, and these gloves were no different.

Sefa stood, dusting loose fabric from her lap. She snorted at my expression. "Rovial's tainted tomb, look at her, Marek. You might think we were planning to bury her in the woods."

Marek frowned. "Aren't we?"

"Both of you are banned from my room. Forever."

I followed them outside, past the row of fluttering clotheslines and the pitiful herb garden. Built at the top of a grassy slope, Raya's keep overlooked the entire village, all the way to the main road. Most of the homes in Mahair sat stacked on top of each other, forming squat, three-story buildings with crumbling walls and cracks in the clay. The villagers raised poultry on the roofs, nurturing a steady supply of chickens and rabbits that would see them through the monthly food shortages. Livestock meandered in the fields shouldering Essam Woods, fenced in by the miles-long wall surrounding Mahair.

Past the wall, darkness marked the expanse of Essam Woods. Moonlight disappeared over the trees stretching into the black horizon.

Ahead of me, Marek and Sefa averted their gaze from the woods. They had arrived in Mahair when they were sixteen, two years before me. I couldn't tell if they'd simply adopted Mahair's peculiar customs or if those customs were more widespread than I thought.

The day after I emerged from Essam, I'd spent the night sitting on the hill and watching the spot where Mahair's lanterns disappeared into the empty void of the woods. Escaping Essam had nearly killed me. I'd wanted to confirm to myself that this village and the roof over my head weren't a cruel dream. That when I closed my eyes, I wouldn't open them to branches rustling below a starless sky.

Raya had stormed out of the keep in her nightgown and hauled me inside, where I'd listened to her harangue me about the risk of staring into Essam Woods and inviting mischievous spirits forward from the dark. As though my attention alone might summon them into being.

I spent five years in those woods. I wasn't afraid of their darkness. It was everything outside Essam I couldn't trust.

"Behold!" Sefa announced, flinging her arm toward a tangle of plants.

We stopped around the back of the keep, where I had illicitly shoveled the fig plant I bought off a Lukubi merchant at the last market. I wasn't sure why. Nurturing a plant that reminded me of Jasad, something rooted I couldn't take with me in an emergency—it was embarrassing. Another sign of the weakness I'd allowed to settle.

My fig plant's leaves drooped mournfully. I prodded the dirt. Were they mocking my planting technique?

"She doesn't like it. I told you we should have bought her a new cloak," Marek sighed.

"With whose wages? Are you a wealthy man now?" Sefa peered at me. "You don't like it?"

I squinted at the plant. Had they watered it while I was gone? What was I supposed to like? Sefa's face crumpled, so I hurriedly said, "I love it! It is, uh, wonderful, truly. Thank you."

"Oh. You can't see it, can you?" Marek started to laugh. "Sefa forgot she is the size of a thimble and hid it out of your sight."

"I am a perfectly standard height! I cannot be blamed for befriending a woman tall enough to tickle the moon," Sefa protested.

I crouched by the plant. Wedged behind its curtain of yellowing leaves, a woven straw basket held a dozen sesame-seed candies. I loved these brittle, tooth-chipping squares. I always made a point to search for them at market if I'd saved enough to spare the cost.

"They used the good honey, not the chalky one," Marek added.

"Happy birthday, Sylvia," Sefa said. "As a courtesy, I will refrain from hugging you."

First Rory, now this? I cleared my throat. In a village of empty stomachs and dying fields, every kindness came at a price. "You just wanted to see me smile with sesame in my teeth."

Marek smirked. "Ah, yes, our grand scheme is unveiled. We wanted to ruin your smile that emerges once every fifteen years."

I slapped the back of his head. It was the most physical contact I could bear, but it expressed my gratitude.

We walked back to the keep and resettled around the extinguished firepit. Marek dug through the ash for any surviving seeds. Sefa lay back on the ground, her feet propped on Marek's leg. "Arin or Felix?"

I slumped on my bed and set to the tedious task of coaxing my curls out of their knotted disaster of a braid. The sesame-seed candies were nestled safely in my wardrobe. The timing of these gifts could not have been better. As soon as Sefa and Marek fell asleep, I would collect what I needed for my trip back to the woods.

"Are names of the Nizahl and Omal Heirs."

"Sylvia," Sefa wheedled, tossing a seed at my forehead. "You have been selected to attend the Victor's Ball on the arm of an Heir. Arin or Felix?"

Marek groaned, throwing his elbow over his eyes. Soot smeared the corners of his mouth. Neither of us understood why Sefa loved dreaming up intrigues of far-flung courts. She claimed to enjoy the aesthetics of romance, even if she didn't believe in it herself. She had wedded herself to adventure at a young age, when she realized the follies of lust and love did not hold sway over her.

I sighed, giving in to Sefa's game. Felix of Omal would not recognize a hard day's work if it knelt at his polished feet. I had listened to his address after a particularly unforgiving harvest. He brought his handspun clothes and gilded carriages, leaving behind words as empty as the space between his ears. Worse, he gave the Nizahl soldiers free rein, reserving his resistance to intrusion for Omalian society's upper classes.

"Felix is incompetent, cowardly, and thinks the lower villages are full of brutes," Marek scoffed, echoing my unspoken opinion. "I would hesitate to leave him in charge of boiling water. At least the other Heirs are clever, if still as despicable."

At "despicable," my thoughts swung to Arin of Nizahl, the only son of Supreme Rawain.

Silver-haired, ruthless, Heir and Commander of the unmatched Nizahl forces. He had been training soldiers twice his age since he was thirteen. I had always thought Supreme Rawain's bloodthirst had no equal, since it wasn't his kind heart responsible for murdering my family, burning Jasad to the ground, and sending every surviving Jasadi into hiding. But if the rumors about the Heir were true, I could only be glad Arin had been an adolescent during the siege. With the Nizahl Heir leading the march, I doubted a single Jasadi would have made it out alive.

The constant presence of Nizahl soldiers was common to all four kingdoms. An incurable symptom of Nizahl's military supremacy. But the sight of their Heir outside his own lands spelled doom: it meant he had found a cluster of Jasadis or magic of great magnitude. I struggled to repress a shudder. If Arin of Nizahl ever came within a day's riding distance from Mahair, I would be gone faster than liquor at a funeral.

"Sylvia?" Marek asked. Marek and Sefa wore a familiar frown of concern. Black strands had drifted into my lap while I unbraided my hair. I rolled them up and tossed the clump into the fire, where I watched it curdle into ash.

"Sorry," I said. "I forgot the question."

As it always did, the thought of Nizahl curved claws of hatred in my belly. I wasn't capable of sending magic flying in fits of emotion anymore. All I had left was fantasy. I imagined meeting Supreme Rawain in the kingdom he'd laid waste to. I would drive his scepter through the softest part of his stomach, watch the cruelty drain from his blue eyes. Plant him on the steps of the fallen palace for the spirits of Jasad's dead to feast upon.

"Ah, yes, an Heir." I paused. "Sorn."

"The Orban Heir?" Sefa lifted her brows. "Your tastes run toward the brutish? A thirst for danger, perhaps?"

I winked. "What danger is there in a brute?"

if you enjoyed
THE SUN AND THE VOID

look out for

THE PHOENIX KING

The Ravence Trilogy: Book One

by

Aparna Verma

Yassen Knight was the Arohassin's most notorious assassin until a horrible accident. Now he's hunted by the authorities and his former employer, both of whom want him dead. But when he seeks refuge with an old friend, he's offered an irresistible deal: defend the heir of Ravence from the Arohassin and earn his freedom once and for all.

Elena Ravence is preparing to ascend the throne. Trained since birth in statecraft, warfare, and the desert ways, Elena knows she is ready. She lacks only one thing: the ability to hold fire, the magic that is meant to run in her family's blood. And with her coronation only weeks away, she must learn quickly or lose her kingdom.

Leo Ravence is not ready to give up the crown. There's still too much work to be done, too many battles to be won. But when

extras

*an ancient prophecy threatens to undo his lifetime of work,
Leo wages war on the heavens themselves to protect his legacy.*

CHAPTER 1

Yassen

*The king said to his people, "We are the chosen."
And the people responded, "Chosen by whom?"*

—from chapter 37 of *The Great History of Sayon*

To be forgiven, one must be burned. That's what the Ravani said. They were fanatics and fire worshippers, but they were his people. And he would finally be returning home.

Yassen held on to the railing of the hoverboat as it skimmed over the waves. He held on with his left arm, his right limp by his side. Around him, the world was dark, but the horizon began to purple with the faint glimmers of dawn. Soon, the sun would rise, and the twin moons of Sayon would lie down to rest. Soon, he would arrive at Rysanti, the Brass City. And soon, he would find his way back to the desert that had forsaken him.

Yassen withdrew a holopod from his jacket and pressed it open with his thumb. A small holo materialized with a message:
Look for the bull.

He closed the holo, the smell of salt and brine filling his lungs.

The bull. It was nothing close to the Phoenix of Ravence, but then again, Samson liked to be subtle. Yassen wondered if he would be at the port to greet him.

A large wave tossed the boat, but Yassen did not lose his balance. Weeks at sea and suns of combat had taught him how to keep his ground. A cool wind licked his sleeve, and he felt a whisper of pain skitter down his right wrist. He grimaced. His skin was already beginning to redden.

After the Arohassin had pulled him half-conscious from the sea, Yassen had thought, in the delirium of pain, that he would be free. If not in this life, then in death. But the Arohassin had yanked him back from the brink. Treated his burns and saved his arm. Said that he was lucky to be alive while whispering among themselves when they thought he could not hear: "Yassen Knight is no longer of use."

Yassen pulled down his sleeve. It was no matter. He was used to running.

As the hoverboat neared the harbor, the fog along the coastline began to evaporate. Slowly, Yassen saw the tall spires of the Brass City cut through the grey heavens. Skyscrapers of slate and steel from the mines of Sona glimmered in the early dawn as hovertrains weaved through the air, carrying the day laborers. Neon lights flickered within the metal jungle, and a silver bridge snaked through the entire city, connecting the outer rings to the wealthy, affluent center. Yassen squinted as the sun crested the horizon. Suddenly, its light hit the harbor, and the Brass City shone with a blinding intensity.

Yassen quickly clipped on his visor, a fiber sheath that covered his entire face. He closed his eyes for a moment, allowing them to readjust before opening them again. The city stared back at him in subdued colors.

Queen Rydia, one of the first queens of Jantar, had wanted to ward off Enuu, the evil eye, so she had fashioned her port city out of unforgiving metal. If Yassen wasn't careful, the brass could blind him.

The other passengers came up on deck, pulling on half visors that covered their eyes. Yassen tightened his visor and wrapped a scarf around his neck. Most people could not recognize him—none of the passengers even knew of his name—but he could not take any chances. Samson had made it clear that he wanted no one to know of this meeting.

The hoverboat came to rest beside the platform, and Yassen disembarked with the rest of the passengers. Even in the early hours, the port was busy. On the other dock, soldiers barked out orders as fresh immigrants stumbled off a colony boat. Judging from the coiled silver bracelets on their wrists, Yassen guessed they were Sesharian refugees. They shuffled forward on the adjoining dock toward military buses. Some carried luggage; others had nothing save the clothes they wore. They all donned half visors and walked with the resigned grace of people weary of their fate.

Native Jantari, in their lightning suits and golden bracelets, kept a healthy distance from the immigrants. They stayed on the brass homeland and receiving docks where merchants stationed their carts. Unlike most of the city, the carts were made of pale driftwood, but the vendors still wore half visors as they handled their wares. Yassen could already hear a merchant hawking satchels of vermilion tea while another shouted about a new delivery of mirrors from Cyleon that had a 90 percent accuracy of predicting one's romantic future. Yassen shook his head. Only in Jantar.

Floating lanterns guided Yassen and the passengers to the glass-encased immigration office. Yassen slid his holopod into the port while a grim-faced attendant flicked something from his purple nails.

"Name?" he intoned.

"Cassian Newman," Yassen said.

"Country of residence?"

"Nbru."

The attendant waved his hand. "Take off your visor, please."

Yassen unclipped his visor and saw shock register across the attendant's face as he took in Yassen's white, colorless eyes.

"Are you Jantari?" the attendant asked, surprised.

"No," Yassen responded gruffly and clipped his visor back on. "My father was."

"Hmph." The attendant looked at his holopod and then back at him. "Purpose of your visit?"

Yassen paused. The attendant peered at him, and for one wild moment, Yassen wondered if he should turn away, jump back on the boat, and go wherever the sea pushed him. But then a coldness slithered down his right elbow, and he gripped his arm.

"To visit some old friends," Yassen said.

The attendant snorted, but when the holopod slid back out, Yassen saw the burning insignia of a mohanti, a winged ox, on its surface.

"Welcome to the Kingdom of Jantar," the attendant said and waved him through.

Yassen stepped through the glass immigration office and into Rysanti. He breathed in the sharp salt air, intermingled with spices both foreign and familiar. A storm had passed through recently, leaving puddles in its wake. A woman ahead of Yassen slipped on a wet plank and a merchant reached out to steady her. Yassen pushed past them, keeping his head down. Out of the corner of his eye, he saw the merchant swipe the woman's holopod and hide it in his jacket. Yassen smothered a laugh.

As he wandered toward the homeland dock, he scanned the faces in the crowd. The time was nearly two past the sun's breath. Samson and his men should have been here by now.

He came to the bridge connecting the receiving and homeland docks. At the other end of the bridge was a lonely tea stall, held together by worn planks—but the large holosign snagged his attention.

WARM YOUR TIRED BONES FROM YOUR PASSAGE AT SEA! FRESH HOT LEMON CAKES AND RAVANI TEA SERVED DAILY! it read.

It was the word *Ravani* that sent a jolt through Yassen. Home—the one he longed for but knew he was no longer welcome in.

Yassen drew up to the tea stall. Three large hourglasses hissed and steamed. Tea leaves floated along their bottoms, slowly steeping, as a heavyset Sesharian woman flipped them in timed intervals. On her hand, Yassen spotted a tattoo of a bull.

The same mark Samson had asked him to look for.

When the woman met Yassen's eyes, she twirled the hourglass once more before drying her hands on the towel around her wide waist.

"Whatcha want?" she asked in a river-hoarse voice.

"One tea and cake, please," Yassen said.

"You're lucky. I just got a fresh batch of leaves from my connect. Straight from the canyons of Ravence."

"Exactly why I want one," he said and placed his holopod in the counter insert. Yassen tapped it twice.

"Keep the change," he added.

She nodded and turned back to the giant hourglasses.

The brass beneath Yassen's feet grew warmer in the yawning day. Across the docks, more boats pulled in, carrying immigrant laborers and tourists. Yassen adjusted his visor, making sure it was fully in place, as the woman simultaneously flipped the hourglass and slid off its cap. In one fluid motion, the hot tea arced through the air and fell into the cup in her hand. She slid it across the counter.

"Mind the sleeve, the tea's hot," she said. "And here's your cake."

Yassen grabbed the cake box and lifted his cup in thanks. As he moved away from the stall, he scratched the plastic sleeve around the cup.

Slowly, a message burned through:

Look underneath the dock of fortunes.

He almost smiled. Clearly, Samson had not forgotten Yassen's love of tea.

Yassen looked within the box and saw that there was no cake but something sharp, metallic. He reached inside and held it up. Made of silver, the insignia was smaller than his palm and etched in what seemed to be the shape of a teardrop. Yassen held it closer. No, it was more feather than teardrop.

He threw the sleeve and box into a bin, slid the silver into his pocket, and continued down the dock. The commerce section stretched on, a mile of storefronts welcoming him into the great nation of Jantar. Yassen sipped his tea, watching. A few paces down was a stall marketing tales of ruin and fortune. Like the tea stall, it too was old and decrepit, with a painting of a woman reading palms painted across its front. He was beginning to recognize a pattern—and patterns were dangerous. Samson was getting lazy in his mansion.

Three guards stood along the edge of the platform beside the stall. One was dressed in a captain's royal blue, the other two in the plain black of officers. All three wore helmet visors, their pulse guns strapped to their sides. They were laughing at some joke when the captain looked up and frowned at Yassen.

"You there," he said imperiously.

Yassen slowly lowered his cup. The dock was full of carts and merchants. If he ran now, the guards could catch him.

"Yes, you, with the full face," the captain called out, tapping his visor. "Come here!"

"Is there a problem?" Yassen asked as he approached.

"No full visors allowed on the dock, except for the guard," the captain said.

"I didn't know it was a crime to wear a full visor," Yassen said. His voice was cool, perhaps a bit too nonchalant because the captain slapped the cup out of Yassen's hand. The spilled tea hissed against the metal planks.

"New rules," the captain said. "Only guards can wear full visors. Everybody else has to go half."

His subordinates snickered. "Looks like he's fresh off the boat, Cap. You got to cut it up for him," one said.

Behind his visor, Yassen frowned. He glanced at the merchant leaning against the fortunes stall. The man wore a bored expression, as if the interaction before him was nothing new. But then the merchant bent forward, pressing his hands to the counter, and Yassen saw the sign of the bull tattooed there.

Samson's men were watching.

"All right," Yassen said. He would give them a show. Prove that he wasn't as useless as the whispers told.

He unclipped his visor as the guards watched. "But you owe me another cup of tea."

And then Yassen flung his arm out and rammed the visor against the captain's face. The man stumbled back with a groan. The other two leapt forward, but Yassen was quicker; he swung around and gave four quick jabs, two each on the back, and the officers seized and sank to their knees in temporary paralysis.

"Blast him!" the captain cried, reaching for his gun. Yassen pivoted behind him, his hand flashing out to unclip the captain's helmet visor.

The captain whipped around, raising his gun...but then sunlight hit the planks before him, and the brass threw off its unforgiving light. Blinded, the captain fired.

The air screeched.

The pulse whizzed past Yassen's right ear, tearing through the upper beams of a storefront. Immediately, merchants took cover. Someone screamed as the crowd on both docks began to run. Yassen swiftly vanished into the chaotic fray, letting the crowd push him toward the dock's edge, and then he dove into the sea.

The cold water shocked him, and for a moment, Yassen floundered. His muscles clenched. And then he was coughing, swimming, and he surfaced beneath the dock. He willed himself to be still as footsteps thundered overhead and soldiers and guards barked out orders. Yassen caught glimpses of the captain in the spaces between the planks.

"All hells! Where did he go?" the captain yelled at the merchant manning the stall of wild tales.

The merchant shrugged. "He's long gone."

Yassen sank deeper into the water as the captain walked overhead, his subordinates wobbling behind. Something buzzed beneath him, and he could see the faint outlines of a dark shape in the depths. Slowly, Yassen began to swim away—but the dark shape remained stationary. He waited for the guards to pass and then sank beneath the surface.

A submersible, the size of one passenger.

Look underneath the dock of fortunes, indeed.

Samson, that bastard.

Yassen swam toward the sub. He placed his hand on the imprint panel of the hull, and then the sub buzzed again and rose to the surface.

The cockpit was small, with barely enough room for him to stretch his legs, but he sighed and sank back just the same. The glass slid smoothly closed and rudders whined to life. The panel board lit up before him and bathed him in a pale blue light.

A note was there. Handwritten. How rare, and so like Samson.

See you at the palace, it said, and before Yassen could question *which* palace, the sub was off.

Follow us:

📘 **/orbitbooksUS**

🐦 **/orbitbooks**

▶️ **/orbitbooks**

Join our mailing list
to receive alerts on our
latest releases and deals.

orbitbooks.net

Enter our monthly
giveaway for the chance
to win some epic prizes.

orbitloot.com